*M*ALIE!" A touch on her shoulder, a hand, a familiar smell—how could he have a smell that she recognized?—"Oh, Malie!" and he was there, looking unfamiliar in field grey, but oh so familiar with his thick fair hair and wide shoulders.

"I couldn't find you!"

"In the restaurant."

The one place she hadn't looked. His arms were round her and she pressed against his coat, hugging him, terrified that it might be the last time she would ever see him.

"Malie, I love you so much!"

Karoly, Karoly. Papa would never understand. Poor, poor Papa.

"I sent a message," she told him. "I said . . . I said I would pray for you."

"I love you so much, Malie."

"And I you."

"Don't let him separate us. Promise me you will remember me."

"Oh, Karoly!" She was laughing and crying—laughing because here, in this terrible railway station, she was able to say what she liked without fear or inhibition. "I would come with you now if I could."

"A camp follower!" He hugged her to him again, wrapping her in his arms and lifting her a little so that her cheek was against his.

"I'll wait," she said. "No matter what Papa says or does. I'll wait."

Csardas

A NOVEL BY

Diane Pearson

A FAWCETT CREST BOOK

· Fawcett Publications, Inc., Greenwich, Connecticut

CSARDAS

A Fawcett Crest Book reprinted by arrangement with J. B. Lippincott Company

Copyright © 1975 by Diane Pearson

ISBN 0-449-22885-1

Selection of the Literary Guild, September 1975

Printed in the United States of America

First printing: July 1976

10 9 8 7 6 5 4 3 2 1

To
Nicholas Vilag, dear friend,
who inspired and encouraged me
to write this book

Csardas

Author's Note

For a writer to tackle a subject in which the country, social background, and temperament of the people are outside his or her inherent knowledge is the height of impertinence. But writers are impertinent. They also frequently become obsessed by themes outside their own experience, and once a writer is obsessed there is nothing to do but give way and indulge the obsession. *Csardas* is the result of my obsession.

The title (the cs is pronounced *ch* as in *church,* the s at the end is *sh,* as in *brush;* thus, phonetically, *chardash*) came to me while watching a very old couple dancing this courtship dance at a village in the mountains of northern Hungary. The old man was very tall, very thin; his wife—dressed in the black skirt and kerchief of the country people—was a diminutive little lady who was as wide as she was high and who barely came up to her husband's chest. They should have looked incongruous and funny together but they were neither, and such was their grace that soon the younger and more energetic dancers stopped to watch and finally applaud. The faces of the old people were marked by years of harsh living—two world wars, innumerable revolutions, foreign occupation, in addition to the general hardship of just being poor (the lot of the Hungarian peasant has never been an easy one)—but as I watched I suddenly saw them, fifty years back, as they once had been: a strong, handsome young man and a neat little brown-eyed peasant girl. And between that young couple and the old people now before me lay the whole brave, bloody, dignified, cruel story of the Hungarian people.

To list everyone who has helped me with this book would be impossible, and indeed, perhaps they would not wish to be listed, for *Csardas* may not be the kind of book they had finally envisaged. So I just offer my warm and heartfelt thanks to the friends I made in Hungary who, in every walk of life, gave me unstinting help and the most generous of hospitality. On my visits there (made as a lone traveller and without any official guide), I found nothing but kindness and a desire to help. Somehow the language barrier was bridged—mostly because nearly all the Hungarians I met were fluent in two or three tongues—and I returned with a notebook full of personal reminiscences from people of all ages, not big reminiscences of epic history (they can be gleaned from the history books) but tiny details of a first ball dress, of a peasant child walking barefoot to school through the snow, of an old coachman who used to fascinate two small boys with wild tales of the Prussian wars.

I have, for ease of reading, left out all the accents over Hungarian words and have also anglicized some of the more difficult names. I hope the Hungarians will forgive me for mutilating their language, and I hope, also, they will forgive any errors I may unwittingly have made. With research and constant questioning I have endeavoured to make the book as authentic as possible, but undoubtedly something will have slipped through.

The bibliography at the end of the book lists my main source references for the historical background, but I want particularly to mention Paul Ignotus's *Hungary*. In a wealth of reading I found this account to be the most balanced and also the wittiest (Hungary may be brave and bloody, but it has never lacked a sense of humour). Mr. Ignotus, a scholar and historian, was also kind enough to indulge my craving for personal reminiscences.

And finally I must mention, with warmth and gratitude, the man who inspired *Csardas,* who during the four years it has taken to research and write it gave me constant encouragement and patiently answered a huge variety of questions, ranging from the effect of the *Anschluss* to what he ate for breakfast as a little boy. To Nicholas Vilag, my dear friend, I say a particularly warm thank-you. You should really have written this book yourself, but as you wouldn't, I have done the best I could.

DIANE PEARSON
September, 1974

demie, his mother had acquired yet a little more money—result of years of frugality—which she had invested quite wisely. There was enough for his fees and for a small bachelor apartment in Budapest, and also enough to buy back a small section of the land she had been forced to sell.

Her hopes, alas, were not to be fully realized. Since Felix did not appear to enjoy military life and continually failed every exam, she was obviously wasting her money. The only other career open to a son of the nobility was local administration. A further large sum of money was paid as a bribe, and Felix was given a senior position in the land registration office of the county town. Madame Kaldy was a little disappointed, but on the whole it worked out fairly well. The apartment in town cost less than the one in Budapest, and Felix received a salary, which meant he didn't require quite such a large allowance from the strained family resources. In addition—as his duties were mostly carried out by a team of underpaid but reasonably efficient clerks—his long absences from the county offices were taken as a natural part of a young nobleman's behaviour. His sojourns from his office were, more often than not, spent in the company of his mama, whom he loved dearly. She had never refused him anything, and she was strong and resolute and the foundation on which his life rested. Occasionally he visited Budapest but found it had little to offer that his own county town did not. In Budapest he didn't know so many people, the balls and parties were more impersonal, the girls more demanding. In his own small town everyone knew who he was and liked him. He could sit for a whole morning in the cafés drinking coffee with his friends, and almost every passer-by would be someone he knew, with whom he could smile and bow and exchange pleasantries. The wine was just as good as in Budapest. The girls were friendlier and more relaxed. And in recent years he had sometimes been able to persuade his mama to come and share his apartment for the winter months, for since Adam had taken over the management of the farm, she had begun to emerge slightly from her impecunious isolation.

Felix, as well as adoring his mama, was also quite fond of his brother. Adam was a good, if dull, old thing, and Felix enjoyed showing him the town when he came up on his monthly visits to buy supplies for the farm. He tried to see that Adam had a good time—took him to the cafés to join the leisurely society there, encouraged him to attend any balls or parties to which he, Felix, had been invited—but Adam was, regretta-

bly, something of a bore and never quite fitted th[...]
he was with. He had no lighthearted conversation
awkward and silent in the presence of young w[...]
thought it was all the result of the Calvinist scho[...]
attended.

At the time that Felix had gone to share his cousin's tutor,
Madame Kaldy had decided that Adam would have to be
trained to contribute to the maintenance and reinstatement of
the family wealth and position. She could afford to raise only
one son as a nobleman; the other must work for his living
and, indeed, work for the living of them all. Adam, having attended the local elementary school until he was ten years old,
had then been sent to the nearest available *Gymnasium*. The
Kaldys were Catholic by birth, and Felix, in the house of his
cousin, was taught the niceties and elegances of that religion.
Madame Kaldy had hesitated only a little when registering
Adam at the Calvinist grammar school but expediency decided her; the Calvinist school could be reached by pony each
day, and Adam was needed to help on the farm before and
after school. To go to the Catholic *Gymnasium* meant permanent absence during term time and also extra payment for
board. Adam, therefore, from the ages of ten to eighteen, rose
at six every morning, supervised milking and the handing out
of grain and meal, ensured that the carters were sent on their
way, then mounted his pony and rode five miles to school.
After school he came home, once more supervised milking,
checked the daily tallies, took part in the allocation of the
morrow's tasks, ate his supper, did his homework, and went to
bed. During the summer holidays he worked at the harvest:
first the grain harvest, then the hay, then the fruit and pepper
crop. Felix always came home for short visits in the summer,
and occasionally he too, in smooth leather boots and a soft
linen shirt, would go out into the fields and toss a few bales up
onto a stack. The summers were always good for Adam.
When Felix was home their mama was happier. She smiled a
lot, was more relaxed, and there was a holiday air about the
farm, even though the work was just as hard.

At eighteen Adam took his *Abiturium* and passed brilliantly, so brilliantly that the director called on Madame Kaldy
and suggested the Imperial Staff College in Vienna or, failing
that, the study of law and economics at the university in Budapest. Madame Kaldy listened with icy courtesy, then informed him that her younger son would attend the Agricultural College in Budapest, as already arranged. He was to be

boarded with the respectable family of a bank clerk for a minimum fee and the promise of free holidays on the farm for the clerk's wife and four children. The transaction was mutually agreeable, lasted for three years, and Madame Kaldy never for one moment during those years entertained the idea that Adam also might enjoy a bachelor apartment in the city.

When he finally returned with his agricultural diploma, she dismissed the farm manager, handed the supervision of the land to Adam, and set about her own financial transactions, which involved cautious investments and the buying back, metre by metre, of the land that once was her husband's and soon must be Felix's.

From her younger son she demanded nothing but diligence and family loyalty. From her elder son she demanded love and also an awareness that the land—this land she had struggled to hold for so long—was Kaldy property, *his* property. She had his love in abundance; how could he not adore a mama who gave him everything he wanted? His awareness of the land was sometimes apathetic. Every time she bought back a small patch of forest or meadows, he was supposed to visit and gloat and stride round the boundaries of their increasing estate. Every new innovation that Adam introduced on the farm was supposed to be approved and noted by Felix, although—as he explained to her—he didn't care at all for soil and pigs and cattle. But he was an easygoing young man who liked to please everyone if he could, and whenever his mama sent for him he came. He listened when she spoke, sometimes rather fiercely, about *his* land and *his* cattle and *his* forests, and then he would say something like "Darling Mama! How hard you have worked for us both. But now you must learn to rest a little, to spend some time with your son who loves you so much. So come now, Mama, drive with me a little, or come to stay with me in town. I would like to take my darling mama to the elegant parties, to the theatre, to the dressmaker and milliner."

And Madame Kaldy would, for a moment, look nonplussed and worried; then, as Felix stroked her hand and smiled and told her little jokes and fragments of gossip about the society of the town, she would relax and promise to come and stay with him in the winter.

So now he was here again—in April; oh, really!—and all because Adam and Mama were excited about a stretch of land which had just been bought back and that Adam was going to plant with a new crop. He had dutifully ridden round the fields, admired the ground, the beet seed, and the new machine that Adam, with his college ideas, was using to sow it. He had spent hours chatting with Mama. He had ridden, with Adam, to the adjoining farms to extend invitations to watch the new machine working. He had read a couple of novels and also the intellectual magazine *Nyugat* which everyone in Budapest café circles had been talking about for a long time but which he had never found time to study before. He went to sleep over the novels and found he could make nothing of *Nyugat*, which he dismissed as clever and literary. He was just dozing into a bored but pleasant sleep when he heard the sound of a carriage arriving. There was a soft flurry of chatter on the steps and then—with delight—he heard the crisp tones of Madame Gizelli Racs-Rassay. He pulled on his coat and hurried into the reception-room, and when he saw not only Madame Gizelli (whom he rather liked) but also the enchanting Ferenc girls his welcome was unfeigned and overwhelming.

"Madame Gizelli!" he cried, bending gracefully over her hand in a warm, eloquent movement. "And Eva and Amalia! How wonderful, how very wonderful. I cannot tell you; the countryside has been so dull. I have missed my friends and our little parties in town. Now we shall be able to make some entertainment—cards, perhaps." He suddenly noticed that Madame Gizelli was looking very angry, and then he saw Kati hiding behind her cousins. Swiftly he clasped her hand with apologetic charm. "Forgive me, Kati. But in a room so full of charming ladies I must be forgiven for overlooking one of them."

Kati flushed, looked awkward, mumbled, "Hullo, Felix," and then stared at the floor. Her mother tweaked unnecessarily hard at the twisted collar of Kati's coat.

"Stand up straight, Kati," she hissed. "What will Madame Kaldy think if you continue to hunch like a peasant woman?"

She was unusually harsh, even for Aunt Gizi, and the girls were suddenly horrified to see Kati's eyes fill with tears. She could not possibly cry now, not in Madame Kaldy's house! It would be too embarrassing. Amalia hurried over and drew Kati to one side. They sat together on a couch by the window and, while Kati swallowed hard and fought for self-control, Amalia stared out at the yard and the fields.

It was not the prettiest of farms. The fields were flat and utilitarian. There *were* fruit trees, but instead of growing in a lush abundance of waste—like their own beautiful Ferenc orchard—they were lined up along the sides of the tracks and looked like rows of tin tacks set round the fields. There was no garden to the farmhouse and the furniture inside was an incongruous mixture of peasant-made objects and beautiful antiques salvaged from Madame Kaldy's better days.

Every field and corner of soil that Amalia could see from her window seat was ploughed in geometric lines that stretched into the monotonous distance. She watched the tiny human specks of the peasants labouring over the sowing, saw one of the specks begin to move towards the house, watched it grow and finally turn into Adam Kaldy. She covered Kati's small, tightly clenched fists with her own hand and whispered, "Look, Kati. Adam is coming," and, as Kati looked up, insecure, defenceless, she addded, "Don't be upset. I'm sure your mama didn't mean to be unkind."

Kati nodded, unbelieving, and swayed closer to Malie, pressing up against her side as though seeking security from the touch of her cousin's body. Sometimes it irritated Malie the way Kati, after a kind word or a little offered comfort, would cling to her. Sometimes she wanted to pull away, but she never did. She always managed to remember that Kati had very few gestures of affection offered to her. Her papa gave her only the occasional duty kiss and her mama never touched her unless it was to straighten her clothes or jerk her shoulders back.

Adam ran up the steps to the door and came into the room. His face was dirty and he smelled of something faintly unpleasant, pigs or cows. He went to shake hands with Eva, then flushed, turned to Aunt Gizi, flushed again, and said, "I'm dirty. Excuse me. I shall wash."

When he came back Madame Kaldy—cool, slight, and with thick braids of black hair wound round her head—was presiding over a small table set with teapot, sugar and lemon. Adam took Aunt Gizi's hand in his, rather too heartily, and nodded brusquely at the three girls. It was hard to believe that he and Felix had hatched from the same nest.

"How is your mama?" asked Madame Kaldy, handing tea to Eva.

"She's . . . she has a headache this afternoon."

Madame Kaldy pursed her lips in disapproval. "I see." She poured, handed, poured, handed, without seeming to move her body at all. "No doubt when her . . . headache has gone she will call." She stared hard at Eva. "You are like your mama. I remember Marta Bogozy. I remember her very well.

We were girls together. I remember her when she was so poor she had to wear the same ball gown for every occasion." Her expressionless eyes ran over Eva's glossy black hair and the voluptuous tiny figure in the rose-coloured dress. "She wore her clothes too tight as well," she added coldly.

Eva sparkled hatred at Madame Kaldy. "My mama had no need of new dresses. She was so beautiful it did not matter what she wore. And now . . . now she has as many ball gowns as she wishes." She stared pointedly at Madame Kaldy's plain grey serge dress, but the older woman had long ago discarded any female vanity and was not hurt by Eva's gibe.

"Not all the dresses paid for either, I hear," she countered dryly.

Again the atmosphere of the room was charged with disagreeable tension. Eva bit her lip and stared hard at her cup. Aunt Gizi appeared to be gratified. Adam made a slight move towards Eva, stopped, and stood rather lost and out of place holding a teacup in his hand.

Amalia, with her arm round Kati's shoulders, was suddenly grateful for their own warm, careless, silly, indulgent mama. Aunt Gizi and Madame Kaldy, two successful, clever women who had the rare gift of making fortunes for their families, also had the gift of deliberately hurting those around them with their astringent tongues and sharp wits. Mama—so foolish, so constantly in debt, so selfish in a thoughtless casual way—would never have said the things that Aunt Gizi and Madame Kaldy had said this afternoon.

"I wondered . . . that is—" Adam coughed and began again. "Would Eva and Amalia . . . would they care to see the farm—the new crop and my seeding machine? The ground is dry and they could walk along the tracks with comfort."

"Splendid!" Amalia jumped to her feet and buttoned her coat, relieved to get out of the house for a few moments. Eva immediately recovered from her bout with Madame Kaldy. She tilted her head towards Felix and gazed at him from beneath long dark lashes.

"Felix," she commanded lightly, "I demand an instant tour of your estate. I want to see *everything*. I shall want a full description of every building and field on the farm."

"Eva, my darling girl!" Both his mother and Aunt Gizi frowned. "I hate to lose your regard, but I don't think I know what every building and field is for!"

"Then you must make it up," said Eva gaily. She was on her feet and had somehow manoeuvred Felix to the door. As they left the room Aunt Gizi was propelling Kati after them. "It will do you good to walk, Kati. You have been sitting down all day." Stubbornly Kati held back, pushing against her mother's arm until Amalia came and joined her.

"Come, Kati," she said quietly, hating Aunt Gizi and wanting to slap Eva for some inexplicable reason.

Outside they set off across the yard. Felix and Eva were in front, arm in arm, dancing lightly across the ground, bending their heads close and talking in silly affected tones interposed with paroxysms of laughter that echoed across the fields. Adam, with Amalia and Kati, one on each side, stumped solidly behind.

"They're so beautiful together, aren't they?" said Kati without envy. "Like two bright birds skimming over the fields. Do you think they know how beautiful they are?"

"I'm quite sure Eva does," said Malie dryly, and then wondered if she was becoming as sour as the two middle-aged women she had just left behind.

They passed the stables and the granaries and then moved onto the track, the bright dresses of the girls giving life to the brown landscape, Eva's rose dress most of all. Amalia noticed that Adam didn't once take his eyes from Eva's slim darting form, and she felt the same pity for him that she felt for Kati.

"Eva is . . . very young, Adam," she said guardedly. "She is young, even for seventeen." She was trying to warn him, tell him that Eva would never, not once, consider including him in the circle of gay young men who constantly surrounded her. Adam turned his face towards her and stared. Vaguely surprised, she noticed what fine eyes he had—she had never really looked at Adam, not properly—they were green, a deep hazel green, set well apart, intelligent, and in some strange way very soft and kind.

"Felix is not good for her," he said, his tone almost disinterested. "Felix is not good for anyone. He is very gay, a splendid fellow to sit in the cafés with, but he is not good for Eva."

Silence descended on the awkward trio, a silence that was emphasized because of the noisy hilarity of the pair in front. Amalia felt a pang of envy because Eva was enjoying herself with a man she adored. She suddenly felt tired of behaving and being grown-up and having to comfort Kati and rebuke Eva. She felt she would like to be walking along with a young man, laughing and flirting, just the way Eva was doing with Felix.

"Kati," she said without thinking, "there was a young man at your party, a hussar from the garrison. Karoly Vilaghy, I think he was called. I never saw him before." She had been unable to ask until now. She didn't want Kati or Eva to share her idle interest. Kati would look longingly at her, dying to share her beautiful cousin's innermost dreams, and Eva would want to giggle and plot. Amalia wasn't sure quite what she thought about the young lieutenant, but whatever she thought —felt—it was private and not to be destroyed by the tongues of her relatives. But now, with Eva prancing along beside Felix and Adam gazing wistfully after her, her usual discretion deserted her. Kati's reaction nearly ruined everything.

"Oh, Malie! Do you like him?"

Malie stiffened. "I don't know him. How can I say if I like him? I just wondered who he was."

Kati's pale eyes fixed themselves onto Malie's face. "He's a cousin of Papa's," she said eagerly. "They're very poor. Papa says they don't even have enough to eat, and Karoly has nothing but his pay to live on. Their background isn't all that good either, Mama says; some of the connections on Grandmother's side are doubtful and the only reason Karoly got a commission was because he passed so high as a cadet. Papa feels sorry for him; he says he won't achieve anything unless he marries well. Certainly his family would never be able to pay the army's marriage fee if he married someone poor."

"I see." She stared straight ahead.

"Would you like me to ask Papa if he can come to the villa for the summer?"

"Of course not. Don't be so stupid, Kati."

Adam turned and stared at her again; this time the gentle green eyes were disapproving and surprised. She was startled —at herself, not him. How could she have spoken to Kati like that, poor, stupid, irritating Kati?

"Oh, Kati, I'm sorry. I didn't mean it."

"That's all right," said Kati stolidly, but she was hurt. Both Amalia and Adam could tell she was hurt.

Adam put his arm round her shoulders and hugged her. "Come along, Kati," he said gruffly. "Let me show you my splendid new seeder that is going to make the fortunes of us all. Felix isn't interested, and Eva certainly won't look at a machine when Felix is there. I shall have to hope that you will pretend to be enthusiastic about it."

Kati's face wreathed into a smile at the affection and attention. Kati-like she leaned into his shoulder. "I shan't have to pretend, Adam," she said stoutly. "I know I shall love it."

Still with his arm around her shoulder, they turned left, along a track that led to a vast expanse of field where two oxen were drawing a weird contraption of metal tubes and a large wooden box. Eva and Felix didn't even notice the diversion. They were so absorbed in each other that they continued straight down the path towards the river. Disgruntled and annoyed, Amalia found herself excluded from both parties, left to follow whichever couple she wished.

"What a perfectly miserable day," she muttered to herself as, after a moment's consideration, she stumped after Kati and Adam. "What a horrible spring and summer it is going to be."

4

There was a curious sense of unease at the garrison. Karoly, in referring to his comrades as irresponsible rakes, had in truth given a fairly accurate description of the young aristocrats who gambled, hunted, and acquired debts while in the service of the Austro-Hungarian army. But even the wildest and most dilettante of his brother officers seemed, during the spring of 1914, to be held under a pall of nervous anticipation, as though waiting for something.

There was no reason—no obvious reason—for the tenseness that possessed them all. Serbia had frightened the Empire over the past two years by daring to prove her strength as a soldier nation. She had succeeded in vanquishing what was left of the mighty Turkish empire and had, indeed, begun to look north and west for an extension of her territories. Karoly, together with his fellows, had been involved in the preparatory moves of the army to keep Serbia from carving out a piece of the Adriatic coastline for herself. It had been prevented, not without distress on the part of the Empire, but it had been prevented. It seemed at last as though everyone's touchy tempers had been assuaged and possible war averted. There should be no further trouble.

And yet the sense of waiting continued. Karoly inspected men and horses, conducted manoeuvres, attended parades, and did more than his share of paperwork. And all the time he wondered what it was they were awaiting.

He had few friends in the regiment—friends meant drinking together, whoring together, hunting together, and he could not afford these pursuits. Neither could his colleagues, but they usually had a family to rescue them at the last moment from the usurers. Those who were not rescued either resigned their commissions or shot themselves. He was not prepared for either of those alternatives. With a few of his brother officers, the more intelligent and moderate ones, he exchanged a form of friendly acquaintanceship. With one, Count Stefan Tilsky, a Pole, he was slightly more intimate. They did not play together (for Stefan played very hard indeed), but their duties often brought them into contact and they worked well, and occasionally—when Stefan was recovering from a surfeit of wild living—they rode together for no more than the pleasure of riding in the open air on their excellent Lipizzan horses.

It was Stefan he asked about the Ferenc girls, tentatively, feigning a disinterest which didn't for one moment delude the wily Pole.

"Ha!" shouted Stefan gleefully as they walked their mounts through a small oak wood on the outskirts of the town. "You too, Vilaghy. You too have fallen prey to the town's chief antidote to boredom, the enchanting Ferenc sisters."

Karoly smiled with good humour. "Ferenc?" he queried.

Stefan shrugged. "Parvenus, of course, but splendid if you are looking for a wealthy wife and not a pedigree. My father would burst an artery were I to suggest marrying one of them. The father is a Jew—banking, I believe. The mother was a Bogozy—good family but no money."

He turned his head and looked at Karoly with narrowed eyes.

"Could do very well for you, my friend. They're pretty girls, bright, too. Which one has taken your fancy, the little dark one who flirts or the tall one with the hazel eyes?"

Karoly smiled again, rather tightly, but determined not to behave foolishly over what was—after all—just a pretty, provincial, middle-class young woman. "I'm not even sure which is which," he lied. "One is Eva, yes? The other I don't know —not her name."

"Eva's the little one," said Stefan jovially. "Great spirit and style, but I think could be something of a handful as a wife. For my money, if you want to treat the matter seriously, you'd take the other one—Amalia. Smiles a lot, but quieter, gentler. I say!" His face began to grow animated as he involved himself in Karoly's domestic affairs. "Look here, my friend, it could well be the answer for you. Old man Ferenc—bit of a tyrant from all one hears—would need some handling, but he could afford to pay the marriage fee for you. Oh. Sorry!" He looked suddenly embarrassed at his lapse of manners in referring to Karoly's financial difficulties. "But—well, I know how it is with you. It would help, wouldn't it? And then you've a great advantage in getting to know the girls; you've a head start over the rest of us."

"How?" He frowned.

Stefan guffawed, then patted his horse as the beast shied at the unexpected sound. "She's a relative of yours, in a manner of speaking. Didn't you say that Racs-Rassay was a distant cousin?" Karoly nodded. "The Ferenc girls are his nieces. Madame Racs-Rassay was a Ferenc before she married." Again his eyes narrowed. "That's another possibility for you, the ugly little Racs-Rassay girl. Excellent family on her father's side, better than the Bogozys or the—"

He stopped, flushed very red indeed, and bent forward unncessarily to fumble with the girth, and Karoly knew, without any doubt, that his friend had been going to add the name Vilaghy to the list of families whose backgrounds were tinged with query.

"Perhaps not," Stefan said when his embarrassment had subsided. "For all she's the plainest and dullest creature I ever set eyes on, I imagine her papa will be expecting a good match. She's something of an heiress. With all that money and the Racs-Rassay name, she has no need to worry about a Jewish mama."

Karoly suddenly found Stefan's conversation in bad taste. He was a kind enough fellow, but his cold-blooded assessment of Karoly's marriage prospects was slightly offensive.

"Shall we race?" he asked coolly. "Twenty korona to the winner?"

A faint spasm of surprise crossed Stefan's face; then he nodded, realizing why Karoly had felt the need to challenge him and stake money on the outcome. He counted to three, then touched his spurs to his horse. Karoly knew his friend would pay him the respect of not holding back. The race would be a true test of horsemanship.

When he received the invitation from Cousin Alfred to

visit the villa up in the hills for the summer, he went straight to the commanding officer for leave of absence. He had taken no leave for two years and assumed it would be granted without question. He was unprepared for his colonel's hesitancy.

"Not too happy," the senior officer mumbled, picking slightly at his moustache. "Like to keep the garrison intact if possible. Never know what might happen."

Karoly's military instincts, born of years of sensing when a regimental move was imminent, were immediately aroused.

"Are there orders coming through, sir?" he asked respectfully.

The elder man shook his head. "No reason to stop you from going. Leave due, most certainly. But there's a feeling. . . . Everything's quiet at the moment—Serbia quiet, Russia quiet—but still, a feeling."

"Yes, sir. I know."

The old man looked at him sharply. "Do the men feel it, Vilaghy?"

"I think so, sir."

"Hmm." He fiddled with the pen and inkwell. "The General Staff are increasing the intake of recruits. Did you know that?"

"I had heard so, sir."

The colonel grunted again and stared out of the window. A line of hussars were wheeling across the parade-ground in ceremonial display, rehearsing for the regiment's summer celebrations. They looked smart and efficient; the horses were magnificent and the men in perfect control.

"You want to visit your cousin, Racs-Rassay, I hear? Up in the mountains?"

"Yes, sir."

The colonel put his pen down. "Yes, well, mustn't behave like old women. Seeing Serbs behind every cautionary move from headquarters. Any trouble and you'll be recalled at once. Leave granted."

"Thank you, sir."

He saluted, clicked heels again, turned, and left the office. He was disconcerted at the degree of informality with which the colonel had spoken to a very junior officer. His leave had been granted and he should have felt pleased and elated. Several weeks in his cousin's luxurious villa, with the strong possibility of seeing Amalia Ferenc again, should have filled him with gratified satisfaction. Instead he felt, once more, the vague sense of disquiet that hung over the garrison.

5

For the little boys it was the best spring and summer they had ever known, and mostly it was because Papa was not there.

They spent much of their time haunting Roza in the kitchen, waiting for cream bowls to lick, for pieces of strudel to pick up from the floor, for honey cakes to steal straight from the oven. Outside were the dogs, and the new lambs and calves, and the orchard to race in and the river to fall in, and there was no one to punish them or shut them in their room.

They were with the people they loved most: Mama, who (when Papa was away) let them do just as they pleased provided they didn't give her a headache; Eva, who was pretty but who, like Mama, didn't always welcome their presence; and Malie, their beloved Malie, who helped them up into trees, who took off her shoes and stockings and paddled with them, who took them on picnics up in the hills, and who—above all —that summer discovered the Meadow.

That was the very best day of summer, the day they discovered the Meadow. Mama had announced on the previous evening that, provided her headache was better in the morning, they would all go for a picnic on the following day. Uncle Sandor would drive them into the mountains, and they would cook a meal, just like gypsies, out in the open over a fire. At first they had been excited, shouting and thumping each other, but when Uncle Sandor's name had been mentioned they had become subdued and silent. They had never confessed, not even to each other, how afraid they were of Uncle Sandor— not in the same way they were afraid of Papa; that was a fear, they sensed, in spite of their years, that was shared by all the family and servants, a fear that had been with them since birth and which they took for granted. No, the fear of Uncle Sandor was more spine-chilling, more supernatural than the fear of Papa. It was like the feeling they had when the housemaid, who came from Transylvania, told them stories about giants and werewolves. Uncle Sandor was huge and black: black boots, black moustache, black eyes, and black hair all over his arms and the backs of his hands. Even the horses he drove were black. And Uncle Sandor rarely spoke; he growled and grunted, and he glared at them when they misbehaved in the coach. Once, when they were very small and were annoying Eva by pulling her curls, she had told them that Uncle Sandor would eat them if they were naughty, and pulling her hair was very naughty. They hadn't taken any notice at the time—Eva was always saying things like that when she didn't get her own way—but the next time they were in the coach they had both stared at Uncle Sandor's huge back beneath the red and black *mente* of his hussar's uniform, and a shudder that started in the soles of their shoes had spread rapidly upwards, completely enveloping them. Neither of them had ever seen Uncle Sandor smile, but they had a horrifying notion that if he did the parting of his lips would reveal long, sharp, pointed teeth.

When Mama suggested the picnic, they were torn between the delight of going into the mountains and living like gypsies and the fear of having Uncle Sandor with them for a whole day. Mama had looked puzzled.

"Don't you want to go?"

"Yes, Mama."

Amalia had grinned and whispered something to Mama, who laughed (how pretty Mama was when she laughed) and said that of course Uncle Sandor would stay with the horses when they arrived and wouldn't follow them to their picnic spot. That was better. They didn't mind Uncle Sandor in the distance with the coach and horses. It was just the thought of being alone with him in the mountains.

They stood on the chairs in Roza's kitchen and watched her packing up the box: a thick woven red-and-black cloth, a big jar of goulash and a pot to heat it in, a jar of sweet-and-sour green beans and another of stuffed cabbage, two long loaves of white bread still warm from the oven, a crock of nut cakes, milk, cups, plates, spoons, and a wet cloth for wiping sticky hands after eating.

"Just like gypsies!" gloated Leo, and then, "Roza, can we carry the box out into the yard?"

"Bim bim bim!" cried Roza. "Such impatience! How can two such little men get that heavy box from the table?"

Puffing and red-faced they tried, determined to punish Roza for calling them little men, and finally by using the chairs (and with a little secret help from Roza) the box was on the floor. "Now," said Jozsef, assuming the authority of the elder, "out into the yard." The box was pushed, pulled, and kicked across the floor. At the foot of the steps they paused. Leo looked as though he were going to burst and one of Jozsef's stockings was hanging round his ankle. "You can rest now, Leo," he panted graciously, and then they both froze because coming down the steps was a huge pair of black boots. Uncle Sandor didn't say a word. He just stopped and lifted the box as though it were made of paper, then stumped up into the yard.

It was glorious outside. They took the track leading from the back of the farm, through yet another acacia wood, and the sun shining through the lace of the young leaves made a dappled pattern on the backs of the moving horses. Then they came to the road where the women from the village curtsied; then, when they had left the village, Uncle Sandor turned the coach onto a track that became steadily steeper and darker, screened on each side by beech and oak trees and with outcroppings of rock hanging over the path.

Finally the track came to a clearing where sunlight lit a patch of new grass. Uncle Sandor turned into the clearing and stopped.

"Now," said Amalia, "we must look for a place to have our picnic. Not too far from the coach, but up a little into the trees."

Mama said she would wait until they had found the perfect spot, and the four of them, one small boy to each sister, began to climb up through the forest. And it was Amalia who found the Meadow that was to become so important to them that summer.

It was a tiny, flat area, hidden from below and surrounded by trees, a secret meadow full of buttercups and with a stream running at one side. Someone had discovered it before because just by the stream a place to light a fire had been built from the grey mountain stone. They raced back to the coach, and Uncle Sandor brought up the box. Then he collected wood, lit the fire, and went to sit at the edge of the meadow on his own.

"Is he going to stay there?" asked Leo grudgingly as the smell of goulash began to pervade the mountain air.

"Just until he has eaten."

"Who will take his food to him?"

"You will," said Eva brightly. "You and Jozsef will take his food to him, and Mama and Amalia and I shall go for a walk and leave you." Two white faces turned and stared at her, and Eva suddenly exploded into laughter. "I hope there's enough

77

goulash for Uncle Sandor," she continued wickedly. "Who knows what he may eat if he gets hungry enough?"

Jozsef swallowed hard. He was the elder, and besides, he felt sure that Eva *must* be teasing. A quick glance at his brother showed that Leo's face had turned very red and his plump cheeks were beginning to quiver.

"Oh, Eva, really!" said Mama crossly. "You shouldn't be so unkind. Now see what you have done. I shall go home if the boys begin to cry. My poor head couldn't bear it."

Malie put an arm around each of them. "When we have eaten," she whispered, "you and I, just the three of us, will go high into the mountains, as high as we can, and I will show which way is Russia and which way is Austria, where the King lives. Perhaps we shall even be able to see a castle."

Amalia, and the plates of goulash, made things sane again. Eva took a large plate of food over to Uncle Sandor and the boys watched very carefully to see what he would do. Uncle Sandor pulled a brown kerchief over the knee of his trousers and took the plate from Eva. Then he proceeded to eat. From this distance it was impossible to see his teeth.

After the food, Mama and Eva went to sleep in the sun. Amalia put her straw hat on again and began to lead them up through the forest, through a just discernible path. There were rustlings on either side, and once they surprised a pair of pheasants which sprang up, shrieking, in front of them. They found the small black body of a dead mole, its hands curled close to its face, and Jozsef discovered a stone shaped like a dog's head. It was a good track and it led to a promontory of rock from where they could see stretch after stretch of mountains all covered in oak forests.

"There. That way is Russia," said Malie, pointing. "If you could walk for long enough, up and over the hills and through the rivers and marshes, you would come to Russia."

They stared for a moment, then became bored and wriggled away from Amalia, chasing off into the trees. "Don't go far, boys!" she cried, but they only giggled and Jozsef made a rude noise with his mouth.

"We'll wait until she goes to sleep—grown-ups always go to sleep—and then we will jump out on her." he said with relish.

They watched her yawn, sit down with her back against a rock, and close her eyes. They waited a moment, then jumped —roaring—out of the trees. But before they came close to her a man in a uniform like Uncle Sandor's walked into the clearing from the track. He ignored them and walked straight up to Amalia. They waited, afraid both for themselves and for Malie, to see what he was going to do. He did nothing—no, not quite nothing, for he smiled a little sheepishly at her and nodded as though they had met before.

"We rode up after your coach," he said, very dignified, and yet there was something shy about him. "Your mama and your sister told me you had come this way through the forest."

Malie stood up. She was awkward—most un-Malie-like—and she began to brush grass and dirt from her skirt.

"Do you remember my name? Do you remember seeing me before?"

"Karoly Vilaghy. At Kati's birthday party."

"I am staying with Cousin Alfred. We called on you this morning, just after you had left for your picnic. Your aunt and Cousin Kati are back in the clearing, with your mother."

Amalia picked an ant from her skirt. "Oh," she said foolishly.

The boys grew bored again. The soldier, in spite of the Uncle Sandor uniform, was harmless, and he and Malie were obviously not going to do anything interesting. Jozsef pushed Leo onto the ground and began to stuff leaves down his neck. Leo roared, surfaced, and chased his brother into the trees.

"You are not to go too far away, boys," Malie cried. "Play close to the track."

They didn't answer. They peered through the trees and saw that she had sat down again, very prim and upright this time. The soldier was beside her, lounging on the earth in spite of his smart red trousers.

Jozsef discovered a hoard of last year's acorns and cups. They had a race to see who could collect the largest number and then they stood on opposite sides of the track (Jozsef was the Austrian army and Leo the Prussian) and hurled them at each other. After a while they saw a glimmer of white through the trees. Malie was walking very slowly down the track with the soldier. They were talking softly, and Leo and Jozsef waited behind the bole of a tree.

"Brrrraah!" they shouted, jumping out. Malie jumped and looked suddenly very cross, so cross that Leo went up and burrowed in her skirt.

"Why don't you run on and find Eva and Kati," she said impatiently. She turned to the soldier and smiled, and Leo

79

was instantly jealous. He moved round to walk between her and the soldier, holding her hand and trying to push her away from the hussar.

"You're pushing me off the track, Leo!"

"I love you, Malie," he said fiercely, glaring at the soldier.

Malie looked down at him, sighing, and then she said kindly, "All right, Leo, you can walk with us if you want to."

He hated the soldier. They had been having a lovely day until he came. He waited until Malie was looking in the other direction and then he pulled a horrible face at the lieutenant, the one where he crossed his eyes and blew his cheeks and nostrils out. When he did it to the dogs they ran away.

"That's quite enough of *that*," said Karoly Vilaghy, and Leo found himself swinging through the air, right up onto the soldier's head. He could see for miles! He could see right down the track into the Meadow and over the trees in three directions.

"I can see the world!" he shouted gleefully to Jozsef, and at once Jozsef began to pummel the soldier's legs and say it was his turn. It had become a good day again.

When they arrived back at the Meadow there was a lot of tedious grown-up conversation with Aunt Gizi and Kati, all about who was related to who and what kind of plans they could make for the summer. Eva flirted with the soldier, and Amalia stood about looking silly with a permanent smile on her face.

They raced away to the stream, had a fight over the dog-shaped stone, fell in, and had to be hauled out by Karoly Vilaghy.

"It is time we went home," said Mama wearily. "Any more of this and my migraine will come back."

Everything was packed into the box. Uncle Sandor came over, lifted it to one shoulder, and vanished into the trees. The late-afternoon sun was warm and golden and they were relaxed, all of them, even Aunt Gizi, and full of the lethargic gentleness of a summer afternoon. The leaves on the trees were small and green, the grass was crisp and new, and all around them it smelled of things growing. Even Uncle Sandor must have sensed the summer for he drove very slowly and didn't growl at all when he had to stop and let the boys take turn and turn about between the coach and a ride on Karoly Vilaghy's grey horse.

Leo was asleep when they arrived home. Karoly lifted him

down from the coach, and he woke up enough to say, "What a *lovely* picnic it was, Malie. Can we go again next week?"

Malie hesitated, smiled, then said, "We'll go as often as we can . . . until Papa comes."

They went many times to the Meadow, sometimes as often as three or four times a week. Once they had a great big picnic with Uncle Alfred, Aunt Gizi and Kati, and Felix and Adam Kaldy, and two servants to make the picnic. It wasn't very much fun. Uncle Alfred complained about the bees and said he couldn't get comfortable leaning against a rock, and Aunt Gizi seemed to spend the day preventing Felix from talking to Eva. Mama said her headache had never been so bad, and the picnic ended when poor Cousin Kati dropped her hat into the stream and, while trying to retrieve it, soaked the skirt of her muslin dress. Aunt Gizi slapped her. In front of everyone she slapped her; even the little boys could feel what a horible, embarrassing thing it was to do. Kati cried and Aunt Gizi scolded her all the way home. The only people who enjoyed that picnic were Karoly and Amalia, but then they enjoyed them all.

Gradually, as people became bored with the Meadow, the picnics dwindled to the very best sort—just Malie and Eva, Mama, and Karoly Vilaghy. Sometimes he came in the coach with them, but more often he would be waiting for them at the Meadow with his horse tethered to a tree.

After they had all eaten the boys would beg Malie and Karoly to take them up to the top of the mountain. They knew that, once away from the clearing, they could run off alone into the woods and Malie and Karoly wouldn't even notice. Once, in the middle of digging into an ants' nest with Leo's shoe, Jozsef asked, "Do you think Malie and Karoly will marry each other?"

"Of course not," said Leo indignantly. "People have to be in love to marry each other."

"Perhaps they are. They talk a lot, don't they?"

Thoughtfully Leo poked and prodded at the heap of earth. Ants ran hysterically in all directions.

"Let's spy on them and see what they're doing," said Jozsef.

They took off their remaining shoes and crept very quietly through the trees. When they were close enough, Jozsef motioned Leo to the ground.

"See," he said. "I told you."

Karoly and Malie were holding hands. He was talking but they couldn't hear his words. At one point he raised her hand to his lips and kissed it, not the back of the hand like Felix Kaldy did but the palm. He took much longer to kiss it than Felix did too.

They were all very quiet going home that afternoon. Malie and Karoly were absorbed in some private dream and didn't talk, and the little boys were worried. They didn't know why they were worried except it was something to do with Papa. Every time Leo thought of Karoly kissing Malie's hand, and then thought of Papa, he began to feel sick.

The next time they went to the Meadow, Karoly refused to take the boys up to the top of the mountain. He said he wanted to stay and talk to Mama.

"Eva will take you," he said.

"I want to read my book."

"Then go and play on your own," he snapped impatiently. "Malie and I have something to discuss with your mama."

With dignity, showing they didn't care, Jozsef and Leo stalked off into the trees.

"We won't go back," cried Jozsef vengefully. "Then they'll be sorry." They played in a desultory fashion for half an hour, then circled back to the clearing. Karoly was still talking. He was angry about something and Mama had her hand raised to her forehead.

"Surely I can ask, Madame Ferenc! Surely I can call on him and explain my situation. It is not unreasonable merely to be allowed to see him!"

Mama shook her head. She looked so distressed that the boys began to move closer. Usually when grown-ups were talking and did not wish to be overheard they either ceased their conversation or told the children to run away. But this time no one noticed they were there.

"I know there are difficulties. I do not even want to ask for a public engagement until some of the difficulties have been overcome—at least until I get my promotion. All I want is the chance to speak with him."

"No, no!" Mama cried. "You don't understand, Karoly. How could I explain to him? It is such a short time! He will blame me, yes he will! He will want to know how all this could have happened in such a short time." She kept clasping and unclasping her hands and gazing first at Karoly, then at Amalia. Karoly was pacing irritably up and down. He passed right by Leo and Jozsef without even noticing them.

"It is ridiculous! Forgive me, Madame Ferenc; surely you are seeing problems when none exist. I am a cousin of your brother-in-law. I am here for the summer. We have been formally introduced. Our two families have met together in both houses. What could be more easily explained? I have met Amalia and I love her. I want to talk to her father, that is all, just talk to him."

"Oh, you don't understand, you don't understand!" cried Mama, wringing her hands. "There's Gizi and Alfred and Kati. I'm sure they don't always know you ride up here to join us. I don't ask you what you've told them because—because—" She faltered, then added feebly, "Because I don't want to know. It was all so . . . so pleasant: the summer, and you and Malie. . . . I didn't think. I just didn't think."

"But what *is* there to think?" he cried angrily. "We have met, and I have fallen in love with your daughter. What is so wrong with me that that brings disgrace upon you all?"

Mama began to weep. "I cannot tell you. I cannot tell you what is wrong. Nothing is wrong, but he will be so angry with me. He will ask Gizi how many times you have met, and Gizi will remember *exactly*, and she will tell him that you and Malie hardly know each other, and then he will say how could the young man want to marry her if they have met so infrequently, and—" Her words drowned in a sea of helpless incoherence.

Karoly was silent. They could see how tense his shoulders were, but finally he put his hand on Mama's and said quietly, "Please do not cry, Madame Ferenc. I am sorry. Forgive me for shouting at you. I do not—cannot—understand. I am helpless before you. I have so many difficulties to overcome. There is the army marriage fee and my family and my future with the regiment. These things are tangible to me and I can overcome them in time. I can also see that your husband might not like me at all, might refuse to consider a long engagement with Amalia. But I cannot see why I must not even approach him. Why I cannot even speak to him!"

Amalia, for the first time that summer unsmiling, said, "Couldn't he call, Mama? Do you think Papa would be cross? Surely Karoly—he is Uncle Alfred's cousin—surely Papa would listen to him, talk to him."

"Oh, Malie!" Mama's eyes were closed, not languidly, the way they were when she had a headache, but screwed up tightly as though she were in pain. "Malie, dear. You know what he would say, what questions he would ask. He would never forgive me for letting it come to this before he has even met the young man. Before he is even aware of his existence!"

Amalia stared into the trees. "No," she said simply. "No. Of course it wouldn't do."

"If only he knew you," said Mama desperately. "If you had visited our house in town when he was there—not alone, of course, but with other young people. If he had grown used to you *slowly,* seen you with Gizi and Alfred, then he would not be so . . . so surprised."

Malie turned to him and clasped his hand. "Couldn't we do that, Karoly? When Papa comes, couldn't we make sure that you call often, with Kati and the Kaldy boys. Pretend that we know each other slightly, then get *him* to know. That way it would be all right."

Karoly stared incredulously at the pair of them. "I just don't understand. Play games? Stand by your side talking about the weather? How long do I have—I am only here for a few weeks. Then I must return to the garrison while you remain here until the autumn. Do I have to continue through the winter, drinking coffee and pretending that we hardly know one another?"

"Oh, Karoly, if only you would! It would make everything so much easier. When you meet Papa you will understand."

Mama's face grew less agitated. "Of course, that is what you must do," she cried. "You can still be together this summer—a little—but you must come with Kati and the Kaldy boys. And you must be very charming to Gizi. You must talk to her about her brother, about Zsigmond; she will like that. Then you may mention Amalia a little, but not too much. She is jealous of my girls—how dreadful it would have been if it had been Eva you wanted! You must mention Amalia very gently, in connection with her papa and his cleverness and the land he has bought and the property he owns. If you talk this way to Gizi then she will tell my husband what a very *good* and *sensible* young man you are. He listens to Gizi. He will take notice of anything she says. And after you have called for a while and when he has grown used to you, then you can talk to him."

"I cannot do this!" he burst out. "I'm a soldier! I do not want to lie and cheat and flatter. I have behaved as a gentleman, why can I not speak to him as a gentleman?"

Malie clasped his hand hard in hers. "Please, Karoly! Do it

this way. It is the only way, I promise you. If you speak to him now it will make such trouble, not just for me but for Mama also."

"Please!" breathed Mama, echoing Malie.

Leo and Jozsef felt they could bear it no more. "Please!" they cried, running forward and tugging at his coat. "Please do what Malie says. Please don't make Papa angry!"

He stood, a perplexed and hunted expression on his face, and then he shrugged and began to laugh.

"Oh, dear, oh, dear!" he cried. "What can I do against the determined weight of the entire family? I must give in, I suppose. No"—he raised his hand in a guarded gesture—"I do not promise to do all you have asked, but I will see Malie in the presence of my cousins more often, and I will call at your home frequently, and I will wait until I have met Zsigmond Ferenc before I decide what to do next."

There was almost a party atmosphere. Mama kissed him on the cheek and Malie smiled, her eyes full of unshed tears. Leo and Jozsef swung on his hands, trying to wind his arms round him like streamers. Eva, returning with her book, was told what was going to happen and said, "Won't it be enormous fun! Like playing in amateur theatricals at school!"

They still went to the Meadow after that, but not so often, and always Aunt Gizi and Cousin Kati were with them. Eva only came when the Kaldy boys were there and those afternoons were very strained and unhappy because Aunt Gizi was not only cross and sharp with Eva, she was angry with Kati as well.

There was much visiting between Aunt Gizi's house and the farm. Nearly every morning or afternoon or evening one family would ride to the house of the other family. A great deal of coffee and lemonade was drunk, innumerable card games were played, and Karoly became more and more strained, more and more impatient with everyone.

As the time drew near for the arrival of Papa a slight air of hysteria seemed to take possession of the farmhouse. The atmosphere in Roza's kitchen became tense, the little boys constantly being scolded while Roza, usually serene and placid, involved herself in vat after vat of cherry jam. Uncle Zoltan began to shout at the labourers, threatening to turn them off the land and replace them with migrant harvesters if they didn't hurry up and do all the tasks that should have been done several months ago. A pig was killed, and Roza prepared salami and *hurka* and the sweet pieces of cured bacon that would later be served at parties and suppers.

Mama had many more headaches and Amalia became very quiet. Leo and Jozsef were noisy and disobedient and usually went to bed in tears. The long spell without Papa had spoilt them, they had relaxed too much, and now, with his arrival imminent, they were unable to control themselves. The only person who seemed unaffected by Papa's approaching presence was Eva. She was just as happy and vivacious as she had been ever since they had arrived. A large part of her time was spent in her room, gazing into the mirror, curling her hair with tongs, trimming summer hats with new bows, experimenting with sashes and collars. Eva didn't seem to care at all that Papa was coming.

Three days before his expected arrival the boys asked at breakfast if they could go to the Meadow for one more time. Malie looked at Mama.

"I don't want to go today," Mama said fretfully. "Gizi and Alfred are coming this evening, and the Kaldys. I shall rest this afternoon." An expression of pained irritation crossed her face. "You know how these evenings with Gizi exhaust me!"

Amalia looked guilty. "Yes, Mama, I know." She played with a piece of bread, crumpling it into a series of small pellets. "Karoly will be coming to call this morning," she said timorously. "Could he not take Eva and me and the boys on a picnic, just for the last time? It would be all right if Eva was there, wouldn't it?"

Eva fidgeted on her chair. "Oh, Malie, I don't want to go to that wretched place again. I'm tired of picnics. And you know how badly the midges bit me last time. You can't ask me to go today. I don't want blotches on my face when Felix comes this evening."

The boys were disappointed. So was Malie. Mama took refuge in a complaint, endeavoring to drown the feeling that she was spoiling the day for Malie and the boys.

"There's no reason for you to sulk, Amalia," she said unfairly. "We have all spent more time than any of us like having picnics in that uncomfortable place. Really! When I think of the times Eva and I have trailed up that terible mountain just to be accommodating—"

"I didn't notice Eva's reluctance when Felix Kaldy was there," said Malie with unaccustomed sharpness. "She never once mentioned the midges when he was there."

Eva flushed angrily. "Malie! How could you be so mean! Well, I'm not coming. If you want to go you can go on your own!"

There was a bad-tempered silence. Jozsef broke it in a noisy whisper. "Couldn't you take us on your own, Malie? Just you and me and Leo?"

"Couldn't you, Malie?" echoed Leo.

She looked miserable, undecided, then said reluctantly, "Oh, I suppose so, Yes, all right, we'll go, just the three of us. But we must wait to tell Karoly. We cannot go until he has arrived."

The boys raced off to the kitchen. Mama and Eva seemed a little abashed. Eva finished her coffee and then hurried out, murmuring that she wanted to change the sash on her dress for this evening. Mama stood indecisively in the doorway for a moment, then followed Eva from the room.

When Karoly arrived the three of them were waiting on the porch with the picnic box, the boys impatient to be gone, Malie looking wistful.

"I cannot see you today," she said tragically—what did a moment now and a whole evening later count for when the day must be spent apart? "I'm taking the boys to the Meadow and neither Mama nor Eva will come."

"Can I not join you?"

"Oh, Karoly, you know what we decided. Mama says we must only meet when others are present."

"There will be others," he said impatiently, gazing into her eyes. "There will be Uncle Sandor and Jozsef and Leo."

Amalia gazed back. "You know very well they don't count, Karoly. We must do what Mama says. You don't understand about Papa; he would be so angry if he even suspected. We must do what Mama says."

Jozsef and Leo thought Karoly was going to lose his temper again, but just then Mama appeared on the porch. She was wearing a lavender dress with flounces round the hem, and with her dark hair piled high on the crown of her head the resemblance to Eva was even more pronounced than usual.

"Oh, dear!" She sighed. "How complicated it all is. But I cannot think of Karoly fretting here all day while you are playing with the boys." She fluttered her hands in the air, and then she smiled, one of Mama's lovely, gay-hearted smiles that made one forget the carelessness and the selfishness. "Dear Karoly!" she said. "How handsome you look in your uniform! Now you will all go on a lovely picnic and we shall say nothing about it to anyone. The last picnic, for my husband will be here in three days' time. But today you will spend together, a gift from Amalia's mother—a present from Marta Bogozy."

She clasped her hands together under her chin, then flung her arms wide and embraced them both.

"Dear, dear children," she murmured. "How happy you are. How wonderful it is to be young and happy, to have such faith in each other, to believe so strongly in the future. . . ." Her face was suddenly old and unhappy, and Leo, the emotional barometer of the family, left the picnic box and came over to hug her lavender skirts.

"You'll be happy too, Mama," he said, a tremor in his voice. "When I am grown up I shall take you on picnics and make you happy. Every day that you don't have a headache I shall take you for a picnic!"

She stared unseeing at her son for a moment, and then she smiled and clasped her hands once more. "Now you must go!" she cried. "Not to be late back. Remember, Gizi and Alfred are coming this evening."

"What will you do, Mama? What will you do all day?" Everything had changed for Malie. Golden hours with Karoly stretched ahead of her, but even now her pleasure was marred a little. Loving Karoly had made everything keener, her sight and sound and senses more acute. The trees stood out brighter against the sky, the noises of the farm were clearer, louder—and her mother's loneliness, only dimly sensed until now, was painfully apparent to her.

Mama shrugged her shoulders. "Today I am feeling very virtuous and noble. Today I shall behave as a real mama—like Gizi or Madame Kaldy. Oh, no, do not be alarmed; I mean only that I shall not stay at home and think of my headache. Today I will think of my children and do things for them. You, Malie, shall go on a picnic with your young man. Eva—" Mama reflected a moment. "I shall go and call on Madame Kaldy. I shall drink lemonade with her. I will talk about her sons and her farm. I will try to remember mutual events in the past that the Bogozys and the Kaldys have enjoyed together. I will try to impress her with our soberness and respectability."

Even in the midst of her happiness Malie could see that her mama would never be able to carry through such a worthy and organized visit.

"And if she is rude to me, as she often is," continued

Mama, warming to the impending visit as other aspects of it occurred to her, "I shall remind her of the time that her husband kissed me at a ball in Vienna. It was in the garden of the Pulszky villa and she had to come and fetch him from me! Ah! Here is Uncle Sandor. Go into the mountains and have a beautiful picnic!"

It was a stolen day. Tinged with the magic was the knowledge that it was their last time together and that it must be kept a secret from Papa and Aunt Gizi. The conspiracy made them comrades, made everything more exciting. They giggled —all four—like naughty children, and when the boys, as usual, fell in the stream and Malie and Karoly got wet pulling them out, no one scolded because it was all part of their last adventure. Malie and Karoly walked a little and came back ruffled and flushed. The little boys just got dirtier and wetter and happier, and by the time they all climbed back into the coach, barefoot because their shoes were wet, they looked and felt like a band of gypsies.

About them was an air of complete invincibility. Nothing could happen to them, nothing could go wrong. They were made strong by the summer day and by their happiness. The differences of age and sex broke down and they shared a communion of rightness, a knowledge that if only they kept this happiness and love alive between them they would always be safe. Sunshine poured down through the trees and formed patches of white on the rutted earth. Even Uncle Sandor had removed his coat and was dozing on the box, letting the horses amble their own way home.

In the acacia trees, just before the farmhouse came into view, Leo saw a flash of yellow darting through the trees. "A bird!" he cried, but the bird turned into a section of a yellow dress fleetingly seen through trunks and leaves.

Eva was racing towards them, darting through the wood, out of breath and holding her skirts up with both hands.

A tiny darting fear, a first unease, made Amalia sit up. Something wrong? No, nothing could be wrong on this most wonderful of days; hold fast to the happiness, the strength, the love; there was nothing Eva could do or say that would destroy the happiness. So why did the darting yellow dress make them all fall silent, make them view with dread the signs of Eva's distress—her hair coming down, her scarlet face, the clumsiness of her running? Uncle Sandor began to put on his coat.

"Stop! Uncle Sandor, stop the horses!"

Eva grasped the bridle of the near-side horse and then stumbled forward to the carriage door.

"Oh, Malie! Papa. He's arrived early!"

A plummeting of the heart, a sense of cold fear, a moment when the news was not believed, could not possibly be true.

"He came . . . in a hired coach. Something happened and Papa thought Uncle Alfred should know, because of the bank. The Crown Prince has been killed . . . in Bosnia. He came to tell him. Oh, Malie!" She was nearly sobbing, holding to the side of the coach for support and drawing breath into her lungs in long searing gasps. "We tried, Mama and I. He wanted to know where you were and when we told him he was cross. He said you shouldn't be out alone in the mountains with only Leo and Jozsef. And then—Karoly's horse was there. He saw it and we had to tell him. . . . Oh, Malie! Why did the Crown Prince have to get killed now? Why couldn't he have waited for three days. . . ." Her words ran out, petered away in an agony of drawing breath.

Malie's face was white but she tried to smile. "I'm sure it will be all right," she said bravely. "Karoly is related to Uncle Alfred. It is all quite respectable. I'm sure it will be all right. . . ."

Her voice faded away and Eva turned to follow her gaze. Coming along the track, quietly, smoothly, at a speed not slow, not fast, walked Papa. He was dressed for summer, the way he always was at the farm, an alpaca jacket and a straw hat, but the holiday clothes only made everything worse, emphasizing his icy face and controlled movements. He stopped a short distance away and, ignoring the occupants of the coach, addressed himself to Eva.

"I believe I directed you to stay in your room, Eva. Return there at once."

"Papa, I was going with them! I was going too. I always go on the picnics, Papa, and so does Aunt Gizi, and Mama, and Cousin Kati—"

"You heard what I said. Return to the house at once."

"Papa!"

"Eva!" It was almost a shout. There was anger in Papa's face; she was afraid he was going to strike her. She turned quickly and, still panting, sobbing, began to trot back along the path. Papa kept his eyes averted from the coach. Looking down at the ground, he said, "You will oblige me, Amalia, by alighting from the coach."

She was shaking. She tried to smile but even her lips were shaking.

"Papa," she said in a high-pitched, strained voice, "Papa, this officer is Lieutenant Karoly Vilaghy. He is related to Uncle Alfred. He has been so kind. He offered to take us on a drive today, as Mama and Eva could not come. . . ." Her voice trailed away as Papa slowly raised his eyes to her face, then to her dishevelled hair, and from her hair to the wet skirts bunched up on the seat beside her. Karoly opened the door, jumped down, and went to lift her from the steps.

"Please stand away from my daughter." The voice was flat, expressionless. As Malie stepped down she swayed a little, lost her balance, and Karoly put his arm out to help her.

"I have told you once, sir. Please stand away from my daughter." A spasm of disgust twisted his face as he stared at Karoly's bare feet and shirt sleeves.

Karoly, fumbling, reached inside the coach for his boots and coat. He had to stand on one leg to pull the boots on and, under Papa's cold stare, he became awkward and clumsy, skipping from one leg to the other and losing his balance.

"Your horse is tethered in my stable. I would be obliged if you would remove it."

Karoly, his boots restoring some of his dignity, stood to attention. He was taller than Papa, but it made no difference because Papa did not afford him the satisfaction of looking up. "I would like to request an opportunity of talking with you, sir. I have asked Malie and Madame Ferenc several times for permission to call and discuss matters with you. Now you are here I can do so. If convenient I would like to call tomorrow."

"Please remove your horse from my stable as quickly as possible," said Papa tonelessly.

"May I call tomorrow, sir?"

"You may not call, neither tomorrow nor at any other time."

Karoly's quick temper began to ignite. "You are extremely uncivil, sir. It would be courteous at least to wait until you have spoken with my cousin before you bar me from your house."

Papa suddenly raised his head and looked into Karoly's eyes. The younger man's temper evaporated immediately and was replaced by a cold sensation at the back of his neck. Zsigmond Ferenc's eyes were a curious colour, a grey that was almost transparent. There was such venom, such hatred in them

91

that Karoly knew a physical revulsion. The cold at the back of his neck turned into a prickling and he felt his hair rise.

"Please go, Karoly!"

She was so small and helpless in her bedraggled wet dress. He tried to ignore the terrible man standing between them and imbue her with strength and confidence.

"I will ask Cousin Alfred to explain, Malie. It will be all right, I promise you. It will be all right."

"Please go! Please, Karoly!"

He looked from her to the man with the colourless eyes.

"Please!" she sobbed. He sensed that as well as fear she felt shame and humiliation. Her father had turned her into a dirty, abject little girl and she hated Karoly to see her like that.

Helplessly, turning back once, he walked slowly down the track. He had no idea what to do, how to put things right. Surely, in these enlightened times, no father in the world would intimidate his family to this extent, merely because one of his daughters had been on a picnic with a young soldier? Perhaps it had been a little improper—he was aware of guilty unease because he had suggested it—but to strike such fear, to crush even the high-spirited Eva the way he had—no, it was not possible. He looked back. Malie was lifting the boys out of the coach and her father was looking, just looking.

"Leo and Jozsef, they have been party to this . . . Roman picnic? They have taken part in these deceits throughout the summer?"

"It was only today, Papa! Usually we all go, but today Eva and Mama did not want to come, and—"

"You cannot tell me, Amalia, that this was the first time you have been alone with the soldier. You have been alone with him several times." He was not asking a question. He was making a flat statement of fact that forbade further discussion.

"The boys have nothing to do with it, Papa. There was nothing wrong. They are only little; they just wanted to play in the forest."

Leo began to sob. The day had been wonderful, and now the terrible fear of Papa was with them again. Noisy gulps shook his body.

Papa's forehead wrinkled in irritation. "Very well. I will speak to the boys later. Sandor! Take my sons for a drive and bring them back in an hour."

Uncle Sandor bowed his head. Malie lifted them back into

the coach with trembling hands and almost at once it moved off, down the track towards the farm. Leo and Jozsef wanted to look back to see what Malie and Papa were doing, but they were too frightened. When they got to the farmhouse Uncle Sandor didn't stop; he drove straight on down towards the river, jolting and rattling quite fast on the bad track and making the little boys, who had no Malie to hold them up, lurch and fall over on their seats.

Leo, with tears coursing down his cheeks, was unaware of what was happening. His first realization came when Jozsef silently tugged on the sleeve of his shirt. Leo looked at his brother, and Jozsef, round-eyed, pointed in the direction of Uncle Sandor's back. Leo froze. The fear—the familiar known-punishment fear of Papa—was suddenly replaced by another kind, a supernatural, wailing, ogre-ish kind. They were alone with Uncle Sandor!

Gripping each other's hands they kept their eyes on his back. Perhaps if they were quiet he would forget they were there and just drive on, gloating over his evil thoughts. Leo tried to think of other things, of honey cakes and Malie. Two kinds of fear wrestled with each other, the misery of Malie and the terror of Uncle Sandor, and in his heart he knew that the misery of Malie and Papa was worse.

They came to the bank of the river and Uncle Sandor stopped the coach. He sat there for a moment, his back to them, staring out over to the opposite bank. Then, ponderously, he clambered down from the box and came towards them. They shrank back against the seat, gripping tightly to each other, knowing that the moment had finally come.

Uncle Sandor opened the door and reached his arms forward. Leo caught one dreadful glimpse of black eyes, black whiskers, and scowling black brows. Then he could see no more for he closed his eyes. To his astonishment Uncle Sandor dropped him on the ground and a moment later Jozsef was placed beside him.

"Go. Play," Uncle Sandor rumbled.

When they felt their legs could carry them they walked away from the coach, found a log by the side of the river, and sat on it, their arms linked in misery, not only for comfort but because the late afternoon had grown a little cold. Leo was shivering. His damp clothes hadn't bothered him before, but now they were clammy on his body.

"What will happen to Malie, Jozsef?"

"Papa will punish her," whispered Jozsef.

"Will we ever see Karoly again?"

"No." Jozsef shook his head. "I don't suppose he will ever dare come to the house again."

Uncle Sandor came towards them with a great armful of wood. He knelt down, placed some large stones in a circle, then criss-crossed the wood on top. With his tinder he caught a twig and then fed small chips into the flames until they were strong enough to place a log on top. Then he sat down on the other side of the fire. They watched him warily to see what he would do next. Tears were still coursing down Leo's fat cheeks, although he wasn't really crying.

"Mustn't cry. Play," growled Uncle Sandor.

In unison they shook their heads. There was no play in the world that would entice them now. Even on a good day, a bright, smiling, happy day, the sole presence of Uncle Sandor would have destroyed their spirits.

Uncle Sandor took a bundle of cloth from his pocket and unrolled it. Inside was a hunk of grey bread, an onion, and a slab of *szalonna*. He unstrapped a knife from the side of his boot and sawed off a slice of the bacon fat. Then he peeled the onion and bit into it, as though it were an apple. Fascinated, the little boys watched him munch, swallow, and bite again. They had never seen anyone eat an onion like that before. Uncle Sandor sliced another lump of *szalonna*, impaled it on his knife, and passed it across the flames to Jozsef, who nervously reached out his hand, took it, and ate. Another piece came over for Leo. Then two hunks of the grey peasant bread. They weren't really hungry, but there was comfort in the shared food, and when they started to eat they realized how delicious it all was. They never had grey bread and bacon fat at home.

"Do you think," whispered Jozsef, "that I could have a piece of your onion, Uncle Sandor?"

Uncle Sandor didn't cut the onion. He knew it wouldn't taste the same that way. He passed it over so that Jozsef and then Leo could plunge their teeth into it. Then he sawed off two more pieces of bread to try and stop their eyes from watering.

"Time was," said Uncle Sandor, sawing and munching, "time was I would have given my life for *szalonna* and bread and onion like this."

The little boys stared.

"Out on the great plain, with the sun beating down and fifty thousand of the King of Prussia's soldiers waiting to ride us into the ground. Yes, what I would have given for bread and onions then!"

Absent-mindedly Leo held his hand out for another piece of bacon, and the old soldier pressed a lump of dirty fat into his hand.

"No food for four days, our bellies hollow with hunger. Seventy leagues we'd ridden, and the lieutenant comes and says, 'Men, there's food for you. The first for four days, and likely to be the last for many more.' "

He threw another log on the fire, nodded, and picked a piece of bacon fat from his teeth with his knife.

"So we are led to a shepherd's hut. And there is a meal, a great pot of meat and beans and peppers. 'Eat,' says the lieutenant. 'Eat well, because this is your last meal of good Hungarian mutton. From now on you will be eating your horses.' "

The little boys stopped chewing and gazed awestruck at the man who had ridden seventy leagues without eating for four days.

"So we eat. And when our bellies are full, do you know what the lieutenant says? Do you know?" He suddenly slapped his great hand down hard on his thigh and roared. " 'Men,' he says, 'I will tell you. You have just eaten your *first* meal of horse, not your last of mutton!' "

Their mouths dropped open. Before them sat Uncle Sandor, who had eaten a plate of horse and beans and peppers. They glanced over at the carriage horses, nice fat cosy black horses gently pulling at odd tufts of grass around the coach.

"Whose horse was it?"

"A Prussian horse."

That was all right then. A Prussian horse.

Jozsef stood up and moved round the fire, next to Uncle Sandor. "Did you have anything else after that?" he asked. "Did they give you anything to eat after that?"

"One day a dead sheep, out on the plain. It was thin, as thin as we were, but we took water from our flasks and made a little soup."

"A dead sheep," breathed Jozsef in admiration. He was leaning against Uncle Sandor's legs now. The fire was warm and that and the largeness of Uncle Sandor offered a kind of comfort. It was possible to forget for a little while that Papa had come home.

"Uncle Sandor," said Leo suddenly, "could I borrow your knife? I have bacon in my teeth." Uncle Sandor didn't even hesitate, the way any other grown-up would have done. He passed the sharp knife across the fire, and Leo scraped the blade experimentally against his teeth a few times.

"The very knife I skinned the sheep with," mumbled Uncle Sandor.

Leo looked at it with added respect. Then he brought it round the fire to Uncle Sandor and pressed close to his other side.

"It is good to have a fire," said Uncle Sandor, nodding. "There will be no wolves while we have this fire."

They gazed around them, at the peaceful river with trees along its banks, at the cultivated fields (theirs on this side, Uncle Alfred's on the other), at the peasants in the distance who were cutting a field of late hay.

"Wolves, Uncle Sandor?" asked Leo, wriggling with pleasure. "Are there wolves here?"

"Bears too, and wild boar, but the fire will keep them away."

Leo reached up and hugged Uncle Sandor's arm. Uncle Sandor lifted him up and sat him on his huge black knee. He felt very safe sitting there. At the back of his mind he knew he had to go home, but Uncle Sandor would be with them.

"Do you think," asked Jozsef, "that when we go home I could sit on the box with you, Uncle Sandor? I would get in the coach before we were near the house," he added hastily.

Uncle Sandor rumbled a bit. He smelled of onion, and his hands were greasy from the bacon fat and dirty from the fire. "I think there is room for two more there," he growled.

They sat for a few moments, watching the friendly flames that were keeping the wolves away.

"Now it is time." Uncle Sandor stood up holding Leo, who was nearly asleep in his arms. He pushed them up onto the box, then clambered up beside them. As he flicked the horses they each gripped a great arm with their two hands, and then the coach moved off.

"I wish we could stay here with the fire," said Jozsef mournfully.

Leo, through a sleepy haze, thought how nice that would be, to stay on the river-bank, watching the sun go down and building the fire up against the perils of the night. But as he clung to greasy, strong-smelling Uncle Sandor, he found his dread of going back to the farmhouse mitigated by a tiny ray of comfort. Uncle Sandor would be in the stables, sleeping in a little cupboard just by the door. The horses would be strong and big and warm, and so would Uncle Sandor, who had fought the Prussians and eaten a dead sheep. Papa had never done those things, and Papa had never eaten an onion as though it were an apple or cleaned his teeth with a sharp-bladed skinning knife.

"Will you say our names this evening, before you sleep? Say our names and we will say yours, Uncle Sandor."

It made a moment of hope in what was going to be a bad, bad evening. They would be sent directly to bed, of course, but Papa's anger would be apparent in every room and corner of the house. And there was tomorrow. Tomorrow Malie would be punished, and Mama and Eva too. The thought that Uncle Sandor, in his cosy stable cupboard, was saying their names gave them a secret point of sanity that would help them bear the night.

"'I will say your names," he promised, and with that they had to fortify themselves for the return to Papa.

6

At first there was concern solely because of the bank. The assassination of the Archduke Ferdinand, said Uncle Alfred, could well provoke some international disturbance on the stock market. Papa assured Alfred that he had anticipated this and had done everything within his power, including telegrams to Switzerland and Berlin, to ensure stabilization. There might be fluctuations, but with firm control right from the beginning there were unlikely to be long-lasting repercussions.

Uncle Alfred also put forward the view that there was bound to be a punitive expedition into Serbia.

"Absolutely imperative," he stated flatly. "We none of us liked Franz Ferdinand and certainly he was no friend to Hungary, but there is the honour of the Monarchy to be considered. Once we allow the subservient races to believe that acts of aggression will be overlooked, we shall have revolution and anarchy within our frontiers."

It was so strange. They were all there, just as they had been invited. Only Karoly and Amalia were missing, and in a little while Roza would bring in a huge dish of meats and cheeses and eggs, all arranged on a bed of red and green peppers. She would offer cake and coffee, all the things that had been prepared for the little party that had been planned. But instead of a party they were sitting round the table, the green-shaded oil lamp hanging low from the ceiling, and talking about the bank and Franz Ferdinand being killed by the Serbians.

"All indications point to a show of strength," Uncle Alfred continued. "My young cousin, Karoly Vilaghy—been recalled to garrison duties immediately—telegram waiting for him this afternoon when he returned." He darted a quick look at Papa, then hurried on. "Wouldn't have been recalled if Vienna wasn't considering some sort of military protest."

It was the only time reference was made to Karoly during the evening, and Papa ignored it. It was as though Uncle Alfred had never spoken. Just for one fleeting moment his face was touched by fury, but it instantly disappeared, blown away in a discussion between Uncle Alfred and the Kaldy boys about the possibility of using force against Serbia.

The women said nothing. They were all subdued, even Aunt Gizi, and they made no attempt at conversation, not even among themselves. Eva had smiled brightly at Felix once or twice, but the smile lacked confidence and fitted ill with her red, swollen eyes. And Felix—surprisingly—appeared to be concerned in the masculine conversation that was in progress. He had returned Eva's smile with his own tender, charming one, but then the smile had been replaced by a frown of concentration as he listened to Uncle Alfred and Papa.

A large moth droned in through the open window and homed directly towards the lamp. It hit the shade, hummed loudly, hit it again, and began a process of alternately circling and hitting. All eyes turned towards it and yet did not really see it.

"They should have been taught a lesson before," Alfred said, rapping his hand on the table to emphasize his point. "Last year they should have been crushed. We should never have let them beat the Bulgars back behind their frontiers. We should have stepped over the border and shown them Imperial discipline!"

Everything was strange and uncomfortable. Mostly it was because of Amalia and Karoly, but in some unaccountable way that was not the whole of the unease about them. The Crown Prince, who was universally disliked throughout the Empire, had been killed and there was an air of unreality about the evening. All the familiar things about them—the rugs hanging on the walls, the rush and mahogany chairs, the well-known night shapes of the trees seen through the unshuttered windows—all these things were alien. It was as though they had never been seen before. And yet, after Papa and Uncle Alfred and Adam and Felix Kaldy had discussed the international situation, looking carefully at every aspect and possible development, there seemed nothing to fear.

When the supper was brought in Adam tried to introduce a softening of the atmosphere, tried to bring the women out of their unhappy silence and make them talk.

"Amalia not here?" he questioned lightly. "Is she unwell, or has she just decided she does not like us this evening?"

The close atmosphere of the summer night grew more oppressive. No one answered him.

"Can someone not destroy that moth?" Papa snapped. "It is extremely irritating.'"

Gizi rose in her chair, cupped her hand over the insect on the shade, and took it to the window. All eyes followed her, then followed the moth as it was thrown into the night.

Just as they were leaving, Kati drew Eva to one side on the porch. "Karoly told us," she whispered. "He wanted to stop here on his way back to the garrison. He was desperate to say good-bye to Malie." Her eyes were glowing with the drama and excitement of Karoly's love for Amalia, and Malie's doomed fulfilment of that love. Kati was completely and utterly involved in all the sweetness and poignancy of their emotion for one another, an emotion she could never hope to experience for herself. "Oh, Eva! He was so angry, and so sad. He was talking to Papa while he was packing. He was crying, really crying, and shouting at the same time. He said your papa was a monster! Oh, Eva, I'm sorry! I shouldn't have told you that, but if you could have seen poor Karoly you would understand."

Dumbly Eva nodded. Tears welled up once more in her bloodshot eyes, and she felt only confusion and misery in her heart. What had Amalia done that she, Eva, would not have wished to do with Felix?

"Papa tried to restrain him; it is due to Papa that Karoly did not come here. Papa explained it would make things worse for Malie. And Papa promised he would try and talk to Uncle Zsigmond, assure him there was nothing wrong with the picnics. Karoly quietened a little, and then just as he was leaving he shouted at Mama. 'Your brother is a monster!' he said. 'I want to marry one of his daughters; what is so wrong with that?' " Kati's eyes grew round as she remembered how someone had actually shouted at her mama. "And she didn't answer him. She was so silent and white I thought she was going to faint—although Mama never, never faints."

Eva nodded again, longing for Kati to leave.

"Oh, Eva! They must love each other so much! What do you think will happen? Will your papa send Malie away? He could send her to your grandparents. The Bogozys live a long way from the town, don't they? He might send her there."

"I don't know," said Eva, slumping wearily against the sweet-smelling leaves of the vine curled round the post. A tiny cluster of hard green grapes pressed against her cheek. "I don't know. I'm so tired I don't know anything any more. I don't understand why Papa is like this. Sometimes he is kind and proud of us, and then—"

"Mama hasn't grumbled at me once this evening." Kati prattled on. "Did you notice how she didn't once speak to me about my hair or the way I was sitting?"

To Eva's relief the Racs-Rassay coach came round from the stable. Behind, led by Roza's eldest son, were the Kaldy horses. The good-byes were said quietly. There was no light-hearted calling through the night, no lingering pleasantries and promises of tomorrow. Aunt Gizi suddenly stood on tiptoe and kissed her brother on both cheeks. The second kiss she held for a moment, with her beautiful long fingers gripping his shoulders and her eyes tightly closed. And Eva noticed that Papa, who was so undemonstrative and lacking in affection with anyone except herself, swayed a little and allowed his head to bow towards Gizi's. There was pain on his face, but Eva was too emotionally exhausted to feel sympathy for him. She said, "Good night, Papa. Good night, Mama," and walked back into the house. She hesitated outside the door of Malie's room. It was now locked, and she wondered whether to whisper through and try to tell her about Karoly leaving for the garrison. Then she envisaged what would follow if Papa overheard, and so she crept into the little boys' room and lay down, fully dressed, on the temporary bed which had been set up for her there.

During the week that followed, while Malie remained locked in her room, the news from Budapest grew more and more disturbing. Alfred's surmisings of a military confrontation with Serbia began to sound not quite so ridiculous. The newspapers, which did not arrive until the afternoon, spoke of alarm and counter-alarm, of what might occur if this were done or that were done, of what and with whom Berchtold and Tisza and the Kaiser and Franz Josef were talking. The arrival of the newspapers became the most important event of the day. Until they came there was silence in the house. Papa spoke to no one, neither at mealtimes, nor in the yard, nor round the farm. His straight, cold figure could be seen inspecting the crops and cattle, with Uncle Zoltan a nervous and supplicating figure at his rear. Eva, Mama, and the boys did not dare leave the farm. Just once the little boys had set off with the dogs down in the direction of the river, and suddenly Papa had appeared before them, not saying anything, only staring at them in fury. Now Leo and Jozsef spent what time they had away from the house in the stables with Uncle Sandor. His small smelly cupboard became a refuge in a house of chilly madness.

Mama and Eva tried to occupy themselves inside the house, but the constant silent presence of Papa suppressed anything but a nervous staring, either at a book or from the window or at each other. They were aware, all the time, of the locked door and the silence behind it. Papa never referred to Amalia either—at least not after the first morning when he had stared at Mama and said, "Your daughter will not be sent away until I have seen how the international situation develops. She will remain here until we know if there is to be a war."

"Thank you, Zsigmond."

"You are not to communicate with her in any way."

"No, Zsigmond."

When the papers came down from the village Papa would immediately settle down to study them and then, as though against his own will, he would read the conflicting reports from the capital aloud. Relieved to hear him say anything, anything at all, they would gather round and listen with great respect and concentration. Eva and Mama would try to pass intelligent comments, and the little boys just listened and nodded, and gradually Papa would unbend. Then he would suggest that Uncle Sandor take them over to Alfred and Gizi's to discuss the news. That was good too, because it got them out of the house to where there were other people. The boys, who were too little to go, would wait until the coach was out of sight and then run screaming all round the farm.

Eva wondered what they would all do when the news and

101

excitement died down and the papers had nothing worthwhile to report.

At the end of a week, when they were returning from Alfred and Gizi's, Mama broke. She had grown thin and tired in the days since Papa's arrival, and suddenly she said to him, quite loudly, "When are you going to let my daughter out of her room?"

Papa stared and did not answer, and Mama began to shout, leaning forward on the seat and looking at him with hatred and fear.

"You have imprisoned her for a week. She has seen no one except Roza, and you have forbidden Roza to speak when she takes her food in. You do not know if she is ill, or starving herself to death, or what has happened to her. If she dies I shall tell your sister what you have done to my child!"

Papa's eyes flickered for a second. Eva knew that sign well, and her heart lifted and became confident and strong again. She always knew when it was safe to try and persuade Papa of something. It could not always be done, but now Papa had returned to them from whatever terrible place he lived in while fury controlled him. Now it would be possible to speak to him again.

"Malie doesn't even know about the Crown Prince," she said, very quietly and carefully. "You have explained everything to us, Papa—all about Russia and Serbia, and France and Germany. But Malie has been told nothing. If there is a war surely she has right to know why."

Papa did not answer, but when he stared out of the carriage window it was in a different way, absorbed and thoughtful. The next morning he went into Malie's room very early and, after an hour, led her out. Silently they sat at the breakfast table. Mama swept from her place and wrapped her arms round her elder daughter. Her voice was trembling as she plied Malie with hot bread and apricot jam. Then she rushed from the room and returned in a few moments with a comb of fresh honey on a plate.

"There! Uncle Zoltan has just taken it from the hive." She smiled her silly Mama smile. "If you listen you can still hear the bees singing in it!"

Malie nodded, her mouth doing its best to smile back at Mama. Round her eyes were large dark circles and the lids were unhealthily swollen. Her hair was limp and dirty and her skin looked bad too; the golden soft complexion was pallid and slightly mottled. "Thank you, Mama," she managed at last. The words were stiff, as though she had forgotten how to speak.

"Your sister has reminded me that you are unacquainted with the historic events of the last week," Papa said quietly. "It is possible that the Empire stands on the brink of war."

Malie stared obediently at Papa, and he began to recite the readings accumulated from the past week's papers. Eva, under the table, squeezed Malie's hand. Leo and Jozsef gazed at her with barely controlled longing. Suddenly all the things they had missed her for seemed unimportant. It was just enough to know she was there again. And they had a surprise for her, a lovely surprise. Malie did not yet know that Uncle Sandor was the most wonderful man in the world.

By the middle of July it appeared that the furore over Serbia and the killing was dying down. It would fizzle out, as these things usually did, in long and dreary talks at diplomatic levels. The harvesters had arrived and the fields were full of big brown men with scythes. It was difficult to take Serbia or the newspapers too seriously when the harvesters were here. The war—anyway—had finished without ever beginning and now the important things had to be carried on: the hay stacked up, wild strawberries picked, the cheeses made for the winter. Everything was still controlled and melancholy, because of Papa, and now that the international situation seemed to be settling there was mention of Malie's being sent away to a school in Berlin famous for discipline. They tried to ignore it, tried to pretend that this was a summer just like any other.

The war happened before they had even caught up with the news. There was an ultimatum, and then a declaration of war from Vienna, and the next time they went into the village a crowd of men and women stood round the schoolhouse door reading the mobilization order. One or two of the peasant women were crying, but the men seemed jovial and noisy. Papa called to Uncle Sandor to drive them straight to Gizi and Alfred's. When they arrived Madame Kaldy, Felix, and Adam were there. Madame Kaldy had two bright spots of colour on her cheeks and her back was rigid. "My sons have their mobilization orders," she said proudly. "They have been called to the reserve, Felix to Budapest, Adam to the garrison in the town. They will go tomorrow." She glared at them all, forbidding expressions of sympathy or offers of help. "I shall manage the farm myself for the next few weeks," she announced.

Alfred was noisy and belligerent. "Just as I said. We'll teach the dirty Balkan shepherds not to tamper with the Monarchy. We'll handle the Russians too if they interfere!"

Even Papa was confident. "Quite the best thing to do," he said. "Get it over before the bad weather sets in."

Adam was silent, Felix gay. Eva gazed at him, imagining how he would look in his uniform. The picture that came to her mind was almost too much to bear.

Everyone except Madame Kaldy decided it would be sensible to return to town where the news could be obtained quickly and where Papa and Uncle Alfred could be within speedy reach of Budapest and the bank. As they pattered back to the farmhouse there was an air of expectancy about them, a taut excitement as though great things were going to be asked of them, splendid and dramatic actions which they would nobly perform.

Just as Uncle Sandor pulled the coach into the yard, Mama looked out of the window at the young peasants bringing in the last of the grain and her gaiety vanished. "All the young men who are going to be killed," she murmured sadly. "We cannot stop them . . . they will be killed." She turned to her daughters, relieved because they were not sons, and saw in their faces the fear of women who love men who are old enough to go to war.

The town was a riot of bunting and flags and martial music. Young men with suitcases and bundles arrived in carts, on horses, and from the station, all converging on the garrison. Mostly they were peasants, because the land around the town was farming country, and everyone suddenly felt proud of the healthy, stocky young men that the land had bred. At other times they were stupid, lazy, dishonest, and dirty, but now, with their bags of bread and sausage, they were strong and reliable and brave. The Russians wouldn't be able to defeat men like that. Several peasant women had come into town with their men. The young ones were smiling and wore flowers in their hair, but the old women, with their black skirts and head scarves and faces like year-old apples, were silent. They pressed extra *kolbasz* and fruit into the bags and parcels of their men and tried to say, with the food they had prepared themselves, what anguish was in their hearts.

Felix and Adam called next day to say good-bye. Felix was on his way to Budapest, and Adam, although he was only reporting to the garrison, did not know if he would see them again either. Papa shook hands with them and told them what a fine and splendid thing they were doing. Mama kissed them both and pinned roses on their coats. Eva laughed and flirted and finally managed to corner Felix for herself.

"You are not to forget me!" she cried playfully. "If you are too dazzled by the girls in Budapest it will quite break my heart." She smiled up at him through her long, dark lashes to show that it was all a joke, that she was flirting the way she had throughout the summer. She couldn't quite understand the tiny pain in her chest. If she could cry it would be better, but she had no right to cry for Felix Kaldy. They had laughed and teased each other all through the long summer days, and the gaiety must be preserved. It was her gaiety he liked so much.

"There will be no time to make new friends!" he cried. "Do you think we shall allow a handful of Serbian peasants to keep us from the hunting season? Dearest Eva! We shall be back for the autumn. There will be your birthday in November; do you think I could possibly miss your birthday?"

He snatched her hand and kissed it with great gallantry. She was still laughing, but the pain grew worse and finally she had to say to him, "There will be no . . . no danger, will there, Felix? You will be careful, won't you?"

He laughed again and pulled from his pocket a watch engraved with the Kaldy crest. "See," he cried, "I shall give you this to guard for me. It belonged to my papa, and it is the most beautiful and valuable thing I possess. If I leave it in your trust there will be no danger of a southern beauty taking it from me!" And Eva, eyes shining, held the watch in both hands because surely he would never have given it to her if she hadn't been very special to him.

Adam was quiet, and Amalia, who was also quiet, sat beside him for a few moments without saying anything. She wanted to ask a favour of him but was afraid that Papa might hear.

"Adam," she whispered. "In the garrison. Could you manage to see Karoly?"

He frowned, irritated. "Malie, how can I? The garrison is only a central mustering point. There will be thousands of men arriving and departing. Karoly may already have left."

"No," she faltered. "None of the garrison have left yet. I asked Uncle Sandor."

"I do not know how I can manage to see him or speak with

him. He is a regular officer of hussars; I am only a mobilized soldier. I do not even know what part of the garrison he will be in." As he saw her face his voice softened. "Understand, Malie, try to understand. Have you any idea of the confusion there? Oh, very well, I will try, but I cannot promise. If I see him I will try to speak. What do you want me to say?"

"Tell him—"

Suddenly there was nothing she could say. Tell him she loved him? She pictured Adam rushing across a crowded parade-ground, saying, *Amalia Ferenc loves you,* and she fell silent again.

"Tell him I shall pray for him," she said at last. "And tell him that he is more important to me than Papa, and I will act accordingly."

Adam nodded, but his eyes were on Eva, sitting laughing with Felix at the other side of the room.

"You will soon be back, Adam."

Malie smiled, and he nodded again, briskly this time. "Oh, yes. I must be back soon to see my sugar crop harvested. There is no one but myself who will care about it."

"Good-bye, dear Adam. You will remember . . . Karoly. Remember, please."

At last he looked at her, his kind eyes understanding and patient. "We don't choose very well, do we, Malie?" he said quietly. "We both seem to be unlucky when it is a matter of loving."

She followed his eyes to Eva, Eva in the yellow dress with her dark hair springing away in tendrils from the braids. She wanted to offer him comfort—the misery in her own heart was such that she was painfully aware of his unhappiness too—but there was only one thing Adam wanted to hear. And even if she said it, said, "Eva cares for you, Adam. I am sure she cares for you," it was so patently untrue he would think her a fool.

The young men left, all the young men with whom they had danced and skated and drunk coffee. They came to say good-bye to the enchanting Ferenc sisters and Papa shook them all by the hand, gratified that his daughters provoked such respectful admiration. The town was still noisy, gay, awash with peasants and horses and more motorcars than they had ever seen in their lives. At breakfast Papa read out the official reply to Russia, which had ordered mobilization too. The reply left no doubt in anyone's mind that Russia was the aggressor and had wronged them. There was still time; if

106

Russia sent her soldiers back to the steppes, the war could be stopped—except that now no one really wanted to stop it. The Russians must be taught a lesson as well as the Serbs.

The first battalions began to march from the garrison—the first men from their town, their county, to go to the front and do their duty. Through cheering crowds and women throwing flowers, the cavalry in their field uniforms clattered to the station against a background of regimental music.

They stood at the window of the upstairs drawing-room watching the men and horses, pointing out to each other the faces they knew. "There's Laszlo, look, leading his troop. He's seen us. He's smiling. And Janni Szabo! And there is Uncle Zoltan's son. When did he come up? He could have come in the coach with us! And there—"

Eva stopped, but it was too late. Everyone, including Papa, had seen Karoly riding ahead of his men. From Amalia's lips came a tiny involuntary moan, and then she pressed close to the window and stared down through the panes of glass. "He's not looking up," she said in a small voice. "He isn't even looking to see if I'm here."

Papa was very angry, both angry and confused. "Come away from the window, Amalia."

"He isn't even looking up. He thinks I do not care. I haven't written and Adam has not delivered my message. He will go away and think I do not care."

"Amalia! Come away from the window at once!"

She moved away from the window, stared uncomprehendingly at Papa, and then suddenly ran from the room. Eva thought she had gone to the bedroom, but a few moments later they saw her running along the cobbled road in the direction of the station, no hat and just a white lace shawl thrown over her muslin dress. Papa, white-faced, turned to Mama.

"Follow her! Get her back! She is behaving like a street woman!"

"Let her say good-bye," said Mama wearily. "What does it matter? He will probably die and then you will not have to make them unhappy. The war will do it for you."

Eva thought Papa was going mad for a moment. He pulled Mama away from the window so roughly that her head swung against the frame. He dragged at the blind; it clattered down and banged hard against the ledge. Then he strode towards the door.

"You'll never find her in the crowds. You have lost her, but

107

she will come home when the train has gone and then you can punish her again . . . and again . . . and again." Mama slumped into a chair, weeping. "Why do you destroy us, Zsigmond? You love us, I know this, therefore why do you destroy us?"

They had both forgotten Eva was there. She cowered in a corner, afraid to draw their attention because already, in these few moments, there was an unbalanced atmosphere in the room. Thin rays of sun slatted through onto the carpet, but apart from that it was dim. She remained quiet and inconspicuous, awaiting a moment when she could leave.

Papa's face was tormented. His eyes darted feverishly from side to side, looking at nothing, everything. "You do not understand. You have never understood, because you are a Bogozy—lazy, immoral, decadent. I have created a class of my own, a family of my own. But I have to guard you, all of you, because you are Bogozys—and Racs-Rassays—useless, idle, proud people."

"Why do you hate us?" moaned Mama. "Why did you marry a Bogozy if you hate us so much?"

"I married you—" Papa stopped. He gazed at Mama in the dim light, seeing her drooped on a chair, still graceful even in despair. "I married you because you were—the loveliest creature I had ever known. And you were a Bogozy. No one believed I could marry a Bogozy. I wanted you."

"Then why do you destroy us, Zsigmond? Why do you destroy your daughter?"

"Because she is a Bogozy too," he answered, suddenly cold again. "She has the bad blood, the carelessness, the . . . the immorality of you all, and I must protect her, guard against the Bogozy influence, the looseness, the immorality."

Slowly, slowly, Mama raised her head and gazed at him. She was as tremulous and helpless as she always was before Papa, not strong enough to fight him but still alive enough to understand him. "So that is why. . . ."

She stretched her hands out before her and shook her head.

"After all these years, that is why you came to hate me. You have never forgotten that night, that one time."

"Never."

"You thought I was . . . careless, immoral."

His face was white and strained and full of hate. "My sister, Gizi—she would never have done it."

Mama's eyes were huge with tears. For a long, long time she had trained herself to live in a world where Papa could not hurt her. And now, because her daughters were growing up, because Amalia and Eva had allowed themselves to tumble down the precipice of emotion, she was once more vulnerable to pain.

"Your sister never loved Alfred as I loved you," she said simply. "You hate me because you think I was immoral. You never considered it was because I loved you."

"No doubt Amalia believes she loves the lieutenant too. But I shall not allow them to be alone together, as your father allowed us."

Mama put one hand to the back of her chair and pulled herself upright. Like a sick, elderly woman she moved across the room towards the door. "I shall be happy again," she said softly, reassuring herself.

Eva was terrified. She did not want to understand what Mama and Papa had been talking of. Already she was burying it away, down in the part of her mind where she buried other unpleasant things. She wanted to get out of the room, because if Papa realized she had heard their conversation he might—she couldn't imagine what he might do, but her skin crawled at something deeper, stranger than she could understand. Silently she moved round the darkened sides of the room to the door. She need not have worried. Papa was staring sightlessly at the shutters and did not hear her depart.

There was a band playing in the large open area before the station. The bandsmen, in red and blue uniforms, puffed and banged and blew, and the noise they made helped to drown the whinnying of horses and the shouting of men. She weaved her way through the crowds: through groups of soldiers who were just standing, smoking, eating sausage and bread; through women holding children in their arms; through harassed officers assembling their men into units. Everywhere was noise, whistles, steam, the cranking of engines and rolling stock, screaming, shouting, and over it all the band playing Strauss marches.

In her stomach were the first stirrings of panic, not because of the noise or people but because, having disobeyed Papa, she might not be able to find Karoly. To risk all this and not be able to see him! A small sob caught at her throat and she swallowed quickly. An officer with a board and pencil in hand pushed hard against her and she grabbed at his sleeve.

"Lieutenant Karoly Vilaghy? Where would—"

"Stand to one side. Excuse me." He smiled briefly and automatically, to show that he was a gentleman albeit a busy one, then shouldered away and was swallowed up in a mass of field grey and rifles.

"Karoly?" She pushed and hunted through a sea of screaming, shouting humanity. An old woman stood, lost and hopeless, but there wasn't time to help her. A soldier with his girl, straight from the country in her long black skirt and stitched blouse, embraced shamelessly and in oblivion. A small boy screaming with delight was riding on the shoulders of a middle-aged soldier.

"Karoly?"

She pressed through the double doors to the rail tracks—four tracks, three of them occupied, one train facing south and two north—how could she know where he would be? Where were the trains going? To Serbia, Russia, or just to another allocation centre? How could she find him when she didn't even know which front he was posted to?

And then there were whistles, shouts, the rumble of engines, people calling from the tracks alongside one of the northbound trains. Flowers were being thrown into windows, flags waved; there were last embraces and tears and soldiers jumping quickly onto the mounting steps, pushing their way into the carriages so that they caught a last glimpse of those left behind. A bell rang and a bewildered guard tried to run along the track and move everyone back. With a mighty lurch, like a prehistoric monster rising from sleep, the train began to move away.

"Karoly! Karoly!" Oh, God, suppose he was on that train! And she was on the wrong side and couldn't even see clearly who was in the coaches. She rushed along the length of the train on her left, to the end where she could cross the track. A ramp was up against a cattle car and horses were being led onto the train.

"Karoly!"

Now she must search systematically: two trains remained, and if she didn't allow herself to panic it was logical that—were he still here—she would find him. Up one side of the train, along the flat, baked earth, look up through every window, then to the side to peer through the crowds. But they would keep moving; that woman she had seen a long way back just a minute ago. She wanted to order everyone to stay where they were so that she could conduct her search in an orderly fashion.

Halfway through checking that train, it too began to pull

away and again she wanted to scream. Now there was only one train and if she couldn't find him it was all wasted; the trouble with Papa would all be for nothing!

She began to run, hurrying to make her way through the crowds and over the empty track to the other line. It was quieter now, with only one train, and some of the women began to melt away. But she still couldn't see him. He must have gone. . . .

"Malie!" A touch on her shoulder, a hand, a familiar smell —how could he have a smell that she recognized?—"Oh, Malie!" and he was there, looking unfamiliar in field grey but oh so familiar with his thick, fair hair and wide shoulders.

"I couldn't find you!"

"In the restaurant."

The one place she hadn't looked. His arms were round her and she pressed against his coat, hugging him, terrified that it might be the last time she would ever see him.

"Malie, I love you so much!"

Karoly, Karoly. Papa would never understand. Poor, poor Papa.

"I sent a message—Adam Kaldy. I said . . . I said I would pray for you."

"I love you so much, Malie."

"And I you."

"Don't let him separate us. Promise me you will remember me."

"Oh, Karoly!" She was laughing and crying—laughing because here, in this terrible railway station, she was able to say what she liked without fear or inhibition. "I would come with you now if I could."

"A camp follower!" He hugged her to him again, wrapping her in his arms and lifting her a little so that her cheek was against his.

"I'll wait, no matter what Papa says or does. Write to me— write to Kati. She will bring me the letters. And if . . . if there is no answer, if Papa finds a way of stopping that too, write to Roza at the farm. She can read and she will find a way of letting me have the letters. Uncle Sandor will bring them to me."

"Oh, Malie! Now I am happy. You have come to me and I am happy. Nothing matters, does it? It will come right—the marriage fee, and your papa. Just love me, Malie. Everything will be all right."

His large body, his arms, his face, his eyes. Remember them all, engrave them on your mind in case it is the last time.

111

Remember the words, remember that he loves you, remember how he looked when he spoke, for now, at this moment, he is wholly yours.

The whistles began again, the engine, the steam, the bells. The frantic guard began his sheepdog tactics up the sides of the train. A last grasping of the beloved body, his mouth on hers—without passion because now there was only the frenzied necessity of expressing their love.

"Darling Malie."

He pulled away and jumped onto the steps of the moving train. The white lace shawl caught in the buckle of his belt and went with him. He tried to unravel it but already he was moving away and she shook her head and waved at him. She saw him smile, lift the shawl to his lips, and mouth the words, *I love you.*

They watched the train disappear in the distance, she and all the other women. There had been so much noise and now, within a few brief seconds, it was silent: no band, no engines, no whistles or bells, just women standing on the baked earth clutching handkerchiefs and bags and trying not to let despair overwhelm them. The station was strange, quiet, uncanny, with, overhead, two doves lifting and falling in the summer air.

Women in lace dresses and expensive hats, women in black peasant scarves, women in cheap coats and mended gloves, old women, young women, ugly, pretty, poor, rich, they drew together because only they understood; not even the men on the train understood. They waited together until their strength united and they knew they could face the world outside with dignity.

Then began a quiet brushing of skirts along the ground as the gentle procession moved out into the street and back to their homes.

7

Resolutely, and with panache, the war began. To the south went the punitive expedition to Serbia. To the north and east, the great armies of Brudermann, Dankl, and Auffenberg prepared to stop the Russian steam-roller before it could even begin. The Germans had obliterated the Russian army at Tannenberg, and now the time was ripe for Franz Josef's military machine to destroy the southern arm of the Czar.

Forward into Russian Poland they advanced—twenty, thirty, forty miles into good rich farming country from which the grain had already been harvested. There were apples on the trees, cattle fat from their summer grazing, and at night when they bivouacked they were able to eat well from the produce all around them—suppers elegantly served by their orderlies of roast pig, butter, eggs, vegetables, and fruit. It was more exciting than the usual summer manoeuvres because here and there was real opposition—not too much, just enough to raze a few village farmhouses and test the magnificent new howitzers from the Skoda Works. Fifty miles in and the weather was still good. In the evening, while the tents were being pitched and the tables laid, it was often possible to bathe in a stream or pool, removing the dust and grime of the day's ride before sitting down to a pleasant supper.

There were cavalry skirmishes. On the skyline could be seen waiting groups of Russian horsemen and sometimes they could be drawn into a minor charge, a little gentle shooting, before disappearing into the landscape. It was exciting, a little dangerous, and a chance to prove that they were still soldiers and could fight.

It was difficult to pin down the first signs of uneasiness. Cavalry reconnaissance reported more and more Russian horsemen in the area, and when the wind blew from the south they could hear very dimly the sound of regular cannon fire. There was hesitation and some conjecture. There was no danger from the north, the Germans had seen to that, but what was happening in the south? They were fifty miles into enemy Poland, and slowly they were becoming aware that their right side was unprotected and exposed. The holiday air began to disperse and, their sense of isolation in enemy territory growing, they scoured the countryside for signs of advancing Russian troops. When they found them it was from the one direction they did not expect—from behind.

They tried to turn the guns, the transports, the mechanized tractors—all the heavy artillery which formed the strength of their army. The skirmishes gave way to battles, to machine-guns in the face of cavalry charges, to murderous stands where it was uncertain from which direction the Russians would attack. The Slavs and Czechs began to desert, not just in ones and twos but in whole companies, vanishing into the countryside where it was impossible to shoot them down.

The artillery companies began to break down the massive howitzers ready for the retreat order, but when it came it was too late. The rains had begun and the roads and farm tracks, unable to support the weight of armies, quickly turned into glutinous mud that swallowed the expensive motorized equipment. Infantry and horses tried, hopelessly, to pull out some of the smaller guns, only to have them sink again farther along the retreat, the retreat which was rapidly turning into a rout.

Karoly had lost contact with most of the rest of his battalion, even Stefan Tilsky, with whom he had managed to stay close during the battle and early retreat. Stefan, the only one of his brother officers whom he had ever considered his friend, had suddenly become very dear to him during the fighting. They had shared men and food and horses, had cheered each other whenever possible, and had discovered, in the curious way of men at war, that they were both better and more human than either of them suspected. When he lost Stefan—last seen charging furiously into a group of Russian infantrymen—he had felt betrayed and abandoned, much more so than when he had first been informed that the army was isolated, almost surrounded, in the heart of enemy territory.

Orders were to retreat over the River San with as little loss as possible. It was the only way they could retreat, and even that was proving more and more difficult as the Russians pushed up from the south. With what remained of his troop he tried to make his way to where the River San and comparative safety should be. They trudged over the soggy plains, leading their horses and spread out as wide as possible in order to pick the firmest ground. A change of terrain forced them to close in again as the open ploughed land ceased at the edge of a wood. A cart track, now half a metre of mud, led through the trees. The sides of the track were scattered with small guns and dead infantrymen.

In a woody morass of mud, with rain drenching men and horses and steam rising from both, he saw an officer of artillery shouting at a hybrid collection of straining men who were trying to clear the axles of a small howitzer from the mud. The officer was swearing, quietly and intensely, and something about the way he stood, moved, shouted, brought to Karoly's exhausted vision a picture of beet fields and meadows and gentle walks in the summer sun. He led his horse forward and waited until the artillery officer had trudged back to the near side of the gun carriage. It was Adam Kaldy.

"Adam?"

His brown hair was plastered flat beneath his cap and rivulets of rain poured down the sides of his nose. His left hand was bandaged, and blood oozed soggily out of the rag. He glared ferociously at Karoly; then the solid features broke into a wide smile which instantly vanished.

"Karoly, old friend! How many horses do you have?"

Karoly looked at the sad, sick beasts behind him, and then at Adam's great gun carriage. "Five that are still fit. The rest are lame or covered in galls."

Adam nodded. "They will do, they will do. Harness them up to the carriage, old friend. I need them for my gun."

Ahead stretched the track, churned mud and water. From the high banked trees at the sides of the road rain poured in a series of tiny falls and gullies. In one or two places the mud had given way to rain-pocked pools.

"Do you think you can get the gun through that?"

Adam studied the track. "I've checked forward. Round the corner the ground rises and it is better. We have saved this gun from the Cossacks for the last three days. On two occasions it has saved us. Do you know how far we are from the river?"

"Soon, I hope."

"An hour away. And we are near a bridge that the infantry are holding for us."

He considered carefully, thoughtfully. His expression was one that Karoly had seen many times on his face, as though he were deciding what crop he should plant on his farm next year. Finally he nodded.

"I think we must try to save the gun. We shall need it on the other side of the river. So many of our guns have gone, we shall have nothing for defence."

Karoly shouted an order to his tiny group of cavalry. They slithered forward knee high in the mud and began to harness the beasts to the front of the carriage. From the rear appeared a group of infantrymen, only half of whom still had their rifles. One was wounded and dragged miserably in the rear, supported on each side by a comrade.

"You men! Here! Collect brushwood from the forest—plenty, enough to throw in front of the horses and under the wheels of the carriages!" The men stared stupidly at him, not moving or answering, and Karoly, driven to frustration, pulled his revolver and pointed it at the largest soldier. "Deserters!" he shouted. "Czech deserters. Obey orders or I shoot!"

He felt a slight touch on his shoulder and then heard Adam repeating the order in German. Sullenly the men began to scramble up the banks of the wood and throw down brushwood. "Moravians," Adam said apologetically. "There is a battalion of them on the road at the moment. They understand only German or Czech."

He felt foolish and annoyed. He should, of course, have realized. He was a regular officer and knew only too well the language barriers within the army. A violent unreasoning hatred of Adam, a farmer who had no knowledge of military matters, overwhelmed him. It was gone quickly, replaced by hatred of the rain, the mud, and the inefficiency of the high command who had led them into this purposeless confrontation with the enemy. The Moravians threw brush under the feet of the horses and then took up the side harnesses of the carriage.

"Pull! Now, heave . . . and heave. . . ."

Straining, sinking into the mud; the axle didn't move and one of the horses fell, screaming and frightened, trying to pull away from the harness.

"Three hours we have been here," said Adam. "How far behind are they?"

"The mud is slowing them too. And they are looting, whatever is left to loot."

"Have you a cigarette?"

He fumbled beneath his riding cape and from his pocket produced a cigarette. It was wet. "There's no way of lighting it," he said, but Adam took it, smiled, and placed it in his breast pocket.

"Thank you. I will light it later. I will enjoy it later." He turned away to shout again, and then he trudged forward and hauled one of the Moravians out of the way, taking his place and pushing at the wheel. He was a good soldier. There was mud on his face, up his arms and legs and down the front of his uniform. "Come and push, damn you!" he shouted at Karoly. "What use are the cavalry except to pull guns out of the mud?" He leaned forward, his brown, heavy face breaking into a grin, and the cigarette fell into the mud and was immediately trodden on by an infantryman. Adam swore descriptively and Karoly, infected by his tenacity, moved forward to join him.

A rifle cracked. A bullet sang through the air at the place where he had just been standing. The Moravians threw themselves down into the mud, gripping their hands protectively over their heads. From the trees opposite came a volley of rifle fire. One of Karoly's cavalrymen dropped into the mud, his face shattered, and hastily they ranged themselves along the side of the gun carriage, sighting rifles into the wood where nothing, and no one, could be seen. The rifle fire from the wood spread out before them, along a wider front. The Russians were intending to surround them.

"I think we shall have to abandon the gun," Adam remarked slowly. "What a great pity."

"Give me back my horses and we will lead a diversion. Draw them off to the left, away from your gun." Karoly was on his feet immediately, thankful to have some purpose, some opportunity of proving himself and his cavalry, of contributing to the saving of the howitzer. Adam pulled him down into the mud just before a fresh volley of rifle fire flew in their direction.

"Please," he said quietly, lifting his good hand in the air. "I grow nervous when you give them something to fire at. And when I am nervous I cannot think. Now." His brow furrowed. "If we give you back your horses, we shall have nothing to pull with. Moreover you will undoubtedly be shot and this would make me very unhappy." His teeth gleamed briefly in his tired brown face. "You would not draw them to the left. They do not want you. They want my gun. Therefore they would just shoot you as you galloped—and how would you gallop in this mud, my friend?—and then return their fire to us."

To Adam it was just like growing sugar beet—logical, painstaking, based on reason uncluttered by anger or pride or any other emotion. Karoly did not know whether to laugh at him or hit him. Their army was disgraced, defeated, abandoned. They lay in mud, rain beating down on them, victims of apathetic despair, and Adam pondered, oblivious of everything except the immediate problem before him.

The fire from the wood ceased. Karoly felt a prickling along his spine. A sense of impending danger alerted every part of his body. Then there was a scream and from the high ground before them, backed from the left by a fresh volley of

117

rifle fire, a troop of Russian cavalry plunged down into the mud, sabres threshing in their hands.

The Moravians began to shout and cry out. Two of them stood, tried to run back into the forest behind, and were picked off by rifle fire. The remnants of the gun crew and Karoly's cavalry fired into the horsemen at random, and the Russians, slowed by the mud, lost three of their men. Adam, crouching behind the gun axle, sighted, fired, sighted and fired. His bandaged hand made him clumsy, but when the breech was empty he threw the rifle down and snatched one from a prostrate infantryman. The Russians faltered, spurred their horses out of the mud as quickly as they could, and scrambled back up into the trees.

Karoly slithered forward to the front of the gun carriage. His troopers and the remnants of Adam's gun crew were cowering miserably against the front wheels.

"All right! Spread out; face the woods. You there, the man at the end, watch the far side of the track as much as you can." He settled himself alongside them, sighting his rifle towards the trees and straining his eyes into the gloomy, rain-darkened forest. Another long silence, disturbed only by the sound of water on branches and the chesty breathing of the man on his right. Then a flash, a movement to the side, and the Cossacks broke cover from the trees again.

"Fire!"

Four horsemen went down. A horse crumpled to its knees and the Russian jumped clear and tried to clamber back up the bank. Karoly hit him in the back of the head. This time the Russians came on, undeterred by the mud or their fire, but now the men round the gun carriage were becoming organized, taking confidence from the presence of Karoly in their midst.

"Sight and fire . . . carefully!"

It was easy to pick them off when they were this close. Moreover the Russians had no protection, no gun carriage to shelter behind. Six more went down; another was wounded and turned, holding to the neck of his horse. Three of them finally came round the end of the carriage, right on top of the men. The watcher, the one who had been told to look to the far side of the track, was hacked to bits by a sabre before Karoly was able to shoot the horseman. The remaining two slithered forward in the mud and were shot at point-blank range by the hysterical artillery men. The rest of the Russian troop vanished back into the trees.

Karoly worked his way back to Adam. The farmer, unruffled, was lying quite alone, sighting and firing.

"I don't think they'll come back," he said. "They will wait in the woods until we grow tired, or they will circle round and pick us off from the rear. I think we must move now."

Karoly stared at the deserted end of the gun carriage.

"Where are the Moravians?"

"Ran back into the woods. Most of them were shot, I think."

Adam crawled forward and began to release the horses from the carriage. One was lying in the mud whimpering with pain. High up on the beast's front leg a splinter of bone stood out through the flesh and Adam stared down, then softly placed his good hand on the creature's neck. "Poor old fellow," he whispered. "Poor, poor old fellow." He gentled the muzzle for a second, placed his bandaged hand over its seeing eye. The horse quietened. Small snorts of pain came from the nostrils, but the touch of the farmer appeared to give reassurance. Adam's face was drawn, no longer impassive or logical. Beneath his sodden hair and cap he looked old, the way he would look when he was seventy. "Poor old fellow," he said again, and then fired his revolver into the back of the beast's neck. Instantly he stood, turning away from the dead animal back to his men.

"Who is wounded?" he asked.

One of the troopers had been shot in the thigh. Adam nodded deferentially to Karoly, waiting for him to organize the escape.

"Can you ride, Kovacs?"

"Yes, Lieutenant."

"Lukacs! Take Kovacs up before you. You two go first; we will cover you for a few moments. Back through the woods behind, then skirt down as you can to the river."

"Sir!" Behind the shelter of the gun carriage the wounded man was assisted onto one of the remaining mounts. His face was white but he said nothing, only gripping tightly to the neck of the horse. Lukacs climbed up behind and the two men bent low over the horse as it pulled its way through the mud. Behind them a sloping incline formed by the boles of a huge oak tree gave a rough kind of ramp for the horse. Spurred, it went as fast as it could. Rifle shots cracked but the men were unharmed and disappeared into the forest.

"Anyone whose horse is lame, start leading."

One by one the walking cavalry, pulling at the reins of their sick beasts, hurried up the ramp, missing rifle fire as best they could and plunging thankfully into the dripping trees.

"Three horses left," said Karoly. "Everyone else must go on foot—now! Three of us will remain to draw their fire for a little while, keep them from pursuing the walking men."

"I think, once they have the gun, they will not follow too far."

"I shall remain," continued Karoly, ignoring Adam's logic again. "We need two more."

"I am a better shot than most of you," Adam said contemplatively.

"'But your hand is injured."

"I am still a better shot than most of you."

"Very well. One other." He was waiting for one of his dismounted hussars to come forward. It was a chance for the cavalry, the outdated, useless, wasteful cavalry, to show they were still the elite corps of the Imperial army, to prove there was still something they could offer in a modern war—courage—the cold drawn-out courage that could stand against a troop of Cossacks for an hour while the walking soldiers made their escape. He stared at the surly faces of his troopers, reflecting that even after all this time he didn't really know any of them. Several of them were Polish, a few Slavs, some but not many Hungarians. They didn't move.

"I will stay, sir. I can ride a horse and shoot."

A middle-aged man, Hungarian, and talking to Adam, not him. One of the artillery team, a swarthy, middle-aged peasant with big square hands and a heavy face.

"Thank you, Marton." Adam nodded at the peasant; they were not unlike each other, Karoly thought briefly. Adam, a Kaldy, younger son of an ancient family, and Marton, the peasant-bred gunner—how strange they should be so similar. He was ashamed of his troopers, humiliated before these two stocky fellows who now, phlegmatically, put their rifles to their shoulders and stared into the wood.

"Very well. Unless anyone else wishes to stay and give cover to his comrades, you may now retreat into the woods. Make your way to the river. We shall re-form on the other side."

They didn't look at him, but they did look at the horses, covetously and with calculation. Karoly placed his hand on his revolver. "Go!" he shouted. They ran up the incline. Shots were fired but no one was hit, and the wood was filled with rustlings and the noise of feet thrashing through wet leaves.

The noise receded and they were alone, three of them, scanning the forest to see from which direction the attack would come.

"'Shall we fire? Just to let them know we are still here, that the gun has not been abandoned?"

Adam screwed up his eyes and stared into the gloom. It was only midafternoon but the leaden sky and dark trees made vision poor. "No," he answered. "Let them grow careless. Perhaps we can frighten them a little."

They waited: five, ten minutes. "Over there," Karoly said softly. There was a glimpse of movement between two trees. Adam fired and a figure toppled forward from behind a beech trunk. A sensed tension: the wood growing quiet again; water, rustlings, the stirrings of the three horses loosely tethered behind them.

"Now!"

They came galloping through the trees. Sabres had been abandoned and each rider was shooting from a revolver in the right hand. The steep slope—no convenient incline on that side, thank God—had been churned by their previous attacks into a treacherous precipice. As they slithered down, the first ones were easily picked off by the three in the shelter of the gun carriage. The riders behind tried to turn and get up again, stumbled, fell. More fire came from the Cossacks hidden in the trees. Bullets whistled close to the gun carriage, the horses whimpered, and Adam, sighting and firing, systematically picked off another two riders. A gasp, a stifled scream, came from close beside them, but there was no time to turn. The last Cossack scrambled up the muddy bank and spurred back to the advancing gloom. Silence.

"My gunner is wounded," said Adam quietly.

Karoly turned from his tense scrutiny of the forest. Marton lay beside him, a bubble of blood welling from a hole in his throat, another from between fingers clasped tightly over his belly. He was alive, and his eyes were brilliant. A sick noise of phlegm and gurgling blood came from his throat.

"Oh, God!" said Karoly. Adam leaned forward and prized the man's hands away from his stomach. He stared, then released them and let them spring back. The bubble of blood from the throat welled out into a thick red mess, and Marton gurgled and heaved. From his mouth issued a spume of yet more blood.

"Take the horses into the forest," Adam said quietly. "Take them now."

"I shall not leave you here! To face the Russians alone with a dy—wounded man for company."

"Take the horses."

"No! We will get him over a horse and leave together. You and he leave and I will cover you!"

The body of the gunner was rigid, like a piece of bowed steel. His hands over his stomach were wet and red; not even the rain could wash the blood away quicker than it seeped from his body. His eyes had now lost their first agonized brilliance and were oblivious of everything except pain as he choked, vomiting blood and bile.

"Please, Karoly Vilaghy, do not argue any longer. This man is one of my peasants, from my land. He is dying. Please leave us. It is my wish."

"Oh, my God!"

He scrambled to his feet, moved crouching to where the horses were standing, and gathered the reins in his hands. "Let me charge them. Draw the fire from you; perhaps one of the men will come back from the wood to help you." His own frustration was making him talk wildly, foolishly. He was helpless, furious, and he felt it could only be relieved by charging into the Russian guns.

Adam's green eyes gazed at him without expression. "Please," he said quietly. "He suffers. Go now."

Sobbing, raging, he ran up the muddy incline, pulling the horses with him. They slipped, fell, righted themselves, but curiously there were no shots from the forest on the other side of the track. He urged the tired horses deeper into the trees, then mounted one of them and waited.

A single shot, a pause, a sound of feet trudging through mud. Adam was stumbling towards him, his face screwed into a mask of misery. In his hand he held his revolver and down the front of his trench cape a stain of blood was rapidly being washed away by the rain.

"Adam?"

Adam walked past him. Some little distance away he stopped immediately before the trunk of a young beech, wrapped his arms round it, and pressed his head against the bark. A violent paroxysm shook his square frame, a shuddering that spread to the tree and made the wet leaves fall to the forest floor. Karoly, all frustration and anger now dispersed by the fear that Adam had become deranged, moved forward with the horses.

"Adam?"

He watched the stocky figure rocking, saw his filthy hands gripping the trunk as though he wanted to make the tree part of him. From the branches overhead rain dripped on both of them. It was gloomy, endless, and, apart from the noise of water, silent. Finally, some alchemy of the forest seemed to quieten Adam; the sheer size and infinity of it pervaded his distress and he rested motionless against the trunk.

"Adam, old friend. It is dangerous to stay here—they will come at any moment. We must try and get down to the river."

"Yes." He turned and climbed awkwardly up onto one of the mounts. As though at a given signal, a burst of firing came from the track they had left behind them.

"Ride!" screamed Karoly. Adam, galvanized into action, bent low over the horse and kicked it into a gallop between the trees. For a few moments they rode together; then the encroaching gloom and the difficulty of finding a clear path made them draw apart. Rifle shots were still coming from behind, and the last glimpse Karoly had of Adam was of him systematically winding over to the left, where the River San was supposed to be.

He did not see Adam again during the retreat. It was impossible to stop and search, to ask and be answered, to examine every haunted face trudging through the mud.

Back to the Wisloka, back to the Dunajec: 350,000 men and Galicia lost, the army broken, the fortress of Przemysl besieged. In November, behind the River Dunajec, they tried to re-form and support the German attack on exultant Russian lines. Forward a little, with the dead littering the field like careless confetti, then back to the Dunajec again. The mud had frozen now and a thin layer of snow hid some of the ravages of 140 miles of battle and retreat. Victor and vanquished, tired, frightened, cold, settled into winter lines, waiting for the spring when the gods who led them would order once more the charges and countercharges across the Polish landscape.

Stefan Tilsky returned, trudged into the abandoned farmhouse they were using as headquarters. He had lost his horse early in the retreat and had walked most of the way back to the Dunajec. They greeted each other with an affection bordering on hysteria. To recognize an old face, to be able to meet up in their right and proper unit after the destruction of

123

the army—surely it boded well for the future, surely it was an indication that the authorities were still capable of organizing and directing the war?

A few days after Stefan returned, Karoly found himself thinking more and more of Adam. His anxiety was out of all proportion to the length of his acquaintanceship with the younger son of the Kaldys. They had met only briefly during the golden summer of the Ferenc sisters, and Adam had inspired little rapport or remembrance. Karoly mostly recalled him wandering round his fields, giving orders to his peasants and playing with a host of modern but inefficient-looking machines. In company, at parties and picnics, he spoke little. He had been an agreeable background figure, nothing more.

But he kept remembering Adam, the bandaged hand, the unruffled sighting and firing, the painstaking logic, the shooting of the horse, the wounded man, Marton. In the cold, lengthening nights, sleeping in the upstairs room of the farmhouse with Stefan and two brother officers, he lay staring at the ceiling, picturing Adam rocking in misery against the narrow trunk of the beech tree. He tried to imagine if he could have done what Adam had done. If Stefan Tilsky, now, were wounded as Marton had been wounded, could he have done it? But then that was not a fair comparison. Tilsky was a fellow officer, an aristocrat, while Marton had been a peasant. Pondering, reflecting, many things became clear. Marton: why did he look so like Adam Kaldy? The resemblance was very noticeable. "This man is one of my peasants." Yes, of course, the man, older than Adam, could have been a bastard son of the old Kaldy grandfather; perhaps he was even Adam's own brother. That might explain why he had done what he had, feeling responsibility towards a peasant with Kaldy blood. But even so, even with that explained away, could he, Karoly, have done it?

As the men froze into their winter positions, both sides content with a little spasmodic firing from time to time, the necessity to find out if Adam Kaldy had escaped to the Dunajec became an obsession. Finally he inquired at battalion headquarters for the whereabouts of Adam's artillery unit. He was sent to company headquarters and there learned that Adam Kaldy was still alive, and from there he tracked down their new position along the river. The following day he rode across to where Adam must surely be. On a slight rise overlooking the river he found him camping with his men—his peasants—in a snow-bound gun emplacement. His pinched face lit into a swift, cheery smile.

"Old friend!"

Karoly was disappointed. It was just Adam, stocky, square-faced, quiet. He was a little thinner, as were they all, but there was no outward sign of the curious courage that had disturbed Karoly's thoughts for so many weeks. The green eyes were gentle and quiet, the smile welcoming, but Adam did not, as Stefan Tilsky had done, run forward tearfully to embrace his friend.

"Ah! They have given you a new horse! Of course. They must; what is a cavalryman without a horse?" He nodded wryly. "And what is an artillery man without a gun? I am still waiting for a new gun, but in the meantime we manage."

He lifted a blanket over the opening of what was their emplacement and beckoned Karoly inside. The gunners had built a most curious construction. To a small hut had been added a fabrication of branches and canvas sheeting spread over a large dugout. On the side facing the river a few men crouched apathetically, holding rifles to holes in the wall.

"This is our gun site. But we have no gun so we are using whatever we have been able to steal from the infantry. It appears to deter Brusilov's men on the other side. They shell us if they see fire or smoke, but otherwise we are left alone."

"We too."

"I suspect, my friend, that they are as unhappy as we are. I hear they have no food. We have food, but no guns. Perhaps we should come to some arrangement."

"Are you—are you well, Adam? Since we parted, in the retreat, I have been concerned. . . ." He wanted to ask so many things: how Adam had managed his escape, if the man Marton was indeed a blood relative, if he had had nightmares about shooting him. But something in Adam's manner, in his withdrawal from intimacy, dissuaded Karoly from probing further.

"Well? Of course. We are all well. We wait for the *gulasch-kanone* so that we may eat. We wait for our letters from home so that we may read. We wait for our relief watch so that we may go back and sit by a fire. Yes, we are well. We are alive, so we are well."

"You have letters from home?"

Adam's cool green eyes stared impassively into Karoly's. "Yes indeed. From my mother, naturally, and from Amalia Ferenc."

He stiffened a little at that. "From Malie? Malie is writing to you?"

Adam smiled. "She writes because Eva does not. They are letters, just letters."

They were both silent.

Then Adam said reflectively, "No one has raised my beet crop. The women tried, but it was left too late. The ground is hard and the first snow has fallen. It is wasted now."

"I'm sorry."

"It is going to matter. Very soon it is going to be important, my sugar crop and the land."

All this time he had been obsessed with the remembrance of Adam. In his mind the artillery man had become a giant figure, a colossus of strength able to bear the war with fortitude. He had forgotten just how dull Adam Kaldy was, how lacking in vision and imagination. Of course, he was not a soldier. He was a farmer, and he could not see the future of war in the way of a soldier.

"Have you spoken to any of the men of the Second army?" Adam asked dolefully.

Karoly was—unreasonably—irritated. "Yes."

"They have beaten us out of Serbia. We are lucky they have advanced no farther than they have. And to the south of us, I am told, the Russians are at the foot of the Carpathians; in the spring they will try to force the passes and enter into our farming lands." He gazed through the opening in the wall at the bleak, ruined, war-scarred countryside. "Our land too will be ravaged," he murmured.

"Rubbish!" Now Karoly was annoyed beyond measure. The army, the administration, was outdated, true, but they had seen what ineptitude and lack of progress had done. Now things would be different. Now the high command would understand. It was going to be hard but they would manage somehow. Men of skill and vision would rise and save the Empire.

"Rubbish?" Adam considered; then his face broke into a grin. "Well, perhaps you are right, old friend. Perhaps we shall win the war and I shall return to my farm and try, once more, to grow and harvest sugar beet on my land." He chuckled, laughing at himself, and Karoly's irritation vanished, to be replaced by a wave of patronizing affection for his unimaginative companion. The war would end, and Adam would sleep on his farm and let the great events of the times sweep over him.

Karoly stood, wrapped his cape round him, and lifted the blanket. "I must go. God be with you, Adam Kaldy."

Adam smiled and lifted a hand in gentle salutation. Then he turned his gaze back to the ruined farmlands of the Dunajec valley.

8

Every morning at breakfast Papa read out the war news to them. Positions were being maintained; along all fronts the gallant troops were holding back the Russians and the Serbians from Hungarian territory, and relations between the German and Austro-Hungarian armies were comradely and courageous. The wounded—those fit to be seen—were received as heroes; there was a picture of a major receiving the Silver Medal for Valour from the Archduke Karl. Sometimes Papa made little jokes about the war—patriotic ones, of course. He was often affable and teased Amalia and Eva about the number of their suitors at the various fronts.

"Now let me see," he joked heavily when the iron window balustrades had been taken, along with the copper and brass from the bathroom, to be used for the war effort. "I wonder which of Eva's admirers will be firing from the bathroom geyser? And who will be riding along on the iron balustrades from the Ferenc sisters' bedroom window?"

They all laughed, perhaps a little longer and louder than was necessary. It was such a relief to have Papa in a good temper, and the war, with all its many ramifications, appeared to both absorb and entertain him.

There was further enforced jollity when Marie brought in the coffee and also the morning post. The pink postcards from the front were easily identifiable, and Eva and Amalia, one or the other, received such a missive on most mornings.

"I hear that the Military Post Office have formed a special unit to sort the correspondence for two young ladies with the surname of Ferenc!"

Laughter again, strained and ingratiating. Sometimes Leo became hysterical; the opportunity to laugh in front of Papa was too much for him and he was unable to control it. On those occasions Papa's mirth could swiftly turn to irritation and a stern rebuke would result in tears and Leo's removal from the room. Jozsef, who had been attending school since September, was better able to cope. The hours spent at school released him from the oppressive presence of Papa and he had developed a certain detachment, a second life away from home in which he could take refuge.

After the jokes came the gentle inquiries—"And what is happening on the Russian front, Eva? Or is it from Serbia?" —and another attempt at humour. "Your father has to rely on military communiqués and reports in the papers. He does not have a network of informants set all round the Empire!"

It was a respectful but nonetheless authoritative command for the postcard to be read aloud or passed to Papa for silent perusal. Most of the cards, from the cheerful young men who used to call at the Ferenc house, were strangely uncommunicative. The censor cast a blight over everything but, more than that, the things that were happening in Galicia and Serbia served to separate Janos and Pali and George and the others from the charming, gracious life they had previously known. Sometimes Amalia wondered why they bothered to send the postcards at all, there was so little on them, but still they came, a silent cry for assurance that the old world still existed, a world of pretty girls and picnics and courteous rituals and formality.

Letters came too, and then the jokes from Papa grew even more laboured, a result of his uneasiness and suspicion. Eva soon discovered that if she read her letters aloud with smooth, unfaltering confidence Papa accepted the sentences without query or demands to read them himself. She became adept at assessing the contents of the page before she started and sliding quickly, without any break at all, over the parts she did not wish to be heard. Alas, only rarely was there need for such subterfuge. She received letters from both Felix and Adam Kaldy. Adam's were strange and made her feel at first uncomfortable, then bored. He told her little of the war or of how much he was missing her, but he wrote at great length about his men, of their humour, of his feelings and reflections on the countryside and rivers and snow, of what it was like to stand on an icy slope and watch dawn breaking over the Galicia plain, of how he longed to be home on his farm. There was nothing in the letters at all that she had to brush over hurriedly because of Papa, and finally, because she really couldn't be bothered to toil all the way through Adam's tedious pages, she would say, "Oh, it's just another one from Adam Kaldy, Papa," and pass it straight over without reading it herself.

Unfortunately the letters from Felix were even more impersonal and were concerned almost entirely with society news from the capital. For some reason Felix had gone no farther than Budapest, where he was attached to Army HQ. The letters, beginning with *Dear Eva* and progressing through accounts of military balls, recruiting campaigns, parades, and parties, to the final *Please give my fondest wishes to your mama, to Amalia, Leo, and Jozsef, and my sincere respects to your papa,* were insultingly harmless. As soon as breakfast was over, Eva would hurry to her room and scrutinize them carefully, searching for hidden intimacy in the bland and chatty sentences. Once there was reference to the watch, a sentence she slid over quickly without reading aloud to Papa. "My dear Eva! I hope you are taking great care of my watch. Sometimes it is inconvenient not to have it when my day's programme is full of appointments and meetings. I think I must ask you to forward it to me, if you would be so kind. It will be all the more welcome as it comes from such safe hands, and indeed such pretty ones."

She hugged that sentence to her for days. All the while she was packing up the watch and taking it to the post office, she gloated over the intimate compliment. He would hardly have written that if he wasn't thinking of her with affection, longing to see her again. She decided to try and persuade Papa to take her to Budapest the next time he went on business. She discussed the whole problem with Malie, the possibility of going to the capital and the significance of Felix's letters.

"He must like me, mustn't he, Malie? To write every week, and to say that about me having pretty hands? It must mean that he is thinking of me almost constantly."

"To write so often . . ." Malie answered slowly. "Yes, of course, darling, he must think of you as one of his dearest friends."

"'I write to him every day. I don't post it every day because that would make me look too eager, but I write a little piece every day, like a diary, and then post it once a week. That's good, isn't it, Malie?"

"Why don't you write to Adam too?"

"Oh!" Eva shrugged irritably. "Oh, Malie, you know how long and dreary his letters are. I sent him one some weeks ago, and a postcard. I cannot find anything to say to Adam; there is nothing at all to answer. His letters are so boring."

Amalia received letters from Adam Kaldy too, long letters from a lonely young man whose world was disintegrating around him. Those letters also were read aloud to Papa.

It was not until the spring that Papa discovered about the other letters, the letters that were brought over by Kati and passed to Malie in the privacy of the girls' bedroom. Kati, excited, enjoying vicariously with every fibre of her being the delight of Amalia's love, took on a brief authority during the winter and spring of 1915 by becoming their official go-between. For the first time in her life she was performing a needed function for someone. Inevitably her new-found confidence led to her undoing. Aunt Gizi noticed her daughter's bright eyes and flushed cheeks, her firmness of voice (sometimes saying things that verged on the impertinent), and she became alarmed. Her alarm intensified when she realized that the changes in her daughter coincided with the arrival of numerous and fat letters from Alfred's young kinsman, Karoly Vilaghy. A brief inspection of her daughter's room revealed a collection of very short notes which were no more than courteous accompaniments to enclosures. Twenty minutes reduced Kati to tears and a full confession. A further half hour was needed to persuade Alfred that it was his duty, not hers, to explain the situation to Zsigmond Ferenc. Alfred, with reluctant heart and heavy step, donned his coat and beaver hat and proceeded to walk (it took a long time, thus delaying the painful interview) to the home of his brother-in-law. His misery and discomfort was increased when for the last ten minutes of his journey he was joined by Amalia, returning home —radiant—from posting a letter.

"Hullo, Uncle Alfred! Are you coming to see us? Isn't it a beautiful day?"

Alfred stared glumly at the narrow street full of melting snow. From the overhanging roofs dirty water dripped. A beggar shuffled through the slush, one sleeve of a ragged coat flapping empty in the wind, his eyes hopeful but not daring to ask. In the midst of the grey day Amalia was a bright and glowing promise of spring. Her soft hazel eyes smiled at him and, knowing what awful thing he was about to do, he looked quickly away.

"Here," he said to the beggar, caring nothing for him but not wanting to talk to Amalia. "Take this and keep away from the thoroughfares of respectable citizens." He pushed ten filler into the beggar's hand and was suddenly appalled when the man lurched forward and pushed his face close to Alfred's.

"It's keep away now: ten filler and keep away from our streets and houses. It was different last August: flags and flowers for us then, wasn't it?" He waved the flapping sleeve in Alfred's face. "Czernowitz, master! Czernowitz! Thirty minutes trapped under a gun carriage, thirty minutes and a pulped arm. You know what I say, master? Let the Cossacks come! Let them force the passes and come! Then we'll see who must keep off the streets, then we'll see!" He spat into the melting snow and Alfred nervously drew back. "Go and fetch the gendarme!" he said shakily to Amalia, but Malie just stared at the man, at his mad face and flapping sleeve. She wore a grey sealskin coat and a fur hat, and against the soft fur her face was soft. The beggar stared back and some scrap of humanity in him, left over from the war, recognized her innocence. "You don't understand," he moaned. "You don't know what it was like." He stumbled away, disappeared through a narrow arch at the side of the street, leaving Alfred shaking but bombastic.

"Disgraceful," he sputtered. "The sooner the war is over the better, if dangerous creatures like that are to be left roaming the street."

"He was wounded, Uncle Alfred," Malie answered slowly. "He was a soldier and now no one wants him."

"Nonsense! The authorities look after the wounded and disabled. It is only a case of applying to the right people. There is no need for anyone who has served his country to descend to that. He is most probably a deserter."

He was dismayed to see tears rolling sowly down Malie's cheeks.

"My dear! You mustn't let it upset you. I will report the matter to the gendarme at once and they will take the fellow in so that he doesn't offend respectable people."

Malie clasped her hands together and shook her head. "It's the war, Uncle Alfred, the dreadful, terrible war! Will they ever come back to us? Will they all be killed? The young men have gone . . . the postcards come, and the letters. Some have already been killed. Pali. Do you remember Pali? He danced

131

so badly and his hands and face were always wet because he was so nervous. He is dead now. Will they all die? Will none of them come back?"

"Malie, my dear!" Distressed, he remembered his mission. He longed to turn and go home, but at home Gizi was waiting. "Malie." He swallowed hard. "I must tell you—it is so difficult, but you must know—your Aunt Gizi has discovered. . . . It is Kati. . . . She didn't betray you. . . . Please try to understand, my child. I have to tell your father. Gizi knows. If I don't inform him, she will. . . ."

White-faced, she seemed almost to have stopped breathing.

"I shall explain to your papa, tell him in my view no possible harm. . . . Could never understand his objection. . . ." He faded into apologetic mumbling. Within a few seconds Malie's brightness had drained completely away. She was a slumped, drab little girl with huge eyes and he felt ashamed of himself for not knowing what he should have said when Gizi faced him with this task.

"I am sure, once he understands—I will explain, you see—I am sure he will not forbid the correspondence. It is just . . . not right that Kati should be concealing this matter." He felt better when he said that, as though reminding himself that he was only doing his best to protect *his* child. He held on to the thought with all the strength he could muster. "Yes. Kati. If your—when your papa knows Kati has shared in this deceit he will be shocked."

Her face screwed into sudden fury. "How could you!" she screamed. "How could you, Uncle Afred? How could you come to . . . to betray me? Oh, you are a bad man! A bad, bad man!"

She broke from him and began to run.

"Amalia! Come back!"

"He won't see them!" she called over her shoulder. "Whatever you say, I'll get there first! I'll destroy them." Sobbing, she ran along the road and Alfred, feeling sick and most unpleasant, took a few feeble steps in her direction. Just before he reached the Ferenc home he turned right, into the square, and entered a café in order to fortify himself with a glass of brandy.

The interview with his brother-in-law was as disturbing as he had expected. Without the brandy he couldn't have managed at all; as it was he tried, feebly, to soften matters for Amalia. Through his halting, stumbling explanation, Zsigmond sat with a face as white as Malie's had been. Then he rang the bell.

"Please have Amalia come to my study," he said tonelessly to Marie, and the plump little Austrian maid hurried away, slamming the door too loudly in her nervousness.

"Only a girlish prank," muttered Alfred. "Naughty, of course; shouldn't have done it. But no harm. He's a good boy, a fine-looking boy, no reason to be ashamed . . . intentions honourable . . . told me so before he departed for the front. Good officer. . . ."

Papa's cold stare fixed itself on Alfred and successfully froze his mumblings. "Karoly Vilaghy is not suitable for my daughter. I have been unable to crush this—affair, it seems. On two occasions it has been necessary to confine Amalie to her room. The last time, with his departure, I hoped the war would solve the matter for me. It appears I have been too lax."

"Oh, yes! But look here," blustered Alfred. "I mean, what's wrong with the lad? Good family—my relatives—"

"Not good enough." Papa's reply cut rudely into Alfred's protestations. "I investigated Karoly Vilaghy. You seem to think, all of you, that I prevented this relationship for no other reason than my own amusement. I demand obedience from my children, but within that obedience I am prepared to consider, where possible, their own peculiar tastes and predilections. My daughter and this—this young man have behaved so—"

Anger brought him to a temporary silence. Colour flooded and receded over his face several times. He breathed deeply, then continued.

"After their behaviour last summer, the idea of a union between them was repugnant to me. Nevertheless, I investigated. The Vilaghys have no money, are mortgaged to the limits of their property, and have no prospects."

"Oh, but really!" blustered Alfred. "You yourself—when you married—that description could have applied equally well to Marta."

"Marta was a Bogozy," said Papa flatly. "The Vilaghys are nothing."

"Now look here—"

"I cannot consider Karoly Vilaghy as a husband for Amalia, any more than you could consider him for Kati."

Alfred's incoherence, his bumbling discomfort, vanished. "Kati is a Racs-Rassay," he replied with dignity, "a Racs-Ras-

133

say and the richest girl in the county. There is a great difference between the status of Kati and Vilaghy. For Kati I intend something better!"

"Then why should he be worthy of Amalia?"

The tension of the morning finally severed Alfred's self-control. The tirade of humiliation poured on him by his wife, the guilt over Amalia, the uncomfortable feeling that the beggar had left, built to a crescendo of indignant pride. A dark seed of inborn aristocracy in him, the unspoken, unadmitted, unacknowleded barrier between him and his brother-in-law finally burst into unforgettable words.

"Because Amalia has a Jew for a father, and Kati does not!"

It was said, regretted instantly but said. Sickness, disgust, shame welled up between them. Crippling things they had pretended never to think of were revealed instead of being left to fester unseen and unrecognized for the rest of their lives. Always it had been there, covered, held down with many layers of family ties, business discussions, shared transactions, and manly conviviality. Now it was said. The facade that had propped them up for so long was smashed. So much was understood and hated, so many nuances of resentment and rank. Alfred had married a Jewess, but his daughter was still a Racs-Rassay. Zsigmond Ferenc had married a Bogozy, and it was not enough. His daughters and his sons would always be the children of a Jewish banker. And even more: all the hate and resentment, so carefully concealed, neither admitting it even to themselves all these years, was now released, welling up in their hearts. Ferenc money: Jewish money that had saved the Racs-Rassays and the Bogozys, money that had built a new dynasty and repaired an old one, money that the effete, overbred nobility could not earn for themselves. And the cleverness, the brightness, the skill: Gizi with her sharp tongue and keen-edged brain doubling her dowry and building Alfred's empire; Zsigmond, providing a fortune, buying land, proving that he could do what Alfred could never do. And beneath that something deeper still, something basic and primeval and more vital than any matters of race or wealth or family: two men, facing each other, two males, one with a feeble and inadequate daughter; the other, a Jew, a patriarch, with four fine, strong children.

"Forgive me, good friend! It was unpardonable. I did not mean it. I am married to your sister; my wife, a good wife. . . . I try to defend my cousin, the young lieutenant, too vehe-

134

mently and lose my temper. I ask you, Zsigmond, to forget my ill words and let our families continue in love together."

He was a Racs-Rassay; even now, flabby and weakened by years of dependence on Gizi, he could summon something of noble graciousness.

"Not myself, you understand, not my attitude at all, Zsigmond. But the world—society, you understand—would not appreciate your objections to the young man, would think it strange. Not me, my friend. You know my feelings of appreciation, the work we have done together, the farms, the estates, most gratifying."

"Yes." Silence.

"I—er—"

All pretence at conversation ceased. Alfred sat down and stared at the Turkish carpet set in the middle of the polished floor. They would have to go on, continue their lives the way they had done before, share things, pretend they were happy together, but it would never be the same. The silence ceased to be oppressive and became pervaded by a kind of misery. The sound of feet outside the door came as a welcome relief to both of them and their heads turned together as Malie, without knocking, burst into the room.

"You cannot have the letters! You are going to make me fetch them here, but you can't!" Her hands, balled into fists, were clenched into the sides of her skirt.

"Fetch the letters, Amalia," he answered tiredly.

"No. I cannot." Triumphant misery burst from her. "It is too late. I have torn them into pieces, and now they are flushed into the water closet!" Her mouth trembled. "All my letters, all I had of him, and they are gone. Because of you they are gone."

"Amalia, you will not write to this young man any more. You will not see him should he return from the front. There is no question of the association developing. I will not permit it, and this continual . . . defiance must now cease. Do you understand?"

It was so strange. For the first time Papa was not in the insane, terrifying fury that disobedience usually induced. He was cold but dispassionate, as though discussing a business arrangement in which he had complete control but little emotional interest.

"I must ask for your word on this, Amalia."

She had nothing of Karoly's now, nothing to hold and read, to say, *This was his; this came from him; his hand has*

135

touched these pages. The letters, drowned in the lavatory, had left her with no tangible evidence of his beloved presence. Perhaps he was already dead and she would have nothing to hold and say, *My love was real; he lived.*

"I shall not give you my word, Papa."

He looked up at her then, but more in surprise than in rage. "You have no choice, Amalia."

"I do, Papa." She was shaking.

"While you live in this house, until you are married and have authority of your own, you have no choice, Amalia. You will do exactly as I tell you. Now go."

He heard her gasp of indrawn breath; then she stepped forward.

"I shall not do what you ask, Papa. I cannot. I shall not marry him, because there is no way for me to do this at present. But I will not stop writing. I will no longer involve poor Kati in this matter. I will ask for the letters to be sent here."

The fury finally began to generate. Amalia and Uncle Alfred saw the stiffening back, the transparent eyes darken. Amalia had a swift recollection of the beggar with a flapping sleeve, and Papa no longer seemed so omnipotent, so invincible. She was still afraid of him, but she was even more afraid that Karoly might soon be dead.

"I can leave home, Papa. I have been reading the papers and talking to the Women's Charity Association. It is all different now; ladies are working and it is respectable because of the war. I can work in a factory, or train to be a nurse, or—there are many, many things. The man who brings the meat. Did you ever notice that now it is his wife who does it? He is dead, her husband, and now she does his job. And at the station, too, a woman is acting as guard." Her knees were trembling so hard she had to sit down. Never in her life had she defied him before. Only her love for Karoly kept the small thread of courage from snapping. "I do not care any more, Papa. I will not disobey you on anything else. I will be good always. But I want my letters from him. And I will go away and work for the war so that I can have my letters. I will live with Grandma Bogozy." That was a pathetic and idle boast. The Bogozys, terrified that Zsigmond Ferenc's money would cease to rescue them, would have packed her home at once. "Or I will go to Budapest and live in a room near a factory."

That was ridiculous too. They all knew it was ridiculous—beautiful, graceful Amalia, with her finishing-school manners and her three languages, her music and dancing, trying to work in a factory and earn her living. It was ludicrous.

"Or if I am no good in a factory, I could work with children," she continued in a shaking voice. "I look after Jozsef and Leo much more than Marie or the nursemaid. I could go into a private home and look after children, be a governess. There are lots of things I can do."

It was still ludicrous, but it wasn't that ludicrous. The war was already beginning to rock the structure that had supported everyone for so long. Of course Amalia couldn't go away from home and find work. She would never survive in a world of strong aggressive people. But a small pocket of disquiet began to stir in both Alfred and Papa.

"You are nineteen, Amalia," he said furiously. "You will do as I say."

"No, Papa." They could see that her whole body was shaking. She sat in the chair, feet, head, hands, shoulders, all quivering in nervous paroxysm.

"Leave the room at once!"

She ran across the floor to the door. They heard her feet hurrying down the passage and sobs, released from tension, breaking from her throat.

The two men stared at one another. The dreadful thing was still there between them, as it would always be, but now other things could be superimposed upon it.

"I think she would do it," said Alfred slowly. "It is bad, the war; things have changed. Look how it is in Budapest now. Women are driving cabs; I even saw a street sweeper, a woman, the last time I was there. In the offices too—my office, the one off Andrassy Avenue—women now, clerks and bookkeepers, all women."

Zsigmond was silent.

"Why not ignore it, good friend? Letters can do no harm."

"She has disobeyed me," he replied stonily.

"Oh, yes, but look here; they are all naughty at that age. Remember how we—"

He stopped suddenly as he realized that whatever youthful indulgences he had been employed in at nineteen, Zsigmond Ferenc, driven by ambition, would already have been involved in a programme of austerity and work. He felt a shaft of pity—unusual in Alfred—for this man who had never had time to play.

"Leave it, old friend," he said quietly. "The war has made everything different. We can only wait; things will change."

Zsigmond Ferenc did not answer. Too many things had happened in the space of the past hour. Alfred studied his brother-in-law's controlled, silent form and wondered, with some fear, what turmoil of emotion seethed beneath the disciplined face. Suddenly he could take no more. He wanted to get out of the study as quickly as possible and return to the café in the square for another glass of brandy.

"I must go. If Gizi and I can do anything. . . . You know how close our families are. Great unity. Good-bye, Zsigmond." He grasped his gloves and hat, waved in an affable, casual way, and moved towards the door. Zsigmond Ferenc nodded but did not speak and, thankfully, Alfred left the room, rushed down the stairs to the courtyard, and was out in the damp, cold air.

When the letter came from Malie telling him that henceforth he was to write directly to her, it seemed unimportant. Everything connected with Zsigmond Ferenc—the humiliation of their first meeting, the terror and secrecy with which his courtship had been pursued—all seemed trivial, as though it had happened long ago to a young boy. His need for Malie was still strong, stronger than ever. But it had changed. The remembrance of the bright shining girl was the only illusion he had left, the only escape in a landscape of horror.

In spite of repeated efforts to suppress bad news from drifting down through the armies, a trickle of depressing items—rumours, counter-rumours, atrocity stories—filtered through to the troops. Przemysl, besieged for so long, had fallen to the Russians. Horrifying tales were told of its surrender, of men so starved that as the victors moved in their horses had been torn to pieces and eaten raw. The Russians were at the foot of the Carpathian passes, then over the passes—it could not be true! Soon they would swarm over the great Hungarian plain, and the granary of the Empire would be lost. The 28th Prague regiment had deserted, run away during the battle of the Dukla Pass, and the King and Emperor had dissolved them in a manifesto to their disgrace. The Serbs were winning in the south—surely not! And so it went on, fear piled on fear, hopelessness upon hopelessness.

When the spring campaign began, everything should have been better. Led by the Germans, the shattered, humiliated Austro-Hungarian armies began to advance, forward across Galicia, across the ground they had lost in the autumn. Fighting forward, winning against the enemy, it should have been better. At least now there was hope, but the hope was accompanied by bitter, savage fighting.

Karoly's regiment had been transferred down to the southern, more hilly stretches of Galicia. It should have looked different, but in some strange way it was the same, only worse. Small, cannon-bleached stumps of trees stood unbudding in the new spring. Round one or two of the burnt-out villages a few trees still survived and, almost invariably, from their branches hung the bodies of Ruthenian peasants. Karoly thought the Russians had done it until he came upon his own men stringing up a farmer who refused to tell them where his grain was hidden. He had ordered the man to be cut down, but he knew that the next time, when they came to another village and needed food, his men would do it again.

He was deaf for four days—from the German guns, not the Russians—and when the time came for him and Stefan Tilsky to lead a charge onto a Russian machine-gun post he was thankful he could not hear the screams of his men being mowed down. They took the post, but his hatred for the enemy was now so intense that he ignored the ragged surrender and began to cut at them with his sabre. After, when he looked at Stefan, he found his friend's hand, face, and clothes were covered in Russian blood, the same as his own.

Night was when he needed Malie. From his memory he took her—quiet, serene, smiling—a girl who made the world about her composed and tranquil, a girl who could still the battle if only she chose, who would hold him and soothe him and wash the blood from his hands. When he had a chance to sleep he managed to do it only by imagining Malie wrapping her arms around him and soothing death from his head.

Forward, forward to Lemberg. The fighting was harder and he killed more. He wondered why he was not killed himself, because the cavalry—as he had told the old general that night in Cousin Alfred's house—was outdated and archaic. Often he found himself on foot, fighting with sabre and rifle alongside a platoon of infantrymen. In a dispassionate way he pondered on the incongruity of himself and the war. When the hatred was upon him he could kill and slash and smash, faces, arms, legs, torsos, cut them all to pieces. But once he came upon a near-mad emaciated dog gnawing at the rotting skull of a child and he had to turn away and vomit onto the earth.

Everything looked the same: shell craters, trenches, burnt-out villages, pieces of bodies, broken carts bearing the remains of homes as the refugees fled, either one way or the other. In most cases whichever way they ran they were killed for being traitors to one side or the other.

In May, through a haze of blood and killing, they heard that the Empire had another enemy. Italy had declared war and was now preparing to wage a battle, different from theirs, an alpine battle but similar in that it was really just a matter of killing.

Przemysl was relieved, but the fortress had been obliterated by German guns and there was nothing worth having or fighting for any more. Lemberg was taken. Karoly's troop, two days behind the advance force, entered the city and for the first time in ten months found themselves in a city of buildings, trees, cafés, hospitals, and homes. Everything was a little battered, a little frayed and sordid, but it was a city still, a city with gardens and flowers, with leaves on the trees. There were civilians, not many but some, who looked normal and walked about instead of hanging from the branches of trees. There was filthy ersatz coffee to be drunk in the cafés, and girls to be bought, if one had any money, and beds to be slept in, if there was time to commandeer billeting quarters.

The collision with civilization turned him once more into a human being, a tired, horrified, disillusioned human being who hated himself, the Russians, the Germans. Malie . . . Malie. Can I be the same again? Can I enjoy a summer in the mountains ever again?

They were finally riding out of the town, still advancing, when a colonel from military headquarters shouted at them to stop.

"You! And you!" He pointed to Karoly and Stefan. "You are to leave your troop here and follow me. I am requisitioning you for urgent and secret military duty. Officers only."

He turned. Karoly shouted emergency orders to his men and spurred his horse after the colonel, who led them out of the town, through narrow thoroughfares, to an area of warehouses and stockyards on the outskirts of the city.

"May I ask our duty, sir?"

The colonel didn't answer. In spite of the sordid part of town they were in, quite a few people were walking, hurrying, in one particular direction. Horse-drawn ambulances pushed past them, all of them tightly closed and driven by men with frightened faces.

"Is it an ambulance train, sir?"

"You will not speak of what you see, do you understand?"

"Sir." A sick depression settled in his stomach. He began to suspect what duty awaited him, something to do with Russian prisoners or possibly deserters from their own army. He hoped, desperately, that he was not being ordered to assist in a mass execution.

They came to a high brick wall set at intervals with gates, some of which were blown off their hinges by recent shellfire. They rode along the side of the wall until they came to a pair of solid metal doors. One or two civilians were drifting through into the yard beyond and were being pushed back by a harassed lieutenant with a rifle. But, strangely, most of the people whom Karoly had seen hurrying in this direction were just standing silent by the wall. They were waiting in the aimless manner of people who sense something is wrong and are drawn to find out what it is: curious, afraid, unable to move away.

"Get back, scum!" The colonel scowled, hitting out with his reins. "Get away, back to your homes! You'll see nothing here!"

Like a large dumb animal the crowd moved back a few feet and then, as the colonel rode through the gates, they closed in again, going no farther than before.

In the yard was a smell. Karoly, used to the smell of battle, blood, and rotting corpses, found himself gagging. It was vile and abominable, more than the smell of death. It was the smell of corruption and sewers and pus. His chest and stomach heaved, writhed, his throat choked and closed. The colonel glared at him.

"If you have no stomach for this, get out. We can't afford women or weaklings in the army."

"Sorry, sir. It was the smell."

The colonel's face was disdainful. "You'll get used to the smell. And please note, this is a tannery. Any questions from the rabble outside, and that is what is causing the smell—the rotting leather and uncured hides. You understand?"

"Sir!"

"The railway line is at the back."

They rode across the yard and then round the factory building. Karoly glanced at Stefan. His friend's face was wrinkled into a grimace of disgust but there seemed to be no fear, no dread of what they were about to do.

They came round the end of the leather factory, and he saw it—he saw, but he didn't believe. It was so horrible that control slipped away from him and, startled, he found he was laughing, a meaningless, uncontrollable, futile laugh. He forced himself to stop and look away, down at the ground, at the line of ambulances, at the soldiers—no, not soldiers—they were all officers who were standing at the openings along the factory walls, trying to block the exits and entrances caused by shell damage.

"Join those officers at the alley there. Don't let anyone through except the ambulances and the medical corps. You"—he pointed to Stefan—"you had better return to the entrance, prevent them from getting in that way."

"Sir." Tilsky was white now, his face no longer unconcerned.

The rail track stretched away into the distance, a little domestic siding that had once been used for bringing the skins straight into the factory yard. Along it, for several hundred metres, stretched out like beads hanging from a black necklace, were lines of bodies, all twisted into hideous grotesque shapes. Just here and there a hand could be seen moving, clawing up into the air, grasping for help. The bodies were so closely packed together they were in some cases piled on one another. A doctor—one doctor—moved along the lines, two orderlies behind him. He moved quite fast, and once in a while he would stop and point. The orderlies would step forward and separate a body from the heap, beckon one of the ambulances forward, and lift it in. Karoly watched them raise a body, pause, then throw it back on the heap.

"Cholera," said the colonel briefly. "Broken out at the front. Carefully isolated. Orders to conceal it from everyone until the sick are in hospital—otherwise panic and mass desertions. It's gone wrong. Something's gone wrong: no medical orderlies on the train, no water, no sanitation. Mustn't let anyone know."

There was a stir from one of the openings in the factory wall, and Karoly spurred his horse over to the officer guarding it. An old woman was trying to force her way past. "It is my son, my son!" she kept shouting. "You have a train of wounded men there! I know it is my son. You have my son."

"Get back, old mother! We have no one's son here, only Russians."

"Russians!" she screamed. "Russians! Why are Russians wearing Austrian uniforms? I can see; there are wounded there. Let me through. I must find my son!"

The colonel, near madness, galloped over and began to

crowd the old woman back up the alleyway. "Out, out, old cow! Out!" She began to scream at him and he raised his whip and hit her across the shoulders. "Back, bitch of a woman!" he bellowed, and finally the old woman began to run in the other direction. The colonel was sweating; large wet patches spread out from his armpits. "How am I supposed to keep the rabble out with no men?" he shouted. "They give me a platoon of medical orderlies and tell me to handle the situation with secrecy. I don't have enough men. I don't have enough orderlies!"

From the distance came a rumbling. It drove the colonel into a greater frenzy. He raced up and down the sides of the track, swearing and shouting, raising his fists and shaking them in the air.

"God help us!" he cried. "God help us!"

A train was moving slowly towards them, one engine with a small head of steam and twelve closed cattle cars. Like a madman the colonel began to run back and forth, screaming instructions. "Start moving the dead away! Get the dead away before the train comes in!"

It was like moving boulders with a table knife. Medical orderlies drifted in and out of the piles of knotted, twisted shapes, lifting a body here, placing one there. They made no gap at all in the avenue of dead and finally, numbed and apathetic, they stood and watched the train coming in from the east.

The driver and the stoker were at the engine and as the train shuddered to a halt they leaned out, mesmerized at the sight awaiting them. The colonel jumped up onto the running board. "Where are the orderlies, the medical orderlies?"

"No orderlies," the driver said slowly.

"How long? From the front, how long?"

"Two and a half days. The track was shelled. We had to go back and make a diversion. We had new orders. They knew it was a hospital train but they said we must go round the long way."

"Have you opened the doors?"

The driver was terrified. He could not take his eyes from the rows of corpses, and although he did not know what had gone wrong he was sure he was going to be blamed for it.

"No, Colonel, sir. They were closed when we took the engine up. We were ordered not to open them and not to take notice if anyone called out." His voice faded into a whisper.

"We were told there were soldiers inside who would look after the wounded. We thought they were wounded. What is wrong with them? Why are they dead?"

Terror in his eyes, he stared at the colonel. He was a middle-aged man with a bald head. He had a plump wife and six children and in peacetime he shuttled to and fro on the passenger line between Miskolc and Lillafured.

"It is the new weapon imported from the Western Front," the colonel lied, suddenly calm. "Gas, poison gas." No one in the east knew anything of the gas attacks, and the colonel had only just heard of their being used in France. But he was safe. Poison gas was a new, unknown horror and the twisted, rigor-set bodies could not be explained by anything other than a new and incredibly evil weapon.

"Poison gas," repeated the driver. "Poison gas."

"Get back to your engine. Stay there until you are told to move off the siding."

The driver withdrew into the train. His pale face looked out once; then at a snarl from the colonel he turned his head. The colonel shouted at one of his requisitioned assistants—a captain of artillery—and they began to take the bars off the doors.

Karoly was trying to watch the alley, but as he heard the metal doors being slid open he turned. He was in time to see the artillery captain jump clear of an avalanche of stick-like forms spilling out onto the ground. He had almost grown accustomed to the stink, but now a fresh wave of it hit him from across the yard: excreta, urine, blood, the sickly sweet smell of death.

Helpless, like automatons, the few officers, orderlies, and ambulance men stood scattered and still among the unburied dead. They were no longer capable of dealing with the situation.

There was a scurry of fresh horses as a major led in a selection of commissioned officers and one middle-aged sergeant of infantry. Karoly, already in this short time feeling old and experienced in how to keep stomach and sanity under control, watched the new "volunteers" gag, vomit, giggle, and turn white. The colonel, having at last found something he could handle, came across and began to shout at the new assistants.

"We have not enough doctors or orderlies. All single men step forward."

The sergeant stayed back; so did a major and two captains

of hussars. All the other officers, the young ones, were unmarried.

"Married men to keep the civilians away—shoot if necessary. The rest of you must help sort the living from the dead. Not enough orderlies." He began to mumble and move away. The sergeant stepped forward.

"Sir, respectfully suggest that the dead bodies should be carried straight into the drying sheds. We can dispose of them later."

"Yes, good," said the colonel dreamily. "Splendid idea."

They moved over to the track and began working from the near end.

Karoly began by counting, merely to keep his mind from thinking about the death grins on the shrivelled faces. But after a while he stopped counting and the bodies became no more to him than things that had to be moved.

There was a fire on the outskirts of the city that night. The civilian population, used to burning buildings and night skies lit by shells, took no notice at first. Then the smell began to seep into parts of the city and there were questions and uneasy glances at neighbours, everyone hoping for comforting words that would explain the things they did not want to know. In the morning it was all right as the news spread rapidly through the streets and cafés. The old tannery had caught fire and some rotting hides had gone up in the blaze. Nothing had happened and the army had been present all the time to see the flames did not spread beyond the vicinity of the yard.

Until now he had not considered the possibility that he would die. He had known fear and blood lust and shame, but some prevailing confidence had assured him that he would not be killed. He had faith, even now, in the power of the Imperial machine. It was creaking and old-fashioned, but it had always worked before and in the final conflict it would survive. In his youthful conceit he knew that he, and men like him, were to be the saviours of the old army—modern, intelligent men who could adapt and reorganize once it was seen that they were needed. He was needed, and therefore he would not die. This was the faith that burnt in him and sustained him through cavalry charges, machine-gun fire, shelling, and fighting on foot when his horse was killed.

Now it was different. Now he knew he was going to die.

145

At the end of the night of the cholera trains they had all been taken by ambulances to the military hospital. Their clothes had been removed, baked, cleaned, and baked again, and then they were shown to a stone-floored room full of steam where silently, not looking at one another, they immersed themselves in tubs of hot water and carbolic disinfectant.

Later, called together by the colonel, they had received a further warning on the question of secrecy and a pass explaining to whatever authorities would be interested that they had been commandeered for special duties. Then they were sent away, back to their units. But the baked uniforms and the carbolic baths made no difference to the feelings they shared. They all knew they were going to die.

The fear of becoming one of those rigid, twisted bodies haunted him. At night he was pleased to be placed on patrols so that he did not have to try and sleep, for sleep brought with it an imagined stiffening of the limbs, a crawling irritation of every inch of skin, and then he wondered what would happen in the morning. Would he be thrown into a cattle train without food or water for two and a half days to be disgorged and burnt in some disused brickyard or factory building? He was careless during the few skirmishes that followed the retreating Russians. He knew he was going to die and he hoped that a Russian machine-gun would cheat the insidious disease that even now must be germinating in his body. He felt unclean, loathsome, sick, and nauseous. He looked into the face of Stefan Tilsky, and they neither of them spoke of the thing that was uppermost in their hearts.

A week, two weeks, passed, and there were no signs of impending death. The advance was surging over Galicia. "Soon we shall be in Kiev!" they shouted to one another, but it seemed unimportant to Karoly. He knew he would never get to Kiev. With apathy he watched and shared in the vast rolling forward across the Polish plains.

One morning, when the artillery were coming through, he saw a unit belonging to Adam Kaldy's regiment, and a longing to see that stocky figure seized him. Vainly he searched the columns of men and guns for a sign of the man who was not his friend but whom he needed at this hour. Once he asked if they knew where Kaldy was, but the confused and varying answers gave him no hope.

When, finally, the first symptoms of illness apppeared—real symptoms that were not products of his fevered brain—there was almost a sense of triumph. "There!" he cried to himself. "I knew the baths and the precautions were useless. Now I am going to die of cholera." And as he said the words, terror smote him, real anguished terror that made him want to scream. He swallowed brandy and fought the violent shudders that rocked his body. For three days he remained upright on horse and foot. The brandy helped, but finally his coated tongue and unquenchable need for water made the brandy abhorrent to him. On the fourth night he removed himself from his men and went to the ruins of a hut on the outskirts of a village. He told Tilsky before he left that something was wrong, and his friend stared and then looked away.

"What can I do?" Stefan asked, and Karoly, shivering and fighting a blinding pain in his head, stepped back a pace from his friend, feeling already that he was one of the dead. He wanted to fall on his knees and beg Stefan to see that he was not lifted into a cattle train with several other bodies. Please shoot me, he wanted to say. Shoot me now—no, not now, for I am still able to think and feel and be afraid of dying. But when I have turned into an insensible creature of dirt and smell, then shoot me. Adam Kaldy would shoot me; he would not leave me to rot to death. If Adam were here he would help.

"Do? Why there is nothing to do, my friend. I am sure it is a minor ailment, of no importance. I must take every precaution, that is all."

He stumbled across rutted earth, sobbing quietly, shaking, holding his bursting head between his hands. By the time he reached the hut he could hardly walk and he slumped onto the cold ground, too ill even to unroll his ground sheet. Later he woke from a hazy feverish daze and took from his pack a soiled white lace shawl. Hands clenched in misery, he clutched the shawl and cried quietly into it, longing for the comfort and love of another human being. The shawl reminded him of sunshine and streams; and Malie laughing and crying, and two small boys afraid of an old coachman. The shawl was innocence, and he no longer believed in innocence, but he cried for Malie and after a while the sadness wore away and numb comfort came from the contact with the lace.

The following morning he felt no better. He was still shivering in spite of being so hot. He looked out from the hut and saw several more artillery units moving along the village street. In their rear came Stefan Tilsky, riding slowly, looking over walls and into trenches and dugouts.

"Keep back," Karoly cried faintly, but Stefan, when he saw him, spurred his horse and galloped over. As he drew near Karoly noticed the growing consternation in Tilsky's face and knew he must already be looking like the men who spilled from the train in the leather yard.

"You cannot stay here alone! We shall be moving on tomorrow. Can you ride or stand?"

Karoly put his hands against the wall and dragged himself upright. The landscape swayed and a burning agony in his back and limbs felled him to the ground again.

"I shall be well tomorrow. A little rest and I will be cured."

"Back in the last village they have a field station. I shall have you taken back there and then to hospital—"

"No!"

Stefan understood, because he had seen it too. Through a haze of images and shapes, Karoly realized it was not death he feared, it was death in a confined space with thirty bodies beside him.

"Please, old friend," he croaked. "Let me stay here until we know. If I am to die, let it be here."

Stefan nodded. "I will bring you water and a further blanket. Your orderly—"

"No. Keep the men away. If they know there will be more desertions."

"Is there nothing you want?"

Stefan was receding and advancing, like the war across Galicia. Now he was close, now he was a tiny figure a long way away.

"Kaldy, Adam Kaldy," he muttered. "Artillery . . . regiment passing through now. If you see him—you know the Kaldys . . . remember the parties. . . ."

"Adam Kaldy? Yes, I remember the Kaldys."

He made one last effort. "Lieutenant Kaldy . . . to come here . . . he will . . . no fear . . . has not seen the leather yard. . . ." He could still see Stefan but it was too much effort to speak, and he waved him away and closed his eyes.

Blurred figures danced in the darkness. Zsigmond Ferenc stood by a coach watching Malie stumbling out, then Zsigmond Ferenc reached up and pulled out a body, shrunk and twisted and clothed in a field grey uniform. "Keep away from my daughter," he shouted, and threw the body at Karoly.

He woke sweating, trying to push the body away from him, then descended again into a world of thirst and pain. Stefan was there; he opened his eyes once and saw Stefan dropping a blanket over him. He heard the name Adam Kaldy, but he no longer cared or understood what Stefan was saying and again he closed his eyes.

That night he had a moment's lucidity, and loneliness and despair engulfed him. He felt abandoned, unwanted, even though it was by his own wish that he lay hidden in the burnt-out hut. He longed for kindness, for the warm touch of someone who cared about him. Malie was a dream now—he was filthy and knew he would never be able to touch Malie again —but someone would come surely: his mother, or Adam Kaldy. If only Adam would come he could die in peace.

It was daylight again, and Stefan was there with two other men. They were lifting him and he began to scream; Stefan had betrayed him. Every movement of his body brought pain but still he tried to struggle. He was terrified of the pressure of the other bodies, the dirty, unclean bodies that would soon be stacked up all around him. "Stefan!" he screamed, and Stefan's face faded guiltily away and was replaced by a square solid one.

"I have found your friend," he heard Stefan say distantly, and then the miracle burned its way through all the pain and fear. He clung to the sight of the burly face, the face that signified strength and sanity, the face that was his lifeline. He felt Adam opening the fastenings of his tunic and the contact with his square, rough farmer's hands brought comfort.

"Into the cart," he heard Adam's voice saying, but he knew that it would be all right now. Adam would not let him suffocate in a sea of dead. Then the green eyes came close and stared into his face.

"Listen, my friend, try to understand what I am saying. I cannot stay with you—we are advancing—but I have seen that you will be taken to the field hospital. You will be cared for, nursed; you are an officer. They do not let officers die as easily as troops. If you are to die it will be in a bed with someone to bring you water."

He reached up with his hand and felt it clasped. Adam was not afraid of catching cholera. Adam was afraid of nothing.

"Into the cart."

He screamed once more when he was in the cart; it was because he opened his eyes and saw a body next to him, two bodies, two faces covered in a dark erupting rash, two faces with mad eyes, two mouths that sang and muttered and shout-

149

ed. He thought the nightmare had come true, but then he remembered Adam Kaldy and felt safe again. Adam and the jolting of the cart were the last things he remembered. . . .

Ten days later, when he opened his eyes, he found he was in a ward of what appeared to be a makeshift military hospital. There were shelves—empty—stretching from floor to ceiling, and a gallery ran round the upper part of the room. In times of peace it must be a library or museum. A medical orderly was filling a pitcher of water by his bed and all round him were the noises of sickness: men shouting, muttering, breathing painfully, and the clink of bedpans and china.

"Kiev?" he murmured, and the orderly turned round, surprised.

"Kiev? No, this is not Kiev. This is Lemberg."

Back to Lemberg . . . where it had all begun. "And the cholera?" he asked weakly. "Has the epidemic spread?" The orderly looked at him as though he were still delirious.

"Cholera? There has been no cholera."

Karoly felt his heart pounding. What had happened to him? Had he been dreaming the nightmare? "I have been ill?" he asked and the orderly nodded and moved on to the next bed.

"Everyone here is ill," he said irritably. "This is a typhus ward. Bad outbreaks all along the front."

Typhus, not cholera. The wrong disease; he had caught the wrong disease. He began to laugh at the joke that was no joke, laughed until he could not control himself, and the orderly used to mad and feverish patients, shrugged his shoulders and moved away.

9

They went to the farm that summer, just the same as always, only it wasn't the same. Uncle Zoltan had been called up and was somewhere on the Russian front. His sons had gone too, and most of the men in the village. Roza and the other women, the old men, and the children tended the fields and animals and got the crops in, but already the land was beginning to show signs of neglect. When they went to call on Madame Kaldy, Adam's beet fields—left untended for a whole year—were a riot of last season's bolters, newly grown weeds, and spindly beet tops that had reseeded themselves.

Malie and Eva had decided that their contribution to the shadowed times would be to relieve Roza from all kitchen duties. With something of the spirit of small girls playing at cooks, they descended into the kitchen beneath the portico and proceeded to experiment with the stove. Malie's approach was one of curious interest. She had watched Roza (and the cook in the town house) apparently effortlessly produce meals for six, seven, or eight, always on time and always well cooked. How was it done? Planning, organization, and strict timing, she finally decided, but it was difficult to put these into operation when one's partner was Eva, who frequently grew bored just when the dough had finished rising and who never, under any circumstances, cleared up after her own messy and chaotic efforts. When in the mood, Eva could, from some depths of talent hitherto unsuspected, produce a well-cooked meal. This, she considered, excused her from any other contribution, and Roza, returning to her kitchen, would firm her mouth into a line of annoyance. She could not, of course, speak to the young ladies as she wished to, and she would proceed noisily to clear up the mess that Eva had left and scrub the floor that Eva had usually covered in grease and sauce.

Mama lay on her bed reading novels, until after three weeks she noticed that her food was not very well cooked and that her daughters were often quarrelling about who had used too much of this or that or who had spoiled the bread. She announced, with frail, rallying charm, that she too would do her very best to help the war effort, and for a few days following this announcement she could be seen wandering about the farmhouse with duster and broom. The novelty quickly faded, however, and the novels and the escape they brought were resumed.

Leo and Jozsef were not seen much that summer. Uncle Sandor, having brought the family to the farm, then went out to work on the land, and the boys tailed after him like sheepdogs. They took sausage and bread and peppers and ate them with Uncle Sandor and were not seen until the sun had gone down.

Papa came only for short spells. Papa's concession to the war effort was a needed and necessary one. The bank was making money for the nation; there were war loans and bonds, and adjustments, and any number of things that none of them really understood. But they did understand—with joy and relief—that, whatever it was, it kept Papa in town for much of the time and took him to Budapest more often. He came up to see them at weekends, but for the rest of the summer they were left alone.

Apart from the conflict with Eva, Amalia didn't mind working in Roza's kitchen; for one thing, it kept her from thinking of last summer. It was impossible to dismiss those memories altogether and often the two girls would find themselves saying, "Do you remember last year when—?" She found that cooking brought a soothing balm to her gnawing anxiety about Karoly. Two letters had arrived addressed to her at the house; since then, silence. Of course she knew that with the wonderful news of the advance into Russia it would be difficult for the letters to be delivered and dispatched, but nonetheless, always, all the time, there was a sick gentle pain of worry in her stomach.

Eva fluctuated between wild elation and sullen, bad-tempered gloom. Every time a letter arrived from Budapest she would rush to her room, eyes bright, bustling with excitement. Later she would emerge miserable and irritable, and in response to queries about Felix Kaldy's welfare would snap, "All right, I suppose," and slam the earthenware jars and bowls so hard that some of them broke.

On a Sunday in September, with Mama resting in her room and Papa sitting on the veranda working with some papers, Malie heard the distant sound of a carriage. It could only be Aunt Gizi and Kati. The war had cast a pall of quiet over the countryside. There were no young men left to come visiting and the women who came—unless relatives—did so only by invitation.

She went and stood on the porch, looking out at the golden sunlit woods to catch the first glimpse of the Racs-Rassay coach.

"Only one horse," she said to Papa. "The army must have taken the other one, just as they've taken ours."

Papa did not answer. He frequently did not answer Amalia. Since her defiance over the letters they had lived in a strained atmosphere of compromise. He no longer locked her in her room or ostracized her completely from conversation and family activities. He remained cold, stern, and unsmiling whenever he had to address himself to her. On all matters other than the letters she was dutiful and obedient, but on the subject of Karoly she had remained quietly stubborn. When the first letter had arrived addressed directly to her, Papa had waited at breakfast for the usual reading aloud. Amalia had not opened the envelope.

"This letter is from Lieutenant Karoly Vilaghy, Papa. I should prefer to read it in my room." She had stuffed the letter into the pocket of her dress and only Eva saw how her hand was trembling.

They waited for Papa to burn into one of his terrible furies. Amalia had stared at him, straight into his face across the table, and whatever he saw there prevented him from taking issue on the matter. He had risen from the table and left the room. He had not spoken to Amalia for three days. But superficially they were still a family. Amalia was still obedient and helpful, she never again referred to working in a factory, and Papa never referred to Karoly Vilaghy.

"Uncle Alfred has come too," Malie said now, on the porch. "And there is somebody else, another man in the coach." And then her hand flew to her mouth—"Oh, no!"—and she was running down the steps and across the yard towards the coach. Papa put down his papers and rose slowly from his chair, looking out after his daughter.

In the coach sat his sister and brother-in-law. Kati on the other seat was not alone. By her side was a young-old man in the uniform of a captain of hussars. He was thin to the point of emaciation and the uniform hung badly over fleshless shoulders.

The coach stopped and Uncle Alfred alighted, then helped the ladies down. The young-old man was the last to climb down and he did so slowly, as though his body was cracked.

"You remember my kinsman?" Alfred asked gently. "Karoly Vilaghy, now promoted to captain."

Amalia was just standing to one side. She didn't run to him or touch him. They heard her whisper, "Oh, Karoly! What have they done to you!" and tears began to run down her face. The young-old man stared at her, obsessed, following her every movement in a dazed, dreamlike fashion, as though she were not real.

Zsigmond Ferenc looked at his sister, then at his niece. It was obvious that both of them had been crying. He was angry but nonplussed. He could not understand why Gizi had permitted Alfred to bring the young man here, and he could not understand why they had been crying. They were all staring at him, waiting for something.

"Yes, I remember Karoly Vilaghy," he said coldly, looking at the young man.

There was a medal ribbon on his breast, and his face was gaunt and sunk around the mouth. The once tall, upright young man was still tall, but he was bent forward and, as Zsigmond stared, a harsh paroxysm of coughing shook his chest and he hunched forward even more.

"May we come in?" Alfred asked. "My cousin is not well. He has been in hospital for many weeks. He has had typhus and pneumonia and the doctors suspected he had developed a disease of the lung. Now he is better and is on leave to rest. But he cannot stand very long."

Zsigmond felt betrayed. He had always been able to cow Alfred, to intimidate him and make him do whatever he wanted. But now Alfred was waiting, quietly and with the dignity of a Racs-Rassay.

"May we come in?" he asked again.

He looked at his sister for explanation. Her dark eyes stared back, devoid of anything except compassion, an unusual emotion for Gizi to reveal.

"The first of our young men, our own young men, to come back from the front," she said heavily.

Karoly Vilaghy began to cough again and his face turned grey. "You had better come in," Papa said at last, and quietly they began to move towards the porch. Only then did Amalia go to him. She glided to his side and placed her hand beneath his arm.

"Karoly."

He stared down at her hand, then touched it with his fingers, caressed it gently, stroking the back of her palm. "Malie," he said, not to her but to himself, "Malie." Like a blind man learning the names of objects he can never see, he spoke her name and stroked her hand with his fingers.

At the porch he had to stop for a moment, then drag himself up by the rail. He was out of breath at the top and began to cough again, and finally Zsigmond Ferenc began to feel ashamed of his tardy hospitality.

"Sit here," he said, pointing to the chair he had just vacated. "We will all sit here, and Amalia shall fetch lemonade for

154

us. Alfred, perhaps you will assist me in bringing out some chairs."

Mama and Eva suddenly appeared from the doorway. They were dragging the cane chairs from the summer parlour and it was obvious they had both studied the arrival of the visitors from the shuttered windows of the house because they had bright, exaggerated smiles on their faces. They avoided looking at Karoly in the way that people do not look at hunchbacks or cripples.

"How wonderful!" said Mama, giving him her hand and still managing not to look at him. "Just like last summer, a wonderful little family party in the September sunshine. So few of our young men have leave—we haven't seen the Kaldys at all since the war began—and so we must make a great fuss over you, dear Karoly! Amalia shall fetch some tea. We still have a little tea left that we have been saving for a special occasion."

"I'll do it, Malie," Eva said quickly. "You stay here and talk to . . . everyone." She hurried inside, as though relieved to be away.

"Karoly is going to stay with us until he is better," Gizi said. "He was discharged from the military hospital at Kassa yesterday—they are short of beds—and Alfred brought him here this morning. His mother and father have closed their home and gone to Budapest, and we think it will be better if he stays in the country with us for a little while."

For the first time in his life Gizi seemed a stranger to him. Always, no matter what their domestic circumstances, they had been, before anything else, brother and sister, Zsigmond and Gizelli Ferenc. This afternoon she was no longer Gizi Ferenc. She was a Racs-Rassay, wife of Alfred and kinswoman to the emaciated young captain of hussars. He was angry with Gizi. She should have understood more than anyone else. She should never have allowed Alfred to bring him here.

Amalia was sitting close to Karoly. Their hands were unashamedly linked and no one, except Zsigmond, seemed to notice. His anger grew more intense. How dare they flout his authority in this manner! How dare Gizi bring the young man here, and how dare he sit blatantly holding Amalia's hand! A pounding began behind his eyes, a cold white fury that he only just managed to control.

"We have letters from Felix and Adam Kaldy," Mama was

155

saying brightly to Karoly. "Felix is in Budapest, but Adam—ah! I remember, he said that you and he had met."

"We have met," he answered; then he looked straight across the veranda into Papa's eyes. "When I am better I shall come and talk with you," he said.

Zsigmond Ferenc felt his anger drain away. He was shocked at the contempt in the young man's voice. No, it was not even contempt, it was . . . indifference. Karoly Vilaghy was not afraid of him, not even bothered by what he might do to Amalia.

"I must get things finally settled before I go back to the front," Karoly continued tiredly. There was a pause in the forced chatter around them; for so long they had talked and thought about the war and the front. They had bought war bonds and the women had knitted socks and comforters and had raised money in all kinds of ways to help the soldiers. But they had, none of them, understood what it was like, realized what was happening to the brave young men they had cheered through the streets a year ago. And now Karoly had returned to them, a cruel and tangible product of a year of war, a horrifying figure with gaunt features and greying hair, unable to walk or speak for any time without exhausting his lungs. His very presence was an uncomfortable reminder of their easy lives—oh, yes, they complained about the ersatz coffee and the meat queues in the town; they grumbled about losing their peasants and servants and horses to the army—but when they looked at each other, and then at Karoly, it was as though death were sitting in their midst.

There was the medal ribbon on the young man's coat; why did it bother Zsigmond so much? And the blue eyes that looked at him and dismissed him as just another unimportant, harmless child who liked to play at dramatizing life—a child who grew angry and shouted and locked people in their rooms, but who still was only a child and not an adult. Karoly had fought with adults. When they grew angry they killed one another.

There was a flurry from the other side of the door, and Alfred jumped up to help Eva with the tea.

"Delightful!" he cried with obvious relief. "Let us hope this will be the first of many family parties together this summer."

The only people in the room who did not seem disturbed were Karoly and Amalia.

Four days later he called, and the interview with Papa was

brief and to the point. He spoke first, not waiting for Papa to intimidate him, and he spoke while sitting, excusing himself because he was still unable to stand for any length of time.

"I shall not disturb you for too long," he said, politely but without interest. "You know, naturally, that I wish to marry Amalia . . . eventually. I cannot marry her now; I do not know if I am going to live or die. But if I survive the war, we shall marry. It will naturally be pleasanter if you are agreeable to this."

Papa's world was crumbling about him, his world where his children did as they were told and where he was stronger than anyone else. "You know I do not consider a marriage between you and Amalia suitable. I have made myself clear on this many times."

"Yes, well—" Karoly paused to succumb to a severe bout of coughing. When he had finished a thin film of sweat stood across his forehead. "Yes, of course. Some of your doubts I can remove. My promotion, for one thing. If I can manage to stay alive I will be promoted very quickly. Already I am a captain." He smiled, but the smile held no humour. "It is no longer necessary to prove one's military abilities or have influence at the staff college in order to be promoted. It is much simpler now; one only has to stay alive. My family estate—no doubt you have already made inquiries into the conditions of our land—this too has been . . . assisted by the war. My father has sold most of the ground to a Jewish grain merchant, enough to clear the debts and establish himself in Budapest. We have been very lucky."

Everything was said in the same flat, toneless voice. A series of facts, no more, no intention to prove a point or remind Zsigmond Ferenc of his origins.

"I am afraid I still do not think such a marriage suitable for my daughter." He wondered where his fury had gone, the anger that had kept his family in check for so long. He hated this young man with the dying face, but somewhere in his consciousness lay the knowledge that if he succumbed to fury he would be made to feel like a small, badly behaved child. He could not risk the contempt, the contempt of a soldier for a civilian.

"We can plan no time for our marriage," Karoly continued, as though Papa had not spoken. "We must wait until the war is over. If it ends soon and you do not give your consent, we must wait until Amalia is of age. Alternatively, if you wish to expel her from your family circle now, I will take her to my

157

parents in Budapest, and she can stay with them until her marriage can be arranged."

It was as though he were talking of someone known casually to both of them, talking of a vague business situation that had to be arranged in a satisfactory manner.

"I—"

"'My feeling is that it would be better if Amalia remained here, with her family, until the war is ended." He began to cough again, very badly this time, and as he held a cloth to his mouth Zsigmond noticed that it was flecked with blood. The coughing went on and on; he was hunched forward in his chair, one hand held to his stomach, the other clasping the handkerchief. Finally it ended and he lay back exhausted, panting a little and with his eyes half closed.

"I wonder," he gasped. "Could I have a little water, please?"

He was about to ring for Roza, and then he remembered that Roza would be working in the fields and that either Amalia or Eva would come. He wanted neither of his daughters to see Karoly Vilaghy at the moment, so he removed himself quietly from the room and hurried downstairs to get a jug of water. When he came back he thought for one moment that the hussar captain was dead. He was lying back on the chair with his eyes closed and his face a sickly yellow colour.

"Water," he said, pouring and passing a glass. The young man drank it slowly, then lay back again in the chair, staring out of the window towards the vines with their heavy crops of grapes, to the peaches and apricots lying on top of the wine press, drying in the sun, to the chickens and geese and dogs, all scratching together in the dust, to the acacia woods that led down to the river.

"How peaceful it is here," Karoly murmured dreamily. "How quiet and peaceful, like Amalia." He was silent for a moment, then continued. "Did you know how close the Russians were last year? I don't suppose they told you: nearly over the Carpathians. All this"—he waved his hand towards the window—"would have looked like Galicia, everything burnt and dead and full of shell holes, the peasants hanging from trees, all the food gone, just guns and soldiers and burnt huts."

He couldn't answer. Too much had happened. He wanted to drive the young man from his house with a whip, hurl him down the steps into the dust of the yard. He could still do it, physically he could still do it; he was a big man, a strong man in spite of his years. But how could he throw a soldier with a medal ribbon and a bloodstained handkerchief from his house? How could he quell him with words and silent threats when the soldier was no longer afraid of him? He wanted to pound his fists on something, or somebody, raise his voice to the heavens and scream his anger, but how could he do this when the cold blue eyes would just stare at him with indifference and apathy?

"I shall go home . . . to Cousin Alfred's." Karoly began to pull himself to his feet. "The coach is waiting and I have stayed too long." As he walked slowly towards the door he added casually, "It is agreed, then. Amalia stays here until the war is over and we can be married."

He opened the door and she was waiting outside. Her face lit into a smile when she saw him and swiftly she slid her arm round his waist in a gesture that combined femininity with the need to support and help him.

"It is agreed," Karoly told her. "We shall marry as soon as the war is over."

She turned back, smiling, said, "Thank you, Papa," and then returned all her attention to helping him through the hall and down the steps.

He watched them from the window—the thin, young-old man bent exhausted over the prop of the girl's body—and dimly he began to understand why Kati and his sister had been crying.

10

It wasn't that she was jealous of Malie—no, not at all. Poor Malie had had a very difficult time with Papa since meeting Karoly, and it was only right that at last darling Malie and dear Karoly should be rewarded for their constancy. She wasn't one little bit jealous; she loved her sister very much. Indeed, in some curious way Malie was more important to her than Mama, who was gay and charming but . . . unreliable. Oh, no, she was very happy for Malie, delighted that at last Papa had agreed that one day they could get married. She wasn't jealous at all.

It was just that it was so unfair! Always it had been Eva first, *then* Malie. Even when they were little girls she could remember Mama saying, "No, Amalia! You must let Eva have the doll because she is your little sister and you must be kind to her." And Malie had been kind. Eva had had the dolls, and the chance to choose first when there were picture books or crayons to be divided between them. And when they were older and the French mademoiselle who made the clothes for the town's gentry began to come and measure them, always it was Eva's dress that was sewn before Malie's, and Eva who was allowed to make the first selection from the festive dress lengths.

And she was prettier than Malie too. They were called the enchanting Ferenc girls, and of course Malie *was* very handsome, but Eva knew she was really the prettier of the two; every young man who had ever danced or skated or walked or drunk coffee with her had told her so. "Oh, yes, your sister is very nice to look at, but you—you are wonderful, Eva!"

She could see it in the mirror. Every time she looked at her delicate heart-shaped face with the bright eyes and thick mass of black curls, she knew she was prettier than Malie. And— she blushed at the thought, but nonetheless it was true—she had more . . . seduction than Malie. She pretended not to notice the way men looked at her, but all the time she was conscious of their eyes; even Uncle Alfred stared overlong at her narrow waist and the curves of her bosom and hips. Whenever he kissed her he always kept his arms round her just a little longer than necessary.

That's why it was so unfair. She had always been first, and now Malie was in love, and Karoly was in love too. Karoly had never even looked at her. Even when Malie was absent and she tried to cheer him up a little by laughing and teasing, he didn't really look *at* her. He was the second young man not to notice how pretty she was, how naughty and *moderne* and seductive, and while Karoly's indifference merely annoyed her, Felix's failure to appreciate how exceptional she was both hurt and humiliated her. She had done everything: flirted, laughed, provoked, sulked, smiled, pouted, pirouetted, winked, giggled, and flattered. She had, in the course of her pursuit of Felix, collected a number of ardent young men who had been shattered by the side effects of her smiles. They had gone off to the war expressing their devotion and hinting that perhaps it would be rewarded once the war had been won. And Felix had gone away too—smiling at her, saying how much he would miss her, flirting with her—and none of it meant anything. She, who had carelessly charmed so often, knew the difference between a heart heavily inflicted with dramatic love and a pleasant but meaningless romance.

She had even forced herself to pay frequent and dreary calls on Madame Kaldy during the summer. She made Malie go with her, and they had sat and conversed stiffly about the letters they all received from the front. She had asked Felix's mother about the farm, about Adam's boring beet fields, about how she was managing with the men all away. The only time she had seen Madame Kaldy soften was when they called on her soon after Karoly had returned. Malie appeared to be living in some euphoric dream world since Papa's capitulation, and when they had entered Madame Kaldy's drawing room the older woman had crossed to Malie and kissed her on both cheeks.

"My dear," she said, quite kindly, "I am happy for your good fortune. I believe you will be happy with the young man."

Malie flushed, shy but gratified. "We cannot marry until the war is won," she said guardedly, but her face was bright.

Madame Kaldy nodded and raised her hand. "There are difficulties. Obviously it is not the match your papa would have wished, but in the circumstances. . . ."

Eva was angry. Driving back to the farm, her wrath exploded. "How dare she say that. How dare she!"

Amalia frowned. "Say what, Eva?"

"About 'in the circumstances.' Because Papa is not of the gentry—that's what she meant—she thinks we are not really good enough for the old families like the Vilaghys and the Kaldys."

"Why no, Eva! That wasn't what she meant at all. She was referring to the fact that Karoly and I—that we love one another and have refused to give in to Papa. That is what she meant."

She was so obviously upset that Eva said no more. But she knew what the old witch had meant. She hadn't been talking to Malie at all. She had been telling Eva that no Ferenc girl was good enough for *her* son, and that Eva Ferenc could forget about Felix Kaldy.

"Well, I don't like her! And I'm not going there again," she said, hitting angrily at a butterfly that had settled on her skirt. "I only visited her because I felt sorry for her, both Felix and Adam away at the war and no one to talk to her. That's the only reason I went, just to be kind, but I shan't go again."

She was annoyed, not only by the "old witch's" remark but

also by the way Madame Kaldy had kissed Malie and wished her well. Everyone was kissing Malie: Mama, Roza, Kati, even Aunt Gizi. Everyone was saying how wonderful it was that she and Karoly were to be allowed to marry once the war was won. Everyone was talking about nothing else but Malie —and it wasn't fair!

At the end of September they had to get ready to return to town in time for the little boys to begin their school term. And then the final unfairness of all burst upon her.

Uncle Alfred and Aunt Gizi came to see Papa. There was a long and loud (although not loud enough to hear exactly what was said) conversation in the drawing-room, and then Papa had come out looking cross and confused. Aunt Gizi had apparently persuaded him to let Malie stay with them in the country until Karoly was fit and well again.

"He will be here for only a little longer," she said persuasively. "Just as soon as the doctor has declared him fit he will return to the front. Malie can stay until then. It will be company for Kati too."

Eva felt as betrayed by Aunt Gizi as her father. Always Gizi could be relied upon to interfere with her nieces' lives, usually to their disadvantage. Always she was ready to persuade Papa that they should not do this or that, should not go to so many parties, or have so many new dresses. And now Aunt Gizi was actually persuading Papa that Malie should stay in the country, having a lovely time at the Racs-Rassay villa and celebrating the grape harvest with Karoly. She was so angry and peeved that she couldn't even say good-bye to Malie.

The little boys were unhappy about leaving Malie too. They never liked leaving the farm at the end of summer, but this year was even worse because Eva was in such a bad temper. She slapped them both when they climbed up in the coach to go home. She said they had trodden on her dress.

The journey down from the hills was miserable and dreary. Mama prattled gaily for a while—all about Karoly and Malie, of course—until finally Papa said coldly, "I do not see the necessity for constant chatter, Marta. I would appreciate it if you could manage to be silent for a few moments."

Jozsef and Leo sat glaring sullenly at Eva. They had not forgotten the slap, and they were already missing their beloved Malie. The presence of Uncle Sandor on the box afforded a small comfort, but it didn't outweigh the gloomy presence of Papa or their resentment of Eva. In silence they trundled along the dusty roads, between woods and farm-lands, until finally the fields flattened out into a monotonous landscape of small holdings and houses that grew thicker as the town approached.

That evening Eva knocked on the door of Papa's study and glided in without waiting for an answer. Papa was sitting with a book in his lap, but he wasn't reading; he was staring straight ahead of him. She hurried across and sat at his feet, resting her head despondently upon his knee.

"Oh, Papa! I feel so miserable!"

He began to stroke her hair, indulgently, as though enjoying the feel of her soft curls against his palm.

"Everything is changing. Mama and Malie seem so . . . so separate from us all. And even Jozsef and Leo can talk about nothing but Karoly and Amalia." She darted a sly glance up at him. His mouth was firmed into a straight line, his eyes wrinkled in puzzled irritation. "I sometimes think, darling Papa, that only you and I care about the family."

The hand stroking her hair ceased to move. In a cold, remote voice he asked, "What do you mean, Eva? We are as united as ever we were, all of us: your Uncle Alfred and Aunt Gizi, Kati, and all of us—"

"Oh, yes, Papa!" she cried hurriedly. "Of course! I know Malie loves us all really; it is just, with Karoly, she has no time for me at the moment. You know how I love to be with the family, Papa. I'm so lonely. Malie doesn't want to be with me any more, and you are busy with the war." Her delicate face, the eyes brilliant with neglect and unhappiness, turned towards him. "I'm so miserable here on my own. The little boys don't want me, and Mama doesn't want me, and you are away in Budapest all the time. . . ." Tears rolled gently down her unmarked face. She felt so sad at the way everyone was mistreating her.

"You have your friends, my darling," he chided gently. "You know I have always encouraged you to have friends."

"But they are not the same as you, Papa," she said, adoring him. "And when you go away I don't know what I'm going to do."

He stroked her hair again, gazing down into the beautiful, entreating face. "How would it be, my dear," he asked, "if I took you on a little trip to Budapest? When I go up next on business, would you like to come with me?"

"Oh, Papa! I don't mind where I go if I am with you!"

"I cannot be with you all the time," he reminded her. "I

have business to attend to and you will be alone for part of the day."

"I don't mind, Papa."

"Perhaps," he said thoughtfully, "we can find some daughters of my colleagues at the bank to accompany you. Little trips, perhaps to the theatre? And we could ask Felix Kaldy to join us for one or two excursions."

"Anything, Papa!"

She was so lovely, the way Marta had been. She was his daughter and she was obedient and dutiful, grateful for anything he arranged for her, happy to do his bidding instead of defying him like his elder daughter.

"That is settled then." He patted her hand, feeling happier himself because he was once more a father with a loving, obedient child. "Now kiss me good night and go to bed. We will discuss the arrangements in the morning."

"Good night, dearest, dearest Papa!"

She kissed his cheek. She was still sad for herself, because she had been so lonely and neglected, but very soon—immediately outside the door, in fact—she began to feel elated.

"I shall borrow Malie's sealskin coat," she said to herself. "I will ask Marie to shorten it tomorrow." She had a moment's guilt at the thought of actually altering Malie's coat to fit herself, but she pushed the guilt away. Serve her right for not caring about me, she thought piteously, and then she did a few mazurka steps down the passage, humming to herself.

The following morning, bright, happy, and loving everyone at the breakfast table, she opened a letter from Felix. He was leaving Budapest that day following a posting—he could not say which—to one of the fronts.

11

The spring should have brought a sense of hope, a rising promise that the war—which was going well—would soon be over. On the Russian front the great victorious armies of last summer held their positions at a line well inside the enemy territory. The Russians, it was generally conceded by everyone who hadn't actually fought them, were finished. As for the perfidious Italians, those betrayers who had dared to stab the Monarchy in the back, news had just filtered through of a large and glorious victory on the Isonzo. The Italians were being punished for their treachery. The fighting was fierce— yes, the Empire's soldiers were falling—but for every icy alpine rock the Italians tried to defend, their soldiers too were destroyed. Soon they would be reduced, with their inferior weapons and bad organization, to the same routed condition as the Russians.

Serbia was crushed. The hated Balkan shepherds who dared to defy and temporarily conquer the Austro-Hungarian armies were now annihilated. Pushed steadily back into the mountainous hinterland of their own country, caught between the troops of the Empire in the north and the brave Bulgarians (who had decided to throw in their lot with the Central Powers) in the south-east, they were finally starved or frozen into defeat. Yes, everywhere one looked, on all three fronts, things were going well. So why was there no hope in the spring of 1916? Why did people walk a little more heavily and look sadder, more worried? Why was there a feeling of depression and apathy in the air?

The meat and bread queues were longer. There were more women in mourning, more wounded seen walking through the streets of the town. And there were rumours—oh, nonsense, of course!—but they planted seeds of disquiet in the most optimistic of hearts. The rumours stemmed from the soldiers returning on leave from the fronts. Leo and Jozsef, habitués of the kitchen, where Marie, who had a brother at the front, presided, reported chattily one morning that all the soldiers fighting in Russia had deserted. Papa rebuked them and sent them from the table, but the rumours persisted, leaking back through other quarters: all the troops, other than those of Austrian and Hungarian origin, were deserting from their regiments, in some cases joining the Russians in order to fight against their former masters.

And there was a sense, too, of this spring's being somehow repetitious of the last. In the early months of 1915 it had been possible to look both back and forward, to say, "Oh, yes! This time last year we were going to poor cousin Kati's birthday party. And this time next year the war will be over and perhaps we shall be thinking of getting married!" But now, in the spring of 1916, one could only look back to last year, when the war had been on, and then forward to some timeless point when, miraculously, it would all be over and, please God, Karoly and Felix would come home unharmed.

Felix had been sent to Serbia, had indeed been part of the victorious army that had vanquished the dirty Balkan shepherds, but Eva took no joy in his achievements for Felix had ceased to write to her at all, not even sending her a pink field postcard. She had to rely on news of him from the still faithful Adam, who wrote, now, from the Italian front. No longer were Adam's letters tossed irritably to one side without being read; eagerly she scanned them, searching hungrily for a message relayed from Felix. Such comments as there were proved to be brief and unsatisfactory. "Mother reports that Felix is well." "Mother hopes that soon Felix will be given some leave." Leave! What good would that do her! Felix would go home to his wretched old witch of a mother and she wouldn't see him at all, not unless his leave was postponed to the summer when they were all at the farm. Bitterness and hurt pride rankled within her, and combined with the rancour was deep and sincere distress. She prayed for him, prayed he would not be killed and prayed that whatever kept him from writing would soon be put right. At night she brooded and pondered any number of possibilities: that he had met and fallen in love with a Serbian girl, that his right hand had been injured and he had begged Adam not to tell her in case she worried, that he suspected she had grown tired of him and was in love with another. Oh, what did it matter if only he would write?

She began to hate Malie, scribbling away every day to Karoly and constantly receiving great bundles of letters in return. Malie was so happy, so proud of Karoly, so . . . smug!

The visit to Budapest had been miserable and a complete waste of time although for Papa's sake she had had to pretend she was enjoying it. She had gone to the theatre, drunk wartime coffee at Gerbeaud, and generally hated the capital, which would have been so different if only she had visited it when Felix was there. There had been only one bright spot in the whole visit, when Papa had taken her to dinner one evening at a restaurant in Buda. He had arranged to meet a business client, a Mr. Klein, and had warned Eva beforehand that Mr. Klein was a very important man to the bank and Eva must therefore pay respectful attention to him.

She had worn her white dress, the one made specially for cousin Kati's birthday party. The roses—so juvenile, how could she have thought they were *moderne?*—had been stripped off, a fall of blue lace added to the neck and sleeves, and a blue sash draped loosely—as was now the mode—round the waist. Mr. Klein had obviously been enchanted with the ravishing little Ferenc girl, and Papa had glowed with gratification. She had flirted (respectfully of course) with Mr. Klein, who seemed to be nearly forty and had a large, drooping moustache and very sad brown eyes.

The following morning a basket of roses had arrived at the hotel for Eva with a card signed by Mr. Klein.

"How lovely, Papa! But how expensive. Roses in November—and while the war is still on."

Papa had smiled. "He obviously enjoyed his evening, Eva. And he is a very rich man. Yes, indeed . . . Mr. Klein is a very rich man."

The admiration by Mr. Klein who was very rich had done something to ease the wound in her heart caused by Felix's absence. But the roses had faded, and Budapest was cold and rather shabby in the wartime November, and finally she had been happy to return home.

This spring of 1916 was not only depressing, it was boring. It seemed wrong to complain of boredom when men were dying, but really, if you were middle-class, young, and female, there was just nothing at all to do in wartime. Evening parties were composed of young girls and their middle-aged parents, with an occasional officer on leave from his regiment to leaven the heavy company. During the daytime they fetched the little boys from school, sewed, wrote letters, and attended—along with Kati—the charity and wartime societies where they met everyone they had met the day before and would probably meet the day after. A large munitions factory had opened on the outskirts of the town and often, when they were going from one boring fund-raising meeting to the next, they passed small bands of factory girls on their way to the work shifts. They were vulgar, of course, loud and noisy, shouting the way no lady ever would, but they always seemed to be having such an enjoyable time that Malie and Eva were envious.

"They make me feel so *useless*," Malie said one day when they had watched two factory girls in dark blue overalls and white caps throwing a *kolbasz* to each other over the head of a third girl. They were screaming with laughter, jostling, and pushing in the warm May sunshine until a loud high-pitched whistle from the factory made them drop the sausage and race towards the gates.

Malie and Eva stood on the pavement in their deep-brimmed hats trimmed with flowers and ribbons, their white gloves, parasols, and bags of wool (it was knitting-for-soldiers day) clutched in their hands, and the boredom of nearly two years of war washed over them.

"So useless," Malie said again. "I wish we could go out and do something!"

"I wish Felix would write to me," said Eva irrationally, not understanding why Felix's refusal to write made the boredom worse but just knowing that it was so.

"Oh, Eva!"

Amalia was sorry for her sister, sympathetic to her devotion to a man who was unresponsive, but surely her gloom and misery were out of all proportion to any expectations she might have had. She had danced with him at a few balls. They had gone on picnics together, had laughed and flirted a little, and that was all. Eva's two years of bad temper and sulks were surely not caused solely by unrequited love?

"Why do you keep fretting about Felix?" Malie asked her sister. "Last week you received seven letters from the front, three of them from Andras, who wants you to marry him, and two from the Pecsi boy, who is longing for a little encouragement. Why do you still brood over Felix?"

"You don't understand," said Eva moodily. She kicked at the *kolbasz* lying abandoned on the cobblestones. "I'm *different* from you, Amalia." The use of Malie's full name indicated that Eva was feeling superior. "I'm more . . . more sensitive than you. I see things more clearly. I have greater . . . greater desires. Yes, that's the difference between us. I'm more intense and imaginative than you, and I need better things than you. You're contented with nothing. I need more from life than that!"

Malie had stopped walking. She turned and stared, stony-faced, at her sister.

"What do you mean?" she asked in ominous tones. "What do you mean, contented with nothing?"

"Oh, I'm not saying anything about Karoly," Eva went on hastily, slightly bothered by her own carelessness. "I mean he's wonderful and handsome and everything. And I think he's just right for *you*, Malie. But you see, I've decided that Felix Kaldy is the only man suitable for me. I want more than you!"

Amalia's lips pressed into a tight line. Then she spun round and began walking briskly back home again. "I see," she said crisply, and, "I hope you get what you want, Eva."

Later, when Malie was still continuing to be very quiet and detached, Eva wondered if perhaps she had been rude. But really! It was time Malie understood how tired they all were of this dreary constant devotion to Karoly. And she had only said what was true; everyone knew the Vilaghys were inferior to the Kaldys. But the tiny grain of guilt persisted in her heart. She began to feel bad about hurting Malie—if she had hurt her. She didn't like the way Malie continued to be so distant and reserved. It wasn't as though she had said anything dreadful; she had only pointed out the difference between them.

She felt worse when the summer came. She knew, they all knew, that Malie had been hoping Karoly would come home on leave. But in June came news of a giant Russian offensive on the eastern front. The streets of the town were suddenly filled once more with walking wounded, more women wearing black, and the family knew that Karoly wouldn't come home unless he was wounded too.

Uncle Zoltan, that solid farmer figure whom they had known and accepted every summer since childhood, vanished in a sea of dead and missing men lost during the Russian advance. When they arrived at the farm that summer they found that Roza, although not as old as Mama, had already undergone the metamorphosis that changed Hungarian peasant women from healthy sloe-eyed girls into shrunken old women in black.

Mama, her volatile emotions moved to heartbreaking grief by this first casualty in her immediate circle, stepped down from the coach and hugged Roza closely to her.

"Oh, my dear!" she cried softly. "My poor, poor Roza! How can we console you? What can one do to comfort you for the loss of your dear man?"

Roza, always plump and strong, was now so tiny that Mama seemed to dwarf her. Tears ran down the leathery cheeks framed in her black handkerchief. She brushed them roughly away with an awkward movement of her hands. "He will come back! He is a prisoner; he must be. Many, many men have been taken prisoner this June. My Zoltan, he is not dead—he cannot be dead!"

Her hands were ingrained with dirt from the fields. Her back was bent, a little from grief but mostly from bending over the soil.

"Madame," she begged, "what will the master do? He will not take the farm from me because I have no man? I am strong, like a man. I can manage. See already what we have done—your Roza and all the other women who are left. We work hard, the children too. And my sons, two strong sons, madame! They will come home soon from the war. They can take their father's place; the master will be pleased with them! I promise you the master will be pleased. Even if my man—" She choked suddenly, her old woman's face crumpled and distorted as she fought for control. "Even if Zoltan is dead—" And now she could not finish. The use of the terrible word had stripped away pretence. It broke from her in a wail of anguish.

"My dear! My dear!" Mama held Roza by the hand and began to lead her towards the house. "Of course you shall not leave here. I will speak to the master. . . ." Mama's voice trailed away and, behind her, the eyes of Eva and Amalia met in dubious communication. Mama must not promise things she could not guarantee. No one was more war-conscious than Papa, no one more prepared to extol the gallant soldiers who were keeping the Russians from the Hungarian plains. But business was business, and Papa would not tolerate for long a farm run inefficiently by a woman.

Uncle Sandor suddenly came forward. He did not speak, but he placed one huge hand on Roza's shoulder and, as she turned, he bowed and nodded his head slowly two or three times.

"May the Holy Mother bless you, Sandor," the old woman muttered. He patted her shoulder very gently, then turned back to the horse and coach and to the boys, who were waiting very quietly at the side of the yard. They were awed and a little afraid. The war had been glorious until now, martial lessons at school and a sense of excitement and patriotism. Now it was suddenly real; Uncle Zoltan was dead. Leo couldn't remember him very well—it was two years since he had seen him—but the realization that the distant figure had gone forever induced a sense of dread round his heart.

He and Jozsef followed the coach round into the side yard and watched Uncle Sandor unharness the horse.

"Was it like this before, Uncle Sandor?" asked Jozsef. "When you rode seventy leagues and fought the King of Prussia, was it like it is now?"

Uncle Sandor flipped the reins over Sultan's nose. "War is always the same," he growled. "And for the women it is harder."

Jozsef had been concentrating on an inconsistency that had been bothering him for some time.

"Why is it, Uncle Sandor, that when you were a soldier you

were fighting the Prussians, and now the Prussians are on our side?"

Uncle Sandor led Sultan into the stable. "It is good to have a change," he answered. "That is the way of war."

"Uncle Sandor," asked Leo timidly, "you won't have to go, will you? Like Uncle Zoltan? You won't have to go and fight the Russians?"

The coachman grinned and Leo, for the first time since their arrival, felt safe.

"I am an old man. I think too old even for the King to use."

That was all right then. The uncomfortable feeling induced by Roza's unstable grief melted away. Uncle Sandor could not be killed.

Inside the house the four women were sitting in the kitchen. It was the first time the girls ever remembered their mama sitting in the kitchen; indeed, she rarely visited it at all. Amalia made coffee, and Roza, her tension and grief released by the support of the three Ferenc ladies, poured out a long and detailed step-by-step account of her bereavement, as though by repetition she could make herself believe it and gradually come to acceptance.

"And after the telegram," she continued in a high-pitched monotone, "I had a letter from his officer—'a gallant soldier' he called him, 'a gallant soldier'—and then Victor—you remember Victor, the carter on the Kaldy estate; he was in the same unit as my man and he was wounded; they have taken his arm off, poor fellow—he came to see me and he said my Zoltan was one of the few men in their unit who did not desert; there were just a few of them in this barn, a few infantrymen and some cavalry officers whose horses had been killed. And Brusilov's soldiers coming at them and they all shooting but with only one machine-gun from the loft of the house. And at night my man and two of the others go out for water. There is shooting, Victor said, and they do not come back. But who is to say if he is dead? Holy Mother Mary! Do not let him be dead!

"The front is terrible. Victor says we cannot know how bad it is from the papers; they do not tell us all. For the cavalry it is worse than the rest; all their horses killed and they have no good weapons. They have to fight on foot and stay with anyone who has a gun."

Malie's face blanched and Roza, even from the morass of her undisciplined outpourings, noticed the girl's stillness.

171

"But don't you worry, my dear little girl," she said quickly, placing her hand over Malie's. "The officers—of course—they will be safe! Officers do not die like soldiers. Your young captain will be away on his horse out of danger; it is the men who die, not the officers. Look now, how many of our peasants have died, but none of our young gentlemen!"

It was said without rancour and accepted in that spirit by the Ferenc ladies. It was natural that the peasants should die quicker than the officers. There were more of them, and they were more easily expendable.

"The young Kaldy gentlemen now, they are both safe! One of them here on leave with his mother. . . . You must not worry, my little girl. He will come home safe."

"Which Kaldy boy is on leave?"

"Why, Mr. Felix. But surely you knew? Mr. Felix writes and—"

Eva was gone. She rushed away and they heard her feet running up the stairs. Amalia, her heart still thumping from Roza's description of the front, ran after her, expecting to find her flung across the bed crying or at least in a storm of anger. Eva, however, was pulling her yellow lawn dress out of the trunk.

"You'll come with me, won't you?" she demanded peremptorily. "You must. It will look bad if I visit on my own." She took pins from her hair and the great dark mass fell round her shoulders. "Can I borrow your cream gloves, Malie? I shall wear my cream hat with the daisies. Papa always says I look well in yellow and cream."

"Eva! We have only just arrived. You cannot go rushing off to Madame Kaldy's without any kind of announcement."

"Yes I can." Eva stopped brushing her hair, and her face, in the mirror, stared back at Malie. "I'm going to find out why he stopped writing to me. And if that old witch had anything to do with it, then I'll make her sorry!"

They had to walk to the Kaldy estate. Uncle Sandor had already put the coach away and was out working in the fields. Even Eva didn't have the courage to order him back to the coach on such a transparently self-indulgent excursion. She grumbled all the way along the hot track as the dust settled round the hems of their gowns and their faces grew red and dirty. She complained about Madame Kaldy, about Uncle Sandor, about the unmade country tracks, and about the uncomfortably high neck of her lawn dress. After the first few moments Amalia ceased to listen and studied the condition of the fields about her.

Madame Kaldy's land, like everyone else's, was suffering from lack of manpower. But even though there were signs of neglect, that indomitable old woman had somehow kept her soil producing more than anyone else's. Adam's beet field had vanished; it was ploughed over and planted with peppers. Already they were turning red and an old woman was hoeing between the lines of plants. The grain had been cut and stacked—cut badly by women, leaving an irregular stubble—but nonetheless the harvest was in. The fruit trees that lined the fields were laden: unripe apples, pears, and plums; apricots and peaches ready for picking. Another old woman was on a ladder, a basket strapped over her back, picking the last of the apricots. As they approached she was respectfully quiet, motionless on the ladder, her black gown and handkerchief outlined against the green foliage. Malie waited for the customary bob of the head, the kindly but deferential greeting that was their right as young ladies. It did not come and, surprised, Malie looked upwards, then became as still as the old woman.

"I thought you were not arriving until today," said Madame Kaldy bitterly. "I hardly expected you so soon. I am not dressed for visitors."

She was angry. She began to clamber down the ladder, and Malie was too embarrassed to offer to help with the basket.

"I'm so sorry—so sorry, Madame Kaldy. We had no idea. . . . Of course we shall go at once. We should not have called so soon. Please forgive us. Mama—"

"Your mama, no doubt, is lying down with a novel after her tiring journey in the coach," Madame Kaldy replied with some asperity. "She will be amused—no, that is the wrong word—she will be incredulous to learn that I have been up a ladder trying to save my apricots."

Amalia was flustered. Madame Kaldy, who had been caught doing something no lady should ever do, had managed to turn the tables and make it sound as though their mama was in the wrong, not her.

"We will call again when it is more convenient," she said stiffly.

Madame Kaldy unstrapped the basket from her back. "Now you are here you can come in," she snapped. "Take the other side of the basket and help me carry it to the house."

173

Awkwardly, moving out of step with each other, they puffed along the path. Eva, unembarrassed and uninvolved, walked behind.

"We've come to see Felix," she said bluntly. "Roza told us he is on leave."

"Yes."

"It would be so nice to see him."

"My son is resting."

Eva suddenly ran forward, trotting sideways and trying to look into Madame Kaldy's face as she moved. "He is not wounded, is he?"

"No."

"Is he ill?"

"He is . . . tired. Felix is very tired."

Her voice, like her face, was non-committal.

"Can we see him? Malie and I would love to see him."

"I don't know. Leave the basket here, on the porch, Amalia. I will spread them for drying tomorrow."

They followed her into the unprepossessing Kaldy farmhouse. The old woman led them into the drawing-room, then hastily withdrew. It was silent and heavy and there was no sign of Felix.

"What's the matter with him?" Eva whispered. "Why didn't he come out to greet us? Surely he should be pleased to welcome us." Malie did not answer and the silence in the room became oppressive. Madame Kaldy had not hung her summer blinds, and the room was dusty and airless behind winter plush.

She returned at last with a tray of cake and lemonade. She had removed the handkerchief from her head and had pinned a cameo and a cream lace collar to her dress. She was, once more, a lady.

She asked after Karoly, and the girls asked about Adam. Then another depressing silence descended and finally Eva could bear it no longer.

"Can we not see Felix, Madame Kaldy? Would he not be cheered by the presence of old friends?"

The bite, the asperity had gone from Madame Kaldy. Her dark eyes were expressionless.

"He is very tired," she said again.

"Just for a few moments."

She looked out of the window, her face set in long, dour lines, and finally she rose from her chair, using the arms to pull herself upright as though she were very tired.

174

"I will fetch him."

They waited again, Eva fidgeting with her hair and dress and arranging her parasol prettily to one side of her. They heard footsteps—slow footsteps—and Amalia, remembering the emaciated aged young man who had returned to her from Russia a year ago, braced herself for a horrifying sight.

"Hullo," said Felix dully.

It was incredible. He hadn't changed at all. He was still olive-skinned, beautifully shaped, black-haired and dark-eyed. He hadn't changed—no—but what was it? There was some imperceptible difference, something so slight it was difficult to define. And then, shocked, Amalia realized what the change was: Felix was unshaven. Previously his soft moustache had pouted from a smooth brown face; now there was a dirty three- or four-day stubble on his cheeks.

And he was in shirt sleeves too. It was all right in the summer, on picnics and outings, for the young gentlemen to remove their jackets, but not for a drawing-room, and in the presence of two visiting ladies.

"Oh, Felix! It is good to see you! I—we—we were worried. We wondered what had happened to you!"

Felix's gaze moved dreamily from his mother to Eva, then out of the window.

"Oh . . . yes . . ." he said, and yawned.

"I—we thought perhaps you were wounded, or ill, or . . . something. . . ."

"Did you? Oh, no. I was all right."

Eva swallowed, Malie could tell from the pitch of her voice that Eva was close to tears.

"Were you away from your supply lines?" she asked. "When you advanced into Serbia, were you cut off from letters and things like that?"

Felix sat down. He wouldn't look at either of them. His eyes roamed nervously over the ceiling, the floor, the curtains, the lemonade glasses.

"Felix! Eva is speaking to you!" Madame Kaldy was distressed. The girls had never seen her so disturbed. Her hands were twisted together in her lap and her brow was arched into nervous lines.

"What? Oh, sorry. . . . No, I wasn't in the forward line at all."

"Was the fighting dreadful?" Eva persisted.

"I didn't have to do any," he answered, and then he shuddered involuntarily as though he were going to retch.

175

"We were worried. When you stopped writing, we wondered what had happened. . . ." Her voice trailed away as she realized that Felix wasn't listening. Piteously, forgetting that Felix's mother was her arch enemy, she turned to Madame Kaldy. "He didn't answer any of my letters," she cried. "He hasn't written to me at all, not since last November."

"And why should he?" snarled the old woman. "Why should he write to you when I, his mother, only received two postcards in all that time?"

"But why?" Eva was nearly crying. The shrill plaintive tones of her voice finally pierced Felix's abstraction; he frowned, irritated by the noise. "Why did you stop writing, Felix?" she screamed.

"Stop? Did I stop? Oh. . . . I don't remember. I'm sorry." He stood and began to pace rapidly forward and back, forward and back, across the room. "So hot in here," he muttered. "I think I shall go and rest."

As he passed, Amalia was disturbed by something else. It took a second for her to realize what had perturbed her. Felix smelled! From his body came a stale, sour odour that was a mixture of dirty underclothes and an unwashed body. She was nauseated, not only by the smell but by the fact that her sister could be so obsessed by this lazy, apathetic creature who lay on his bed while his mother picked her own fruit crop like a peasant woman.

"Come, Eva! It is time we left," she said angrily, rising from her chair, and the unaccustomed note of authority in her voice made Eva obey. "We are sorry to have interrupted your afternoon, Madame Kaldy," she continued. "We shall not call again unless by invitation. In these troubled times it is not always convenient."

Madame Kaldy shook her head. "Come when you like," she murmured. "Come when you like. Who knows, you may be able to cheer him; I cannot."

They could not say good-bye to Felix. He had already disappeared without speaking to them or even looking back. Malie glared at Eva, who seemed to be hesitating over whether or not she should follow him.

"Come, Eva," she said again, firmly, grasping her sister by the arm. "We will go home now."

"Malie?"

"We must go home now. We can call again later, towards the end of the week; Madame Kaldy has said we may. And we can bring Mama. Felix always enjoyed Mama's visits. Perhaps Mama will cheer him."

Eva allowed herself to be led to the door and out into the hall. "Yes," she said loudly, "we will come again at the end of the week, with Mama."

As they began to descend the veranda steps she looked out at the long hot path shimmering in heat haze.

"Oh, Malie!" she sobbed. "It's such a long, long walk back to the farm and I'm so hot!"

Amalia pursed her lips, tightened her grip on Eva's arm, and began to march her firmly over the baked track.

They visited the Kaldys again many times that summer, with Mama, without Mama, and on one occasion with Papa as well. It made no difference. Felix was apathetic and disinterested to the point of rudeness. On some days he was cleaner than others, but this was almost certainly due more to the promptings of Madame Kaldy than to any returning self-respect. All efforts at cheering Felix were met with the same gloomy abstraction. Picnics up in the hills, a tennis party at the Racs-Rassay villa, the harvest celebrations on all three farms—every distraction proved pointless and depressing.

In August everyone was roused to fury by Romania's declaration of war. Transylvania, long coveted by Romania, was invaded, and Hungarian citizens were forced to flee from their mountain farms. Papa and Uncle Alfred spent long hours raging against the iniquitous Romanians, and even Mama shed some tears for the land they had lost (the Bogozys had once possessed a small estate close to the River Arges; it had long since been gambled away, but Mama felt a family affection for what had once been theirs). Felix received the news of the invasion of Hungarian soil with a mild flicker of interest which quickly evaporated into apathy.

In September he returned to Budapest; his posting had been changed and he was no longer with the army of occupation in Serbia. And at the end of September when they had all returned to the town once more, Felix was again on leave.

"How strange," said Malie thoughtfully. "It is almost as though the army has no use for him."

On his way back to the Kaldy farm he called to see them, the first sign of a desire to be sociable he had shown for several months. In his uniform he looked slightly more like the old Felix, handsome and smooth, but the edge had gone; the wit and sharpness that always made Felix such a delightful com-

177

panion was no longer there. And sitting in the drawing-room of the Ferenc town house, he paid little attention to either Eva or Malie. His conversation was all of Mackensen's recovery of the Romanian territories.

"No one can stand against Mackensen!" he said, and he stuttered slightly in a wild, unnatural kind of way.

Papa strode over to a small table that stood near his desk. Since the outbreak of war a map of Austria-Hungary and her neighbours had lain permanently open with flags marking the fluctuating progress of the war. The western fronts were not so important (it was obvious that the war was going to be won here, in central Europe, where it had begun) and if necessary could be briefly looked at in Papa's *geographia*. But the Russian, Italian, and Serbian fronts had to be kept within easy reach so that everyone could acquaint themselves with the situation at a moment's notice. "Yes," he said ponderously. "It seems obvious that Mackensen will lead his armies straight across Romania to the Black Sea, and then"—he paused dramatically and moved his finger on the map—"and then, what is to stop him driving north, directly into Russia?"

"I've seen him." Felix stuttered again. "I've seen Mackensen advancing—not him, you understand, but his armies. In Serbia . . . I saw . . . I was there . . . the soldiers . . . I saw . . ."

He was suddenly embarrassingly uncontrolled. His eyes were shining and a slight nervous tic began at the right-hand side of his mouth. Eva and Malie looked away from him. Mama was staring out of the window, not paying any attention, but Papa had noticed Felix's strangeness, and he looked at him and frowned.

"Yes. Well, Felix, I am sure you have a very good idea of our allied commander's tactics. One would like"—Papa rolled back on his heels and addressed the room authoritatively—"one would like to study in detail the brilliant manoeuvres and techniques of Mackensen. Not for nothing is he called the Lion of Lemberg. Further, he seems to have the gift of leading armies of mixed nationalities and welding them into a loyal and patriotic unit. I believe he commands Germans, Bulgars, and Turks as he advances into Romania."

"They were the worst, the Bulgars!" Felix cut straight across Papa and failed to notice the tightening of Papa's mouth. "But we were just as bad . . . we . . . and I couldn't stop them. An officer, so I had to pretend it was my orders. . . . The same in Romania. . . . It must be—I'm not there, though, am I?"

Everyone in the room was silent. Mama had stopped looking out of the window and her face was turned in astonishment to Felix. The tic had spread right over his face and a thin stream of saliva trickled from the corner of his mouth.

"Are you ill, Felix?" Eva asked, frightened.

Felix rose suddenly and walked to the door. He made a noise that could have been anything and fumbled for the handle. Then he made another noise which sounded vaguely like good-bye and was gone. There was a coldness in all their hearts, the same coldness as when Karoly had stepped down from Uncle Alfred's coach like a sick old man. Sometimes the war was too frightening to understand.

12

There were so many ways of measuring time. You could measure it by the mounting piles of letters: from Karoly if you were Amalia, from Adam Kaldy if you were Eva. You could measure it by the way the little boys had changed. They were no longer round, terrorized lumps of childhood but leggy independent young boys whose lives alternated between school and the stables. At seven and nine they seemed to be divorced from the family, spending much time plotting in corners and chasing out of the house on mysterious boy's errands. Sometimes they returned and, for no apparent reason at all, sought out Malie, pressed her hands or hugged her, and then were away again. Leo came to her secretly when his end-of-term tests were due to take place, and slowly and painstakingly she went through sums and spelling with him and calmed his tendency to tearful nerves.

You could measure time in big, important ways too. Franz Josef was dead and a new Habsburg stood in his place. The Czar of Russia had abdicated and a revolution was taking place. The war had virtually ceased on the eastern front.

Several times a day Malie thanked God for the Russian revolution. She was sorry for the Czar and she supposed Papa was right when he said that it was a dangerous thing to overthrow an established authority. But oh, God, if there was no fighting on the Russian front, then Karoly was safe. His letters throughout the autumn of 1917 spoke of stationary positions and forays that became idle excursions. No fighting, no killing, none of that hideous advancing and retreating across the Galician plains with cholera and typhus ravaging the armies as well as the Russian guns. If he could only stay there, safe on a non-active front until the war was over! Now that Serbia was finished, and Russia almost so, there was only Italy to defeat. She dreaded hearing that he might be posted to the Isonzo as Adam had been. The fighting in Italy was brutal, the casualty lists long. It was a war of rock, ice, and front lines so close they sometimes blew themselves up as well as the enemy. Adam had lost three fingers of his left hand with frostbite. They had thought he might be invalided out, but after a long stay in an Austrian hospital he had been sent back to his unit without even being allowed leave.

Every night she prayed that they would leave Karoly there on the harmless Russian front: please, please, dear God! Everything else was working so wonderfully. Papa, in between bouts of preoccupied depression, seemed at last to have forgiven her initial disobedience. He was gracious, comparatively so, when she told him Karoly had been promoted yet again. Their marriage prospects, once so hopeless, now seemed within reach—if only they would leave him on the Russian front. She could bear the boredom, the worry, Eva's bad temper, Mama's vagueness, and Papa's gloom if only Karoly remained in the east.

Papa's severe moods had made them all a little afraid, until it had been ascertained that, after all, it was nothing that any of them had done; it was the state of the war which was apparently affecting the state of Papa's bank. The strikes in Budapest, the reports of famine in Vienna, the mutiny of the Austrian fleet, all sent Papa into periods of black anxiety. He spent a lot of time closeted with Uncle Alfred and Aunt Gizi in his study, and then Aunt Gizi, and finally Uncle Alfred, too, began to look worried.

The morning came when Papa informed them that a visitor would be coming to stay for a few days, a visitor from Budapest—Mr. Klein.

There was a shocked silence around the table. Never before had Papa invited a visitor to stay in the house. Mama's Bogozy relatives occasionally turned up uninvited but were usually dealt with hastily by Papa (a monetary transaction in the study) and left the same day. Papa had no relatives other than Gizi, and permission for friends of the family to stay had never been granted, either to the girls or to their mama. Papa was either impervious to the air of astonishment or chose to ignore it.

"I wish Mr. Klein to be given every possible welcome in our house. Marta, I know you concern yourself very little in matters of the household, but I would like you to conduct affairs a little more splendidly than usual. Some formal dinners, an extra maid perhaps, just for the visit, and the china and silver I bought from your father, the Bogozy silver—I will have it removed from the vault at the bank and I would like to see it used at table."

"Yes, Zsigmond."

"Is it the same Mr. Klein, Papa? The Mr. Klein who sent me roses in Budapest?"

Papa stared coolly at his daughter, eyeing her in a dispassionate, almost calculating way. "The same Mr. Klein, Eva."

Mama began to sparkle. Life would have motivation again, if only for a few days. She knew she didn't run the house very well—why bother when Marie was so capable?—but she was perfectly able, and would enjoy, arranging a few splendid days: luxurious dinners with musicians and hired servants, crested silver trays carried in and out of bedrooms, bowls of flowers, special dishes and the Bogozy monogrammed glasses (one hundred and fifty years old) filled with vintage wines. Her back straightened and she ran one thin, elegant hand up the back of her hair.

"He is important, this Mr. Klein?"

Papa gave her the same look that he had given Eva, an assessing, considering look, as though wondering how much support he could rely upon.

"He is very important indeed, Marta. He has just returned from Switzerland. Mr. Klein is one of Budapest's leading bankers and does a great deal of business in Switzerland."

"Oh!" Mama fluttered. "Zsigmond, how can we compete? A traveller, a cosmopolitan, he will be used to exotic foods, clever conversation, exciting programmes and people." She wasn't really bothered at all; they could all see that. She was a Bogozy—shiftless and disorganized—but a Bogozy who knew quite well that she was capable of entertaining, graciously and with charm, the King and Emperor himself. Papa ignored her and began to roll his table-napkin.

"Send Sandor up to the farm," he ordered. "He is to bring down meats and poultry, plenty of eggs and butter, whatever delicacies are available."

A festive air began to permeate the room. They hadn't really suffered too much from the deprivations of the war. Hungary was the larder of the Empire and they had their own provisions carefully stored from the farm. Nonetheless the war had brought economies, and now it seemed a gargantuan series of repasts was about to be prepared.

"You have some pretty dresses? Some gowns suitable for formal dinners? Something graceful for day wear?"

Malie hesitated and was about to say yes, when Eva intervened. "We have the dresses we wore for Cousin Kati's party, Papa. And the coats and day dresses we had made last year. We have had nothing new since then." She managed a smile, wistful rather than plaintive. It had recently been a distressing fact that Papa had forgotten about their dress allowances. No one, not even Eva, had had the courage to draw Papa's attention to this fact, nor to the other curious economies that he seeemed to be practising. Papa stared at them yet again.

"Yes. Take the girls to the dressmaker, Marta. A dinner gown each, and a morning dress."

"Yes, Zsigmond!" She wasn't going to ask if she were included. She would order the same for herself without asking. Papa rose from his chair and began to leave the room. At the door he paused.

"Mr. Klein is very important to the bank," he stated tonelessly. "He is to be treated as an honoured and privileged guest."

"Yes, Papa."

"Yes, Zsigmond."

He left the room.

Mr. Klein was exactly as Eva remembered him, tall, dark, with a drooping moustache and sad, dreamy eyes. He didn't look a bit like a financier, more like a professor or a writer of history books. His clothes were beautiful though; both Eva and Mama noticed that and remarked on it to each other. He had a quiet, drawling voice and an amazingly warm and friendly smile. He was enchanted with them.

He arrived late in the afternoon, met at the station by Papa (Uncle Sandor, the coach, and the horse, all groomed to unprecedented splendour), and was escorted home for a brief introduction before retiring to his room to bathe and change.

Glorious smells drifted through the house, soups, pike and mushrooms, goose, venison, stuffed cabbage, and cherry *retes*.

Mama had graced the dining-room as only a Bogozy could: the table was covered with Bogozy lace, French porcelain, and Venetian glass, all bearing the crest of that flamboyant family, and an abundance of silver candlesticks, dishes, cutlery, vases, and an epergne which Mama had decorated with fresh spring flowers. She was pleased, not only because it was a party but also—humanly enough—because Gizi, who had just as many beautiful Racs-Rassay objects to use, would be reminded that she, Marta Bogozy, could present a glorious table when necessary.

They came, Alfred and Gizi and poor Kati, flushed into ugly blotches by excitement; and the advocate, who was important; and the editor of the town's paper, who was not important but Mama needed an extra man; and then the girls came into the drawing-room, and finally Mr. Klein. And Mr. Klein was enchanted.

He was placed next to Eva and opposite Amalia. If he looked two places to Amalia's left he could see Kati Racs-Rassay, and the comparison did everything for the Ferenc girls and nothing for Kati. In their new dresses, Amalia in pale green and Eva in yellow, they were again the enchanting Ferenc sisters. Amalia was pretty because Karoly, dear beloved Karoly, was still on the Russian front where it was safe, and Eva was happy (momentarily) because the hairdresser had wound a coronet of freesias into her dark hair and the freesias were exactly the same colour as the dress.

Mr. Klein didn't speak very much but he smiled a lot, and he paid compliments to the ladies, including Kati, and he listened to Mama, who, sitting at the end of the table, was his other neighbour.

And suddenly everyone, even Gizi, could see why Papa had fallen in love with Marta Bogozy so many years ago. She was graceful and provocative and flattering and proud. Her table was exquisite, her food splendid, her daughters beautiful. She was a Bogozy, an aristocrat, and Mr. Klein was enchanted. After dinner Eva played the piano, rippling her way through Mozart and Strauss with dash and expertise. And Mr. Klein didn't take his eyes from her once.

The evening ended, and Mr. Klein was taken into Papa's study for a last glass of brandy. Upstairs the girls removed the gowns and the flowers and gold lockets, wrapped kimono-type robes around them, and began to brush their hair.

"Do you think Papa was pleased?" asked Amalia.

"He was smiling when he took Mr. Klein into his study."

"I suppose Papa wants him to invest money, or whatever it is that financiers do."

"He didn't stop staring at Mama, did you notice? All through dinner he was looking at her, staring into her eyes and looking at her hair and hands and dress." Eva giggled rudely. "Wouldn't it be funny if Mr. Klein fell in love with Mama, and instead of lending any money to the bank he ran away with Mama instead?"

"'Don't be so unpleasant, Eva!" Amalia turned sharply away from the mirror, feeling suddenly sick at what was really only a vulgar joke.

Eva looked at her in surprise. "Don't be stuffy, Malie. I was only making fun."

"Yes, I know."

She didn't like it, just the same. It was true that Mr. Klein had stared at Mama; he had also stared at Eva and at herself. The melancholy eyes with their heavy lids had studied them each very warmly, and although it was flattering, it had also sent a tiny disquieting ripple up Malie's spine.

There was a scuffle at the door and Leo's face appeared. "Did you bring anything up for us?" the face asked.

"Oh, Leo, darling! We didn't!"

The face crumpled. Four years ago it would have cried, but now the face was eight years old, and men of eight who were training to be sergeants of hussars did not cry.

"Uncle Sandor had some of the banquet," said the face reproachfully. "Ica gave him a big plateful in the kitchen."

"I'll go down now," said Malie, retying the sash of her kimono.

"Oh, Malie! Don't bother," said Eva, yawning. "They can have the bits and pieces in the morning. Ica or Marie or someone will be sure to let them go through the dishes."

"It won't be the same." Leo glared balefully at her.

Malie slipped past him and hurried down the stairs. In the kitchen Marie, the cook, and the hired maid were sitting at the table drinking wine. Between them lay the ravages of the feast and they were staring, satiated, at the remains of the venison.

"It seems wicked, Miss Malie. All this food and in Vienna they're starving."

"And at the front too," said the cook.

Malie filled two plates with a selection of bits. "It is only while Mr. Klein is here," she explained. "He is very important to Papa. After, we shall return to normal."

They nodded solemnly at her. "Important to the master," Marie murmured, and took another sip of wine.

Upstairs the lights had been extinguished in the drawing-room, but from under the door of Papa's study a strip of light played out onto the floor. Just before she got to the study the door opened and Mr. Klein came out. She was conscious of her unpinned hair and of the thin silk of the wrapover kimono. She was also conscious of the two plates in her hand.

"For my brothers," she explained defensively. "The little boys."

"Ah, yes," said Mr. Klein softly. "The bedroom banquet at midnight, the very best kind of party there is." He paused and then added, "It is never quite the same when one grows up."

"No." She waited for a moment, then said shyly, "Good night."

"Good night."

She went swiftly along the passage towards the boys' room. And all the time she was aware of Mr. Klein staring at her back.

Every night there were guests for dinner. The gowns worn for Kati's party four years ago had to be utilized as well. One could hardly wear the same dress every evening. In the mornings Mr. Klein spent all his time with Papa, either in the study or at the bank. Some days they lunched out; Papa would take Mr. Klein to the Marie Thérèse and there they would meet some of the town's important investors. On the remaining days they all ate "informally" at home. Informally meant only that the Bogozy silver and glass were not used; the food was just as splendid, and served by Marie and the hired maid. In the afternoons they took Mr. Klein for drives a little way out of the town, showing him all the rich farmland which was only a little neglected because of the war. Papa didn't come on the drives. Now that he knew Mama was managing so beautifully, he was happy to leave the afternoons to her. And so Mr. Klein and Malie and Eva and Mama trotted out every day in the spring sunshine, and Mama sparkled and shone and enchanted, and Mr. Klein stared and smiled. They called once or twice on Uncle Alfred and Aunt Gizi and everything was just as beautiful as at home. Gizi and Alfred were playing their part in whatever schemes it had been found necessary to carry out.

Once, when they were leaving Alfred's splendid baroque mansion, Mr. Klein looked up at the window where Kati was standing. Kati waved and the girls waved back, and Mr. Klein smiled up at Kati and murmured softly, "What a pity!"

Mama flicked him lightly on the hand with her glove and scolded him. "Now David"—when had Mama started calling Mr. Klein David?—"you are not to be cruel about my little niece. She is a kind girl and we love her, do we not, Malie? Eva?"

"Oh, yes, Mama!"

"Kati is a dear."

Mr. Klein raised one of his dark eyebrows. "Is it necessary only to be kind for all the Ferenc ladies to love one?"

Eva flushed and dimpled, Mama smiled and raised her white hand reprovingly, and Malie felt again that tremor—or something—that moved up and down her spine.

Mr. Klein stayed for ten days, and at the end of that time they were all sick of rich food and evening entertainments. Mama was growing more beautiful, Papa more complacent, and Eva more flirtatious. They all went to see Mr. Klein on the train for Budapest. He shook hands with Papa and then in turn took the ladies' hands in his and raised them to his mouth. Malie was surprised to find his hands were warm and, in spite of the manicured grooming, very hard and strong. The lazy brown eyes stared at each of the ladies—caressingly, flatteringly—and then Mr. Klein climbed up into the train behind his expensive leather suitcases and was gone.

Papa was extremely amiable on the return drive. "I think—yes, I am sure—we can say that Mr. Klein's visit was a tremendous success. He was impressed. Everything impressed him: our standing in the town; the wealth of the county, which he could see was undergoing only temporary difficulties; our . . . solidarity; our accumulated wealth; Gizi and Alfred, not financially inconvenienced too much by the war as yet, and very close to us, united by land and marriage."

Mama did not answer. She had suddenly grown very quiet. The sparkle had left her and she was slumped a little, hands huddled in her muff, over to the side of the carriage. Papa paid one of his rare, uncomfortable compliments.

"Mr. Klein was also impressed with my family," he said awkwardly. "Gracious and enchanting, was the expression he used. Gracious and enchanting."

"Will he come again?" asked Mama.

"Possibly. We shall meet later in Budapest. Maybe—perhaps it will be necessary to invite him again."

A sad, resigned smile drifted across Mama's face. "It was such fun," she murmured. "It was like it was before—when I was a girl."

Papa stared at her, and Malie said very quickly, "You mean the silver and glass and all the entertaining, Mama? The dinners, the splendid food, the guests every night?"

Mama faltered a little and then blinked nervously. "Of course, that's what I meant. We entertained the way we used to, when I was a girl."

They all sighed and settled. There was a relaxing—sad on Mama's part—and a relief from the tension that had gripped them all over the last ten days.

"It will be nice to return to normal," Malie said softly to herself.

When they arrived home the Racs-Rassay coach was outside. Mama was quite cross. "Oh, no! Can't Alfred and Gizi give us a moment's peace? We have only just said good-bye to Mr. Klein. Can they not let us collect ourselves before calling?"

She flung out of the coach and led the way upstairs, unpinning her hat as she went and throwing it on the chiffonier in the hall. In the drawing-room sat Alfred, Gizi, Kati, and—Felix Kaldy!

"Felix!"

Eva was so pleased that she was wearing her new morning dress, the one that had been bought for Mr. Klein. She looked beautiful; she knew she did. The dress was violet and her dark eyes took reflection from the colour.

"Felix! Dear, dear Felix! When did you arrive here?"

"I came . . . ye—yesterday."

"Yesterday!" Eva frowned. "Why did you not call?"

"I heard you—you had someone important staying. And—and I had a message for—"

"He wanted to see us. It was important," interrupted Gizi abruptly. "He came from the war office in Budapest to see us."

Uncle Alfred had been staring out of the window, his back to the room. Now he turned. His face was crumpled and distressed, blurred somehow as though he had been left out in the rain.

187

"Is something wrong, Alfred?" asked Papa quickly. "Is the war news worse? Has something happened on the Italian front?"

Alfred shook his head. He tried to speak but only odd noises came from his lips.

"N-n-not Italy," stuttered Felix. "Russia." Felix was odd too; even for Felix he seemed strained and unnatural. The stutter was worse. It had started when he returned from Serbia and now it was continual.

"What has happened in Russia?" asked Papa.

No one answered. Felix's mouth began to twitch. Alfred turned back to the window. Kati, who had been standing quietly in a corner of the room, began to cry.

"What has happened?" asked Papa again, and then Gizi—how strange it should be Gizi—crossed over to Amalia and put her arms round the girl.

"Malie, my dear, it is Karoly. He has been killed in Galicia."

The only thing she was conscious of was that Aunt Gizi's arms were round her, and that was very odd. She could never remember, even when she was tiny, having Aunt Gizi's arms around her. She felt vaguely sorry for Kati. Aunt Gizi was Kati's own mother and yet she never put her arms round Kati.

"Felix took the message at headquarters. It was forwarded to Karoly's parents in Budapest, and then Felix came to tell us as we are—were—Karoly's relatives. He—he was shot a week ago. Dear Karoly . . . dear Malie. . . ." Aunt Gizi's eyes were filling with tears, brimming over, running down her cheeks.

"Oh, no, Aunt Gizi," said Malie sweetly. "Karoly couldn't possibly have been shot in Galicia. The war is over in Russia. They signed the treaty. At Brest-Litovsk. Haven't you heard of Brest-Litovsk, Aunt Gizi? It was in the papers. The war is over. It must be a mistake. Why would the Russians shoot Karoly when the war is over?"

"It wasn't the Russians," whispered Gizi. "It was our men: deserters, revolutionaries, Slavs, Croats, Czechs. . . ."

"Oh, no! No, Aunt Gizi! Please, no!" She wrenched away from Gizi's arms and clenched her hands by her sides. A long keening wail broke from her. "Oh, no! Not Karoly! Not my Karoly! Not to see him any more, my Karoly, my love, my love!"

Her hands tore at her hair; then she held her forehead as though trying to stop pain.

"He can't be dead! I love him. I was going to marry him; I was, I was! Papa said we could—you did, Papa—I'm going to marry him." She was quieter then, tears choking in her throat, coursing down her face. "The first time he went I was prepared, I thought he might die, but he came back and we made him well again. Didn't we, Aunt Gizi?"

Gizi's face was screwed into ugly lines of pain. Her mouth and chin were trembling. "Yes, child, we made him well again."

"The army thought he would die, so they sent him home . . . and we made him well." She began to sob. "We nursed him and loved him and we made him well.'"

"Yes, child."

"Now—he's dead—"

"Yes, Malie."

She stared round the room, eyes wide and uncomprehending. "What am I doing to do? Mama, Eva, what am I going to do?"

Mama had closed her eyes and was quite white. So was Eva.

"Mama, help me. Karoly is dead. . . ."

She felt someone's arms round her. They weren't Gizi's, they were strong, warm, protective arms like Karoly's had been. Like Karoly's had been when they said good-bye at the station. Warm, strong arms that one could hide and die in.

"Little one," said Papa, "come with me. Come and be quiet with Papa."

He hugged her and she buried her face in the side of his coat. "Papa?"

"Come with me, little one. Come with Papa."

"Karoly—"

"Yes, little one." She cried very quietly across the room, clutched against Papa's side, holding tightly, whimpering a little.

Gizi and Papa, how strange they should be the two who helped her. . . .

Later that night, she sat in the chair by the window, gazing out at the night sky, at an owl drifting across the moon, at the minaret-shaped spire of the church, and remembering, remembering—

"Malie. Come to bed."

"Soon."

Remembering, because now she must learn everything by

heart, every moment they had shared together. To remember was agony; each image evoked said, "No more, no more! That was the end!" But still she must go through them, step by step, train her mind to remember clearly so that later, years from now, when the sharpness had gone, when the sorrow did not corrode, she could be happy with the memories. "Lieutenant Karoly Vilaghy," he had called out, running beside the coach, and later she had looked out of this same window at the young men and been disappointed because he was not there. The balcony was boarded off now. The iron balustrade had been taken away and planks had been nailed over the bottom of the window to prevent them from forgetting and carelessly walking out. Four years ago, and she had seen him so little: two summers. One summer of picnics at the meadow and another of Karoly spitting blood and lying exhausted in Aunt Gizi's drawing-room. Two summers, two farewells at the station. The terror, remember the terror when you couldn't find him in the crowds? And then he was there and he kissed you and rode away on the steps of the train with your white shawl held in his hand. Karoly, Karoly—

"Come to bed, Malie." Eva's voice was trembling, and Malie could hear she had been crying. She had known Karoly too; he was her sister's sweetheart and now he was dead.

"Soon."

Since they had told her, since that one terrible outburst when they told her, she hadn't cried, but there was a pain in her body, a tight, unnatural pain and she felt she would never be able to walk, or talk, or eat, or be natural ever again. They told her—Mama, Aunt Gizi, Papa—that she would be happy again one day, that the sense of tearing away a part of herself would go and she would be left with a warm, sad memory. But some strange age-old part of her senses, something timeless and out of herself, made her aware that whatever happened to her she would never heal, never be once more self-sufficient or complete. She would be happy, yes, probably she would, but something had gone. Her youth? hope? energy? She knew she would always carry a pocket of melancholy in her heart.

Eva's breathing had steadied to a slow gentle sound. Exhausted from crying she had fallen asleep and now, in blessed solitude, Malie could grieve quietly for him.

The sky was beginning to pale behind the church spire when she heard the door leading to the boys' room open and close. Leo padded over and quietly climbed onto her lap, putting his arms up around her neck and placing his cheek against hers. His face was wet and soundlessly they wept together, her sorrow eased by the feel of his young body against hers.

Two days later Eva knocked on the bedroom door—she had knocked ever since the news had come—and entered bearing a huge basket of pink roses.

"For you, Malie. See how beautiful they are."

She put her hand out and fingered the petals.

"They're from Mr. Klein."

"Mr. Klein? But how would he know?"

"Oh, no!" Eva flushed and hurriedly shook her head. "It's nothing to do with . . . with Karoly. He sent roses for all of us, pink for you, yellow for me, red for Mama."

"How kind." They were beautiful and . . . unnatural. Roses in March, when men were being killed and people were starving in Vienna?

Eva stared at her anxiously. "I thought they might cheer you. I thought you would like them."

"I like them."

Eva's shoulders slumped forward a little. "I wish you would not stay here in the bedroom so much, Malie. Just sitting in the chair and sewing. Why don't you come out with me, come for a walk, sit in the drawing-room with the rest of us? Felix Kaldy came to see how you were. He was worried; he wanted to know if there was anything he could do."

Malie put down her sewing. She had been repairing the Bogozy lace that had covered the table during Mr. Klein's visit. It was intricate work that required maximum concentration and she wondered what she would do when the tear had been mended.

"I would like to stay here, Eva. It is quiet, and I can be aone." Her voice raised a pitch. "They mean to be kind, but I cannot bear them: Mama, Aunt Gizi, Kati, Uncle Alfred, Marie, even Cook. They all talk and sit with me. They won't leave me alone."

"Do you want me to go?" Eva asked timidly, and Malie smiled and placed her hand over Eva's.

"No, you stay if you wish. This is your room too."

"You don't want to see Felix either?"

Malie was silent. She didn't want to see Felix, but there was something she wanted to know that only Felix could tell her.

"Will you do something for me, Eva?"

191

"Oh, Malie, anything you like. I'll do anything. And—please forgive me, what I said that time. I cannot"—Eva began to cry, rubbing her knuckles into her eyes just like Leo did—"I cannot forgive myself. . . . That time, when I was rude about Karoly, said he wasn't as good as Felix. I didn't mean it, really I didn't."

Malie patted Eva on the shoulder and smiled. "No, of course you didn't."

"I'll do anything you like, Malie."

Malie pushed the cloth from her lap and let it fall to the floor. She stared out at the March sky, a pale, pale blue sky with wispy clouds coming down from the mountains. She took a deep breath and tried to control her voice.

"I want to know . . . I want to know how he died."

"But—"

"They told me he was shot . . . by his own soldiers. Why?" Her voice broke on a sudden sob and her forehead began to crease into lines. "Why did our soldiers shoot him? What was wrong? The war was over in Russia. They were all coming back. I want to know everything. I want to know exactly what happened, how and why and when. Please, Eva!" She sobbed again and twisted her hands together. "Promise me you will talk to Felix. He'll know. Ask Felix."

"Oh, Malie! You mustn't think about it. You must try to forget."

The days of kindly platitudes, the softened sympathy, the unreality of everything suddenly snapped in her head.

"But I can't forget," she screamed at Eva. "Don't you understand? I can't forget!"

She covered her face with her hands, not crying, trying to hold the pain behind her eyes from spreading.

"Please, Eva! If you ever loved me, do this thing for me. Ask Felix how it happened, and why, and where. Everything."

Eva was frightened. Malie had always been the calm one, the capable one, and now she was shrieking just like—like she herself did on occasion.

"If that's what you want—"

"I do. Ask him. And you must promise me—promise me—that you will tell me *exactly* what you learn. I will know if you are hiding anything. I always know when you are hiding things from me."

"Yes, Malie."

"Ask him, Eva."

192

"Yes, Malie." Eva sniffed and wiped her handkerchief across her swollen nose. She would have to bathe her face in cold water before she could talk to Felix Kaldy.

In fact she had to wait a few weeks for the difficult conversation with Felix. He had been recalled to Budapest; there were so many rumours and counter-rumours circulating that it could be for any number of reasons. It was said that the Czechs had demanded independence, that the King and Emperor was suing for peace, that there were strikes again in Budapest, that cholera had broken out in Vienna. But whatever of the now-taken-for-granted disasters it was, it kept Felix away some time. When he came again he called immediately to inquire after Malie.

"I don't want to see him, Eva. You talk to him. You ask him . . . about Karoly . . . the things I want to know."

Eva, now that the moment was imminent, became nervous. Felix had been different ever since he had returned from the Serbian front, and she wasn't sure how to talk seriously to him.

"You come too, Malie," she pleaded. "Hear for yourself the things about . . . the things you want to know."

But Malie shuddered. "I don't want to talk to him."

"Please, Malie."

"No."

And so she had to go into the drawing-room alone, and when Mama had finally left them she had to broach the difficult subject herself. Felix was restless. He kept bounding up from his chair and pacing to and fro.

"I haven't seen Amalia since that . . . the day I brought the news."

"No," she said timidly.

He stared at her, eyes piercing and the muscles in his cheek tensed. "Is she ill?"

"No, it's just . . . she's not like Malie at the moment. She doesn't talk very much, and she doesn't seem to want to see any of her family and friends, even though we all love her."

"Does she think about it much? About Karoly being shot?" She didn't like the way he asked that question. He didn't say it with any concern for Malie; it was said with curiosity, an unhealthy kind of curiosity, as though he wanted to share Malie's emotions for all the wrong reasons.

"She thinks about Karoly all the time—I believe she does although she never mentions him." Then she remembered what she was supposed to be finding out from Felix. "That is, she doesn't mention him very much." She cleared her throat. "That day, when you came, you said he had been shot by his own soldiers?"

"That's right."

"She—Malie—she wants to know why, how it happened. I think"—and now Eva tried to put into words what fears she thought Malie had—"I think she is afraid that something terrible happened to him, that he was tortured or was ill or something. She said you would know."

Felix's eyes were brilliant. The pupils had retracted into pinpoints and they stared straight ahead into the air.

"No, he wasn't tortured—although he could have been, Eva! He could have been! You don't know, none of you, what it's like out there! It isn't like a world of people; it's a wilderness that goes on forever: killing everywhere, death everywhere. . . ."

Eva tried to look away but couldn't. She was fascinated by the sight of his tall, slim figure striding up and down, his hands clenching and unclenching by his sides.

"Everything's broken up on the eastern front. There's no discipline any more, just a great wilderness of soldiers trying to go home, trying to find food, trying to find women. Russian soldiers, our soldiers, prisoners, Poles, Slavs, Czechs. It's the revolution. All the troops know what it means and some of them, the revolutionaries, those who hate us even though they have been fighting for us, they just want to kill. They want to kill everyone who made the war."

"But Karoly didn't make the war!"

A thin stream of saliva was beginning to trickle from the corner of his mouth and with just a trace of the old Felix, the gay pre-war Felix, he flicked his handkerchief from his pocket and wiped his lips. His hand was trembling. "He was an officer. That was enough."

"How do you know he wasn't hurt . . . tortured?"

"Tilsky—you remember Stefan Tilsky—they tried to shoot him too but he got away. Karoly and Stefan were trying to requisition transport, trying to get back home, here to Hungary. And a group of soldiers on horses—Russian horses —came up and he ordered them off the horses. And they just surrounded him and Tilsky and shouted 'Death to the tyrants!' and they shot him. Tilsky killed one of them with his sabre and then jumped on the man's horse and rode away."

"How could they do such a thing? How could they shoot a man who was one of their own officers?"

"You don't understand, Eva. You don't understand what horrible things happen! That wasn't bad. What happened to Karoly wasn't bad!"

He was like a madman, a controlled madman, and that made it worse.

"I've seen the bad things. I've seen them, Eva! Men together, advancing, retreating, it's all the same. Mad, terrible, bad things." He sat suddenly and began to rock to and fro. "Eva, I've done those things . . . terrible things . . . I've done them." He gazed at her imploringly, and she, not understanding, tried to comfort him with all the senseless phrases that she had ever heard or read.

"Yes, Felix, of course. You are a soldier. You had to kill the enemy. It was part of your duty."

"Not soldiers, Eva," he moaned. "I didn't kill soldiers. They were civilians—don't you understand? Women. . . . Old men. . . . Children. . . ."

She was cold, icily, clammily cold, and she wanted to get away. Malie shouldn't have forced her to ask these questions; it was making Felix tell silly lies.

"I couldn't control the men," he cried, staring up at the ceiling. "We were advancing behind the front line and they learned that the Serbs were to be punished. Mackensen, victorious Mackensen, he conquered Serbia, and we—I—came behind. I couldn't control them, Eva. The soldiers . . . every village . . . I wanted to stop them but I was afraid because they weren't my men any more. I was afraid."

Horrified she watched him drop his face into his hands and sob. She felt sick, ashamed, frightened.

"I'll go to Malie now," she cried shrilly, but before she could rise from her chair he was kneeling beside her, gripping her hands in his, gazing up at her.

"Don't leave me now, Eva! Don't go away now! Nobody knows, and I can't sleep at night! We burned them, Eva, burned them alive! They stood round laughing, and . . . I had to stand there too. They wouldn't stop so I had to pretend it was my orders."

"Don't tell me any more! I don't want to know any more!" She placed her hands over her ears but Felix pulled them away.

"We cut them into pieces, little pieces, and then they pegged some of the women out—"

"Stop!" she screamed. "Stop, Felix!"

"They—we—pegged the women out, and after they had used them they cut them in pieces too . . . and it went on and on, village after village. Sometimes we just tied them up and left them without water. Everything died: the cattle died, and the dogs and horses. . . . It went on and on. I was an officer and I had to pretend. Don't you understand, Eva? I had to pretend."

"I don't want to hear any more!" she sobbed. "I don't want to know any more."

"Oh, Eva! Don't turn away from me!" He began to cry into her lap. "I'm afraid to go to sleep at night. And they know, the authorities know that I was no good. I ran away in the end, I ran back to the supply lines with a silly story I made up, but they all knew. I wasn't a proper officer. Mama had to go to Budapest and speak to some friends. I don't have to go to war any more, but I can't sleep. I can't sleep and no one understands, and I can't tell anyone, not even Mama!"

She felt sick. Her stomach was turning and twisting and there was a sharp, hideous pain in her bowels that made her want to run to the water closet. She tried to get up again but Felix, on his knees, stumbled after her, holding her skirt and crying into her hands.

"Please, please, Eva! Don't despise me like the rest do! If I'd gone to Russia, like Karoly and Adam, it might have been different, just an ordinary war, shooting at the enemy. But they made me do this. What would have happened to anyone —Karoly, Adam, anyone—if they'd had to punish the Serbs!"

He raised his face to her and curiously, in spite of the tears and the misery, it was more like the old face of Felix, before the twitch and the trickle of saliva.

"Eva, I needed someone! I needed to tell someone—if only Adam had been home; if only I could have seen Adam! I'm like a madman, I can't stop thinking about it, seeing them roasting, bleeding, the bodies cut—"

"Stop!"

She took a deep, deep breath and then, because it was obvious that Felix was not going to let her move, she sat down again. She closed her eyes and tried to think of Malie. How would Malie have dealt with this horrible, sick, vile confession? What would Malie have done?

"Children too, Eva." He was gasping, sobbing. "Children too, broken to pieces and—"

"Stop, Felix! You must stop! I promise you I will stay here.

I will not run away. But you must stop telling me these things. I understand what . . . what you did"—she was trembling, shaking with nervous movement—"but now you must stop talking of them."

"I can't, Eva! I can't!"

"Yes you can, Felix. If you stop talking I will stay here with you. See, I will hold your hand." Yes, that was good. Malie would have held his hand. Malie always held people when they were wild and hysterical. "I will hold your hand, but if you go on telling me—telling me . . . the things, then I will go away."

"Oh, no," he sobbed. "Don't go away, Eva. Everyone has gone away. In the office, at Budapest, they don't talk to me; they put the papers on my desk but they don't talk to me. I have no one, Eva. No one!"

It was too much. She didn't want the responsibility of this helpless, disintegrating man. She was sorry for him, but she didn't know what to do.

"Eva, how can I sleep without dreaming? What can I do? The pictures in my mind . . . the time that—"

"I shall go away," she screamed. "I shall go away."

His mouth trembled and he clenched his lower lip between his teeth. "I'll stop, Eva. I won't talk any more."

"No. Don't talk any more."

He was gripping her hand very tightly. His head was close to her knee and as she looked down she could see the beautiful tear-stained profile, the dark lashes wetted into spikes, the high smooth cheekbones, the lips trembling like a child's.

"Oh, Felix!" she said piteously, and at the sorrow and kindness in her voice he looked up into her face.

"You'll help me, won't you, Eva?

"How can I help you? What can I do? I don't know what to do." She remembered Malie suddenly, Malie upstairs, waiting to know how Karoly had died. "It's all too much: the war, Karoly, now you. . . . I don't know how to help anyone. I—"

"But you'll pray for me, Eva, won't you?"

"I'll pray, but what good will it do?" she cried. "Malie prayed for Karoly, and your mama prayed for you all through the war. What good did it do?"

"Mama doesn't understand," he said, frustrated and desperate. "Mama is good, and she is always there, and she will make things come right for me; she stopped them from discharging me from the army. But she doesn't know why they think I am a coward. And I can't tell her. She wouldn't understand." He gripped her hand again, gazed up, then frenziedly kissed her fingers. "You understand, Eva. You understand and you'll help me! You'll make the dreams go away. You'll make me stop thinking about it!"

Beneath the horror and the great weight of responsibility she felt a tiny throb of acid satisfaction. At last there was something the old witch hadn't been able to do for her son. He had come to her, Eva, hadn't he? He wanted Eva, not Madame Kaldy.

"How can I stop, Eva? How can I stop thinking?"

"You—you can think of nice things: the farm in summer, the picnics, the dances. . . ."

It was a futile suggestion and she knew it. Felix wrinkled up his face and moaned, "No, no!"

"You can come to see me, Felix." She was groping, fumbling in the dark for a way to help him combat a nightmare she could hardly cope with herself. "You can come to me, or if you are in Budapest and the dreams . . . then you must sit down and write to me."

"Yes," he cried eagerly. "Yes, if I share it with you, if I tell you—"

"No!" She swallowed hard, then tried again. "You must not talk of—of the . . . things. You must just write, or come and see me, and you will say, 'Eva, I am afraid and unhappy, and I am lonely,' and then I will know what is troubling you and I will think of you and pray for you and talk to you—not about Serbia, just talk. And after a little while you will feel better.'"

"Yes, Eva." His eyes were fixed on her face, in their depths the same faith and hope that she had seen in Leo's when Malie was promising something.

"We will never talk of . . . specific things again, but you will know that I am sharing your . . . unhappiness, and then it will be better."

"Oh, yes!"

"Now get up, Felix. You must try to start living as a gentleman again. You must try to have nice manners and be polite, and then, you will see, everyone will like you again."

He looked miserable and unbelieving, and so she hurried on.

"And soon the war will be over and you can come back to town and your post in the land registration office, and everyone will forget the war and what has happened."

He smiled uncertainly and then rose slowly to his feet and began to dust the knees of his beautifully cut trousers. Even in grief and despair and humiliation, he was still incredibly handsome.

"You must go now, Felix. Say good-bye to Mama, and I will go and tell Malie—" Oh, it was all too much! She still had to tell Malie.

"You won't tell your sister about—about us, and . . . everything?"

"Of course not."

In his face was trust, and hope, and dependence. It was flattering, the very thing she had longed for, but now it was all mixed up with women being pegged down and . . . stop!

"You must go now, Felix."

"Yes. Good-bye, Eva." At the door he stopped and said humbly, "Could I call this afternoon? Could we go walking together? We could have tea—coffee, that is—at the Marie Thérèse. That would be nice, wouldn't it, Eva?"

"All right then."

He smiled, like a child, but the smile made his face the same beautiful face that she had always worshipped. He left and she sat, drained and weak on the chair. Spasmodic shudders made her jerk and finally she rose and went across to the window, opened it, and breathed deeply. Down in the street, just turning into the square, she could see Felix. He was tall and wide-shouldered, his legs were long and strong and he moved as only a young Hungarian aristocrat could move, with strength and grace. It was strange that he should look just the same as he used to look.

She closed the window and went upstairs to talk to Malie.

13

When, on the morning of October the twenty-ninth, Adam looked from his trench dug into the side of a mountain and saw English tanks advancing over the Livenza valley, he knew they had lost the war.

They were terrifying, the English tanks. It was the first time he had seen them, although he had heard other men describe them. Ponderous, inhuman, monstrous, they drove forward over mud, rock, fallen trees, bodies, and guns and a terrible

199

fear stopped his breathing. Nothing could stand against them. They were invincible. No amount of courage or strategy could achieve any kind of success against them. These paleolithic giants of destruction, above everything else, were the reason they had lost the war.

He looked back into the dugout, seeking human reassurance, the sight of men instead of vast machines that were nothing to do with soldiers, machines that could swallow, crush, and digest. They were still asleep, the three of them. Only three: Nemeth, who had miraculously survived Russia and Italy and was the only one of his old men still with him; Kovacs, who was forty-five and had a gastric ulcer; and the boy, Fekete.

The boy was pathetic in sleep. When he was awake he tried to behave like a man, to swear and smoke and talk with relish about killing the hated Italians, but in sleep he was a child, smooth-cheeked and with dark, unhappy stains under his eyes. He had been apprenticed to a tailor in Budapest and his hands were small and neat. He had handled the gun very well, when they had had a gun.

"Wake, wake!" He shook them, kicked them lightly as their exhausted bodies refused to move. "Get up!" We must move quickly before we are cut off. Look."

One by one they stumbled to the edge of the dugout. Nemeth urinated, his eyes still closed in sleep. Kovacs and the boy looked over the plain and saw the tanks. They were both silent, and Adam saw chill fear spread over their faces.

"Will they come up here?" asked the boy. His voice broke. It often did, but this time he was too afraid to bother with disguising it by coughing.

"No." In fact he didn't know whether or not the English tanks were capable of climbing the side of a mountain. They were so terrible to look upon, even from this height and distance, that he was prepared to believe they could do anything.

"Let's go."

They picked up rifles and packs and began to climb. Their legs were stiff, but the fear of the tanks drove them up into the cold October wind. The ground was rock and sparse grass, but as they climbed the grass ceased and it became just rock, wet with early morning mist.

Every so often they would look back, down at the valley, and then stand immobilized, gripped with fear that was unlike any other fear they had known in battle. Gunfire was bad, yes; it kept one constantly on guard. The next shell might be yours and the muscles in the back of the neck were always tensed, the body listening. Infantry attacks, machine-guns, all turned the bowels to water, made some men cry and others run. But the tanks were the invention of something other than man. *And God created a tank in his own image.* It was almighty and if man *had* made it he would be unable to control it. Like Frankenstein's monster it would destroy everyone.

The boy had not moved for several moments. He was staring hypnotized down into the valley. Adam punched him in the stomach.

"Move. We are nearly at the top."

The ridge was just above them. Behind that a small high valley, another ridge, and then a battalion post. There they would be given more hopeless, useless orders. They would obey them because there was nothing else to do.

Nemeth, old soldier, old friend, trudged quietly at the front. His pace was good; two and a half years up and down the splintered rock and ice of the Italian Alps had taught him a measured stride suitable for climbing. The other two, Kovacs and the boy, still walked like civilians. Hurrying, then pausing for breath, sweating in spite of the cold, rubbing the insides of their thighs where the muscles ached.

"Nearly at the top."

Kovacs's belly rumbled. His face had the bluish tinge common to people with gastric ulcers. "Any food, Lieutenant? My ulcer—"

"I have none." In his knapsack he had half a sausage and a piece of black bread but he knew they were going to need it later more than they did now. Also Kovacs complained before he needed to. His ulcer wasn't as bad as he pretended. The boy didn't complain at all.

At the ridge they paused for breath. Kovacs collapsed on a rock and slumped over. Nemeth stood, relaxed and still. He and Adam had discovered in two and a half years that it was better not to sit after you had climbed. One rested standing, and the muscles didn't have time to slacken again.

To the north, in the distance, the peaks were covered in snow. The sun shone up here, but even though they weren't very high there was a thin mist just below them. It blocked out the valley in front and, mercifully, the valley behind. Shellfire reverberated round the hills.

"Now. It is time to go. We must hurry. The next ridge isn't so high and behind that we are at the command post."

Down, easier this side, quite fast. The boy was still nervous but high spirits and an incline made him hop and run, career a little, like a child. Adam almost expected him to throw his arms wide as he ran and whoop with excitement.

In the valley it was raining, a fine drizzle that gradually soaked everything. They forded a couple of streams and then began to climb again. It was midday and he called another halt and this time took the sausage and bread from his pack. Kovacs gazed at him reproachfully as he took his two slices.

"Keep some if you can, Kovacs. It may be a long time before we get more."

Kovacs ate it all; so did the boy. He and Nemeth divided their tiny portions yet again, ate half, and put the rest in their packs. The shell-fire was growing louder and, to the south, they could hear the rapping of a machine-gun.

Over the second ridge and then, coming a little way behind them from higher up, five infantrymen, two of them without boots, their feet bleeding on the rocky ground.

They were too weary, all of them, to talk to one another. The infantrymen just fell in behind and they stumbled down the mountain.

The village, the hut where the post was supposed to be, was deserted. Inside the hut a table with a plate and cup, in the corner a heap of ash with some papers not quite properly burnt through, a map hanging from one pin on the wall, and for the rest, nothing.

Two more infantrymen joined them, from the south end of the valley, torn uniforms, thin dirty faces, one without a rifle.

"What has happened?"

"What has happened," said Adam soberly, "is that the retreat is no longer being ordered. We must just go, the best way we can."

"Can't we rest?" grumbled Kovacs.

"If you wish. I estimate the Italians and English are three or four hours behind us."

He stepped straight out of the hut and didn't even bother to give an order. All the men fell in behind, and as quickly as their tired bodies and sore feet would allow, they began to walk back to Austria.

They were just ahead of the enemy. The next day a stranded hussar told them that the town of Vittorio Veneto had fallen but they didn't really need to be told. They could hear the gunfire and see the pall of smoke in the sky behind them. The hussar also told them that it was thirty miles to a railway line. Their faces numb with apathy and fatigue, none of them answered, and he rode away in the direction of home.

The track broadened into a country road and the soldiers multiplied, a great line of dirty, silent figures trudging away from the distant shell-fire. Sometimes their lethargy was interrupted by shouting and the hooting of a staff vehicle. Silently they opened to let a car go through, then closed again.

Despair . . . despair. When had he known the war was lost? Finally and irrevocably when he saw the English tanks, but long before that in actuality, in the spring when the recruits and supplies ceased to come for the simple reason that there were no more men and no more supplies. Through a tired, bitter summer's fighting and an autumn's retreat, he had known that the war was lost. Perhaps he had known even earlier, in Russia when their soldiers had deserted, and perhaps he had even known when he went to the garrison four years ago, leaving a good crop of sugar beet to go to seed.

He tried never to think about what he was doing, what great schemes he was part of. He was a farmer, he liked to see blossoming and fruiting, and if he thought about the rape of the land—the land of a whole continent—he knew he would lie down in a ditch and let the rain wash over him and never get up again.

Becuse he was a farmer he tried to accept the huge catastrophe about him in the same way that he had to accept cattle sickness or crop failure or the burning of a barn. One must not rail against God, or fate, or whatever it was that decreed natural disaster. No, one must not rage in impotence; one must tackle the small area close around: segregate the sick cattle, use the wasted corn as compost and buy seed for next year, rebuild the barn. And he had tried to treat the war in the same way. He had men to lead and a gun to guard. He had tried to keep his men alive. He had tried to stop his gun from being captured or blown up. In neither had he succeeded, and now he was reduced to three men—everyone else dead, dying, in hospital, or invalided out, the lucky ones—and no gun. And now he did not care any more. The war was over. The natural phenomena had succeeded. Four years of waste.

When at last they hit the railway line there was a semblance of order. A bad-tempered major, his arm in a sling and his head bandaged, told them to march up the line to the next village. It was rumoured there was an engine and some rolling stock there. If they would get the engine going, and provided the Italians didn't advance too quickly and blow up the line, they might get to Krainburg.

"After Krainburg—if you get to Krainburg—you are on your own." The major was standing on a wooden crate beside the railway line. It was raining, and pools of dirty water lay in the ruts between the lines. The major stared at them, not seeing them, miserable, failed. "Get to your homes, any way you can. The Empire has disintegrated. No one is responsible for anyone else any more. Just get home and protect your families from whatever is about to happen."

They heard him, and some of them were afraid, but mostly they were too tired, too hungry, too sick to care.

As he led Kovacs and Nemeth and the boy along the line he clung to one thought, one small instinct of survival that the war had not extinguished. If he could only get home to the farm, to his land, he would be all right. He would get these three men, the last of the army that he commanded, inside the frontiers of Hungary and then, his duty done—the cattle cared for, the crops in—he would fight his way back to the farm, where he could weep quietly and in peace.

It was over. Incredibly, frighteningly, the war—which only a few weeks ago hadn't seemed to be going too badly—was over. The government, the King, the railways, the law, all was finished. The Serbs and Croats had demanded autonomy; so had the Czechs and Slovaks. Count Tisza had been shot in his own house by a group of revolutionaries, and crowds of refugees were flocking into the country away from the advancing Romanians.

There were ugly rumours from Budapest, and Papa hastened up at once to see what was happening. He gave strict instructions that they were to lock the doors of the house and not unbar the gates to the courtyard. Uncle Sandor carried his gaming gun with him in the yard, and the servants huddled together nervously in the kitchen. (Afterwards they learned that Papa had waited for nine hours at the station. There were no trains and when, finally, one did come it was full of soldiers, undisciplined scarecrows who clung onto the sides and roof of the train. Papa had managed to find a standing place only by giving the guard several korona, and the journey, which usually took only about two hours, lasted all night.)

It was November, but if they stared out from behind the shuttered windows of the house they could see wild and hungry-looking men in tattered uniforms, walking the pavements in bare feet. There was no order, no one to tell them what to do. The world had been destroyed.

Papa finally got a message through to them. It was pushed under the door of the courtyard one morning by an unseen hand. Uncle Sandor found it when he came to sweep. It was addressed to Mama, but the instructions were for all of them.

My dear Marta,

Things are dangerous and unsettled here. Karolyi is trying to form a government, but what kind of government it will be I am afraid to guess—revolutionaries and poets, I imagine. No one knows what will be the ultimate terms of our surrender to the enemy and at the moment we are more concerned with the disorder in the city. I am sleeping at the bank with some of the so-called Civic Guard defending us. I want you and the children to go up to the farm with Uncle Sandor. You will be safer in the country; Gizi and Alfred were wise to stay on at the end of the summer. Alfred will help you once you are up there and our own peasants who know us will protect you from the bands of killers who are plundering and looting. Go early in the morning in the big coach and wear your oldest and shabbiest clothes. Stay there until I come.

Zsigmond

And so they had done exactly what he ordered. Locking the house behind them, they had started out very early one morning when the streets were empty and the dawn was just breaking. Sleepy and cold they huddled together in miserable silence. Even the boys were not cheered by the thought of an unofficial winter visit to the farm. They did not understand the full implication of the journey but the general fear and gloom penetrated their youthful indifference.

"Malie," Leo asked after an hour's silence, "will losing the war make any difference to us? Will we have to go away from Hungary and the farm?"

Malie's nose was red about the edge of her scarf. She wanted to comfort Leo the way she had comforted him all his life, but what could she say? She hugged him and re-wrapped a blanket round his legs, but she couldn't assure him of the future.

Halfway to the farm Uncle Sandor was stopped and they all held their breath, frightened in case their luggage was about to be stolen, the coach attacked. But it was only a soldier trying to get home and begging a lift. Sandor, after a moment's hesitation, took him onto the box and they all fell silent again.

As they neared the hills patches of thin snow appeared on the ground, and finally, when they entered the acacia woods, the track was covered. The trees looked pretty, delicately festooned in white, and for a moment the reason for their arrival was forgotten.

"Oh, how pretty!" cried Mama, clapping her hands together. "Look boys, see how pretty the snow is!"

"Can we sleigh, Mama? Can we come out and play? Uncle Sandor and Sultan could take us out in the sleigh."

"Why, yes." And then they all remembered, remembered the war and the uncertainty, and the fear of things that might or might not happen.

The farm was silent, covered in a pall of snow with just a small area cleared round Roza's kitchen entrance. A dog barked from inside but there were no other sounds, no cackling of hens, no plaintive cries from the cattle, nothing. Roza's face, white, guarded, peered through the slightly opened door.

"Madame! Oh, madame! You have come to help poor Roza!"

She staggered forward through the snow and flung her arms round Mama, then kissed and hugged them all. Roza was even smaller now, thin and wizened, her black eyes sunk deep into her skull.

The kitchen was warm. There was still wood to burn and the stove was hot and welcoming. Roza put a tiny spoonful of coffee into the pot and poured on water for all of them. "There is no cream," she apologized. "The cows have gone to your uncle's villa. He still has a man to care for them and protect them. He sends a little milk to me once a week."

"Where are the chickens, the geese, the ducks?"

Roza's eyes filled with tired tears. She wasn't really unhappy, just relieved that now she had someone to talk to and confide in. "All gone." She shrugged. "Some soldiers came—not from this district—a band of them. They demanded food, banged on my door but I would not answer. And so they took the poultry, and the grain and potatoes from the barn, whatever was there. We still have a little grain left here, inside the house, but we have no eggs."

"But Roza, why did you stay here alone? Why did you not go down to the village, to your sister, or over to the Racs-Rassay house? Aunt Gizi would have been pleased to use you."

Roza stuck her hands inside the sleeves of her black woollen blouse. Her dark eyes, dumb, patient, long-suffering, gazed into Malie's.

"I shall remain here, for as long as the master says I may. My sons—where else would they come when they return from the war? My sons, all I have, I must be here for them." She nodded slowly. "I shall stay here. And now—now I have my young ladies to help me and my two small mountain devils to curse." She smiled at the boys, revealing broken teeth and sunken gums. How had that happened? Roza had always had such strong white teeth.

They tried to settle in the farmhouse, but it was cold and there was not enough wood to heat all the rooms. Finally they lived in the kitchen and used the rooms immediately above— the drawing-room and Papa's study—as places to sleep in. They were warmer than the other rooms.

They sent Uncle Sandor over to Alfred and Gizi's and he came back with milk and eggs and bread. Somehow Alfred had managed to keep more servants than anyone else. He promised to send them whatever they needed. He offered them shelter under his roof, but the Ferencs had been hit by the same animal homing instinct as everyone else. Whatever had to be faced would be better faced there.

Once, from the direction of the village, they heard shooting and then a scream. Roza bolted the door and they all remained very quiet. The distant shouting died away and then it was still again.

They grew tired, tired of waiting, of doing very little, of watching the snow drop from the acacia trees and then come down and cover them again. One morning Eva said she would drive with Uncle Sandor to collect the milk and eggs from Uncle Alfred. Roza protested, Mama and Malie tried to deter her, but Eva was bored and fractious.

"I can just as easily be killed here as with Uncle Sandor," she stated. "And anyway, why shouldn't I go? I shall be safer than Malie is when she goes out walking on her own!" That had provoked a fresh outburst because no one had known that Malie went out of the house early every morning and walked alone in the forest. Eva, watching through half-closed sleepy eyes, had seen her steal quietly from the room and vanish into the morning gloom.

"I just walk," said Malie quietly. "Just walk to be alone."

"Well, I want to go out and see people," Eva grumbled. "Even Aunt Gizi and Kati are better than no one at all. I'm tired of not seeing anyone." She wrapped a shawl round her head and the boys, bored also and seizing a chance of freedom, begged to go too. Finally they set off, the four of them. How good it was to be out, trotting through the snow, the trees, feeling the crisp air and feeling also a slight tingle of fear that something might unexpectedly happen.

At the Racs-Rassay villa they were all so pleased to see her that she felt like a heroine, plunging through the snow to collect provisions for her family. She talked and listened and allowed Uncle Alfred to spoil her a little. Then she hurried home with all the news.

"Uncle Alfred is actually working with the animals! Can you believe that! And Aunt Gizi is helping too. They will come to see us soon. And Kati is learning to cook—she is thinner and even uglier, poor Kati—and, ah, yes, Kati told me that Madame Kaldy is all alone in her house, just a couple of old peasant women with her. And she is looking just like her old peasants, milking the cows with them and milling grain and baking bread. Uncle Alfred invited her to stay at the villa with them, and she was quite rude. She said she would stay to welcome home her sons! Fancy, Mama, that is exactly what Roza said!"

"Poor woman." Malie's voice was quiet. She was looking out of the window at the snow. "She has two sons to pray for, to worry about, to cry for. She does not know if they will come back. Even Felix is not necessarily safe in Budapest."

"Nothing can happen to Felix," said Eva emphatically. "Felix will be safe." She wasn't always very good at judging people, at knowing what they would do or how they would react. But she knew, beyond all doubt, that Felix would come safely home. All through the summer, every time he had come from Budapest, they had spent hours together, walking, playing the piano, drinking bad coffee, talking, and during that time Eva had begun to know the real Felix. And because she knew him she also knew he would come home safely.

"You cannot be sure, Eva, no one is ever sure. We think the danger is past and then—" Malie's face was sad and Eva did not want to look at it. Their positions had been reversed. Now Malie had no one, while she, Eva, was bound to Felix by ties of confession and need and reliance. Felix was hers at last.

"Perhaps we should go to see her, Eva. Madame Kaldy. Perhaps we should go."

"I don't want to go!" She didn't want to face Madame Kaldy at the present time. She wasn't sure why. It was something to do with all the hours she had spent with Felix this summer, all those hours and all the things, the bad, horrible things they never spoke of.

"It would be kind, Eva."

Eva turned away and began to unwind her shawl. "I don't want to be kind to Madame Kaldy. She is spiteful and patronizing, and I don't want to spend my time with her. I don't like her."

"Then I shall go."

Eva shrugged. "Go if you like, Malie. She won't be pleased to see you. Remember the time we walked over there in the hot sun and she was quite rude and made you help her with the fruit basket."

Malie didn't answer. She wondered what kind of reasoning functioned in Eva's mind. It was obvious, from the events of the past summer, that Eva had at last won Felix Kaldy. They spent a lot of time together sitting in corners, holding hands and looking unhappy. How could Eva be planning marriage with Felix when she wouldn't even talk to his mother?

The following day she climbed into the pony cart with the boys, and Uncle Sandor turned the horse's head in the direction of the Kaldy farm.

It was peaceful, so peaceful and quiet it was difficult to remember that these were bad times, that millions of men had died, that the old world had been torn up by its roots and nothing planted in its place. The snow was sad, the icicles on the trees, the fleeting back of a deer seen bounding away from the track, they were all sad and . . . finished. But there was peace too. Eight months since the news had come, eight months facing up to a life without him. She was still desolate, the pain was still there, but it had deadened a little. She sat outside the problems and turmoils of those around her, watching as a disinterested stranger might watch, knowing that their emotions, their joys and pains, would not—could not—touch her any more. She was free from involvement. And now, sometimes, she took melancholy pleasure from things unconnected with people: from the deer bounding through the forest, from the snow covering the trees, from the horse's breath steaming in the cold air.

"There's a soldier in front of us," said Jozsef quietly. He was almost twelve and understood some of the ramifications of the present situation. Soldiers were no longer gallant saviours of the Empire. They were unstable men who might possibly be dangerous. Uncle Sandor grunted and put his hand reassuringly on the rifle beside him.

"Only one soldier," he growled. "Nothing to fear."

But the soldier's behaviour was unnatural. He had been walking very slowly ahead of them, with his pack slung over one shoulder and his head bowed low. As they grew closer to him he suddenly stopped. He didn't look round at them, the way he would if he had been begging a ride. He just stood quite still at the edge of the wood, looking ahead at the fields. His pack slid to the ground and he didn't stoop to pick it up. Malie put her arms round the boys and gripped them to her. "Just take no notice of him," she whispered. "We shall go straight past and pretend we have not seen him."

Uncle Sandor flicked Sultan very lightly with the whip and the old horse moved a little faster. Staring straight ahead they drove past and only at the last moment, drawn by curiosity, did Malie glance swiftly at the motionless figure.

She couldn't believe it, but it was Adam, Adam Kaldy with a torn uniform and no coat, Adam Kaldy with boots split down to the soles and paper packed in the sides, Adam Kaldy standing, just standing, staring at his land, with runnels of tears flowing unchecked over his bearded face.

14

Things settled a little. There was law and order of some sort but the future was uncertain. The enemy—only now they were no longer the enemy but the victors—had still to decide what punishment should be meted out to the defeated. There was no king. Hungary was a republic. Some frightening innovations were about to take place.

She sat, the "old witch," her hands idle in her lap, staring out at the snow and ice of a bitterly cold February. Was it colder than usual? Or was it just that now there was no coal and they had to be careful with the wood? Or was it the death of her dreams that made this February colder than any other?

A lifetime spent rebuilding an estate, planning, scheming, gaining a reputation for meanness and sharpness, all so that one day she could leave her son in possession of the land his father had frittered away. Economies, humiliating work, begging from rich relatives for help in educating her children, all so that bit by bit, piece by piece, she could buy back the land, rebuild the Kaldy heritage, and now—with much of her ambition realized—it all threatened to vanish. Count Karolyi was running the country and he had promised the people land. He had promised to start with his own land—all to be given to the people—and, after his, everyone else's land would go into the same destructive abyss.

All this land—hers! Hers by her toil and misery and hate, hers to give to whomsoever she pleased!—all this would be split among the peasantry, the scum she had chased and harried for so many years, the men and women who had cheated her and idled on her land. Now it would be given away to the stupid, the poor, the lazy.

She had tried, just once, to talk to Adam about it, to relieve the welter of bitter burnt-out hope that was corroding her heart. But Adam was silent, going about his tasks, watering and feeding the cattle with whatever fodder he could beg or borrow, mending the barns and grooming their one remaining horse. Adam was a recluse. He wouldn't talk about anything.

And, in any case, what use was it to talk? She had never shared her problems, never asked for help (unless it was to further her plans of re-establishment), never wept helplessly (as that stupid Bogozy woman was prone to do) when things were not going well. It did no good to talk. Keep your secrets; worry them out yourself; let no one know what you are doing or why.

And so she sat and brooded and hated—hated the Bolsheviks who had begun the disease, hated the Austrians who had led them into a war and then lost it, hated Count Karolyi who deemed himself a saviour of the poor, hated her husband who had squandered his birthright. She had been so close to completion. Just the manor house and a large track of forest and it would all have been hers again—hers to give to Felix.

The manor; she had never looked at it again since the day she left twenty-five years ago. She had handed the keys to the bailiff, climbed into the hired coach with her two small sons, and ridden away without looking back. But every feature of the house that had been her home for five years was ingrained on her soul; every room, every mosaic floor, every painted fragment of ceiling and walls, every chandelier, tapestry, and door was catalogued in her mind. And now, nothing. They would lose it too, the bourgeois who had bought it from her, the bourgeois who had nothing to commend them except the money they possessed.

As the February days iced to a close her brooding took an illogical twist. She did not understand why, but the desire grew to go once more and see the manor—see it before it was irrevocably lost to her. It was an hour away, at the far end of the estate she had slowly bought back, and between their farm and the old house was the river and the land she rented out (at a very high rate) to tenants. The wish grew, and as it grew so her despair retreated and a thin flame—of chance? hope? —glimmered in her mind. She wanted to see the manor. Why? Because even now she had not given up. Even now there might be a way. She could not fight an entire government—a law, a new decree, no—but why not take a chance? Throw everything on one last speculation. What could she lose? Her land? Karolyi and his Communists would take that away from her anyway. And governments changed; wars broke out again; times were still unsettled, restless.

She turned in her sleep at night, fretting, brooding, wondering if her courage was failing because she was growing old. And finally, knowing that if she revisited the old house it would prompt her to action, she took the horse and trap and, refusing Adam's offer to accompany her, drove along a road she had not travelled for twenty-five years.

The farms were just like any farms at this time, cold, snowy, lacking animals and men. But they could be good again! Imagine the estate owned entirely by Felix, with Adam superintending a huge staff of drovers and shepherds and labourers, all working to unite the Kaldy lands in one profitable, money-making venture.

The idea that had lain dormant for so many weeks took a little more shape, a little more fire in her heart. As she grew near the old house she began to feel excitement mounting, a wild, gay, exhilarated excitement, the excitement of a young girl going to meet her lover.

It was there, shabby because of the war but otherwise just the same, standing on a rise of grassland, a line of birch trees hiding one side of the lower storey—they had grown so tall!

—the colonnaded porch peeling a little, but the roof was good. Yes, she could see there was nothing wrong with the roof.

The trap came to a halt and she stared, devouring the jewel in her crown of rehabilitation. There were huge stables at the back; Felix could have as many horses as he wished. And parties and balls; the big doors could be thrown open and the music would echo over the gardens, through the trees, and down to the ornamental lake.

She had dreaded that perhaps the bourgeois had changed things. So many of them did, throwing on a wing here or converting a stable into a garage if they wished to indulge in a motorcar. But this particular bourgeois, a cloth manufacturer who had invested with great wisdom, had left things as they were.

She sat unheeding of the cold, or the time, and then she saw a nervous face at one of the downstairs windows. Erdei! That was their name. And the old man was still alive, and so was she, and now she had a proposition to make to old man Erdei, the cloth manufacturer, the bourgeois who had lived in her house for too long.

She tied the reins to the seat and climbed down from the cart. She moved lithely, like a girl again, as she stepped daintily onto the terrace and walked towards the door.

It took only an hour—an hour of incredulity, shock, and finally acceptance on old Erdei's part, and of nerve on hers. She was shaking when she came out of the house and stepped up on the cart; her hands were trembling and there was an uneasy palpitation around her heart. She wasn't a young girl, she was an old woman, and the years of strain, culminating in this one last throw, were making her aware of her frailty. She wished she could go back to the farmhouse—she never thought of that utilitarian place as home—and rest for a while in her room. But the day's tasks were not over yet. Now she had to visit Alfred Racs-Rassay.

She'd known them all in the old days, of course; the Racs-Rassay, the Bogozy, all of them. Alfred had not been married then and his father had still been alive. She had danced and drunk and hunted with them, before her world had smashed to pieces.

She saw them sometimes even now—Alfred, who had grown even sillier and weaker with the years, and Gizi, whom she secretly admired, and their ugly little daughter. She saw them and they were polite to one another. And now she was going to make a proposition to Alfred Racs-Rassay. . . .

The afternoon was growing dusky when she arrived at their villa, and her tiredness nearly overwhelmed her. But she braced herself, and the old servant woman took her in and left her in Alfred's study. She sat in a leather chair and closed her eyes, trying to recuperate her wits and strength, and then she heard the door open and Alfred came in. He was surprised. She never paid social visits.

"Madame Kaldy . . . Luiza!"

She resented the familiarity but supposed it justified from someone with whom she had once danced.

"It is so enjoyable to see you here. Some refreshment—?"

God, how she would have loved a glass of tea, the good tea that one got before the war. There was almost no tea in the country now and what there was had to be bought on the black market. But she straightened her back, tweaked her skirt, shook her head.

"'No refreshment, Alfred. This is not a social visit. I have come here to see you on a matter of business."

He was polite but puzzled. "What business can we have, Luiza? No one is doing business at the moment. It is too dangerous for people like us. It is better to stay quiet and hope that the masses—the proletariat they call them—do not notice us."

"Business," she repeated firmly. "Rumour has it that you are still the richest man in the district, that the war has not entirely crippled you, that your interests, some of them, were cleverly invested outside the country."

Alfred looked slightly uncomfortable. "Ah, well, my brother-in-law, Ferenc, he is a banker; his advice—"

"From all accounts he has not done himself any good," she countered dryly. "Rumour has it that Zsigmond Ferenc is in financial difficulties at the moment."

Alfred floundered and hemmed and looked anywhere but straight at her.

"And in any case, Alfred Racs-Rassay, it is not Zsigmond Ferenc I am asking to lend me money. It is you."

"You want to borrow money?" He gasped, not from the shock of being asked but because it was Luiza Kaldy—proud, untouchable, autocratic Luiza Kaldy—who was asking.

"I have just been to see the Erdei family," she stated flatly. "For a sum of money—which I do not have—they are pre-

214

pared to sell me back my manor house and the forest that was part of my land."

Alfred's mouth dropped open and his pale blue eyes bulged. "You are mad!" he cried rudely. "You are utterly mad!"

"What is so mad about buying back my land and house?"

"You—my God!" He began to splutter. "Where have you been for the past few months? Don't you know what has happened? We have a socialist government! At any moment we—you, I, people like us—will be removed from our property, our land will be taken away. And you—you choose this time to go and buy back your house!"

"And my land."

Alfred blew his cheeks out and let the air escape in a hiss of irritation. "What on earth are you doing, Luiza Kaldy, buying something you may only have for a day!"

"You think Erdei doesn't know that? He thinks I am mad too. A private transaction, I suggested. A private one with the papers kept secret, and finally he was happy to agree!" She paused, glared at Alfred, and said, "Do you think, in normal times, he would ever have accepted the figure I offered? He would have asked for six—seven times as much! But he thought he could swindle a mad old woman, take her money and sign away a house that would belong to neither of us for long."

"What would you expect him to do? You offer him a gift, a sum of money for something neither of you may keep, and—"

"How do you know we may not keep it? Are you so sure, Alfred Racs-Rassay? Are you absolutely, completely sure that we will not keep our land? If you are so sure of this, why are you and your family still sitting here, waiting in your big house, instead of going to Switzerland where your money is?"

"Well, of course," Alfred blustered, "we shall not move one inch until the law actually comes to pass. But the government's intentions have been made plain. And staying on one's own property is one thing; buying more land is another. None of us would invest in land that we almost certainly are going to lose."

"I am prepared to invest," she said bluntly. "I am prepared to invest—with your money!"

She thought Alfred was going to explode. He coughed, shouted, and raged and finally, when he did calm a little, he spent several minutes explaining why she was mad and why he wouldn't let her be mad with his money. At last he quietened, talking himself into rationality, and then he began to treat her not as though she were wilfully mad but just senile.

"Luiza," he said with great patience, "you are in trouble, great trouble. I know, because you are a proud woman, that you would not come here asking me for money if it was not that you had some great need. Now, my dear"—he patted her shoulder and she bore the pat with fortitude—"if it is food, or your passage to another country if times make it necessary, then you must tell me. Together we will solve your problem. I will speak to Adam, and we shall see that you are provided for—"

"Don't be more of a fool than you can help, Alfred!"

"I—"

"I know exactly what I am doing. I am risking all on a throw of the dice. Something I have never done before: gambled. My late husband"—her lip curled in a derisive smile—"it was something he did many times. He rarely won. But I am gambling just once, and I may win—if you will give me the money."

"Give, now, is it?" screamed Alfred, his control snapping again. "Now it is 'give me the money.' A short while ago it was 'lend.' And my answer is still the same. I am not mad, even if you are. I will neither give nor lend you my money to throw away on a hare-brained scheme! Nothing will make me give you the money!"

"Not even as a dowry for your daughter?"

Fleeting expressions chased across his face. He was slow-witted, Alfred Racs-Rassay, for all his intellectual pretensions, slow and dull when it came to grasping a point. Fury, bewilderment, conjecture, doubt flew over his face and he did not answer.

"You have a daughter, Alfred. You wife has been trying to find a husband for Kati for four years. You know, and I know, that Felix was once a very favoured suitor."

"Kati—"

"Kati is the richest girl in this area. Even now, with the war and the troubles that threaten us, Kati is still, will still be, a wealthy bride, a catch for any young man—or she would have been."

"Would have been?"

"The young men are all gone now, Alfred. They are dead,

or maimed, or lost forever in Russia. The few who have come back are very precious. They can pick their brides as they wish. Your wife was always aware that Felix was the most suitable husband for Kati. Yes, Kati is the richest girl in the country, but Felix"—her voice softened—"Felix is a gentleman, a Kaldy, an aristocrat! We are of the old stock, Alfred. You know it. Why, my father was once concerned because you danced with me too often at a ball! He was worried that I would fall in love with you . . . and he considered you, a Racs-Rassay, unsuitable as a husband."

Alfred flushed. He resented the reminder, but the old laws of caste and strata were imbedded as deeply in him as in her, and what she said was the truth.

"My father even now, if he were alive, would spit at me if he knew I were contemplating allowing my son to match with your daughter—my son, Felix Kaldy, to wed with the little Racs-Rassay girl—and remember, Alfred, Kati's antecedents are not too desirable on her mother's side."

He was bewildered and helpless. Somehow he was convinced he was being tricked but he could not see where.

"If—if these things are true," he faltered, "if I admit these things are true, if I say that Kati's marriage with a Kaldy would bring great credit to her—if I admit these things were so before the war, I cannot admit them now. What difference would it make to Kati now, married to a Kaldy, when neither of them will have any land or money?"

She had trapped him! A surging of confidence pumped blood through her body at a speed that set her heart fluttering again. She had won. A few more points and she had won.

"But if they *do* have the land, Alfred, then Kati has made a brilliant match!"

Alfred looked puzzled and unhappy again.

"A bargain, Alfred. Give me the money to buy my house back, and even as that transaction is private, so shall the engagement between Felix and Kati be private. We need not even tell them too definitely. If we win our gamble—if the dice fall our way—then I have the Kaldy estate, complete as it used to be, and Kati will be married to the head of that estate and will bear a noble and honourable name."

"And if we all lose our land?" he muttered unhappily. "If the government takes it away from us?"

"Then I have lost my house, you have lost your money—but only a little of your money—and Kati is still free to make a more suitable match." Her lip curled again. "To a Swiss

217

watch manufacturer, perhaps. Or even a socialist if they are to be Hungary's new lords."

Alfred was trying to follow, trying to see where the snags lay.

"You see, Alfred," she explained patiently, "you are spending some money on a chance. If you lose, you have only lost your money. If you win, your daughter is mistress of an estate and will bear the name of Kaldy. Her . . . antecedents . . . will be forgotten. She will be a Kaldy who was once a Racs-Rassay. And your grandsons will be the inheritors of the old lands."

He was floundering, helpless, puzzled, but dazzled by the logic of it all.

"I will call Gizi," he muttered at last. "These things are for Gizi to decide."

And then she knew it was all right. Gizi Racs-Rassay, whose "antecedents" she had been forced to dwell upon in order to press her point, was a woman of her own brand. Gizi knew exactly what she wanted, had always known. She wanted Felix for her daughter, and when money was the only stake she would be happy to spend it. Money was easy to make. She had created Alfred's fortune for him, and now some of it was going to be spent on the things that were important.

The interview with Gizi was smooth, efficient, crisp—two clever women settling a bargain to their mutual advantage. There was only one moment of unease and it came when she was on her feet ready to leave.

"I have one point," Gizi Racs-Rassay said softly, "and it is about your son."

She stiffened. Had any rumours leaked back? Had the news of Felix's . . . difficulties . . . during the war been made public? He had done something wrong; even she wasn't too sure what it was except that he had apparently left the place he should have been in and gone somewhere else.

"Yes?" she said guardedly.

"All last summer, in the town and here in the country, it was observed that your son spent much time with my niece, the younger Ferenc girl. I think it would be most unwise for this . . . friendship to continue. The engagement is secret for the time being—I shall hint only lightly to Kati; she is foolish at times and might well confide in her cousins—but secret or not, Felix should not spend his leisure with Eva."

Of course the woman was right. She would see that Felix was kept away from the Ferencs. And yet—the memory of Felix as he had been came to her mind—the zombie-like, catatonic creature who had lain on his bed unwashed. He had never really been cured until the little Ferenc trollop had taken a hand last summer. Whatever she had done, Felix was more human, more like the son she used to know. What would happen if she kept him away from Eva Ferenc? She felt the flutter round her heart again. She did not want Felix to be—ill—like that again. He was her pride, her hope, her firstborn. He was his father again, but his father with the deceit and fecklessness ground out.

But the land . . . the house . . . the bargain with the Racs-Rassay family. . . .

"I will do my best," she promised. "I will see that the friendship is . . . restricted."

Gizi smiled. "I would prefer that it ceased altogether," she said sweetly and the two women tensed, waiting to flare, each wanting to exert the ultimate authority over the other.

But the bargain meant too much to both of them. The moment passed and the demands were not emphasized. They said a careful farewell and then, at last, she was free to go back to the farmhouse and lie exhausted on the bed.

15

And now the real revolution broke over their heads in a red cataclysm of terror. This was no moderate socialism, as—they soon realized—Karolyi's had been. This was the raw, brutal stuff born in the Soviets, bred in Siberian prison camps, and matured finally in the misery and despair of the Hungarian poor after four years of war. Count Karolyi, aristocrat and idealist, had tried to create Utopia out of a country broken by war. He had promised free elections and land reform and had been cheered in the streets of Budapest, but when his dream had not turned into an instant miracle, when he had failed to prevent the victors of the West from exacting their pound of flesh, the people's hopes turned to Russia. If Karolyi's republic could not save them, Bolshevism would. This was the triumph of Bela Kun, prisoner of war in Russia and a disciple of Lenin.

They were still in the country, where they had been all through the winter. Papa was in Budapest, a Budapest that was unstable and violent. Mama, who had at first been afraid but who was now bored, had written and asked if they could return to their house in town. Their own little country town was not like Budapest; it was quiet and calm and fairly settled. Felix had reported on his last visit to the country that, although there was no fuel, and little food in the restaurants, some attempt had been made to establish a social life. Mama couldn't see why they should have to stay in the country where it was cold and miserable. She wanted to go home.

Papa's reply had been swift and adamant: they were to stay where they were. And a postscript had added, "Also, my dear Marta, it is possible that the future may see the need for more serious economies. Opening the town house is an unnecessary expense at this time. On the farm you have fuel, food, and servants, and the company of Alfred and Gizi if you need it. I wish you all to remain there."

And so, when the revolution burst over their heads, they were alone on the farm.

The boys were the first to bring back news. Throughout the winter they had been receiving lessons from the schoolmaster in the village. It was unthinkable that they should attend classes with the peasant children, and so every day after school hours were over they went to the master's house for rudimentary private tutoring. And the news they brought back was that a real revolution, like the Russian one, had broken out and that they were not to go for lessons any more.

"Men came and sat in the schoolhouse," Jozsef said. His face was very red and flustered. Leo was silent. "They said they were from the revolutionary tribunal. What is the revolutionary tribunal, Malie?"

"I'm not sure, dear. It's something to do with the government." She was uneasy but not really afraid. This was their farm and all their peasants knew them, and everyone in the village knew them too. They could hardly come to any harm.

"Everyone in the village was going to the square to listen to them. And the schoolmaster said it wasn't safe for us and we must come back here and stay here."

"I see." Of course it was safe. Their own peasants would hardly let them come to any harm. And anyway, everyone in the village was too cold and tired and hungry to be fired with revolutionary ideas. They would do what peasants always did, listen and neither agree nor disagree.

But nonetheless they all stayed close to the house for several days. No one was really afraid, but perhaps it was wise to be careful. Roza walked into the village to see her sister. When she came back she reported that something called a committee was being formed and that the village was full of strange men, most of them in ex-military uniforms. And then Uncle Alfred came over and what had been no more than uneasiness began to grow into fear.

"The land has been nationalized!" he shouted. "We've lost! All of us—your papa, that foolish Kaldy woman, Gizi and myself—we've lost everything we have. All gone, all taken away by the Bolshevik rabble!"

"But Uncle Alfred, we're still here! What have they done if we are still here?"

"For the moment you're still here. At present it is the big estates that are being divided; soon it will be ours. The Kaldy woman . . . she fooled me, trapped me." His face was red, his words incoherent, and none of them really knew what he was talking of. But the fear he generated spread to them all.

"What shall we do, Alfred?" asked Mama shrilly. "What *can* we do? Oh! Zsigmond was so cruel to leave us here! We have no man to protect us and now we shall be murdered, murdered like they were in Russia!" She began to cry and Malie had an overpowering desire to smack her. If only Mama would *help* sometimes instead of being so very feminine and helpless.

"Do?" shouted Alfred. "What we must do is go back to town, all of us. We have homes there and we have friends. We can group together for protection. And Zsigmond must come back from Budapest and guard our interests. Yes, we must go back to town at once, all of us."

Malie felt someone touching the back of her skirt. She didn't turn round because she knew it was Leo. He was too big now to look for reassurance from her openly, but she was familiar with his slight touch, seeking the comfort that contact with her brought.

"Yes!" Mama's tears ceased. "Yes, we shall go home! Everyone is in the town. Only we remain here—stupid creatures that we are—to be murdered in our beds!"

"Mama, don't you think we are safer here? Papa said—"

But Mama was already halfway towards the door. "Papa!" She waved her hand in the air. "Papa said we must stay here

221

until things are settled. Well, they are not settling, they are growing worse. And Alfred has said we must go, so we shall."

"Tomorrow!" bellowed Alfred. "Be ready in your coach when we come by and we will travel together!"

"Is that wise, Uncle Alfred? Surely a procession—two coaches—would be more likely to attract attention than single travellers?"

"Oh, yes!" cried Mama. "We will go alone. Too many together—I'm sure it is dangerous . . . and we have Sandor."

"Mama, I still think we are safer here. We should remain here. No one would attack us. Everyone knows us!"

"What about the strange men? The men—the councils or whatever they are called? They do not know us. And they are the ones who will turn us from our land!"

Amalia gave in. They packed their clothes and took all the food that was available, and finally, because Mama would not wait, they agreed to start at once, that day, instead of waiting for Alfred and the Racs-Rassay coach to be somewhere on the road with them.

Roza was crying, standing at the door rocking to and fro, not understanding but not wanting to be left alone. Finally her weeping penetrated through to Mama, who patted her shoulder as she passed her with an armful of petticoats. "Don't weep, Roza dear. Nothing can happen to *you*. You are safe. You are one of them. They wouldn't dream of hurting their own people."

"But madame—"

"Roza, dear," interrupted Malie quietly, "go to your sister's. It will be better for you there. And if—when—your sons come home and you are not here, where else would they go but to your sister in the village?"

She was persuaded, and weeping, screaming farewells, she set off through the trees, a basket of sausage and bread on her arm, a black shawl wound tightly over her head. The farm without Roza was frightening.

"Come. We must leave very soon. Otherwise we shall be travelling in the dark."

They climbed into the coach and Uncle Sandor flicked the horse. Malie looked back through the acacia trees that were covered in tight green buds. The dogs were staring after them, sad and not understanding. The farmhouse had never looked so bleak.

"Malie, we can't leave the dogs. What will happen to the dogs?"

"They'll be all right, Leo. There's water in the stream and the weather is warmer now. We can't take them with us."

"But what will they eat?"

"Roza will send someone to feed them, and they will forage for themselves."

Roza wouldn't feed them. There wasn't enough food to go round among the people for anyone to worry about the dogs. But she was tired, oh, so tired of having to find answers to all the problems and questions. Eva and Mama seemed already to have forgotten why they were leaving; they were just pleased to be going home, Mama because she was bored with country life, Eva because she would be closer to Felix.

The spring countryside was quiet, uncannily quiet. There was hardly anyone working in the fields, and they didn't pass another person or cart or coach anywhere on the track. There was no sound—not even that of the birds—except for the clopping of Sultan's hoofs and the noise of the wheels. They passed the boundary of their land—only it wasn't to be theirs for very much longer—and then the Kaldy land. Everything was the same: quiet, deserted, and somehow . . . ominous.

"We should have waited until tomorrow," Malie said sharply. "There is something wrong and we've left it too late. We should have waited and begun early in the morning."

No one answered. Mama and Eva, at first oblivious to the atmosphere about them, now seemed to be aware of the tension. Mama tapped her hand restlessly on the side of the coach. "Can't Sandor drive any faster?" she said irritably.

They were on the good road when they saw the men in front of them. It was the level road on the lower land, running between flat fields bordered with larch trees. The men were waiting in a silent, threatening line across the road.

"Ugh!" growled Uncle Sandor, and brought the whip down on Sultan's back. The old horse went a little faster.

They had scythes and shovels, one or two rifles, clubs of wood. They were dressed mostly in old army uniforms, and one or two had red bands on their sleeves.

"Stop! In the name of the People's Republic!"

Sandor took no notice. He whipped Sultan harder and growled again, louder.

"Oh, God!" It was only a whisper and she wondered who had said it. The men had put their rifles and shovels and scythes in front of them, across their bodies, so that they formed a chain of weapons across the road. Sultan faltered.

"Stop!"

Uncle Sandor swore, a violent outpouring of epithets culminating in a stream of saliva that he ejected into the face of the nearest man. He whipped Sultan again, and the old horse screamed and plunged forward into the line of men.

"Oh, God!" The whisper again. By her side Mama began to cry, not loudly, but the noise was frightening because it contributed to the lack of control and the hysteria that was thick about them. Sultan struggled and reared up, and the men closed in. Two fell to the ground, but there were several more to leap up and pull on the reins, to drag on the side of the coach.

"Stop! You have been ordered in the name of the People's Republic!"

"Get away! Scum!" Uncle Sandor thrashed out with the whip, hitting several faces, shoulders, arms, but the whip was grasped and he was dragged down from the box.

A thin, dirty hand pulled the door open and Eva was wrenched out of the coach. Sobbing, she fell onto the ground but the men didn't touch her. They stood in a little circle round the coach, thin, ugly, sick-looking men.

"We have orders to search your coach."

The apparent leader was even thinner than the rest. He had the high red cheeks and gaunt features of the consumptive, and half of his left hand was shot away.

"Stop the old woman from screaming!" he shouted. They were dragging boxes and baskets out of the coach. Like starving dogs they rifled through the food, stuffing it into their mouths and passing it back to others on the outer edge of the circle. "Stop her from screaming!" he shouted again.

"Mama! For God's sake try and be quiet! You're making them angry!"

Mama screamed louder, and the consumptive suddenly thrust his body into the coach and clutched her shoulder, shaking her back and forth and shouting, "Shut up! Shut up!"

There was a roar, a loud guttural bellowing roar, and Uncle Sandor was up from the road. His black eyes were nearly closed and blood was running from his mouth. His great bulk hurtled towards the consumptive, and the scarecrow leader was suddenly tossed from the coach and thrown to the surface of the road.

"Filthy scum! Keep away from the Bogozy!"

Shouting . . . Eva screaming from the roadway . . . Leo fighting to get out of the coach, calling to Uncle Sandor, someone holding him back—me, Malie: "You cannot help,

Leo!"—Leo shouting . . . all the boxes emptied onto the road . . . Uncle Sandor still bellowing, rearing his mighty body up from a heap of thin dirty ones, like a bear being baited by dogs.

There was a shot, and the noise—the noise of final violence —drowned everything else so that suddenly there was no other noise; everything was hushed, still.

The screaming—oh, God, Mama, be quiet, do be quiet!— fell to a keening and sobbing. Someone had been killed. . . . Leo? Where are you, Leo?

"Leo!"

Another moment of unnatural, chilled silence, and then the men began to run. The leader, the thin consumptive with half a hand, shouted at them to come back but they were beggars, peasants who needed food, and now they were frightened because they had killed someone.

"Come back!"

"Leo! Leo!"

It was all right. Leo was alive. She could hear him. And she could see him. He was crouching by the torn body of Uncle Sandor. There was a small hole in the side of Uncle Sandor's head and a trickle of blood ran onto the road. Jozsef was out of the coach before her. He ran over to Uncle Sandor and she followed, trying to prevent Jozsef from seeing what Leo had already seen.

Leo was crying, sobbing piteously, desperately. One of Uncle Sandor's huge great hands was held in the boy's tiny palms.

"Oh, don't die, Uncle Sandor! Please don't die!"

Jozsef turned white features towards her. "Malie! Don't let Uncle Sandor die!"

Oh, dear God! Is this how Karoly had looked? Clothes torn from his body, his face bruised and smashed, a hole through his head?

Leo was nearly hysterical. He pulled Uncle Sandor's great thick hand up to his face and rubbed it against his cheek. "Don't leave us, Uncle Sandor! Don't leave us!"

"He's dead, Leo. Uncle Sandor is dead."

"No!"

"He's dead, Leo. I can't do anything. He's dead."

Leo fell forward over Uncle Sandor's body. Rich, adult pain assaulted his boy's senses. "I won't let him be dead! I won't let him!"

"Jozsef, find something to cover Uncle Sandor with."

Jozsef stared at her, tears running down his face; then he stumbled about the road, looking for something among the garments that were strewn there.

"Malie! We can't leave him here! We must take him back with us! We can't leave him! We can't, we can't!"

She began to feel sick. She couldn't cope any more. There was no one to help her and she didn't know how to manage.

"We can't lift him, Leo. He's too heavy."

"Don't leave him here, Malie! Please don't leave him!"

Her hands began to tense and tremble. She looked back at the coach. It was slewed halfway across the road and Sultan was whinnying and trying to pull free from the harness. Eva, sobbing, had managed to pull herself forward and was holding the reins. She was talking to Sultan, trying to calm him and sobbing at the same time.

"Can you help me, Eva?"

Eva tied the reins to a larch tree and came over. It was done slowly, and all the time she was sobbing. When she saw Uncle Sandor she just went on sobbing.

"We can't get him up into the coach, Eva."

"No."

"Will you help me bury him?"

Eva nodded.

There were shovels and scythes, wooden bars and pieces of iron scattered over the road. They took up spades and went to the side of the road. The soil of the field was fairly soft and it wasn't too difficult to dig.

"Cover him, Jozsef."

Jozsef had found a petticoat of Mama's. He pulled it over Uncle Sandor's head.

"Jozsef, take Leo into the fields on the far side of the road, right across the fields—there—to the woods. You are to—to find something to put on the grave. Tell Leo to look for violets and primroses, a very big bunch, and then you are both to make a cross with branches. Don't come back for a long, long time."

They were both crying, but Jozsef took Leo's hand and they stumbled away. She could hear them from a long way off.

She had never seen a dead man before, neither had the boys, but already the battered hulk of Uncle Sandor was no longer strange to them. And she was suddenly able to understand that when they dragged that great torso to the shallow hole, when they tipped him in and began to throw earth on

226

top of him, it would be a final desecration, a hideous violation of identity.

As though two other people were doing it and they were watching, Malie and Eva dragged, pulled, pushed, and finally thrust the old man into the grave. Neither of them could bring themselves to throw soil on top of him and so they collected all the stray clothes, the shawls and undergarments and nightdresses (all the warm things had been taken), and covered his body many times with layers of cloth. Then they were able to put soil on him and bang it hard with the shovel.

When the boys came back with flowers and a cross, Uncle Sandor was already in his grave.

Eva took the reins for the first part of the journey. It was dark and they gave Sultan his head, but the horse knew his master was absent and it was hours before they reached the outskirts of the town.

Mama, crying quietly and moaning, sat in a corner. Malie left her alone. She was too tired to comfort Mama. There was nothing to hope for, nothing to rebuild. Was it always going to be like this? A year since Karoly had died, a year of pretending to be brave and cheerful, of seeking comfort in small things, and now this. Oh, Uncle Sandor, forgive us! Foolish Bogozy women who should have waited until tomorrow, who should have stopped screaming when they were told; so many things the foolish Bogozy women should have done. And now the old man was dead, packed into a shallow trench at the side of a field. Wet soil . . . worms . . . oh, God!

The boys were silent. They sat on each side, holding her hand.

"Malie."

"Yes, Leo?"

"Malie. I saw him, the man who killed Uncle Sandor. He was thin and dirty and he had a red armband. I saw him."

"Oh, Leo. They all had red armbands. And they all looked alike. They were all thin and dirty."

"I'm sure I'd know him, Malie. I'm sure!"

But his shrill boy's voice faltered. He wanted to avenge the old soldier who had been his friend, he wanted to swear an oath that he would find the man who had shot Uncle Sandor and kill him too, but the face in his mind, the face of the killer, was already blurring.

"Malie."

"Yes, Leo."

"Malie, I don't think I can live without Uncle Sandor. He

227

was the most important person in the world. How are we going to live without him?"

How indeed?

They lived carefully and quietly in the town. Papa came back from Budapest, a tired, despondent Papa. The banks, the insurance companies, the large industrial works had all been taken over by the state. Papa was still working in his bank, but it wasn't his any more. He went there every day, and every day he waited to be told not to come again.

They had closed off most of the house. Marie was still there, but they couldn't afford any of the other servants. They couldn't afford new clothes, or black-market coal. Food was expensive, and there was no Uncle Sandor to send up to the farm for provisions. Indeed, it might only be a little while before the farm was officially taken away from them.

Everything seemed transitional. There was no more violence, but they were all uncertain of what was going to happen next. There was still a war, but now it wasn't clear who was supposed to win. The Czechs in the north, the Romanians in the east, were battering once more against them, but this time perhaps it would be better if they won and brought back the old government. In the south it was rumoured that some of the old Imperial officers had formed yet another army and were fighting against the Romanians *and* against the regime of Bela Kun. Who was fighting whom? And for what? Would the troubled times ever cease?

The only one who was happy was Eva; the news, the shortage of food, the depressing outlook for the future seemed to leave her spirits untouched. Felix was pottering happily in his office. He had to work now, something he had never done before, but there was still time to call, to take Eva for walks, to sit with her on the terrace of the Franz-Josef drinking coffee or, as the warm weather progressed, diluted ersatz cordial. So Eva was happy, not the wild ecstatic happiness of her first adoration of Felix, but a contented pride that lent her dignity and quietness.

One afternoon Papa came home early from the bank. Malie watched him walking from the square and realized, shocked, that Papa was turning into an old man. He wasn't as big or as dark as he had always seemed. His shoulders were stooped and his coat hung loosely from them. And his hair was quite grey at the sides. He walked slowly, with a plodding motion, as though every step were an effort. They were all in the drawing-room when he came in.

"Good afternoon, Papa."

"Papa."

"Zsigmond."

Papa nodded and walked over to his favourite chair. He sat down, leaned his head back, and closed his eyes for a moment.

"What will become of us all?" he asked despairingly. "How can I provide for my family when all I have worked for is lost?"

Never, never had they heard Papa speak like this. He had been angry, proud, sad, puzzled, but never hopeless.

"My wife, my children, all the land I bought, everything I built—nothing." He placed one gaunt hand over his face and bent his head forward, a tired old man. Papa, old?

"I have been trying to think of something to save us," he said. "We could try and get to Vienna, but Vienna is crowded and conditions there are worse than in Budapest."

"Papa. . . ." Malie spoke diffidently. The years of habit, of not interrupting, were deeply ingrained and she was nervous of making any kind of comment. "Papa, could we not wait a little longer, wait and see what happens? All the armies . . . if they defeat Bela Kun everything will be just the way it was before the war."

"No, Amalia. Things will never be like that again."

He was so sad, so slow, so . . . kind. He had been kind once before, when Karoly died. The hatred she had felt for Papa had begun to fade then. She could never love him—he was not a man who needed love—but she was aware of a strange sensation in her breast. Pity? Affection?

"We could also try and get through the frontiers to Switzerland. If we could get to Berne I think Mr. Klein would help us. Mr. Klein has many business houses in Switzerland and, possibly, he would help us."

"Leave Hungary, Papa?" asked Eva. "Leave our friends and our family—Uncle Alfred, Aunt Gizi, our Bogozy relatives?" *And Felix Kaldy* was in everyone's mind as they looked at her. She had worked so hard for so many years to win Felix. And now Papa was threatening to take her away.

"We have to live, children. We have to live."

It was all speculation, suggestion, but the seed had been planted and Eva was afraid. Later that night she waited until

Mama had gone to bed and then she joined her father in the drawing-room.

"Papa, if . . . if we—you—go to Switzerland, or even Vienna, I—"

"Yes, Eva? What is it you are trying to say?"

"Papa, Felix has a post. Even in the new government he would probably have a post."

"I expect so. As much as anyone can tell—and who can tell anything in these times?"

"Papa, if Felix were to ask me to marry him—if he were to ask you—would you let me stay here as his wife?"

Papa looked at her, his face so sad she had to turn away.

"To lose you, Eva? To lose my little Eva?"

"Oh, Papa! It would only be until things were better."

"Of course." He slumped in his chair and nodded. "Felix Kaldy. A fine young man, a fine family. But they have nothing now, even as we have nothing."

"He has his post, Papa! It pays only a little but we could manage."

"Has Felix suggested this?"

She flushed and shook her head. "No, Papa, but how could he? You have just said that he has nothing. But I know he wants to marry me. He is waiting for something to happen before he asks me."

Papa bowed his head. "Then we shall wait, either until he comes to speak to me or until we decide to go to Switzerland."

"But, Papa!"

She crossed over to him and knelt by his chair, the way she had done so many times in the past. She had always managed to get her own way with Papa, and now, with this new, softer, tired Papa she didn't see any difficulties. She put her small, soft hand into his palm and pressed her cheek against his hand.

"I promise you, Eva, that I will come to no decisions without first discussing it with you and Felix."

"You like him, don't you, Papa?"

He smiled at her. "A fine young man," he repeated. "In other times—but there, we cannot dwell on what might have been." But he was dwelling on it, thinking how magnificent it would have been: his younger daughter married to the head of the Kaldy estate, all that land linked with his—and Alfred's on the other side of the river—and the name, the Kaldy name, putting yet another seal of respectability on the dynasty he was building.

"If Felix comes to see me," he promised, "I shall be happy to speak to him. And together we will see what can be done."

She was satisfied. At least she was satisfied with Papa. Now all she had to do was convey, tactfully, to Felix that if he wanted to ask her to marry him it was quite all right.

They were defeated. The Hungarian Red Army was defeated by the Romanians, pushed steadily north until there was no-where for them to go except into the mountains where they could disperse and vanish.

Leo and Jozsef were returning from school when they heard the distant rumble, the *thud-thud* of an army marching in orderly retreat, and just as they turned into the square they saw them, line after line of soldiers, the same ones who had been fighting for the last five years. Even the uniforms were the same old Imperial uniforms, except that now they had red stars or armbands instead of the insignia of the King and Emperor.

Tired men, disillusioned men, they had believed in an ideal and the ideal had turned sour. The dream of an Eldorado state had died.

Leo stared hard at every face, looking for the one that haunted his dreams, the one he wanted to denounce and destroy. Two nights ago Uncle Sandor had appeared in one of his dreams. He had lifted him up onto his horse and had said to Leo, "Now we must go and kill the King of Prussia!" They had whooped and galloped, and Uncle Sandor had been popping bread and onions into his mouth as they rode. Then, in the middle of an acacia wood, they had come to a bench and there was the King of Prussia. "Shoot him," said Uncle Sandor, and Leo threw the onion at the King, who rolled over and died. The King was thin and hungry and he had a uniform with a red armband. Then he and Uncle Sandor rode away and Uncle Sandor was singing, bellowing out a folk song in his great bass voice.

When he woke up he felt happy and safe for a moment. And then he remembered and everything crumbled and he was lost. There was no one to seek for reassurance. But then he remembered the King of Prussia's face and he said to the ceiling, "I'll kill him, Uncle Sandor. I'll kill him."

The soldiers, surprisingly, were marching in step and their

rifles were held at a uniform angle over their shoulders. Leo squinted into the column.

"There he is!"

"Where?"

"That one! In the middle, with the torn coat—oh, he's gone!"

"Are you sure it was him?"

"It was him." But he wasn't sure. For a moment he had been convinced, but the face had blurred again in his mind. How could he catch the man when the face moved and changed? He had seen the man more than once, in the street, serving in the Franz-Josef, and always the memory blurred before he could be sure.

"Let's go home," said Jozsef tiredly. "I'm hungry. And it wasn't him. I'm sure it wasn't him."

They turned and began to trudge back along the street.

"This is the first summer we shall not be going to the farm." Images chased across their minds: the sheepdogs, the orchards, the river, Uncle Sandor.

"Perhaps Malie will take us into the country for a day," said Leo hopefully. "We could drive Sultan ourselves and go a little way into the hills."

"I'm fed up with going around with a lot of women!" Jozsef was at middle school now, but because the last year had been so disruptive, so dangerous and confused, he had not been able to make new friends. Now they were breaking up and he wouldn't have a chance to develop his acquaintanceships. The holidays loomed ahead, empty and dull. He was tired of being continually in the company of Eva and Malie. He wanted male talk, male doings, horses and tales of hunting and old wars. Uncle Sandor.

All the houses in Petofi Street were shabby, none more so than theirs. The stonework was chipped and the shutters peeling. They trudged into the yard, their bulging schoolbags clasped to their chests.

There was a carriage in the yard, a pony cart that was neat and shiny with smart black wheels and polished harness. It shone, misplaced and incongruous in the dust and dingy surroundings of the yard.

"Visitors!" They ran into the house, chased upstairs straight into the kitchen. Marie was stirring goulash at the stove and even she seemed cheered and stimulated.

"Go and wash," she called brightly. "We have a visitor. Mr. Klein is here!"

Mr. Klein, incredibly just-the-same Mr. Klein, tall and sleepy with beautiful clothes and gracious manners. The last Papa had heard he was in Switzerland, but now he had, in some mysterious way, travelled unharmed and with affluent dignity through two frontiers, through a Budapest rent by yet another government on the point of falling, through a country rife with a disintegrating Bolshevik army and advancing Romanians and White Hungarians. Mr. Klein didn't even mention how he had done all these things. They asked him once and he waved his hand deprecatingly in the air and said softly, "A little inconvenience at one or two places," and after that it seemed discourteous to question him about his journey.

The difference in Papa was amazing. His tiredness had evaporated and though he still looked old and shabby (especially compared with Mr. Klein, he seemed shabby) all his old authority as head of the tribe was back.

"Mr. Klein believes that soon we shall return to economic stability," he said. "A new government is being formed at Szeged. It has the approval of the enemy"—Papa coughed and corrected himself—"of the English and French. Mr. Klein says it is almost certain that eventually the Romanians will be forced to withdraw and then the country will be restored to peace and order."

Oh, what a difference Mr. Klein made to everyone! The room seemed full and yet there was only one extra person there. Mama was smiling and running from drawing-room to kitchen to superintend the goulash—oh, the shame, to offer peasants' food to Mr. Klein!—Eva was bright and vivacious, and even Malie felt the old stir of fascinated interest that she remembered from Mr. Klein's last visit.

Mr. Klein and Papa spent the afternoon in the study, and when they came out Papa was still confident, although now his confidence was more controlled, more orderly and systematic.

The goulash was apologized for, but even so there was a festive note about the table. There were candles and flowers and some wine that Papa had saved for a special occasion. Mr. Klein toasted Mama and Amalia and Eva and then the entire family.

"And soon, madame," he said smoothly to Mama, "when the world is once more tranquil, you will be giving little parties, little occasions for your daughters, yes?" His lazy brown eyes slid from Mama to Eva, from Eva to Amalia. "Your

233

daughters are very beautiful. Soon, very soon, the young men will come to take them away."

Papa, in an unusually expansive mood, picked up Eva's hand and caressed it with his own. "They have already come for this little one," he said benignly. "I think Eva already has a suitor, do you not, my dear?"

Eva flushed prettily and managed to look embarrassed and gratified at the same time. Mr. Klein stared hard at Eva; then his gaze moved to Malie and she felt the assessing eyes wandering over her hair, her face, her body.

"Indeed," murmured Mr. Klein. "Is an old friend permitted to ask—"

"Oh, no, Papa! Please. You know nothing is settled. We must not talk about it yet."

Mr. Klein raised his hand in the air and smiled. "A secret, of course, and we must not pry, Zsigmond. The young must be left to enjoy the delicacy of their emotions alone." Back and forth wandered the speculative gaze, from bright, dark-eyed, glowing little Eva with her pouting chin and provocative breasts to Amalia, serene and graceful but quiet, so quiet.

Papa laughed. "Perhaps she is right, my friend. It is too soon to discuss, but"—his voice deepened—"I am happy for her. The young man is a splendid choice. The family will gain nothing but credit from Eva's match."

"Oh, Papa!" She smiled and blushed. How lovely it was to be the centre of attention, and for such a happy reason. If everything that Mr. Klein said was true, if the country was going to be at peace once more, if better times were coming, perhaps Felix would feel that at last he could ask her to marry him.

The evening ended happily, on a note of hope that none of them had experienced for a long, long time. The next morning Mr. Klein took Eva and Malie out for a little drive in his pony cart, and the following day, because the boys had loitered in the yard looking envious, he took just Malie and the boys.

Somehow, in spite of the times, Mr. Klein managed to find gifts, welcome gifts of a goose, of eggs and cream, that he presented to Mama with such graciousness she could hardly refuse. It was difficult to refuse Mr. Klein anything. It always seemed to happen—in a lazy, gentle way—that one was doing exactly what Mr. Klein intended. And because Mr. Klein always wanted to go for drives, or for leisurely strolls, or to

234

drink coffee at the Franz-Josef, that was what they did. And increasingly, because Eva did not always want to come if Felix was visiting, Amalia and Mama went out with Mr. Klein on their own. It was pleasant, and entertaining, and . . . disquieting.

When Mr. Klein left, everything was flat and drab for a little while, but the hope he had brought remained. The Romanians occupied much of the country now, but rumour said that it was only a prelude to the establishment of a permanent government. And, after all, the Romanian officers were not so bad; they came into the town and were handsome and quiet and well-behaved.

When the flowers arrived from Mr. Klein no one was surprised. But Eva stared a little at the baskets. Pink roses for her and Mama, and red ones for Malie. Malie refused to discuss why she had been treated differently and later, in the bin in the yard, Eva saw that the red roses had been thrown away.

16

"And so," said Aunt Gizi, "we thought we should have the wedding at the end of the summer, up at the villa. We shall give a party for the farm labourers as well. It seems at last that the country is settled and at peace, and Kati's wedding shall be the occasion of a double celebration!"

She spoke quickly to try and hide the fact that for twenty minutes, ever since she had broken the news, no one had spoken. Amalia looked stunned and incredulous, Marta Bogozy puzzled, and Eva—Eva was just sitting, her face completely drained of colour and the pupils of her eyes frozen to tiny points of darkness. What bothered her most, though, was her brother. Zsigmond was staring at her with a face of compressed fury. His nose suddenly seemed extraordinarily thin and prominent in his now pinched face.

"Madame Kaldy has already put the repairs and refurnishing of the manor house in hand," she went on, deliberately not looking at anyone and trying to chatter happily, the way any mother of a newly betrothed girl would. "Naturally we

235

shall invest a little money in the manor, such a beautiful old house. It is, after all, to be the home of our little girl and we shall try to make it as splendid as we can."

She began to feel she would scream if someone didn't speak soon. Alfred was no help either; he just stood by the window and fiddled with the blind. When he wasn't looking smug he was looking bored.

"I never believed, Marta," she said desperately, trying anything to gain a response, "that our little Kati would be married before your daughters. It seemed inevitable, from when they were very small, that Eva and Amalia would naturally be married first."

Mama finally managed to rouse herself from incomprehension. "It is so . . . surprising, Gizi! No one, not one of us, had any idea that Felix and Kati were growing close to one another. Friends, yes; we have all been friends together for many years, but—"

"Ah, yes!" Gizi interrupted with heightened colour. "Well, of course, since the war—for the first year after the war—Felix had to work hard here, in the town. And we were mostly in the country, so no one really saw them together. But lately, since things have become settled, Felix—and Madame Kaldy —have paid several visits to us and Felix has taken Kati out on several occasions. Hasn't he, Kati?"

Kati nodded. She was wearing a tan jumper suit—it was new as behooved a girl just engaged—but, Kati being Kati, the suit didn't seem to fit. It looked too large and the white linen collar stuck out awkwardly at the back of her neck. On her right hand shone a gold signet ring with a diamond embedded in a graven K. Madame Kaldy had kept her part of the bargain magnificently, even to parting with the last remaining pieces of Kaldy jewellery that she possessed.

"We could see what was happening, couldn't we, Alfred"— Alfred grunted and continued to fiddle with the blind—"and when Kati came to us and said that Felix had proposed to her, we weren't one little bit surprised, no, not at all."

Kati looked more confused than any of them. Her small, colourless face hovered between a smile and tears. The smile was because her mama was being so nice to her and seemed so pleased about everything. The tears were because she felt something was wrong. She didn't really want to marry Felix Kaldy; she had always thought of him as belonging to Eva. She had been astonished and embarrassed when, during one of their awkward and silent walks together, he had suddenly proposed to her. No one had ever proposed to her before so she had nothing to compare it with, but Felix's stilted and pompous proposition had seemed wrong and unnatural. The atmosphere between them had been so formal and withdrawn she hadn't liked to say no; not just like that. They had turned round and gone straight home without her making any answer at all, and then her mama had come rushing into her room, hugging her and kissing her and saying how happy she was and how happy Kati was going to be. And overwhelmed with Mama's warmth and excitement, with the feeling that for the first time in her life she had done something right, she had succumbed to the avalanche of excitement and flurry and visits to Madame Kaldy that immediately ensued. But now, with Eva and Amalia looking so strange, she began to feel utterly miserable again. She swallowed hard and blinked, trying to fight back tears. Her mama was still chattering, rather too loudly and shrilly.

"'As soon as the manor house is finished, Madame Kaldy will move in and leave the little farmhouse to Adam and the foreman. Felix and Kati, of course, will live with Madame Kaldy at the manor.''

Malie, in the middle of shocked sorrow for Eva, was still able to feel pity for poor Cousin Kati. Even in marriage she was not to know freedom or peace, not to have her own home. She was just exchanging Aunt Gizi for Madame Kaldy.

"Madame Kaldy has been so gracious! She intends to re-open the old house and entertain the way she used to in the old days. And our little Kati will have all the help and advice she can possibly want on how to run a big house. Madame Kaldy —Luiza—has promised to help her in every way.''

Still no one spoke and Kati, rejected by her beautiful cousins, could control herself no more. Two large tears welled out of her eyes and oozed down her cheeks. Instantly Mama was on her feet.

"Kati, my darling! Here we sit, so overwhelmed by your good news that we are too stunned to speak!'' She glided lightly to Kati and kissed her warmly on both cheeks. "My child, may you have all the happiness that you deserve.''

"Thank you, Aunt Marta.''

"Yes, of course, Kati,'' echoed Malie. "We hope you will be happy and we shall love to visit you in your grand manor house, shall we not, Eva?'' She was trying to help Eva, to give her a chance of saving at least her pride. When Aunt Gizi had first announced the news she had been terrified that Eva would fly at Aunt Gizi, or even at poor Kati, and shriek and fight and scream. Eva was never very good at hiding her emotions. But shock had kept her silent, and now all Malie wanted was for Eva to escape from the debacle with dignity.

"Your girls will lead Kati to her wedding, Marta? It would be natural and what we all expect. Kati has no sisters; your girls are her dearest and closest friends." And how bad it will look if they do not lead her into church, her eyes pleaded. What speculation might ensue if Kati's beloved cousins refused to participate at her wedding.

Eva stood up. She gazed at Kati and took several deep, gulping breaths, and then suddenly she crumpled. Her shoulders and head sagged and she turned and walked towards the door, feet dragging, hands hanging loosely by her side. Everyone was quiet as they watched her open the door and leave the room. Then Mama followed unobtrusively, saying to no one in particular, "Eva has been feeling unwell all day. I expect she had gone to lie down."

Papa stood also. His face was still white and pinched and he crossed to Gizi and said icily, "I would like to speak to you and Alfred alone, please. Shall we talk in the study?"

Alfred harrumphed by the window and began to drum his fingers against the frame. Gizi stared her brother down but then, seeing Kati hunched miserably in the corner, said, "Come, Alfred, come with me," and swept ahead of her brother, trying to show by her manner that she had no intention of being intimidated.

Malie, alone with Kati, tried to make a pretence that everything was all right. Two attempts at bright conversation died, defeated by Kati's obvious misery, and finally she was forced to ask, "Are you pleased, Kati? I mean, do you want to get married?"

Kati shrugged. "I don't know," she said pathetically. "Mama says I do. Mama says I will be very happy once I have my own home and husband."

"But what do *you* want, Kati?" It was possible to love Kati, to feel sorry for her, and yet at the same time to be exasperated by her. Why did she never fight back?

"I don't know what I want," said Kati bleakly. "I suppose that's why Mama doesn't like me very much. And why Papa ignores me. I've never known what I want, except—"

"Except what, Kati?"

"Except I would like Mama to stop grumbling at me. I would like"—she paused and sighed with resignation—"I would like to be left in peace. Perhaps if I were left alone I would begin to discover what I want."

"Do you like Felix Kaldy?" She couldn't bring herself to say the word *love*. It was so obvious to everyone that Kati didn't love Felix it seemed an obscenity to mention it. Kati flushed.

"I don't really know him, Malie."

"Then Kati, why?"

Kati's face, a picture of misery, began to twist in anxious distress. "Oh, Malie, you know how Mama was always trying to force us together, Felix and me, and I didn't take any notice. It was all so stupid when it was obvious that he and Eva —right from the beginning, before the war even—it was obvious they were happy and . . . suitable! I never even thought about it, not for me, and then suddenly Felix proposed and Mama told me how right it was that we should be married, and—oh, Malie!" She clasped her two small hands together in unhappiness. "What can I do except what Mama tells me to do? I don't want to go and live with Madame Kaldy, but what would happen if I said no to Mama?"

The sheer, appalling disaster of it all smote Malie afresh: Eva betrayed and humiliated, Kati frightened and bewildered, Felix—who knew what Felix's desires or emotions were, but it was certain that the present arrangements had been hatched between Aunt Gizi and Madame Kaldy.

"But Kati," she pleaded. "You cannot marry someone just because your mama tells you to! You are casting your whole life away. If you do not know Felix, or do not like him, you must not marry him. If you marry him it means you will have to spend the rest of your life with him!"

"And if I don't marry him," she answered miserably, "I will have to spend the rest of my life with Mama."

"Oh, Kati!"

Her pity for Kati began to outweigh her sympathy and indignation for Eva. In fact, secretly she was beginning to feel relieved that Eva had been rejected.

Two more large tears squeezed from Kati's eyes and fell onto her jumper suit. "And I'm so miserable about Eva. I don't want Eva to hate me. You and Eva, and Aunt Marta, are the nicest people I know. I don't want Eva to stop being my friend."

"Of course she won't," said Malie, speaking with a confidence she did not feel. "She did like Felix at one time, but over the last few months she has hardly seen him." It was true. Since Horthy had ridden into Budapest and the land had returned to some kind of post-war settlement, Felix had been seen less and less in the town. He had spent most of the winter and early spring up on the farm because "his mother needed him." And whatever she needed him for, it had finally culminated in this.

"You don't blame me, do you, Malie? You and Eva, you will always be my friends, won't you?"

"Of course, my darling. We're family, aren't we? How could we be anything else but your friends?"

She vowed she would do anything to make Eva gracious and kind to Kati in spite of the disappointment and misery she must be feeling. Every instinct she possessed told her that Kati was going to need friends in the years that lay ahead.

Eva still couldn't believe it. She lay on her bed alternating between absolute and complete misery and the optimistic belief that it was all a mistake that would very soon be put right. He couldn't possibly be going to marry Kati! Beautiful, handsome, smooth, charming Felix, tied in wedlock to lumpy old Kati? Why, it was disgusting! And whereas at one time she had despaired of ever coming close enough to Felix to believe he would share intimacies with her, since his revelations about the war all the formality and unnaturalness had vanished from their relationship. She reflected briefly on Felix's confidences, a subject she forced herself never to dwell on too often. Felix had turned to her in shame and fear. Since that time he had turned to her again and again, seeking reassurance and sanity from her acceptance of his confession. She had watched him and helped him become normal and happy again. She had cheered him when he was depressed, flattered his declining confidence, and once held him in her arms when he cried. He had told her all the things he never told anyone else, and he had told her that he didn't know what he would do without her. And now, this. It was a mistake! They couldn't have spent all that time together, shared all those things if he hadn't meant to marry her!

And in the midst of knowing it was a mistake, an error that Kati and Aunt Gizi had made between them, her confidence would plummet and other memories would force their way into her miserable heart. He had never asked her to marry him. In all that time, over a year, he had never actually said, "Marry me, Eva."

He had said that she was the dearest friend he had in the

whole world. He had told her he thought he would go mad if it wasn't for her. But he had never, not once, actually mentioned the word marriage. She had hinted that it was all right to ask Papa, that there would be nothing but gratification from her family, and still, somehow, Felix had continued to call, to monopolize her time, without ever saying he wanted to marry her. And he had never, not once, tried—well, what other young men tried when no one was looking, the impertinent squeeze and caress, the kisses that were more than the kisses of friendship, the careless but calculated brushing of her body when walking or dancing. Felix had often held her hand and gazed into her eyes, and she had loved it because it was just like Felix to be so romantic. But why had he never tried to kiss her? There had been opportunity enough. Why had he never spoken of love but only of friendship?

Between tears and anger, between believing she would kill herself and believing she would kill him, she finally found a suspicion growing, the suspicion that Felix had used her and that he had never, at any time, had any idea of marrying other than for the very best and most advantageous of reasons.

In an interview later with Papa it seemed she was right. Papa, sad for her, humiliated for his family, told her something of Gizi's revelations to him in the study. Madame Kaldy and Gizi between them had hatched up a monstrous plot to their mutual satisfaction. The details were not entirely known, but obviously an exchange had been arranged between money and good name. The idea had come from Madame Kaldy, and Gizi had been delighted to respond.

As she listened the misery in her heart turned to disgust and venomous dislike—not for Felix, surprisingly enough, but for Madame Kaldy. The old witch had used her, used her to cheer Felix and make him well again, and then when the need for the little Ferenc girl was over, she had forced him into a marriage she had chosen herself. Felix was weak and vacillating—oh, yes, she had learned that, and had discovered that it made no difference. She had still wanted him; she could have made him happy and herself too. But the old woman had taken him away, and the seed of resentment in her chest turned gradually to rancour and hatred.

Papa droned on, wanting to comfort his little girl and at the same time show the world that none of them had wanted Felix Kaldy.

"I consider, Eva, that the young man has behaved abomin-

241

ably. He has abused our hospitality and hurt us all. But there is no way that we can avoid him; he is marrying Kati and we shall be forced to include him in our family gatherings. For that reason, my dear child, you must try to hide your disappointment; you must try to show him that you care nothing for his bad manners and treachery. In time you will come to care nothing for him and we shall perhaps be able to forgive him. But until that time, you must remember you are my daughter, a Ference, and behave with pride and independence."

Papa paused and took her hand in his.

"We don't need anyone, Eva. We are Ferencs." He paused again and continued haltingly. "I . . . I have been rejected in various ways throughout my life, Eva. And I was enabled to bear my rejections because of pride, and that pride finally carried me to a point where I no longer needed the friendship and approval of others. It is possible to stand alone, if you are a Ferenc."

She supposed it was meant to help her, but she didn't understand at all. She knew Papa intended to comfort her, and she smiled and said, "Yes, Papa," and then went to bed. And on the way she reflected that as well as being a Ferenc she was a Bogozy, and that was why Madame Kaldy hated her. And so she would go on being a Bogozy, and she would continue to make Madame Kaldy hate her. It was a decision made coldly and with finality. But decisions regarding the emotions are difficult to keep, and later the hatred drowned in a welter of loneliness and despair, and like any other discarded girl she cried herself to sleep.

17

When the summer of 1920 came Papa said they would have to hire a coach to take them to the farm. They still had the carriage and the pony cart, but Sultan had been sold. (The boys had remained silent for several days afterwards and Leo, particularly, wouldn't go into the stables at all.)

They hadn't been to the farm since the spring of 1919 when Uncle Sandor was killed, and Malie found the thought of the journey there a depressing prospect. Uncle Sandor's body had been removed and buried properly in the graveyard, but the spot where everything had happened still had to be passed for the first time.

At the eleventh hour they were saved, from the hired coach at least. Mr. Klein sent word from Budapest that he would like to see their country property and offered to drive them up himself. The invitation was graciously accepted. And when Mr. Klein arrived at the house they found they were not being taken in a carriage. Mr. Klein had a motorcar!

He said there wouldn't be room for all of them in the vehicle, so Papa, who had business to conduct in town, said he would follow in a day or two. And as Papa was constantly tired and worried these days, Eva offered to stay with him for company. In truth she was not looking forward to the country this summer, a country swarming with Kaldy and Racs-Rassay relatives all preparing for the wedding. She was relieved to delay her departure for a few days, and Papa's preoccupation was a selfless and noble excuse.

Mama, Amalia, and the boys climbed nervously into the motorcar. It was huge and had brown leather upholstery and polished brass fittings. The boys were awed for a short while, and then the novelty, the speed, and the anticipated envy of their schoolfellows drove everything else out of their minds. They sped along the road, out of the town, with passers-by standing gawping at them. Leo and Jozsef were blatantly boastful, waving and grinning out of the windows and finally even Malie felt herself smiling, wanting to laugh at the grandeur and foolishness of it all. Mama was hysterical with excitement and floods of reminiscences poured forth: how she had raced her brother's coach against one of Vienna's leading horsemen, how she had once ridden all night after a party in order to reach Baden for breakfast, how she had staked a large sum of money at the races and had fainted from excitement as her horse passed the winning post. Her eyes sparkled, and her face glowed. She had, during the last two years, begun to look older; the small heart-shaped face had become pinched and the black hair was streaked with white. But now she was young again. She looked like Eva.

Malie, uncertain and nervous of Mr. Klein, nonetheless felt gratitude for the help he was unwittingly giving them. The place where Uncle Sandor was killed grew closer. Mama and Jozsef didn't appear to be noticing, so lost were they in the rush of wind, but Leo was suddenly quiet and Malie put her hand over his and squeezed it. Before they had a chance to be unhappy the place had vanished, obliterated by the speed of the motorcar. Mr. Klein had certainly proved useful.

Once they had left the good roads, Mr. Klein had to drive much slower and they bumped and slid over the dirt surfaces, but even so it was far, far smoother than riding in a coach. They turned into the acacia woods, and for the first time Malie couldn't smell the flowers around them or the delicate blossoms in the air; everything was subordinated to the smell of petrol and machinery. It was a new and rather exotic experience.

The day, begun so well, continued with surprises. When they drove into the yard of the farm, geese and ducks flapping away from the noisy machine, there was an old man, a cripple, with two crutches and a leg severed just above the knee, waiting at the bottom of the steps. They stared politely at him, wondering what function he was fulfilling around the yard and house. Roza came out and stood beside him.

"He has come back to me!" she whispered tremulously. "My Zoltan has come back."

They looked at the old man who smiled and nodded and said, "Madame Ferenc, children, it is good to see you. And it is so good to be home again!" His face was phlegmatic but the eyes were pleading and sad: Recognize me! Show me I have not changed!

Mama swept forward—she was always so good on this kind of occasion—and placed her hand on Uncle Zoltan's cheek. "Zoltan, old friend! How we have missed you! And how the farm has missed you!"

Malie kissed him, but the boys were shy and embarrassed. They had only the dimmest memories of Uncle Zoltan, and this dried-up old cripple bore no resemblance at all to the large farmer of distant time. Their withdrawal was swallowed up in Roza's explanations.

"All these years in a Russian prison camp! And three days ago I received a letter telling me that my Zoltan was alive and would be sent home again, and hardly have I finished reading the letter when there is a cart in the yard, and I look, and there"—her face twisted with renewed emotion—"there is my Zoltan!"

They sat round the kitchen table, just like old times, and Zoltan told them all the things that had happened to him: the prison camp, and getting his leg shot while trying to escape, and how the Bolsheviks had not told them when the war had ended but how they had somehow known, and finally how the Russians had turned the prisoners loose at the frontier.

He was a sad old man now. He had come back to a wife grown unrecognizably old like himself and to the knowledge that one of his sons was dead. But even so, the return of Uncle Zoltan was a contribution towards the reinstatement of the past, the past that meant stability and a return of the old world.

Malie realized, after several moments had passed, that Mr. Klein had gracefully vanished from the domestic scene as soon as they had arrived. When she went to the door and looked out into the yard she saw him standing by his motorcar, gazing round at the farm and woods and land in a contemplative way. She began to walk towards him, then changed her mind and went to fetch Mama so that he could be shown to his room.

When they had first known Mr. Klein would be coming to the farm, Malie had tried to imagine how he would fit in, but her imagination had failed. At the farm they lived casually, simply. There was no grand entertaining and everyone behaved and dressed in a relaxed and informal way. The thought of Mr. Klein with his smooth well-cut city suits and his sad sophisticated manners adapting himself to country life was completely incongruous.

Indeed, when he came to breakfast on the first morning he did look wrong, but not as wrong as she had expected. He was wearing riding breeches and boots, as expensive as everything else he wore. They looked wrong because there were no horses for riding any more, only the poor old things left from the war that pulled the carts around the farm. But Mr. Klein obviously didn't expect to ride. He walked round the farm, studying the fields and animals, and in the afternoons he changed into a cream tussore suit and took everyone for drives in the motorcar. Once he suggested a picnic.

"We could go up to the Meadow, Malie!" Jozsef said eagerly. "We haven't been to the Meadow for years!"

"No!"

"Oh, Malie, why not?"

But Leo remembered. He remembered the golden afternoons with Karoly and the times they had fallen in the brook. He didn't want to go there either, any more than he wanted to go down to the river, to the place where Uncle Sandor had taken them that first time.

"'I don't want to go either," he said stoutly.

Mr. Klein gazed upon them, each in turn, a reflective gaze, studying their faces, thinking.

"So," he said at last. "Then we shall not go."

Malie found Mr. Klein something of a strain at first. She couldn't say what was the matter except that he was always there. Sometimes—most times—Mama was there too, on other occasions the boys were present, but Malie always felt that she must be the one to entertain, to listen, to talk, to see that Mr. Klein was not bored. But gradually she came to realize that Mr. Klein was quite happy not to be entertained. Walking through the acacia woods, driving in the motorcar, watching the hay being cut, he was content to remain silent and have her silent also.

When Eva and Papa came up she felt slightly relieved; now the burden would no longer be on her. But Eva was not much help. She was subdued and irritable and not even the flattering attentions of their guest—he flirted equally with Mama and with Eva—could lift her spirits.

The day came when they had to call on Uncle Alfred and Aunt Gizi. Eva's small face was white and her mouth was pinched into a grimace of self-control. She had not seen Felix for a long time and now, in the presence of hated Aunt Gizi, she had to greet the betrothed couple as though nothing had happened. At the last moment she declared she would not go.

"I can't, Malie. I can't go and have them gloating over me! Have Aunt Gizi preening and—"

"Oh, darling! She won't!"

"Yes, she will. And supposing Madame Kaldy is there. I couldn't bear it if she were there. I can't go, Malie! I can't go. I—" Tears welled up again. "I don't want to see Felix with Kati," she whispered.

Malie tried to persuade her, but it was Mr. Klein who finally solved the dilemma, or rather it was Mr. Klein's motorcar. He came into the drawing-room, ignoring Eva's unhappy face, and said, "I trust I shall have the privilege of escorting you to your cousin's in my motor. Your uncle, I am sure, would be most interested in seeing the vehicle, and I would like to pay my compliments once more to your relatives."

His voice was droll, amused, as though making fun of his own formal way of speaking.

"I feel it would enhance my reputation if I were to arrive with the adorable Ferenc ladies in my motorcar."

And immediately Eva saw how it would look. No longer would she be the discarded sweetheart arriving to brave it out before her cousin and her erstwhile suitor. No! She would drive up in a new and splendid machine that even Uncle Alfred didn't possess, in spite of all his money. And at the wheel would be smooth, elegant, rich Mr. Klein, on whose financial transactions Uncle Alfred relied. And she and Malie and Mama, dressed as beautifully, as *moderne* as they could manage, would descend from the motor, full of their exciting ride and talking about speed and danger instead of Kati's wedding.

It was even better than she thought. Mr. Klein pressed down on the accelerator just before they arrived at Uncle Alfred's villa, and they pulled swiftly into the drive and braked to a sensational halt. The car was polished and gleaming, and so was Mr. Klein in his pale linen suit and silk shirt. Papa had come with them, and so the ladies were assisted from the car and then escorted to the steps before an admiring and slightly awestruck audience. Eva, on the arm of Mr. Klein, was able to laugh and make little mock gestures of relief at being out of the dangerous machine, placing her hand on her breast and making provocative moues with her mouth.

"Well!" enthused Uncle Alfred. "How splendid, David! How magnificent!"

They all crowded round the machine—Felix too—admiring and envious and somehow Eva managed to give the impression that the motorcar was hers as well as Mr. Klein's and by the time they went into the house the horror of meeting them all together for the first time was over.

Aunt Gizi talked of nothing but the wedding. She was overwrought but rapturous. Alfred seemed affable but talked of nothing but Mr. Klein's motorcar. Felix and Kati talked of nothing. Felix looked bored and unhappy, Kati frightened and unhappy. The gayest people in the room were Eva and Mr. Klein.

Under cover of conversation Felix finally worked his way round the room and sat beside Eva.

"Such a long while since I saw you, Eva," he said wistfully.

Eva laughed.

"I suppose you were . . . surprised . . . when you heard about Kati and me."

Eva laughed again.

"Mama says it will be good for me to be married," he said, resigned. And then, cheering a little, "And Eva, you should see the old manor. I am making it look quite beautiful. I am having bathrooms added, two bathrooms! And—you will

247

hardly believe it, Eva—there was no modern lighting! We are having electricity installed, but in the most tasteful way. I cannot wait for you to see how beautiful it all is. I know you will love it."

"Yes," said Eva, smiling. "I'm sure I shall."

"You will come, won't you?" he asked eagerly. "You are such a dear, dear friend, I could not bear to think you wouldn't come to see us often. Mama is so fond of you, I know you would be welcome to visit us."

Eva smiled, sweetly and dangerously. "Of course I shall come, Felix, if Kati, your wife, invites me."

"Kati?" he asked, puzzled.

"Why, yes! Kati, the new mistress of the Kaldy house."

"Oh, yes." His eyes rested on Kati across the room, then moved hurriedly away. "Mama intends to give parties and dances once everything is finished. You must promise me that you will come."

And Eva laughed again and said she supposed she would have to come as Kati was so fond of her.

They climbed into Mr. Klein's motor, Malie, Eva, and Mama in the back, and as they moved away Eva's smile cracked and tears began to roll down her cheeks. Mr. Klein blew his horn and threw the car into a stylish whirl so that they left the house in a flurry of exciting noise and movement. Malie put her arm round Eva's shoulder and reflected, as Eva's control finally disintegrated altogether, that it was the second time Mr. Klein and his motor had saved them from a distressing situation.

The harvesters arrived. One or two of the old people, the pre-war ones, were there, but mostly they were new people, some wearing their old army uniforms. The songs were the same though. All the tall grasses fell before the scythes, the choruses echoed over the fields. Leo and Jozsef, old enough now to understand the ribald verses, giggled with the reapers and then, when they came into supper at the end of the day, daringly hummed the tunes of the songs they dared not sing.

Mr. Klein rolled up the sleeves of his shirt and his arms turned brown in the sun. His beautiful riding breeches and boots began to look worn and more familiar. He watched the hay being brought in, saw the apricots and peaches ripening on the trees, and spent much time with Papa walking over the farm and talking in the study.

At the end of the harvest the gypsies arrived and Roza haggled with the leader over a price for the harvest music. The money was agreed upon, and the band—two violins and a *cimbalom*—set up on the veranda. A fire was built in the yard, the huge black pot suspended over it, and Roza began to heat goulash.

Mama, looking extraordinarily pretty in a white cotton dress that was daringly short and showed five or six inches of ankle, set out loaves of bread on the wine press and pretended to help Roza. She was usually rather bored by the harvest festivities—she was expected to dance with the reapers and most of them, by the end of the afternoon, were drunk and ungainly—but this year the presence of Mr. Klein made it different. This year she was Madame Ferenc, showing how enchanting she could be at a pastoral festival.

The head man of the harvesters, dressed in his best clothes, came formally up the steps to Papa. "Sir—God be praised—it is my happiness to report that a good crop has been gathered."

Papa nodded affably. The two men shook hands with great ceremony; then Papa turned to the gypsies, raised his eyebrows, bowed, and the music began.

Smiling and pretty, Mama was led down the steps by the chief harvester. Gracefully, to the melody of an old waltz, they circled once on the baked soil of the yard as the onlookers, waiting for the free goulash and wine, murmured appreciatively.

Most of the wives were dressed in formal black, but some of the young girls from the village were wearing the old festival garments of weddings and feast days. When Malie and Eva were younger they had worn them too. Roza had made the costumes for them, the embroidered bodices and caps sewn painstakingly during the winter months. Just before the party began Malie, seized by a sudden lightening of the spirits, a relief that she was, after all that had happened, still alive, had suggested that they get the old skirts and bodices out and wear them again.

"It's the first harvest party for so many years, Eva! And it would make us realize . . . make us realize that the war is over." It would be the first time that she had felt any gladness, and joy, since Karoly had died. She was not happy, but a slow contentment was creeping round her heart—an acceptance, mingled with sadness, of all the things that had happened—and at last the grace to find peace and tenderness had returned.

"Oh, no! No one wears those silly costumes any more."

"Some of the village girls might."

Eva shrugged. "It isn't worth dressing up just for the harvesters. I would rather wear something fashionable."

And so they had worn pale cotton dresses, short like Mama's, with lace collars and contrasting sashes. When Malie saw the occasional coloured skirt whirling among the dancers she felt sad about Eva's lack of enthusiasm.

Uncle Zoltan, propped on his crutches, stood by the wine cask. In the old days he had been the first to ask Mama to dance. Now his self-respect demanded some kind of authority, and so he said from time to time, "Fill your cups! As much as you like! Good farm wine for everyone!"

As the wine flowed the reserve of the reapers melted a little. A young one—there seemed to be so few young ones now— took courage and asked Eva to dance. He was strong and brown, the column of his neck straight, his arms firm. He was only a peasant and was very respectful while dancing, but his brown eyes were like those of any other young man, warm, challenging, admiring. Eva began to revive. Her smile arched a little, her head went back, and she began to dance as though she were one of the enchanting Ferenc sisters.

"It is many years since I have danced a *csardas*. I think I would like to try."

Malie, absorbed, had been watching the dancing couples, and now Mr. Klein was in front of her, smiling, sad, laughing at himself. Automatically she began to refuse, then remembered that it was Mr. Klein, so smiled and descended the steps. Her body instinctively withdrew from his as he placed his arm round her waist, but then, as they danced, the wildness of the music made her relax a little.

"You should grip me a little firmer. Otherwise you will spin away."

She forced herself to tighten her arm around Mr. Klein. Through his silk shirt she could feel sweat on his body; did Mr. Klein sweat like other men? They spun, twisted, then balanced gracefully for the slow steps. People of Mr. Klein's age usually only survived a few movements of the *csardas,* unless they were peasants who were capable of controlled stamina when dancing. To her surprise Mr. Klein didn't even seem to be out of breath. He gripped her firmly when it was necessary, guided her when their dancing should be stately, and never once fell out of step with the violins and *cimbalom.* A pang, a foolish whim swept over her. How she wished she were wearing the old embroidered bodice and cotton skirt. Dancing here, on the soil of their own farm, with the harvest in and the war over, how she would have loved to be dressed in the colourful clothes of their childhood, their innocence!

They were well matched, she could feel it; their height was balanced and they moved well. Suddenly she was able to see, as though from an onlooker's angle, how pleasing they looked together, how handsome and graceful, even though he was so much older. She was gratified, and then the feeling vanished and she thought, *What am I doing, dancing with this stranger? Oh, Karoly, Karoly! You are my partner, no one but you!* And she knew a renewal of the old feeling, the old voice that said, *You will never dance with, or speak to, or see Karoly Vilaghy again.*

"I'm sorry. I can't dance any more."

She pulled away, and her arm slid through his hand. She had enough sense of courtesy not to snatch her hand away too, and Mr. Klein held it, staring at her, puffing a little, with beads of perspiration standing out on his brow.

"It is enough," he agreed. "Come, we shall walk out a little, to see the harvest."

She was suddenly tired. She wanted to go back to the veranda and watch—observing others brought her peace and contentment—but obediently she followed Mr. Klein onto the track that led through the acacia woods.

Mr. Klein was very quiet. He walked and hummed a soft little tune to himself. Shocked, she realized what the tune was, the bawdy verse sung by the reapers. Mr. Klein must have picked it up without appreciating what the words were! She gazed sideways at him and was disconcerted to see him wink very slowly and deliberately.

"So," he said at last. "What are you going to do with the rest of your life?"

"Do?"

"Mmmm. You are . . . how old? Twenty-four. And your fiance has been killed and the world is no longer the same place that it once was."

"But it will be," she said quickly. "Everything is returning to normal now. Horthy is bringing the old ways back."

"At what a cost, Amalia," he said slowly. "At what a cost. Do you hear nothing of what has happened in the south, or even in Budapest?"

Of course she had heard—a little, as much as she wanted to hear: stories of the dreadful revenge exacted by Horthy's soldiers on the Communists who had been running the country a year ago, the Communists who had killed Uncle Sandor. But the stories came from the south, and who was to say how true they were?

"They did no worse than the men who murdered Uncle Sandor. You don't know about Uncle Sandor, our coachman, he—"

"Oh, yes, I know about your coachman. He was murdered by frightened rebels. And now it is the turn of the soldiers, the old Austro-Hungarian officers who are executing Communists, socialists, liberals, intellectuals, Jews—"

"All that is over," she said loudly. "The war is over, and so are all the revolutions. I don't believe any of the stories you tell me!"

But she did believe him. She knew he was right; the red terror had been followed by the white. But she didn't want to hear about it. They were safe, safe on their mountain farm with all the killing and punishment taking place in the south. She didn't want any more. It was over. It must be over!

"So." He stared at her, considering, making her feel ashamed. "So," he said again. "Perhaps you are right. Perhaps the rumours are exaggerated. And, in any case, perhaps the killing is the price of peace. But you see, my little Amalia, the world will never be the same place again, because you are no longer the same person. Now you know of man's evil and cruelty. You know that life is the briefest turn of a wheel and that happiness and the good things can be destroyed in a moment. Your sister, she has not learned this lesson yet. Perhaps she never will. But you—you understand how rare it is to capture contentment. You can never be as you once were: Amalia Ferenc, content to go to parties and visit with your mama. What are you going to do?"

She felt panic gripping her. The question, buried deep in her heart, was one she had fought against asking herself. What was she going to do? Spend the rest of her life bickering with Eva, paying visits to relatives, watching Papa and Mama grow more estranged as they got older?

"Something will happen," she said defiantly, angry with him for spoiling her earlier happiness. "Something will happen to me, and then I will know what to do."

"Would you like to marry me?"

All the uneasiness she had felt about Mr. Klein suddenly

congealed into a knot of dread within her stomach. She longed to run, to shout, to vomit, to hit him. Instead she stood like a paralysed rabbit.

"You will notice I did not say, Will you? I said, Would you like to?"

"No."

Mr. Klein laughed, a low soft chuckle. "How fortunate it is you are not in business," he mused. "It does not do at all to be so direct."

"I am sorry." She was floundering, anxious not to be rude to Mr. Klein, who ran the bank, but also terrified that he come near her.

"Sorry? No, you must never be sorry until the bargain is closed, one way or another. And now . . . now I think it would be pleasant to return to the festivities. I have not yet danced with your charming mama, and as I can see, she still has much grace and ability."

She was confused, angry and puzzled. Had she been proposed to or not? What kind of game was Mr. Klein playing? Why was he so serious one moment, trying to make her face up to unpleasant truths, and mocking and ironical the next? Her pleasure in the day, in the festival, was destroyed. She stood once more on the veranda and watched them all dancing, but now there was disturbance in her heart. Mr. Klein danced with Mama and then with Eva, and it was obvious that both her mother and her sister enjoyed his company completely. Mama was young again, laughing up into his face and tapping him reprovingly on the shoulder at some impertinent comment he had made. And as Malie watched Mr. Klein flattering and *playing* with Mama, her distaste renewed itself, and with it embarrassment that Mama could behave so badly. She finally looked away from them, vowing that she would only speak to Mr. Klein in a cool and detached manner from now on.

But then, that same evening, she watched him walking alone and a curious sense of fellowship overcame her. She had gone into the orchard when the evening was still light, and she saw him strolling beneath the trees, a slow, solitary figure who suddenly appeared to be older, heavier than he normally was. He was staring out at the fields beyond the trees and once he put his hand up and ran his forefinger lightly along the underside of a branch. His shoulders were slightly stooped and there was an ageless and familiar quality about him that she recognized from somewhere a long, long time ago.

She tried to remember, failed, tried again, and was rewarded by the memory of a visit to an old man when she had been small, an old man lying in a bed, a black hat on his head, an old man with a long beard and side whiskers. He had spoken to her in a language she did not understand and Papa—yes, Papa had taken her there—had answered in their own language that she did understand. The memory, dredged from her subconscious, had some curious significance. She remembered a feeling of identity with the old man. She felt it again now with Mr. Klein, and so she turned quickly away because the feeling was one she did not want to encourage. Neither did she want Mr. Klein to see her in the dusk and resume their bantering conversation of the afternoon. She hurried back into the house, confused and beset by emotions, puzzled by things she felt she ought to remember.

A few days later, when she was alone with Papa, she asked him about the old man. She had begun to wonder if perhaps she had dreamt the meeting: the small room, the bed, the old man with the shawl over his shoulders and the black hat on his head. Papa said slowly, "How strange you should remember. You were not even three years old. He wanted to see you, the old man. He was dying, and though he never forgave me for marrying your mother, he still wanted to see his grandchild."

"Ah, yes!"

Of course, it had been Papa's own father. One never thought of Papa's parents. He and Aunt Gizi had somehow thrown aside their old roots and lowered new and aggressive ones into the ground. But she remembered her affinity with the old man and sometimes—oh, very, very occasionally—she sensed this same affinity with Papa.

"Why did you ask, Amalia? What made you think of the old man?"

"It was . . . Mr. Klein," she said slowly. "A feeling that I had seen him before. And I remembered him—my grandfather—and that was whom Mr. Klein reminded me of."

Papa smiled. "No. Mr. Klein is no relative of ours, not even distantly." He paused as though considering something and then continued, "Amalia, I have been intending to speak to you about Mr. Klein."

"Yes, Papa?" The old familiar pounding in her breast, a

nervous excitement that anything to do with Mr. Klein always precipitated.

"Mr. Klein—David—has indicated to me, most tactfully, that he finds you personable and admirable in every way." Papa cleared his throat. "He asked what my reaction would be if he asked you to marry him."

"I see, Papa." It hadn't been a joke. That day at the harvest party he hadn't been joking or teasing.

"I explained," said Papa haltingly, "about Karoly, that it was just over two years since— Mr. Klein said he knew about that."

"Yes, Papa."

"Amalia, I do not want to force you to do anything against your will. I remember my sorrow when you and Karoly— But there, that is past and the war changed everything and had he lived I would have accepted your wishes. But no. I do not want to force you again. It is only that I ask you to think about this. Mr. Klein is a good man."

"I know, Papa." She closed her eyes, swallowed, and opened them. "I know he is a good man. But I do not want to marry him."

"I see." Papa picked up the inkwell and absent-mindedly smoothed the top of it with his thumb. "Could I ask why?"

Why? How could she explain to Papa the mingled emotions Mr. Klein induced in her?

"I do not wish to marry anyone, Papa. Karoly was to be my husband, and now he is dead I don't want to marry anyone, ever." She knew it sounded foolish, the kind of thing every young girl bereft by the war was saying, and so she added something that Papa would understand. "And, Papa, if I were ever to think of marriage again, it would not be with someone of Mr. Klein's age. He is far too old."

"He is eighteen years older than you, Amalia," said Papa, for some reason nettled. "And even if the disparity in age is rather pronounced, just remember that Mr. Klein's age enables him to offer more in marriage than another, younger man. You would have a secure and assured place in society. You would be superbly maintained. You would travel, if you wished. You know him well, Amalia. He is a generous man, a responsible man. Many women would envy you."

"Then let one of those women marry him!" she cried nervously, feeling that, for all his assurances, Papa was going to try and coerce her. "Eva, for instance. Oh, yes, now she is miserable because of Felix, but in time Eva would adore to be the wife of someone like Mr. Klein. She likes him and he flatters her; she would love to be rich and travel and live in Budapest. Why doesn't he wait and then ask Eva?"

"Because he has chosen you, Amalia. If he had wanted Eva, he would have said so."

"He only chose me because he thought Eva was going to marry Felix," she cried. "He would have *preferred* Eva at the beginning. Oh, Papa, she is so much more suited to him than I—she likes to flirt and laugh and tease—why doesn't he wait and then ask Eva!"

She had lost control. At the beginning of the discussion she had been determined to remain calm, to answer Papa's comments with cool reason, but now the fear of being forced to marry Mr. Klein made her panic and say foolish, ill-advised things.

"No, Amalia," said Papa slowly. "Mr. Klein spoke to me a long, long time ago about his feelings—the first time he came to stay with us, in fact. I was not certain then just how serious he was. And in any case Karoly was alive—or we thought he was alive—at that time, and I told him of your commitment to that young man."

She was shocked. She supposed she ought to feel flattered, but she was only aware of shock. All those visits, when he had flirted with Mama and Eva, when he had indulged in sharp witticisms and sophistications with the two exquisite little Bogozy women, all that time he had been watching her, considering, comparing. But it made no difference. She didn't like Mr. Klein and she couldn't marry him. Papa had said he wouldn't try and force her again, and so she must remain firm, like she had before when Karoly had been the crisis in her life.

"I would rather not marry him, Papa," she said quietly.

Papa sank down into a chair and rested his hands on the desk. His shoulders were slumped and under his eyes deep folds of skin made haggard stains on his cheeks. He was old again, thin and old and worried.

"Amalia," he said, almost choking, "I have no right to ask this of my daughter, but please, consider it carefully. Do not reject Mr. Klein without thinking a little, without giving him some time. If I did not know he would be a good husband, I would not beg you to think again. But I do ask you. For all our sakes I ask you."

"I don't understand, Papa." A cold sensation in the pit of her stomach warned her that she was being steadily cornered.

Papa looked terrible. With every passing moment he looked infinitely worse. And there was something degrading about seeing Papa, who was stern and cruel and could be hateful, broken and begging his daughter to reconsider a matrimonial decision.

"It was the war," he mumbled, and then he turned red-rimmed eyes up to hers. "The war, and the revolutions after the war. I did everything I could. If only I had possessed a little more capital I could have invested the way Gizi did—I might have saved us—but it just got worse. If it hadn't been for Mr. Klein I would have had to close the bank . . . our bank."

"But we're all right now, Papa, aren't we?" she asked, fighting away a sense of dread. "We all knew it was bad just after the war, but we're all right now, surely?"

"We are all right because Mr. Klein has not pressed for his money or demanded his securities," Papa replied heavily. His hands were trembling and she had to look away, it was so dreadful to see—hear—Papa making such a humiliating confession. "Mr. Klein owns virtually everything we have, Amalia. The bank, all my securities, our house, this farm—"

"No, Papa! Not the farm!" The one place they were inviolate, the place where so much had happened, where they had all been so happy. And it belonged to Mr. Klein! It wasn't theirs. They were all living there, enjoying the summer, giving parties for the harvesters, and none of them had any right to be there! The house belonged to Mr. Klein; the land, the harvest, the food they ate, all was his. She felt humiliated, and then she felt lost and homeless.

"Not the farm, Papa! Oh, no, not the farm!"

Papa looked down at the top of his desk, an unhealthy flush staining his face. All his life he had set incredible standards for his wife, his daughters, his sons, his employees. He had applied those standards cruelly and rigidly and had felt justified in doing so because he set standards for himself that were equally severe. And he had proved unequal to the task he had set himself. He had failed to provide for his family.

"Can't Aunt Gizi and Uncle Alfred help us? Uncle Alfred is part of the bank. Surely he could help us!"

"Gizi and Alfred backed the bank right at the beginning, and it was not enough. We were all . . . in danger. And then Mr. Klein took over the affairs, and since that time I have preferred to do business with him rather than with Gizi and Alfred."

Through her own distress she was vaguely aware of his, sensing a little of his humiliation at not being able to save Gizi's investments as well as his own. No, not Gizi's; he wouldn't have minded so much if it had only been Gizi. It was Uncle Alfred—a Racs-Rassay—whom he could no longer bear to ask for help.

"Gizi has recouped her losses," he continued hoarsely. "Mr. Klein helped her too, and she invested wisely and suffered little loss overall. I have not been so fortunate—no, I must not say fortunate, as though luck were part of it. I have failed through my own lack of foresight. I have no excuse, no excuse at all."

"Oh, Papa." She wanted to comfort him suddenly, to reassure him that it didn't matter. But it did matter, it mattered very much that Mr. Klein owned the very chairs they were sitting on.

"In time," he said, "and with Mr. Klein's patience, I shall be able to redeem the securities, rebuild as Gizi has done . . . but it will take time."

The cold clutch of fear in her breast again. "But Papa, surely Mr. Klein wouldn't demand his securities just because I refused to marry him."

"No, of course not, Amalia." He tried to smile at her, then reached across and patted her hand. "Of course not, and in time I shall repair the crisis myself. I am not asking you to marry Mr. Klein in order to save the family fortune. No father has any right to expect another man, even a son-in-law, to do what he cannot do himself. But Mr. Klein would be so happy if you could bring yourself to even think of his proposition. I only ask you to *consider* it, Amalia. Just *consider* it."

She could no longer bear Papa's pleading, his humiliation and lack of authority. She wanted to get away and try to sort out the implications of what she had learned. She wasn't even sure of her own reactions to the news. Certainly she was no longer prepared to state with final authority that she would never marry Mr. Klein. She could think of many situations in which she *would* be prepared to marry him; the war had taught her that lesson, that it did not do to set high and rigid rules for oneself. But . . . Mr. Klein . . . as a husband?

"I will not say no at this moment then, Papa. I will think about it."

He nodded, but that was all. His shame prevented him from smiling or speaking on the subject further. As she walked away from him she caught sight of his reflection in the mirror set into the back of the server. He too resembled the old man she had seen so many years ago.

In September, Kati—small, afraid, wearing a white silk dress that became her as little as anything else—was married to Felix Kaldy. Bride and groom spoke to each other hardly at all, and if Kati seemed frightened, Felix failed to notice it, his attitude throughout being one of boredom with Kati and delight with all the guests who thronged to the Racs-Rassay villa.

Gizi had excelled herself, providing not only a magnificent repast for the county inside the house but unlimited food, wine, and a gypsy player outside for the estate workers.

A succession of carriages and a sprinkling of motorcars brought relatives and influential friends of the Kaldy and Racs-Rassay families from halfway across the county. The farm servants and their wives walked to the villa, and by the end of the evening the numbers in the yard had grown, swollen by people from the village who had wandered up and by farm workers from other estates who had somehow heard of the party and found means of joining it.

Inside, during a gargantuan wedding feast that took no cognizance of the fact that food was in short supply throughout the land, they toasted the incongruous couple in champagne and congratulated them on the uniting of two sound old families. Outside, Kati and Felix were toasted in rough wine straight from the barrel, and the good wishes ranged from the merely lewd to the downright obscene. Kati appeared not to hear or understand any of the greetings, and as Felix never once stepped out of the house, he heard only the elegant comments of his friends.

Everything was bright, everyone—except the bride—vivacious. Eva drank, flirted, teased Felix unmercifully—which Felix adored—and danced every dance, a great number with Mr. Klein, an even greater number with Adam.

Uncle Alfred, who along with one or two Racs-Rassay relatives and several distant Kaldy kinsmen wore the velvet tunic and dolman of the Hungarian gentry, quickly became very drunk and remained in a condition of loud, semi-boisterous gaiety for the remainder of the evening. Since the war he had grown much heavier and more florid. When young he had looked handsome and romantic in his lavish costume, but now, drunk, his tight trousers and boots looked uncomfortably strained and his complexion had turned to a dull red that was both unattractive and alarming.

Aunt Gizi, brilliant in a fashionable new gown of pink crepe trimmed with osprey at the hem, was outshone by only one figure, that of the triumphant Madame Kaldy.

Amalia, gazing round the huge drawing-room, her eyes drawn repeatedly back to the central figures of Aunt Gizi and Madame Kaldy, realized that it was as though it were *their* marriage, two dominating women who had accomplished their hearts' desires. They had both submerged their entire lives and personalities to the fulfillment of those desires, and on this day their success and happiness was assured.

Madame Kaldy, more restrained than Gizi, nonetheless overpowered the room. Tall, fine-boned, her dark eyes glowing and feverish and her farm-stained hands covered in lace gloves, she moved from group to group of old friends, people she had deliberately avoided for years, families who had witnessed her humiliating downfall and who now were there to see her triumph. She bowed graciously to Mama, remembering but no longer caring about her husband's long-past flirtation with the Bogozy woman. She bowed more coolly to Papa; he was an upstart, but nonetheless the brother of Gizi, and it was Gizi's money that had finally rebuilt the Kaldy estates. She smiled, slightly, at Eva, then ignored her. And strangely enough she also appeared to ignore Kati—no, not ignore her; it was as though Kati, having performed her function, wasn't there any more.

Amalia watched Kati move farther and farther back into a corner. Once the right things had been said to her, everyone preferred talking to all the old friends and acquaintances they had not seen for a long time. There was so much to discuss: the war, the losses, the decline of their properties. The little bride was really too dull to waste a good party on. Amalia weaved through the guests towards Kati.

"Are you all right, Kati?"

"I've spilt champagne on my dress."

Amalia looked down at the pale stain on the white silk, then up into Kati's bewildered face. "It doesn't matter," she answered gently. "You are a married woman now. You can spill anything you like."

Kati smiled half-heartedly. "I hate parties, Malie. I wish I could go away. I mean, away from all these people."

"You will be going soon, Kati. In a little while you'll be going to your new house."

"Madame Kaldy's house, you mean," answered Kati with a rare flash of irony. "And there'll be even more parties there, parties and dinners and lunches and ladies coming in the morning and afternoon—oh, Malie!"

Amalia sought consoling words and found none. Kati's lot was completely unenviable.

"It will be . . . nice to have a husband, won't it, Kati?" she asked feebly.

"I don't know." Kati flushed suddenly and Malie felt even more sorry for her. Any number of girls—Eva, for one—would have envied Kati's happy lot and the fact that tonight she had to climb into bed with Felix. Kati, who was innocent but not so innocent she didn't know, vaguely, what was supposed to happen, could only view the ordeal with awkward embarrassment. There was a moment's silence in which Malie desperately wanted to say something to the effect that it wouldn't be too bad. But what right or experience had she to try and reassure Kati? Whenever she thought of loving a man, she thought of Karoly, the long hot kisses and embraces, furtively stolen and always interrupted by Mama or Eva or Aunt Gizi, embraces that, she imagined, would have progressed naturally to a shocking and ecstatic fusion of bodies. But how would it be with someone like Felix? How would it be with someone like Mr. Klein? She pushed the thought quickly away and transferred her thoughts from Mr. Klein himself to Mr. Klein's motorcar.

"We'll come and see you very, very soon. We'll ask Mr. Klein to bring us in his motor, the day after tomorrow. There, that's not too far away, is it?"

"Oh, Malie, you will come? It will give me something to look forward to if you say you'll come. Eva too?"

They looked across the room at Eva. She was enchanting—pale pink voile in soft drapes and frills—twinkling, sparkling up at Adam Kaldy, who appeared to be completely absorbed in her.

"Eva's so beautiful," Kati said wistfully. "I thought at first she would be angry with me for taking Felix from her, but she doesn't seem to mind, does she? And she looks so happy. . . ." Her voice trailed away. Amalia was struck afresh with the foolishness of it all. Kati, longing to be Eva who was pretty and free, and Eva, raging with hurt frustration and

261

anger because she was not going to live with Felix in Madame Kaldy's old house.

"Eva will come too. Of course she will." Eva looked across at them, laughed, and waved her hand. "You see, Kati, Eva's not a bit angry with you. She wants you to be happy." And Kati, deeply touched at the thought that anyone might care about her happiness, gave a tremulous and uncertain smile.

Eva, like everyone else in the room, had hardly noticed Kati. Just once, when Kati was being greeted by a distant relative—standing stiffly while being kissed on both cheeks—she had thought, Oh, why is it her? Why not me? I would have done it all so beautifully! I would have been so charming to everyone! I would have looked and behaved so well! Why is it terrible old Kati and not me!

But the thought had not been directed with any resentment towards Kati. Felix didn't like his new wife. That was obvious. She didn't even think he would *talk* to her very much. She wasn't jealous of Kati, so why was she still so hurting inside, why the pain, the jealousy, the humiliation? After all these months when she had tried so hard to convince herself she didn't care, why did she want to scream and cry and pound her fists on the body of the hateful old Kaldy witch?

A fresh wave of anguish smote her, and she smiled even more brightly at Adam, who hadn't taken his eyes from her for the whole day.

"Adam! How strange it is that your eyes should be green when Felix's are brown. I wonder what happened!" She glanced naughtily at him. "You are not alike at all, are you? I don't think I ever met two brothers so unlike before."

"Felix is tall and slim and elegant. I am short and square and clumsy," Adam answered briskly, without taking his eyes from her face. "Nonetheless, Eva Ferenc, I feel flattered that after several years you have looked at me long enough to notice the colour of my eyes." She hardly heard him. There was a pain in her stomach, a twisting, bitter agony of misery. She fought the pain, straightened her body, and held out her glass. Adam filled it and pressed the glass back into her hand.

"And so now you must live all alone in your little farmhouse. How sad. Whatever will you do there, all alone without your incredible mama to arrange your life?" That was better, much better. She was still teasing, still flirting, but she was able to do it better when she could speak scathingly about his mama.

"I shall do all kind of things," Adam replied coolly. "I shall get drunk a lot, of course, and I shall not bother to wash or change my clothes, and I shall have girls from the village to come and sleep with me every night."

She was shocked. Even through her misery she was shocked. Felix would never have spoken that way, not even when they were in their most suggestive and flirtatious moods. Adam had never spoken like that before. He had spoken very little at all, and when he did he was always stilted and boring. How could he be so crude and vulgar?

"It would be nice to have someone to get drunk with when I am all alone," Adam continued blandly. "Have some more champagne, Eva." He handed her his own glass, scarcely touched, took the empty one from her and refilled it. She drank, feeling that she was somehow being mocked but unable to work it out properly. There was a fuzzy feeling in her head but it helped to blur the pain and anger of Felix and Madame Kaldy.

"You are very coarse!" she rebuked, forgetting to flirt with him.

"Yes. I feel it incumbent on me to be coarse. I have a family reputation to maintain. My father—you must have heard—was a roué who spent all our money at the gaming tables and in bed. I believe he gained little return at the tables. I can only hope his mistresses proved more rewarding."

She was so astonished she couldn't answer. He had always been dull but he had behaved like a gentleman, his manners at least a poor imitation of Felix's.

"And then there was my grandfather. His tastes were not so expensive. He slept with peasant girls who were pleased to do as they were told. You may have noticed several stolid faces on the land that bear a strong resemblance to mine?"

He was insulting her. Just because she had been discarded by Felix, humiliated by his horrible old mother, he thought he could insult her, speak to her like a factory girl. How dare he! Tears of rage choked in her throat and she hiccoughed.

"I have a reputation to uphold, Eva: the last of the Kaldy philanderers."

"You . . . you are not the last of the Kaldy anything!" she said angrily. "Felix is the last of the Kaldys! Felix is the gentleman, the head of the estate. You are only a younger son!" Careful, a little warning bell in her head cried, if you argue with Adam people will notice and see that you are unhappy.

Madame Kaldy will note it and be pleased, and everyone else will snigger and feel sorry for you. You must flirt and laugh with Adam, the way you have been doing all day.

"True. I am only the younger son. But just look at Felix. Do you think he will be able to sustain the reputation of the profligate Kaldys? Quite apart from anything else, Mama would not allow it."

"How dare you!" She trembled, trying to keep her voice quiet and controlled. "How dare you say things like that about Felix! Speaking of him as though he were . . . stupid. Or weak. What of you? You do what your mama tells you as well as Felix!"

"No," said Adam, suddenly still. "I do what I want to do, Eva. No one, not even you, can make me do things unless I wish to."

The misery welled up again. Now even Adam was turning against her. He wasn't much, but he served to flirt with; his adoration, bovine and uncritical, had been useful. Suddenly he had become vulgar and boorish, and his adoration had turned to contempt and a rebuke. She looked in desperation round the room. Where was Mr. Klein? He would do; he would flatter her and look after her. She felt lonely and unloved and the pain of losing Felix was as strong as it had been several months ago. She couldn't be brave any more. The fight had gone. She didn't want to scream or claw at Madame Kaldy, she just wanted to rock to and fro crying, not having to be brave and show people she didn't care.

Her shoulders slumped and she didn't try to hold them straight. She felt the taut lines of brightness on her face begin to slip and she didn't care. Adam's hand suddenly gripped her arm.

"Outside," he said. She felt herself propelled through the company, her legs forced to speed, people looking at her curiously but gone before they could really see what was wrong. The doors were open onto the veranda, and Adam hurried her out and then round to the side of the house. She could hear the violin—beastly, wretched violin—scraping and wailing in the distance at the back. Once Felix had paid a violinist to stand beneath her window playing for her. She had comforted him and loved him and he hadn't even noticed her love. She slid to the ground, a heap of soft pink voile and pale arms and face.

"Up!" said Adam crossly.

"Leave me alone," she wept. "Leave me alone to die!"

He placed his hands under her armpits, heaved, and she came up like an awkward, floppy doll.

"I'm so miserable!" she sobbed. "I don't think I can go on being as miserable as this. What can I do! Oh, what can I do?"

"You can be quiet."

"You don't understand. You don't know what it's like to be so unhappy. No one knows except me!"

"Oh, Eva, Eva!" He shook her reprovingly. "You are drunk, and so I will not be too hard with you. But you are a selfish, ungrateful girl! Have you forgotten your sister? Have you forgotten Karoly who died? Have you forgotten all the young men who died? All the girls who will never have husbands?"

"It would have been better if he had died," she wept. "At least he would have been mine!"

Even while she said it, shame was creeping into her heart. Adam didn't let her fall again, although she half expected him to. He stared with his penetrating green eyes deep into her face, and the shame and guilt grew.

"I didn't mean it," she cried, looking away from him. "I'm wicked to say that. I didn't mean it. And I know about Malie, how dreadful it was for her. I think I know. I hated it too when Karoly was killed. I'm sorry. . . . Oh, but I'm so unhappy! I'm so unhappy I don't know what I'm going to do!"

"I think the best thing you can do is marry me."

She heard him, and vaguely it made sense. She leaned against his chest and he was strong and comforting; her eyes closed and she felt that she could sleep and the pain would go away.

"You can come and live in my farmhouse, and we can get drunk together, and I will be saved the inconvenience of getting in girls from the village to sleep with me."

She felt another brief surge of anger at his lack of respect, but she was weary and her tears had left her drained of fight. His arms round her were warm. She felt safe and relaxed. One good thing about Adam was that she didn't have to make any effort. He was so ordinary anything was good enough for him.

"Why should I marry you?" she asked lazily.

"Because I love you more than anyone else is likely to love you. And because I'll put up with you: your tempers and your extravagance and your selfishness; your cruelty too. Yes, you are cruel sometimes, Eva. You have been cruel to me many

265

times but I have not minded; your brothers and sister are used to you, I suppose, and I have forgiven you that. Kati. That nearly made me turn away from you; Kati has so little and you so much. You could have been kinder to Kati. But I came to see it was thoughtlessness more than cruelty, and I forgave you for Kati as well."

"How pompous you are, Adam Kaldy!" She pulled away from him.

"Yes, I'm pompous. But if you think about it when you are sober, you will see that marrying me is a sound and sensible idea. Who else can you marry?"

Even in the midst of her months of misery, the idea had once or twice crossed her mind. Whom could she marry? Where were all the wonderful young men from before the war? One or two had come back, but they weren't the same young men any more. They were all quiet, old. Adam was quiet and old too, but then he had always been that way.

"I could marry Mr. Klein!"

Adam began to laugh, a gentle, affectionate laugh, and she began to giggle too. "Mr. Klein wouldn't consider asking you to be his wife," he said, and abruptly she stopped giggling. "You think Mr. Klein, a man in his forties, would be willing to bear with your capriciousness, your whims and fancies, your bad manners in public, your moods and tempers? Good gracious, Eva. He is an intellectual, a cosmopolitan, a man of culture. He doesn't have the patience to cope with a fractious child."

She began to cry again. Now he was insulting her. First he had been vulgar; now he was being deliberately unkind. "If that is what you think of me, why do you want to marry me?" she wept.

"I love you."

It was said in a flat, bored, expressionless voice. He was quite still, utterly controlled; no movement of hand or face showed any emotion whatsoever. There was something tense, unnatural, about his stillness. Oh, how differently Felix would have said it! How warm and exciting a proposal from Felix would have been! But Felix hadn't proposed—not to her—and again a wave of lonely misery swept over her.

"How could he do it!" she sobbed. "He told me I was the only person who could help him. When he came back from the war—he was so ill and I was the one who made him better—he said I was the only person who understood, who was dear to him. How could he! How could he do this to me?"

"Felix doesn't think he has done anything to you," Adam answered slowly. "You don't understand Felix, Eva. He is not emotional, not in the way the rest of us are emotional. I think the only person he really loves is Mama. And she would never have allowed you to marry Felix. She will not allow you to marry me. But you will, just the same."

Suddenly she knew she would marry him. It was strange and not at all what she had ever expected. He was dreary, boring, and she didn't love him. But he was safe, comforting. When she was miserable she wouldn't have to pretend to be gay and bright with Adam. She wouldn't have to bother to be charming, to flirt and laugh. She could just let him take care of her, console her. The thick, muzzy feeling in her head was still there and she leaned forward and placed her head on Adam's chest. How nice it would be to go to sleep.

"All right, Adam."

"You'll marry me?"

"Mmm."

He lifted her face with one hand and kissed her. It was not unpleasant, but it disturbed her lethargy a little.

"Shall we go and tell them now, Adam? Shall we go in and make an announcement?"

"No."

"Oh, yes! Let's tell everyone now! It will be such a surprise!" And such a way of convincing everyone that she didn't care, of making them all crowd round her, smiling, congratulating, paying her compliments.

"No, Eva. We shall wait until we have told your father and my mother."

"Oh, Adam!" She pouted. "Don't be so stuffy and dreary. I want to tell everyone now. Come on!"

The hand on her arm was like a vice. She could feel his hard farmer's fingers bruising her tender flesh.

"Adam! You're hurting me!"

"Eva, you will not go in there and tell everyone. Do you hear me? This is Kati's day, as much as any day can be Kati's. In a smaller way it is also my mother's day. You can do what you like tomorrow, but today you will behave as a guest at my brother's wedding should behave."

"I—"

"If you insist on running in there, with your face swollen

from crying and your dress crumpled and dirty where you have been lying on the ground, if you insist on going in like that to tell them of our marriage, I shall deny it."

She was about to flare back at him when she became aware of a queasy sensation in her stomach. The ground tilted upwards and the queasiness became a violent pain. "Oh, Adam!" she groaned, and quickly he bent her forward, holding her head over the grass while she retched.

Later, feeling slightly ashamed, she consoled herself with the thought that if there was one man in the world she didn't mind seeing her vomit, it was Adam Kaldy.

In the yard outside the house and gardens there was more than one being sick. Leo and Jozsef, who had left the sedate party inside the house as quickly as they could, watched fascinated as one by one the farmhands passed out or were carried away on the shoulders of more sober friends.

As the afternoon wore on, the scene in the yard became less and less orderly. The food on the trestle tables had vanished (some of it under the aprons of peasant wives and daughters who knew there wasn't very much at home) and the violinist, although still playing with verve and passion, was swaying with both his eyes closed. There was a fight going on in the far corner where the gate led into the orchard: a carter from the Kaldy estate quarrelling with a carter from the Racs-Rassay land. Here and there bodies—male—lay scattered across the ground. All the women had left, vanished discreetly long since to the sobriety of their own cottages.

"Look," said Leo, fascinated. At one end of the trestle the wine tap had been left open. A thin trickle poured directly into the open mouth of a snoring figure lying on the ground. At frequent intervals the peasant would gurgle and spew back some liquid that collected in a puddle by the side of his head. Once or twice, nearly choking, the man would heave, stir, then swallow and relapse comatose again. It seemed impossible for a man to go on absorbing wine while unconscious, and the two boys stared in awed disbelief.

In the centre of the yard a large group of men, arms round each other's shoulders, circled in a sedate dance—sedate because none of them could move too quickly. Someone's hat fell off and was crushed by the progression of booted feet.

Leo suddenly froze.

The man without a hat broke away from the circle, cursed at his fellows, fell on the ground, and grovelled for his hat.

"That's him."

"That's who, Leo?"

"Him."

The man was unable to rise. Dancing, supported by his friends, he had remained upright. But once on the ground he stayed there, trampled by the careless steps of the dancers.

"He killed Uncle Sandor."

"Are you sure, Leo?"

"That's him!"

All the times he had thought he recognized the killer it had been when men were marching, moving, standing. So often had he glimpsed a figure that resembled the murderer, and always the figure had moved and he wasn't sure. But now he could see him. The body rolled over; the man was sick, then insensible; and the more Leo looked, the more certain he was that he had found the killer. Fury welled up inside him. Uncle Sandor was dead, and his murderer danced and drank and ate the food provided by Aunt Gizi and Uncle Alfred. Hatred began to choke him, hatred and renewed grief. Uncle Sandor! Uncle Sandor!

"Killer!" he screamed, and launched himself forward into the melee of drunken revellers. "Killer! Killer! You shot him! You shot Uncle Sandor!" He began to sob, to sob and kick at the sodden body. The men, still drunk and moving, laughed a little and then grew quiet, sensing that something was not right.

"You shot him! I saw you! I hate you, hate you!" His feet, in beautiful well-polished wedding shoes, pummelled the drunkard's side. The man groaned and was sick again. His head was lying in a pool of vomit.

"Come away, Leo." Jozsef was nervous. He was quite prepared to believe Leo but he was afraid of the drunken men and also a little afraid of Leo's sudden unbridled wrath. "Come away." He tried to pull his brother away from the body on the ground.

"No!" Leo jerked his arm away. "Go and tell someone, Jozsef! Get the *pandur!* Anyone! Tell Papa!" He began to kick again, screaming and sobbing with frustration because no one would help him. He felt Jozsef pulling at him again, pulling hard, then hitting him, and he looked and saw that it wasn't Jozsef this time. It was a small, dirty, ragged child who seemed to be as agonized, as insane with fury, as he himself was.

"Stop!" screamed the child. His face was thin and filthy; blazing blue eyes glared from a peasant's face.

Astonished, Leo stood still.

"You go away!" sobbed the child. "You! Do not kick him. This is my father. Go away!"

Everyone in the yard was silent now. Soberness had swiftly returned and with it fear. The peasant's son had attacked the younger of the two young Ferenc gentlemen. Only a childhood game, perhaps, but it did not do for peasants' children to attack the sons of gentlemen. They backed away, not wanting to be involved with the incident in case someone should decide to investigate and mete out punishment.

The small boy was standing defiantly over the body of his father. He wore no shoes and his feet were covered with scabs and sores. He was half the size of Leo, and now that the yard had suddenly become silent his sobs seemed too loud for such a puny body.

Leo's anger abated, dispersed in surprise that anyone at all could want to protect the peasant who had killed Uncle Sandor.

"Your father is a murderer!" he said, but the child didn't understand or even hear him.

"Go away!" He lifted one of his father's feet and began to pull. Sweat broke out on the dirty face, but the insensible man was too heavy. The child dropped the foot and moved round and grasped the collar of his father's shirt. It was wet and disgusting but he took no notice. He heaved and strained, trying to drag his father's head away from the mess of stale food and wine. "I'll get him away from you!" he gasped. "I'll get him away."

Leo wanted to cry—with despair because, though Uncle Sandor's killer was found, no one would do anything to arrest him, but also because the child dragging his father away confused him and made him miserable. He stood helpless, watching, his emotions a tumbled mass of indecision. The small boy slipped and fell.

"I'll help you," he heard himself saying. "I'll help you drag him away." His words seemed to galvanize everyone to action. The child spat at him and several of the men came forward to lift the drunkard and carry him out of sight.

Jozsef pulled again at his arm. "Leave him, Leo. It is only a peasant! They are all only peasants!"

"He killed Uncle Sandor, Jozsef."

"Are you sure? Are you quite sure?"

Was he sure? He had been mistaken many times before, but this time he *was* sure. Always before there had been doubt, but now he was sure.

"Yes. I shall tell Malie. She will know what to do. She will see that he is arrested."

The yard had emptied save for those too sodden to move. The boys began to walk away.

"Did you see the boy's feet, Jozsef? They were all bleeding."

"No. I didn't notice."

"They were very bad."

And then he was overwhelmed by everything, not least by his own emotion. He ran away from Jozsef, into the villa to tell Malie.

A wedding was no place to investigate a murder, but Malie could see that Leo was disturbed enough to wreck the day if she didn't do something quickly and quietly. He burst into the wedding chamber and began to shout at her, a story about Uncle Sandor's killer and a boy with sore feet. She led him quickly back into the garden and there, with the help of Jozsef, pieced together a story of drunken brawling and high tempers.

"But darling," she explained patiently, "how could you be sure it was the same man? You didn't *really* see him that day. You didn't really see him any more than the rest of us did. You saw a man firing a rifle, but you can't say definitely which one it was, not after all this time!"

"I can! And it was him! I tell you, Malie, it was him! You must believe me. You must do something about it. He must be punished, killed!" Colour flamed in his face and his voice was high and loud. She couldn't quieten him and finally she went in search of Adam, a search that took longer than she expected and that ended, rather surprisingly, with the discovery of Eva—white-faced—sitting with Adam on a stone seat at the end of the garden. He came, and the questions began all over again.

"How can you be sure, Leo?"

"I am sure."

Adam turned to Malie, then to Eva. "Could either of you identify the man? Could your mama? Could Jozsef?"

"No. None of us could. That day was so confusing, so terrible. Everyone—anyone could have killed him. I don't know how Leo can be so sure."

"I am sure."

"Very well. Let us try and find the man, but discreetly and quietly. Remember this is a wedding, Leo. Your father and your Uncle Alfred will be very angry indeed if you make scenes or unpleasantness."

"Yes, Adam." He was more subdued now. The grown-ups, with all their authority and common sense, had taken over and he was suddenly a little frightened of the results of his declaration. His heart was thumping and he couldn't understand Jozsef's exhilaration in the search for the drunken peasant.

"We're going peasant hunting, peasant hunting," chanted Jozsef, and Leo felt sick.

"Shut up," he hissed.

Jozsef looked hurt. "I'm only trying to help," came the pained reply, and Leo, once more a victim of confused emotions, turned away.

They didn't have far to go, just through the yard of slumbering forms and round by the stables. They found him where his comrades had dropped him, pillowed on a pile of straw with the scrawny child crouched protectively by his head.

"That's him!"

He said it, but all the time he was conscious of blazing eyes, of vitriolic hatred, of fear.

"Marton," said Adam slowly. "That's Marton, one of my peasants. His father . . . his father was with me on the Russian front, right at the beginning of the war."

"That's him." His confidence was faltering now. What was Adam going to do? What would happen to the man? What would happen to the boy?

"I see. Yes." Adam didn't move. He stood looking down at the man, at Marton. No one seemed to notice the small boy, no one but Leo. Their eyes met and held. Leo looked away first.

Adam sighed, a tired, weary sound. Then he put his hand on Leo's shoulder and pushed him away from the others. "Leo, you realize that you are the only one who says this man killed Uncle Sandor?"

"It's him. I know it's him."

"But no one else does. It is your word against his."

"But he is a peasant!"

Adam crouched down so that he could talk quietly to Leo. His face was only a little distance away and he looked old again, the way he had looked when he first came back from the war.

"Leo, if you are right we must call the *pandur*. And they will beat the man, Marton, in order to make him tell the truth. Do you understand, Leo?"

Leo swallowed.

"I want you to understand what you are doing."

"What will happen? If they beat him and he tells the truth, what will happen to him?"

"They will hang him."

Leo looked over to the pile of straw. The child was still staring at him. "Does he have any other children?"

"Yes. That boy is his eldest, Janos. He is not very old, Leo, no more than five or six. He must have been born soon after his grandfather died." Adam had drifted away a little and was talking to himself. "He was a good man, the old Marton, nearly fifty but he came with me to Russia. A brave man."

"His feet are bleeding."

"Hmmm?"

"The little boy. His feet are bleeding."

"Do you want me to call the *pandur*, Leo?"

Uncle Sandor, tell me what to do. He shot you, I'm sure he did. But if they beat him, if they hang him, the little boy will cry.

"Leo?"

The little boy—Janos—was still crouching, spitting hate, on the pile of straw, but finally the strain of scrutiny, the tension of something happening but not knowing what, broke him. He put his head down between his legs and began to cry. Marton turned his head and was sick again. Some of it went on the boy's foot.

"No."

"What do you mean, Leo?"

"Don't get the *pandur*." *Forgive me, Uncle Sandor. I promised I'd find him and punish him. Perhaps I will later on, when he's bigger and I can fight him. Then I'll punish his father.*

"I don't want them to beat him. It is him—he shot Uncle Sandor—but I don't want . . . the little boy, you see. I can't—"

Adam stared at him, his face solid, impassive, no expression at all.

"It's all right, Leo. I understand."

"The boy—"

"Yes, Leo. I understand. I think you have chosen the right thing to do. Uncle Sandor—would he want you to hurt the little boy?"

"No." But all the same he felt he had betrayed the old coachman. What should he have done? What should he have done?

"Come, Leo, we'll go back into the house now. The wedding is over and the guests will soon be leaving. We must forget all about this. Don't mention it to anyone, eh?"

"No, Adam."

They walked away and the others followed. Once he looked back and saw that the peasant boy had stopped crying and was watching them furtively, like a nasty little animal.

They filed back through the yard, into the garden, and up to the terrace. He was too old to cry and so he clenched his fists and pressed them into his side. The attempt to control his misery was only just successful.

18

To think upon something, to consider and brood over a possible course of action, is frequently the first step towards acceptance.

The thought of marrying Mr. Klein—anathema to Malie—came to be a daily game of imagination. Where would they live? What were his friends like? Did he have any family? How could she marry someone whom she still addressed as Mr. Klein? And so on. And in some way living with the speculation, considering (frequently with distaste but occasionally with levity) this particular aspect and that especial possibility, removed the shocked horror that Papa's revelation had produced. Of course she had no intention of marrying Mr. Klein

—David—but she had promised to think about it, and it was an interesting exercise to wonder what kind of marriage it would have been.

Mr. Klein—David—went back to Budapest in the autumn, and throughout the winter and spring she *thought* about the idea of marrying him. Nursing Eva through a stormy, uncertain engagement, watching Papa grow more and more worried and seeing the household economies increase, she let the thought drift through her mind. What would it be like to marry Mr. Klein? She didn't like him, but then she didn't dislike him either. And, even though she couldn't bear to be married to him, there would be advantages, great advantages.

She realized how rarely now she went to the theatre or to a concert. She had so loved music and she remembered with pleasure their year at school in Vienna, the concerts and operas they had attended. She had never spoken to David Klein about music, but somehow she knew he would enjoy it as much as she did. To marry him would mean concerts, ballet, theatre: in Budapest, almost certainly in Vienna—that is if Vienna ever managed to recover from the war—and possibly even Paris or London. On other days she would reflect that perhaps it would be better *not* to travel about with him when they married; she could stay on her own and enjoy his absence.

Listening to Eva protest that her engagement was all a mistake and that she didn't want to marry Adam Kaldy, Malie would, between making sympathetic noises, acknowledge the fact that marrying David Klein would also mean escaping from Eva's constant emotional crises.

Watching Papa grow fretful and old she would consider how good it would be to make sure that Papa's securities were safe, to guarantee that every summer the boys could go up to the farm.

Once, in a mood of dull cynicism, she even found herself reflecting that Mr. Klein would obviously die long before she did. However unpleasant marriage to him might be, it wouldn't last forever.

And permeating everything was one final question: If she didn't marry Mr. Klein or someone else (and who else was there?), what would she do for the rest of her life? What was there for girls like her and Eva to do? Out of all their friends, all the girls they had grown up with, one and one only had accepted a working post. Juli Glatz taught French in the local girl's school, which was considered an acceptable if rather second-best occupation for a young woman. It was acceptable only because Juli was extremely plain, not very rich, and twenty-five years old. The town generally acknowledged that with the shortage of young men it was unlikely that Juli would find a husband. Poor girl, at least she showed some kind of courage in accepting her inevitable single state and settling for a "vocation" instead.

Amalia, when she wasn't thinking about marrying Mr. Klein, thought a lot about Juli Glatz. She thought about the freedom Juli must have: her own money, the chance to mix with people in the school whom she would never have met socially. She wondered why Mama and Papa (and Aunt Gizi and Uncle Alfred too) had spent a great deal of money educating their daughters when at the end of it all they were not expected to use any of it. One day, when Eva was sobbing theatrically that the engagement to Adam Kaldy must be broken, Amalia tried to talk to her about it.

"Very well, Eva," she said brutally (it was the second time that week Eva had made her dramatic announcement), "break the engagement. And then, as you can't marry Felix, which is what you really want, go out to work instead—like Juli Glatz."

"What?" Eva's tears vanished and two patches of red appeared on her cheeks.

"You—we—don't *have* to get married. Why should we? Lots of girls go out to work now. Look at Papa's office. Even Papa has lady typists."

Eva was appalled. "But they are shopkeepers' daughters, clerks' daughters! Don't be ridiculous, Malie! How could we go and work as typists?"

"We couldn't," said Amalia bitterly. "We don't know how to type. We can speak German and French beautifully. We have studied Shakespeare and Tolstoy and Goethe. We know a little Latin, a little English, and we can play Beethoven sonatas quite well. But we cannot type or, indeed, do anything that would enable us to go out and find employment."

"But why should we? We were the most popular girls in the town! We still are. Remember how they called us the enchanting Ferenc girls, that summer before the war? Do you remember?"

"I remember," Malie said softly. "Oh, yes, I remember."

"Well, we don't need to find employment! Oh, I know they keep saying there are too many women and not enough men, but *we* don't need to worry about that. Not us!"

276

Malie stared at her sister, her pretty, capricious, stupid sister.

"Eva, don't you ever think about the future? You don't want to marry Adam—you say you don't love him—so what will you do? Will you break your engagement and live with Mama and Papa for the rest of your life, just waiting, hoping that someone else will come along? Don't you see, Eva? Why should we *have* to get married? Why is there no choice for us when even a shopkeeper's daughter has a choice? Why can't we go out into the world and see what exciting things might happen if we didn't get married?"

"That's silly," said Eva, bored. "You know very well we shall get married. I shall marry Adam and"—her face brightened—"I shall infuriate Madame Kaldy, who hates the thought of having me in her family. She has spent her whole life keeping Felix away from me. And now I shall be related to them. She will be forced to ask me to join every single family occasion. I will be Felix's sister-in-law and she will hate it."

"Oh, Eva!" She gave up, knowing it would be useless to try and make Eva understand. And indeed there was no need for Eva to understand. Eva was intended for matrimony. It would make little difference to her life style. She would continue to go to parties, buy pretty clothes, meet her friends for coffee, flirt, dance, tease. Look at Mama. Mama was forty-five and still enjoying these frivolous pursuits.

Mr. Klein came for short visits, brought little gifts for the three of them, was charming, entertaining, and left as elegantly as he had come. But the visits were not quite the way they had been. There always seemed to come a moment when she and Mr. Klein were alone together, just talking, and Mr. Klein would drop his bantering, amused manner and ask her all kinds of things, forcing her to think, to voice opinions and contradict him. He wanted to know her views on Horthy, on the emerging political system, on the economic crisis, on the anti-Semitism that was taking shape. He asked very few questions about her, about her emotions or feelings, but wanted to know everything about her ideas of the world. Once, roused by a slighting remark that emphasized her ignorance of topical matters, she flared into an attack on the system that didn't allow women to know too much about current affairs or allow them to work without the stigma of "matrimony—failed" being attached to them. Mr. Klein had listened attentively to her and then asked, "So, my dear Amalia. And if you wanted

277

to work, if you were a man and could choose any profession, what would it be?"

And, disconcerted because she expected a defence of the matrimonial system, she had floundered around seeking to choose a living for herself and had failed to find one. She had no vocation. The years of doing nothing had enervated her and now she didn't know what she could do.

She wasn't aware of when her acceptance of marrying Mr. Klein occurred. They never spoke of it when they were alone together, but sometime during the year that passed between Kati's wedding and Eva's, the thought of marrying him became no longer an imaginary exercise but an inevitability. Without either of them speaking of it, it came to be recognized between them. No details were mentioned, no dates or feelings were dwelt upon, but they both knew that at some point Amalia Ferenc would become the wife of David Klein.

As she watched Eva preparing for her wedding, sweeping herself into a frenzy of excitement where she could forget her misery over Felix, Amalia found a peace within herself. Karoly's death no longer hurt, but the sweetness, the poignancy, the utter faith and sincerity of that first love still remained with her. Marrying Mr. Klein meant that she could keep that love inviolate. There would be no intrusion of passion into the memories of Karoly. Marriage to Mr. Klein—a sedate, calm, business-like arrangement where Mr. Klein got a young bride who was related to the nobility and she got a financial backer —meant that Karoly would be untouched. Eva, alas, was to know no such peace. Adam was young and in love with her. Felix was young and definitely not in love with her. Caught between the two, the one who did not want her and the one who did, she was in a state of nervous unbalance by the time her wedding day arrived.

The ceremony was smaller and more chic than the great pastoral Racs-Rassay feast of the year before. It was held in the house in town, the Bogozy silver and glass being once more removed from the vaults of the bank. The bridegroom was happier than the one at the previous wedding, and the bride far lovelier than poor Kati had been. Felix was just as excitable and charming, Kati just as nervous and unhappy (in some curious way they didn't seem to be like a married couple; there was a lack of the bonding that even the most ill-matched couples acquire after a year of marriage). Madame

278

Kaldy was angry but aristocratically controlled, showing her disdain for the match by wearing the same clothes that she had bought for Felix's marriage: Adam, who in spite of orders to the contrary had insisted on marrying the little Bogozy trollop, did not deserve new clothes for his wedding.

And it was at the marriage of Eva and Adam that Mr. Klein acknowledged at last the unspoken arrangement between Malie and himself.

He was seated a little apart from everyone—legs elegantly crossed, one hand stretched casually across the back of his chair—and his dark, heavy-lidded eyes slid in amused contemplation from couple to couple, from coldly furious Madame Kaldy to Mama, who was excited, unbelievably happy, and a charming and delightful hostess. Malie found her eyes drawn repeatedly to him, and finally, because the secret smile annoyed her, she went across to him.

"How very strange, the mating habits of the young," he murmured. "There is your poor little Racs-Rassay cousin—inconsequential, is she not?—married to the most attractive man in the room and obviously unimpressed. And now your sister—quite enchanting!—adored by that rather stolid young fellow and equally unimpressed."

"Eva is very fond of Adam!" said Malie, nettled.

Mr. Klein turned his bland gaze upon her. "Come now, Amalia. You and I know very well that she cares little or nothing for her unfortunate bridegroom. But I think fate is with her. Unwittingly she has chosen the right husband. He is solid, a little dull perhaps, but he will be to her what your father has been to your mother."

"Papa has not always been good to Mama," she blurted out.

"No, perhaps not, but you see, your papa has many conflicts to overcome within himself. He has protected and guided your mama. She has never had to face reality—unlike the estimable Madame Kaldy over there—and in fact I believe she would not be able to face reality. Your papa has given her the things she needs most from life: loyalty, stability, financial security, and discipline. And perhaps, because it has not been easy for him to give her these things, a little surface emotion has been lost on the way."

She was fascinated. Mr. Klein had never spoken to her like this before, not about people and their feelings towards one

279

another. In a different way from Papa he too often seemed cold and dispassionate, but now here he was, discussing love and human relationships with her.

"Do you ever think about your origins, Amalia?" he asked suddenly.

"My origins?"

"The room is full of Bogozys, your mother's charming and delightful family. Do you ever think about your father's family?"

"There's Aunt Gizi," she said slowly. "And once, when I was very small, Papa took me to see an old man, my grandfather. Papa said the old man never forgave him for marrying Mama."

"No," Mr. Klein replied quietly. "He wouldn't forgive that."

"You reminded me of him a little—the old man, I mean."

"I too, like your papa, have thrown away my origins. In Hungary it is necessary if a man is to make a special kind of impact. But I think, Amalia, I am not prepared to shout my betrayal from the rooftops. To slide gently away from one's roots is possible without too much inner conflict, but to say aloud, 'This is finished; now I am a new man with new manners and customs'—this I cannot do."

"I'm not quite sure—"

"I am saying, Amalia, that I do not think I can bring myself to marry you before a priest. For our children—yes—I can watch them at the altar even as your papa watches Eva, but my blood is not yet sufficiently diluted to accept the cross as the authority for our marriage."

"We could not be married by a rabbi!" she cried, suddenly alarmed. "I am not—I do not . . . no! It would be terrible!"

Mr. Klein raised a sardonic eyebrow. "Really, Amalia, how very foolish you can be sometimes. Do you think I would even contemplate such a thing? No, we shall be married in a civil ceremony. And I would suggest that we go to Budapest. I shall hire a suite in a hotel and we shall give a very smart and graceful party. I am told that to be married in a hotel is considered the very latest fashion!"

She liked the idea. He was being a little patronizing, a little arrogant, but unwittingly he had selected the right way to do things. There would be no thoughts of Karoly, no "might have been" in a smart civil ceremony in a Budapest hotel. It would be the symbol of their entire . . . arrangement: in good taste, undemanding, civilized, pleasant.

"That seems to me admirable," she said calmly, and he smiled, the warm, affectionate smile that she had seen only rarely on his face. He reached for her hand and held it for a few seconds.

"Amalia," he whispered, "do not forget your origins entirely. Remember the old man sometimes."

There was confusion in her breast, a stirring of unease, and then as the warmth of his hand communicated itself to her, the sense of affinity overcame her again and she felt at peace —secure, safe, and at peace.

"I think we shall be very . . . comfortable," she said, and Mr. Klein nodded.

It was some time later that she realized they had both accepted the fact that no proposal had been necessary. All they had done was to confirm the engagement.

And it was also some time before she realized her physical aversion to Mr. Klein had vanished some months ago.

Mama was dreadfully upset. Her face blanched when she was told and it was several moments before she could speak. She managed to smile and murmur, "How surprising. David and my little girl, my last little girl. All my children leaving me," and then she had put her hand to her mouth and left the room. The three of them, Malie, Mr. Klein, and Papa, had been left in uncomfortable silence.

"She is overwrought," said Papa finally. "The wedding tired her; she grows too excited with these affairs. And she relies on Amalia. I think she hoped that Amalia would stay with her for some time yet."

"Of course." Mr. Klein was frowning.

"And she has to face the fact that you will take Amalia away from the town. You will live in Budapest for much of the time and Marta will not be able to see her too often."

"We shall come here many times," said Mr. Klein, still frowning. "I have invested greatly in the town, as you know, Zsigmond. We shall live in Budapest, yes, but there will be many, many business visits here. And in the summer we shall be together up in the mountains."

"I think I will go and speak to her," Malie said, rising from her chair. "I'm sure it was just that she had no idea. . . . Eva has always confided in Mama, whereas I—she had no idea at all, you see. I will go and speak to her."

"Yes, Amalia. That would be wise." Soberly they watched her leave the room. She was aware of their silence long after she had left them.

When she reached Mama's room she listened and heard the distressing sound of Mama crying. She knocked, and when there was no answer she went in. Mama was lying across the bed with a handkerchief clamped to her eyes.

"Oh, Mama! You mustn't be upset! I'm not going away forever!"

"He's far too old for you!" Mama sobbed. "And he's . . . he's not suitable for you! You're not suitable for him! He has no right to marry a girl!"

"Mama, I'm not a girl any longer. I'm twenty-five. I'm nearly an old maid!"

"You're too young for him!" Mama cried. "He needs an older woman, a mature woman who knows the world and could entertain him, amuse him, someone who would appreciate his presents and his manners and his—oh, everything!"

"I appreciate him, Mama," she said slowly.

"No! No, you don't. You're too young to appreciate a man like that. Why, you even threw his roses away. Eva told me. And you can't talk the way—other women can talk. You're too serious!" She sat up and flung one arm out into the air, trying to say with a gesture what she could not say with words. "Oh! You're just too *young* for him, Malie!"

She couldn't answer. She just stared at Mama, her face growing white. Mama burst into tears again and flung her arms round Malie.

"Darling! I love you and I want you to be happy. I didn't mean to hurt you. You are lovely. Karoly—he thought you were lovely and you are, my dearest, you are! But—oh, no, not David. You cannot marry David, Amalia!"

She didn't reply. There was nothing she could say. She sat feeling pity for Mama but, as well as pity, an emotion verging on dislike.

"How could he!" Mama sobbed. "Humiliating me this way, marrying my daughter. We are practically the same age, Malie! Do you realize that?"

"Yes, Mama."

"He will be my son-in-law!"

She sat by the bed and watched Mama sob and rage and finally quieten. She went and fetched smelling salts and coffee, and she closed the blinds and left Mama to sleep her distress away. Later Mama tried to put it right. She explained that she wanted Malie to be happy and have a young, energetic husband. She didn't want Malie to marry an older man just because she didn't think a young one would come along. But of course, if Malie had set her heart on it, then Mama would give her blessing, her fond and loving blessing. She got up and bathed her face and dressed with great care. And by the time she came down to dinner she was nearly back to normal. She laughed and flirted with David and said how very naughty he was, stealing her daughter from under her nose. She said a great many gay and foolish things, like telling him he must call her Mama and pay great respect to her. Mr. Klein didn't laugh. He was very serious, and he stared at Mama with a small frown on his forehead.

By the time dinner was over everything was natural again and they began to talk about the wedding, and whether Mr. Klein and Malie should have a new apartment in Budapest or use Mr. Klein's present one. Mama was charming and gracious, and everyone relaxed, everyone except Malie.

That night, overwhelmed with a sense of complete isolation, with the knowledge that she was, in spite of all her rationalization, marrying a man who was a stranger, she cried for Karoly for the very last time.

Part 2

19

The boy, Janos, accepted without question the manner of his living, which was, with a few gradations, a few varying niceties of very poor, poor, and not quite so poor, the manner of living of those all about him.

His home was a room in a single-storied hut made of sun-baked brick. Between this room and the room at the other end of the hut was a kitchen containing two stoves. One was his mother's, the other that of Mrs. Boros. Between the Boros family and the Martons was a strong social distinction which was the sum of several factors. In the Boros room slept Mrs. Boros, her eight children, her mother, and her sister whose husband had been killed in the war. Mr. Boros, who was a carter, slept in the ox stables. There was nothing strange about that. Mostly the men did sleep outside in the stables, away from crying children and old women's snores. In contrast to Mrs. Boros's room, which was noisy and disorganized, Janos's home was luxurious and contained evidence of education and culture. There were lace curtains at the window. The earth floor was brushed into patterns, and on the walls were pinned two pictures which had been cut from magazines. One was a fashion plate of ladies and gentlemen dancing together; the gentlemen wore gloves and the ladies had feathers in their hair. The other picture, the one Janos liked better, was of a stag drinking from a stream in the Bukk Mountains. When he was very small he would lie in the bed he shared with his mother and grandmother and stare up at the stag. It wasn't just the animal that intrigued him, it was the great misty background of hills and forest. He had never been away from the farm and, although on clear days one could see the mountains, he had no first-hand experience of the landscape shown in the picture. Janos's mother had acquired the picture when working as a sewing girl in the Kaldy farmhouse before her marriage. She had never forgotten the things she had learned there or the things she had read, for there were books in the Kaldy house and she had, in stolen moments, sampled them all. The curtains, her most treasured and valued possessions,

286

had been given to her by Madame Kaldy and represented all that she wanted for her family. They were not new, and a close inspection revealed delicate repairs, but to Janos's mother they were a symbol of how she must strive never to descend to the level of the Boros family. Mrs. Boros had no curtains, no pictures, and the floor of her room was sometimes never swept at all. Also, Mr. Boros frequently beat Mrs. Boros, one time so badly that Mrs. Boros broke the glass of her window in order to alarm the neighbours, an unprecedented and incredibly expensive alert signal that so shocked Mr. Boros he immediately stopped.

When Janos's father had first returned from the war he had tried to beat his wife too. Unlike Mrs. Boros, Edina Marton had not screamed or tried to defend herself. She had remained quite still, taking the blows across her face and shoulders with silent fortitude and staring—her blue eyes wide and brilliant—straight into her husband's face so that finally his hand fell and his fury abated. He mumbled something awkward and ineffectual and then stumbled, ashamed, out of the room. After that he beat her only very rarely.

Mrs. Marton's blue eyes—eyes that, of her four children, only her son inherited—were a rarity and an object of both discussion and envy on the farm. They placed her apart in the same way that the lace curtains and the pictures on the walls placed her apart. There was talk that she must be the byblow of a farm manager or a bailiff, but no one could be quite certain, for she had come to the farm as a child with her uncle from some place on the other side of the county.

Janos did not know his father until the war ended. When he was three, or perhaps it was four, a soldier had walked into the hut one day. His mother had been working in the fields and Janos had been husking maize with his grandmother. The soldier had stared and then disappeared even as Grandmother cried out and reached her arms towards him. Later he had returned with Janos's mother and she had given him bread and soup and told Janos that the soldier was his father.

The soldier had come and gone after that; sometimes he was gone for so long that Janos thought he had gone forever and the thought made him happy. Then, late one night, his father had returned looking thinner and more ragged than usual. His mother had begun to cry, saying she was afraid, and the soldier, his father, had sagged wearily as though he too would have been afraid if only he had had the energy. Janos had been turned out of his bed that night and put to sleep with his grandmother in a small bed in another corner of the room. All night there were whispers and sobs, his mother asking why Janos's father had done something and his father growing more and more afraid. Towards morning the whimpers and scoldings ceased and there was suddenly another sound, the noise of a creaking bed and strange grunts and breathing. These noises had disturbed the boy much more than his mother's tears or his father's fears.

In the morning his father had polished his boots and taken him to see Mr. Adam at the farmhouse. He told Janos to wait outside and that was the first time the boy saw that not everyone lived as he did. He had often seen the farmhouse from a distance, but now he was close and had a clear view right down into the kitchen—a kitchen in which the floor was not earth but some shiny, flat stuff, a kitchen with only one stove, but that stove stretching along one entire wall and bigger than both his mother's and Mrs. Boros's put together. There were chests and chairs and tables, and the tables were covered with food. He had never seen food like it in his whole life and his empty stomach began to gurgle at the sight of the sausages, the ham, the noodles, the cabbage. An aroma wafted up the kitchen steps, delicious but strange, a brown smell, rich and exotic. He had closed his eyes and the smell had luxuriated throughout his body, giving him the same sensation that lying in the sun gave him. He breathed the heady scent deep into his lungs—and then felt himself knocked down the steps by a giant hand. Just before he tumbled against the kitchen door the hand jerked him back and set him on his feet in the yard. It was his father, standing angry and red-faced and twisting his hat round and round. "Miserable dog!" he shouted at Janos. "Peering into his honour's kitchen like a mangy hound. Bow to his excellency and ask his pardon!"

Janos had felt himself wrenched forward by one ear. Mr. Adam stood before him. The child bowed and muttered something apologetic.

"Forgive him, excellency!" His father was sweating a little. "This is what happens when a man's son is left to grow without menfolk to correct him."

"No harm, no harm," muttered Mr. Adam. He was staring at Janos and finally he said, "So this is the grandson of old Marton. He was a fine soldier. You should be proud of your father, Marton. He was a brave and loyal man."

"Yes, excellency."

Mr. Adam stared at Janos again. "The child is slight, Marton, and the blue eyes—they are not like those of your father."

"No, excellency. The boy looks like his mother." He puffed proudly a little. "Edina worked for your mother, Mr. Adam, sir. She was your mother's sewing girl before the war."

Mr. Adam made a non-committal noise. He looked away from Janos, past him and out towards the fields and pastures. "Indeed, Marton, indeed. Get along, now. Your place is restored to you, and there is much to be done. The land has suffered in the last years, with only women and children to tend it."

"Yes, excellency." He cuffed Janos round the ear. "Bow to his excellency." Janos bowed.

"I have not forgotten that your father, old Marton, was overseer of the threshing barn," Mr. Adam said. "We shall see how the crops progress." He turned away and was nearly back in the house when he suddenly turned again and rummaged in his pocket. He extracted a *filler* and threw it down the steps onto the ground. "For the child, old Marton's grandson," he said, and went into the house.

"Pick it up."

Janos couldn't pick it up. He wanted it, but he couldn't pick it up. His father had called him a dog and that was what he felt like, a blue-eyed dog.

"Pick it up."

"No."

His father felled him to the ground with one blow. He picked the filler up.

When they got home his mother was burning a strip of red cloth in the stove. She looked up and asked, "Well?" and then she jabbed hard at the red cloth with a piece of stick until it took light and vanished.

"All well. I am to have my old job back and we can stay here. He promised me Father's place one day, overseer of the barn."

His mother's smile, the easing of lines on her face, was like the transformation the sun achieves on a black day. She looked so happy Janos forgave his father for the lie—not lie but exaggeration—about the threshing barn.

"We are safe then! I have burnt the. . . . No one need know."

They smiled at one another and Janos was unhappy. That night the bed creaked and rustled again and he wished his father had never come home.

His father went to work in the granary, and his mother began to have children, girl children. Grandmother nursed them while his mother hoed their strip and tended the pig and the chickens. Every day six eggs had to go up to the farm-house, and once a week his mother took what eggs were left and walked three miles to the market to sell or barter them. The girl children took what little leisure his mother had left, and now she had no time to tell him the stories she had gleaned from the Kaldy house, no time to tell him about the world according to her interpretation, no time to draw letters in the earth with a stick and tell him that once he had mastered them he woud be able to read for himself.

He had his work to do, fetching water, picking caterpillars from the crops, husking maize, but when these tasks were done there was still time left and he wandered away in search of company—and the nearest company was the Boros family. He was fascinated by them. Their room was dirty and they ate (not often but they did eat sometimes) from bowls without spoons or knives. They didn't even sit at a table to eat because there was no table. The women sat on the bed and the men took their food outside to eat from the carts. The children just squatted where they were. At first appalled, later envious, he saw that the Boros children were allowed to do many things that he was not. They spat and blew their noses on the ground. They did not wash at all when the weather was cold, and not very much when the weather was warm. They gambled, imitating the young men playing for money on Sundays, only they used pebbles instead of *filler*. And they swore —how they swore!—rich, earthy epithets that shocked and thrilled him. It was the swearing that finally led to his downfall. The baby was in his charge and she was crying, crying, crying. He rocked her and patted her the way Grandmother did and finally—because he resented having to watch her when he wanted to play with the Boros boys—he became irritated and called her "the poxy mother of a whorehound," a phrase he did not really understand but which relieved his feelings because he knew it was coarse. His mother, entering the room at that moment, was suddenly still. She didn't beat him, but her face was sad and her shoulders, already tired from the day's work, slumped a little more.

"Why did you say those things, my son?" she asked.

He stammered some reply about the Boros boys, his face red, knowing he had done wrong. His mother sat down. She was expecting another child—he knew how to tell now—and as she pushed her legs out in front of her he saw that her ankles were thick and puffy.

"This is my fault," she said, speaking quietly to herself. "I have allowed the family to slip back, and this is my punishment."

"I'm sorry, Mother." He wanted to cry.

"It is time you were at school; that is my error. Tomorrow I go to see the schoolmaster. You will come with me."

He had looked forward to going to school, but now it was tinged with unpleasantness. Instead of the exciting world his mother had promised him it was to be a punishment because he had sworn at the baby.

That night his father thrashed him and the next morning his mother asked permission of Mr. Adam to walk the three miles into the village and see the schoolmaster. Mr. Feher was fierce and large and barked questions at Janos: how old was he, how many maize heads could he husk in an hour, could he pick beans, and so on. Mother stood, humble and quiet, knowing her place before this man of learning. She was aware of their good fortune in that the farm children were allowed to attend the village school. Many farms had their own classes, but the Kaldys did not have sufficient farm servants to warrant a *puszta* school and an arrangement had been reached with Mr. Feher in the village. To go to school in the village, to mix with the children of sophisticated families, some of whom had small portions of land of their own, this was honour indeed.

On the way back from the school he began to notice the village, and for the second time in his life he observed that not everyone lived as he lived. The houses were different, spaced apart, and some were big and some small. Each house had its own vine trained along the portico and there were grapes hanging, all belonging—so his mother said—not to Mr. Adam but to the people themselves. The chickens in the yards were fatter. There were as many as three pigs to a house, and two houses had cows. And the people, so many! So many it was frightening. They were fatter than the farm servants. There was a shop too, a shop with a glass window that he was afraid but compelled to look at. It was a bakery, full of confections—cakes and creams and loaves which seemed unreal.

"Is it a picture, Mother?"

"No, Janos, it is a bakery, where people buy food to eat."

They watched, saw a boy enter, select a confection, pay, and leave. As he walked along the road he bit into the food, and cherries welled out of the side of the dough. Janos swallowed. Beside him he heard his mother's stomach rumble.

"Come, my son, we must go home. We can tell Grandmother what we have seen."

They began the long walk back to the farm and were still on the village road when a frightening, repetitive noise jerked them into the brush at the side. An incredible contraption was coming towards them, a coach without horses, a coach that rattled and banged and was covered in brass.

"A motorcar!" breathed his mother reverently. "A motorcar, and with the young Ferenc ladies inside. Bow, Janos!"

Janos bowed, his mother curtsied. She was still graceful, in spite of her swollen legs and the heavy stomach. The people in the coach didn't see them. No, one person did see them; a boy with black curly hair stared out and raised a hand in lofty salutation.

"There!" His mother smiled, a radiant, excited smile, the same smile she wore when speaking of her time at the Kaldy house. "We have seen so much, Janos! A bakery, and a motorcar, and the young Ferenc ladies! So much!"

She took his hand and he was happy. She was his mother again, the way she had been during the war. On the long walk back they sang together, the old songs of the country people, and he picked her a bunch of wild scabious to wear in her kerchief, "flowers the same colour as our eyes, Mother!"

At home the baby was crying and there was no flour left. It was nearly quarter day when Mr. Adam would allocate the next payment of grain, but the Martons, like all the other families, could not make their grain last three months however hard they tried. They had turnip soup for supper, and his father was angry because the trip to the village had meant that no work had been done on their strip. He shouted at Janos and then stumped away to the stables to talk to the men. Janos wished his father had never come home.

Suddenly the farm was seething with rumours and counter-rumours. There was to be a party, a wedding party for his honour, Mr. Felix, who was to marry the daughter of the Racs-Rassay family. A big wedding! And after the wedding the manor house was to be reopened and the old madame was to retire there with her son and daughter-in-law. Madame Kaldy and Mr. Felix were distant and lofty figures; even

292

though the women said that Madame Kaldy had worked on her own land during the war, she was still lofty and distant. She and her son were real gentry. Mr. Adam was gentry too, but he was different because he was also the farm manager. The fact that he ran the farm and knew about crops and animals removed some of the aristocratic aura from him. Rumour had it that the wedding of his honour, Mr. Felix, was to be celebrated with a party at the Racs-Rassay villa, a party to which the workers on the two estates would be invited.

Speculation, incredulity, cynicism, and faith wrestled with each other until the matter was finally decided with the arrival of a carter from the Racs-Rassay estate who had brought seed for Mr. Adam. It was true, said the carter. There was to be food and drink and dancing for anyone who could get to the villa. More speculation, this time as to the quantity of the food and drink, what would be served, and who would be able to eat the most. The men looked out their wedding jackets and best hats. The women took their black dresses from chests which had stored the selfsame garments for three or four generations. A little exchanging was done—someone's grandmother had been taller than her granddaughter; this one was bigger at the waist and could be lent to a girl just pregnant whose own dress wouldn't fit her. For days the women of the farm slipped in and out of the Marton room—"Just a favour, Edina. My mother's old dress, it is too tight here, too loose there, the sleeve is torn"—and his mother stitched and sewed and was somehow happy even though she had too much work to do.

Mr. Adam called them together and told them how it was to be arranged. Some must go early and return early to care for the animals. When the first party came back, the second could leave. He divided them into two shifts and Janos's father was in the first. He must go early but return in the afternoon.

When the day came his mother could not go at all—her legs were so swollen she had to hoe sitting on the ground—and so his father set out alone, looking clean and cheerful. The farm was quiet when he had gone. The baby had stopped crying and the silence from the Boros room was incredible and unusual; even that noisy brood had been affected by the brilliance and unprecedented generosity of their employers.

Grandmother had gone to look after the children of the Ladi family, and Janos sat with his mother, worrying about her tired white face and stroking her hand. After a while she

293

began to talk, mostly about his going to school, about how she was trying to save the egg money so that he could stay on into the fifth and sixth class. She told him about her own schooling, years ago, and then she made him get the stick and write in the earth whatever letters he could remember. He could remember them all—since the affair with the Boros boys he had been practising the letters for just such an occasion—and now, when he saw her gratified face and hopeful eyes, he wanted to burst with endeavour and success, to show her that he would be able to read quicker than anyone else in the school.

She was worried by four o'clock. His father hadn't come home. All Saints' Eve was approaching, when the staff would be re-employed or dismissed, and now—so near the fateful day of reappointment—was not the time to disobey the master's orders. At half past four she was twisting her hands with nervous anxiety and finally she asked Janos if he thought he could find the way to the Racs-Rassay villa on his own.

"Of course," he said stoutly. He knew roughly what path to go on, and because his mother trusted him he didn't doubt he could find the place.

"Listen now," she said, her voice high-pitched with worry. "Listen while I tell exactly how to get there."

He listened carefully, then repeated it to her, and she put her hand on his shoulder and pushed him gently out the door.

"Run as much as you can," she cried. "Not all the way, but as much as you can," and because he was both proud and hurt for her he began to run at once, puffing his way between the fields and then down into the woods, stopping when his breathing was beginning to hurt, then on again when his wind had returned.

It was a long way, longer than the walk to the village. His legs began to feel wobbly and his head began to float, as though he were standing up high somewhere watching himself running along the track. He stopped at the river, drank, and bathed his sweating face and hands in the cool water. He longed to bathe his feet too but there wasn't time.

Finally he heard the wedding, violins and voices, a long long way off but at least he was not lost. He began to walk, growing nervous because now he must enter an estate not his own, and far grander than the Kaldy farm, or so he had been told.

There were iron railings round the grounds, and big double gates. He was afraid but he followed the railings and gradually the music grew louder and louder and finally he came out into the yard. In the distance he could see the house—a palace!—but he had no time to be awed because he was immediately frozen into horror at the sight that awaited him.

His father was lying on the ground, apparently dead, and the boy who had waved from the car was screaming and kicking at his body. Janos was petrified. Thoughts flashed through his mind with the speed of an ox whip. How could he tell his mother that his father was dead? Where would they go to live? Was this the punishment meted out by Mr. Adam to those who had not returned at the specified time? Panic, confusion, nearly choked him. He looked for familiar faces to help but even though he knew the men they all looked different; they were bloated and red and mad-looking. He clenched his fists by his sides, fighting the desire to turn and run, and then his father moved and groaned and was sick. Relief, and then a strange burning sensation filled him, a fury, a white anger that snapped, a hate for the beautifully dressed boy who was kicking his father. He flung himself forward, not caring, just angry, wanting to kill and hurt. He shouted at the boy; he didn't know what he said and later he couldn't remember if he had hit him or just wanted to. The anger faded, a little, and was replaced by a terrible anxiety. Somehow he had to get his father away. He had to pull him from his vomit because his mother would be so ashamed if she knew.

He tugged and heaved and finally felt panic again, panic that grew when the mad boy suddenly offered to help him. He could hardly understand what the boy was saying, his accent was so unlike anything he had heard before.

And then they were gone, all gone, and he followed Uncle Pal and Uncle Andras when they carried his father to a pile of straw and dropped him. He stayed with him, and later the boy came back with his brother and Mr. Adam. He was frightened because now he knew Mr. Adam would punish them all, would evict them from their home and dismiss his father on All Saints' Eve. There was nothing more he could do. He had failed his mother and he began to cry. His feet hurt and he was tired. . . . Tired.

They all talked, and then they went away and he was left with his father, his father whom he did not like but who had suddenly, for the first time, *become* his father, someone who belonged to him, who was his in the same way that his mother was his.

Presently Uncle Pal and Uncle Andras threw a bucket of

water over his father and when he had roused they staggered away, the three of them, back down the track towards the woods that led to home. Numb with exhaustion the boy Janos dragged behind.

They were not evicted. His father was not dismissed. The men who had failed to return on time from the wedding party —which meant all of them—were called together the following morning. When they returned they were subdued and crushed but no more was said about dismissal and for a while all the men were quiet and behaved kindly to their wives and children.

The following week he went to school to receive an education from Mr. Feher.

20

It was one of those amusing little family reflections—the kind of cosy domestic comment women especially like to make— that Malie, who was the last of the three cousins to be married, should be the first to have children. When Aunt Gizi remarked on it her comments were slightly acid. "Quite extraordinary!" she said to Mama, smiling. "Amalia, married only three years and already the mother of two sons—and with a middle-aged husband too."

Mama, who had almost recovered from the shock of David Klein's becoming her son-in-law (the rise in their financial circumstances had done much to reconcile her) smiled winsomely back. "I'm sure it won't be long, Gizi, before you have a grandchild. Kati and Felix—they have so much to give a child, do they not? The manor house, and all the land, and the Kaldy name, of course. I'm sure it will happen very, very soon."

"I hope so." Aunt Gizi spoke with a commanding note in her voice. Kati had been so obedient until now, doing exactly as she had been told, marrying Felix and settling unobtrusively into a life regulated by her mother-in-law. But after five years of marriage she and Felix should have produced some kind of offspring. It worried Gizi considerably. She was always slightly aware that Madame Kaldy felt she had reneged on the bargain. After all, what was the point of saving the Kaldy estate if there was no heir to inherit it?

"I wonder," she mused reflectively. "I wonder if I should take Kati to Lake Balaton. A holiday by the water, some swimming and healthy walks . . . perhaps she is anaemic."

"Perhaps she is bored," said Mama, yawning. "What does she do with herself, your little Kati? Girls, especially married girls, can get bored so easily and Kati—Kati never *enjoys* things very much."

"What do you mean?" snapped Gizi defensively.

"Well, Eva goes out and drinks coffee and dances and buys clothes. And now she is married she has parties at home and buys new furniture. And Amalia runs her home—beautifully, quite beautifully!—but Kati doesn't do any of those things, does she?"

Gizi stared, angry but concerned.

"I mean," Mama continued delicately. "If you don't enjoy doing anything—well, you don't enjoy doing *anything* . . . if you understand me, Gizi?"

Gizi was aware, only too aware, of the imperfections of her daughter, but nonetheless she was a mother and she swung feebly to Kati's defence.

"She has her painting," she said quickly. "She was always good at her little flower pictures, Marta, you remember? And Madame Kaldy has given her the summer house at the end of the garden to keep her paints and pictures in."

Mama sniffed. "It doesn't sound very . . . vibrant, Gizi. I think you should try to make her lively, take her to Budapest and buy her some pretty clothes, or let her go on her own. Yes, that would be far better!"

"It would be most improper."

"She can stay with Malie and David." Mama clapped her hands. "Oh, what a delightful idea! Kati adores Malie. You know very well, Gizi, that Kati would be most happy to go and stay with Malie in Budapest."

Gizi didn't answer, but the idea took root. Even while she was thinking that perhaps a visit to Amalia with her two small sons would be quite a good idea, she was also wishing that her sister-in-law didn't behave quite so girlishly. Marta Bogozy was nearly fifty, and still using the mannerisms of a girl in a pre-war ballroom. She was too old to clap her hands and giggle.

"And perhaps," continued Mama excitedly, "perhaps Eva

297

could go up as well. My poor Eva so hates it in the country during the winter; she should never have married a farmer, poor darling. But if she went too, then our three lovely girls could have a little holiday together! Just like they used to; do everything together the way they always did!"

And my daughter will be the odd one out, just as she always was, reflected Gizi bitterly. Not that it mattered now. They had all found husbands, and Kati had made the best match of them all. Except sometimes, in the middle of the night when Alfred's snores from the next room woke her up, she would begin to worry about Kati. At first, just after the wedding, she had felt a sense of relief. Kati was married, a splendid marriage, a marriage that had all the security of money and name, land and possessions. There was no need to worry about Kati's future any more. And then, only occasionally at first but more frequently of late, a faint sense of unease would overcome her. When she was watching Felix and Kati together she would feel that something was wrong. Oh, she didn't expect an ecstatic or even a happy marriage—there wasn't any such thing—but it seemed as though Kati was nothing to do with Felix or Madame Kaldy. It was as though she was living with them but they didn't know she was there. And recently, in the night, at the bad time when one woke and thought about the pains in one's stomach, wondering if it were cancer, she would also think, What will happen to Kati when I die, when Alfred dies? And she began to worry. Who would protect her daughter when she was dead?

"Yes," she said slowly. "Yes, Marta. Perhaps it would be a good idea, if Amalia doesn't mind." For she had also begun to realize that when she and Alfred were dead the only ones who would care about her daughter were Marta Bogozy—irritating Marta—and her two daughters. Family. The only ones who really ever cared were family.

And—again in the night—she remembered the old man, her father. Two children he had had, herself and Zsigmond, and both of them had sacrificed their birthright to ambition. The old man had lost both his children, sucked into an alien culture, and yet he had sent for them when he was dying. Family.

"Wonderful!" twittered Marta, clapping her hands like a girl again. "I shall write to Malie at once. She will be thrilled."

The pattern of their family life had changed. No longer did

they gather in the town every winter and spring, exchanging invitations to parties and meeting each other nearly every day. Malie now lived in Budapest, Eva and Kati in the country (although during the winter months Eva visited her parents in town whenever she could). In the summer it was much more the way it had always been. Malie and David Klein stayed with Mama and Papa at the farm, and carriages and motors rolled continuously between it and the other three residences, the Racs-Rassay villa, the Kaldy manor house, and Adam's farm. In the summer it was picnics, summer dances, tennis parties at the Kaldy manor and what seemed one long somnolent sun-drenched gathering of friends and family. The summers were glorious, especially for Eva, for she was now the undisputed centre of the family network.

Malie, married and busy with her children, had grown quieter, calmer, and somehow *older*. Kati didn't count at all. Madame Kaldy, Mama, and Aunt Gizi were relegated—now that a generation of new young wives were present—to positions of gentle but disregarded authority. So Eva, Mrs. Adam Kaldy, was the undisputed queen of the district's society. Marriage to Adam had brought many surprises. One was that although Felix and his mother in their renovated manor house were the most aristocratic figures in the area, Adam was considered the soundest and most progressive, the greatest authority on land and farming and finance. Adam was asked to sit on committees, to represent various bodies, to act as adviser on any number of local matters. And Eva, basking in Adam's reflection, found that her role—smart, attractive, *moderne*—was very much to her liking. Time and time again, at a dinner or party at the Kaldy manor house, she was aware that she, not Kati or Madame Kaldy, was the leader of their social set. And always it was she and Felix with their gay smart talk who made everything so successful, who kept the parties lively and fun.

In the winter it wasn't so good. With every year of her marriage she hated the winters more and more. Nearly all the entertaining people went back to the town. The manor house, which was the farthest away of all the dwellings, took longer to get to when the weather was bad and, in any case, Felix and his mother paid long visits to the town, sometimes taking Kati and sometimes not. She wondered—not very often, just occasionally—how Kati could bear the winter months up at the manor without company or parties and once or twice in a mood of high endeavour she had the coach brought round

(Adam still wouldn't buy a motorcar however much she asked) and made the cold winter journey to see her cousin. If Malie had become more mature since marriage, and Eva more vivacious and beautiful, Kati had become quieter and even more insignificant. She was never in the house when Eva called, even when the snow was thick and the mountain wind blew from the north. She was invariably to be found in the little summer-house at the end of the garden, wrapped in an old fur coat of her mother's, her hands so cold she could hardly hold her crayons and brushes. But her pinched face would leap into animation when she saw her cousin and Eva always left feeling gratified and extremely magnanimous.

But even with odd visits to the manor and little family parties where she could flirt with Felix, the winters were unbearable. She begged Adam finally to take an apartment in town, somewhere they could stay throughout the winter months.

"And who would look after the estate?"

Eva shrugged. "Why can't you do what everyone else does? Put a manager in. Or come back during the week and just stay whenever you can with me in town."

"I have explained to you, Eva," he said patiently, "that the reason our estate is so successful is because I do not leave it in the care of a manager."

"Then travel back and forth between town and here," she said petulantly.

"No." They were having dinner in the room that had, in Madame Kaldy's time, been dusty and unused. Now it was lavish and slightly vulgar in gold plush and with a modern serving-table and chairs.

"I think you are mean." She pouted prettily. "You know how I hate the winters here. I am a town girl. I'm not used to this primitive life."

"You should not have married a farmer, should you?" he asked quietly. "You can have whatever you like to make you happy here, Eva. You can furnish and entertain and rebuild to your heart's content. You can have as many servants from the estate as you need. But I am staying here. It is my home. And you are staying with me."

That was another surprising thing about Adam, surprising and disconcerting. She had thought when she married him that his adoration would cover any whim of hers, any behaviour however outrageous. And indeed he was indulgent in many matters. But there were times when no matter how she wheedled, cried, and pleaded, she could not get her own way. The visit to Malie in Budapest was such a case.

When she received the letter from her mama telling her of the wonderful idea, that she and Kati should go to Budapest, she couldn't wait to tell Adam.

"'How exciting, Adam! I am going to stay with Malie in Budapest!"

She should have recognized the stillness, the sudden tensing of his shoulders, but she didn't.

"Kati and I will go at the end of the month and stay until spring when we all come up to the country. Oh, Adam! I can't wait to stay in Budapest. It seems years since I was there!"

"You were there on your honeymoon," Adam said quietly. And then he turned, fastening his tie and fixing the studs in his cuffs. "I'm afraid, Eva, that you must decline your sister's invitation. I see no reason why you shouldn't go for a few days if you wish. But you are not staying away from me for three months."

She was amazed. Amazed, but not unduly perturbed. "But Malie is my *sister!*" she cried. "You let me visit Mama and Papa in town. Why won't you let me visit my sister?"

"You may visit her for a week. That is quite long enough."

"But it isn't long enough!" She was so cross she nearly stamped her foot. Then she remembered the way she used to handle Papa and she glided over to Adam and curled her head against his shoulder. "Please, Adam. I should so love to see my sister—and her babies too."

"You shall see them. For a week."

"But I stayed with Mama and Papa for a month last winter!"

"It was a mistake. Too long. You won't be away from me that long again."

"Why?" She was nearly crying with frustration.

"Because you are not old enough or responsible enough or sensible enough to be away for too long. And anyway, I need you here." He turned away to the mirror and began to brush his hair.

"But—you don't need me! I'll tell the servants how to look after you. They did it beautifully last winter. They'll cook for you just the same!"

Cool green eyes regarded her quizzically in the mirror. "I wasn't thinking of my food," he said dryly, and he grinned in such a common way that she flushed.

"You are so very vulgar," she said stiffly.

"Yes. But you are not going to Budapest for longer than a week."

"Then I shall not go at all!"

"As you wish."

"I think you are mean and selfish and—" Frustration proved too much and angry tears burst from her.

Adam patted her shoulder affectionately, dried her tears with his fingers, and said consolingly, "You'll feel better when you've cried, Eva. Then when you've finished we'll go and have our supper."

She screamed at him, hit him, cried again, allowed herself to be soothed, and later that night tried to bribe him with her body, all to no avail. And because she didn't wish to lose face with Mama, she had to write and say she couldn't bear to leave Adam for so long and would just spend a week in Budapest. Then she sulked and spoke only when necessary to Adam until the time came for her departure, trying to force him to relent. Her fury was increased because Adam didn't even appear to notice he was being punished.

Both girls were quiet when they arrived in Budapest. Kati seemed overawed and unable to believe that she was away from her husband and mother-in-law. But Eva—when she saw the way Amalia lived—was consumed with a bitter and corrosive envy.

Malie and David Klein had a nine-room apartment in the fashionable Fifth District, in Pannonia Street. Set round a courtyard of trees and flowers, with a red stone fountain playing in the centre, the whole block was elegant and expensive. So was Malie. Since her marriage they had only seen her up at the farm, and mostly she had been pregnant. Now, in her own setting, the new, luxurious, cosmopolitan setting her husband had provided, she suddenly seemed . . . what? Sophisticated? No, not that, but—grown up.

The apartment was so beautiful it made Eva hate her own country bungalow that she had spent so much money in refurnishing. Malie's apartment was filled with pictures and hanging carpets, with books, even a grand piano. And the people who came to the apartment were different from any Eva had ever met before: painters and writers, politicians, the editor of an intellectual left-wing newspaper, a psychiatrist, an English actor, a Polish pianist, all gathered together eating and drinking and talking, and in their midst Malie moved with friendly ease, warm, witty, gracious, as though she had known these people all her life.

The bitterness grew because she—the enchanting Eva Ferenc—didn't seem to be as popular with these smart city people as she was in her own provincial society. She looked beautiful, she knew that. Since marriage she had fined down, and the short skirts now worn revealed that Eva's legs were as well shaped as the rest of her. She even went out on the second day and had her hair bobbed, wanting to prove by such drastic action that she was still the more fashionable, the more lively, the more *moderne* of the Ferenc girls. And that evening as she walked into Malie's sitting-room, waiting for praise and compliments and admiration, she found nothing but politeness and the chance to sit and listen to more of David Klein's boring friends talking about the economic situation.

It was the same whomever she talked to. She, who knew so well how to flirt, how to make society conversation fascinating, how to tilt an ordinary commonplace remark into something amusing and vaguely naughty, found she didn't understand the way these people spoke. She became bored and irritable, and finally she ceased making an effort to join in the evening and went and sat beside Kati, whispering in her ear about clothes and Felix and what parties they would give this summer.

The whole week was like that, more and more disappointing, so disappointing she could have cried. Wherever they went—coffee at Gerbeaud, cocktails at the Bristol, tea on Margaret Island—it was the same. People, men and women, would rush over, kiss Malie's hand, and talk about dreary, uninteresting, boring things like picture exhibitions and articles in the press, things that were nothing to do with *people* at all.

Her depression and disgust grew with the realization that Kati—dull, dreary old Kati!—was enjoying it more than she was. Oh, she didn't talk or join in anything, but she listened. And when Eva tried to gain her attention at a luncheon because she was so bored, Kati hushed her because someone was talking. When, at the end of the week, Malie said how sad it was that Eva must go home she was unable to control her rancour.

"Heavens!" she said, laughing shrilly. "I'm glad it's Kati staying for three months and not me! Kati doesn't seem to be quite as bored as I am. Who would have expected Budapest to be boring!"

When she saw Malie's distressed expression she felt even worse.

"Oh, darling!" said Malie. "I did want you to enjoy it all! I felt so sorry you were only here for a week, that's why I arranged so many parties and invited all these people for you to meet. I know how much you love company and meeting people."

"It's been lovely seeing you and the boys, Malie," she replied feebly. "And David has been kind. It's just . . ."

It was all too much—the disappointment of the holiday, the fact that she had to return to the country in February, Malie's apparent happiness and contentment with her married life—it was too much and she burst into swift, heartbreaking sobs. Instantly Malie's arms were round her, all concern and anxiety. "Oh, darling! What is it? Are you unhappy? Don't you want to go home? Are you missing Adam? What is it, Eva?"

"It's nothing." She scrubbed a handkerchief over her face. "Just—oh, I don't mean to begrudge you anything, Malie. I'm sure you deserve it all, but you seem to have . . . to have everything!" She bowed her head and sobbed louder. "You have everything! And I have nothing!"

"Nothing?"

"Oh!" Eva waved a deprecating hand. "That horrible old farmhouse isn't anything like this, you know it isn't. And we began so differently, didn't we? You had a honeymoon in Vienna and Paris; I came to Budapest. And Adam won't buy a motorcar or a flat in the town for the winter! He's no fun, Malie. You remember how stodgy he always was; can you imagine how dreary it is living with him all the time? And Madame Kaldy doesn't like me. Every time I go and see Felix she's rude and unpleasant to me. I hate it there! If it wasn't for Felix—" She felt Malie's arm leave her shoulder and looked up to see that Malie was staring at her, an expression of disbelief on her face

"Oh, no, Eva, not after all these years! Married to Adam, and still you carry that absurd obsession for Felix in your heart. How can you? You see how unhappy he has made poor Kati, how he ignores her, and still you hanker for him."

"You don't understand," she mumbled. "He didn't want to

marry Kati. He told me so himself. It was because of the estate. If Papa had had the money he would have married me. I know he would."

"But he didn't marry you, Eva," Amalia said slowly. "He didn't ask you to marry him, and Adam did. You had a choice. No one forced you to marry Adam."

"It was the only way I could be with Felix!" she screamed. "Kati didn't count. He only wanted her money, and I had to be with him the only way I could!"

She was sobbing and crying so loudly she didn't hear the little moan that was almost a grunt from the other side of the room. But Malie heard and looked across. Kati, smiling painfully, apologetically, was standing inside the door. "I'm sorry," she stuttered. "I heard Eva crying and I wanted to do something. I shouldn't have come in. . . . I'm sorry. . . ."

Amalia's face was white and Eva felt a faint twinge of unease. Suddenly Malie looked like Papa in one of his rages.

"Of course you should have come in, Kati. When Eva makes enough noise to disturb the entire house, anyone has a right to come in."

"I didn't mean—" began Eva.

"Eva has been behaving very badly and feeling sorry for herself, Kati. That is why she spoke so unkindly about you. She didn't mean to be rude or vindictive, did you, Eva?"

Suddenly Eva was really afraid. Malie's usually gentle eyes were blazing and she was looking at Eva as though she hated her. Malie, her own sister, the one person in the world who loved her no matter what she said or did; now Malie had turned against her. Nobody understood. Nobody sympathized or wanted to help her.

"It's all right," said Kati, staring down at the carpet. " I understand. I understand about everything."

They were all quiet. Even Eva ceased to make a noise; she just sat on the edge of her bed picking at her handkerchief. The traffic outside seemed particularly loud, the noise of wheels sloshing through melted snow echoing in the ravine between the tall buildings.

"I'm sorry, Kati," Eva said finally.

"It's all right."

"I mean—I don't suppose it was true, the things I said."

"I don't mind."

"I—" She began to cry again, because she didn't like the feeling that Malie and Kati were cross with her. She relied on

Malie so much, and in a curious way Kati's adoration was also necessary. "I'm sorry to have been so horrible," she wept. "It's just—oh, Malie, you seem so *happy*. You have your two boys, and David *adores* you."

"I am sure Adam adores you," Malie replied, melting slightly.

"Yes. But I was married before you—and I have no children." Inspired, she turned to Kati, anxious to enlist Kati as an ally in any cause at all. "And we get so tired of Madame Kaldy being spiteful because she has no grandchildren, don't we, Kati? Really, Malie, you have no idea of her continual goading: 'Two daughters-in-law, neither of whom seem prepared to provide me with a grandchild'—that's all we hear, isn't it, Kati?"

Kati didn't answer, but the ruse had worked because Amalia could understand that Eva might be unhappy about not having any children.

"I'm sure you'll both have children soon," she comforted.

"I shan't."

They both turned to look at Kati. Her lumpy, plain face was expressionless.

"Of course you will, darling. One day—"

"It's impossible."

The traffic noise had ceased; a momentary lull of cars and carriages made the room silent again. This time the silence was ominous and neither Eva nor Amalia were able to move or say anything. Malie had a swift backward recollection of the three of them together in a bedroom once before, all looking in a mirror: Eva and Kati both in white dresses, one so lovely, the other so plain.

"Madame Kaldy blames me. She says I am infertile. And I cannot bring myself to tell her that there is no way of knowing if I am or am not."

"What do you mean?" breathed Eva.

Kati folded her arms round her thin rib cage, as though trying to protect herself from an unexpected blow.

"You know very well what I mean, Eva," she replied evenly. "You were quite right. They married me, Felix and his mother, for my money. Felix dislikes me so much he has never even kissed me in private. His kisses are reserved as necessary public formalities, on my feast day and at Christmas. At first I was puzzled, then hurt. I don't care any more. But I still don't want Madame Kaldy to know." Kati shuddered suddenly, looking small and afraid. "I would rather she thought me infertile than that—than that she should try to arrange that particular matter, the way she has arranged everything else."

She sat down on the bed beside Eva, looking drawn and yellow. The narrow short dress she wore didn't suit her any more than the old styles had done.

"So it is for you to provide the heir to the Kaldy wealth, Eva!" she said bitterly. "And I do not envy you when you have a son. She will requisition him, just as she has everything else."

They were shocked, not so much because of Kati's revelation as the fact that she had told them at all. Kati had always been a failure in whatever she did, but they had taken it for granted; even Kati had taken it for granted. Kati was silent, inconspicuous, and did not speak of her failures. And now Kati had not only announced that her marriage had never been consummated but had also told them her thoughts and wishes on the matter. They were both silent, not knowing what they could say to this new Kati who had developed a small skin of defiance.

"Kati, I—"

"You don't have to be sad, Malie. I'm very happy at the moment. I couldn't believe it when I first came here to stay with you. I was so happy I was frightened to believe it would work out right. Three months with you on my own, and then back to the country with you all for the summer! I was afraid to believe it. I kept thinking something would happen to make it go wrong. But I'm here, and I have all the spring and summer to look forward to. No Mama, no Madame Kaldy, no Felix. I'm free, aren't I?"

"As free as you like, darling. You can do just what you want!"

Kati smiled, nodded, and looked strangely composed—for Kati. "That's what I found hard to believe when I first came. But I believe it now."

Silence again. Finally Amalia went to the wardrobe, anxious to lighten the heavy atmosphere of the room. "Let me help Eva pack her things. Then we will ask David to take us out for our last evening. Would you like to dance, Eva? I believe there are some bars, rather daring places, where it is possible to dance."

"Oh, Malie! I would love that!" All traces of tears had vanished. The little faerie face, even more piquant beneath the short hair, was alive and flushed.

"Very well. I will ask David to arrange for some partners."

"What a wonderful last evening!" exclaimed Eva. She felt happy, excited, and not altogether sad about going home on the following day. Kati's revelation—now that she was thinking about it—made her heart pound a little. He had been true to her! He loved her, desired her so much that he had been unable to bring himself to embrace Kati even once, even when his mother, the old witch, wanted an heir. The suspense, the anticipation that preceded dances and balls in the old days, was back in her heart and she began to look forward to going home to the country—where Felix was.

The summer that followed was a strange one. An atmosphere that was almost unreal pervaded each and every one of them, even the older generation. The pace was quicker, the laughter shriller, and the cars that traversed the routes between farmhouses, manor, and villa went faster and more furiously. Afterwards Malie often thought about the summer of 1925. It was as though some enormous event lay ahead so that, like birds before an earthquake, they were all behaving in an unnatural manner. What the something was she couldn't say—something wonderful, awful, stupendous, dreadful; it was impossible to tell. But afterwards she reflected that it *should* have been like that in 1914; they should have felt that sense of impending events then instead of dancing through the pre-war summer as though the world was going to last forever.

It would have been easy to attribute the changing atmosphere solely to Eva. Certainly she was different that summer, wilder, gayer, slightly hysterical. Her short hair style was only the first of many changes. She began to use eye make-up, then lipstick, and her dresses became shorter, flimsier, more daring. She lost weight too, and now she looked like some mythical wood sprite, a beautiful but insane creature from an old forest legend. Even Mama, that indulgent good-natured hedonist, was troubled and spoke tentatively to Eva about her latest dress, an affair of silver transparent gauze that showed her knees at the hem and was cut nearly to the waist at the neckline. Every time Eva moved it clung and rippled over her body, revealing the fact that she was wearing very little underneath. Mama, vivacious and clothes-loving, was perturbed by her near-naked daughter.

"Eva, my darling," she faltered one day when Eva had called to collect her for a summer evening party at the Kaldy manor. "That dress. Is it—is that what the fashion says must be worn now? It seems so . . . so vulgar."

Eva slid her naked arms down the side of the dress. The armholes were cut so low it was possible to see her rib cage as she moved. "Of course it is fashionable, Mama," she snapped. "Would I wear it if it wasn't?"

"But . . . it just doesn't seem suitable for a simple summer party among friends. And why—" Mama stammered, uncertain of herself. "Why does Amalia not wear such a dress? Amalia lives in Budapest and goes to Vienna and Paris once a year. Why does she not dress in the latest fashion?"

"Because she is dowdy and because she has an old husband!" snapped Eva. "What point is there in comparing me with Malie? She has surrendered her life to dreariness. You forget, Mama, I have visited Malie in Budapest. Her friends are all insufferably dull, the friends you would expect David Klein to have. And what does she do all day? She talks to the boring friends and looks after her boring children."

"Eva!"

"They are boring," said Eva defiantly. "All children are! That is why Malie dresses like an old woman. You might as well compare me with Kati."

Mama looked unhappy but said no more. She was sensitive enough—even Marta Bogozy was sensitive enough—to be aware of the disapproval of Madame Kaldy and Aunt Gizi. Eva, darting through the crowd in her silver dress, was like a provocative tropical bird, or a piece of white fire that would soon burn itself out.

In the old days they would all have expressed displeasure and Eva would have felt reproved. But she was a married woman now and she anticipated any disapproval by calling across to Felix as soon as she entered the room, "Felix, my darling! I hope you too are not going to reprimand me about my dress! Mama has scolded me, and just look at Aunt Gizi and your mama. I can tell that no one approves of my delightful, delightful gown!" She pirouetted and pulled a streamer of silver gauze over the lower part of her face, clowning, sensual, bizarre. Felix adored the whole performance.

"Where is Adam? Where is my son?" barked Madame Kaldy, and Eva barely bothered to turn when she answered. "Oh, cows . . . or sheep . . . or something." She shrugged. "He hates parties anyway, you know that."

"Well, I *love* parties," declared Felix enthusiastically. "And

I love the dress. How daring! No one, but no one, has worn a dress like that yet, I am quite sure. And the material! Eva, my darling! When did you buy it?"

They were away, the pair of them, chattering and exquisite, a pair of sharp-set magpies darting through the room, and everyone was silent and bothered without knowing why.

But although it would have been easy to blame Eva for the unnatural atmosphere of the summer, it wasn't just Eva. Everyone was different.

Aunt Gizi didn't talk very much, unlike Gizi; she spent a lot of time staring into the middle distance and staring also at Kati. She sat down a lot, ate little, and as the summer progressed she became thinner. It was all the more noticeable because Uncle Alfred had become fatter and noisier. When his attention was drawn to the fact that his wife didn't look very well, he was full of loud solicitude. He was insistent about her resting and could be heard whispering noisily about "women's difficulties." The old Gizi would have silenced him with a waspish comment, but now she seemed glad of the excuse to rest away from the others. She said she wasn't really ill, just suffering from digestive troubles. She sucked a lot of carbon tablets and no one bothered too much because obviously Aunt Gizi wouldn't allow herself to be seriously ill. Nonetheless, the lack of scolding, the subduing of her sharp tongue, added to the general strangeness of the summer.

In June a ghost arrived to see Malie, a Polish ghost, unbelievably handsome and carrying in his hand a bundle of letters nearly ten years old. It was Count Stefan Tilsky, ex-hussar officer from the old Imperial army, friend and comrade of the lover she had nearly but not quite forgotten. He drove, in a black shiny car, up to the farmhouse one hot afternoon, bent over her hand—the old manners of the Empire were still there—and smiled, a deep, warm smile that held sympathy but also curiosity in its depths.

"Amalia—Mrs. Klein now, I believe?—how strange. I have not seen you for eleven years. You will forgive me for coming unannounced."

"I am happy to see you." She spoke the formal words, but she wasn't happy at all. Stefan Tilsky brought back memories: balls at the garrison; the first csardas, when the men picked the girls they wanted instead of the ones they had to pick; picnics with Karoly; the war.

"I meant to come before to see you, to talk to you—that is

if you wished to talk—and to give you back your letters. But I have not been able to visit Hungary or see my old friends and comrades until now. We have had a little war of our own." He smiled a trifle. "You may have heard?"

"I am happy for you, Stefan. We thought of you many times. We thought of all our old Polish friends while you were fighting Russia. And we were happy that you became your own country again. You—I suppose you have your land restored?"

He nodded and smiled again. She had forgotten just how handsome Stefan had been. Now, in his middle thirties, he was even more attractive. His body had filled out—wide shoulders, strong legs—and his face had the interesting marks of a man who has discovered how to live with himself.

"After the Germans and the Russians there was little land left, Amalia. It took time to rebuild and somehow, because one was never sure of what would happen next, it seemed unwise to go visiting. But I always intended to come back. My friends, the few left after the war, were here." His brown eyes twinkled and mocked himself. "My youth was here."

"Are you married?"

He shrugged, raised an eyebrow, and smiled. "A little. You too, of course. I hear that you are both married, the enchanting Ferenc girls. How long ago it seems!"

It was long ago, and she didn't wish to be reminded. That girl was dead, the girl who had waded barefoot in a stream with a young man, who had kissed him at a crowded railway-station in 1914. That girl was dead.

They were both silent, staring out from the veranda into the gentle trees of the acacia woods. She was startled to feel her hand taken.

"Amalia. I took your letters from Karoly's body. After he was killed I went back. I wanted to be sure—anyway, I took the letters. I thought you would prefer that no one else read them."

He had been carrying a smooth leather briefcase, and now he opened it and took a bundle of shabby envelopes, meaningless paper, from the case. "At first I thought I should send them, then somehow it was too soon after the war and I was afraid of disturbing you. But last year I heard that you were married, with children, and were happy and settled, so I thought now would be the time to return the letters."

"Thank you."

He placed them in her lap, crumpled fragments of tragedy. Karoly, that brave, first, yearning love. She had defied Papa, lived in hope for three years, survived his death, and married someone else. Where had that girl gone? Where had Karoly gone?

Stefan pressed her hand and she looked up, surprised to see that his eyes were moist. The emotional Poles, she thought disparagingly to herself, and wished he had not come, bringing pain with him.

"You are very lovely, Amalia. You are more beautiful than you were as a girl."

She shrugged. "I am an old married lady now—nearly thirty, Stefan—with two sons."

"Their names?"

She hesitated, swallowed. "Jacob . . . and Karoly. The elder is Karoly."

How to explain, how to account for the curious scene by her bedside when her first son had been born? Her husband in his shirt sleeves, ruffled, unlike himself and with a thin film of sweat across his forehead, kneeling by her bed with his arms stretched round her shoulders, watching her face, searching for something.

"We have a son, Amalia. A strong boy, a strong dark boy like his father."

She was tired, pleasantly tired, relieved that the ordeal was over and that she had done her duty according to the unwritten marriage contract between them. She had smiled at him, patted his cheek, wished he would go away so that she could sleep.

"Would you like to name him, Amalia?"

"I thought we had decided," she had murmured sleepily. "Jacob if a boy, Julie if a girl. We will call him Jacob, after your father."

"Would you like to call him Karoly?" It had jarred, hurt and disturbed her, and her face had twisted into a frown, a small moan of denial issuing from her lips. But the pain had disappeared almost immediately. She had felt her husband's arms tighten around her. "Karoly, yes?" And she had nodded, not understanding but content that he would not let the memory hurt her. It had been as inexplicable as many of the things he did; her wedding present had been the deeds of the farm, purchased in a private transaction from her father and handed to her as a security for all of them for all time.

Stefan Tilsky stared curiously at her, a beautiful Polish

aristocrat, so handsome, so warm and charming it would have been easy to tell him everything, if only she had understood it herself.

"Ah, yes," he said softly, "Jacob . . . and Karoly. You married well, I hear, Amalia? Mr. Klein is a banker. Jewish. The very best bankers . . ."

It was said pleasantly, flatteringly. There was no reason why she should have felt annoyed, defensive even. He was disturbing, Stefan Tilsky; she wished he had never come.

"Your sister, the ravishing Eva. She married one of the Kaldy boys?"

"Adam."

"Ah, yes."

A noise behind her, a hand on her shoulder, a firm comforting hand that made the tension evaporate from her body. "This is my husband," she said, leaning back into the hand. "David, this is Count Tilsky, an old friend from before the war."

The usual noises of introduction, friendliness, polite inquiry. She noticed but did not comment when David reached down and took the letters from her lap. "I will take them to your bedroom," he murmured. "And then we must arrange a little party for your friend, Amalia. He must meet all the old ones from the war. He must stay with us for a day or two."

Polite negations, remonstrances, protests, and a reluctant acceptance. And then she was a wife again, organizing bedrooms, dinners, sending messages to the others to come and meet Stefan. The girl of several summers ago, the ghost who flitted by her side, was under control, still there but not too disturbing, a strange elusive creature who seemed just another part of the fantasy summer.

Stefan made the summer strange too. He was dazzled by Eva—dazzled, but in a different way from Felix. He stared at her a lot, he listened to her a great deal, and he smiled frequently, a smile directed at Eva and no one else. Eva teased and encouraged but it was no more than a game to her. Amalia wasn't sure just how much of a game it was to Stefan.

At the Kaldy manor she watched the two men, Felix and Stefan Tilsky, playfully arguing about who should fetch Eva an ice, and it struck her that though the two men were much of an age, Felix was somehow unformed, innocuous, beside the handsome Pole. Even though the gentle feuding was in fun there was an undercurrent between them that had nothing to do with getting Eva a strawberry ice. Eva, stretched out on a wicker chair, laughed and applauded their antics, but there was a wildness about her, a near hysteria that lent unhappy tension to the hot afternoon.

Amalia looked across to Kati to see how the "game" was affecting her. Kati was seated beside Madame Kaldy, ready to take and pass the teacups as Madame Kaldy filled them. No one, not even Kati's mother, thought it strange any more that Kati should not preside over her own teapot—or kitchen, or table, or household. Now, with quiet composure, she passed cups and honey cakes, smiling only at Malie. Kati had changed slightly since spending the early part of the year in Budapest. The change was so imperceptible that no one except Malie had noticed it. She was still quiet, obedient, inoffensive, but the quietness was no longer the result of nervousness. Kati had simply withdrawn into a world where she could not be hurt. When she had finished helping her mother-in-law she came over to Malie. "Come to the summer-house, Malie. I want to show you what I've been doing since I returned from Budapest."

The two cousins set off up the long sloping lawn. They crossed a stone bridge set over a sunken shrubbery (Madame Kaldy always maintained that the shrubbery was the remains of a moat that had once surrounded the manor) and then followed a flag path through the herbaceous garden.

"No one ever comes to the summer-house unless it is a servant sent to fetch me."

They came out to another grassy slope that led to a knoll where the summer-house, a hexagonal structure of wood and plaster, had been built.

"I hope you will like it," said Kati softly. "No one else has seen it."

She led the way to the little house and opened the door. She looked over her shoulder at Amalia and smiled. Her plain, lumpy face was placid and content. Malie had never seen her cousin look so sure of herself.

"Come in."

The summer-house had two windows, gothic in shape, and a small circle of glass set into the roof. When Malie had called there on previous summers there had been a table on which rested Kati's paints and sketch-books, and a small easel to take Kati's little flower pictures.

The easel had gone. The table was still there but it was difficult to see because Kati had painted it—painted an intricate web of brilliant vines and leaves up and over the legs of the table and covered the top surface with vivid flowers and ferns and creepers. And the table was the least part of the summer-house's transformation.

"Why, Kati!"

They had all accepted Kati's one little talent, her small, tight gift for painting flowers: a single rose, a bunch of violets resting on a piece of silk—delicate colours, timid sizes, pretty but unremarkable.

"Oh, Kati!"

The six walls and the ceiling of the summer-house were smothered in creepers, birds, exotic flowers, flowers completely different from anything Kati had painted before. Hibiscus and sunflower, peony, poppy, orchid and morning glory rioted over the walls, curled up round the windows and to the edges of the glass room. A few tendrils of vine even curled onto the glass itself. Laws of nature, of colour and proportions, had been ignored. Velvet-skinned plums fell from the stems of hibiscus; apples grew from the same stalks as orchids. A gigantic poppy dropped petals onto a flight of minute brilliant blue birds. Everything was colour—green, red, yellow, purple; no part of the original wall showed through at all.

"Do you like it?"

She stood in the middle of her creation, her brilliant, breathtaking creation, and just for a second the old Kati was visible, unsure of herself, vulnerable to hurt.

Amalia felt as though the breath had been knocked from her lungs. Frightened of destroying Kati's confidence, she said, "It—it's incredible. I can hardly believe it!"

"But do you like it?"

"I don't know, Kati. It's beautiful. But it is so . . . different, so unlike you."

"You think it beautiful, though?"

"Yes. Beautiful, and exotic, and . . . a little frightening."

The answer seemed to please her.

"I worked with oils for this, Malie. I hate my water-colours now. I'm never going to use water-colour or pastel or crayon ever again. If I hadn't come to Budapest I would never have done this. It was that man, the artist, he talked to me about painting—oh, not how to do it, the art master taught us that, but the *feeling* it should give you. And the fact that you

315

should try to do *more* than you think you can. I showed him my flowers, Malie, and do you know what he did? He tore them up. Just ripped them out of my book and tore them in half."

Amalia stared speechless at her cousin. Kati's face was animated and flushed, her hitherto colourless eyes were bright, her small, shapeless body taut and alive.

"I was so upset. You remember the day I would not come to Margaret Island with you? It was the day after he tore them up, and I was so upset I didn't want to go anywhere. And while you were out he came round again. Remember he was there when you came back? And he said that he had torn them up because anyone who *could* paint, even a little bit, should try to do better than that. And then he invited me to his studio—you remember we all went, David too—and he showed me his work. Some of it was bad, Malie, and I told him so. The first time in my life that I told someone what I thought of them. And he didn't mind. He showed me how to *try*. Try to do something really hard, he said; some of it will be bad, but some of it will be wonderful. He made me promise to paint something different—not different but more *honest*. Oh, Malie, I do wish he could come and see this and tell me what he thinks. Will you speak to him when you go back to Budapest? Will you tell him what I've been doing?"

Malie stared at Kati, stunned and confused. She had no idea which, of the many artists who visited them, had been responsible for Kati's metamorphosis. The flood of words, the assumption that Malie knew of her friendship with the artist, was all so out of character for her faded, nondescript little cousin. And anxious not to destroy this new Kati, this positive and involved Kati, she was frightened to say anything at all.

"I would really like your husband to see what I've painted." Kati looked nervous again: shy, afraid, ashamed. "There's only you and he who would be interested, who know about painting and who—who wouldn't think of me as just Kati—who would look at my paintings and think about them instead of me."

Kati's loneliness suddenly overwhelmed Malie. In a community of friends and relatives there was no one at all to whom she could talk about the most important discovery of her life.

"Would he come, Malie?" she asked timidly. "If you asked him, would he come?"

"Darling, he would love to see them. I'll fetch him now."

"Don't let the others know," said Kati, alarmed. "I don't want the others to see."

There was no one she trusted enough to let them see her exposed, undressed, all her hidden nakedness on view before the disinterested and the disdainful.

"I'll be careful."

She left the summer-house and began to walk back towards the lawns, glad of a period alone. She was aware that she, Kati's "dearest friend," had failed her cousin too. Kati had stayed in her home for three months, and during that time she hadn't been at all aware of Kati's interest, or distress, or excitement. She didn't even know the name of the artist who had made such an impression, even though he apparently visited their home quite frequently and had invited them to his studio. She hastily ran through the names of the artists in their circle. It could have been any of them.

Walking back with David she tried to explain what had happened, to warn him not to say anything that would hurt Kati, and to try and remember the name of the artist. David raised one dark, humorous eyebrow.

"I don't have to remember. It was Dominic."

She paused, then continued towards the summer-house. "How can you be so sure?"

Her husband shrugged. "They spent much time talking together, and your cousin ceased to be afraid when she was with him. And they were always showing each other books. He gave her a small canvas of his before she left."

"She didn't tell me any of this."

"No. Well, I think she believed that you knew."

He wasn't surprised inside the summer-house either. He examined, nodded, examined again, stood back by the door, and stared at the ceiling. "Good, Kati," he said finally. "Very good. You have avoided the pitfall of many new artists; you have not abandoned your technical knowledge to create a new medium. It has all the perfection and detail of your old work —see, Amalia, how finely the stamens are drawn?—and the courage of a new venture."

Kati was unrecognizable. Her face was engrossed, intent, almost beautiful because for the first time in her life it was alive.

"Of course"—David held up a reproving finger—"you have been blessed with an excellent canvas: no limitations on size, and this interesting six-sided room. Now, my little Kati, what are you going to do when you have to work on board and canvas like your good friend Dominic?"

"I'm not sure *what* to do next," said Kati happily. "I had an idea for painting on linen—making tapestries that would fold and hang, not oils, of course. I would have to experiment with dyes, I suppose. . . ." Her voice and face faded back into the old Kati. "It might be difficult to do that here," she whispered.

"Walk before you run, my Kati! I think you now try to discipline yourself. Do some canvases, not too small but not too big either. When you come up to Budapest next you can bring them with you and—well, we shall see."

Malie watched them, listened to them talking of textures and colour and form. She had loved Kati and had tried to be kind to her, but she had never managed to bring her to the normal exchanges of human contact. She had never brought Kati to life the way David was doing now. I have never treated Kati as an adult, she thought suddenly. I have always treated her as a child, an unfortunate, under-privileged child. David—and Dominic too, I suppose—have accorded her the respect due another adult. They have praised, criticized, and been honest with her.

They finally went back, all three of them, to the lawns in front of the house. Felix and Stefan Tilsky were still paying court to Eva, who was squealing with laughter under the jaundiced eyes of her mother-in-law and her aunt. Kati retreated behind a blank face and a blank silence, and David went to flirt a little with Mama, who had been sitting rather disconsolately away from the others. Malie stared round, sensing tensions, knowing secrets, and wondered again why this particular summer was not the same as all the others.

In July Papa and the boys came up. Papa was taking a month's vacation from the bank, and the boys had finished at school. Jozsef was preparing for his last year before going to Berlin University. He was seventeen, tall, and rather like Papa to look at, although he was softer and less energetic than Papa. He was supposed to be working for his *Abiturium* but had not received a very good report, and Papa was a little cross, believing that his elder son would have done better if only he had tried. There had been some considerable discussion about the choice of university. It was thought that the *numerus clausus* which restricted the number of Jewish stu-

318

dents entering Hungarian universities would not apply to Jozsef (he was, after all, only Jewish in origin and not registered as a Jew), but nonetheless it was decided not to risk the possibility of refusal. Anti-Semitic organizations abounded, and one was never sure when they might decide to "make a case" of some obscure Jewish question. Jozsef should go to study economics in Berlin, where the *numerus clausus* did not apply.

Jozsef behaved reasonably well when Papa was about. Papa had made it quite plain that he disapproved of Jozsef's idleness in the matter of examinations. There were a great many avowals that he was going to do better this last year before going to university and, when Papa was around, Jozsef was often to be seen sitting on the veranda frowning over a book. He was hoping for a generous allowance once he got to Berlin. When Papa was not around Jozsef spent a lot of time lying underneath David Klein's car peering up, or standing over the engine peering down.

Leo, at fifteen, had become incredibly tall and incredibly thin. The chubby little boy of infancy had entirely vanished into a willowy and rather frail-looking youth. He had shown an aptitude for languages but had missed his winter term at school and now was worried about catching up. Just after Christmas he had been ill: a cough, a temperature, pains in his chest. He had recovered but was left with the cough and a feeling of constant lassitude, and finally the doctor had recommended that he go into the mountains or the country for a couple of months.

He had been dispatched immediately to Eva and Adam and had spent the rest of the winter staying at their farm. A tutor in French and English had been employed to spend time conversing with him, but when he went back to school he was three months behind with his work. Now he lay awake at night worrying about his studies. He spent the daytime alternately dreaming and studying, and as the days grew hotter and the air balmier, he dreamed more and studied less and then spent the night worrying again. He had decided that he was a failure, both mentally and physically. His body couldn't stand a normal bout of influenza, and his brain was unable to come to a decision about work and then persevere with it. He realized he would fail in practically everything he did and, in addition, he had spots.

He was too old to seek comfort from Malie, but nonetheless he felt happy when they were all together, the whole family, gossiping and drinking lemonade beneath the acacia trees. He felt safe but found he was unable to talk to any of them in case they realized what a disgusting mess he had made of his life. So he would listen, and roll and wrestle with little Karoly and Jacob on the ground, and feel miserable and happy all at the same time. That summer was a strange and disturbed one for him too. And it became even more disturbed.

He had driven Malie and the little boys over to Adam's farm in the trap. There had been no special invitation, but one of Adam's cows had just calved and they had suddenly decided that young Karoly should see the calf. They arrived in the morning, were taken by Adam to see the calf, and then sat on the veranda trying to decide whether to have a picnic or eat at home. Just below the veranda Eva had slung a hammock between two smallish trees, and she swayed to and fro, waving flies away with her handkerchief and saying that it was really too hot to go anywhere.

Leo, staring out at the distant fields, saw a ball of dust moving slowly towards the house. Idly he watched it grow bigger, then turn into two dust balls; a woman and a boy emerged. Suddenly, his body tense, he sat upright on his chair.

"Someone coming." Eva yawned and then she too sat up, nearly tilting herself out of the hammock. "How extraordinary! Why has the woman come here?"

At the far end of the concrete path a peasant woman waited, by her side a boy, thin but fairly neatly dressed. Leo knew at once who the boy was.

They continued to wait, humbly knowing that it was not their place to cross the boundary that separated the farm from Mr. Adam's home. Eva finally beckoned them forward. The woman hesitated, put her face forward and covered it with her hand, then shuffled up to stand a few feet away from the veranda.

"What do you want?"

"His excellency—if I could speak to your noble husband, madame? I am Edina, wife of Marton who works on your husband's land. Before my marriage I was sewing girl here, in this house." She paused. Her nervousness was still apparent, but the mention of being sewing girl seemed to give her a little confidence. "I beg forgiveness, madame. If I could just speak to his excellency?"

"Why do you not go to the yard with your husband? You know when it is possible to see the master."

The woman stared at the ground. "My husband would beat me if he knew I wanted to speak to his excellency. It—it is private, madame. It is private from my husband."

No one knew what to say or do. Never before had a peasant come to any of their houses begging requests for private audiences with their masters. It was unnerving and made them all feel uneasy. Through Eva's mind flashed the absurd notion that Adam had been messing about with this woman. The thought made her giggle as soon as it came into her head; the woman was thin, old and unattractive. Brilliant blue eyes shone out of a face lined with work and leathered with too much sun and wind. The child also had blue eyes.

"Do you want your sewing job again?"

The woman raised her head, a spasm of hope crossed her features. "No, Madame Kaldy. I know you have a girl, a young girl. If you needed extra help I would work for you." She bit her lip and looked down at the ground again. "I would like to speak to his excellency."

Eva, puzzled, interested, turned swiftly to Leo.

"Go and fetch him, Leo. He's still with the calf, I expect."

He stood up and tried to move quickly down the steps, but his ungainly legs got tangled in the chair and he stumbled and arrived at the bottom awkwardly. The boy was staring at him and he wanted to get away from the watching blue eyes. He hurried round the house to the farm buildings, already trying to decide whether he would return with Adam or whether he would stay out of sight until Janos Marton and his mother had retreated.

During the winter months he had spent with Eva and Adam, he had seen the child twice. Every morning Adam had to fetch the post from the village and, once Leo had recovered a little, he had taken this task upon himself. Riding on one of the farm horses across the morning snow had become one of his greatest pleasures. He looked forward to it from his first waking moment: the crisp snow, the clean morning air with his breath blowing out in a cloud before him, above all the solitude, the delicious pure solitude when he was no longer aware of comparisons with other boys and his spots were temporarily forgotten.

When the weather was bad the farm children didn't go to school. It was three miles to the village, only a few of them had boots, and those who did were usually told not to waste them on travelling to school. But one morning—going to fetch the post earlier than usual—he had overtaken a figure trudging through the snow. As he grew near he saw that the boy had no boots, just pieces of old grain sack wrapped round his feet. He reined in his horse and was confronted by the blue eyes he remembered from Kati's wedding.

When he had stopped he had fully intended to offer the child a ride to the village school, but faced with that thin, passionate body, and with the confused memories—Uncle Sandor and the killer lying drunk on the ground, the boy defending the killer, sobbing, his feet, always the wretched child's feet, covered in scabs and sores—his words had died in his throat. The boy stared at him—how could a child hate anyone that much?—and finally, too embarrassed to put his offer into words, he had ridden on, the morning ride spoilt by his own guilty conscience.

A week later he had seen the boy again, but this time he was being carried on his mother's back. His feet were still wrapped but there had been thick falls of snow in the night, too thick even for several layers of grain sack. He hesitated, wanting to help, hating to see the woman trudging three miles carrying her son. Without waiting to think what he would say, he galloped up to them. "I'll take the child to school," he shouted, but he saw that he had frightened them both. Perhaps the child didn't hate him; perhaps it was fear? She had shrunk away, and he had a swift image of how it would look in her eyes—her son riding on the young master's horse, accepting favours from one of the people who should be feared and respected. She shook her head violently, and the motion was reflected in the young face that looked over her shoulder. He had ridden away and after that he took the longer route to the village, a route which was never used by anyone in the winter.

He told Adam that the woman was here to see him, then reluctantly stayed with him, impelled by curiosity and a kind of misery. When they arrived at the front of the house the woman was sitting on the bottom step talking to Amalia about little Jacob. She seemed easier talking to another woman about her baby, and Leo guessed at once that Malie had told the woman to sit and had found a subject that would put her at ease.

"Mrs. Marton?"

She rose instantly.

"Why do you want to see me?"

Misery crumpled her face as she stared at Eva, Amalia, Leo, and the baby boys. Malie stood up and handed Jacob to

322

Eva. "Time to make the little ones rest, Eva. Come now, you can help me find a place inside that will comfort them." She herded them indoors, as though it were her house, not Eva's, and silenced them both when they began to speculate on the extraordinary behaviour of Mrs. Marton.

"You will know soon enough. And in the meantime remember that everything we say can be heard outside."

They fidgeted and peered between the shutters. Adam was reading something given to him by Mrs. Marton. She was talking, explaining and drawing her son forward to face Adam. When she and the boy finally left, Adam was still holding the piece of paper in his hand.

"I cannot believe it," he murmured, after they had hurried out to join him. "She has asked me to speak to the director of the school in town. She wants him to allocate a free place to her son!"

They were all so shocked they couldn't speak. Then Eva began to laugh.

"She brought letters for me to see, one from the priest, another from Feher in the village."

"Why didn't she ask them to find a place?" giggled Eva.

Adam stared at her. "She did. Feher, of course, has no influence at all. The priest told her to take the boy to the Catholic *Gymnasium*. She did, but they wouldn't give him a place."

"Of course not!" snapped Eva. "How can a peasant's child go to secondary school? It is unheard of."

"No, Eva. Remember the child on Grandfather Bogozy's estate? The priest found a place for him."

Eva shrugged. "Oh, him! Everyone knew it was because Grandfather Bogozy was his father. He looked so like Grandfather it was embarrassing. They were all pleased when the child went away."

"It was her courage," Adam said slowly. "She was so frightened. She was terrified that I might dismiss her husband because of her request. She was shaking and said he would beat her if he knew—and how will he not know when the servants here begin to talk?"

"I just can't believe it! Where did she get the idea that her son should go to secondary school?"

Adam held the letters out. "Feher says the child is outstanding considering the limitations of his background. Apparently he excels at almost every subject and is brilliant at mathematics. The priest is even more impressed."

"What did you tell her?"

"That I would consider the matter."

"You must be mad! What will happen if you find a place for this child? Every peasant on the estate will come shuffling up here asking for favours. They will all expect their children to go to secondary school!"

"No." Adam's gaze wandered out over the land, the lush, well-cultivated land, the harvest just about to be brought in, the trees heavy with fruit, the maize stalks standing high and green. "No. This child will be different. This child is the grandson of old Marton. He was with me in '14; he stayed to help the retreat over the San; he died there. I shall let it be known that any privileges reaped by this child are the result of his grandfather's loyalty and courage."

Eva frowned. She was always uneasy on the rare occasions when Adam mentioned the war. It was bound up with a memory she had pushed to the back of her mind, a memory of Felix, mad and dishevelled, confiding his miseries of Serbia to her. She tried never to think of those revelations, and neither did she want to hear of Adam's war.

"Oh, well." She shrugged, apparently losing interest. "As you please. I suppose it might be quite interesting to see what happens."

Leo remained silent. What would he do if by some horrible freak Janos Marton was sent to his school? There were free places at his school, usually filled by sons of smallholders who were little better off than the farm peasants. The free boys were alien, despised creatures; they spoke differently, dressed differently, and were alternately obsequious and belligerent. How could he cope if Janos Marton was in the bottom class of his own school? The burden of yet another worry pressed down on him and he wanted to cry. As he went into the house for lunch he felt another spot breaking out on the back of his neck.

21

All summer she was aware of something happening between Felix and herself. The heat emphasized it. In sleeveless, low-necked dresses, with bare legs turning brown in the sun, she was conscious not only of her own body but also of Felix's. They seemed to collide much more than usual when they were playing tennis, to hold each other a little too long, a little too close when dancing; their kisses of greeting and farewell were quick but intense. Sometimes, after an evening when the danger—delicious danger too heady to avoid—threatened to explode betweeen them, she would go to bed with her body so tense she was unable to sleep. Lying beside Adam she would dig her fingers into her own flesh, wanting to scream with frustration but afraid to move in case she roused Adam. The work on the farm during the summer was so hard that he usually slept without being aware of her tension, but when he did wake she couldn't bear it. Invariably he would reach out for her, his square hands and body claiming her patiently but doggedly. And with the memory of Felix's slim, smooth, sensitive hands still with her, it was as much as she could do not to shudder and push him away.

Before this summer she wouldn't have hesitated to have pushed him away, but now she dare not, for Adam appeared to be completely oblivious of what was happening between her and Felix and she wanted to do nothing that would alter that condition. He watched them laughing and flirting together and dismissed it as boring nonsense, just the way he had always done. But it wasn't that way any more. Night after night she thought of Felix, lying in his own room, untouched and untouching. When Adam demanded her body she felt disloyal to Felix. If he had managed to remain faithful to her, why couldn't she do the same? But acquiescence to Adam was the price she must pay if he was to remain ignorant.

Madame Kaldy was not ignorant. She missed nothing. Her sharp eyes watched them, followed them, saw every touch and look between them. The whole of that long summer she made sure they were never alone together, not even for one moment.

When Stefan Tilsky came the tension grew worse. She cared nothing for Stefan, but the admiration in his eyes seemed to raise to burning point her hunger for Felix. During one incredibly hot afternoon, when they were pushing her back and forth on the swing, she forgot which man was which. There were just two male bodies, dark, scented slightly with sweat, and they ceased to be two bodies and became one. She was thrown from one part of this masculine hydra to another and she felt moisture breaking out on her own body, running between her breasts and collecting in a damp strip round her waist. She had a thick red mark on her stomach when she undressed that night.

No one else really existed that summer. She was vaguely aware of Papa, Leo, and Jozsef coming up, but they were all dim, shadowy figures, part of the great dangerous audience before whom the game of hide-and-seek had to be played. The only ones who existed were herself, Felix, Stefan Tilsky, and the dark destructive eyes of her mother-in-law.

Towards the end of the summer Adam suddenly emerged from his work preoccupation and announced that he was going to the autumn agricultural fair in Budapest to buy a tractor. Papa, David Klein, Uncle Alfred, even Felix were all fascinated by the thought of the tractor, but all she could think of was that Adam would be gone and she would be alone—apart from Madame Kaldy and Kati—with Felix. Almost at once began a sparring game between Eva and her mother-in-law.

"Felix must go too," said Madame Kaldy curtly. "He is the head of this estate, and if we are to invest in machinery he must share in the knowledge and the responsibility. Felix and Adam will go together."

And so that night she was all smiles and passionate acquiescence to Adam and the next day was able to report that she too would be going to Budapest with her husband and brother-in-law.

Madame Kaldy's eyes narrowed; then she smiled. "A splendid idea, Eva. A little second honeymoon for my two sons.

"Can we stay at the Bristol?" asked Eva quickly, already thinking how easy it would be to make individual plans in a Kati shall go too. The four of you will be able to go everywhere together."

large hotel, but Amalia—for God's sake why did Malie always have to be so *kind!*—forestalled her.

"You can have our apartment. There's plenty of room and the servants will look after you exactly as you wish. We shall be in Vienna until the middle of November."

"Thank you," said Eva bleakly. She and Felix wouldn't have a single chance to be alone together, not even to slip outside and meet in a restaurant for cocktails or coffee. A hotel was impersonal; you could get lost in lounges and dining-rooms and even in corridors travelling from one room to another. In David and Malie's flat they would be within constant communication, and Malie's wretched cook and maid would be there all the time, just waiting to gossip.

They packed, the four of them, all pretending that it was going to be great fun—theatres, dancing, the fair—but all she could think of was how hateful it was going to be, sleeping with Adam every night and knowing that Felix was only a few yards away from her.

On the morning of their departure, Aunt Gizi stepped out of bed and collapsed into an insensible heap on the floor. Uncle Alfred arrived at the Kaldy manor just as Felix and Kati were stepping into their motor.

"Kati!" he shouted in terror. "You must come immediately. Your mama is terribly ill. Oh, what are we going to do? What are we going to do?"

His face had turned into a shapeless red blob. He was soggy and frightened. On the way home he recounted seven times how he had heard a thump and gone in to see his wife on the floor. He burst into tears, asking God what he would do if Gizi was taken from him, and finally he turned in fury on Kati because she had not spoken a word. Why was she not crying like a loving and dutiful daughter?

Aunt Gizi was conscious, pale and drawn but still able to snap at Alfred and tell him to be quiet. She lay in bed, a well-organized invalid with smelling salts, brandy, lemonade, and aspirin on the table by her side. The doctor had not been— Uncle Alfred had rushed out of the house forgetting to fetch the doctor—but she said firmly that she was all right and did not wish them to miss their train.

"Please go, my dears," she said firmly. "I am quite well, and the doctor will prescribe whatever medicine I need."

"You can't go now and leave me here when your poor mama is dying!"

"Be quiet, Alfred, do! And stop putting me in my grave before I am dead."

Alfred started to whimper again, and Gizi, in weak but tolerant affection, waved him away.

"I'll stay, Mama." Kati frowned. She had never been called upon to make decisions before, she had always done what Mama had told her to do, but she had seen a glimpse of something unfamiliar in her mother's face, a passing flash of fear. "I'll stay. But there's no need for Felix to stay too. He can go and buy the tractor with Adam." A small positive voice trying to grow up and do the right thing.

There were protestations, over-concern, promises of a present from Budapest, and then Felix kissed Aunt Gizi's hand

and Kati's cheek and raced for his motorcar and the station while Kati began to try and calm her father.

Three of them on the train. She hardly dared speak directly to Felix in case Adam should recognize the hunger in her voice. Lunch was brought to them in their first-class carriage and they spoke of poor Aunt Gizi and then of the tractor and of what they would do in Budapest. Finally she sat back and pretended to be asleep, sheltering and brooding behind closed eyes.

They did all the things they were supposed to do in Budapest. They went to the Vigszinhaz Theatre, just strolling distance from the Klein apartment. They walked in Buda. They visited the fair. Every night they went out to dine, sometimes just the three of them, sometimes with business people whom Adam had met during the day. Afterwards, with coffee and *barack* inside them, they would go back to the luxurious apartment on Pannonia Street and there Felix and she would drag the evening on, drinking, talking, not wanting to go to bed, forcing Adam to stay awake and join in their strained festivities. It grew worse. The tension grew worse; how could Adam not sense it, smell it, hear it in their voices every time they spoke to one another? She knew something must happen; the control between the three of them was only just holding.

Right in the middle of the fair, just after breakfast one morning, Adam received a telegram. He read it, looked vaguely irritated, and then, not knowing what turmoil he was causing, said casually, "It is really quite incredible how incompetent even the most worthy overseer is. I only have to stay away for a few days and there is an emergency in the grain shed. Someone has been stealing grain and Rigo does not know what to do. I shall have to go, I suppose; the telegram is quite hysterical." He studied his watch, then snapped it shut and replaced it in his pocket.

How could he not hear the noise her heart was making? She swallowed and coughed. "Do you have to go, Adam? Can't it wait until we all get back?"

"You know what Rigo is. If I leave it he will have the county militia rounding up every gypsy and migrant in the area. It's sure to be one of our own men anyway. No, it's a nuisance but I don't see what else I can do."

"Shall we come back with you?" she asked brightly.

"No need. I must return tonight to arrange the tractor payment. We have to buy some other things too; I've been think-

328

ing about new stock. Felix, you go along to the fair today and see if you can charm a bigger discount out of Roth."

"Yes."

"You'll be all right, won't you, Eva? Felix can take you shopping or something this afternoon."

"Yes, I'll be all right."

"Must hurry now. Get a cab, Felix, there's a good fellow."

Felix, not looking at her, jumped from his chair and left the room. Adam picked up some papers and bundled them into a satchel. He kissed her peremptorily on the cheek and rushed out. A few moments later Felix returned. He sat down, watching her make patterns in the sugar with a spoon. She tried to say something, couldn't, looked at him, and saw he was smiling. "Oh, Felix!" she choked, and then the door opened and the girl came in to clear away the breakfast.

"Shall we go to the fair?" asked Felix. She nodded and went into the bedroom to get ready.

Strolling arm in arm with Felix through the fair she was able to delude herself into a dream of what-might-have-been. If they had married, this was the way it would have been—such a smart, stylish couple, the women envying her both her looks and her man, the men smiling appreciatively. This is how it would have been if only she was Mrs. Felix Kaldy and not Mrs. Adam. They took the tractor manufacturer to lunch. It was a long, protracted lunch which she enjoyed at first because both men made much of her. But the coffee dragged on and on and Felix appeared to be taking Adam's instructions about discussing terms seriously. She began to fidget. Surely he appreciated that this was the one day they could be alone together. He could haggle with Roth any time but please, Felix, don't waste this precious day we have.

She lit cigarette after cigarette, powdered her nose and re-applied her lipstick. Irritation turned to anguish. It was vanishing, the beautiful long day was vanishing and at the end of it they would have nothing to show except a beastly percentage on a tractor. She could hardly stop herself from crying and when, just before four o'clock, they finally rose from the table, she was too ill to feel happy any longer. They said good-bye to Mr. Roth and then stood waiting for a cab.

"Are you all right, Eva? You look pale."

"How could you?" She turned on him, furious. "How could you waste our day on that horrible man! We could have gone

329

to Margaret Island and had lunch at the Grand, or—oh, we could have gone up into the hills. Anything, we could have done anything. But you've wasted it all talking to that horrible man about a tractor." She was sobbing, and Felix, looking slightly embarrassed, began to walk her along the pavement.

"My darling Eva. I had no idea it would take so long. I had to do it, didn't I? I promised Adam I'd help if I could. And after all it is because of Adam's beastly tractor that we're here, you and I, having a lovely time in Budapest."

"I'm not having a lovely time. It's been hideous!"

"It won't be hideous any more. We'll do something exciting now. Shall we go dancing? There's sure to be a tea dance somewhere."

"Where?" she asked, mollified.

"Oh, the Bristol perhaps. We'll go and see. We've still hours before Adam comes back. We can do whatever you like."

Dancing was better than nothing. They could dance forgetting Adam, oblivious of everything except each other. But it wasn't enough, it only made things worse. Pressed together on the tiny dance floor, her body became an agony and she tried desperately to think of a way they could return to the flat and get rid of the servants. This was the hour when they settled with their friends in the kitchen of the apartment. She'd heard them on other afternoons, giving their permanent tea party. She wanted to go back and be alone with Felix. For years she had wanted to be alone with Felix, and now they had the opportunity it was vanishing because of petty irritations that should have been swept aside. She was aware of annoyance. Surely a man of the world knew how to handle these things. She was a well-brought-up girl, a respectable wife who was prepared to break all the teachings of her background and commit adultery with the man she loved. Surely the very least he could have done was arrange it properly. What did other people do?

"Come on, Eva darling. You're all strung up. Let's go and have a cocktail."

That was better. In a quiet corner, softly lit, her anguish abated. Felix sat with his arm loosely around her waist and began to talk.

"It's so marvellous with you, Eva," he said wistfully. "Everything is better, more fun, alive. Thank God you live in the country too. Sometimes I think I couldn't bear it if you weren't living near me."

330

"I feel that way too. I only married Adam to be near you."

"Eva darling!" He snatched her hand from the table and kissed it. "You've no idea how I hate being married to Kati. Oh, she isn't a nuisance or anything, but does she look like my wife? Can you imagine how I feel? Every time you walk in the room, Kati seems even worse than she is. You're so bright and beautiful. You're like quicksilver when you come into a room. I hate ugly things. I can't help it and I'm sorry for Kati. But I can't bear ugly things and I hate being married to her."

"Felix!" She squeezed his hand. The desire had momentarily left her aching limbs and now, helped by the cocktails, she was warm, filled with love and happiness at his declaration.

"You're the only good thing in my life, Eva. Sometimes I think you really are the only one who understands me. Oh, Mama loves me, of course . . . too much. And Adam is fond of me. But you and I are the same. We think alike, feel alike."

"Oh, yes, we do," she breathed. "Felix . . . why did you marry Kati like that? Why?"

"There was no choice, Eva. You know that."

He looked so beautiful in the soft light. Age had given him a style that made him even more attractive. The face was still smooth and well-shaped, but now there was a small network of lines at the corners of his eyes. When he smiled they crinkled into bewitching maturity.

"My poor Felix." She squeezed his hand, then, greatly daring, kissed him softly on the cheek. Felix stared down into his drink, twisting the glass on its stem.

"We wanted the house back, Mama and I. And it seemed the only way. But sometimes I think the price was too much: my whole future for the Kaldy estate. It was too much."

She wasn't listening, not to the words, only to the meaning. Felix was unhappy because he had Kati, not her. She was unhappy too, but not at this particular moment. She was pleasantly drunk, and Felix had declared his love for her. Somehow, sometime, they would be together. It was impossible for two people to love as much as she and Felix did and not be together.

Felix's soft voice murmured on, saying how wonderful she was, how dreary Kati was. They had several more drinks, and in the warm intimacy of the cocktail bar they felt close to one another, full of peaceful understanding. It was not until the waiter was bringing more drinks that she suddenly caught sight of the clock over the bar.

331

"My God, Felix! We've been here over three hours. It's nine o'clock! Adam will be back at the apartment wondering where we are. Come on, quickly!"

While Felix was paying the bill she wondered if they ought to phone the apartment and tell him they were coming back at once. But she was too nervous to work out what to say. They hadn't done anything wrong—she suddenly felt relieved that she needn't face Adam with the knowledge of guilt—but she still didn't relish the idea of walking in late with Felix when they were both a little drunk.

They were quiet in the cab. She was nervous. Affable, easygoing Adam was sometimes unpredictable. Supposing he was angry. Supposing he suddenly saw that his wife and his brother were in love. What chance would they have then to be together?

They hurried through the stone arch and entered the apartment. It was empty.

"He's gone out looking for us," she said foolishly, and then the girl came out from the kitchen with a telegram in her hand.

"It came at seven, Madame Kaldy," she said. "Cook and I didn't know what to do. We weren't sure where you and Mr. Felix had gone." She paused, her face avid with curiosity.

"That's all right. You can go now."

She read it in silence, although she knew even before opening what it would say.

"He's not coming back this evening. He'll return in the morning."

"Would you like me to move out to a hotel? It would be the proper thing to do."

"No."

"Are you sure?"

"Yes."

"We'll go and have dinner then."

She dressed with the care of a bride. She had packed the silver gauze dress, not knowing if she would have an opportunity to wear it, and now she was able to drop the few shimmering fronds about her body, knowing that she looked as desirable as any woman could look. They crossed the river and went to a restaurant in Buda; there were too many of David and Malie's friends in the Pest cafés. Felix ordered champagne—just like a wedding—and the sad confidences of the cocktail hour vanished and were replaced by laughter and risqué jokes. They were the way they always were together, gay and happy people.

They ate little, but had more champagne and then a light Alsace wine that suited their mood. At midnight they left the restaurant and walked, hand in hand, across Margaret Bridge. The lights from the Buda and Gellert hills shone down onto the Danube, and the faintly tangy smell of the river made them feel fresh and incredibly young. On their left Margaret Island stretched, a dark mysterious mass of trees with lights flickering from the far end. A waterfowl croaked; the river splashed gently against the embankments.

"I think this is the happiest evening of my life," said Felix wistfully, and the great swelling ache in her breast threatened to engulf her completely.

They let themselves quietly into the apartment, knowing that the servants were already in bed. She went straight to her room. Felix called after her but she turned and hushed him, pointing towards the servants' quarters. Then she slid out of her dress, combed her hair with a passing regret that it was no longer sweeping over her shoulders, and wrapped a silk kimono over her naked body. She was excited, but there was no dilemma in her mind about whether she should or should not go to bed with Felix. At some point during this last insane summer, the decision had been made for her. Even if the rest of her life was a torment, she knew she had no alternative on this particular night. And she wasn't going to think about what came after. She was beautiful and loved. Her body was perfect and she had wanted Felix for eleven years. Nothing was going to spoil this night.

She slipped quietly out of her room, crossed the hall and dining-room, and opened Felix's door.

"Eva—"

"Ssh."

His light was out but the moon was bright through the unshuttered windows. Sounds of the Budapest night flowed in: cars, horses, a distant train. Felix was still dressed. He was sitting on his bed gazing out of the window.

"Your room is farther from the servants, Felix. It will be better here than in mine."

In the moonlight she could see him staring at her. The silk of her wrapper was so fine it was transparent. He was staring at her body, unbelieving, rapt. A tremor ran through him.

"Felix!" She could think of nothing else but lying with him, feeling that smooth strong body pressed up and into hers, his chest against hers, belly to belly, thigh to thigh. A small moan escaped her and she tore the sash of her wrapper loose. It was a pain, a tight constricting pain that now at last she didn't have to control any more.

"Oh, Felix, please!" She threw the wrapper away and moved towards him, waiting for his hands, his mouth, his body. "I know you have never slept with Kati. I know why. That's the reason I'm here."

The tremor ran through him again. He moved and she waited for his touch. But it didn't come. He moved again, but it was to the foot of the bed, away from her.

"Go away."

"Felix, what's the matter?"

"Please go away." He trembled again and suddenly she was frightened. She remembered him shaking once before, kneeling at her feet holding onto her skirts, telling her of the things he had done to Serbian women.

"Is something wrong, Felix?"

"Just go away!" His voice was shrill.

"Please don't make a noise. You'll wake the servants."

"If you go away it won't matter if they wake! For God's sake go away and leave me alone. You're like all the rest, rapacious and greedy, horrible. . . ."

He covered his face with his hands and shudder after shudder racked his body. Stunned, she could only watch. What had gone wrong? What had she said to destroy their love?

"You don't understand. I thought you were my friend, my dearest and most beloved friend, more to me than my mother, or my brother, or anyone in the world. I trusted you, believed you. You weren't like the others. And now you've done this . . . this horrible thing. Cover yourself! At least cover yourself!"

Shocked she stooped and fumbled for the kimono. Her hands were cold and clumsy and one sleeve was inside out. She thrust her arm into it any way she could and wrapped it awkwardly round her.

His face was still bowed into his hands and he was half crying, half shouting. "Even Kati never did this to me. She was modest and quiet and kept to her room. She never coarsened herself, made things disgusting and vile. . . . I thought you were beautiful, my dearest, dearest friend whom I loved, and you're just like the others."

"But Felix." She wasn't crying, but tears ran down her face.

She only half understood, even now, that the shudders were not the movements of desire but of revulsion. "You said you loved me! In the bar you told me how wonderful I was, you danced with me, you held my hand, you loved me!"

He jerked his head up and looked at her, spite and loathing in his face. "Yes," he spat out. "I loved you then, because I thought you were my friend and understood me. But I don't love you now! You disgust me! Horrible great heavy body . . . like a cow!"

"Felix!" She screamed and fell sobbing against the bed. "Felix! I don't understand. I thought you loved me! I've wanted you for so long. Even as a girl I wanted you, and you married Kati and I was unhappy. Oh, Felix, you don't know how unhappy I was!" She wiped her sleeve across her face. Her eyes and cheeks were wet; her nose was running and she didn't have a handkerchief. She tried to grasp his hand but he snatched it away. "I wanted you. I just wanted you!"

"Well, I don't want you," he shouted. "I shan't ever be able to look at you again without feeling sick. You think I'm like all the others! Panting and sweating, always thinking about women and their bodies. I never thought about you as one of those hot dirty creatures. You were just my friend. But now you're like all the rest . . . and you don't have the decency to keep it to yourself."

"Felix," she moaned. "Don't, please, don't."

"Then go away! Go away!"

She tried to stand but fell against the bed. With one hand against the wall she stumbled round the room, crying, clutching the wrap tightly over her body. The terrible humiliation of being naked before him was almost worse than her grief. She paused at the door, leaning against it, sobbing, thinking even now that he would give her just one word of kindness, one gentle phrase to cling to in the welter of misery and shame. But all she could hear was a curious low keening, a sound like a sick animal or a . . . a madman. And all her other emotions were replaced by fear. She twisted the handle and ran from the room, not even stopping to shut the door after her. In her room the light was still on and she saw herself in the mirror. Her face was a swollen mess and her body was slumped and sagging. She looked like a revolting middle-aged woman, ugly, coarse, like a . . . cow.

She was gone in the morning, her clothes packed and vanished and no trace of her at all. There was just a note for

Adam that Felix dared not read because it was placed on the breakfast table and the servants had seen it. They stared at him curiously when they brought breakfast in, and he hated her even more. But he was afraid, too, because of what she might have written in the note.

22

Amalia never confessed it to her husband or her family, but she had always preferred Vienna to her own capital city of Budapest. Even post-war Vienna, which was unsettled, slightly dangerous, and filled with sick-looking people, still had a charm that the Hungarian capital lacked. Perhaps it was because of her girlhood—the year at school before the war had been a happy one—or perhaps it was the cosmopolitan atmosphere of the city. Vienna was never quite as provincial as Budapest. And there was the Opera House and the Volksoper, feast upon feast of music; every night she and David indulged themselves, gorged themselves on music and then clopped home in a fiacre humming fragments all the way. They had rented an apartment complete with staff and took only the nursemaid for the little boys with them. During the day David was working and she and the nurse would push the boys through the Stadtpark or into the Volksgarten. She was entirely happy. Vienna always had made her happy, and not even the presence of Stefan Tilsky could mar her pleasure.

He seemed to be indulging in a banking transaction with her husband. During the summer months David had arranged to meet him in Vienna and assist him with business matters. Seeing him in Vienna, engaged with lawyers and bankers and financiers, put Stefan Tilsky (who had referred a trifle patronizingly to "Jewish" bankers) in a nice, settled, and non-disturbing niche. He was gradually becoming less of a remembrance of the past and more of a business colleague of her husband's. Once or twice she found she was still defensive with him, such as the day he bumped into her on a golden afternoon in the Volksgarten. She was feeding the sparrows and the little boys were delighted because she had discovered how to sit very still until the birds came down and pecked the food from her hands. Stefan had strolled along, looking handsome and tall, had smiled and said, "How very charming—a sweet little family scene," and for some reason his tone had annoyed her.

Another time he came home to dinner, invited by her husband. David, not waiting until he was alone with her, had handed her a small package.

"Something you wanted, I believe, Amalia," he had said casually, and when she opened it she found a long, long string of old Bohemian garnets, held together on gold silk.

"Do you like it?" She had learned in three years that her husband's coolness, his suavity, concealed a boyish delight in giving pleasure. He loved to find out special gifts that she wanted, perfume she had admired on someone else, a length of silk that was unique, a book on some subject she was especially interested in. The gifts were tossed nonchalantly at her, but then he would watch and, as she once teased him, sometimes forget to look dispassionate when he saw her pleasure.

"Oh, David! It's the necklace I admired in the little shop behind the Cathedral. It is so beautiful!"

"I thought it would look very handsome when you wore your cream silk dress . . . perhaps to the opera tomorrow?"

"Tomorrow? No, I must wear it now." It was so easy to be genuinely thrilled with David's gifts. Always they were different, special, and in superb taste. She turned, flushed, gratified, towards their guest. "Stefan, have you ever seen such beautiful old garnets?"

"Delightful," he murmured. "A most expensive gift—especially for a wife!" His eyebrow raised, he laughed, and they laughed with him. But again it grated because it was not said entirely in fun. Stefan obviously considered wives, like Jewish bankers, slightly inferior persons.

She was most relieved he wasn't there on the morning when her sister arrived, unannounced and unexpected at the apartment. She had answered the door herself (David didn't like her doing that but it seemed foolish when she was passing the door just to let it ring) and for a fleeting second of time she didn't recognize the woman standing there.

"Eva!"

"Can I stay with you for a while, Malie? I won't be any bother, I promise you."

Eva had sagged. That was the word that came immediately

337

to mind. Her neat little figure, her face, her hair, even her clothes all seemed to sag. The pert, pretty features had degenerated into a series of perpendicular lines. Her hair had lost its curl, her shoulders slumped, and she appeared to have thickened round the waist.

"What's the matter, darling? You look so . . . unlike yourself. And where is Adam? I thought he was taking you to Budapest for the fair."

"I've left him." Eva crumpled and began to cry.

"Come in, quickly, dear!" Even while she soothed Eva, took her hat and coat and made her coffee, she was aware of a slight depression. Eva was such a restless person to live with. During the summer she was just bearable because they had different establishments and were not cooped up together. But Eva staying in her Budapest or Viennese apartment was altogether a different thing. Feverish excitements, dismal glooms, spitefulness, abject apologies and tears, overwhelming affection, critical dislike, all could happen within the range of a day. She and David were so happy in Vienna— She stopped, suddenly astonished because she realized she *was* happy: happy with her home, her children, her interesting friends, the luxury and the trips abroad, and above all with her husband. Guilt overwhelmed her because she, who had not expected happiness, had been given it, while it was obvious that Eva had not.

"Of course you can stay here, darling. It isn't as big as the apartment in Pannonia Street, but I know David would love you to stay as long as you like."

"I shan't be in your way, Malie. I'll keep to my room."

"There's no need for that, unless you want to."

"That is, if you have a room you can spare for me?"

"You can have Hermin's room and she can share with the children."

"Thank you, Malie."

She sat completely lifeless, with all the fight, all the old spirit gone from her. Even when Felix had left her to marry Kati she hadn't been as broken as this.

"What's happened? Do you want to tell me? Has Adam done something to you?"

Tears seeped from Eva. There was no other way to describe it. She didn't cry; wetness just seemed to ooze out of her face. She began to talk, rambling and unintelligible words, about not being able to live with Adam because of Felix, and of hating Felix, and hating men, and hating herself.

"What did Adam say when you told him you were leaving him?"

"I don't know. I left a note—in your Budapest apartment. I said I couldn't bear to see him for a while and I was coming to stay with you."

"But why can't you bear to see him? You've been living with him for four years. Why can't you live with him now?"

Eva's tears flowed again, amidst a welter of self-reproach which culminated in the fact that she was ashamed of herself because Adam had been so kind and that she didn't like men any more.

"I see." Malie was alarmed. She had never known her sister to be ashamed or blame herself for anything. And she had never known Eva to lack fight. She decided to wait until David came home and discuss it with him. Poor David, once again his home invaded by his disturbing sister-in-law.

Eva stayed in her room all the afternoon. She wasn't crying, just lying on her bed, curled on her side and alternately sleeping and picking at the sheet. She came out for supper, then went back to her room and said she would read in bed. Amalia asked David what she ought to do.

"Write to your brother-in-law, first of all. He must be concerned, poor fellow. Even though he is obviously used to Eva's lack of discipline this is a new and bothersome venture of hers. And then—I am not sure. Perhaps wait a few days and then take her out and buy her some clothes." He took his cheque book from the desk and scribbled a cheque. "Spend a little money on her. It will help."

"Thank you, David. I am sorry . . . sorry she's come. She is my sister but I'm sorry. She disturbs your life I think."

"Mmm . . . Perhaps a little." His dark brows raised in a mocking gesture. "And perhaps it is good for me. Certainly when your sister is here I appreciate anew the fact that I chose the more suitable of the Ferenc girls."

She wrote to Adam, assuring him that after a little holiday Eva was sure to have recovered and they would bring her back to Hungary with them. Then, after two dreadful days had passed, days when Eva stayed in her room, lying on her bed, she persuaded her to come out for a walk with the children. The first person they saw was Stefan Tilsky.

"The ravishing Eva!" he exclaimed, staring perplexed but courteous. Eva smiled as though she didn't believe a word of it. "You are ravishing, but I dislike your hat. Grey is not a colour you should wear."

To Malie's horror Eva began to ooze tears again. Stefan Tilsky, who was kind if supercilious, was immediately contrite.

"Eva! My darling girl. Forgive me. See, I crave your humble forgiveness."

He knelt on the path, right in the middle of the Stadtpark. Two old ladies stared and nearly fell over as they walked backwards watching him.

"I shall remain here on my knees until you say I am forgiven."

"Oh, do get up," said Eva, looking tired and embarrassed.

"Say you forgive me."

"All right."

He stood, brushed dirt from his knees. Then he reached over and took Eva's hat from her head. "You are much prettier without it," he said, and threw the hat in the river. Eva was so surprised she forgot to be miserable.

"That's my hat! Get it back."

"You look better without it."

He reached forward and fluffed her hair out a little. When his hand touched her cheek her face suddenly burned and she pulled away. Stefan took no notice. He put his hand up again and continued to arrange her hair.

"It was a perfectly horrible hat," he said quietly. "And you are too beautiful to wear such a thing."

Eva flushed again but ignored him. She took her nephew by the hand and walked away from Malie and the Pole.

"Something has happened to your little sister."

"I think so."

"Hmm. She was such a pretty woman—ravishing indeed." He smiled at Malie, a charming, warm, open smile. "We must all do what we can to cheer her, must we not?"

For days she couldn't think about anything else but the nightmare scene in the Pannonia apartment. She tried to push it away but it leapt into her head with the clarity of a photograph at repeated moments—at meals, in bed, in the middle of conversation—and each time the humiliation grew, the shame, the degrading spectacle of herself, naked, and the disgust on his face. And when the sharpness of that memory had blunted itself slightly, she began to see the longer and wider humiliation, the years of adoration, of faithfulness, of believing he was a man like other men. Eleven years worshipping a hero who did not exist. Was she a mad, mindless creature?

Had she no instincts as other women? Did they all know? Had they been watching her throwing herself at Felix all these years, knowing that the affair was moribund before it even started? His mother didn't know, she was sure of that. Otherwise why the continual hints about a grandchild? But Adam? Is that why Adam had never minded them flirting, playing together? Her head ached as, hour after hour, every permutation and alternative presented itself. It was with her all the time; whatever she was doing she was conscious all the time of the terrible mistake she had made.

Malie was there, that was nice. She and David (did they know?) were kind, and little Karoly and Jacob were useful to take on walks. And Stefan Tilsky (oh, God, did he know? had he known all last summer when they were making such exhibitions of themselves?) seemed to be there a lot, hovering around on the walks and coming with them to make up a fourth at the opera. She didn't like him. He was handsome enough, but he was too like Felix with his flattering jokes and charming interest in female matters.

She began, as she became a little calmer, to spend the mornings wandering about Vienna on her own. It wasn't at all like the old Vienna; it was poor and scruffy and all the children seemed to have rickets or sores. Once she passed a charity kitchen where lines of sour-smelling women and small children waited for bread and a mug of some steaming liquid. It was dispensed by women who were apparently ladies, and she watched for a long, long time, then walked away, wondering if something like that could be her panacea for disappointment and humiliation. But the poor—oh, dear, one was sorry, of course, but since the war there were so many of them, so many children suffering from malnutrition and tuberculosis, so many men wandering about the streets with arms or legs or eyes missing, so many people lacking money and health and food and warmth—that it didn't seem worthwhile to even try. And she was so miserable anyway that the first unhappy child she had to serve would be sure to make her start crying again.

She walked up Mariahilferstrasse, smelling the rather nasty coffee they were still serving in some of the cafés. She came to Mariahilfer Kirche by Haydn's statue and, moved by a sudden impulse, she went in.

Mass was in progress, and she sat enjoying the peace and music. Her religious upbringing had been spasmodic. Papa had taken no hand at all in their spiritual tuition and had been content to let any necessary instructions in the Christian faith

341

take place when they were on visits to their Bogozy grand-parents. She had taken her first communion at the Bogozys', but since then she had bothered only on rare occasions. But it was pleasant to listen and gaze up at the painted ceiling of the old church. The stillness, the formal movements of priests and acolytes, slowly cast a sense of peace over her, a temporary lulling of the pain that she felt would always be with her.

Someone was staring at her and the peace was jarred a lit-tle. She did not turn to see who it was but, as the conscious-ness of eyes fixed upon her grew stronger, so the tranquillity vanished completely. She picked up her gloves and bag and turned to leave. Stefan Tilsky was standing at the end of the pew, his face turned towards her, smiling, brown eyes looking in admiration. The eyes, once they had observed that her at-tention was drawn, changed direction. With a flattery that verged on insolence, Stefan Tilsky studied the entire length of her body, slowly and with lustful concentration. Even she, lost and unsure of herself where men were concerned, could not fail to interpret the desire in his face. She slid quickly from her seat and left from the end of the pew farthest away from him, but when she got to the church door he was waiting for her.

"Come and drink a glass of wine with me?"

"No thank you."

"Or coffee?"

She shook her head and began to walk across the cobbles back to Mariahilferstrasse.

"Continue in that direction and you will come to the sta-tion, unless you are contemplating walking all the way to the Schönbrunn."

She was suddenly tired, not physically but spiritually weary. She wondered if she would ever be able to enjoy the company of a man again.

"Please—" he said softly.

She felt his hand beneath her elbow. Her body was being gently drawn towards the narrow street that ran down the side of the church.

"There is a charming café nearby, very discreet and shel-tered, and picturesque too."

Listlessly she let herself be led down the street. They turned right through a wooden doorway, and she found she was in a stone courtyard set with tables. In the middle of the grey cob-bles a huge chestnut tree formed an umbrella of gold and crimson leaves.

"It is warm enough to sit here, yes? And much pleasanter than inside."

He ordered wine and coffee and she sipped both. An old woman selling flowers came in and he beckoned her over and took a rose from the basket.

"For you," he said, smiling his warm and devastating smile.

"Thank you."

"May I fasten it to your coat?" Without waiting for an answer, he reached across and slid the flower into the top buttonhole of her jacket. His hand lingered, then his fingers touched her throat, ran up her cheek and down again. "You are very beautiful, Eva Kaldy. I remember you as a girl. You were pretty then, but now—"

She smiled and tried not to remember Felix's face as he looked at her naked body.

"What is so fascinating about married women?" Stefan mused softly. "So much nonsense talked about young girls, virgins, about their appeal and sexuality when they really have no sexuality at all. Virgins are for very old men or for youths, similarly virgin, who are obsessed with a romantic image. I think I was in love with a virgin once, many years ago." He twinkled at her, mocking himself. "Married women fascinate me. I cannot help it. It is their . . . mystery. One never knows, does one, with a married woman. Obviously she understands about men, but how much? And how many?"

"Really, Stefan!" she protested, faintly shocked and also faintly embarrassed because she wondered if he knew of her own recent willingness to take a lover.

"Now you, Eva, grow more beguiling every time we meet. In the summer—oh!" He drew his breath in suddenly and across his face spread an expression of greed. "In the summer you were tempting—oh, so tempting. Every time you moved or spoke or even looked at me I wanted you. I cursed your family and friends, all clustered around you like fat cats around a cheetah. And I came away, annoyed but resigned. And now I meet you again, and this time you are even better. This time the crispness has gone. Now you are a little sad, quieter, because you are thinking. Now it is possible to approach you and say, 'Eva Kaldy, I want to make love to you. I desire you in every possible way a man can desire a woman.'"

It was like a poultice, a soothing, healing balm on the agonized wound that Felix had left. Blatant, vulgar, impertinent—all those things too—but because of that very vulgarity

343

it healed where a subtler, more sensitive flattery would not have done.

"You have no right to speak like that," she said unconvincingly, and Stefan reached over the table and took her hand in his.

Felix had beautiful hands. She shuddered and then looked down at Stefan's. Well-shaped but square. They were bigger than Felix's. They were also very warm.

"May I see you again?"

"Of course. We are meeting this evening I believe."

"Aach!" He shrugged irritably. "You know very well what I mean. I want to see you alone, without your sister and her husband in attendance. Will you meet me here tomorrow? Tell your sister you are going out for lunch and eat here with me."

"I can't," she said feebly and he made the "aach" noise again and then swore softly in Polish.

"Of course you can, and you will. I'm asking you to eat a meal with me. That is all I am asking, for the moment."

"Perhaps. . . . I'll try."

"Good." He stood up, held her chair back for her, and, as she rose, he pressed his hands, one each side of her waist. "God!" she heard him say, and she turned round to see a film of sweat on his upper lip. The pressure of his hands, the sweat, triggered the hunger of the summer once more in her body. It was gone as swiftly as it had come but for the first time since the scene in the Pannonia bedroom she felt like a woman again. Outside the restaurant they separated, already acknowledging guilt although they had done nothing to be guilty of. She climbed into a cab and went down into the city, to Kärntnerstrasse, and there she spent the rest of the day buying a new dress to wear to the opera that evening.

All through the performance she could feel him watching her. His eyes rested on the slashed silk of her neckline and on the places where the silk clung. She dropped her programme once and as he leaned forward to pick it up his hand brushed against her thigh. The game they were playing seemed sordid and coarse, but nonetheless it was exciting and for the first time she began to look at Stefan Tilsky, seeing what a magnificent body he had, huge-shouldered, strong-thighed, flat-bellied. He was big, very big. A pulse in her throat began to throb as she realized how very big he was.

Felix. Felix was not a man, and he had nearly destroyed

her. Why had he hurt her like that? Why had he been so cruel, to encourage her and then destroy her?

When the opera ended Stefan wrapped her cloak around her and his hands bore down on her shoulders. For a brief second his body was pressed against her back and she could feel every muscle straining to keep control. Her own hunger leapt up again and she had a wild impulse to turn her body and thrust back against him. They fought against lust, won, and left the opera with the two gentle, happy people who had brought them. The rest of the evening was a delicious, agonizing torment of desire for both of them.

A week later, oblivious of everything except Vienna, Stefan Tilsky, and Felix, she went to an apartment close to the Belvedere Gardens, a luxurious apartment with a marble bathroom and a bed covered in purple satin. Stefan had arranged everything with the smooth ease of an experienced philanderer, and this time she did not feel ashamed of her body.

Malie was delighted to see Eva getting back to normal again. Her sister was never easy to live with, and as she got older she became less easy, but the quiet, subdued Eva who had arrived in Budapest had distressed Malie immeasurably and she was almost relieved when Eva borrowed her squirrel wrap without asking and snapped at the children for making a noise in the morning. Eva's restoration to health was, Malie was forced to admit, largely due to Stefan Tilsky. He paid court, flattered, and was attentive in the way Eva loved. After a while Malie began to grow a little afraid that perhaps he was *too* attentive. After all, she had written to Adam assuring him that she and David would look after Eva and now—well, there was something disturbing in the way they looked at each other, the way Stefan kissed Eva's hand and brought her flowers whenever they were all going out for the evening.

She grew really alarmed when she saw Eva alighting from a cab that had come from the direction of Schwarzenbergplatz. Eva had said she was going to visit an old school friend who lived near Turkenschanz Park. How could she possibly have come from Turkenschanz via Schwarzenbergplatz? She was so uneasy that she was unable to bring herself to ask Eva. She sat and fretted all evening about it, watching the two lovers playing a game she didn't understand but that she sensed was dangerous. Stefan Tilsky was a masculine and attractive animal.

She herself had occasionally found his nearness disturbing, even though his arrogance annoyed her. He had the unquestionable charm that all Poles had, gaiety, sincerity, and an ability to make a woman, any woman, feel beautiful and desired. Her silly headstrong sister, who had spent her life rushing from one thoughtless deed to the next, was quite capable of falling out of love with Felix and in love with Stefan Tilsky in the space of one night.

So it was with infinite relief that she granted Eva's surprising request one morning for the loan of enough money to take her home to Hungary and the Kaldy farm.

"Of course, my darling. You can have what you like. You would prefer to go now rather than return with us in November?"

"I want to go this morning." Eva stared down at the tablecloth. She was quiet, but it wasn't the quiet of her arrival in Vienna. That Eva had been crushed, listless. This Eva was controlled and tense.

"This morning! But we were all going to the theatre this evening! Surely you can wait for one day?"

"No. I must leave this morning. Adam—" She paused and swallowed. "Adam hasn't written to me and I don't know if he's going to be cross because I ran away. Do you think he'll be cross?"

"Possibly," replied Malie dryly.

"I'll go now, if you don't mind."

She was quiet, but Malie could sense the springs that were waiting to thrust her from the chair and precipitate her onto the Budapest train. Having spent the last few days worrying about Eva's visit, she now began to worry about her erratic departure.

"Is something wrong, darling?" she asked gently.

"Nothing at all." Eva was poised, wary. "Why? Does it seem as though something is wrong?"

"Well, no, but you were enjoying yourself so much here. It seems a little strange to leave so suddenly."

"I just think it's time to go home to my husband."

Amalia asked no more. Whatever had prompted Eva's arrival in Vienna had now been replaced by some equally urgent need to go home. She was a trifle concerned at the urgency and at the mystery, but overlying everything else was the relief of having peace descend once more on their household. She went into their bedroom and asked David for enough money to send her sister home. When she came out Eva was back in her room, already packing.

They got her to the station just in time to catch the Budapest train and then they returned to an apartment in the total disorder of a frenzied and unplanned departure. Eva, amongst other things, had inadvertently packed the garnet chain and the squirrel wrap. She had also omitted to send Stefan Tilsky a note, and that evening Malie had the somewhat uncomfortable task of telling a startled and angry Polish nobleman that her sister had fled back to the country.

It was almost impossible to reach the farm from Vienna in one day, but Eva knew she couldn't bear to wait overnight, either in Budapest or with her parents up in the town. She just *had* to get back to Adam and the farm that night. She couldn't stand the torment of going to sleep not knowing what her reception would be. She arrived in Budapest that afternoon and had to wait for two hours before she could catch a train out. She sat in the station restaurant, ignoring the interested and inviting glances of male passers-by and trying to look composed in spite of the turmoil raging in her head. What shall I do if he won't forgive me? Supposing he turns me out. What shall I do? But he won't turn me out, he loves me! But remember how stubborn he can be? Remember how he wouldn't let you go away for longer than a week? He said you were irresponsible and undisciplined. Oh, what shall I do if he won't forgive me!

In the train going up to the town she shed a few tears, tears of anxiety and strain but also rehearsal tears. She couldn't eat anything when food was brought round and, after a few sips of coffee, she threw the rest out of the window. It was dark when she arrived and she was tired and dirty. It would have been sensible to have gone to Mama and Papa's for the night and travelled up to the hills next day. But a self-induced panic was driving her on. She had to know. She had to know if Adam would forgive her.

After three quarters of an hour she found a cab driver who would take her along the country roads up to the hills. He insisted on payment in advance and she had to empty her purse before he was satisfied. She sat on the edge of the car seat, tense, feeling sick with anxiety and with the constant jolting over the bad roads. What could she say? What could she do that would put it all right? Should she say she was sorry?

What explanation had Felix given of her flight from Budapest? She took her hat from her aching head and stuffed it into her bag. There were spasms of blinding light across her eyes and she pressed the fingers against the lids, trying to drive the pain and tiredness away.

"Can't you hurry?" she snapped at the driver. "I've paid you enough. Surely you can drive faster than this!"

The driver didn't answer, but he opened the window of his cabin and spat out into the night. He was already regretting the avarice that had made him agree to drive this madwoman out into the country at night. He steadfastly ignored the impatient noises she was making and began, ruefully, to estimate what time he would get home again.

The drive through the acacia woods was nightmarish. The lights on the car made a dark and eerie tunnel out of the trees, and several times they saw the red eyes of animals gleaming at them from the side of the road. The driver was swearing quite blatantly now but she was past hearing or caring. In her stomach was a huge hard ball of fear that pressed down on her bladder, making her feel sick and uncomfortable. She resolutely blotted out from her mind any other explanation for feeling so ill. Why hadn't she waited overnight at Papa's? Then she would have arrived looking clean and pretty. She would have been able to win him then. What would she do if he wouldn't take her back? What would she do? Where could she go?

Screaming directions at the driver she got them at last to the long flat stretch that led to the farmhouse. A light was showing in the bedroom window. God! Supposing he was doing what he had once threatened to do! Supposing he had a girl from the village there with him! The car squealed to a halt and, ignoring the cries of the driver, she was out before the engine had stilled and was running up the steps into the house.

"Adam! Adam! It's me! Eva!"

The bedroom door opened and he stood there, outlined against the light.

"Adam!" She began to cry, to sob piteously with fear and tiredness. Adam slowly reached his arm out and pressed a switch. The hall was flooded with light and she was able to see his face, stern, immobile except for a small muscle twitching at the corner of his mouth.

"It's me," she wept. "I've come home, Adam!" She flung

348

herself forward and then felt his arms go round her, gripping her so tightly that for one terrible second she thought he was going to thrust her away. But then the tightness changed to a violent trembling and when she looked at his face she saw tears filling his eyes.

"Darling Adam!" she cried, relief draining through her body.

She could handle all the rest, the questions and explanations, the sorrow and tears and pleadings. She could handle all that, providing he still wanted her. And he did. Oh, it was obvious he did!

"I've come all the way from Vienna in one day. The car driver was angry, I think he wants some more money, but I had to see you. I couldn't wait another night. I missed you so much, Adam! I had to see you!"

He buried his face in her neck, and suddenly she realized he was sobbing. Not the way she was sobbing, frightened and tearful, but with deep, wrenching movements that shook his body. For the first time since leaving the apartment in Pannonia Street she felt shame for what she had done to Adam. The shame lasted for a brief moment, and then relief drowned it once more. I'll make it up to him, I promise I'll make it up to him. He doesn't need much. It will be easy to make him happy.

The driver blew his horn and all the dogs began to bark. "I'll go and see what he wants," Adam said. He left her and when he came back he was calm again, the old, unruffled, stolid Adam.

"We won't talk tonight, will we, Adam? I'm so tired! It was such a long journey and I was afraid you wouldn't want me back. I was so worried! Can we just go to bed and talk in the morning?"

He nodded and drew her forward once more into his arms. He wiped her face gently with one hand as though she were a child. "Oh, Eva, why did you do this to me?"

"In the morning," she said. "We'll talk in the morning."

He went down and put fresh coal on the stove himself so that there would be hot water for her to bathe in. And later, tired but refreshed, she crawled into his arms prepared to do what she must do if her return and her future were to be safeguarded. She discovered, to her surprise, that Felix and Stefan Tilsky had made no difference to the way she was with her husband. The Eva who had offered herself to Felix and had

349

subsequently been possessed by Stefan Tilsky seemed to have
nothing whatsoever to do with the dutiful wife of Adam
Kaldy.

Six weeks later, she was able to tell him that she thought
she might be pregnant. He stared for a moment, his green
eyes unfathomable, and then he kissed her and said that he
was satisfied. Fear shot through her when he said that. Satisfied. Why should he choose a word like that? But his behaviour during the months that followed lulled and soothed her
anxieties. And when her child was born the following July her
relief was absolute, for little Terez resembled only her mother. The black curls and the tiny heart-shaped face were those
of Eva and no one else.

23

When the day came for him to leave the farm and go away to
school, he awoke with a scalding sensation in his bowels. He
had to rush outside, and when he came back and lay down
again he felt weak and afraid.

In their corner of the room his mother, grandmother, and
three sisters stirred and made little grunting snores. There was
a rustle, and then his mother slid from the bed and came over
to him.

"All right, my son?"

He tried to speak and couldn't. To his shame he found that
his voice cracked, and he stopped trying to speak in case he
cried. Eleven years old, nearly a man, and here he was about
to cry. His mother sat down beside him on the straw mattress
and hugged him close.

"Only a few months and you will be home again," she said
softly. "Home—and with what tales of learning! What stories
of the town and the school, and of Uncle Lajos! We shall
think of nothing else while you are gone but the tales you will
have to tell us when you return."

He put his arms round her waist and buried his head
against her side, still not daring to speak. His mother smelt of
wood ash, of cabbage soup, of sunflowers, of sweat. He didn't

even recognize it as a smell; it was his mother, warm and secure, his mother whom he was leaving.

"And what pride you have brought to the family," she murmured. "Why, even Mrs. Boros spoke with great respect to me yesterday. My son is to go to the school to receive an education."

"I shall come back the very moment I have finished the education," he said, finding words at last. "The minute the school is finished I shall come home here back to you."

She hugged him, stroked his hair (newly cut by Aunt Ilonka, ready for school), and said, "Of course, Janni! That is why we have tried so hard to find a place for you in the school. When the education is finished you will come back, and perhaps you will be the accountant or the man in charge of the engines. And then what lives we shall lead!"

"You will have a bed to yourself and as many pictures as you like, and you will have the best house on the farm!"

He felt his mother nod. It wasn't light enough yet to see her, but he could feel her body move. "That's right, Janni. And I shall be so proud of you!"

The misery that overwhelmed him channelled itself. Everything must be borne so that soon he could come home and buy the family meat every day. This must be the thing he remembered above all else. He was going away so that soon he could return and buy his mother all the things he had seen in the village.

And then the fear washed over him again, driving high intention far from his mind. It wasn't just the fear and misery of leaving his family, it was fear of the unknown, of a world totally unfamiliar to him in which he would be a stranger without friends or family, at least no family that he knew.

Uncle Lajos was a second cousin of his father, a man who had done well for himself and had been a credit to the sacrifices made by his parents. He had been apprenticed to a shoemaker and now had his own business in the town, that distant, legendary town where the Kaldys and the Ferencs and the Racs-Rassays came from, the town that included incredible things like the school and factories and hundreds of houses stretched out in rows. Uncle Lajos had married the daughter of a factory hand and their children were all grown up and all placed in brilliant positions of unbelievable sophistication: one was a railway guard; one, who had attended the secondary school, was a government clerk; and another had trained with his father as a shoemaker. Three daughters had all married well to affluent town dwellers. Uncle Lajos had been applied to for lodgings during the term time while Janos was at school. An arrangement had been made: Uncle Lajos and Aunt Berta would take a minimal fee for his keep, and he would have to earn the rest of his food and lodging by working for Uncle Lajos in the evenings and at weekends. At the back of everyone's mind was the thought that, if the education failed, perhaps Uncle Lajos would keep the boy as an apprentice. So while Uncle Lajos and Aunt Berta were relations, he didn't know them other than one brief meeting and they were also touched with the Olympian mystery of the town, the mystery that made them distant strangers and not part of the family at all.

For several months, during the time the arrangements for his departure had been going on, he had been the object of awed envy from everyone on the farm. Not only his schoolfellows but even the adults had spoken to him, of him, as one touched with divine blessing. No one talked of anything else, and his fame had spread from the Kaldy farm to the Racs-Rassay and the Ferenc. He had been pointed out by carter and ox herder, field worker and shepherd, from all the lands about, as the boy who had achieved the impossible and was going to the secondary school in the town. The respect, the reverent humility had been contagious, and for some time he had begun to believe that he was indeed set apart from his friends and relatives. But now, with departure imminent, he was shocked to realize that he was unworthy of the greatness and did not have the courage to grasp it.

"Mama, what shall I do if"—he choked, fought, and recovered—"if I get lost, or if no one will speak to me?"

"You will not get lost because in your pocket you have a paper with the address of Uncle Lajos written upon it. And everyone at the school will speak to you because his excellency, Mr. Adam, has arranged for you to have a place there."

She had the firm note in her voice, the note he knew meant she would brook no change of plan and weakening of courage. He had heard the note in her voice many times during the last year, when she was talking to Director Feher at the village school, to the priest, to Mr. Adam Kaldy, to any number of relatives all round the county who might be coerced into help, to the Father at the Catholic *Gymnasium* who said he had no place available for a peasant child. He had heard it above all when she was talking to his father.

The day they had returned from Mr. Adam's house, his father had been insane with rage. Subsequently Janos had realized the rage stemmed from fear. His mother's impertinence could have cost his father his job in the granary. Undeterred, she had stated that Janos was going to receive an education, no matter how impossible it seemed. Through arguments and battles that ended in blows, she had maintained the firm and positive tones that all of them were coming to recognize. She had divulged the amazing news that she had saved money—how and what she could have saved it from was a mystery—to provide clothes and lodgings for her son, enough for one term at least. And finally his father had fallen before a spirit stronger than his own. He had capitulated, and gradually his chagrin had turned to pride. What a wife he had, to accomplish the impossible! And what a son, to receive a place at the grammar school! Once the decision had been reached he had done everything to further his wife's crusade, dictating the letter to his cousin Lajos and begging rides for his son on carts going towards town on the day that the entrance examination had to be taken. He was proud of his son, and proud of himself. Did not men point him out on three farms as the father of the boy who was going to the secondary school? It was a pride shared by every servant on the Kaldy farm. It put them above all the other farms. There were, it was true, brilliant children on the Racs-Rassay land and on the smaller Ferenc farm; some were fortunate enough to be apprenticed, one or two even spent a little time in the town acquiring mechanics' qualifications. But on no other farm was there a boy who was going to receive an education at the grammar school.

Their chauvinism had reached unsurpassed proportions. Uncle Istvan had made a school box for Janos's clothes. It was of beautiful grooved and fitted wood and the top was carved with his initials. Aunt Rozi had given him a pair of boots that were nearly new, even though it meant that her own son would have to go without during the winter. From Uncle Pal a comb, from Aunt Nansci two handkerchiefs, and so on. He had felt like a prince until this morning, when he felt like an exile.

His mother left him and went out into the kitchen. He followed her because this was the last morning he would be able to help her get the wood in for the stove. She prodded and blew and finally the full embers glowed again and she moved the pan of soup over to the hot part.

Yesterday he had been sent down to the river to wash and

then had gone in company with his father to thank Mr. Adam
Kaldy for the great kindness he was receiving. He was no
longer afraid of Mr. Adam Kaldy. During the year since his
mother had first gone there he had seen Mr. Adam many
times. Once, in the estate office, Mr. Adam had made him
stand by the desk and had shown him the account books for
the estate. He had explained the columns and the entries and
then asked Janos to take a separate piece of paper—beautiful
white paper!—and copy the entries and then work out how
many hectares of land provided the wheat and the maize and
how much milk the herds could be expected to give and what
proportion of that could be used in the dairy and so on. Janos
had been nervous, but not of the task set him. He had been
nervous in case he made the white paper dirty, and in case he
disgraced himself by speaking disrespectfully to his excellency. He had begun working on the columns of figures and had
finally forgotten about Mr. Adam. This was a far more brilliant and exciting problem than any set by Mr. Feher. He had
raced through, checking and calculating and pointing out an
error that had been made in the book. When he gave the result to Mr. Adam, his excellency had appeared to be surprised, and Janos wondered if perhaps he had not been careful enough with the paper. But Mr. Adam had said nothing,
just sent him home again and told him to return on the same
day in the following week.

Frequently after that Mr. Adam gave him problems to do
out of the estate books. Sometimes he also told him not to use
certain words as the people in the town wouldn't understand
him. When the time came for him to go to the school and
take the entrance examination, Mr. Adam had given him a
letter addressed to the director. On the way to the town with
his father (they had started before dawn and it had taken
four different carts to get there), he had asked a question that
had been troubling him for some time.

"Papa, why is it that there is so much maize and wheat and
beet grown on the estate and yet we do not have enough?"

"How do you know what is grown?" his father growled.

"I have seen the book, in Mr. Adam's office. He showed me
only one book, but I have seen the others when they were
open. Many hectares, much hay and wheat and milk—so
much milk Why is there not enough for us?"

Usually his father was uncommunicative, sometimes boastful, but mostly terse. That day he seemed to be searching for
words, trying to explain something.

"It is the law," he had said finally, and then added halting-ly, "You must never talk like that in front of other people. It will bring trouble. You must remember that his excellency Mr. Adam is sending you to school because your grandfather fought with him in Russia. That is all you must remember."

Yesterday he had thanked Mr. Adam, who had given him three *filler*. He'd offered the money to his mother when he came home, but she had told him that this time he could keep it. Now it rested in his pocket and the feel of it gave him a small security. With money he wasn't quite so defenceless.

He drank some soup and then his mother wrapped a shawl round her head. He kissed his grandmother and sisters good-bye, and he and his mother walked over to the ox stables, where the cart was ready to depart, the oxen already yoked.

"Good-bye, Janni. Be a good boy." She gripped him close and he wrapped his arms round her waist again, smelling the dear beloved smell of her for the last time. She was crying; he could feel her body shaking and he could hold his own tears no longer.

"I wish I wasn't going! I wish I wasn't going!"

"Hush now!"

She wiped her face with her apron, then wiped his tears away. "Remember, you and I are different, Janni. We have blue eyes. No one else on the farm has blue eyes. So we'll al-ways be different—different and together—and that is why you must go away to school now and why you won't cry."

Light was beginning to break. He was lifted onto the plank across the front of the cart.

In the back was a load of manure, which caused his mother to call anxiously, "Don't lean back and dirty your clothes, Janni. Remember you must be better, cleaner, more industri-ous than anyone else!"

He nodded, unable to speak again. He saw his father hurry-ing from behind the sheds, taking a moment from his work in order to say good-bye.

"God bless you, my son." He lifted the new wooden box up onto the plank beside Janos, and then Uncle Andras stirred the oxen and the cart began to rumble away across the yard. He looked back to see his mother standing alone. She raised her hand and then the cart turned and he saw her no more.

Aunt Gizi was growing worse. Her complaint, diagnosed as "female trouble," did not right itself with the passing of time, and finally an appointment was made for her to go to a hospital in Budapest. An abdominal operation resulted in the announcement that she was cured, but all through the winter that followed Aunt Gizi lay in her bed and grew more and more skeletal.

Kati, who had at first commuted between the Kaldy manor and her parents' house in town, now moved permanently to look after her mother. Silent—and surprisingly efficient—she washed, fed, and administered drugs.

Uncle Alfred alternated between drunken tears and drunken optimism.

"She's getting better, isn't she?" he demanded of Malie, who was visiting. "She had a little food today. That's a good sign, isn't it?" And then, as he so often did, he collapsed into a confession of self-mortification, recounting all the things he had always meant to do for Gizi but had never done. If only she would get better so that he could do all those things! Every day he went into Gizi's bedroom and endeavoured to cheer his wife with jovial and noisy humour. Watching her mother's face grow even more drawn, Kati did her best to hasten his departure and would prepare herself for Alfred's collapse as soon as he stepped outside the door.

Malie, during her visit, tried to console the maudlin Alfred as best she could. "But what will he do when—if anything happens to Aunt Gizi?" she asked Kati.

Kati smiled, a bitter little smile that was unlike her. "No 'if,' Malie. There's no need to pretend when Papa's not here. She's dying. She knows she's dying. She told me two weeks ago."

"Oh, Kati!" Malie placed her hand over Kati's stubby fingers. "I'm so very sorry."

Kati stared out of the drawing-room window. She, more than either of her cousins, looked her age. She was thirty-one, as indeed was Malie, but Kati's years had given her a dried-up, unlived-in look. Now, pinched and white through hours of nursing, she could have been anyone's spinster daughter.

"Hasn't Felix—or your mother-in-law—suggested helping?"

The bitter little smile again. "Madame Kaldy has done all the proper things. She has written, and sent flowers and fruit from the hothouses. And she has made three visits with Felix and has sent a nurse to help (Mama won't have the nurse near her). Madame Kaldy also told Papa that he wasn't to feel one bit guilty at keeping me here away from my home and husband. I was to stay as long as I was needed."

356

"I see."

"How horrible marriage is, Malie. How hypocritical and . . . expedient. Everyone living in pairs because it is arranged that way, and everyone so lonely."

Malie was shocked. Even allowing for Kati's curious marriage, she was still dismayed by her cousin's cynicism.

"Oh, Kati! That's not true! Your own marriage, it was wrong, but not all of them are like that."

"No?" Kati picked at the tassels on the velvet curtains. "I suppose not. You seem happy enough, although we all knew you only married David Klein because Karoly was dead. And Eva? Is she happy? I don't think so. And my own mama and papa: all those years of marriage, all those years, and he cannot help her now she's dying; she just wants him out of the room. She never asks for him. And all he does is think of how he's going to manage when she's gone. I don't think he really cares for her. And I don't think Mama cares for him. I don't think Mama has ever really loved anyone in her whole life."

"Kati!"

"No. She's felt responsible for me. But she's never loved me. Even now, even while I'm nursing her and helping her, she doesn't love me. How can someone die without loving someone, Malie?"

She could give no answer and, indeed, she was too ashamed to answer—ashamed because she was so very loved, by her husband, her sons, her sister, brothers, and parents. And Kati had never been loved by anyone.

"Can I see her today?"

Kati shrugged. Her shoulders were slumped in exhaustion and she sat badly, the way a woman sits when she is too tired to care about being graceful.

"Go in. She was sleeping just now. Don't wake her."

Aunt Gizi's room was hot, the air sickly with disinfectant and medicaments. She lay, her arms outside the covers, with her face dropped in, like a skull. She wasn't asleep and her eyes followed Malie across the room.

"Hello, Aunt Gizi," she whispered, dropping a kiss on the emaciated cheek.

Aunt Gizi stared.

"Are you feeling a little better?"

It was eerie to see Aunt Gizi, sharp, snappy, astringent Aunt Gizi, lying helpless and disinterested, waiting to die.

"Kati will be along soon," she said. The lids over Aunt Gizi's eyes lowered and raised again.

357

"Look after Kati," she croaked. "She only has you, only the Ferencs. Look after Kati."

Ice ran down her spine. She longed to feel pity or affection for Aunt Gizi, but there was something macabre about this cold, dying creature that repelled her.

"I made a mistake," whispered Gizi. "It was a bad marriage." Her eyes closed and she drifted away. Malie, with relief, started to leave the room, but suddenly Aunt Gizi's eyes opened again. "Eva too," she continued, "a mistake, a bad mistake. You were the best, Malie. You married the way we all should have done. . . ." The whisper trailed away and she could hear the sudden noise in Aunt Gizi's chest, a quick, heavy breathing. "Where's my brother?" she rasped. "I want to see my brother."

Malie fled. Outside she told Kati that her mother was worse, much worse, and they had better send for the doctor and get Alfred into the bedroom too. Then she sent one of the servants for her papa; he had been coming every day to see poor Gizi but Gizi had never specifically asked for him before. By the time he arrived Alfred was blubbering all over the library with his arm clutched round a bottle of brandy. The doctor was in Aunt Gizi's bedroom and Papa waited until he came out and then spoke to him about Alfred.

"You had better give him a sedative or something," he said sternly. "My brother-in-law is unable to control himself in the sick-room, and he is upsetting my sister and her daughter. Can you do something to quieten him?"

The doctor nodded and disappeared into the library. Papa waited for a second and then went in to his sister. The breathing was even sharper and faster. Amalia watched her father take Aunt Gizi's hand in his and bend over the pillow.

"Gizi."

He said a few words that she did not understand, and suddenly she was back in the bedroom with the old man dying and herself only a child.

"Gizi?"

Aunt Gizi opened her eyes and tried to smile at Papa, and Malie saw that Kati had been wrong about one thing. Aunt Gizi had loved someone in her life; she had loved the brother who had trodden the same harsh path to success that she had.

The two hands clasped against the coverlet tightened against each other, and then Gizi's slender fingers went slack, the rasping stopped, and Papa turned away from the bed.

After the funeral Kati made no attempt to go home, back to the manor and Felix. She sent a message saying that her papa needed her and she would be up in the country with him during the summer and would visit her husband and mother-in-law then.

She spent the summer at the Racs-Rassay villa and went "home" only once, to collect her paints. She left her clothes and the expensive wedding presents that had flowed from all parts of the county. On social occasions she met her husband and Madame Kaldy with dignified cordiality. Madame Kaldy did not seem too happy with the arrangement, or rather she did not seem happy with Kati's composure and disinterest. She tried to speak to Alfred Racs-Rassay, intending to ask him if some compromise could be arrived at where Kati spent at least some time being a dutiful wife. Alfred and she had come to a very fair arrangement once before and the result was the restoration of the Kaldy estate and an aristocratic husband for his daughter. Something could surely be agreed upon again. But Alfred, the widower, was not the same man as Alfred, the man of affairs and business. He was now permanently drunk and bloated with too much food. His hands shook all the time she was talking to him and he kept saying, "I agree, my dear Luiza, I agree," without having the slightest idea of what she was saying.

She finally had to tackle Kati herself and was chagrined to discover that Kati, although still quiet and respectful, was no longer the docile creature who had come to the manor as a bride.

"I cannot come home, mother-in-law," she stated flatly. "As you can see, my papa needs me. Felix is quite happy with you and his horses. I see no necessity at all for me to hurry home."

Madame Kaldy fidgeted. "A wife's place is with her husband," she said sanctimoniously. "Your dear mama would have agreed with me, I know. When she was ill it was different—a special need—but your papa is just drinking because he feels sorry for himself. Your place is with your husband, not your father."

"I cannot leave him." Kati's voice was without expression, and she stared blankly at her mother-in-law. Madame Kaldy fidgeted again.

"You should come home," she urged. "You are, what, thirty-one now? And no sign of children. And how will there be if you do not come home?"

Kati stared again, coolly, almost pityingly. Without knowing why, Madame Kaldy flushed. She knew there was something wrong between her son and Kati, they did not behave as other married couples behaved, but she blamed Kati for that. Look how devoted he had been to Eva. There was nothing wrong with her son, for with Eva he had behaved just like any other young man. It was all Kati's fault. She made no attempt to be pretty or vivacious. How could she capture a man as sensitive and fastidious as Felix when she never even tried to be feminine? Sometimes she wondered if perhaps she should have let him marry Eva Ferenc after all. Then there would have been an heir but no estate. She sighed. How difficult and complicated it all was.

"You need not worry about an heir, mother-in-law." Kati smiled. "Eva will give you all the heirs you need."

Eva, this summer, had announced smugly that she was pregnant again. She seemed to have settled into marriage at last and was overheard to say that she hoped this child would be a boy as she "owed it to Adam." Madame Kaldy didn't understand that remark either and it made her uncomfortable. What did she mean, owed it to Adam? When questioned, Eva had flushed and mumbled that she had remained childless for five years before Terez was born, so she thought she ought to hurry up now. It all seemed strange, and Madame Kaldy didn't like it.

"So you won't come home?" she pressed.

Kati smiled politely and shook her head.

"When will you come home?"

"When Papa is better."

And, frustrated, Madame Kaldy had to be content with that.

It seemed that her problem might quickly be solved that winter, for just before Christmas Alfred stepped out of bed one morning and dropped dead on the floor. No one was really too surprised. He had become enormous and dropsical and a post-mortem revealed that, although he had died of a heart attack, he also had cirrhosis of the liver. Kati, wooden-faced and dry-eyed, followed the coffin of her parent to the Racs-Rassay tomb for the second time in a year. After the funeral Malie invited her to come and stay in Budapest for as long as she liked, and Kati, for the first time in months, showed a little warmth and enthusiasm.

"Oh, Malie, could I?"

"Of course, darling! You know we love to have you. The boys adore you, and you can see your artist friend again. Dominic, wasn't it?"

"I shan't stay for long. Just long enough to make arrangements to go to Vienna."

"Vienna? Why do you want to go to Vienna? You know so very few people there."

Kati suddenly leaned forward and took Malie's hands in hers. "Malie. I haven't told anyone yet, but I'm going to live in Vienna. I'm never going back to Madame Kaldy or Felix. I'm going to live in Vienna, and maybe I shall study painting, or maybe I'll just live like a lady with servants and a carriage. But I'm never, never going to do what anyone tells me again." She shook her head. "I'm never going to allow myself to be in a position where people *can* tell me what to do. I'm free, Malie! For the first time in my life, I'm free!"

Malie, about to ask how Kati was going to live, stopped, realizing suddenly that Kati was an extremely rich young woman. She owned a house in the town, a villa up in the hills, and any number of interests in various factories and coal mines.

But Kati . . . all alone in Vienna?

"You shouldn't go and live alone, Kati. Not now, not after this year with your mama and papa dying. If you want to leave Felix—"

"I do . . . and have."

"Then come and stay with us. You can study painting if you wish, and meet our friends. You can do everything in Budapest that you can do in Vienna."

Kati smiled, the old Kati smile that was shy and timid and grateful. "I'll come for a little while, but I'm tired of being 'poor Cousin Kati,' and that's what I'll always be if I stay forever in the family." She clasped her hands together and closed her eyes. "I'll never know what I could be unless I go away, where no one knows me, where no one is sorry for me. I want—I want to be a *person*, Malie, a real person. Don't you understand?"

She understood, and she promised to take the letter to Madame Kaldy and answer the questions that would ensue. It would all be arranged very discreetly. It would be announced that after nursing two parents Kati's own health was in jeopardy and she was going to a convalescent hospital in the Austrian Alps. Eventually people in the county would realize that she was not coming back.

Malie, who knew more of Kati's marriage than anyone else, privately decided it was more than either Felix or his mother deserved.

24

In 1929, just as Jozsef completed his courses in Berlin, Leo set out for that vibrant and urbane metropolis. Their studies should have overlapped by a year, but Leo, cursed with the weak chest of his boyhood, had been forced to spend another winter up in the hills with Eva and Adam. Now, pronounced cured, finally and completely, he set off to meet his brother in Berlin. They had arranged it so that, before Jozsef finally left, Leo would spend two weeks settling in Jozsef's apartment and being generally eased into Berlin life by his experienced elder brother.

The girls in Berlin were slim and lovely. French, English, American accents could be heard in the restaurants and bars, and Leo nervously, but with admiration, watched Jozsef's easy camaraderie with the crop-haired young women and their noisy companions. Jozsef had filled out into a square-shouldered, heavily built young man. He looked a little like Papa but had none of Papa's sternness and rigidity. On the contrary, his face had already become a little full round the jowls from German beers. He seemed to know everyone by name and was constantly calling across to people. "Hi, Lisette, Gunther! Come and meet my little brother from Budapest. He can speak four languages fluently. What do you think of that?" One of the slim, bright young girls came over and kissed Jozsef, leaving a bloody smear of lipstick over his mouth and chin. Leo blushed, but the blush didn't signify disapproval, only envy and a certain degree of erotic sympathy in his own body.

"Hey, Jozsef, look at your little brother! He's blushing. Who would expect a Hungarian to blush because he sees a girl kissing a man!"

Jozsef laughed and answered in some Berliner slang that Leo did not understand. He was, as Jozsef had said, fluent in four languages, but this was a quick-fire colloquialism that he couldn't grasp. He wondered if he would ever have the temerity to kiss a girl in a public restaurant.

Later, in the apartment on Savigny Platz, he tried to question his brother on the subject of women.

"It's been difficult for me, Jozsef," he said earnestly. "You know what it's like at home, Papa knowing everyone in the town, and up in the hills it's worse, all the girls full of county pedigrees and looking for husbands. And the peasants—I don't think I could with the peasants." How to explain that while he found some of the peasant girls smooth and brown and pretty, he couldn't bring himself to ask favours of them, even though many of his schoolmates had. On the rare occasions when his desire had been roused by a farm girl, the fear and the humility in her brown eyes had killed his overtures.

Jozsef opened the bottle of brandy that Leo had brought from home. He sat down on the opposite side of the table and poured two glasses.

"It's easy in Berlin," he said expansively. "You can go out and buy a girl if you want. No one to spy on you or report back. You must be careful about making sure she's clean, though. A fellow in my second year had to leave the university and go home for medical treatment. His father made no end of a row about it."

"I don't think I'd like to buy a woman," said Leo, although a faint surge of excitement caught him at the *idea* of such an arrangement.

Jozsef preened himself a little. "No. Well, I've never had to do it—buy a woman. There was a girl last summer. That's why I didn't come home for the vacation. She came and stayed here with me for three months, did all the cooking and washing too. She was crazy about me. Said she'd never known anyone like me in her whole life."

"What happened to her?" asked Leo, fascinated.

Jozsef looked crestfallen. "She went back to Frankfurt when my allowance ran out," he explained. "She couldn't be bought, you understand, but she had to have something to live on and I'd used all my money up. I couldn't write to Papa for any more."

It seemed incredible, exciting and tremendously cosmopolitan. To think that his own brother had lived here, in this apartment, with a ravishing creature whom he could possess whenever he wanted. A kaleidoscope of fantastic images chased themselves through his head: Jozsef and the girl in bed, on the bed, under the table, in the bath, on the floor in front of the stove. . . . Sweat broke out on his forehead.

"But," he persisted, "how do you find girls like that? Girls who love you, girls you can talk to as well as . . ."

Jozsef shrugged, the careless shrug of the man who isn't pressed by urgent bodily needs in contrast to the man who is. "Oh, they just come along. Some you'll meet at the university or at parties. I met Gerta at a bar in Friedrichstrasse. She didn't have enough money to pay her bill, and I helped her. She came back here and that was that." He regarded his brother's glum face with idle affection and then said good-naturedly, "Look, old fellow, I'll tell you what we'll do. Do you have any money?"

"I've my first term's allowance from Papa."

"Right. Then we'll go out on the town this evening, your first evening in Berlin. I'll show you the bars and the bright lights, and who knows what might happen?"

They went to about four bars and drank a lot of beer. Jozsef kept seeing people he knew, and they all talked and shouted and bought more beer until Leo felt that if anyone squeezed him the liquid would burst from both ends the way it does when you squeeze a rubber tube. After the fourth bar there was much whispered conversation with an unshaven young man called Theodor, and then they went through a door at the back of the bar into a small overheated room with a rostrum at one end. A jaundiced pianist was thumping out jazz on a piano.

"You can dance here," said Jozsef affably. "Over there, you can pick anyone you like." Through the smoke and gloom he could see a wooden partition with, over the top, a row of female heads. "Come on," said Jozsef, pulling him across the room.

On the other side of the partition were five plumpish young women, naked except for silver fringes strung just below their navels and several matching silver chains round their necks. Leo began to giggle.

"Shut up," hissed Jozsef.

One of the girls stood up and walked toward Jozsef. Her fringe came to the top of her fat thighs and rustled when she walked. "Want to dance?" she asked professionally. Leo couldn't stop giggling. Every time he looked at the fringe he began to giggle again.

"What's the matter with him?" asked the girl sharply.

"Doesn't he like girls? He shouldn't come here if he doesn't like girls."

"He's shy."

She glared at him, then at Leo. "You want to dance?" she asked again, belligerently.

Jozsef pushed him towards her, and he found himself competently gripped by a pair of heavy Teutonic arms. There was a smell of stale powder about her, and close up he could see that the pores of her skin were clogged with make-up. They jiggled up and down to the music, Leo doing his best to keep a distance from her so that her powder-covered breasts wouldn't smudge his suit. He caught sight of Jozsef dancing with another tasseled beauty, and the sight of the fringes bobbing up and down over her buttocks made him giggle again.

"What's so funny?"

"My brother. He—look at him."

She looked. "What's so funny?" she asked again tonelessly, and then suddenly she pushed him away, with a remark that he only half understood but which he knew was insulting. Her voice grew louder and Jozsef left his dancing companion and hurried over.

"We'd better get out," he said, annoyed. "She thinks you're some kind of freak or police spy or something. Come on. If she shouts for much longer we'll get thrown out."

In the street Jozsef walked along, sulking a little. "Complete waste of money," he grumbled. "What's the matter with you? First of all you say you want to see some women, then when I take you all you do is laugh."

"I'm sorry, Jozsef."

"What was wrong with them?"

"They—I don't know, they just made me laugh. It wouldn't have been so bad if they were completely naked. It was the tassels. They reminded me of Aunt Gizi's curtains up at the villa!"

Jozsef, always good-natured, grinned a little, then flung his arm round Leo's shoulders. "Okay. We'll try something else. Maybe you were wise. I expect it would have cost most of your allowance."

They stumbled on into several more bars until after a while Leo found he could no longer even see them properly, all neon lights and red lamps and, everywhere you looked, fringes: on the lamps, on the curtains, on the foreheads of girls in the bars. And photographs; every third bar seemed to be full of photographs of naked girls. First he was shocked, then titillated, and finally he couldn't see them at all.

Jozsef pushed open the door of yet another establishment, which proved to be a hall with a curtained stage at one end. The floor was filled with tables and chairs, and sweating waiters pushed their way between customers.

"Hi, Jozsef. Come over here!" It was the girl who had kissed Jozsef earlier in the day and they fought their way to her table, where Jozsef ordered more beer. She was there with another girl, crop-haired and fringed like all the others. She wore a green dress, and that too had a fringe across the neck.

"This is Hanna Weiss."

Jozsef stood up and kissed Hanna's hand (he told Leo later that he always tried to live up to the reputation of being a romantic Hungarian; the girls loved it and it gave him a head start over his home-brewed German rivals). "Enchanting," he murmured. Leo wanted to say and do something equally effective, but he could only blink owlishly. He was afraid to stand up in case he fell over.

"Hanna works in the bookshop just off Friedrichstrasse."

"You're here alone?"

"Gunther brought us, but he's passed out. He's in the washroom, I believe." Lisette shrugged thin naked shoulders. "Got a cigarette?" she demanded of Leo.

He flushed drunkenly and shook his head.

"Get me some cigarettes, darling."

"Sorry, Lisette, my allowance has just about run out. We're celebrating on my little brother's money this evening."

Lisette fixed Leo with a speculative eye; then she began—fully and explicitly—to swear. Leo stared. He had never heard a woman swear before. He looked at the girl in the green dress, who stared back coolly and flicked ash from her cigarette straight onto the table.

The noise of piano, clarinet, and drums crashed from the stage at the end of the hall. The curtain rose and four tall blondes in split evening dress did a few high kicks and sang a little song about wanting to please the boys. The audience was appreciative, calling out and passing comments on the shapes of the women. Then three of them left the stage and the remaining one sang in a husky and curiously attractive voice, something about her lovers: what she did to the old ones and what the young ones did to her. Halfway through the song she coyly removed her skirt. She had long beautiful legs. Leo tried to focus his eyes a little better.

"You like her?" asked Jozsef. Leo nodded, and for some reason Jozsef and Lisette burst out laughing. Lisette whispered into Jozsef's ear, and they laughed again. The fringed girl wasn't laughing, but she was interested. She was staring at the blond singer in an absorbed and inquiring manner, as though wondering how the performer put her act together.

The blonde on the stage turned round and thrust her hips back at the audience, which roared and clapped. Then she took the top of her dress off. She had a narrow waist and small, high breasts covered in a silver brassiere. Leo's fuddled eyes ran the length of her beautiful body. How did you get a girl like that to come and live in your apartment, do the cooking and the cleaning, and be available whenever you wanted?

"She's beautiful," he muttered, and his brother and Lisette roared again, leaning against each other and heaving together.

The song continued, built towards a climax, and suddenly the girl stripped off the brassiere, revealing to Leo's surprise a completely flat chest. He was puzzled. "She's got no breasts!" he complained drunkenly. "That's cheating, not to have breasts!"

Lisette and his brother were hysterical. Jozsef had his head on the table. He was laughing so hard he couldn't even lift it. Hanna stared at him, curiously.

"You're very drunk, aren't you?" she asked coolly.

"No." He tried to straighten his back and took another gulp of beer just to show that he wasn't drunk. The girl on the stage, with a final flourish, ripped off the tiny strip of cloth over her loins. Underneath was a support—made of silver lamé—as worn by male athletes.

"It's a man," said Leo blankly. Jozsef and Lisette fell on each other's necks, wiped each other's tears away, tried to speak and couldn't. Leo's disappointment changed immediately to another sensation. The floor rocked up at him and nausea gripped his stomach.

"Get him out! Quick!"

Lisette and Jozsef, one each side, bundled him out through the door and he was sick on the pavement, conscious of shame even while he was vomiting. Suppose his papa or either of his brothers-in-law were to walk past now. How disgusted they would be. How disgusted he was himself.

"All right now, old chap?"

He nodded, was sick again, and suddenly felt better, subdued but better. "I think perhaps I'd better go home."

"Do you think you can make it on your own while I take the girls back?"

"Oh, yes."

They began to walk along the streeet, Jozsef and Lisette in front. They were still giggling and Jozsef had his arm round Lisette's shoulders.

"I'm very sorry," he said to the silent Hanna by his side, "for spoiling your evening, having to leave so soon."

"I'd about finished anyway."

If only he had managed to get to the lavatory instead of being sick before this self-possessed young woman. What was the name of her bookshop? He must remember never to go there. He couldn't bear to see her looking at him and remembering him drunk.

"Why don't you come and visit me in the shop?" she said suddenly. "It's all quite different in daylight, isn't it?" She smiled slightly. Her mouth was narrow but she had nice eyes. They were friendlier than the rest of her face.

"I . . . perhaps . . . thank you."

"You'll need books at the university. I might be able to let you have damaged ones cheaper."

"Thank you."

"I live here." She stopped before a three-storey apartment house. "Your brother and Lisette have disappeared. I expect they've gone back to Lisette's room. You'll be all right, won't you? Savigny Platz is only just round the corner."

He wished, so much, that he could have kissed her hand with all the style that Jozsef had exhibited. If he could have done that it would have helped to blot out the miserable memory of his being sick on the pavement. He took her hand in his, looked at her face, and thought better of it. "Good night," he said briskly, pumping her hand up and down in a fierce shake.

"Don't forget to come and see me in the shop."

She walked up the three steps. She had long legs like the girl—man—in the cabaret. Would she take her brassiere off to reveal no breasts? He began to giggle at himself as he walked back to the apartment.

When he returned to Berlin for the university year, he went and called at the bookshop. He wore his best suit and had brushed his hair back from his forehead, shaved, and put on a clean collar. He wanted to remove the impression of the

368

drunken student. He didn't recognize her at first. Her hair was still combed down over her eyes, but she was wearing a neat white blouse and navy-blue skirt. She looked very clean and efficient, not at all like a girl who went to bars and was experienced in sexual matters.

"Hello."

"I'm back . . . for the university."

"What are you studying?"

"Literature. And I'm thinking of learning Russian as well."

"Is that why you've come here? To buy books?"

"No, I didn't come here to buy books. I wondered. . . . Could I see you?"

It was strange how attractive her smile was. Her mouth hardly moved but her eyes crinkled. They were pale and she had long dark lashes that stuck out straight. "I expect so."

"When?"

"This evening. The shop closes at seven. You can meet me here."

He hurried back to Savigny Platz, deciding to miss his lecture and prepare himself for what lay ahead. He tidied the apartment and bought a bottle of wine, some sausage, jellied eggs, and a small pot of caviar. He made the bed and covered it with a Chinese shawl that he'd found in the bottom of a chest. Of course, he considered while soaping himself thoroughly in the bath, it might not be here; it might be in her apartment. But it would be better here, an intimate dinner, wine, bed. . . . He tried to remember all the things that Jozsef had instructed him on during the summer: not to be in a hurry, to spend plenty of time talking first, to say nice things about her intellect as well as her appearance. He put on clean underclothes and went to meet her at the bookshop.

They spent the entire evening drinking coffee at a restaurant in Friedrichstrasse. It was a terrible evening because he didn't know how to arrange things so that eventually they would end up on the Chinese shawl in his apartment. He suggested a drink to begin with, thinking that from then on everything would progress to an increasing warmth that would float them along to Savigny Platz and an evening of passionate fulfilment. Hanna said she would prefer coffee, and instead of inviting intimacies she proceeded to question him about his university course. After the fourth coffee he tried to change the subject.

"Do you often go out with Lisette? To bars and cabarets, like the one we met at?"

369

She shrugged. "Sometimes. I knew her in Hamburg. We were at school together. She was very bright and her family were quite rich. She came to the university but dropped it after a year. She was reading Literature too."

He refused to be taken back to that theme and asked, "Do you enjoy that sort of cabaret? That sort of place?"

Her pale eyes narrowed slightly. "It's very interesting," she said tonelessly. "Please, could I have another coffee?"

Should he offer to buy dinner? But if he did, what of the carefully prepared seducer's dinner laid out in Savigny Platz? He could hardly buy dinner here and then take her back to his apartment where the other one was spread, complete with flowers and candles.

He tried again. "You must find Lisette an exciting girl to go around with. She's so popular, and she knows so many people. My brother liked her a lot."

"Oh?"

"I expect you have much fun together?"

"We don't see each other all that much," she said glacially. "I work during the day and Lisette sleeps."

He felt he could have approached her more easily if she had been wearing the green fringed dress. There was something very forbidding about her white blouse and navy skirt. Several times he tried to say, the way Jozsef would have said, "Would you like to come and eat at home with me?" but always the buttoned-to-the-neck blouse deterred him, that and the row of coffee cups between them.

At ten o'clock he gave up. "Shall we eat here?" he asked bleakly after the seventh cup of coffee.

"Thank you, but I should really go home now. I have to get up early, so I like to go to bed at ten thirty."

"I see."

In silence they waited for the *Stadtbahn*. And equally silently they sat next to one another on the train. At the steps of her apartment she thanked him politely for the seven coffees, then waited. For a wild, incredulous moment he thought she was going to invite him in. Perhaps she was waiting for him to ask to come in.

"May I come—" he began, and was interrupted by her eager reply.

"Oh, yes! You can come to the bookshop any time. I'm always there! You'll find me whenever you like!"

Her eyes were curiously defenceless, shy, pleading a little, so unlike the rest of her face. He didn't have the courage to ask again. He just said, "Thank you. Good night," and walked away, his mouth sour with too much coffee and his stomach rumbling because he hadn't eaten all day. He consumed several frankfurters at a pavement stand on his way home and vowed he wouldn't bother to see her any more.

A week later he went into the bookshop again, and his confidence was slightly restored when he saw her give that funny smile that lit her eyes but not her mouth. He was wearing his ordinary clothes and he knew his shirt needed changing. This time he was determined. "Are you free this evening?" She nodded. "Would you like to have dinner with me, in my apartment?" The words suddenly sounded loud in the shop, as though he'd shouted them at the top of his voice. He flushed but refused to give ground. "I've bought some wine," he finished aggressively.

"I—er—"

"You just said you were free."

"I'm free for the first part of the evening. I could meet you for coffee in Friedrichstrasse."

"What about the rest of the evening?" he asked doggedly.

"I—I have a friend coming round to see me. An old friend I haven't seen for a long time. I can't ask her not to come. She's coming at—at nine."

He was caught. She hadn't got a friend coming; she'd lied. But how could he say he only wanted to see her providing she was coming to his apartment for the whole evening? It might give the impression he was a lecher, a seducer.

"Can't she come another evening?"

"Oh, no," she said in firm tones.

"Could you come to dinner tomorrow then?"

For a moment she looked trapped. "No. Not tomorrow. But I could have coffee with you this evening, between seven and nine, in Friedrichstrasse."

He gave up. "All right." He sighed. "I'll meet you here, and I'll make sure you are home by nine."

The smile again, the happy, glowing, secretive smile that was really quite gratifying if you weren't trying to arrange the preliminaries to a great passion.

They drank coffee for two hours—four cups this time—and then went back on to the *Stadtbahn*, home to the friend who didn't exist. Again, at the steps, she paused, waiting for him to say something. As he began to walk away she called, "Will I see you again?"

"Perhaps." He looked back. She was watching him. She was small and had a dejected look about her. Serve her right, he thought. Let her go in and sit on her own for the rest of the evening, waiting for her friend who isn't coming. But the picture of her, drooping and small, stayed in his mind, and four days later he went into the shop just before lunch and suggested they eat together.

It was in November, after countless evenings of coffee in Friedrichstrasse, a few lunches, and some visits to the cinema, that she finally consented to come to the apartment in Savigny Platz and eat with him there. He could hardly believe after all this time that he had finally won and he was surprised to find that all the excitement and anticipation of the evening ahead had gone, vanished into gallons of coffee and dozens of formal farewells outside her apartment. He bought all the same things as before, except for the candles. He felt the time for obvious seduction props was past and he thought the candles might make them both nervous.

She was nervous anyway when she arrived. He helped her off with her coat and wished, not for the first time, that she wasn't wearing the white blouse and navy skirt. She didn't smile at all. She looked rather the way she had the first time they met, very cool and disdainful, a worthy companion to Lisette. She sat and smoked, not even trying to talk while he darted round the screen that separated the sink and the gas ring from the rest of the room and tried to open the bottle of wine.

"Shall I do that for you?"

"No, of course not. I can manage." He wrestled and felt the corkscrew bend under his neurotic pressure.

"Oh dear! You've pushed the cork into the bottle!"

Enraged he stared at the cork fragmenting into the wine. Then he poured it into their glasses and tried to remove the cork from hers with a fork.

"It's all right I like it with cork in." She raised one eyebrow slightly disdainfully, and he drank his own wine noisily and filled the glass again.

She ate very little, picking at the food he had bought as though each morsel were smothered in aphrodisiac. Several times he tried to speak and gave up under her cool, analytical stare.

She drank sparingly, also, and finally she put her fork down and said, "Shall I make some coffee?"

"No!" he shouted. The composure left her face and she was

suddenly nervous again. "I've spent weeks sitting with you drinking coffee when all I've wanted to do is bring you back here. For God's sake don't start making coffee now in my apartment! I've had enough coffee to last me a lifetime!"

"I'm sorry. I—"

"You're not sorry! You know very well why I wanted you to come here, and you've done your best to spoil it. And you have! I don't know what's so different about me. Why you can't treat me like all the other men you've known? What's wrong with me that I'm only good enough to drink coffee with? Is it because I'm Jozsef's little brother? Is that it? Because I'm a joke? I don't understand about men dressed up as women on a stage? Is that what's wrong with me?"

She began to cry, curling back away from him into a corner of the armchair.

"What's wrong with me?" he asked again, disconcerted and a little ashamed of himself. "If you don't like me, why have you gone out with me?"

"I do like you." She muffled the words with her hand. "I do like you, but—"

"But what?"

She raised her face and stared anxiously at him. "I'd like to be the same as Lisette, but somehow I can't seem to be. And you all think I am, and I'm too ashamed to let you know that I'm not."

"What?" He tried to follow her through the labyrinths of explanations.

"You obviously thought I was wild and daring and . . . everything that Lisette is. That's what everyone thinks. When you didn't understand the cabaret and you were sick outside I thought it would be all right with you. You didn't understand about how necessary it is to be *fashionable* in Berlin. I thought you would be happy if I was just . . . ordinary, not fast or exciting. And when I realized that you did want me to be like Lisette, I didn't know what to do."

Her pale eyes were huge under the ragged hair. Her thin small hands were trembling and he was sorry for her, sorry and also a little repulsed. She had seemed so self-possessed, so mature, and suddenly she was a nervous, unhappy little girl, asking his pardon.

"I've spoilt it all, haven't I?" she asked tremulously. "You don't like me any more, do you?"

"Of course I do." He just wanted to get her out of his apartment now. She seemed to be growing tinier every minute, tinier and more helpless and dependent on him. She was making him feel mean and dirty when all he had wanted to do was to be a man, like Jozsef.

"You won't want to see me again, will you?"

"Of course I shall."

"I shan't always be so—dull. I'm sure it will be different later on."

"I expect so."

"I've spoilt the evening, haven't I?"

"Of course you haven't. But it's getting late now so I'll take you home We'll both feel different in the morning."

She allowed herself to be comforted and talked into her coat and beret He walked her back to her apartment and all the time she was talking, clinging to his arm and humiliating herself asking him to continue seeing her, offering half promises of her body in the future. He kissed her cheek very gently when they reached her home and she suddenly stopped talking, staring up at him with her pale eloquent eyes.

"Good-bye then, Leo," she said quietly. "Good-bye."

"There's no need to say good-bye."

She was already walking away from him. She closed the door of the house and didn't look back at all.

He never wanted to see her again.

25

When he went home for the winter vacation it was like stepping back fifty years. He'd never realized how old-fashioned Hungary was and how out of date the members of his own family were even Eva who prided herself on being the harbinger of current fashions and trends. Good heavens, she was still referring to herself as *moderne*, which alone was enough to date her terribly.

Hungary even Budapest, had a stately, old-world feel about it and a sense of constriction caused by the censorship of press and politics. Berlin, capital of a new republic, with its heady air of freedom, made Budapest seem restrictive and the Hungarian people oppressed. A world war, a revolution, and a counter-revolution seemed to have made little change in the iron-handed methods with which his native land was governed. There wasn't the vibrant sense of events that there was in Berlin. Everyone seemed sleepy and slow, and in addition Papa and David Klein were worried and depressed about the Wall Street crash.

He spent his vacation commuting aimlessly between David and Malie in Budapest, Mama, Papa, and Jozsef in the town, and Eva and Adam at the farm. And everywhere he was struck by the smallness of their worlds, their parochial attitudes. Even Papa and David Klein, worrying over the stock markets, were more concerned with what it would do to the credits and debits of their particular banking concerns than with its effect on the world. He had come from Berlin where the crash was already beginning to make itself felt. In Budapest it was the same: more poor, more unemployed, longer queues at the soup kitchens. Two students who had begun with him last October had already been compelled to drop out of their courses because their parents could no longer afford to give them an allowance. He watched his family. There was Malie—whom he loved, yes, he really did—happy and complacent with her two sons, her luxurious Budapest apartment, and an adoring husband. What did Malie know of suffering? And Eva, indulged not only by her husband but now—as mother of a son, heir to the Kaldy estate at last—by her mother-in-law also. What did Eva care for the hungry and unemployed?

He raged in silence, and when he could be silent no more he tackled Jozsef on the subject.

"Don't you see, Jozsef? Don't you see how wrong it all is, that we don't care? Everyone concerned about where they will go for their holiday, and Mama still buying dresses like a girl, and none of them thinking about all the people in Budapest and Berlin who haven't enough to eat!"

Jozsef blinked and lit a cigar. Since he had become an employee of the bank, he had adopted man-of-the-world ways. He sported a walking stick too, which he swung most professionally on his way to and from work. "I remember all that from my first year as a student," he said, bored. "It was quite the thing when I first went to Berlin. I suppose it still must be. Do you have discussion groups about it?"

Leo wanted to hit him. His anger was all the more pronounced because he had been going to the discussion groups.

"It's that kind of attitude that produced the Russian revolution," he blazed. "People like you . . . and 'Let them eat cake.' "

"Surely that was the French revolution, old fellow?"

"It's the same thing! Unless we do something now there'll be another bloody revolution. It's poverty, not politics, that makes bloodshed!"

"Oh, but look here." Jozsef flicked ash from his cigar. "No one wants to see people hungry, but how can we stop it? We just go on working, all of us. It's not our fault if the system breaks down every so often. And anyway, if you feel this strongly about it you shouldn't be taking an allowance from Papa. If it's middle-class bourgeois money you're angry about, why are you having such a good time on it in Berlin?"

He was so angry and ashamed he had to turn away. All the time he had been aware of his hypocrisy, raging about the unfair division of money when he himself was enjoying the fruits of that unfairness. In Berlin he had been swayed by the fiery logic of Communist agitators. He knew there was something wrong with the world, and sometimes, not always but sometimes their doctrines seemed to make sense. Deep in his heart he carried conflicting memories that grew worse as he got older: memories of Uncle Sandor being killed by a group of ragged beggars one of whom he thought he knew; memories of Janos Marton trying to defend his father from attack and, again Janos Marton, walking through the snow to school, thin and poorly clothed with sacking wrapped round his feet; memories of the woman, his mother, humble and supplicating, asking a place for her son at school. All these things bothered him more and more as he grew older, when by right they should have bothered him less. He felt sick and angry when he saw fear in a peasant's face as an overseer went to strike him. He hated the ragged, thin children and the pregnant women carrying those same children to school when the snow was too thick for unshod feet. And yet communism was what had killed Uncle Sandor. He was desperate, searching for a cause he could espouse that would ease the unhappiness he felt when he saw poverty and misery around him.

He saw the boy Janos Marton, once that winter. He went into the kitchen of their town house and the boy was waiting by the door, standing to attention, his cap in his hand.

"Oh . . . er . . . hello."

"Good morning, sir," the boy said tonelessly.

"Are you waiting for someone?"

"I've brought the shoes, the repaired shoes."

"I see."

In the old days he and the boy had always glared at each other, blue eyes blazing at brown whenever they met. But they were older now and had learnt to dissemble. Now there was embarrassment and tension between them, an embarrassment made worse by the fact that Janos was wearing an old jacket of Leo's. He was surprised at his own reaction to that. The jacket was patched and thin and indeed no longer fitted him, but he had to fight a longing to leap forward and tear it from the peasant boy's back.

"How are you enjoying school?"

"Very good, thank you, sir." Up at the farm he would have addressed Leo as "excellency," but three years of school in town had already removed deference and humility from his manner. In another three years he probably wouldn't even call Leo "sir."

Marie bustled back into the kitchen and gave the boy some money. "That's for your uncle, for the shoes," she said. "And here. The mistress found an overcoat for you, and also some more of Mr. Leo's old schoolbooks."

"My schoolbooks!" How dare Mama give his old books away? She had no right to go through his school chest and sort out his things.

Marie looked surprised. "Why, yes, Mr. Leo. She didn't think you'd have any more use for them." She held out the bundle. Most of the books had one or both covers torn and they were battered and ink-stained. *"Third Year Mathematics,"* she said doubtfully. *"The Structure of Hungarian Grammar.* Your mama thought you wouldn't have any more use for these. Mr. Leo."

He forced himself to laugh. "No, of course not. Thank heavens I'm through with all that nonsense. If they're of any use to young Marton here, he's very welcome to them."

"Thank you, sir." The voice was humble, a little afraid, but the blue eyes glared resentment.

"Off you go then, Janos Marton. . . . Here, wait." Marie waddled over to the stove and took a piece of hot strudel from the top of it. "Take this."

The boy hesitated. His tongue came out a little and moistened his lower lip. He picked up the bundle from the table and walked back to the door. "No, thank you," he said distantly. "I'm not hungry."

377

Marie stared, astonished. "What are you saying? Boys are always hungry!"

"No, thank you!" He opened the door and left.

Marie faced Leo, puzzled and slightly hurt. "What of that, Mr. Leo? He's never refused food from me before."

"It must be as he said, he's not hungry."

"Pah!" She shrugged and returned to the sink. "You've only to look at him to see he's hungry. He doesn't get much to eat at his uncle's. He's a mean man, the cobbler. He only gives the child enough to keep him from starving. Still"—she shrugged—"he's a peasant child. He's used to being hungry."

He left the kitchen, disturbed because he hated the thought of Janos Marton wearing his old clothes and using his old books. And disturbed too because his presence had prevented the boy from accepting a piece of strudel.

It was cold when he returned to Berlin. There was thick snow that turned quickly to slush in the streeets. It was disagreeable to go out and he found more and more that he was shutting himself in his room, studying, thinking, growing depressed about things he couldn't quite sort out in his mind. And finally, not really knowing why he did so, he went to the bookshop off Friedrichstrasse.

Hanna wasn't there. The manager told him that she didn't work for him any more, and he looked uncomfortable when Leo asked why and mumbled something about "changes." She wasn't at her apartment either. That was in the possession of two large, handsome young men with S.A. armbands on their sleeves. The room, which he had never seen before, was full of papers and files and there were two desks and a picture of Adolf Hitler on the wall. He couldn't imagine how it must have looked when she was there.

He finally found her, through Lisette, in a lodging house in the Centrum district. She was much thinner and her hair had grown out a little.

"Oh. It's you." She held the door open just enough to show herself, but she made no attempt to ask him in.

"I—I wondered where you were. I went to your apartment, and to the shop."

"I lost my job," she said in a hard, unpleasant voice. "Business has been so bad Herr Gruber said he couldn't afford to pay an assistant."

"Where are you working now?"

She hesitated; then her hand suddenly fell from the door handle and she leaned wearily against the wall. "I don't have anything at the moment. Most of the shops are cutting down on staff, not taking more. A friend of Lisette's told me they were taking waitresses at the Garten, but I didn't get anything. There were too many out-of-work waitresses for a shop assistant to stand a chance."

She looked very small, very vulnerable. He felt a wave of emotion, a gentle protectiveness, the same that he felt whenever Terez, Eva's little girl, put her hand in his. He placed his hand against the door and gently pushed it.

"Can I come in?"

She sighed, then shrugged her shoulders again as though she didn't care any more.

The room was horrible, tiny, damp, and dark. There was a bed, a chair, and a cupboard. Under the window a brown fungus flowered into a Frankensteinian creation. She followed his eyes and said apologetically, "It comes back. I keep scrubbing it off but it comes back."

"Don't you have any money? I mean, why did you give up your other apartment and come to this terrible place?"

"Don't be stupid!" she flared suddenly. "Don't you know anything about money or earning a living? The other apartment cost me forty marks a month. This one costs me sixteen. If I'm lucky I'll find another job before my money goes."

She had seemed so cool and self-possessed before, except for their final evening. She had seemed older than he was, groomed, self-assured, able to take care of herself in a way that he, with his over-protected, middle-class background, was incapable of doing. The pale eyes with the long dark lashes were enormous in her white face and when he looked down at her hands he saw they were quite still, the blue veins standing out vividly. He reached out, touched them, and found they were icy.

"Come and have supper with me," he said, and saw a spurt of greed in her eyes. "We'll go to the Vienna. It's not luxurious, but the food is good and we can talk there."

Watching her eat he thought of the boy Janos again. Food . . . food . . . what a difference it makes, he reflected. There are really only two kinds of people in the world, those who have enough to eat and those who don't. He saw a faint flush of colour creep back slowly into her cheeks as the hot meat and soup settled in her stomach. Her tiny face was almost bird-like, and for the first time since he had knocked on her apartment door she smiled at him, the funny smile that began in her eyes and barely touched her mouth.

"How long have you been out of work?" he asked.

"Two months."

"Can't your parents help you, or don't you have any parents?" He was slightly shocked to remember that he had been contemplating going to bed with her and he'd never even bothered to find out if she had parents.

"They live in Hamburg. My father worked in the shipyard. In my mother's last letter she said he had lost his job and could I send some money home."

"I see. Couldn't Lisette help you? She has a good big apartment and plenty of money——" He stopped, realizing that the way Lisette earned her money was not likely to appeal to Hanna.

She smiled at him and patted his hand. "Lisette has been very kind," she said. "She would lend me money if I asked. But that's not fair, is it? I could earn money that way too. It isn't fair to take Lisette's money when I won't earn it myself."

Ethics, principles; his head was pounding with the problems of poverty and pride. He'd left Hungary believing he could get away from the confusion, and now he was involved again, emotionally involved when all he wanted to do was approach the problem in a clear, abstract, impersonal way.

"I could stay in her apartment if I asked," she continued, "but it would be awkward for her. She needs the room for herself."

"You can't stay in the place you have now."

"What else can I do?"

"Come and live with me," he blurted out, astonishing himself with the suggestion. "It's only one room, but it's a big room."

"No," she said bitterly. "I've not come to that yet. If I do I'll let you know."

"There's the couch," he continued. "You can have that, and if you like we'll fix a sheet round it so that you will be private. You can clean and wash my clothes instead of rent, and if you do the cooking I will buy the food." He was doing something, at last he was doing something instead of talking and theorizing about poverty and the masses. Oh, yes, he would still be taking bourgeois money from his parents, but this way he would at least be sharing it, helping someone who otherwise might starve. He knew a fleeting regret for the things he wouldn't be able to do if the allowance had to support two of them, and he also felt a deeper regret because his freedom would inevitably be curtailed. What kind of relationship they would have, he didn't know, but it was obvious he couldn't behave exactly the way he wanted if Hanna was there all the time.

But these things were minor compared with the fact that, for the first time since returning from Budapest, he felt constructive and conscience-free. He was *doing* something about the world.

"What do you say?" he enthused, and then fell silent when he saw that Hanna was crying quietly into her coffee.

In March, for the very first time, he encountered political violence. He was listening to a speaker at the Red Student Group of the University when there was a commotion at the back of the hall and suddenly several brown-shirted men burst in screaming, "Avenge Horst Wessel!" He just had time to pick up a chair when the fight was all round him. He thrust the chair into the stomach of a S.A. man, who doubled over and tried to slide round the edge of the chair. He jabbed it again, viciously, because he saw that the S.A. man had a club in his hand and was about to use it. Then he raised the chair over his head and brought it down hard and the S.A. man rolled onto the ground screaming for his comrades. The chair was the worst thing he could have done because suddenly they were all on him, clubbing him down and kicking, screaming, shouting, swearing: "Avenge Horst Wessel! Kill the bastard Communist." He felt blood in his mouth and by some superhuman effort managed to rear up like a wounded beast in the middle of the clump of S.A. men. "Gunther! Otto!" he shouted, and then there was help, six or seven or them bashing and fighting and bloodlust finally taking him over so that he screamed with delight every time his fist smashed into a Nazi mouth or belly. In the distance he heard the police horns and sensed, vaguely, that the fight was thinning out, but not for him: blood, pain, the crunch of wood on bone, whose bone he wasn't sure. Bastards! Nazi bastards! Screw their legs off and beat their brains out with them!

There was cold water, a jet of it, and they all went sprawling on the floor where, one by one, they were picked up by the police and taken to the vans outside. The police made a mistake and put an S.A. man in the van with them, and the fight started all over again until they came and pulled him out. At the police station he was charged, and then a doctor came and looked him over, strapped up two ribs, and pulled out the rest of a broken tooth. He was still flying high on excitement and pain and the sense of comradeship with his young fellow students. There was Gunther, good old Gunther, with two rapidly closing eyes and a hand bound up in a splint. And Lajos, a Hungarian like himself, with blood streaming from his skull and a smile of maniacal delight upon his face.

But in the morning he was ill, very ill. His body hurt and when he coughed saliva and blood came up and his chest was an agony to him. At about ten a policeman came down and unlocked the door of the cell. They were taken upstairs and then—surprisingly—thrown roughly out of the yard onto the pavement. He staggered along drunkenly for a few paces, leaning against the wall, and with relief saw Hanna running towards him.

"Oh, God! Leo!"

"Give me an arm, there's a good girl," he croaked.

"I've been so worried! I couldn't think where you'd been all night, and then I heard what had happened at the meeting and I came straight here."

She propped her small shoulder under his and he winced as it jerked his chest.

"Sorry," she said nervously, and then, "Do you think just this once we could afford a taxi?"

At home she helped him into bed, and then brought a bowl of hot water and washed the blood from his body. His mouth was swollen to several times its normal size and from the waist up his body was one livid bruise.

"Oh, God! How awful!" she kept saying while she was washing him. "How awful! How could they do it? How could any of you do it?"

He knew he couldn't bear it if she began to cry, because he felt so ill he might cry himself. He'd tried to joke instead.

"At least they didn't hit me below the waist," he mumbled. "They've left the important bits unharmed. They couldn't have known about the curtain."

"Oh, Leo!" She laughed a little, but the sight of his injured body had shocked her too much. She covered him over with the blanket and then went out to buy some aspirin for his pain.

A week later, when he was tossing and turning one night, reliving the battle in his mind and sweating with the effort of fighting it again, he heard her leave the couch and cross the room. Then he felt her bird-like body slipping softly into bed beside him.

For him even the ecstasy of loving for the first time was double-edged; every time he moved too violently the pain in his ribs forced him to stop, catch his breath, and begin again. It was, altogether, quite a poignant sensation.

He didn't go home that summer. He managed to get a job doing a few translations for a press agency, French, English, and Hungarian. The agency was run by a middle-aged Jew called Heinlein whose obsession, to the point of paranoia, was hatred of Hitler's propaganda paper, the *Völkische Beobachter*. At least once every week he would get Leo to translate a section of the paper into French, Hungarian, and English, together with an editorial written by himself. Whether or not the editorials were ever used Leo did not know. He found the pieces he was forced to translate so crudely and blatantly anti-Semitic, so over-dramatic, that he didn't see how anyone could take them seriously. He dismissed Herr Heinlein's fanatical opposition to the paper as the obsession of an unhappy Jew whose own journalistic career had ended in a second-rate translation agency. As he explained to Hanna, no one of any intelligence could possibly take the screaming editorials of *Völkische Beobachter* as anything but cheap journalism, appealing to just a few illiterate thugs, the thugs who had beaten him up in March. He was shocked and slightly alarmed when, in the September elections, Hitler's party returned 107 seats to the Reichstag. How could so many people vote for a party that was unbalanced and had no economic policy at all? The following week at a meeting of the Red Student Group he got up, for the first time in his career, and made what he considered to be a rather well-planned speech on the best way to educate people against Nazism. He received moderate but well-selected applause and was feeling pleased with himself with the door burst open again and in came the S.A. again.

His group were more prepared this time. They had formed a fighting unit of their own, armed with truncheons and staves. This time he came out of it with no more than a black eye, and that night he and Hanna bought a bottle of wine and celebrated what they decided was their anniversary. The S.A. had brought her to his bed in the first place, he remarked wryly; therefore this second attack could be considered a sentimental reminder of a happy occasion.

The ripples from the Wall Street crash spread wider and more devastatingly. On May 31, 1931, the Kreditanstalt, Austria's largest bank, collapsed and, like current travelling along a wire, sent disaster to the German banks and thence to the Hungarian. A panic—controlled, but still a panic—spread through the financial quarters of Budapest. When he arrived at the Pannonia apartment on his way home that summer it was to learn of disastrous family news. David Klein broke it to him, quietly and with a distant restraint, as though the catastrophe was an inconvenience that had occurred on the other side of the world.

"I am telling you, Leo," he said softly, "because your father is still a very proud man. Once before he failed his family—or considered he had failed them—by his financial losses. This time he is older and not so resilient. I think if he has to tell you himself it will break him."

"But what—how—what will he live on? He and Mama, and Jozsef too; Jozsef works for the bank. What will Jozsef do for a living?"

"We can salvage a little. By some judicious . . . rearrangement we can preserve your father's interest in the bank and protect Jozsef's position there. Amalia and I will be giving up this apartment."

"Giving up the apartment! But why?"

Malie, who had said nothing until now, moved across the room and placed her hand on David's shoulder. She didn't look shocked or strained, not as strained as David did. She looked, extraordinarily enough, contented and cherished.

"We are going back home, Leo. We shall live near Papa and Mama. David—" She smiled down at her husband's head and then raised her hand and stroked his hair in a gesture so affectionate that Leo suddenly felt his throat constrict and a longing for Hanna, for the comfort and affection she gave, swept over him. "David has come to Papa's rescue again. He thinks he can manage to ease Papa's situation if we give up this apartment and reinvest in the town."

"But—but surely," stuttered Leo, "your business is here, in Budapest. Surely—"

David smiled, a rather wry, self-deprecating smile. "I'm afraid that I too have sustained losses, Leo. Large ones. You look surprised? Yes, well, I was aware that for many years

384

you all looked upon me as the financial genius of the family, but I am afraid that your genius has betrayed you. Most of my international investments have crashed, and my interests here in Budapest have only just survived. What, at the moment, seems to be unimpaired is the money I spent twelve years ago to save your father. I invested heavily in the town's factories and steelworks." He raised a quizzical eyebrow. "My altruism has been rewarded."

"But why go back? You know you will hate it. You and Malie, in a provincial town? Oh, no, you will hate it!"

David frowned. "Many things are happening that people hate, Leo. People will hate being unemployed, will hate to starve because they have no work. We are fortunate because we can still live in some kind of comfort."

"But surely—all right, so you cannot afford to keep this apartment, but there are less expensive places in Budapest."

"The reason we are returning, Leo, is because David is good and generous and kind," Malie said very loudly. "If we sell this apartment we can buy Papa's house—he must sell it to someone—and he and Mama can remain there. We shall turn it into two apartments; it is far too big now anyway. We shall live in one, and Papa and Mama can remain at their old address. Remember how Mama was always so adamant about a permanent address?" She smiled a little. "With what David can save for Papa, and with our own financial interests in the town still reasonably intact, we shall be able to see that they live in not too changed a manner."

"I see." He was beginning to see a great deal, chiefly that David Klein, who appeared to be no more than a worldly wise sophisticate, was doing more for his father-in-law than could possibly be expected of him. He was doing more—far more—than Zsigmond Ferenc's own sons were able to do.

"Why are you doing all this, David?" he asked quietly. "Why are you going to live in a provincial town that you will hate, merely in order to save my father's pride?"

"Because they are my family. Because your father is also the father of my beloved wife."

The longing for Hanna struck him afresh, and the longing brought loneliness; even if Hanna were here, their relationship wouldn't be like that of the two people in front of him. He was envious and his sense of isolation grew. He felt he had no one in the world to whom he could reach out. He used to cry for Malie when he was a little boy, but now Malie, even though she still loved him, was welded into intimacy with this gentle, sardonic, good man. One can only give completely to one person, he reflected, and Malie's being was given to David. She wasn't "his" Malie any more.

"There's one more thing, Leo," she continued softly. "The farm. The farm has to go."

"Oh, no!"

"We have no choice, darling. But it will not be too bad. There is still Eva and Adam's farm; we can go there, any of us, whenever we wish, and you always liked it there with Adam. You spent a long time with them when you were ill; you were very happy there. You can always go there again."

She spoke calmly, but he knew that of all the losses this one would hurt her most. She had loved the farm as much as he had.

Later, when David was absent, he spoke to her about it again. "Is there no way the farm could be saved, Malie? Is there nothing else that can be sold?"

Slowly she shook her head. "David tried. It is not possible. He knew how much I loved it, how much it meant to the family. It was the reason I married him. Did you know that, Leo?"

"I heard Jozsef mention something once."

"Oh, that wasn't the only reason. But he held the deeds to the farm and I couldn't bear to let it go. So much had happened there. We were all so very young and happy at the farm. You wouldn't remember it all, Leo; you were too young to remember how it was before the war, the picnics and parties. Eva was silly about Felix Kaldy in those days, and I—" She paused and stared out of the window, smiling a little. "I suppose I was silly too, and I suppose I wasn't happy a lot of times. Papa was stricter then—oh, so much stricter!—but you wouldn't remember that either."

"Yes, I do," he said quickly. "I remember the day when war broke out and Papa came and you were with Karoly."

She turned away from the window and looked at him. "How strange you should remember that. You were such a little boy then."

He remembered, and now, because he was grown up himself and in love and concerned about the person he was in love with, he asked, "Was it very bad, Malie? When Karoly was killed, was it very bad?"

She nodded. "Oh, yes, Leo, it was bad. It's always bad losing someone you love."

"How could you bear to marry someone else then?" he

blurted out. "I don't understand. If you loved Karoly then, how can you be so happy with David now?"

She smiled, a little wistfully. "I didn't love him at first, but he was kind, and he held the deed to the farm, and I didn't know what else to do with my life. Karoly was dead and I knew I would never fall in love like that again. But when you live with someone every day, and grow to know them, then something happens to you. One day I found that because I lived with David and shared his friends and tastes and life, I was happy with him. You'll understand when you live with someone, Leo. You'll understand how living with someone is nothing to do with falling in love."

He nearly told her then—about Hanna. Sometime, soon, he was going to have to tell the family about Hanna because he had one more year at university and at the end of that time he couldn't possibly leave her. He had fully intended this summer to break the news to the family that he was "engaged." He had prepared himself to withstand the family's shock when they learned that a Ferenc son was going to marry the daughter of an unemployed German shipyard labourer, but the financial disaster blocked his efforts. How could he say he wanted to get married—to anyone—when he hadn't even begun to earn his own living?

Papa, over sixty now and trying to hide his humiliation behind coldness and disapproval, had an embarrassing talk with him.

"I had hoped, Leo, when your studies were finished, that David and I would be able to find a niche for you in one or another of the businesses. Literature and languages—well, you know how disappointed I was when you elected to read those subjects instead of something a little more useful, but nonetheless I hoped we might find something for you to do. However"—he looked tormented for a moment—"at this time I can see no prospects for you. I can just manage to see you complete your course, but that is all."

"That's fine, Papa." He wanted to say that nothing on earth would have dragged him into the family combine. Long ago he had decided he didn't want to join the comfortable, dull, financial set-up in which they all lived.

"In fact, Papa, I already have a job in Berlin, translating for a press agency. I can manage without my allowance next year."

The relief on Papa's face was obvious, even though he tried to hide it. "Are you sure?"

"Quite sure." And why did he not tell Papa his reasons for refusing the allowance? He had decided on this course of action before he knew anything of the financial crash. Why did he not tell Papa that his new principles forbade him to accept bourgeois money that had been earned at the expense of others? He had rehearsed his speech all the way home from Berlin but now, hypocrite that he was, he let Papa think he was refusing the money for the sake of the family.

"We will do everything we can to help you find a position when you've finished in Berlin. But it's very difficult now, so little work available—"

"That's all right, Papa. I'll manage."

They were all so small, so wrapped up in their tiny lives (Mama crying over her diminished dress allowance!) that he wanted to shake them, make them wake up and see what was happening in the world. He longed to shout, "Look at me! I've been living with a girl whose father is a labourer and I've been in prison and I've been beaten up by S.A. men at Communist meetings!" He still wasn't a Communist yet, not officially. The memory of Uncle Sandor hovered at the back of his soul.

He wandered like a miserable estranged being through the summer, writing long letters to Hanna and finally accepting Eva and Adam's invitation to go to the country.

Adam too was concerned about economy. He hadn't been hit like David, but he was anxious and worried about produce prices and also about the fact that his pepper crop had failed. He was short-tempered with the farm servants and irritable with his wife and children, even Terez, who could usually charm him into humour.

On the morning that the overseer of the granary came and told him several sacks were missing, Leo, for the first time, saw his brother-in-law lose his temper.

"Again? Haven't we stopped that yet? It's enough. I've been lenient long enough. Get the *pandur* and we'll settle this question of stealing the way it should have been settled long ago."

"It must be the granary workers, excellency," the overseer said, afraid of the wrath he had unleashed.

"Of course it is, you fool! How many in the granary these last months?"

"Two men, excellency, Dezso and Marton."

"Well, which of them is it?"

"I think Marton, excellency. He has a son away at school,

and they sell all their food to send money to him. And yet they do not starve."

"Fetch the *pandur*. Leo, you come with me."

"I don't—"

"Come with me! If an example is going to be made, it must be done with a show of authority. You will come with me!"

He knew before they even started for the farm cottage that the boy was going to be there; he felt it in his blood and bones. Janos was a constant reproach in his life, but a reproach for what? He hated that thin blue-eyed boy, hated him as much as it was possible to hate a human being. At each profound moment of his life it seemed that Janos Marton stared at him, making him ashamed of what he was, what he could not help being.

It was as he thought. When they walked into the Marton hut the boy was there, standing defiantly by the bed in the corner where his mother lay.

"Where is your father, boy?"

He pointed, out through the door and across to the ox stables. Adam turned and strode away, followed by the overseer, two *pandur,* and Leo. And behind him, Leo could feel Janos Marton following, feel the eyes staring into his back and imagine the breath of the skinny youth on his neck.

Outside the ox stable Marton was unloading a cart. When he saw them hurrying toward him he dropped a sack, swore, and then stood waiting beside the cart. Adam nodded to the policemen. "Go ahead, question him."

They stepped forward, towering menacingly over him. One forgot how small the peasants were until one saw them close to ordinary people. The *pandur* were thick, big men, and Marton seemed to shrink back into the cart as they came near him. Neither of the policemen spoke. The bigger one slapped Marton across the face several times with one hand—across, back, across, back, *slap, slap*—and the peasant's head flew from side to side. He cringed and put his hands up to save his face, and the other *pandur* hit him on the side of the head, then pushed him hard so that he fell against the first man.

"Stand up!"

He began to whimper, shielding his face again, whining and crying into his hands, begging his excellency for mercy. His face was marked in vivid red and white patches and a stream of mucus came from his nose. Leo looked down at the ground, but behind him he sensed the boy.

389

"Where have you hidden the grain?" barked the *pandur*. "The grain you have stolen from his excellency's barns. Where have you hidden the grain?"

"I have taken no grain!"

Slap, slap again, and the hands trying to protect the face, the pushing. jostling the man to and fro, frightening him more than hurting him. Leo felt the boy moving and then saw him standing by the oxcart as near to the policemen as he dare go.

"No grain!"

Slap, and a boot was thrust roughly against the man's leg. One policeman grasped his shoulders and swung them towards his colleague. They played thus for a while, pushing him to and fro between them with what amounted to good-natured indifference. "Where is the grain?"

"No grain!"

Slap. His nose began to bleed. A final push caught him off balance and he toppled over, cringing into a heap on the ground.

Leo watched, helpless, but with nausea turning in his bowels. It was degrading, shaming; it was also customary and nothing out of the ordinary, and before he went to Berlin he would have accepted it—unhappily—as the law of his country.

"Where is the grain?"

"In my house! Beneath my wife's bed!"

Leo darted a glance at the boy, expecting to see the blue eyes blazing hatred at him and was shocked when he met blankness. veiled passivity that told nothing. Janos Marton looked at him and nodded, his face and eyes empty—carefully empty. There was no hint of defiance or arrogance in the nod; it was a careful and guarded token of respect and Leo was inexplicably alarmed.

The policemen released the man and turned to Adam. "We will get the grain, excellency."

Janos came forward. "I will get it. My mother is ill in the bed. I will get the grain." He vanished, hurrying away, revealing nothing except respect and obedience.

"You wish to charge, excellency?"

Adam shook his head. "The lesson has been learned. He will not steal again."

Marton had pulled himself up and was leaning against the cart wiping his nose on a handful of straw. He blubbered a humiliating excuse which Leo could still hear as they walked away from the stables. As they passed the cottage they saw Janos dragging out a sack of grain which he heaved onto his shoulders and began to carry back to the grain sheds. Adam was very quiet. "It is unpleasant to have to do that," he said, "but it is better to punish and then forget the whole affair than to bring him to court where his wife and children would suffer also. Now it is over. I shall not dismiss him. He has been punished and we shall continue as before."

Leo could not answer. He felt they had all lost something—dignity, he supposed—by the scene he had just witnessed. And he began to feel there was something sick and wrong with his country.

He went back to Berlin earlier than he needed to. He wanted the freedom of Germany again, the liberty and the right to make anything public that you wished. It was noisier, rowdier, there were more street fights between the Communists and the S.A., but the noise and the fights were at least a symbol of Germany's freedom. He looked forward to discussing it with Hanna. He had so often found her a clever and provoking sounding-board, helping him to define his thoughts. Her first words when she saw him were, "Did you tell them?"

"Tell them?"

"Your family. About us."

He had forgotten that that was to have been the purpose of his visit. He tried to explain what had happened, the crash, the depression at home, his father, but none of it sounded convincing. It was hard to make her, an emancipated daughter of Berlin, appreciate the heavy atmosphere of Hungary, of his home and family.

She looked hurt and said little, but later that night in bed she asked him quietly. "Are your family very rich?"

"Not now. They were."

"Why do you speak of them so little? Is it that you like to keep us in separate boxes, me here as your lover in Berlin, and them, rich and respectable, the part of your life which you do not wish me to share?"

"Oh, Hanna, no! I don't talk about them because . . . because there is nothing to say."

"I have spoken to you of my family."

And every time she had he had been aware of the gulf between the Ferencs and the shipyard worker's family. He was embarrassed not because of her but because of *them*, his family—snobbish, conservative, self-indulgent—and yet they were his family and he didn't want to betray them to Hanna yet.

She said nothing more, but the next day there was a tension between them a slight strain that was carefully concealed beneath scrupulous consideration and politeness for one another. Finally, in the afternoon, he went out, deciding he would go to the press and translation agency and tell Mr. Heinlein he was ready to work at whatever was available.

As he came near the agency he saw a crowd and heard the noise of fighting and breaking glass. He began to hurry, and when he heard someone screaming he pummelled his way through the crowd to the pavement in front of the agency. Mr. Heinlein was in the arms of two S.A. men and a third was in the process of smashing his face with his fists. The windows of the agency were broken and "Jew" was written on the brickwork underneath the frame. Mr. Heinlein was screaming and the S.A. men were swearing at him. He couldn't believe it. Fighting, yes, at meetings when the students and the S.A. punched each other with sticks and truncheons and all went off happily to the police station together. But this was cold and vicious, and what made it worse was the crowd, standing silent staring and not doing anything.

"Mr. Heinlein!" he shouted, and rushed in, diving for the legs of the attacking S.A. man and bringing him crashing to the ground There was the familiar sensation of a boot in his side and then the three of them were on him, kicking and punching "Help you bloody cowards, help!" he bellowed to the silent crowd, and was aware of a rustle through its depths that settled down once more into frightened stillness. He stood, punched and was punched in turn, right into the broken window It was his salvation. His hand closed around a jagged sword of glass and he stood up.

"Right!" He grinned hatefully. "Who's coming in first?" The spike of glass was eighteen inches long and he jabbed it viciously in the direction of the nearest S.A. man. Heinlein had somehow managed to crawl to the shelter of the window and from some hidden source of courage suddenly reached up his hand and snapped off another shard of glass.

"Two of us Come on!" snarled Leo, his legs bent and the glass held in front of him. "Come on, boys! Whose eyes are going to come out first?"

The crowd rumbled and began to move, hurrying away,

frightened because something had changed, and anyway if glass was going to be thrust about there was no knowing who might get hurt.

"Jew lover!" one of the S.A. men shouted and advanced a step forward. Leo raised his arm, an expression of fiendish pleasure on his face. He had forgotten everything but the soul-satisfying pleasure. Too much violence, at home and here, had bred a need to assert himself, to strike back at the striker, to kill and draw blood.

"Come on, Heinlein," he encouraged. "You've a big piece of glass there. Good. Go for their eyes or their throats. Or try to dig right through the cheeks." He was almost insane now, loving it, enjoying it. He couldn't wait for them to come closer and suddenly he jumped out of the broken window and advanced towards them, blood streaming from his hand.

One of the S.A. men walked away, just turned and strode swiftly up the street. The others hesitated and then looked again at the madman bearing down on them, a spear of bloodstained glass in his hand.

"Jew lover!" they shouted again, and ran. He found he was running after them, the attacked suddenly becoming the attacker. He couldn't bear to let them go without maiming them.

"Leo!"

The voice penetrated his consciousness but he couldn't stop. They were nearly out of sight now and he could have cried with disappointment.

"Leo, stop it! It's me, Hanna! Put the glass down before you get arrested!"

Through a white-red haze he saw her, breathless and trotting beside him, trying to snatch at the arm holding the glass.

"Hanna." He stopped and stared back. Mr. Heinlein had crawled into the agency window and was lying on the floor.

"We'd better help him," he said, staring down at his bloody hand. "I wanted to help him. I wanted to kill those men."

"Someone's gone to him now," said Hanna, pointing to the agency. "Someone has gone in there; look, they're getting a chair for him to sit on."

"Why didn't they help before?" he said bitterly. "Why did they just stand and watch?"

"Come on, Leo. We'll go home."

He walked back to the agency. Mr. Heinlein was sitting, covered with blood and one arm hung useless by his side.

"We've rung for his brother and an ambulance," said a fat man in a raincoat and homburg. Leo had noticed him in the crowd, watching. He ignored him.

"You'll be all right, Mr. Heinlein. I'll come and tidy up here and see about new glass. I'll answer the phone and stay here until something is sorted out."

Mr. Heinlein nodded, trying to speak words that were inaudible between his battered lips. Leo bent his head down and caught the words *Völkische Beobachter*.

"I expect you're right, Mr. Heinlein, I expect you're right. They can't forgive the things you write about them."

There was a gleam of satisfaction in the little man's rapidly closing eyes. Someone pushed a glass of schnapps into Leo's hand and said, "Drink this, son, and then we'll get you to the hospital too."

He ignored the schnapps and the kind words. Berlin, the free, emancipated city, had sickened him and at this moment he could only see Hanna and Mr. Heinlein.

"You'll be all right until the ambulance comes?"

Mr. Heinlein nodded.

"I'll go home and come back later to sort all this out." He patted the little grey man on the shoulder and saw him wince. "We did well, Mr. Heinlein, didn't we? Just us and some pieces of glass!" And again he felt the pang of disappointment that they'd got away before he could gouge out his hate on them. "You did very well, Mr. Heinlein."

The frustrated press man gleamed and nodded.

Leo succumbed at last to Hanna's gently pulling hand and allowed himself to be led away. "So much violence, fighting," he muttered to her, and she squeezed his arm comfortingly. "Nothing but hurt and violence, wherever I go," he continued.

They climbed the stairs to their apartment and he drank coffee and schnapps and felt a little better. He began to talk about it, the crowd standing watching, the senseless unreasoning cruelty, the urge to kill that had overtaken him. And then he began to explain what he had wanted to explain before: the other scene of violence, the orderly controlled one at home when two policemen had intimidated a grain thief. He tried to tell her what he felt about his country, what was wrong, and why he hadn't been able to tell his family about her and about the life they led together.

This time it was all right. Maybe he was explaining better or she was understanding better, but at least the artificiality of the morning vanished and she smiled at him, the smile that still moved him profoundly every time he saw it.

"I'll come with you tomorrow and help you run the agency for the old man," she said. "Maybe he'll give you an increase when he comes out of hospital. Maybe he could even find me a job!"

They were together again, loving one another, close, reaching out for comfort and consolation. He was glad because he suddenly realized that vibrant, emancipated Berlin was not a good place to be alone in.

He couldn't sleep that night, and it wasn't just from the bruises. So many things were wrong, and now he knew the time had come to do something about them. A blaze of revelation burned in his head. For so long he had drifted, doing a little of this, hoping that temperance and moderation would put things right. The scene outside the agency showed him that from now on one must fight back, any way one could. "Uncle Sandor," said the old voice, and this time he was able to answer, "a victim of people's misery," and even though it sounded like vulgar propaganda, there was no doubt in his heart.

Everything was resolved, and not just the big things, the burning causes that he could now espouse. Another excitement was leaping in his fevered brow. He pulled a sheet of paper toward him and began to write: *In the last week, in two widely differing countries, I have seen two men of varied state and circumstances being beaten by uniformed bullies . . .*

The words flowed, balanced and exciting. He didn't even have to try and marshal his thoughts. The story came out, a clear, concise piece of reportage and when he read it to Hanna next morning she was critically enthusiastic, praising both his style and his handling of the subject.

When he went to the agency he took advantage of his temporary authority to translate it into French and English and sent it out on the agency transcript.

26

Just before the end of his studies in Berlin he wrote to Malie about the problem of Hanna. He and Hanna were going to get married and nothing was going to stop them. But his family had to be told—told that their son, a Ferenc, a Bogozy, was going to marry the daughter of an unemployed Hamburg shipyard worker. He had decided the best thing to do was to take Hanna home for the summer. Once they saw how she was, how quiet and restrained, they would have to accept her. He knew that of all of them Malie would be the only one to understand, the only one who would support him. He wrote and told her everything, except that he and Hanna had been living together for two years. He knew that even Malie would be shocked at that. Her reply came a week before he was due to leave Berlin.

My dearest Leo,

I cannot think why your letter surprised me, but it did; of course you are a man now, living a man's life, and it was inevitable that sooner or later you would meet a girl you wished to marry. I am happy for you, but a little sad for myself. Forgive me. It is hard to realize that my little brother who was so unhappy whenever he was away from me has now grown up. How very much harder it will be for me when Karoly and Jacob go away and find women of their own. I must try very hard not to mind.

You have a problem, dear Leo, but you know that. Papa appears to be a little softer, a little more lenient now he is older, but he is neither so soft nor so lenient that he will accept your marriage without question. The problem will be, as you very well know, that of your Hanna's family. I know things are different nowadays and we have lost our land. But this will make Papa—and Mama too, I fear—more defensive than ever of family standards. You told me that you remembered the time when I was betrothed to Karoly Vilaghy. Leo, I do not think you know all the things that happened to me because

Papa considered Karoly and the Vilaghys were not suitable partners for the Ferencs. How much more he will declaim against your poor Hanna's family who, as well as being poor, are also German. I cannot perform miracles, but I will do my best to prepare Papa, and of course I will take your Hanna into my heart and love her. It is better, I think, that she stays in our apartment rather than Papa's, even though it is one house. Later perhaps you can go to the country, to Eva and Adam's, although Eva may not welcome her too much either. Leo, my darling, if you wish to marry her, then make up your mind that she is the *only* one who matters. It may well be that the family will not forgive you, and in that case you must accept that you will have no family, only a wife and, of course, a loving sister.

To change the subject entirely, I am increasingly worried about something and I want you to help me on your way home from Berlin. Cousin Kati seems to have vanished—no, that is silly and melodramatic—but for eighteen months she has not answered my letters or communicated in any way at all. In the old days it would have been easy for me to make a little trip to Vienna and see how she was, but we are no longer able to afford little trips to Vienna, at least not for such a purpose as this. I still have her last address and I want you to try and see her when you pass through Vienna on your way home. It is four years since she left us, and she has never been home during that time and now has ceased to write. Something has happened to her and I am worried. I enclose her address. Please find out what is wrong.

I shall be so pleased to see you home again, little brother. We hear such frightening things about Berlin now—two elections already this year and a third about to take place and every one of them accompanied by fighting and murder. Who is this man Adolf Hitler? How is it he can make Germany such a disturbed place to live in? I hope you take no part in these political upheavals and keep away from all the Communist and National Socialist meetings. I shall be happy when you return home with your degree and your fiancée, safe once more in Hungary.

Your little nephews send their love—but they are not little any more! They are happy at school. Ah, yes, one more piece of news. Remember the peasant child, Janos Marton, whom Adam found a place for in the school? Apparently he is so gifted that his education is to continue —not university, of course, that would be unthinkable, but his teachers are endeavouring to find a college vacancy where he can train as a teacher. We all think it most suitable and possibly he could go back to the village at the end of his studies and take over the post in the village school. We feel that would be a most fitting conclusion to Adam's kindness and generosity.

All our love, dearest Leo. Please help me with poor Kati.

Your sister,

Malie

He wasn't sorry to be going home, even with the problems that Hanna's presence would bring and even though a long period of trying to find employment lay ahead. Berlin was making him feel angry and impotent. Political persuasion had degenerated into nothing but street fights, and with each fight he grew a little angrier, a little more bloody, more anxious to inflict pain on his brown-shirted opponents. Now leader of his own particular Red Student Group, he was also aware of being ineffectual. Berlin was not his city; he could not influence votes. He wanted to get home and right the wrongs in Hungary.

He didn't show Amalia's letter to Hanna. He just told her that his sister was most anxious to meet her.

"What about your parents?" she asked. "Why don't your parents write and say they are looking forward to meeting me?"

"My parents are old-fashioned," he said guardedly. "They have very fixed ideas of the kind of girl I should marry. They will be happy when they meet you—they will love you, Hanna—but I have asked my sister to explain the situation to them. It will be a shock for them that I have found a wife who is someone they do not know."

"You're afraid they won't approve of me?"

"No." And then, realizing that she was too intelligent to be deceived, he continued, "And even if they don't, it makes no difference."

"It does if we're to live in Hungary." She sat down on the bed and reached out for his hand, as though trying to take comfort. "Leo, couldn't we get married and stay in Berlin? You could get a job. Mr. Heinlein gives you quite a lot of work at the agency, and perhaps he could recommend you to others. And now that I have work, we could manage. We've been so happy here." She stared round at the apartment that had been their home for over two years, the screen in the corner, the high marble mantelpiece, the Chinese shawl pinned up on the wall. "Couldn't we stay here, settle in Berlin, keep away from both our parents?"

"No."

"Why not?"

"I must go home. Hungary is my home. And I'm beginning to hate Berlin, Hanna. I think if I stay here I'll be killed. . . or I'll kill someone." He rose from the bed and paced restlessly over to the window. On the wall opposite, a weather-stained picture of Hitler stared out from a hoarding, a relic of the second election campaign. Someone had thrown mud at it and the top left-hand corner had torn away and flapped down over the eyes. "Hitler, Hitler," he mused. "I'm tired of translating pieces about Hitler and elections. I want to go home and try to find a job in Hungary."

Hanna sighed. "All right, Leo. But what shall I do? Am I supposed to stay with your sister until you find a job and we can get married? Or do I just stay—and then come back to Berlin and wait?"

"You can stay with my sister as long as necessary. If you want to come back, you can." He sounded more abrupt than he meant to and she was annoyed. She went behind the screen and began to fuss with coffee and bread. He followed her round and pulled her close against him. "It will be all right, Hanna. I promise you it will be all right."

Her arms gripped him hard. "I'm so afraid something will happen to spoil everything," she whispered. "I'm afraid of your family. You speak of them so little, you tell me nothing about them: their habits, their customs, the things they like. You mention them so seldom and when I ask you about them you do not really answer me. No, Leo, you don't tell me the things I want to know."

"It doesn't matter about them," he murmured into her hair. "If they don't like you, it doesn't matter. We'll never see them again if they aren't good to you."

They had one of the happiest weeks together they had ever had, and then Leo left for Vienna. In two weeks she would follow him to Hungary.

Approaching Kati's apartment he prepared himself for the worst. He remembered seeking out Hanna after her "disappearance." He remembered the shoddy room with the fungus under the window and he supposed that—for whatever reason —Kati too had somehow been forced to live in destitution, although so far as he knew there was still plenty of money from the Racs-Rassay estate.

She was not at the address Malie had given him, but the new tenants had been in residence only six months and they told him where Kati was now living. He jumped onto a tram going to the Sudbahnhof and there, just off Wiedner Gürtel, he found her apartment.

He didn't even have time to prepare himself for the worst. Kati opened the door herself and he could see at once that the apartment was pleasant, large, and clean. Kati looked astonished, pleased, then nervous.

"Leo!"

"Hello, Cousin Kati. Can I come in?"

"Well—"

He stared at Kati, astonished. Poor Cousin Kati had always been so grateful for attention, any attention. What was she doing hesitating about letting him in?

"Yes, of course," she said finally, opening the door a little wider. "Come in." And then, with a touch of the old Kati, "Oh, Leo, how good to see you. How very good! And how changed you are. I would hardly have recognized you, so big and square. And have you finished at university now? So strange . . . so strange. Little Leo grown up, a great big man now."

He had always been aware that Kati was small, but now he felt as though he were towering over her. She hadn't grown any smaller; it was he who had changed. He was large; for the first time he realized just how large he was.

The apartment was . . . interesting. A large window was open onto a balcony packed with geraniums and sunflowers. The floor was covered in linoleum, but that was obviously because the room was also a studio. An easel and stacks of canvases littered the floor. Orange curtains draped the windows and there were shelves full of books and china. Kati saw his eyes staring at the china.

"Do you like that?" she asked cheerfully. "I made them, made them and painted them. They are good, don't you think?" Vases, cups, jugs, plates, all painted in different designs of poppies and sunflowers. They were bright and exciting.

"We wondered, Kati—at least Malie wrote to me and said she was worried because you had stopped writing to her. She asked me to come and see you on my way home. I think she thought you might be ill or dead. She's been very worried."

Kati stared down at the table and picked at a white fringe round the edge of the cloth. "I know," she said without looking at him. "I've wanted to write. I just didn't know what to say." He frowned, but before he could ask her any more questions she jumped up and cried, "What am I thinking of! Here you are straight from Berlin and I haven't even made you food to eat. What would Malie think of me! Come now, sit by the window while I get coffee and cheese and cake. Later, we will go out to eat and you shall have some good Viennese food."

She disappeared into a kitchen on the far side. There were four doors leading from the studio. It was obvious, from the comfort and size of the apartment, that whatever troubled Kati it was not shortage of money.

She chattered back through the open kitchen door, telling him of her painting, of what small success she had achieved.

"You know, Leo, when I first came to Vienna I was going to be a great artist, the first female Rembrandt!" She laughed, a pleasant, amused laugh that contained no bitterness. "I think I had lived in my dreams for so long that when at last I had a chance of freedom I thought it would be easy for the dreams to come true. Can you imagine how bad it was when I discovered I was not a great artist? Oh, Leo!" She came through the door bearing a tray. "It was such a shock to me. For years I had been nobody, and I wanted so much to prove that I was good at something. And here I was in Vienna and I had failed!" She poured coffee and piled a plate with strawberry cake and cream.

"I nearly went back to the loving comfort of Malie, who accepted me as poor Cousin Kati and loved me just the same. But I didn't. I stayed and I discovered that even though I couldn't be a great artist, I could be a good one, yes? The china is good, very delicate in design, and yet the painting is colourful, is it not?" She held the cup towards him. "You will see it is good to drink from too."

He didn't know Kati intimately or well. To him she had always been the subject of pity and, more recently, of speculative whispers. Vaguely he had gleaned the knowledge that she had been forced into marriage with Felix Kaldy. Her desertion of her husband caused no little disapproval in his home town. Even his own family, other than Malie, seemed to think that Kati had disobeyed certain rules. He knew little of her past, nor cared to know, but he did recognize that this Viennese Kati who designed china was totally different from the cousin he remembered.

She was still small, still plain. Her hair was still colourless, her nose large, her eyes pale and uninteresting, but in some indefinable way Kati had become a person, someone you would notice and remember. Her hair had been hacked off short, like a man's, and her face seemed bolder because of it. She was wearing a black cotton tunic—completely unfashionable—that had been painted across the bodice with bright red flowers. On her arms were several coloured bangles. Kati looked odd, ugly but interesting.

Aware of his scrutiny she looked up and smiled. Of course, he thought, that was why she seemed different. The old Kati had never smiled, at least not like that.

"How long are you staying in Vienna, Leo?"

"I shall go home tomorrow. I've missed the afternoon train now."

She hesitated. "Do you have anywhere to stay?"

"No. But it's quite all right. I'll find a hotel and—"

"You may as well stay here," she interrupted, staring down at her plate and mashing the cake into a mess with her fork. "I didn't want anyone from home to know—oh, but why does it matter? I'm never going back and I don't care what they think of me any more. I'm happy here, so what does it matter if you all know?"

"Know what, Kati?"

She smiled at him again. "You'll see in a moment," she said quietly. "I wanted to write and tell Malie. I knew she would understand but I kept waiting, and the longer I waited the harder it grew. It is so hard to shake off all the old conventions, all the old restrictions and disapprovals."

He heard feet on the stairs and wondered for a moment if Kati, like himself, was living with someone. A key turned in the lock and a rosy-cheeked Austrian girl walked in, carrying one of the most beautiful small boys he had ever seen.

"This is Ingrid," said Kati, reaching out her arms to the small boy. "And this is Nicholas, my son."

He stared, not knowing what to say, slightly shocked but more concerned that Kati should not see his surprise.

"He's two years old."

"I see." He searched lamely for some commonplace remark. "He's a very handsome child."

402

Kati stared hard at the little boy's face. "Yes, he is," she agreed. "I look at him carefully every day to see if there is anything of me in him, hoping that just because I am his mother I am not biased about his beauty. But no, I am satisfied that he is nothing like me at all, not to look at. He is quite beautiful, is he not? And he is mine, Leo. My son."

"Where—I mean, who—you are still married to Felix, of course. But—"

Kati flushed, just a little. "His father?" She paused, then shrugged. "What does it matter who his father is? It is enough that for a while I was very happy. When I knew I was to have a child I was even happier."

"But why is he not with you? Don't you want to marry again? You could get a divorce, I am sure. Felix would divorce you."

"No, you know little of Felix or his mother if you think that. They will continue to pretend. They will pretend their lives away in that horrible mansion up in the hills. They will never admit . . . what they ought to admit. But it means little to me. If it helps them to believe that Felix still has a wife in Austria I don't care. I have finished with them and shall never go back. They can believe what they like!"

"But what of him, the child's father?"

She made a funny little gesture with her hands. "There was never any pretence between us that we should marry. He was not a man to tie himself to one woman. When he returns to Vienna we meet and are happy together like old friends. But we have never considered that we have an obligation to each other." She shuddered. "Leo, you are young and will not understand this, but I never want to be tied to a man again. I never want to remarry or feel that my life is surrendered to someone else. Now I am myself, and I shall remain like that for the rest of my days. I am happy and I shall never entrust my happiness to another man. I have my child, and my life here in Vienna, and that is all I want."

He felt a warm gush of affection for her, this strange cousin whom he had never really thought about before. He had a fellow feeling for her, both renegades, rebels against the family. He decided that if an opportunity occurred he would confide in her about his own life in Berlin.

"You can stay here tonight," Kati said. "You can share Nicky's room with him. You'll like that won't you, Nicky?" The small boy chortled and beamed. It was incredible that

403

Kati could have such a beautiful child. He had large, warm brown eyes and a wide engaging smile. His cheeks were round and red, and dark curls covered his head.

"May I tell Malie?"

Kati considered. "Why not? I suppose it doesn't matter who knows. I'm never coming back so it doesn't matter."

Later that evening, in a small restaurant in Wiedner Gürtel, he told her all about Hanna and that he was a Communist. He told her about having his ribs broken in the street fighting. He explained his fears about the family not accepting Hanna and the fact that he must try and find a job fairly soon so that they could marry. He told her about seeing the peasant beaten on the Kaldy estate and about conditions in Berlin and of his worries and concern for the world they lived in. Kati—poor Cousin Kati—listened and answered and asked questions the way he had longed for someone to do all these years.

When he left her the next morning, it was with regret. He was twenty-two, she was thirty-six, and they had always known each other. But now, for the first time in his life, he felt he had found a friend who was intelligent and sympathetic, a friend whom he could talk to.

He told his sisters but no one else. Eva had come up from the country in order to welcome Hanna and he waited until they were together, he and Malie and Eva, before telling them about Kati. They were stunned.

"I can't believe it! Not poor old Kati!"

"It's true," he said, slightly nettled. "And she is not poor old Kati any more. She's a bright, interesting woman and Nicky is a bright and very handsome boy. You would be surprised."

"I certainly would," chortled Eva. "Where on earth did Kati get a handsome child from?"

"Oh, don't be so vulgar, Eva," cried Amalia, distressed. "Poor Kati. I should have found a way of going to see her before. If only I could have helped her!"

"She doesn't need help." He was beginning to grow angry. Somehow Kati's life style was his life style and his sisters' attitude towards Kati was a criticism of his own conduct. He resented not only Eva's ribald jeering but Malie's pity. "You don't really understand, either of you. I've never seen her so happy. She has a large and pleasant apartment with a servant. She has plenty of interesting friends and work she likes doing.

She adores her child and says nothing would ever make her marry again or give up her freedom. She is completely and utterly happy!"

"How can she be?" faltered Malie. "How can she be happy with a child and no husband to look after her?"

"She never had a husband to look after her," Leo snapped. "And now she doesn't want one. She is free to do as she pleases. She paints when she likes; she goes to parties or concerts when she wants to. She has friends of both sexes whom she can see whenever she likes. She is fulfilled and happy."

They were both silent. Malie looked doubtful and Eva resentful. "Well, she has no right to be happy," she said angrily. "It's disgraceful, what she's done. What about the family? Our name and reputation? What would poor Aunt Gizi have thought? And Mama and Papa, just think how distressed they will be when they know!"

"They won't know," said Malie quickly. "We're not going to tell anyone else, do you understand, Eva?"

Eva didn't answer.

"Eva! You are not to mention this to anyone! Papa has enough worries at the moment and this would be just another burden for him. And have you thought what might happen if Madame Kaldy learned of her daughter-in-law's escapade? Don't forget that Kati is our cousin. Madame Kaldy might well decide she wanted nothing more to do with such a family. And then where would you and your son be?"

Eva, since the birth of her son, had been accepted into the good graces of Madame Kaldy. There were battles, many battles, which Eva usually won, but nonetheless between the two women a truce had been declared. Eva was the mother of the Kaldy heir and they were both aware that they needed one another.

"I suppose you're right," Eva said slowly. "It wouldn't be very kind to tell the old lady. But I still think it's quite disgraceful of Kati. How could she behave in such an immoral way! Having a child with just anyone!"

Malie was staring at Eva, a curious expression on her face, and Eva slowly began to flush.

"Why are you looking at me like that?" she said, and then continued hurriedly. "Well, I won't tell anyone. As you say, Malie, it would be worrying people unnecessarily." A sharp tone entered her voice. "What a shock it would be for Felix, wouldn't it?"

405

"Yes. But he is not going to know."

Leo was suddenly bored by his two sisters. He didn't understand the undercurrents in their conversation, but he was aware of smallness, of petit-bourgeois bickering, and he felt a swift yearning to go back to Vienna, to settle there with Hanna in an atmosphere of freedom and friendship. How nice it would be to introduce Hanna to Cousin Kati and not have to worry about whether the family approved of her or not.

Malie came with him to the station and brought the boys, Karoly and Jacob, in order to ease what might be an awkward moment. They stood beside the track, small replicas of their dark, heavy-eyed father, clothed in clean white shirts and newly pressed grey trousers. Neither of Malie's boys resembled her at all. They were quiet, studious children, the delight of their father and of their grandfather, who found them obedient and willing to listen. Leo, watching their solemn faces, wished that little Terez was present instead. She was merry, noisy and naughty, and would have provided much more diversion for this awkward occasion.

"Here comes the train, boys," said Malie brightly. "Uncle Leo's friend will be here any moment."

"What are we to call her?" asked Jacob politely. Malie stared helplessly at her son. "Are we to call her Aunt Hanna?"

"No," Leo replied quickly. "That won't be necessary, boys. You can just call her Hanna."

"Very well. Uncle Leo."

He was incredibly nervous, and he hated himself for being so nervous. Two weeks ago he had held Hanna in his arms, slept with her, eaten with her, quarrelled with her, and now he felt as though he were meeting a stranger. He should have gone to meet her in Budapest. Just a few hours together on the train might have helped.

When the train stopped he couldn't see her and for one wild second he thought she hadn't come, and then at the far end of the track her neat little body appeared on the ground. She looked small and afraid, and a sudden wave of love for her drove everything else out of his mind. "There she is!" he cried and hurried to meet her.

She had a new suitcase and she looked fresh and clean, even though she had been travelling for over a day. Her tight, controlled face looked about her and then the large grey eyes flooded with relief when she saw him. "Darling Leo!"

They didn't even kiss, they were both so tense. He just squeezed her hand and said, "It's fine, Hanna. My sister has come to meet you and I know it's going to be all right."

"Have you told them about me?"

"I've told them you are my girl friend and that I want them to meet you."

At Malie's suggestion he hadn't mentioned the shipyard worker lurking in the background. When asked what Hanna's father did, he said he didn't know. Let them meet her first; then all the other things would come right.

"That's my sister. You'll like her. She's the good one of the family." He put his arm around her shoulders and steered her up the track. Malie—oh, kind, blessed, wonderful Malie!—smiled and came forward and put her arms round the girl.

"Dear Hanna!" she said warmly. "I can't tell you how much I have waited for this moment. Leo talks of nothing but his Hanna, and now you are here and I can see why."

Hanna tried to smile back. It was a tight little smile and a muscle at the corner of her mouth twitched.

"These are my boys, Karoly and Jacob."

The boys stared sombrely at her, then politely held up hands for her to shake. Hanna tried to unbend. "Twins?" she asked.

"No, though I suppose you could think that. Karoly is nine, Jacob eight."

"Oh."

"You will be staying in my apartment, Hanna, but you will not be far away from Leo. He and his parents and his brother live in the apartment below. But you already know Jozsef, don't you? Surely you have met in Berlin?"

"Just once."

They climbed into a cab and made desultory conversation all the way home. He was aware, as he had never been before, of the language difference between Hanna and himself. In Berlin they had spoken German together without his even being aware of it. But here he was conscious of having to speak in German, and he was also conscious of Malie and the boys trying to remember they mustn't lapse into Hungarian.

It was all right when they arrived home. Eva and little Terez made a great deal of noise and there was bustle and confusion that masked any strain. Mama was having one of her good days, one of her gracious Bogozy days, and if there was any coolness in Papa's manner it was not too noticeable. Hanna was whisked upstairs into Malie's apartment to "lie

407

down and rest." He longed to ask them all if they liked her but was terrified in case they said no. So he followed Eva into the drawing-room and said tentatively, "Do you think it will be all right, Eva?"

"Will what be all right?"

"Well, her staying here for the summer. Do you think she will fit in with everyone?"

Eva shrugged. "I suppose so. I don't see how anyone could be *bothered* by her. If she continues to be like she is today we won't even know she's here."

"Oh, God!" he said, annoyed. "You're always so spiteful, Eva."

"I am not!"

"Yes, you are. You never used to be like this. You're always cruel and sarcastic nowadays."

Eva stared at him, open-mouthed. "Well, really!" she exclaimed. "I've trailed all the way down from the country, just to show that your German girl friend is welcome here, and that's all you can say, that I'm spiteful and sarcastic!"

They began to bicker, childishly and noisily, degenerating into all kinds of complaints and arguments that had nothing to do with the present crisis, and their quarrelling didn't stop until Malie came into the room.

"Why are you shouting?" she demanded. "Have you forgotten the windows are open? I can hear every word upstairs!"

Eva looked angry and flounced towards the door. "I only hope *she* can hear every word. Then she'll know exactly what she's getting if she marries our delightful little brother." She slammed the door and they heard the heels of her expensive shoes tapping along the passage. Leo stared glumly at the carpet.

"I'm sorry, Malie," he said finally.

His sister sighed. "When I was very young I used to long for us all to grow up," she said tiredly. "I grew so weary of Eva's temper and I thought that when she grew up it would all go away. Alas, it is worse." She smiled a little wryly. "I hope you have not inherited that temper, Leo."

"No." He paced moodily across to the window, then came back and flung himself onto the couch. "No. It was my fault as much as Eva's. But she does seem sharper than she used to be. I don't remember Eva always being so . . . so sour."

"It has something to do with Felix, I think. Remember what great friends they used to be, how funny and gay they

408

were together? And then Eva became pregnant and for some curious reason Felix changed towards her. I suppose he was jealous and resentful, anxious in case his mother diverted some of her attention to her grandchildren. Have you never noticed how he and Eva still joke and talk but how spiteful it all is?"

"I do hope she's going to be nice to Hanna. She's not going to be sharp with Hanna, is she?"

Malie chuckled. "What an old mother hen you are, Leo. One would think that no one ever brought a girl home to meet his family before. Now just relax."

He tried. He tried his very best in the days that followed to behave naturally, both with his family and with Hanna. He realized how much Berlin had changed him. He was two people, the boy who had grown up in this comfortable middle-class home and the man who had lived with Hanna in Berlin. He found it difficult to fuse the two. It was made more difficult because of the charade that he and Hanna had to enact. Each evening she went upstairs to her virginal room in David and Malie's apartment and the separation drove a gap between them. She grew prim and even more silent, and as Hanna withdrew into herself the family became more positively gracious, as though they were saying, Look how hard we are trying to like your young woman. Even though she is not responding, just look how charming we all are.

Even Papa was checking his disapproval. David Klein had obviously spoken to him, asking him to control his resentment and remember the changing times. But with all that, with Papa's control and Malie's warmth, with Jozsef's genial acceptance and Eva's heavy attempts at friendship, it was obvious that the visit wasn't working. And it was obvious, even to Leo, that the barrier, the stiffness, was mostly Hanna's.

Strangely, the only person she seemed to relax with was Mama. Silly garrulous Mama and carefully controlled Hanna —it was an incongruous relationship, but the only time Hanna smiled was when Mama was prattling on about clothes and about her girlhood in Vienna.

At the end of two weeks Hanna said she thought she would return to Berlin. He was stunned.

"I know it's difficult for you, Hanna, but couldn't you try a little longer? I'm sorry about Papa, but he really is trying hard to be pleasant and it is very difficult for him. He is old-fashioned and—"

"I think it's better I return to Berlin," she said, not looking at him. "If I go now I shall be able to return to the office. I will get a smaller room and wait for you to send for me."

"Hanna, you don't have to spend the whole summer here. We hadn't planned it that way. We could go to Eva's farm in the mountains. It's beautiful up there and you'd love it. We could ride and walk and lie out in the sun—lie out on our own somewhere." He tried to pull her close to him, but she was stiff and unyielding.

"It's no good, Leo. I'll go back to Berlin."

Her face was pinched, her mouth seemed even smaller than usual. Beneath her cream cotton dress her neat little body was taut. He realized that for several days the strain between them had been so great he hadn't even wanted to make love to her.

"You know I don't care what they think. You know that, don't you, Hanna?"

"Your family are very important to you. Otherwise why are we doing all this?"

"They're important, yes. But I am not prepared to risk losing you, and if you are not happy with them, if you think you can never be happy with them, then you need never meet them again. We shall live in Budapest or wherever I can find employment—and we will begin together, two people without families."

"Oh, Leo!" For a moment he thought she was going to capitulate, but then she drew a deep breath and stiffened her body against him. "I'm sorry. I'm confused and disturbed. It was all so simple in Berlin and I think if I go back there I shall be able to sort everything out . . . about your family."

"It will be simple when we are married," he insisted. "All right, go back if you must. But don't go back to worry about my family. Just remember that once we are married there will be only the two of us, no one else, and then it will be just the way it was in Berlin."

He tried once more to persuade her; then, when he could see the tension and constraint in her, he ceased to plead. He tried not to notice how relieved the family were, and then he took her to the station to bid her a miserable farewell. Just before the train pulled out he had a brief glimpse of the old Hanna. Her eyes filled with tears and, standing on the step of the train, she said suddenly, "We were so happy, weren't we, Leo? In Berlin we were so happy."

"We will be again! I promise you, we will be again." And

then the train began to move and she stepped up and vanished into the corridor, appearing once more, just briefly, at a carriage window before the train pulled away. He walked back home feeling more despondent than he had for a long time, but also determined to find work as quickly as possible so that he could send for Hanna and be happy again.

The slump began to hit him for the first time. Until now it had been a vague threat lying somewhere in the future; now it was the barrier that kept him apart from Hanna. He wrote to every publisher, every newspaper, every press agency in Budapest, sending clippings of his work for Mr. Heinlein and references from a variety of sources in Berlin. Most of them didn't even bother to answer. He applied for a post as teacher at any number of grammar schools and was told that there were experienced teachers who were looking for work. He realized how useless a qualification in literature was, although he took comfort from the fact that students of science and economics and mathematics were having just as difficult a time as he was. In desperation he even put his name forward for a position in government administration—although he didn't know how he was going to bear working in a government office—and was told that his name would be added to the list of other waiting applicants.

He earned a little money that summer and autumn. He wrote a few miscellaneous pieces for the local press—nothing controversial, just critiques of plays and books. And while the summer lasted he earned a little more at coaching schoolboys in tennis. He wrote long encouraging letters to Hanna, assuring her that soon he would find a job and then she could join him and they would marry. Hanna's letters were short and there were longer and longer intervals between them. They ceased to be intimate, and panic grew within him because his lack of work was driving her away; he knew he was going to lose her if he didn't find something soon. In December, although he wrote several times, she didn't answer him. He looked for a letter every day, but December slid into January and there was still no news from her. He began to wonder if she was all right, if the hideous year of elections and street fighting had somehow claimed Hanna as a victim; the figures were growing increasingly frightening in the papers. Finally, in February, he swallowed his pride and asked Papa if he could borrow a little money for his fare to Berlin. His anxiety was now so acute he knew he had to go and see her and find out exactly what was wrong. He had a little cash saved from the coaching and from a recent article on a visiting violinist. Grudgingly Papa gave him the balance of the money.

On the morning that he was about to depart, he received two letters with Berlin postmarks. One was typewritten; the other was addressed in Hanna's neat script and he tore her envelope open first, his hands shaking a little.

Dear Leo,

This is the most horrible letter I have ever had to write. It is horrible because I know it is going to hurt you, and it is also horrible because I have to confess to something in my character which is shameful. I don't think you will ever understand—or perhaps, remembering those years in Berlin, you will understand a little and just be shocked that the girl you thought so highly of could be like everyone else.

Leo, I know you thought I shared all your beliefs, all your ideals. I thought I did too and I was so proud when you fought the fascists and defended Mr. Heinlein outside the agency. I was proud, not only of you, but of myself because through you I was part of everything you were fighting for. I used to lie beside you at night unable to believe how lucky I was, that I, Hanna Weiss, the daughter of a shipyard labourer, should be loved by a man of your background who was also an idealist. I knew you came from a wealthy family, but it really didn't matter to you. You didn't care about it at all and it made no difference to you that I was who I was.

I was so frightened of meeting your family. You spoke of them so little and yet I knew the kind of people they were. I used to see them when I was a child in Hamburg, people with cars and houses and good clothes. I was so afraid when I came to Hungary and then—oh, Leo! why did you never tell me you were Jewish? Why did you keep it a secret? If ony I had known before, right at the beginning, everything might have been all right. I tried not to let it make any difference. It *shouldn't* make any difference, but it does. I don't ask you to forgive me, or even understand why I was so shocked when I realized (it was your brother-in-law, David Klein, he looked so Jewish, and then I asked your mother about how she met your father and she told me the whole family history).

412

Right from a child I have been taught that the worst thing to be in the whole world is a Jew—no, not taught it, but it was always there as though one didn't *have* to be taught it. One didn't play with Jews or go to their houses, and it took me years to realize that this was wrong.

I prided myself that I really had thrown off all my old prejudices and narrow attitudes, and then I came to Hungary and I was shocked, most of all with myself. Leo, I loved you. I still love you. But obviously I don't love you enough, because when I think of leaving my family, my country, my friends, and coming to live in Hungary with a Jew, I cannot do it. That is about the ugliest way I can think of putting it, but the facts *are* ugly, the fact that I am still bigoted enough, prejudiced enough, not to be able to accept your race. In the months since I returned to Berlin I have tried every way I can to become the idealist I thought I was, the person I really want to be. I have told myself that nothing matters except that you and I love one another, but it isn't true. I am unhappy now, but I know I would be even more unhappy if I married you, and I think I would destroy you.

I deserve to be hated, Leo. I hate myself. The only redeeming aspect I can find in this whole situation is that at least I have, from somewhere, found the courage to write the truth to you. But perhaps even that was wrong.

Please don't answer this letter or try to contact me. I hope that God, and you, will in time forgive me.

Hanna

He began to laugh. He laughed until tears streamed down his face and when Jozsef came into the room he laughed even more, stopping only to gasp, "Did you know we were Jews, Jozsef? Did you realize that we were Jews?" Before his brother's puzzled, anxious face his laughing continued and then faded away into a heavy silence.

He had forgotten the other letter. He discovered it the following day tucked beneath the clock where Marie had placed it. It was a short, terse communication from Mr. Heinlein.

The report he had written more than eighteen months ago had just been syndicated by an American, English, and French press group. Adolf Hitler's appointment as Chancellor had produced a flurry of retrospective interest in his political growth. The article, lying fallow all these months, had become

413

a piece of historical news, and Mr. Heinlein listed the papers in which it would appear. They were impressive. So was the cheque that accompanied the letter. It was enough to take him to Budapest and keep him there while he looked for a job.

27

In every family there is one child, not necessarily the most beautiful or the most intelligent, who has some magic alchemy that makes him or her the favourite and best beloved of parents, grandparents, uncles, aunts, and cousins. Such a child was Terez, the daughter of Eva and Adam Kaldy.

She was able to leap straight through the prejudices, fears, and cautions of every adult in the family so that when her name was spoken an indulgent smile would spread over the face of the listener, banishing bad temper and anxiety. She was able to charm such widely diverse characters as Grandpapa Ferenc and Grandmama Kaldy. She managed to be the pampered favourite of her Aunt Malie and Uncle David, and yet her boy cousins, Karoly and Jacob, were never jealous of her. Her Uncle Jozsef always gave her a handful of *filler* whenever he saw her, and her Uncle Leo—the one she loved best—was never too busy or too tired to tell her stories and explain things that she wanted to know. She could make her silent father talk and her chattering mother be silent. She could make her Grandmama Ferenc give up an afternoon at the hairdresser just to come and play with her. And with all this, with the total of love and affection and indulgence that was heaped upon her, Terez never became precocious or greedy or complacent. She was most truly a child of love.

She had had the good fortune to inherit her mother's looks but not her bad temper, and Marta Bogozy's gaiety but not her fecklessness. She had also been blessed with Malie's warmth and cursed with her sensitivity.

Of all those in the family who loved and petted her, there was just one person who didn't like her, and as she grew older she accepted unconsciously that not only did her Uncle Felix not like her, he actively disliked her. Her first unpleasant

414

memory of Uncle Felix was when she was very small and visiting her Grandmama Kaldy up at the manor house. When she and Mama went to visit there she knew she had to do all the right things: refrain from getting dirty, drink her milk carefully without spilling or making a guzzling noise, accept only one honey cake, and speak quietly instead of shouting as she usually did when she grew excited. She had done all these things most carefully, and was feeling tired with the effort, when the door of the drawing room opened and Uncle Felix came in. He stared at her and then laughed.

"What an extremely fat child she is, Eva," he had said with distaste.

She didn't mind being fat, but she did mind that Mama was so upset. She couldn't see what was wrong with being fat but obviously it *was* wrong, otherwise Mama wouldn't have been so angry with Uncle Felix.

Another time at Grandmama Kaldy's, sitting at the window, bored and wishing she could go out and play, she had been fiddling with the tassels of the curtain. Uncle Felix had rushed over and slapped her quite hard.

"Don't do that, little girl! They are very expensive curtains and you will spoil them." The slap had hurt and she'd begun to cry. Mama had shouted at Uncle Felix, and even Grandmama Kaldy had rebuked him and had pulled Terez onto her lap and given her a bonbon.

She had noted, with a child's keenness but at the same time with disinterest, that when her little brother George was there, Uncle Felix disliked him too, but not as much as he disliked her. And as she grew older she became aware that the reason Uncle Felix disliked her so much was that she resembled her mama—and he hated Mama.

It didn't worry her too much. Uncle Felix never came down to their farmhouse, and often when they went to pay their weekly visit to Grandmama he would be out. The rest of her childhood was so happy that Felix slid away into the hole reserved for things like water snakes, dead rats, and heavy rain that stopped her from going out to play.

Until she was six she had a nurse, a German *Fräulein* who looked after her and at the same time taught her to be as fluent in German as the rest of the family were. When she was six there had been a long family consultation between Mama, Papa, and Grandmama Kaldy. Grandmama wanted her to go and live at the manor house with a governess who later would also teach George. Grandmama Kaldy had been very insistent and had banged her stick several times on the floor. Mama had screamed a little and Terez was beginning to feel quite alarmed, worrying about how she would survive in the huge, stuffy, formal house with a governess whom she didn't know, with Grandmama Kaldy who was so old she hardly ever moved from her chair, and with Uncle Felix who disliked her. But finally Papa, who was usually so silent they sometimes forgot he was there, said very loudly, "Under no circumstances at all will Terez come to live here, Mama. And neither will George when he is old enough. We shall have another *Fräulein* at the farm until Terez is old enough to be sent away to school."

Going home in the car she had stolen a glance at her father and then snuggled up close to him. "I didn't want to live there," she confided. "It isn't like home, is it?" He had chuckled, kissed her, and made some comment to Mama that she didn't quite understand. "I don't think I ever want to leave our farm," she continued anxiously, "not even to go to school. Will I have to go away to school, Papa?"

His hands on the wheel of the car were very positive and controlled, even though he only had two fingers on his left one. Whenever she looked at her father's hands she felt secure. Those hands had carried her, tended her childhood wounds, opened gates for her, lifted, fed, held gifts, and on one occasion chastised her. Her papa did not talk very much, unlike Mama, who talked all the time, but he was the solid basis on which her life was built. "Yes, Terez, you will have to go to school, but I expect we will arrange something with the family. Most probably you will stay with your Aunt Malie and Uncle David and go to school in the town."

That didn't sound too bad, and when the time came (once the shock of leaving the farm had been survived) she had been very happy living with Aunt Malie. In fact she had enjoyed the feeling of having the whole family all about her. Uncle David *seemed* to be solemn, but when you really looked at him he was secretly laughing much of the time and there were always little presents hidden—or not quite hidden—in his pockets. Her cousins were solemn too, really solemn, and they provided her with endless opportunities for amusement: frogs in Karoly's bed and Jacob's bootlaces tied together. She teased them unmercifully, and whenever they were roused to wrath her Uncle David would rebuke his sons, telling them it was unchivalrous to fight back against a little girl. They were good to her, though, and even when she had been particularly irritating Jacob would still help her with her homework in the evening.

Downstairs lived Grandpapa Ferenc, who was very strict and cross with everyone else but never with her; Grandmama Ferenc, who would chatter for hours about balls and dresses and other people's business; and Uncle Jozsef, who was a bit pompous but very generous with presents, especially at the end of the month when her allowance was running out.

At weekends she went back home unless the weather was very bad. Home was the most wonderful place in the world. She could *smell* home when the car was still some way away, smell the river and the hills and the fields all planted with peppers and wheat, smell the oxen and horses, and, just vaguely in the distance, smell the misty tops of the great hills.

"Isn't the farm the most wonderful place, Papa?" she would sing happily. "Isn't our farm the very best there is in the whole county?"

Papa always smiled and said, "The best in the county, Terez? Why it's the best in the whole of the Danube valley!" It was a joke between them because when you looked at the map and saw how huge the Danube valley was you couldn't imagine how many farms must lie along it. But theirs was the best.

When Uncle Leo came home from Budapest she was torn between missing a weekend at home or missing Uncle Leo. Whatever decision she made always seemed the wrong one. Uncle Leo was the most exciting, the most understanding man she knew and she found it difficult to understand why no one quite approved of him. She asked him one day and he had chuckled and said, "Because I have different ideas from everyone else in the family, Terez. Indeed I have different ideas from nearly everyone in this town."

"Does everyone in Budapest have different ideas?"

"Quite a few of us."

"Aunt Malie says I am not to talk to other people about your ideas. She says, if people know, you could be put into prison. I wouldn't like that, Uncle Leo."

"I don't think I'd like it much either."

"Could you be put into prison, Uncle Leo?"

"Perhaps." He grinned and hugged her. "But I am very careful, Terez. I don't suppose anything will happen to me."

She sighed a little to herself. She was eleven years old and in love for the very first time—with Uncle Leo. At night she lay in bed and made up a story where it was discovered that

417

she was a foundling and not really related to Uncle Leo. Then she could declare her love and marry him.

"I wish I could come to Budapest with you, Uncle Leo." She sighed. He remained silent, staring reflectively at her. "I've never been to Budapest and I think it's disgraceful. My own capital city and I've never seen it! I'm the only girl in my class who hasn't been there." That wasn't true, no more than six or seven of her classmates had visited the city, but it *felt* as though everyone else had been there except her.

Leo frowned a little. "I wonder if your papa would allow you to come with me, just for two days. Your birthday present. How would you like that, Terez? A trip to Budapest for your birthday."

"Uncle Leo!"

"Now don't get too excited," he said hastily. "It may not be possible, not just for you but for me too. I may be too busy."

"No, you won't be!"

She couldn't think of anything else, and she was so excited that in spite of trying to keep silent about it she finally blurted her hopes out that night at family supper. Grandpapa and Grandmama Ferenc were there, so was Uncle Jozsef, and they all turned and stared, horror-struck, at Uncle Leo.

"What insanity is this, Leo!" demanded Grandpapa Ferenc.

"Terez says she wishes to visit her capital city. I have offered to take her."

"You think that I—any of us—would allow you to take our granddaughter to that hornet's nest of Marxists in Budapest? Do you think we are deaf and blind, Leo? Do you think we don't know what you're doing up there, hanging around with Paloczi-Horvath, Balint, Kelemen, all that tribe who write for *Gondolat?*"

"It happens, Papa, that I too have had the honour to write for *Gondolat!*"

She could tell that Uncle Leo was growing annoyed. Uncle Leo was the one person who never seemed to be intimidated by Grandpapa's tempers and she was struck afresh with love and admiration for his courage.

"Indeed? Then I may point out that you will have no one but yourself to blame when you are arrested. Terez, however, is innocent of these political machinations, and neither I nor her father have any intention of exposing her to them!"

"Really, Papa!" said Leo in irritated tones. "What kind of man do you think I am? Do you really believe I am going to take Terez to the Balasz to discuss the future of our country?

418

I was thinking of the Fine Arts Museum and possibly a river trip."

The Fine Arts Museum sounded very dull. She thought the Balasz much more promising, and in her mind the idea of a jolly underground restaurant took shape, a warm place lit with candles and draped with red velvet, packed with Uncle Leo's exciting friends all waiting for the police to come and arrest them.

"You are dangerous, Leo. It matters not where you take Terez or where you take yourself. You have chosen to associate with dangerous people and I cannot let Terez—or any of the family—be exposed to the risks that your company might bring."

"Good God, Papa!" shouted Leo. "Do you think I spend all my time plotting in cafés? I am a hard-working journalist and translator. I work for a respectable newspaper—a right-wing newspaper, I might add. If occasionally I submit an article to some other journal, or mix with people who dislike our clerical state as much as I do, does this make me a criminal?"

"Please don't shout or blaspheme in front of your mother and sister!"

Leo threw down his knife with a clatter and stood up. Terez stared in wonder. He looked so tall and his dark eyes were flashing with temper. Surely they could all see how magnificent and handsome he was. She darted a swift glance round the table. Most of them were staring down at their plates. Grandmama, her hand trembling a little, was crumbling her bread into pellets.

"Leo, my darling," she whispered. "You mustn't be angry with us because we are old-fashioned and don't understand the new ways. Your papa is quite right. You are not the person to take a little girl to Budapest for the first time. What if she were ill?"

Uncle Leo pursed his mouth and closed his eyes for a split second. Then he sat down again at the table. "I'm sorry, Mama," he said tersely.

"Later, perhaps, Eva can take her. You know how Eva loves little holidays away from the farm. Or possibly Malie could manage it, and then you can meet them in Budapest and go to some galleries together. That would be much better, would it not?"

"I suppose so, Mama."

Terez didn't think it would be better at all, and she was bitterly disappointed. She debated with herself as to whether she should try and coax Grandpapa into letting her go with Leo, but somehow she knew it would provoke a family dispute and would end without a visit to Budapest at all.

"I suppose I have no choice," he continued bitterly. "It seems I am not considered responsible enough to take my own niece for a little trip on her birthday."

"It isn't that." Malie interrupted quickly before Papa could lose his temper again. "We know you would look after Terez, but—oh, Leo, if you only knew how we all worry about you! It is so dangerous to be a Communist these days, and you seem to make no secret of the fact. Sometimes I wonder how you have escaped imprisonment."

"Disgraceful!" muttered Grandpapa to himself. Terez thought he looked exactly like the old bloodhound at home on the farm when he said it. She giggled, turned the giggle into a cough, and smiled at everyone.

"And we cannot spare her!" cried Grandmama gaily. "We cannot spare her even for two days; otherwise we shall grow old and morose, just like Luiza Kaldy in her great mausoleum up in the hills."

Grandpapa's attention was diverted from Leo and directed towards Grandmama, who was reprimanded for speaking thus of Madame Kaldy when "the child" was present. No more was said to Leo about his views. She could tell he was angry though, and later, when no one was looking, she put her hand under the table and squeezed his leg. He jumped, looked up, and smiled when he saw it was her.

"Never mind, dear Leo," she breathed. "I shall come to you later. As soon as I have left school I will come to Budapest whether they let me or not."

Uncle Leo smiled again, but in a way that showed he wasn't really listening, a way that hurt her because it showed that he still considered her a child and she wanted to be his dearest and closest friend.

When he went back to Budapest, Grandpapa spent a lot of time grumbling about him. He called him a wastrel and a disgrace to the family. He said he was irresponsible, immature, and lazy. Uncle David, who was usually silent on these occasions, stirred himself and, to her infinite delight, came to Leo's defence.

"No, no, my dear Zsigmond," he drawled in his deep, soft voice. "No, we cannot permit you to call him a wastrel or think of him as lazy. He may be a disgrace to the family and possibly immature, but lazy—no."

"What else is he? Sitting in cafés drinking coffee with a bunch of idle, head-in-the-cloud dreamers who can only bring ruin on themselves and those about them."

"But he works very hard, my good friend. In these times would he keep a post if he did not work hard?"

Grandpapa muttered and grumbled something about the work not being respectable, and Uncle David laughed very gently.

"Come, Zsigmond," he chided. "You know he has done very well indeed to find a job on a newspaper, and secretly you are proud of him, no? What other young man do you know who has gone to Budapest with a pocket of press cuttings and a little money and found himself a job? And not altogether an easy one. No, my friend. He is the same as we were when we were young. Remember how we went our own way, regardless of our families? Remember how we were determined to do the things we most cared about?" He was suddenly silent, and then he said reflectively, "Sometimes I think that Leo's ambitions are more worthwhile, more noble than ours. We were driven by ambition, determined to be accepted by a society that had never accepted us. I do not think Leo's ambition is for himself. I think he believes that what he is doing is right, even though we know it is not right."

She was so proud of her Uncle David she went across and kissed him. He had called Leo noble and her heart was swollen with pride and love. Grandpapa muttered again, but she had the feeling that secretly he too was fond of Leo and even admired him a little.

"I suppose a man cannot expect all his children to be as he wishes," he grumbled. "Amalia . . . when she was young I had much trouble with her—defiance and disobedience—and now it is the same with Leo. And yet Jozsef and Eva have never troubled me. They have been such good children. Eva has always done her best to please me."

"Hmm." Uncle David's eyes narrowed a little. "Eva and Jozsef are Bogozys, my friend. Amalia and Leo are Ferenc, pure Ferenc."

"Am I a Ferenc or a Bogozy?" Terez asked, interested.

Uncle David pulled her black curls. "You are Terez, and no one else, and you are also disappointed because you are not going to Budapest for a little holiday, no?"

She smiled, happily, confidently. When Uncle David spoke like that, and Grandpapa absent-mindedly held his hand towards her, she knew that she was yet again going to have something nice happen to her.

"Zsigmond. Do you think I am a fit guardian for your granddaughter?"

"Hmm?"

"The next time I have to go to Budapest, shall I take this young lady?"

"Oh, Uncle David!" It wasn't quite the same as going with Uncle Leo, but it was still very, very good. Uncle David was not as exciting as Leo but he was very nice and sometimes he could be adventurous. He wouldn't make her spend all her time in museums and galleries. And he would make sure that she saw Uncle Leo.

Leo had a large, untidy room in Pest, in Kiraly Street. It was a glorious room and Terez knew that Malie and her mama would not have approved of it at all. For one thing there was nowhere to sit. When she and Uncle David walked in, Leo had to clear a space on the bed for them. There were books and newspapers all over the floor, and on Uncle Leo's desk was a very old typewriter and a great stack of foreign journals. She knew her mother and aunt wouldn't have liked the jar of apricot jam that stood on the floor beside a bottle of *barack*. Nor would they have liked the scuttling sounds in the corner of the room beneath the piles of paper. Uncle David didn't seem to mind the room too much, and she thought it was beautiful!

Along the front of the shelves were rows and rows of apples, and a salami hung from the ceiling. On the walls were drawings and pictures, some of them signed by Uncle Leo's friends, and a beautiful Chinese shawl that he said he had stolen when he was in Berlin. She gazed about her with envy and awe, realizing that this was exactly the kind of room she would like to have. In a tin bucket in the corner several hyacinths were growing and their sweet, heavy scent mixed deliciously with that of goulash and mice.

Uncle Leo stared round, puzzled, and finally said, "I'd meant to tidy things a little before you came but I've had so many translations to do. The Austrian business—everyone wants to know what the world is saying before they decide on their own editorials."

"Ah, yes."

"It is frightening—Austria. I cannot believe that we—anyone—will let the Germans walk in. Surely France and England will try to stop them!"

Uncle David sat on the bed, took a cigar from his case, and lit it. "I hope so, Leo, I hope so," he said softly. They were both silent, and because at that moment Uncle David seemed sadder than Leo, she went to him and held his hand.

Leo grinned "Would you like an apple, Terez? Or would you rather wait until we go out to lunch?"

"Are we going out to lunch, Uncle Leo?"

"Anywhere you like. Your Uncle David and I have all the best places at our fingertips, have we not, David? There is the famous Gerbeaud, where your mother and aunt came when they were girls. There is the Berliner, close to where your uncle used to live. Or we can go over to Buda, to the really elegant cafés on the hill."

"Can I pick anywhere I like?"

"Anywhere."

"Then I should like to go to the Balasz."

The two men looked at one another; then Uncle David laughed and said, "We are beaten, Leo. We promised the young lady we would accept her choice, so the Balasz it must be."

She was very disappointed at first. It wasn't a bit as she'd imagined, just a very ordinary café with rather ordinary people sitting there. They didn't look like revolutionaries or Marxists. But then people began coming to their table, jolly people who slapped Leo on the back, drank a cup of coffee, and went on their way. They all seemed to like Leo and to know him well, and after a while she began to feel not only proud but also very affectionate to all these people who thought so highly of him.

Uncle Leo was very different here from when he was at home. He was more . . . grown up. He talked and argued, laughed, and bought glasses of wine for his friends. When he spoke about Austria and the plebiscite, everyone listened more attentively to him, as though he knew more than anyone else about it.

Because it was her first visit to Budapest, she was allowed a very small glass of wine. The flavour was curious, but it was warming, and people began to look more interesting. There was a very small but very round little man with a bald head and a huge nose whom Leo pointed out as a Member of Parliament. When the little man had finished his lunch he rose very solemnly from his seat, paid his bill, and walked out of the restaurant past their table. When he was level with them he bowed slightly to them, said "Ferenc" in acknowledgment, and then left.

"He spoke to you, Uncle Leo! That Member of Parliament spoke to you! You cannot be a renegade like Grandpapa says if a Member of Parliament spoke to you!"

"Ah, but perhaps he is a renegade too."

"I think everyone here is very nice, very nice indeed," she said warmly, and then lowered her voice and continued. "I cannot think why Communists have to be put in prison. I think they are lovely people!"

Uncle Leo was suddenly very serious. "These are not Communists, Terez. These are people who have come to eat lunch. Some of them talk about things they do not like in Hungary, but you must not go home and say they are Communists, not until you are older and have found out for yourself."

"I think, my dear Leo, it is time we left before this young woman absorbs any more heresies or any more wine."

"I don't want to go."

Her uncles rose and each of them grasped one of her hands.

"I don't want to go. I like it here!"

She was outside on the pavement before she could properly rebel. She felt bad-tempered and scratchy and yet was ashamed of herself for feeling that way. One part of her wanted to apologize and hug them both, thank them for giving her such a lovely time, but the other part was angry and wanted to shout at them. She allowed herself to be dragged along the pavement, scowling and kicking any obstacles that lay in her way. Then suddenly she felt her hands released. She tugged them back to her sides and glared up at them, chagrined to realize they hadn't noticed her, indeed appeared to have even forgotten she was there. They were standing quite still, staring at an old woman at a newspaper kiosk. In a rough, cracked voice she was shouting, "Austrian plebiscite cancelled! Schuschnigg surrenders to Nazis!"

"Uncle Leo?"

He was lost in some private world, staring at the newspaper kiosk, his eyes impenetrable and black.

"Uncle Leo, I'm sorry I behaved so badly."

He took a step forward and stared again at the old woman; then he faced Uncle David and said quietly, "We are finished, David. This will be the end for Hungary."

Uncle David didn't answer. He just looked terribly old and tired. His face and body seemed to sag and all the grey in his hair was suddenly more noticeable.

"What's the matter, Uncle David?" she asked timidly. "Is something wrong?"

They neither of them spoke. They both groped for her hands and then continued their walk along the street, slowly and in silence.

When Leo arrived back at his apartment building the caretaker's door was open and the old man was waiting just inside.

"A woman—lady—came while you were away, Mr. Ferenc. She said she knew you well and that you would want her to wait. She had luggage. She has come from Vienna—and a boy with her."

"Kati! It is Kati! Where is she?"

"In your room, Mr. Ferenc, sir." He half extended his hand but Leo was too disturbed to proffer the customary gratuity. He ran up the stairs and unlocked his door. In the midst of his chaotic room Kati, exhausted and white, was sitting on the corner of the bed that he had cleared for Terez and David. The boy, Nicky, was curled up asleep on the floor.

"Hello, Leo," she said wearily.

"Kati! Dear Kati!"

"I got out as soon as I realized what was going to happen. The trains were being stopped all the way to the frontier. I don't think many will get through at all now."

"My God, Kati! What's happening in Austria?"

She shook her head. Her face and hands were smudged with dirt from the journey. "Austria is finished," she said tiredly. "The Germans have taken over completely. The plebiscite was to have been on Sunday, but the Nazis didn't wait for that. Schuschnigg surrendered rather than have the German army attack. They're moving in anyway." She placed a hand up to her eyes and pressed, as though the pain in her head was too much to bear. She was as he remembered, thin, small, ugly, and yet interesting and, even at this time, with a gentle composure which was attractive.

"I'll make you coffee. And food—I'll send the caretaker out for food." He raced to take coffee from the cupboard, then left it and ran downstairs to the caretaker's apartment. The old man's face cleared when he saw Leo taking money from his pocket.

"My cousin is hungry and exhausted. She has just escaped

from Austria. Could you very kindly fetch a meal from the restaurant? And something for the child too."

"I don't—"

Leo pressed some extra coins into his hand and, grumbling, the old man reached back for his coat and hat. Leo didn't wait for him to go; he ran back upstairs to Kati. She was in exactly the same position he had left her, hands pressed tightly against her eyes.

"Forgive me for coming here, Leo," she said wearily. "I can go to a hotel, and I will. I have plenty of money once I make arrangements with the bank. But it has been so bad, the last few weeks. When I arrived here I was suddenly afraid, lonely. I wanted to see you, any of the family, but especially you, Leo."

"I understand."

Even in the midst of the fear and depression he was aware of pleasure, gratification, that Kati had sought him out for comfort. Their friendship, a curious one, had grown in the six years since he had visited her in Vienna. He had begun to write to her during the period of emotional despair after Hanna's desertion. He had been able to confide in no one else. His family, even Malie, were too curious, too tactful and determined to help him get over it. He couldn't bring himself to refer to the matter at all in case his carefully guarded composure collapsed into unhappy anger. He had written to Kati then, telling her everything that had happened, every tiny detail that he could remember from his life with Hanna. She had answered, a warm dignified letter that sympathized but did not pity, and the letter had served to soothe one thousandth part of his pain.

During the first few months in Budapest, jobless, with his money running out and the family constantly rebuking him for foolishness and irresponsibility, he had written to her many times. And always the answers had been affectionate, confident, and yet practical and lacking in patronage. When he finally found employment, as an underpaid clerk and translator for an agency, she had been the only one who was not ashamed of his inferior position. She appreciated his independence and the difficulty of getting work, any kind of work, and she appreciated, too, the minor advancements that he made in the following years: the transfer from the agency to the newspaper, the acceptance of occasional articles to journals and magazines. Kati was the only one who really knew how hard and difficult his endeavours had been.

"What was it like in Vienna, Kati?"

She shrugged dispiritedly. "I don't have to tell you, Leo. You were in Berlin in '32. You know it all: fighting, broken windows and shops, swastikas, suicides. Exactly the same."

He went over to the spirit stove and began to make coffee. The smell and the noise woke Nicky. He stared about him, frightened, then saw Kati and smiled. "Where are we, Mama?" he asked in German. "Are we in Hungary at last?"

Leo came forward with the coffee. "Yes, young man," he answered in Hungarian. "Now you are in Budapest, and here you must speak Hungarian."

The little boy stared, round-eyed. At eight he was still an incredibly handsome child. Something of him resembled Terez—the eyes—yes, he had very warm, glowing dark eyes, like Terez's.

The caretaker knocked on the door and came in with food. Nicky ate hungrily, but Kati picked listlessly at first. Eventually, however, as the warmth and the coffee seeped into her blood, she began to revive a little, colour flowed back into her face, and she ate her food with some enjoyment.

He found a bottle of wine and opened it. It began to grow dark outside and they covered Nicky up on the bed and lit the fire. It was warm and deceptively safe, an oasis of peace and friendship that it seemed impossible to disrupt. He tried to remember what was happening over the frontier, a country being smashed into political subservience by the Reichswehr, but for the moment he was able to delude himself that the gentle cocoon of this room was reality, not the world outside.

"What do you think will happen to us . . . to Hungary?" Kati said quietly.

"God knows."

"Where do you think Hitler will strike next?"

"Poland, perhaps, Czechoslovakia, Switzerland—no, I don't think Switzerland, not yet."

"Not the western countries, France, Belgium?"

"I don't think so."

"And here. Hungary. Will Horthy be able to keep a permanent alliance with Hitler? Enough to keep the German army out of the country?"

"Maybe, for a little while." The safety had gone from the room and the flavour from the wine. He took her hand and held it, both seeking comfort and giving it. "What will you do, Kati? Will you stay here, in Budapest?"

"No. I am a little afraid of Budapest. I know so few people, and I have been away for ten years."

"You can stay here, Kati. I'll see if we can find another room in this building."

She smiled. It was the first time she had smiled since she had arrived and her pinched, ugly face looked a little younger. "Thank you, Leo. But no, I think I shall go home, not to the country but to the town. Our house is still there, the old Racs-Rassay house. We shall stay there, Nicky and I, and perhaps the family, Malie and Eva at least, will be kind to Nicky."

"Of course they will!"

She smiled again, a gentle but slightly whimsical smile. "Dear Leo, you always see everything with such simplicity. You have accepted Nicky because your life too has changed since you went away from home. But the others have not changed so much."

"Of course they will accept you," he said doggedly. "There is no time now for the old habits, the old prejudices. We have only a little time left, Kati. Surely everyone will see this?"

"No, very few people will see it. To them I will be Kati Racs-Rassay, who married a Kaldy and brought disgrace to both names. But still, I shall go home. I do not like big cities any more. I do not like the shouting crowds and the violence, and the fear that cities breed." She shivered. "Perhaps Budapest is not like this . . . yet. But I shall not stay here."

He began to tell her about the changes that had taken place, to warn her that Hungary was a different country from the one she had left ten years before. There were more restrictions, a greater need to be careful if you held "rebellious" views. And there was the Hungarian Nazi party. Kati stared at him.

"Here too," she said softly. "Why am I surprised? How foolish of me to expect that the disease had stopped at the frontier."

"It is the Arrow Cross Party. You will know the symbol when you see it. And green shirts; they all wear green shirts."

Nicky whimpered in his sleep at some childish dream and Kati leaned over and stroked his head. "What will happen to him, Leo? What will happen to all of them, Malie's sons and Eva's children; what will happen?"

She was afraid, a fear he could not fully understand because he had no children and therefore was not vulnerable in this way. But his affection for Kati made him sound more positive and cheerful than he felt.

"They will survive, Kati. We have bad times ahead, but they will survive."

They finished the wine in silent friendliness. It was cosy and relaxed, and when he went to speak again he saw that Kati had sunk down by her son and was asleep. He took his coat from behind the door and spread it on the floor in front of the fire. It was a hard bed but a warm one, and on this particular night it was comforting to have others in the room with him. Like animals in a cave, he reflected, seeking comfort and security through the physical presence of others.

Just as he was dozing off to sleep he realized, dreamily, that Kati had not once asked how her husband and mother-in-law were. Nor had she mentioned the dilemma that her return with an illegitimate child would pose for them. He was faintly uneasy. Both Madame Kaldy and Felix were slightly unbalanced these days. "Poor Cousin Kati" and her son, in spite of the Racs-Rassay fortune, were going to be defenceless strangers against the neurotic anger of the Kaldys.

28

The Kaldy manor house stood, on its rising knoll of land, like the bastion of a forgotten world. Even in a country that was still imperialistic and clerical in style and administration, the house and its weird inhabitants stood out as anachronistic oddities, paid homage to by the countryside because of rank and wealth but still the subject of much gossip and speculation.

Madame Kaldy was largely unaware of the gossip. Arthritis incapacitated her to an increasing degree and she rarely left the house. She entertained a lot; she had never ceased to delight in the reacquisition of her husband's family home and she displayed it lavishly on every possible occasion. But when the county came to receive her hospitality, the whispers were muted and the amused conjectures were kept for later.

Felix, who went out into society and also kept an apartment in the town, was aware of the gossip, and his resulting resentment and venom grew more paranoiac with every passing year. He had changed—in appearance as well as in character—from the beautiful young man who had charmed the county in his youth. The smooth olive complexion was the same, but the profile was not. The cheeks had become plump and puffy, the result of indulgence in all the rich food and wines that he enjoyed so much, while his nose, for some reason, had missed the fattening process and became sharper. It gave his face a slightly mean look that was emphasized by the gold-rimmed pince-nez that he wore.

For a long time after they had first moved into the manor, he had been content. He had his beautiful things about him, the pictures and the silver, the tapestries and porcelain that he loved and that now—with the money from Kati's dowry—he could afford to collect once more. He had enjoyed being a witty, admired young married man in a society not particularly noted for its ebullient characters. He had enjoyed the admiration of his mama and of his sister-in-law, whose good looks were a perfect complement to his own.

After the trip to Budapest, everything had changed. He began to hate Eva with a virulence that was later to be surpassed only by his hatred for his wife. If the scene in the Pannonia Street bedroom had left its scars on both of them, at least with Eva the years had slightly blurred the memory. For Felix the scene grew sharper and more hateful every time he thought of it. He heard the sniggers, the speculations of his "friends," and he became convinced that Eva had told them everything. In his more rational moments he knew that she wouldn't—couldn't—have done so, but his rational moments became fewer as he grew older.

When Eva's children had been born his relationship with his darling mama had changed too. Before the children she had, it was true, hinted at her hopes for a son of Felix and Kati's. He had shuddered at the thought and ignored the hints but then, after Kati had left, Mama had tentatively, almost distastefully, mentioned divorce.

"It is a disgrace for people of our substance, Felix. But a wife is necessary for the owner of—all this. If there is no other way you must divorce."

He had refused, mentioning their reputation, their family traditions, his own reluctance to bring vulgar publicity on their name. It had taken little to dissuade her, and in any case Eva had at last produced a son. With amazing speed Eva's children had suddenly become the most important things in his mother's life. She still indulged him, pandered to his whims and extravagances, but he was no longer the sun of her firmament. Eva had ousted him from his rightful position, sometimes his mother even took Eva's part against him, and there had been one frightful moment when it was suggested that Terez and George should be brought to the manor to be reared in their ancestral home. All night he had turned in disturbed hatred, resolving that he would sooner see the house burnt to the ground than have Eva's children living in it. The idea, thank God, had been rejected by Adam and he had been able to relax again, but his reprieve was a bitter one for now his mother constantly referred to the day when little George would be the new Kaldy. "Not until after your death, my love. But at least now we are assured that we have a son to love this place and live here."

Live here, in the house that he had re-created so beautifully? Sticky, pudding-faced George and the other simpering brat who resembled her mother so much, in his house, fingering his carpets and Bohemian glass, enjoying his pictures, sitting in his chairs? What did it matter if he was dead then? It was now that mattered, and now was being corroded by the knowledge the Eva's children were going to inherit his birthright.

He knew they laughed at him, the county. Oh, yes, he knew the things they said. "Nearly fifty, and still living with mother. Two old ladies together, counting the silver! And why did his wife run away? The ugliest creature—did you ever see her? But he couldn't even keep an insipid little thing like that. Can you think why?"

He had his friends. He had always been popular, the most popular man in the town when he was young, and he still had his friends, his good friends. Mostly they were just a little beneath his level of society; his equals were the ones who laughed most and he could not forgive them. But he had good friends all the same—an advocat in the town, a couple of the officers at the garrison, these were the people who admired him and knew him for his real worth. His mother objected to their visiting the house other than on occasions when large parties were given, and so he entertained these wise and intelligent men at his apartment in the town. Without his friends, particularly Miklos Egry, the advocat, he would have been lost and desolate. He felt he had no family, his place in his mother's heart had been usurped. His brother? Adam had never seemed like a brother. They had lived apart as boys, had been educated separately, and had lived as strangers for too many years. Adam had completed the estrangement by marrying that bitch. She had probably told him all about the night in the Pannonia apartment. That was why Adam treated him with contempt and spoke to him so rarely.

But his final humiliation did not occur until the spring of 1938. The speculative whispers, the gossiping, the giggling had grown worse. He could feel people looking at him, especially when he came up to the town to pass a few days with his very good friends. He had grown into the habit the last few years of suddenly spinning round whenever he was in company or walking down the street. One day he was going to catch them looking at him and whispering; he would see who the traitors were and he'd be revenged in some way. He'd cut them to begin with, never ask them to a party or dinner at the manor ever again. And after that he'd find something else to punish them. He'd find out their secrets and whisper back at them. He was walking to his apartment one day when he heard someone whispering and spun round in his usual way. Miklos Egry was behind him, talking to a man he hadn't met before.

"Felix, good friend. I was bringing this gentleman to meet you. He is a colleague from Budapest, Mr. Jeno."

He was disconcerted, but when he had recovered he decided that it was nice to see them and he invited them to the Grand Hotel in the square to take coffee with him.

Mr. Jeno was full of the good news about Austria and was also full of promises about Czechoslovakia. The injustices of Trianon would be righted, he was sure. The portion of Hungary that had been stolen by the West and given to the Czechs would be restored. He was full of praise for the Germany which would bring the miracle about. Perhaps, later, the rest of Hungary would be reclaimed. A new empire was being created out of Germany's strength!

The talk was exciting, patriotic and fervent, and Felix responded dramatically to Mr. Jeno's words.

"You are right, Mr. Jeno! You are right! For twenty years our country has borne the decapitation thrust upon it by the West. And now it is Germany, Germany alone, who will right our wrongs."

"Not just Germany, my dear Kaldy. No, not just Germany, but the one man who *is* Germany! Adolf Hitler will perform the miracle for us."

Felix hesitated. He was full of praise for the Germans, but he was a little guarded in his views of Germany's Chancellor. The man might be competent, but he was of plebeian origin, a Viennese tramp who had risen on the baser desires of his subjects. Mama always spoke dismissively of him as "a vulgarian who dresses without style," and there was also the distasteful affair some years ago of his niece. No one knew the truth of that matter, but it appeared to be unpleasant and vulgar. So in answer to Mr. Jeno's paeans of praise he gave an inaudible grunt and stirred his coffee.

"Hungary can only be restored to her former greatness if she follows the example of the German nation," Mr. Jeno said excitedly. "All the weakening elements, the corrupt and decadent, must be rooted out and then Hungary can be what she once was: the land of Arpad, the people who conquered the Turks!"

"You are right, Mr. Jeno, you are right."

"Mr. Jeno is a member of the Arrow Cross Party," said Egry smoothly. "He has persuaded me, by the sense and force of his arguments, to join the organization. I am convinced, Felix, that the future of our country will be proved through the Arrow Cross. We must cleanse ourselves of Jews, Marxists, revolutionaries—the dangerous elements of our country —and the Arrow Cross has enough strength and purpose to do this."

"Yes, yes!" Felix answered excitedly. "I do not associate myself personally with any party, Miklos; you know that. My mother believes, and so do I, that it is not the duty of the nobility to associate with political factions. We rest above parliamentary bickerings. But I am convinced that *you* have done the right thing. For you I think it a splendid notion."

Mr. Jeno leaned forward across the table. The corners of his mouth were filled with fragments of coffee coloured saliva. He spat a little as he talked but Felix was too engrossed to notice.

"But Mr. Kaldy, it is precisely because you are of the nobility that we want you to join our movement. People like you are important to us, all important. We cannot tell you how much we need you, your name and wit and reputation in this community. I feel, most sincerely, that it is your duty to support us with your presence."

Mr. Jeno spoke with respect and reverence, and Felix was warmed. He called the waiter and ordered a bottle of wine.

433

He was with friends, dear, good friends who valued him and thought him important. He was raising his glass to his friends when Egry dropped his bombshell.

"I hear your wife is back in town, Felix. She has opened the old Racs-Rassay house again."

The wine plummeted down into his bowels and he knew he must go immediately to the lavatory. He tried to stand but before he could move Egry spoke again.

"Am I right in believing that your wife is Jewish?"

"No. Well, partially. Jewish in origin, not in religion or up-bringing."

"I ask because her son looks Jewish," Egry said smoothly. And then he waited.

Felix felt a pounding over his eyes. It took several moments for the shock to be absorbed, digested into a part of his mind which could cope with hiding reactions. They were looking at him! Laughing! Everyone was looking at him and now he knew the reason. This is why they sniggered and whispered! He must try and pretend that he had known all the time. He must act like a man of the world and pretend to disinterest, not let them see the shock, the horror that possessed him.

"Really," he answered, as coolly as he could. His hand was shaking and he saw that Egry noticed the trembling fingers and the spilled wine.

"You knew, of course?" Egry eyed him watchfully. "You knew she was back in town?"

"Of course," he lied.

"I was surprised to learn that her family have received her," continued Egry with an assumed blandness. "Old Mr. Ferenc and his wife—I would have thought they were too old-fashioned to accept such a situation. But no, it seems they have taken her into their home. I hear, even, that your own sister in-law—yes, your brother's wife—has met her."

Rage began to well up from his disordered stomach, rage that Kati and the Ferenc family should do this to him. Here with his friends, his good friends, he was being humiliated, scorned, and it was all their fault. The wine and coffee curdled into bile and he wanted to scream and spit.

"Mr. Jeno and I were distressed when we heard all this," whispered Egry. "Surprised and distressed. But condoning such behaviour, encouraging it—a man's own sister-in-law encouraging it—is only a symbol of the corruption and decadence in our country. These things are what must be controlled, disciplined, destroyed!"

His mind was a mess of whirling reflexes: Kati . . . a son . . . Eva . . . the Ferencs . . . his mama . . . Terez and George . . . his beautiful manor house . . . Terez and George . . .

"Why, it seems that it might not be impossible for your own brother to take your wife into his home. And from there who can say where it would end?"

Kati's son. Yes, he knew very well where it could end! His own mama, who had rejected him because Eva had spawned, would take this new child into her home and give his beautiful house and possessions to a bastard! She would flaunt the child and they would all laugh and stare. He would lose his friends.

"You are pale, my friend. Have some more wine." Egry poured and watched. Felix drank, and the wine tasted of gall. The scalding sensation in his stomach spread out and consumed him, spreading up into his chest and throat and eyes so that he could hardly see. His fingers curled round the stem of the empty glass, gripped, and snapped it. The two men were watching him. They had given up all pretence of believing his fiction and were waiting to see in which direction his fury would explode.

Through the rage of blood in his head a single thought began to crystallize. It was the Ferencs who had done this to him! Gizelli Ferenc had plotted with his mother to marry him to her vile daughter. Eva Ferenc had displayed herself, offered herself, humiliated him, and then ousted him from his mother's love. The old Ferencs had taken Kati into their home and finalized his degradation. The Ferencs had ruined his life, robbed him of his birthright!

He stood and stared out across the square, unseeing and mad. His friends did not try to stop him when he lurched between the tables and started to run.

"Wait," Egry said softly, "just wait. I know him, know the functioning of his mind. He will return. He needs us."

Mr. Jeno nodded and emptied the rest of the wine into his glass.

Malie had made the first move. Leo had telephoned her from Budapest and she went to the station to meet Cousin Kati. In her mind she had shelved the problems that must be faced. She had left David to inform Papa of the news, which was cowardly, but wise, because with the passing years she had discovered that Papa listened more and more to David, indeed had become a little dependent on him. David would be able to break the news in the best possible way.

When they alighted from the train, Kati and a small figure beside her, Malie ran up the platform, forgetting everything but the affection of blood for blood, of family for family. "Darling Kati!"

Stupidly her eyes filled with tears. So much had happened to them all and still it was not over. Still the upheavals of emotion brought conflict into their lives.

"Kati! Oh, I'm so pleased you've come home!"

Kati was clinging to her, clinging, and suddenly she was sobbing too. "Home, Malie? Yes, I suppose it is home."

They drew away, ashamed of their outburst, smiling at one another, reassured because whatever had happened, whatever was going to happen, their loyalty and affection was as strong as ever.

"And this is Nicholas?"

"Hello, Aunt Malie." He smiled shyly at her, and Malie raised a querying eyebrow at her cousin.

"I told him his Aunt Malie would meet us at the station. I knew you'd come," Kati said simply.

"I have been to your house this morning. I've told the caretaker to light a fire and air two of the bedrooms. I didn't have time to do anything else."

"Do they know? Uncle Zsigmond and Aunt Marta, do they know?"

"David is telling them now."

Malie observed, as Leo had done, the changes in Kati. Age had not given her beauty, but it had given her confidence and a personality that was arresting. The old Kati would have been trembling at Uncle Zsigmond's probable reaction. This Kati just asked and nodded.

"And the rest of the family?" she asked.

"Jozsef will do whatever Papa says."

"Eva and Adam?"

"I telephoned Eva this morning. She said very little, but I think she will come to town this weekend to see you."

She wasn't at all sure of that. Eva had sounded dismayed on the telephone and there had been long awkward silences. She knew it was more difficult for Eva, living in the shadow of the manor house and having Felix for her brother-in-law, but nonetheless she felt embarrassed that Eva might betray the bonds of family that had always held up until now.

Eva, at that moment, was sitting drumming her fingers against the window, consumed with indecision. She was staring out through the rain, waiting for Adam to come back for the evening so that she could tell him the news. When she finally saw him trudging towards the house her patience broke and she hurried to open the door.

"Adam, Malie telephoned me! What do you think has happened? Kati has come back to live in the town, and she's brought the boy with her!"

Adam stared, then began to peel his wet raincoat from his shoulders. The maid came forward to take it but he waved her away.

"What are we going to do, Adam? How could she do this to us? She knows my position! How could she embarrass us like this?"

"I would like to enter the drawing-room and dry myself, Eva."

She hustled to one side and followed him in. His hair was very wet and rain trickled down his face. He held his hands out towards the fire and a few droplets fell into the flames and sizzled. For years his silence had irritated her and on some occasions it drove her to a frenzy of rage. She could feel herself growing angry with him now.

"Don't you hear what I say, Adam? Kati's come back with her bastard! What are we going to do?"

"Do? Why, she is your cousin. You must go and see her."

"Oh, Adam!" She was so cross she stamped her foot. "How can I? With your mama being so gracious to us now, and George to inherit the estate! How can I upset your mama—and Felix—by being friendly with Kati? How can I condone what she has done?"

"How can you not?" asked Adam quietly.

A chill moved over her. Once every five years or so Adam said something like that, something that shook the roots of her security. She was never sure if he knew. When she saw him with Terez she was convinced he could not possibly know because he obviously loved the child with a deep, abiding devotion. But occasionally he stared at her or said something that made her afraid and unsure of herself.

"Well, of course I'm not going to sit in judgment on my cousin," she went on quickly. "But obviously your mother and Felix are going to be very distressed about it. We cannot aggravate their embarrassing situation by being friends with Kati."

"There is no need to invite her here," he answered. "I think she would not wish to come in any case. She has her own house by the river if she wants to come up here. But I think you should go to town and see her."

"Oh, Adam! Don't be so dull and stupid! What happens to us if your mama is angry? What happens to George, to me and Terez?"

"Nothing can happen to any of us. My mother knows very well who manages the estate. Sometimes she behaves like a madwoman, but when it comes to the running of the farms she is practical and astute. In this house rests everything my mother needs for the future. Here is her grandson, and here the best bailiff she has ever had."

"But what of the future?" she screeched. "Supposing she dies tonight. What will happen to us then?"

"We shall remain here."

"Ha! With Felix in charge, hating both of us because I have taken the part of his unfaithful wife!"

Adam's slow green eyes considered her. Once those eyes had cried because she had left him, but nowadays they only considered her, as though she were an interesting phenomenon growing on his land.

"We shall stay here," he repeated. "Felix can do nothing to us. When Mama dies everything is left to George, but Felix has the use of the house and an income until his death."

"Oh," she said, nonplussed.

"I arranged it that way when George was born."

"You arranged it?"

"I told Mama I would leave unless provision was made."

"I see." The uneasiness returned. Adam frequently did things, important things, without telling her or, indeed, anybody. One jogged along for years, growing accustomed to his dullness and lack of ambition, and suddenly a veil was pulled away and a rather frightening, powerful Adam was glimpsed.

"I think you should go to see your cousin," he said quietly. "And if the farm can be left, I shall come with you."

She was jealous. For some stupid reason she felt a twist of envy in her breast. Jealous of poor old Kati with her illegitimate child? How foolish! But the jealousy persisted. "You always did like Kati," she said sourly.

"Mmm."

"I suppose you think it's all very admirable, what she's

438

done—living like a Bohemian and then coming back to flaunt herself."

"I think she has been brave . . . and honest."

What did he mean? The uneasiness stirred again and she forced herself to relax. She crossed over to the fire and slid her hand through his arm.

"All right, Adam," she said softly. "If you think it's right for us to go and see Kati, then we shall."

They welcomed her in different ways. Mama burst into tears and clasped Kati to her breast in an orgy of emotion. Jozsef looked embarrassed and asked her if she had made her bank transfers yet. David Klein just smiled at her and then—with an expression of shocked dismay on his face—produced a peach from his jacket pocket. The peach had a face and a little hat on it. Nicholas stared in disbelief, then grinned widely and reached up his hand.

Papa, frail and unhappy, stood apart from the others. He was uncertain, at sixty-eight too old to accept such things. He wanted to help his dead sister's child, but his every instinct told him that her behaviour had been immoral and that he was condoning things his sister would have hated. He closed his eyes and thought of Gizi, remembered her when they were young and poor, remembered the old man dying, ashamed of both his children, remembered Gizi lying stretched and yellow on her bed, her hand in his. He crossed the room and kissed Gizi's child on the cheek.

"You should have come home to us much sooner, Kati," he said sternly. "Indeed, you should never have left us."

"Thank you, Uncle Zsigmond," Kati said, but she wasn't meek or frightened, just quiet.

The young ones all stared at each other, like animals staking a claim. Jacob, Karoly, and Terez saw one of the most beautiful boys they had ever known, soft gentle brown eyes, a smiling mouth, and tight black curls just like Uncle Leo's. Nicky saw two solemn nearly grown-up boys who looked exactly like the nice man who had given him the peach, and a leggy girl who looked familiar.

"You look like me," the girl said, and then he realized what she reminded him of—his own face in the mirror.

"I'm Terez. And this is Karoly, and Jacob. They're Aunt Malie's sons."

"Yes," he answered.

"I'm twelve. How old are you?"

439

"Eight."

"My brother George is ten. He's up in the country with the *Fräulein*." She smiled at him, and he offered her the peach. Later the big boys took him out into the cobbled yard and showed him the German car that belonged to their papa. They were very serious boys, but he liked them, and gradually the wariness left the four children and they sat in the car, pretending to drive, already relaxing into casual friendship. Inside the house it took longer. Kati had done something dreadful: she had betrayed not only her moral standards but also the honour and reputation of the family. They were saddened or embarrassed or confused, according to their varying ages and temperaments. They welcomed her because she was a member of the family, but there was a reservation, a tiny barrier that separated her and her child from the rest of them.

Later she began to talk of the *Anschluss*, of the Germans marching into Vienna, of Jews being terrorized in the Graben. "I had to come back," she explained, a hint of apology in her voice. "I had to bring Nicky home because it is unsafe in Austria for anyone who is even half a Jew."

A sliver of fear insinuated itself between them, reached out, touched, moved on. What if—? Supposing—?

"I would not have come home if I had not been afraid," she whispered.

They drew together, bonds of blood and family tightening against the alien threat. The barrier of respectability that separated them from Kati dissolved, swept away by a greater and more urgent emotion.

Two weeks after their return, Eva came up from the country. She remained for only a couple of hours and her greeting to Kati was restrained. Kati didn't seem to notice. She was as admiring, as pleased with Eva's vague courtesies as she had been when a girl.

"You haven't changed, Eva," she said warmly. "You're still so slim and lively, just the way you were when we were girls."

Eva was gratified and tried to make up for her cold greeting. She had been nervous, and she had also been a little confused by the changes in Kati's appearance. Kati was more . . . alive than she used to be. She looked around for something nice to say to atone for her lack of graciousness, but when the saw the little boy she didn't have to search for compliments. She was incredulous. "He's beautiful, Kati! What an extraordinary thing! He really isn't one little bit like you, is he?"

"No." Kati looked proud and pleased. In the old days she had never expected compliments for herself. She had always been pleased to bask in the glamour of her two beautiful cousins. Now she was content to have her son admired.

Eva fidgeted with her gloves and made a few inconsequential remarks and then she blurted out, "Have you seen or heard from Felix?"

"No."

"You know that he has an apartment here, in the town?"

"No."

"It's possible you'll meet him. What will you do if you meet him?"

"I—I don't know. I don't want to meet him."

"But if you do?"

Kati looked distressed. "I shall do nothing. Look away . . . just nod . . . then look away."

Eva fidgeted with her handbag, then took out her compact and studied herself in the mirror.

"Kati, I don't—I would love to see much of you, but you understand—for me, it is difficult. Felix and Madame Kaldy, living so close, and little George to inherit the estate. . . ."

"Oh, yes," Kati replied slowly. "I see. Yes, of course it would be difficult."

"I shan't tell them I've seen you. I think it better that I don't."

"Yes. Of course."

"But you know I'm *thinking* of you all the time. And if there is anything you want. . . . You won't be opening the country house, will you?"

"No."

"That's all right then. I expect it will soon settle down and everyone will be happy."

Kati didn't answer, and Eva found she was unable to look at her cousin's face. She was disconcerted because suddenly, in the midst of talking to Kati, she felt ashamed. She didn't like the feeling and she pushed the shame away, concealed it in a warm embrace that, in the old days, would have brought a happy flush to Kati's face.

"Good-bye, dear Kati," she said, but Kati turned away.

"Thank you for coming, Eva."

On the train going back she was irritated, restless. Everything that was happening these days seemed wrong. The world wasn't a wonderful place to live in any more.

29

To Leo, the Munich pact was yet another disturbing element in his growing confusion. Part of dismembered Hungary was restored. No Hungarian could fail to delight in the return of a portion of the land that the West had wrenched from her after the war. But Hitler had done it. Hitler had given them back their lands and had, at the same time, taken a large piece for himself. Uneasily he waited to see what would happen next, positive that the German juggernaut would not stop at the provisional borders she had newly carved out of Eastern Europe.

In the spring the emasculated remnant of Czechoslovakia succumbed, as Austria had the year before. And in the spring he received notification that he was likely to be called for national service at any time. It surprised him, although it shouldn't have. He had been available for call-up ever since his return from Berlin. He had ceased to think about it and now, even with war imminent all over Eastern Europe, he still felt faintly indignant.

He reported his news to the editor of the newspaper and was disconcerted yet again when the editor told him he could leave straight away.

"I haven't been given my dates yet, Mr. Kertesz," he protested. "I can stay until I have my posting."

Kertesz for some reason refused to look at him. "No, no, Ferenc, go now. Who knows how long you have? Why not take a little holiday before your military service. Go home and see your family."

"That's kind of you, but truly, sir, I would prefer to stay until the last possible moment. I'm sure with all that is happening now I can be useful."

The editor made some abstract outlines on his blotter with a pencil. He still refused to look directly at Leo. "We can manage, Ferenc. You have done well with us and I'm certainly not sorry I gave you the job in the beginning. But we can manage enough to let you have a little vacation before your military service."

"I'm very happy to stay, sir."

Mr. Kertesz looked a little harassed. He still kept his eyes averted, and now he began to flick the end of the pencil back and forth with his other hand. "I'm sorry, Ferenc, but frankly it would be better if you left."

Leo was angry. He had worked hard, accepting low rates because he was thankful to get a job at all. He worked evenings and on Sundays, giving more time to the paper than anyone else on the staff, partly because he liked his work and partly because he was still hoping to be transferred to one of the group's bigger newspapers. He knew that unemployment always hovered in the background, but he also knew that at the present time there wasn't a necessity to cut the staff. And Kertesz was telling him he didn't need him any more.

"Are you trying to tell me I'm dismissed?" he said angrily. "Are you trying to tell me my work is unsatisfactory? Or that there isn't enough news to keep an extra translator-reporter occupied?"

"No, it isn't that," the editor answered, looking unhappy.

"Is my work not speedy enough for you?"

"No, it's—it is disagreeable to have to speak of but—it has been . . . indicated to me that it would be advisable if you didn't work for this group any more. I didn't know how to tell you, and your call-up seemed a perfect answer for both of us. I wish you hadn't pressed me into this ridiculous situation."

His anger evaporated and he felt defenceless, insecure, and uncertain of himself. Who had thought it advisable that he didn't work for them any more? And why?

"Some of your . . . connections," continued Mr. Kertesz, reading his unspoken thoughts. "They are not popular with the owners. You haven't concealed some of your views too well. And of course you've mixed quite openly with those who frequent the Balasz. This and one or two other things have placed me in a very difficult position, my dear Leo."

His voice grew more bland, more fatherly, as the content of what he was saying grew more disturbing. Leo didn't ask what the "other things" were that made him undesirable on the staff. He was afraid to know.

"I can't think why you have never tried to conceal your opinions, Leo. You know how dangerous they are."

"If less people had concealed their opinions in the last few years, we shouldn't be where we are now," he retorted. "Waiting like prisoners in the condemned cell to see if we are next on Hitler's list!"

"Ssh." Mr. Kertesz, afraid, stared in the direction of the

partially open door. "Quiet, Leo," he whispered. "Someone may hear—and you know as well as I that it is dangerous to talk of the Nazis like that. We don't know what may happen in the future, and someone may remember words spoken carelessly in anger."

Leo closed his eyes for a brief moment, disgust racing through him. Kertesz had given him his first full-time job. He had helped him, guided him in the principles of journalism, taught him how to be a professional. And now Kertesz, like everyone else, had succumbed to the spectral fear of Adolf Hitler. He turned, went back to his desk, and began to pack up the flotsam he had collected in five years.

At the Balasz he said a gloomy good-bye to old friends. This very ordinary restaurant had been his spiritual home ever since he had arrived in Budapest. Here, for the first time he had met gifted and talented men who expressed concern over the condition of their country, not Bolsheviks and bloody revolutionaries, as his father described them, but highly respected artists, playwrights, musicians, even a Member of Parliament, men who had wanted to introduce by legitimate means the simplest aspects of democracy, men who had spoken of freedom of the press, secret ballots, and the right to hold varying political views as the sum of their ideals. The Balasz had kept him sane, had given him the companionship and trust that Hanna's betrayal had destroyed. He felt that once he had left the café for the last time and returned home, he would walk out of the light into a dark and stifling paper bag.

When he announced that he must return home, he was greeted with regrets and repeated glasses of wine. And almost immediately he was given information and names and addresses of people he must contact in his own town, people he had never realized existed, who believed, like himself, that the world's salvation and freedom lay in brotherly love and the teachings of Karl Marx.

"Some bright men there!" Roth had shouted jovially at him. "The top man—very young, but gifted—contact him and offer your help. Hitler is only weeks or months away from us. We must fight him, not with guns, for we have none, but with our minds, Leo, with our minds!"

The *barack* had flowed and the evening that was to have been so desolate turned into a triumphant farewell. Drunkenly his friends accompanied him home, and drunkenly he promised he would lead the intellectual revolution in his home town. Hot, boastful words were spoken; enthusiasm for the cause grew strong with the increasing level of alcohol in their blood. They were nearly all young men and they had spent the idealistic period of their lives in controlled frustration. Now, for a few hours of drunkenness, they indulged in the fantasy that their visionary dreams might one day come true.

When he awoke the next morning he had all the depressed remorse of the drunkard, now sober. His head ached and every time he raised it from the pillow the room tilted at a sickening angle. He tried to remember what his elation of the night before had been and finally recalled that it had been no more than a list of names and addresses of people he could contact at home. Just another collection of people, he supposed bitterly, who went to their favourite café when work was over and whispered of the reforms they would like to make.

By his pillow was the crumpled piece of paper that had been thrust into his hand upon leaving his comrades. With his eyes screwed against the light from the window he smoothed the paper and read the names. The one at the top of the list was Janos Marton.

30

They met in a café on the poorer side of the town, between the garrison and the steelworks. He had lived a large part of his life in this town but he had never visited this particular street or café before, and he stared curiously at the shabby apartment houses opposite the café—chipped stone buildings with stairs covered in litter leading to the upper floors. A girl selling matches and bootlaces hovered outside the café entrance.

Janos Marton stood up as he entered. He was a polite young man. He held his hand out and Leo, after a moment's pause, took the proffered palm in greeting.

"How nice to see you again, Mr. Ferenc," said the young man brightly. He had nearly, but not quite, lost the accent of the *puszta*. He waited for Leo to sit, then sat himself and ordered beer.

"I would prefer coffee," said Leo disagreeably, and the young man smiled and said, "Of course," and changed the order.

They sat in silence until the waiter returned. Janos Marton was still very thin, but now his thinness had a hard whipcord quality about it. His dark blond hair was cut and combed neatly about a strong but finely boned head. Blue eyes, carefully guarded, gazed from beneath long, almost girlish lashes. He could have been good-looking were it not for the tenseness, the feeling of muscle drawn against muscle in preparation against constant attack.

"I hope it was not inconvenient for you when I telephoned your home," he said politely. "I had a message from Mr. Roth in Budapest. He said you were coming home for a short period and that you would be exactly the right person to meet our requirements."

Absolutely self-possessed, the little peasant boy whose father drank and stole, whose mother carried him to school on her back and begged for a place at the *Gymnasium*. Self-possessed . . . and inhumanly cold. Leo suddenly longed to smash the self-possession.

"How are your parents?" he asked cruelly. "Are they still working on my brother-in-law's farm?"

"They are dead. Thank you for your inquiry. My mother died just before I qualified as a teacher. She had cancer. My father died last year. He drank too much, fell in the river, and subsequently died of a chill—pneumonia, I imagine. Your parents are well, I believe, Mr. Ferenc? I see them occasionally when I am in that part of the town." The face was dispassionate, the eyes blank, the lips drawn back in a controlled mask.

"I'm sorry to hear of your mother's death. I believe you were very attached to her."

"All only sons are attached to their mothers."

"I heard from my sister that you were intended for the village school. I believe they were all most disappointed when you refused to take that post?"

"I believe they were."

"And now you are teaching here? In the town?"

Janos Marton bowed his head in acknowledgment. "There is much to be taught here," he said lightly, "which is why I contacted you, Mr. Ferenc. I organize one or two little educational schemes in this part of the town, and we would like you

446

to give a series of informal—secret—lectures if you would. Mr. Roth said he could think of no man better informed for our needs."

"What kind of lectures?" Leo asked sullenly.

"On Marxist doctrine. To the workers in the steelyards."

There was a little damp clutch of fear in Leo's stomach. Janos Marton was serious. He was quietly asking Leo to preach heresies against the government in a steel factory. This was different, very different, from all the other things he had done. The articles in *Gondolat*, the boisterous conversations at the Balasz, the defiant declaration of his views before his reactionary colleagues on the paper—all these things were like the bragging of a child compared with Janos Marton's request.

"Are you aware of the risks you're running, organizing this kind of thing?" he asked, trying to appear as cool and distinterested as the young man on the other side of the table.

"Of course, Mr. Ferenc. But you have more to lose than I. It would not be sensible for you to agree to do this unless you are sure of your principles."

Principles? What were his principles? In Berlin he had had many of them. He had gone raging into the streets with his principles emblazoned on a banner and had got his ribs kicked in and his mouth bloodied in order to defend them. He closed his eyes—always his way of thinking deeply—and called back a vision of himself at twenty-two, standing with a spear of glass in his hand, ready to fight the Nazis singlehanded. And what had he done since then? Written a few leftwing articles in intellectual magazines and talked theory with his friends. He was twenty-eight. Had the fire left him already? He opened his eyes and stared at the young man before him. Controlled, tense, clever, Janos Marton would never fight in the street, would not let emotion carry him tearfilled into passionate causes.

"You are very disciplined for one so young," he said tonelessly.

"Thank you, Mr. Ferenc."

"You were not always so disciplined. There were many times, when we were young, when you hated me, would have killed me if you could."

"But surely, Mr. Ferenc, one learns that violent emotions are cruel things to carry about. They can so rarely be released."

447

"It is not always easy to be that rational."

The blue eyes flickered very slightly. A glimpse of fury—anguish? what?—stared out and was instantly controlled.

"One learns to be rational, Mr. Ferenc. One learns very quickly when one is a peasant child, especially the only peasant child in a school of middle-class pupils. Nothing teaches self-discipline so quickly, or the power of intellect over emotion."

Twenty-two years old and a monster, a machine of cold calculations.

"You don't hate me then? For kicking your father when he was drunk, for seeing him beaten by the *pandur,* for riding on a horse when you walked through the snow without shoes, for eating when you were hungry?"

"I don't hate you, Mr. Ferenc," Janos Marton said quietly. "I hate the system that made you."

Twenty-two and a man, while he was twenty-eight and a spoilt child compared with this soul-scorched creature who had learned to live with himself and his passions.

"I will give your lectures, Janos Marton. Until I am called to the army, I will help you in any way that I can."

Again the blue eyes flickered, not in warmth but satisfaction. "We speak to no more than nine or ten at a time; otherwise it is not safe. We use the room behind this restaurant and if anyone asks why we gather on certain evenings it is to play cards and gamble a little."

"I understand."

"I shall be with you at first; then we work separately. It is safer that way."

"I understand," he said again, although a flux of fear suddenly made him long to back out.

Janos Marton rose from his chair and again extended his hand. "I must leave you now. School begins again in a few minutes. I will telephone you when we are ready to begin." He hesitated as though weighing the wisdom of imparting further knowledge. "Your name—your family name—is important to us in this town, but that is not why I have asked you. I have read your articles in *Gondolat* and I recall what they said of you in Budapest. Your beliefs are sound, Mr. Ferenc. And you are honest. Also your way with words is skilled, highly skilled."

"Thank you."

Janos called the waiter over and paid the bill. Leo let him, although he knew the schoolteacher earned a pitifully small wage. He realized it was a way of righting the balance. It wiped out the child with sores on his feet and the frail woman carrying that same child to school on her back.

"I'm sorry about your mother," he said again as they stood to leave. "I remember her very well, a tall, blue-eyed woman. My brother-in-law was impressed with her courage."

The face of the other was turned away so he could not watch to see if the blue eyes moved. There was just the toneless voice. "Yes, she had courage, especially at the end."

Leo sensed suddenly that the tense body was too tense, the stillness too still, and he was alarmed in the way he had been alarmed when small by Papa's silent rages. "I will wait for you to phone me," he said hurriedly, and the other nodded and walked through the door of the restaurant.

Leo watched the schoolteacher walk away, strong and lithe, like an animal. His suit was cheap and badly cut, and it hung shapeless from square-boned shoulders. Above the frayed collar Janos Marton's neck was pathetically thin. It was the neck of a vulnerable, defenceless child who has no friends. Leo felt sorry for him as he had felt sorry several times in the past. But this time his pity was tempered with caution.

Three weeks later, packed into the back room of the café with eight men smelling of sweat and salami, he began to talk on Marxist doctrine. His audience was sincere but ill-educated. It was a radical change from the intellectual exchanges at the Balasz, for now he had to simplify, and simplify yet again. Janos Marton had impressed upon him that they did not want fiery rhetoric or impassioned calls to the blood. These men were to be educated in sound, practical theory that they could understand and use in argument. Leo did his best, but by question time he was sweating with the effort of thinking with their minds and talking with their tongues. They were very nervous and respectful at first. He was a Ferenc and they called him sir, and on one occasion even excellency. But as the evening progressed, and the stink of sweat and sausage combined with that of cigarette smoke, their hereditary respect faded and they bombarded him with stolid, sometimes stupid questions. He stood it for two hours more, then drew the evening to a close with the final authority of the teacher. In the street outside the café he drew a deep breath and shook his head.

"The smell of the proletariat is unpleasant, is it not?" asked Janos Marton behind him, but he was too tired to reply and he just said good night and walked away. He sensed Marton looking after him, could almost feel the cold eyes on his back.

After the third lecture Janos didn't come any more and, curiously, he felt lost and a little helpless, shut up with eight or nine men from the steelyards and no interpreter to help him. Marton explained when they next met that he now considered his presence unnecessary at the talks.

"You don't think, from the question of morale—for them and also for me—that your presence might be useful?"

Marton considered. "No, I have listened to your talk—the same talk—for three nights, and now you are quite capable of dealing with them. Morale is not necessary."

At the sixth lecture there was a man whose face, for some reason, stayed in Leo's mind. Mostly the faces of the steel workers were the same, heavy and square-jawed with hair receding from temples and eyes blunted with tiredness and the effort of understanding Leo's words. The new face was different, sharper, with bright alert eyes. Leo waited for the questions, certain that this man would ask things that he could enjoy answering. The face was keener, more alert, capable of reasoning and calculation. He was disappointed when, at the end of the talk, the man just rose and left the packed room. Leo, smitten already with the conceit of the inspired teacher, felt betrayed. His gift of knowledge, imparted with patient care, had been rejected by a man who obviously understood what Leo was saying. Despondent, disillusioned with the task he had been given, he walked home through the warm summer rain, hoping illogically that his call-up papers would come soon so that he could leave this town he was beginning to hate.

The following morning, as he opened the door of Papa's apartment to leave the house, he discovered the man with the bright intelligent face standing outside the door. With him were three policemen.

"That is him," said the keen-faced man. "I do not know his name, but he gave a lecture on Marxist doctrine to nine men from the factory last night, in a restaurant on Vorosmarty Street."

One moment later, without even having time to tell anyone in the house, he found himself in a car being taken to the police headquarters.

Through the days that followed he wanted desperately to ask if they had arrested anyone else, but he dared not. They were watching, questioning, waiting to see if another political dissident was involved. He knew it was only his family name that prevented them from beating further information out of him. He said he had been approached by a stranger and asked to talk to the factory hands. He described the stranger again and again, taking a wary, private amusement from his description—a short swarthy man with a German accent—which exactly fitted the town's leading magistrate. He knew it was possible that Janos Marton was lying in another cell also awaiting trial, but he dared not ask in case his query led to Marton's arrest.

At the end of the week he was called into court, and there, in the presence of David Klein and a stranger from Budapest, he was released on bail. David drove him home, but even then he found he was unable to mention Marton's name. He had, in the last days, denied all knowledge of the man to himself, and now he could not break his self-erected barrier.

Papa did not speak to him; Mama cried all the time. Jozsef was out, deliberately out, Leo thought with idle amusement. He was taken straight upstairs to Malie's apartment and here he was told that the stranger from Budapest was a barrister, a friend of David's, who was going to handle this case.

"If we keep matters here, in the town," David explained carefully, "you should receive no more than a heavy fine. It is a local matter, a provincial matter, and we are known and respected here. Mr. Elek is the top man for this kind of case. With the town feeling lenient towards us, and Mr. Elek's brilliant record in court, we should be able to prevent a sentence of imprisonment. But we must keep it local. We cannot vouch for what might happen if it goes to Budapest."

Only then did Leo manage to ask, "Was anyone else arrested with me? Was anyone else involved?"

"Seven other . . . Marxists. There has been a sweep in the town. You are the only one connected with the factory."

"The seven?"

David, in a dry, toneless voice, named the others. Two of them Leo recognized from the list given him in Budapest.

"Did anyone come forward while I was in gaol?"

"No one."

Illogically he felt betrayed. Why had Janos Marton not come forward to share his danger? And then he remembered the cold logic, the reason that mastered everything else, and he knew that Marton would never risk practical considerations for a quixotic gesture of sacrifice.

At the trial he saw the schoolmaster once, standing at the back of the court studying with dispassionate interest the process of legal machinery. He stared at Leo as a stranger stares, without interest, and the coldness of the blue eyes generated a sudden chill in Leo's heart. Was it possible he had been the victim of a malicious, vengeful plot? Had the peasant child carried hatred in his heart all these years, in spite of his avowals to the contrary? Leo tried to discard the notion. No one could be that bitter, that unintelligent, but every time he looked at Janos Marton the idea festered. Why had the spy come on a night when he was alone? He pushed the thought away but the seed was there.

Mr. Elek proved to be worth the large sum of money David was paying him. Leo was fined, released, and informed by the court that during his military service he would be barred from the promotion usually given to people of his background. He had forfeited his privileges and must now take his chances with the proletariat he had sought to befriend.

He gave David Klein the remainder of the savings he had managed to accumulate in Budapest, insisting that it would pay part at least of the legal fees. The only aspect of shame he felt in this entire business was the fact that family money had been used to free him from trouble. If he had been Janos, what would have happened? Gaol, he supposed, for an undefinable period.

A month later he received his papers and reported to barracks, pleased to be out of the house where Papa's disapproval and Mama's tears coloured every moment of the day. Once more he was informed, this time at the barracks, that he had no possible chance of promotion, not even to non-commissioned ranks, but by now he no longer cared. Hitler had moved into Poland and the refugees were pouring over the border. Beside that everything else seemed unimportant.

31

Nervously, casting worried glances over the borders towards the three newly conquered vassal states of Austria, Czechoslovakia, and Poland, Horthy's Hungary began to tread the delicate path between preserving its independence and placating the monster of the Third Reich. It was necessary to be not so stalwart an ally as Italy, but not as defiant as Poland, to offer a little but not too much, to support in theory and brave words their gallant German allies, but yet refrain from actually declaring war on Hitler's enemies.

The balancing act was assisted because of the very nature of Horthy's parliament. For nearly twenty years the land had been governed by a strict and rigid regime, set in traditional lines. It was easy to tilt just a little more and convince Hitler that this particular country of Eastern Europe was safe in the Axis block. The Arrow Cross men, now a strong Hungarian Nazi group, were given a little more prominence. So was anti-Semitism and the crushing of moderate and left-wing elements. It was the price that had to be paid to keep Hitler from swallowing their land as he was rapidly swallowing all the other lands of Europe.

Leo made the curious discovery that it was very comforting to be a soldier. All his adult life he had been tortured by making decisions of principle, trying to decide if this loyalty preceded that loyalty, if it was right to fight this particular evil in that particular way. And now as a soldier he was not asked to make decisions or think about his actions. He was absorbed into a great machine that kept him busy every moment of the day and never once gave him a chance to decide if he was doing the right thing. After a lifetime of agonizing and searching after truth, he sank back like a convalescent into the poultice of obedience and non-thought that was army life.

Everything was diminished. Before, he had hated the oppression of the poor, the cruelty of the *pandur*, the lack of freedom. Now he hated Szabo, who had the bunk above his and who snored all night and never changed his underclothes. As a journalist he had wrestled daily with his conscience, wondering how far he dared risk his liberty in the cause of professional integrity. Now he was concerned with seeing that his ration of soup was as large as that of everyone else.

Szabo was the abrasive element in his cushioned existence, because Szabo's favourite pastime was in pointing out to the unit that here was Ferenc, an educated man from a wealthy family, now the lowest and most inferior of them all. "And why?" taunted the ex-factory hand. "Why is his excellency less than we are? Because he is a convicted Communist. And most probably a few other things that he pretends not to be.

Ha, Ferenc, I should like to see your secret files at head-quarters. There's interesting information there about you, I'll swear!"

The remainder of the company were mostly peasants, phlegmatic and nervous of being drawn into an argument involving one of their hereditary overlords, but sometimes Szabo was able to sweep them into mirth at Leo's expense and at those times he wanted to murder Szabo. He had to force himself into restraint, knowing that if he ever struck the man he wouldn't stop, and then he would almost certainly find himself on a charge that would lead to gaol. Szabo was a devout member of the Arrow Cross Party and painstakingly plodded through its news-sheet whenever he could get it. Leo knew, in his saner moments, that a fight between them would be immediately construed as a political conflict, which it was not. Szabo was too stupid to rouse intelligent antipathy in Leo. When he lay on his bunk reading his paper out loud, it wasn't the political content that infuriated Leo, it was his adenoidal voice and the fact that he collected phlegm in his throat and hawked it out every few seconds, once hitting Leo on the leg. Hitler, the impending war, the future of his country, all faded into obscurity beside his hatred for Szabo.

He would have been lonely, in spite of the panacea of army life, if he hadn't struck up a vaguely amiable relationship with a little merchant's clerk from Pest. In the ordinary way they would have found they had little in common, but in the enforced atmosphere of army life they turned to each other in relief, seeking comradeship that was born of necessity.

He was in the artillery unit of a hussar regiment, and for eighteen months he drilled, groomed the regimental horses, cleaned stables and barracks, and learned how to assemble and dismantle a gun so that it could be loaded onto three horses. He kept his uniform clean, queued for meals, washrooms, and evening passes, and in his off-duty moments brooded a little about his changing values, and a lot about the general unpleasantness of Szabo. His enemy's latest manifestation of hatred was in drawing attention to the fact that Leo was almost certainly a coward. "All Communists and Jews are cowards. Everyone knows that."

Leo clenched fists, mouth, and temper, and said nothing. He knew, they all knew, that Szabo wanted more than anything else to goad him into violence. "Wait until we get into battle, my friends, wait until we ride against the enemy! Then you'll see the proud and mighty Mr. Ferenc run!"

"How interesting," drawled Leo. "What enemy did you have in mind? To my knowledge we are not yet at war with anyone. Could it be your friends the Germans we may be battling against?"

Szabo's eyes protruded from their sockets. "You'll see!" he shouted. "Soon there'll be mobilization like the last time! We shall fight beside Hitler's armies and destroy the Bolsheviks and the Jews! That's who the enemy will be!"

"Fascinating," murmured Leo, and felt ecstatic when Szabo's face purpled with rage. He thought Szabo was going to hit him and decided that, charge or no charge, he was going to hit back. He squared up, but the rest of the unit, the ex-peasants and factory hands, thronged between them with bedding, equipment, and clothing—anything to restore normality to the barrack-room and avoid the trouble that a fight would inevitably bring.

The wrath of the two men fizzled out into a state of tumescence. They did not speak for two weeks, and when they did break silence it was Szabo's victory. He burst into barracks, panting with the exertion of running across the parade square. "We've taken Serbia!" he shouted. "Hungary and Germany, fighting together, we've moved in and conquered the filthy Serbs!"

"What are you talking about?" Leo asked, the old clutch of apprehension low in his stomach. "Serbia? Invaded Serbia? What rubbish are you talking?"

"No rubbish," he shouted, spitting with excitement. "Serbia, Yugoslavia, call it what you like, we've invaded and taken it! We are allies of Hitler's Reich!"

"Oh, no," Leo whispered.

"You're afraid now, my fine excellency," gloated Szabo. "Afraid and well you should be. I've heard we are to ride south, down to the border to take part in the invasion. Now we'll see, Ferenc, we'll see how Communists fight in battle. And be careful, for if you don't get an enemy bullet in you, you might get one of mine!" He spat again, and this time it was deliberate. It flew onto Leo's wrist, a thick gobbet of liquid that hung there before dropping onto the ground.

"Filthy pig!" Leo screamed, his temper breaking at last. He began to swear, calling Szabo every foul name he had ever heard. He leapt forward and grasped the man's neck, determined to bend him down into the dirt and rub his face in his own phlegm, but Szabo punched him hard in the stomach, and when he doubled over he felt the factory worker's hard fist chop viciously into the side of his head.

They were wrenched apart by their comrades just in time to avoid the attention of the company sergeant, who strode in and began shouting orders for the regiment's move. They packed battle kit and rations in silence. Szabo's was the silence of a nervous victor, while Leo was only just able to stand after the blow on his head. Outside, the fresh air made him reel for a moment; then the chill April wind served to cool him and quieten his nausea.

They rode for five days, sleeping at night in specially requisitioned barns and stables. They were not even aware of the exact time when they rode over the border. They were in gentle, wooded farming country when the news spread through the lines that already they were in occupied Yugoslavia. At one point a messenger rode up to them on a bicycle with the information that a party of Yugoslav resisters were waiting just outside the village a few kilometres away. They were moved up, then the guns unloaded and assembled. A party of riflemen on horseback thundered past, and there was some desultory shooting in the middle distance, then silence, a wait of a couple of hours, and an order to move forward again.

Up and over the soft, undulating countryside. Whatever fighting had taken place in this part of Yugoslavia, it did not appear to have affected the crops or destroyed the vegetation. The damson trees were in blossom, and the grain and maize showed a healthy growth in well-cultivated fields. The sun grew hotter as the morning advanced and flies began to buzz around their heads. Apart from the flies, it was a pleasant and surprisingly unwarlike progress.

At a bend in the road, just before the village, the progress stopped, then moved again. Littering the path were several bodies: Yugoslav soldiers, all dead from rifle or machine-gun fire. They had been there only a little while but already flies were clustering thickly over the puddles of blackened blood.

Leo darted a quick glance at Szabo, wanting to see what his first reaction would be to men dead in battle. Szabo had a curious avid look on his face that Leo found distasteful and he looked hurriedly away. Farther along they passed the body of a woman. Her throat was cut and her skirts were bundled up round her waist. She wasn't young, about forty, old enough probably to think herself free from the danger of rape. Szabo was staring hard at the corpse, so hard that he turned round as they passed and rode with his head twisted back. The hatred in Leo's heart grew more and more virulent. Nothing would exorcise that hate except his fingers round Szabo's fat neck, squeezing, squeezing. . . .

When they came to the village they were ordered to dismount, and a major assembled them together and told them what they were to do.

"We are billeted here as occupying troops. You will be told by your company sergeants where to go. The village is composed of three national groups: Swabians, Hungarians, Serbs. The Hungarians and Swabians are friendly, the Serbs are not. Many of them have been killed, and tomorrow you will superintend the clearing of the dead from the road so that the rest of the troops can pass through. Can anyone here speak German?"

Leo stepped forward.

"You speak German? Well enough to understand the Swabian dialect?"

"Sir. Also a little Croat."

"Good. You will report to headquarters for special duties. You are excused company drills and will be billeted near headquarters at the centre of the village."

"Sir."

The company was dismissed and allocated to stables and farmhouses. He followed the major to the centre of the village. Their billet was the village inn, closed and shuttered now against the advent of war, but Leo could see how very pleasant it was going to be when the shutters were down and the tables placed outside again. His delight with his special duties was centred almost entirely on scoring over Szabo, who had come south to fight a gallant war but who was, instead, going to clear bodies from a road and then, most probably, act as supply convoy for slicker, smarter troops in the active areas. And while Szabo was cleaning, fetching, and carrying, he, Ferenc, would be liaising between the officers and civilian population.

On the following day he was told to "acquire" a bicycle so that he could travel between all the various occupied villages in the area. One was "requisitioned" from the village, and Leo began to pedal happily along the country roads. The very first person he saw was Szabo, standing over a group of old men and boys, directing the lifting and disposal of bodies from the road into trenches that had been dug at the side. Szabo looked hot and frustrated. He was having to explain himself in sign language and shouts, neither of which were very efficient.

"Need any help, Szabo?" Leo gloated as he pedalled past. "Want me to translate for you?" Szabo glared but did not answer. "No? Very well then. I'll leave you to your task. It seems you won't be fighting in battle after all, doesn't it?"

He was delighting in Szabo's humiliation, feeling compensated for the spit on his wrist, the blow on the head, and the months of taunts and insults in the barracks. Smiling, his eyes slid past Szabo to the road behind, and then his smile faded. He forgot Szabo, forgot the feud, and for a moment even forgot the army.

In the trees at the side of the road were corpses, but these were not the bodies of soldiers or even a lone raped woman. Old men, women in aprons, black kerchiefs and children— young children: the bodies were stacked in rows ready to be put in the ditch when it had been dug deep enough. They were all stretched in attitudes of supplication, clutching hands and taut bodies showing that they had fought death at the final moment, even the little ones. They were poor, all of them, badly dressed and with no shoes, and their bodies were pathetic and hopeless, as though they had never expected anything but death.

He felt no horror, only despair. He multiplied this little group of victims and saw similar groups in Poland, in Czechoslovakia, and in all the countries that had not yet fallen but were inevitably going to. He saw the path his own country was taking, had been taking for years, each step towards self-destruction following inevitably on the one before. He saw the foolishness, the futility of his or anyone's efforts to avert national suicide, the suicide of Europe. All these months he had been dormant, unaware of what was happening. Now he understood only too clearly the way things were to be. War, death, the annihilation of a people—his people, the people of Hungary.

"Frightened of dead bodies?" jeered Szabo, and he looked at his erstwhile enemy and felt no hatred, only pity, because Szabo, like the rest of them, was being led to his destruction.

"Don't you understand what has happened, Szabo?" he said gently. "We have fought with Germany against Yugoslavia. Now all Germany's enemies will be ours. And whatever happens, Hungary will be vanquished. Either Germany will devour us, or Germany's enemies. There is no place for a little land like ours, Szabo. We shall be destroyed between the giants."

A faint flash of fear crossed Szabo's face, a brief realization that his personal wars and dislikes, desires and opinions might count for nothing in a national holocaust. His unaccustomed clarity stemmed not from Leo's words but from Leo's manner. The hated aristocrat had suddenly ceased to be an aristocrat. He had spoken with the voice of a prophet. Then rude joviality reasserted itself. The moment's chill passed.

"Bah! Foolish talk! You are afraid of the bodies, afraid because it might be you next time."

"It might be both of us, Szabo," said Leo quietly, and then they were silent.

Two months later Germany, dragging Hungary behind her, marched into Russia. And by the end of the year the declared enemies of the Third Reich were also the enemies of Hungary.

32

The policy of appeasing the Third Reich began, almost imperceptibly, to make its impact on the people. Providing a few of Hitler's requests were granted—food from the granary of the great plain, partial mobilization to support his Russian war, some gestures of anti-Semitism—their internal independence was left intact. They became an island of semi-autonomy in Hitler's vast European empire. Poles, Jews, religious refugees from all the countries about them streamed over the border, knowing that for awhile, at least, they were safe—as long as Hungary continued to tread the tightrope and make placatory gestures. But even the gestures began to affect the country. Rationing was enforced, and husbands and sons began to disappear into the maw of Russia. And the anti-Semitic laws began to make themselves felt.

Malie didn't know when dread began to grow in her heart, a dread that descended upon her within a few seconds of waking each morning, dread that was carefully hidden from everyone during the day and that, at night, kept her staring into the darkness until her confused thoughts finally collapsed into sleep.

She remembered her anguish of the last war, hoping and praying for the safety of her lover at the Russian front, but this fear was different, born out of unknown terrors that vanished as soon as she tried to grasp them. *We are known and respected in this town,* she thought to herself a hundred times a day. *The Ferencs, the Bogozys, the Racs-Rassays, Kaldys, and Kleins, what harm could come to us providing we stay where we are known?*

No one else seemed to share the fear, or at least there was no indication of it in the family. Papa was absorbed by the continuing inflation brought about by the forced trading with Germany, Mama by the lack of materials to make clothes. Jozsef, who had been called up into his regiment, visited them on leave, looking proud and rather foolish in his lieutenant's uniform but apparently unconcerned by any deeper implication of the war.

Her sons, nearly grown up now, were such serious, silent young men that she could not bring herself to voice the dread in her heart. Against all common sense, all reason, was a conviction that if she ignored the fear it would go away. *My age,* she said to herself, *that's what it is all about. I'm forty-six, the age when women begin to grow nervous and worry unnecessarily. That is all that is wrong with me.* And she would throw herself into a frenzy of household tasks, determined to give herself no time to brood on what might happen. *Two fine sons, a sixteen-year-old schoolgirl niece, and a hard-working husband to look after, and I spend my time fidgeting like a neurotic woman over nameless fears.* Sometimes, when she had time, she would look at herself in the mirror and think how impossible it was that anything dramatic or dreadful could happen to someone so ordinary. She saw a tall, well-built woman with brown hair growing a little gray at the sides, a healthy, serene, *ordinary*-looking woman. It was ridiculous to suppose that anything could happen to ordinary people.

Towards the end of 1942, David began to make several trips to Budapest. It was like the old days when he had travelled up to the capital every week, but now he did not ask her to accompany him and he never talked about what he did there. He looked tired, a little drawn, and sometimes she caught him staring at his two strong sons with an expression of ineffable sadness in his eyes, and then she felt the fear clamping down over her senses again.

Just after Christmas he went, yet again, to Budapest, even though he had a feverish cold and was coughing very badly. It was soaking wet outside, snow that thawed into slush even while it was coming down. Their cobbled street and courtyard had always looked its prettiest in the winter, but on this particular day everything was misty, wet, and dirty. He had gone up by train, leaving his car at the station, and she waited anxiously for his return, concerned about the cough and yet almost pleased to be able to worry about something as normal and everyday as a cough instead of the other thing.

She heard the car at last—driving into the courtyard, the place where once old Uncle Sandor had driven his horse—and she hurried to open the door of their apartment, anxious to welcome him before he arrived at the top of the stairs.

"David!" she cried. "Come quickly into the warm and . . ." Her voice died away. The fear swept over her, receded, returned. David lifted his face to her, a face that was exhausted and as afraid as hers. His smooth olive skin had faded to the colour of parchment and every line was drawn down in haggard despair.

"What's wrong?"

He dragged himself to the top step, then silently put his arms round her and laid his head on her shoulder, like a child needing comfort. He had never, in all the years of their marriage, asked her to be the strong partner. He had always been the capable one, the self-possessed husband who coped and made provision for every eventuality. His arms held her tightly and the weight of his body leant down on her.

"What's wrong?" she said, hysteria mounting in her voice. "What is it?"

"Let us go inside, little one. I have matters to tell you."

"Money? Have we sustained more losses? It doesn't matter, David. You know we managed last time. It isn't important."

"Not money, little one." He still, after all these years, called her little one. In some respects, when they were alone together, she was still the child bride, still the young wife he had been so proud to acquire. The endearment suddenly hurt her. She saw how old he was and realized how infinitely precious he was to her, this kind, gentle, sophisticated man whom she had not wanted to marry.

461

"Tell me! Please tell me what is wrong, David!" The panic in her voice made him straighten his tired body. Immediately he was the old David, the cool, competent man who always had every situation well in control.

"Calm, Malie. We do not want to disturb the boys or Terez. Come now, we shall sit by the fire and talk."

With difficulty, disciplining herself against hysteria, she took his coat and hat from him, rang the bell for coffee, and poured brandy. He was almost the old David, almost composed and assured, but not quite.

"I have some news of Leo. It is not good."

"He's dead!"

"No. Not dead. Or injured. But he was transferred . . . to a labour battalion, the White Labour Corps. That is why we have not heard from him for three months."

There it was, the fear, and now almost with relief she let it swamp her. No point any more in fighting it. Now the gnawing anxiety could be openly exhibited. Leo Ferenc, her brother, was in a labour battalion for Christians of Jewish extraction. It was on record. Someone, somewhere, had noted officially that the Ferencs were not pure Magyar. Whatever followed was inevitable.

"So," she said quietly.

David put his hands over his eyes. His head sank forward a little.

"You understand, Malie, there is nothing to be ashamed or afraid of in joining the White Labour Corps. It is purely to comply with regulations."

"I understand."

"Malie, that is not all. Karoly has to go too."

"Oh, no, David. No!"

"I was told privately . . . by a friend at the ministry."

"Not my son! No! Not my son!" The fear exploded inside her. Her son, nineteen, not even to go in the army—that would have been bad enough—but the Labour Corps! First Karoly, then it would be Jacob, swept away, branded . . . and if the worst happened, if the Germans came in. . . . She clenched and unclenched her fingers. "There must be something we can do. We are people of importance in this town, respected, responsible for the livelihood and welfare of many! And look how we are related: to the Bogozys, the Kaldys, the Racs-Rassays. Why must my sons be sent to the White Labour Corps?"

"Only one, Malie, only Karoly."

Karoly, named after her dead love. She rarely thought of that bright, golden young man any more. Now the name Karoly meant a tall, dark boy with soft brown eyes who sometimes called her Mamalie, who was demonstratively affectionate to both his parents, her firstborn, a plump solemn little boy who had always preferred to read rather than play games. Very quietly she began to cry.

"Malie, Malie." He came across to her chair, knelt, and put his arms round her. "It is not so very dreadful, not like prison. It is the army, just a branch of the army. And if, by forming labour battalions—white, or yellow—we can keep Hitler out of our country, surely it is better. . . ."

His voice was bleak, lacking in conviction, and abruptly she ceased to cry. Karoly was his son too. The implications were as clear to him as they were to her. He knew only too well the danger of possessing Jewish blood. She rested her head against his. The feel of him was so familiar it was only rarely she thought of him as another being. His body was as well known to her as her own. And suddenly the anxiety of her sons receded into a greater anxiety for this man, her husband. "There is nothing else you have to tell me, is there?" she asked, afraid. "You are safe, aren't you? You don't have to go away, do you?"

"What would the Labour Corps want with a sixty-four-year-old banker?" he said dryly.

"David, whatever happens, however bad things become, you and I will stay together, won't we? It doesn't matter, what happens, but you and I will be together?"

"For as long as we can."

The fear receded a little, settled into a gentle ache that was never again to leave her. "Is there nothing we can do?" she asked softly.

David shrugged. "I have been trying to find a way of getting us out of the country, all of us: your mama, papa, the boys, even Kati and her son. I thought I might be able to find a way; I had influence in the old days. But there is no way out. We should have gone before, in 1938; it is my fault that I did not foresee all this happening. I should have made provision for you all."

"Oh, no, my darling! You have done everything for us, always. You saved us after the war, and you saved us again in 1929. You have always looked after us, protected poor Papa's pride and shown kindness to my silly mama. We owe you everything."

They rocked against each other. She felt her tears surging up and swallowed them away. What would I do without him? she thought. How could I face life without him beside me?

They took comfort from each other, and the peace that flowed between them formed a brief illusory defence against the fear. Nothing could harm them when they were as close as this.

Later, when emotion had been swallowed into ordinary things—the eating of the evening meal, preparations for bed, the necessary nightly rebuke to Terez and Jacob, who always called to each other from their rooms long after it was time to sleep—they spoke again, but this time more rationally.

"How is it that Jozsef has not been transferred? Why is he still a lieutenant, and Leo in the Labour Corps?"

"I suspect it was too late to do anything about Jozsef. I think his regiment is probably already in Russia. I have not mentioned this to your papa."

At any other time the news that Jozsef was fighting in Russia would have filled her with anxiety. Now, beside all the other news, it seemed just a minor unpleasantness.

"Why us?" she asked, puzzled. "Why have we been picked out so quickly? There are others like us in town, the Maryks, the Glatz family. They are like us but nothing has happened to them yet."

"I think—suspect—someone has drawn attention to us, Malie," he said into the darkness. "Someone has pointed to the Ferencs and the Kleins a little before it is our turn. I received the same feeling every time I approached the matters of special papers for getting out of the country. Someone was there before me, making sure we are blocked."

"Who would do such a thing?"

"I spoke to Leo on his last leave. He had a theory. He hardly believed it himself, it was so absurd. But do you remember the peasant child your brother-in-law befriended?"

"Janos Marton? Of course, we all befriended him. We gave him clothes and Leo's old textbooks. Marie even used to feed him sometimes. And he did well. He became a schoolteacher here in the town. You have seen him, David."

"Yes, I took little notice of him. Perhaps I should have done."

"But why should he hurt us? He owes us everything."

"Sometimes it is the very ones to whom we owe the most that we hate the most. Leo told me that he was always aware that Janos Marton hated him, has hated him from childhood."

"It sounds so foolish," she said despairingly. "And how could he harm us? A provincial schoolteacher, a peasant."

"He writes for the newspapers. He has friends who are minor officials, bureaucrats. It is easy to do. Just a whisper, a name dropped. . . ."

It was insane, mad. Impressions, memories, raced through her head in disorder, trying to weave logic out of a sequence of irrational events. She was tired and her head ached with trying to understand, trying to reason what they could do to save themselves. She felt David's hand in hers finally begin to relax. Let him sleep, poor darling; he has worked and worried for us for so long. Let him sleep.

The turmoil in her own brain continued, grew worse. One thought emerged clearly, a piece of good common sense. Terez must go home. If the Ferencs and the Kleins were marked, Terez would be safer up at the farm with her father's people. Adam would be able to protect her better than David, for the simple reason that Adam was not Jewish. Terez, whatever the hazard to her education, must go home.

"But why must I go home? I've only just come back for the new term! I need to study for my *Abiturium!* And the school play. I was to have the lead in the new play, and Jacob has promised to take me skating when the lake freezes. I don't want to go home!"

She looked so much like Eva that Malie had a sense of time telescoping: Eva at the end of a ball—"Uncle Sandor has come, Eva"—"But I don't want to go home!"

"Darling, you know Uncle David and I love having you here. We shall hate to lose you. But we feel you will be safer with your papa. The war—"

"You mean because Uncle David is Jewish?" asked Terez slowly. Her brown eyes stared hugely into Malie's, trying to be brave but showing the first glimmer of the now recognizable fear that hovered over all of them. "Nothing could happen to us, could it, Aunt Malie? Everyone at school says we'll be all right if Horthy can keep the Germans out. I think he can, don't you?"

"I hope so, dear. But I still think you should go home. It isn't just your Uncle David; there is Grandfather Ferenc too. You do understand, don't you, Terez?"

The girl was still. She sat lifeless in the huge carved chair they had brought with them from their Budapest apartment. Everything around them was rich, luxurious, in perfect taste. It seemed ridiculous to be talking about danger in this comfortable drawing-room.

"Terez, if you go home to your papa and your grandmother Kaldy, people will not be constantly reminded of . . . of the other side of your family."

"I understand, Aunt Malie, they wouldn't hurt Uncle David, would they? I couldn't bear it." She choked a little and stared hard out of the window. "No one would want to hurt Uncle David, would they?" All the youth, the spirit, was drained away from her. She looked at Malie, her face entreating the comfort she had always been given as a child. But now she was no longer a child and there was no comfort to offer. Malie turned away, unable to watch her destruction.

"When you get home, Terez, try to talk to your papa about . . . everything. Your papa will know what to do, and you must help him. Your mama—your mama isn't very sensible. You must try to see that she does everything your papa tells her to do. It's important now."

Terez didn't answer. Her face, over the navy-blue school skirt and blouse, was white.

"What about the rest of you?" she asked suddenly. "Grandpapa and Grandmama and Karoly and Jacob. And little cousin Nicky, what will happen to him? He has only Aunt Kati to look after him."

"Uncle David will look after all of us." She choked. "He will care for us all. You are not to worry."

Terez rose, put her arms round Malie and hugged her once, very fiercely, before running out of the room. Malie heard her feet on the stairs and then the door of the house slammed. She crossed to the window and watched her hurrying under the branches of the bare wet trees, down the street towards the square. Going to meet Jacob from school, she thought tiredly. Perhaps it's as well she's going home, quite apart from the war. Foolish to have cousins, only two years apart, living in the same house. Perhaps that's why she's so upset.

She watched the two of them that night at dinner. They were quiet, sitting next to each other, as close as they could without disarranging the placing at the table. Jacob, her son, was always quiet, but now his stillness had a heavy despondency about it. Terez had obviously been crying.

So that's it. Now it begins all over again, the loving and the suffering. You think your children will never feel pain the way you felt it, and it happens all over again.

When Adam came the following Sunday to take his daughter away, she noticed that Jacob wasn't there with the rest of them to wave the car on its way. She glanced up and saw his face at the window, staring with all the intensity of an eighteen-year-old about to be bereft of his love. And she felt only relief that Terez was going away before the affair could spring into something violent. This was no time to have to cope with the problem of cousins falling in love.

She thought a long time before going to see Janos Marton. She spent hours at night, brooding, imagining, trying to get inside the mind of a man who could hate the very family who had helped him to rise from the poverty in which the rest of his kind lived. What kind of man could hate like that, sustaining it over the years, waiting for revenge? She tried to relate it to herself. Whom had she ever hated? Papa, yes, during the first war, oh, how she had hated Papa for the pain and hurt he had caused her, the cruelty and the punishment he had inflicted on her because she had fallen in love. But she did not hate Papa any more. As she grew older she had begun to understand him, and now she felt sorry for him, for him and for her silly mama. She tried to remember what she could of Janos Marton. He and Leo had had some extraordinary feud that had begun with the death of Uncle Sandor. Leo had been unbalanced about that. She recalled a scene at someone's wedding—Kati and Felix's—Leo kicking the child's father, the child hitting back. But what could have turned a boyish skirmish into a man-sized desire for revenge?

It was easy enough to find out where he lived. She was a Ferenc. She had only to telephone someone at the County Office and within a very short time a courteous clerk called her back with an address on the industrial side of the town. At the last moment she asked Kati to come with her. If Janos Marton hated her family because he felt underprivileged, because he considered that Leo had ill-used him in some way, then Kati might be able to help. No one had been more ill-used than Kati, and all it had done to her was make her detached, given her an air of abstract isolation that only a few people could penetrate.

She took a tram to the Racs-Rassay house. It was shabby and run-down now; how ashamed Aunt Gizi would have been. Kati and her son had a bedroom each, ate in the huge old ground-floor kitchen, and lived in the room that had once been the old drawing-room but was now Kati's studio. All the other rooms were shut and draped in dust-sheets. A woman came in once a week, tried to clean, and took their clothes away to wash. Kati and her son went out to lunch on week-days in a rather weird café close to Nicholas's school, and on Sundays they came to lunch with Malie and David. When Malie saw Nicholas at her luncheon table she wondered if he had enough to eat the rest of the week. She suspected Kati was an unreliable and erratic caterer. But whatever their private living arrangements they seemed to be devoted to one another and very happy.

When she arrived at Kati's she felt a faint twinge of embarrassment. Kati was getting so odd, shut away with only her paints and her son for company, that sometimes, as on this particular occasion, she didn't seem to notice what she had put on. She was wearing an old fur coat of Aunt Gizi's, a seal-skin that had been fashionable thirty years ago. Her feet were thrust into leather boots and round her head was a red silk bandeau with a bunch of poppies pinned at the side.

"Will you be warm enough, Kati?" she asked carefully, staring at the bandeau. "It is very cold outside and you really need a hat."

"Red is a lovely *warm* colour." Kati smiled. "Nicholas is coming with us. I thought on the way home we could go and have tea somewhere. He loves having tea with you, Malie." Her eyes clouded over a little, then brightened again. "You don't mind, do you?"

She did mind. She was tense and worried enough without having to think about what she was saying in front of Nicholas. But Kati's face was so eager and confident she could do nothing but nod and smile back.

Nicky came racing down into the kitchen and flung his arms round her. He was a demonstrative and affectionate child, the way Kati had always wanted to be but never had. Every time Malie saw the boy she felt the same sense of shock that Nicky was so very handsome. Even at twelve he didn't seem to suffer from the legginess, or the awkwardness, or the skin ailments of most boys. He was neat and handsome, with a soft endearing smile and a permanent expression of excitement, as though he was always expecting something nice to happen to him.

"I've had a letter from Uncle Leo!" From his pocket he took a worn, creased envelope and waved it at her. "Uncle

Leo is serving with some *very* interesting people, Aunt Malie. He has a doctor with him, and a man who was in the government, and a newspaper owner. He says after the war he will take me to Budapest to meet them all!"

Leo, dazzling the younger generation again, even from a labour camp. He had enchanted Karoly, Jacob, Terez, and George, and now Kati's son was going to be bewitched by the family rebel.

When they went outside Nicholas took the letter very carefully from its envelope and walked ahead of them, reading it silently to himself. The two women shuffled along in the slush, Malie, tall and neatly dressed, still smart and attractive in spite of her pre-war clothes, and Kati, clinging to her arm, slipping and laughing, with the red poppies becoming damp and bedraggled as the damp got to them.

"Sometimes I wonder why I'm so happy," she confided to Malie. "I shouldn't be, not at all. I'm a 'disgraced' woman and no one really wants the embarrassment of having me in their home. And the war is frightening for people like us; we don't know what is going to happen—oh, Malie, don't shiver like that—and yet I am happy, very happy."

"You understand why we are going to see this boy, don't you, Kati? I explained on the telephone."

"Yes. I understand. Leo tried to tell me once the way he felt about Janos Marton. He was always convinced that Marton hated him."

Malie felt a slight twist of jealousy. Leo had always been so much *her* brother, and yet he had talked to Kati about things he had never discussed with her. "I thought it a foolish notion," she continued, pushing the envy away from her, "but David—David says someone is making things difficult for us. He would be angry if he knew what I was doing, visiting the young man, but I'm so afraid! And I feel I must try to do everything I can. I feel as though I am living all the time in a bad dream. You know the dreams you have, Kati, where nothing horrible actually happens, and yet you are walking through something that is ominous. That's what it's like now. Every day is like that."

"I know."

"But you just said you were happy."

"I'm happy now. But that's what it was like when I lived with Felix and his mother. Every day was like that." She gave a quick, small shudder. "Everything is good now. I have Nicholas, and I have you and the family. But I remember what

469

it was like. That's why I'm coming to Janos Marton with you."

The fear lifted a little from her heart and she felt comforted, not quite alone. There were things—vague, intangible things—that she could not share with David because she loved him in a very special way. But Kati was a woman; she was not ashamed to tell Kati about her fear. Always in the past Kati had been the one needing protection and assurance, but now Kati seemed older and more experienced than any of them, more experienced and more honest, more sincere. She looked down at the funny little figure clinging to her side and a wave of affection brought the never-far-away tears to her eyes. "Oh, Kati! What would I do without you! What would any of us do without you?" She fought the tears away, ashamed. Always crying. What was the matter with her? Was it her age? She must try and keep control.

On the tram Nicholas got the letter out, read it again with an expression of smug pride on his face, then stared out of the window at the darkening streets.

"How's school, Nicholas?"

"All right." The pride vanished from his face and she wished she hadn't asked. She knew from Jacob, who was in his final year at the school, that Nicholas's position was not particularly happy. He had been registered as Nicholas Rassay, but inevitably someone had found out just who he was and who his mother was. She never saw him walking to and from school with friends, and he never played with his fellow pupils. His friends were his cousins, and his family were his aunts and uncles. He never spoke to any of them about what happened to him at school.

She looked from him to Kati and wondered if the time would ever come when he was ashamed of his mother—not of what she had done but of her curious appearance and her increasingly odd manners. They were such a devoted pair, but inevitably Nicholas would grow, like her own sons—Karoly, next week, to a labour camp!—away from her. Tears, fight them back, swallow them, remember who you are, Mrs. Klein, Amalia Ferenc.

When they alighted from the tram it was Kati who with assurance led the way through the bleak industrial streets at the southern end of the town.

"We come here walking sometimes," she said explanatorily. "It's interesting. We often have ideas when we walk here, don't we, Nicky?"

470

They found the house, a tall brown-brick building with a flight of stairs leading up to a succession of landings. Mr. Marton was out, said the caretaker. He was out but would be back very shortly. The two women and the boy waited while the slush rained down on them, partly from the sky and partly from the leaking gutters along the front of the building. The caretaker stared at Kati. The stain from the poppies had smudged onto her face, giving her a curious raddled look, like an old whore who had only put rouge on one side of her face. He looked from her to Malie, every inch a lady. Quality.

"I could let you into Mr. Marton's room and you could wait there," he said. He didn't like Janos Marton. He wasn't friendly and he never gave him presents like the other tenants did. Furthermore he was a peasant. You could always tell; the accent came through however hard they tried. He was a jumped-up peasant and he had cold blue eyes and cold manners to go with them. If he was annoyed when he found two ladies and a boy waiting in his room, so much the better. All the rooms were in the caretaker's charge and he could do as he thought fit.

"That would be agreeable," said Malie, fumbling in her purse for the right amount of money. The caretaker led them up three flights and unlocked the door. He bowed, pocketed the money, and left them.

They were in a small bare room that was more like a prison cell than someone's home. An iron bed, a desk and chair, a wardrobe, a sink—everything was scrupulously clean, immaculately tidy. There were no curtains, just blinds drawn up to the ceiling. The only signs of human habitation were a row of books on the desk and a yellowed, torn picture pinned onto the wall opposite the bed. It was a picture of a stag drinking from a stream.

"Why, look!" said Kati from the desk. "You didn't tell me he was a poet!" She didn't touch the book, just pointed to it in the row. Malie bent down and saw a thin blue-bound volume. *Poems*. Janos Marton. "He's been published," said Kati, surprised. "How strange we never knew. Adam has always been so interested in his progress. We must read them, Malie. Not here; we'll buy the book in the town and read them."

Strangely the poems didn't make her feel any easier. If he was clever enough to write poems, he was clever enough to be a dangerous enemy. She sat on the edge of the bed and tried to think what she should say. What could she say? What proof did she have that he was giving their names to someone in au-

471

thority? And if she said the wrong thing she might make it worse. Her hands began to tremble and she was overwhelmed with a sense of inadequacy.

They heard feet on the stairs, quick, angry feet, and then the door burst open and a thin young man, vaguely familiar to both of them, came in. Malie could tell he was angry. There were two bright spots of colour on his cheeks, and immediately he was inside the room he darted a quick glance toward the torn picture of the stag, as though assuring himself that they hadn't stolen it.

"Mr. Marton," she said, trying to rise on trembling legs. "I am sorry if we have intruded, but the caretaker said we could come in out of the rain."

"He had no right!" He turned away suddenly and his body tightened and then went limp. He walked to the window and let down the blind, then returned to the door and switched on the light.

"I beg your pardon," he said coolly. "I was perturbed. Please sit down. Mrs. Klein, perhaps you would take the chair. Mrs. Kaldy, the bed."

"You remember us?"

"Of course." He bent his head forward into the merest suggestion of a bow.

"This is my son," said Kati, timidly.

"I know."

Nicholas smiled, and stretched out his hand; then faced with a blast from the blue eyes, his smile faded and he went and sat close to his mother on the bed. Kati put her arm round him. They formed a little island of security together, leaving Malie feeling curiously alone on her chair.

"Why have you come?"

"My brother—that is, my husband and I, we thought—I thought I would like to talk to you, to clear up any misunderstandings over the past. In these terrible times we must try to understand one another, help one another."

The words dried in her mouth. What would happen if she suddenly screamed at him, accused him of seeking revenge, betraying them?

"My brother Leo is concerned because he feels he has wronged you in some way, that we have all wronged you. We are at war and it is not a happy condition . . . to feel a sense of wrong, of injustice." There, that was better. That sounded logical, the beginning on a sensible discussion when they could

472

talk things out between them. She moistened her lips and tried to continue. "If my brother is right, if you do feel that we have harmed you in some way, I—we—would like to know how we could put it right. . . ." Her voice trailed away, swallowed into the realization that he wasn't even listening to her. She was useless, stupid. He had hardly noticed she was there. He was staring at the couple sitting on the bed, staring at Kati with her red smudged face and the sodden poppies hanging over one ear, staring at Nicky curled up by Kati's side, holding his mother's hand, resting his head against the sleeve of the old sealskin coat.

"It has not been easy to come here."

"Why have you come?" he asked without interest, not even looking at her because his whole body seemed to be absorbed with watching Kati and Nicholas.

The sense of inadequacy swamped her again, making her slow and inarticulate. Why had she come? What had possessed her to humiliate herself to a clever peasant child? She was a Ferenc, her mother a Bogozy! Temper flashed through her because the Marton child wasn't well trained enough to listen to her. *Careful. Next week Karoly goes to a labour camp. Leo is already there. In July your other son will be old enough to go too.* She closed her eyes and fought against rising panic.

"My cousin, Mrs. Klein, thinks you hate us so much you have been giving our names to the authorities, drawing their attention to our family background," she heard Kati say coolly. *Kati! How could you be so stupid, so blunt and offensive? What will he do to us if you talk like that?* She opened her eyes. Janos Marton had turned back to her now, but his face told her nothing—hard, thin, expressionless, the blue eyes carefully veiled.

"What reasons have you for thinking that, Mrs. Klein?"

"No reason, except my brother says you hate him, have always hated him."

"Did he say . . . anything more?" Watchful blue eyes, guarded, wary.

"About when you were young, your father—"

"Ah, yes. Nothing more? No details of anything I am supposed to have done because I hate him?"

"Nothing more."

The taut body loosened a little, so little she hardly saw it, just sensed it because her own body seemed to be symbiotically tuned with his.

473

"I think you overestimate my influence, Mrs. Klein, Mrs. Kaldy—"

"Don't call me Mrs. Kaldy," said Kati softly. Like her flowers, she had wilted a little. She was smaller, crumpled and old-looking as she sat on the bed.

Nicholas put both his arms round her waist and hugged her. "We'll go and have tea in a moment, Mama," he whispered loudly. "We'll go from here in a moment." Janos Marton stared at them. Stared? No, devoured the couple on the bed with his eyes.

She couldn't talk to him. He couldn't—wouldn't understand. He was keeping something back, hiding knowledge. She would do anything if only he would talk honestly, tell her he hated them all. Why wouldn't he be honest and then ask for something? He could have whatever he wanted if only he would forget about them.

"My brother says you hate him. We don't want anyone to hate us," she babbled. "My brother has been sent to a labour camp and next week my son, my first son, and soon my younger son. I want no enemies. You understand, I am sorry about whatever we have done, but what did we do? I don't understand. Marie fed you and we gave you our old clothes and books and Adam spoke to the directors of the schools and colleges and—"

"I have nothing but gratitude for you all," he said tonelessly.

"Then why—?" Something huge and warm inside her began to swell, out from her ribs, down into legs, arms, breast, head. "Leave us alone," she wept, as the huge warm thing completely enveloped her. "Leave us alone!"

Kati and Nicholas were miraculously one on each side of her, leading her out through the door as she wept. A last semblance of dignity made her turn at the door. *Must say goodbye courteously. Thank him for receiving us.* But the sight of his cold blue eyes disintegrated her brain and she wept again, all the way down the stairs she wept, past the startled caretaker and out into the street.

They took her back to Kati's house, and she drank thin wartime herb tea and *barack*. After a couple of hours the warm thing in her breast shrank and she was able to control it enough to go home and be with her husband.

Kati and Nicholas watched her walking along the street. When she looked back to wave they had their arms round

474

each other. Nothing had really worried them, the way it had worried her. What could she do? What could she do to stop the world from crumbling all round her? What could she do to save her family from Armageddon?

33

Rumours of a collapse on the Don began to circulate. They were wild and spasmodic at first; then the feeling that something serious had occurred became more prevalent. The newspapers and the broadcast bulletins reported "difficulties" and "heavy fighting," but the whispers said it was worse than that: the army was destroyed and left to forage for itself, abandoned by the Germans who had left them without arms or transport or warm clothes. There had been no letters from the front for a long time, no letters from Jozsef, serving as a lieutenant in the hussars, and no letters from Karoly, serving in a Labour Corps in Russia. Silence. Silence and a gnawing anxiety.

There were letters from Leo, and finally a visit. He arrived in town toward the end of February, thin, a little drawn, but otherwise unhurt.

"Demobilized," he explained. "Our unit disbanded. They said they were overdrawn and we would be recalled when necessary. The truth is that there's no need for the airfields we were building in the north, now the Russian front has collapsed."

They sat round the table in the downstairs apartment, Mama and Papa's apartment, and it was as though a hero had returned instead of the Communist renegade, Leo, who had always brought disgrace on the family. Mama sat beside him, stroking his shoulder, laughing and crying, plying him with food that Marie kept producing from the kitchen as a sign of her own particular love and welcome. Even Papa hung on his words, respectful and attentive, thanking God that at least one son was temporarily safe.

"We built a radio in the camp that picked up foreign broadcasts; we heard the Russians and the British. The Germans are drawing back in Russia. They've been caught by the winter and the Russian counter-offensive."

"What about our soldiers?" faltered Mama. "What about Jozsef and Karoly?"

Leo put his arm round her frail shoulders. She still had the figure of a girl, a slight and delicately boned girl, but her face was old. No amount of cosmetics and visits to the hairdresser could keep her young. "We must wait, Mama darling. We must try to be brave and wait."

"Is it bad, the Labour Corps?" Malie was staring down at her plate. She was trying not to let him see how afraid she was, how worried for her son.

"It is just like the army, Malie," he said gently. "We had to work very hard and there wasn't too much to eat, but that was all."

"Not like prison?"

"Not like prison at all." He glanced round at the silent heavy faces and tried to make a joke. "And I should know, because I'm the only one of the family who has ever been in prison."

How loudly they laughed, even Papa, who hated to be reminded of Leo's flagrant past. He was shocked at the change in them all, especially Malie. She had lost her tranquillity, the peaceful calm that had spread serenely over the whole family for so many years, soothing and helping and putting things right. She was nervous and her left hand trembled nearly all the time. He had expected to see Mama and Papa aged, but it distressed him to see Malie in the throes of some apparent illness. He stayed with them for a week, then said he must go to Budapest and try to pick up some kind of work. Their pleas only made him more determined to go; he had to get away before he was drawn into the miasma of hopeless gloom that surrounded them. He was also aware of his duty to the Group. In many ways the labour camp had been the best thing that could have happened to him, for they had formed the Group and now he had contacts in Budapest. They said they could use him; a translator was particularly useful in times of war and especially useful if he knew how to operate a wireless transmitter. He wanted to get away and start fighting again. Perhaps they were all going to die; certainly if the Germans came in there seemed little doubt what their fate would be. But until that happened he was going to fight. He left them, promising to come back whenever he could but secretly feeling nothing but relief that he was returning to his beloved Budapest.

He was, of course, unemployable. The restrictions had tightened since he had joined the army, and the combination of Jewish blood and Communist record barred him from any of his old contacts. Undaunted, he sold a few articles under a different name to one or two of his old papers and put up an advertisement in the café downstairs announcing that he would give tuition in languages at specially reduced prices. He survived.

A few remnants of the Second Army began to trickle back from Russia. But there was no sign of Jozsef and no sign of Karoly. Every other month he went home, afraid to look at the pale questioning faces. He began to feel that his presence was a reproach because he was alive and they were . . . where?

News came at last, in the early spring of 1944, exactly a year after his own return from the labour camp. When he went home at the beginning of March he knew, as soon as Marie opened the door, that it was bad news.

"Jozsef or Karoly?"

"Jozsef, Mr. Leo." She didn't cry, but her face was swollen and filled with despair. How little they ever thought about Marie. She had always been there, looking after them when they were small. They had never paid her much attention and yet she loved them enough to weep when a son was lost.

The two old people were broken. For the first time in his life Leo saw Mama and Papa united. They sat side by side on the couch, two sad, bewildered parents, not understanding, staring out at the world, trying to absorb the fact that their son was dead.

"The Maryk boy came and told us," Malie said later, when they were alone. "He has only just returned. He was a prisoner; then he caught pneumonia and the Russians left him in a field to die. Somehow he was one of the lucky ones. He just got back; he walked most of the way."

"And Jozsef?"

"A shell splinter in the stomach. They carried him back behind the lines, but he died the next day." She put a hand over her eyes and choked. "I haven't told them this. I wish Maryk hadn't told me, but he was screaming for several hours, screaming, *I don't want to die. Don't let me die!*"

"Oh, God!"

"I asked Maryk to tell them that he died instantly and that

he was buried properly, in a grave. He told them, but I don't know whether they believed him."

He was overwhelmed with a sense of loss, ridiculous because he and Jozsef had had little in common. They had scarcely seen each other since they left Berlin. And now the thought of his good-natured, slightly foolish brother dying made him feel that a part of himself had been torn away.

"He shouldn't have died like that," he murmured to himself. "He should have died like Uncle Alfred died, easily and indulgently. He couldn't stand violence or emotion. Poor, poor Jozsef!"

"He's not the only one," Malie replied harshly. "There are others."

"Oh, Malie! I'm sorry. But if you haven't heard, then it isn't necessarily bad. Karoly may have been taken prisoner. He may be safe."

"From all we hear he doesn't stand much chance of survival if the Russians have him." Her left hand began to tremble again.

"Malie, Malie!" He leaned into her, burrowing his head into her side the way he had when a child. "Is there anything I can do?"

"You can come home and help me!" she cried. "I can't manage any more. I know you hate it here because we're all afraid and because we're old and tired and despairing! But if you came home you could help us not to be like that. Don't you understand? I'm having to keep everyone together, just me. David is old and afraid too. I need you here, Leo. I need you here to help me." She slumped forward, her head in her hands. "You and I, we always kept the family going. Didn't you ever realize that? Me because I was strong, and you because you were bright and had vitality. But my strength is running out, Leo! You must come home, just for a while, until the war is over. It can't last much longer and however it ends I want you here with me." She collapsed into frenzied weeping, and because he had never seen her like this before, he was shocked.

If I come home, what of my work, he thought, the work of the Group? We are supposed to be ready in case the worst should happen. They need me to help form the resistance in case the Germans move in. He looked at Malie and thought of the two old people sitting downstairs and knew that he had no choice.

"All right, Malie," he said slowly. "I'll come home for a

478

while. I shall have to return to Budapest and clear up my things, finish my work and give up my room. But I'll be home as soon as I can, in a couple of weeks."

"Oh, Leo! If only you would!"

"I promise. You're quite right to remind me of my responsibilities, especially now with Jozsef gone. Mama and Papa—it will probably help them to have me here."

It didn't register with them when he first told them. They looked at him with the lost, bewildered look of children. Only when he was leaving them did they come to life, frightened. "Where are you going, Leo? When will you be coming back? Soon? How soon?" They watched him from the doorway when he walked across the yard with his bag in his hand.

"I'm coming back," he called. "Two weeks, no more, and I'll come home and stay."

The two helpless old faces pleaded. Insecure, afraid, they watched their one remaining son walk away. And Leo always remembered that his last glimpse of them was framed in the doorway, like two gentle children who did not want to be left alone.

When, on March 18, rumours of an imminent German invasion began to circulate through Budapest, he decided to delay his return no longer. He packed, cancelled his outstanding lessons, and burned some of his more incriminating papers in a tin standing on the stove. Then he tried to telephone home to Malie, to tell her he would be arriving on the following day. There was something wrong with the line; the operator tried for an hour and then told him there must be a fault and he should try again next morning. He decided not to bother. He would go straight to the station and catch the morning train. There was no need to telephone.

When he arrived at the station he knew it was hopeless. There were troop trains blocking the rails, German troop trains. The station was full of Gestapo, and three grinning Arrow Cross men strutted at the entrance, demanding to see the papers of anyone entering. As he hurried away he saw a convoy of trucks bearing down the middle of the road through the quiet Sunday street, making their way towards the river. He went back to the café deciding it would be safer to sit there, until some kind of public announcement was made over the radio. He wasn't surprised, just resigned to the inevitable, but there was a sore, sad place in his heart when he thought of Malie trying to explain to the old people what had happened to Hungary.

479

Malie, forgive me, he thought. I've left it too late, and now I can't get to you. But I'll come as soon as I can. I'll find a way of getting to you somehow.

34

Isolated in splendour, the splendour of a dinosaur left over in a later age, Madame Kaldy presided over a manor house empty of everything save servants and the spasmodic presence of her son.

Felix, when he was at home, was as adoring, as solicitous as ever, bending over her wheelchair with care, calling her "Darling Mama," bringing her posies, and only sometimes did she detect the patronage, the impatience in his voice. At one time he always used to tell her long before he made a little trip into the town. They would discuss together what he would do, how many nights he would stay in his apartment, what purchases and little luxuries he should acquire. But now she didn't even know when he had gone. His chair would be empty at breakfast, or she would see his motorcar vanishing down the drive, and then a few days later he would return just as unexpectedly, looking bland and smug and wearing that ridiculous green uniform she hated so much.

"The costume of the vulgarians!" she shouted at him one Sunday when he wore it to lunch, deliberately to affront Eva and her children, she supposed. "We are aristocrats! We do not ally ourselves with upstarts and bullies."

He gave her a curious, secretive look, a look that she remembered seeing on his face when he had returned from the Serbian front twenty-eight years ago.

"The uniform of a new Hungary, Mama," he taunted. "A new, refined, strong Hungary."

Her friends ceased to visit them any more and she tried to pretend that it was because she was old, infirm, tied by arthritis to the life of a semi-invalid. Her friends did not wish to disturb her gentle life with their presence. But as the months passed she confessed bitterly to herself that it was because of Felix that they did not come. The old nobility despised the Arrow Cross men. It was considered bad taste to be a fascist, and because they did not wish to insult an old friend, they just removed their presence from her life.

What had happened to Felix? she asked herself tiredly. Why had he changed? When had he changed? She couldn't remember, could place no mark on a time when suddenly he had been this instead of that. After the first war? Yes, he had been strange then, and Eva had helped to restore him to normality. His unfortunate marriage? Perhaps, but he had seemed happy enough, restoring the mansion to its previous splendour, giving parties and receptions, flirting with his sister-in-law. Or were the seeds of corruption—for as such she now recognized it—deeper in the past, in his childhood, in the very genes he had inherited from his father? Waves of despair, hatred, resentment washed over her even after all these years. He, that other Felix, had been handsome, charming, ebullient, and he had hidden his nasty, guilty secrets away, just like her son was doing now.

She had a single guideline to salvation, a hope for the future that was none of her contrivance and yet was her hold on sanity—she and the Kaldy land had an heir. George was young and strong and healthy, and he was the recipient of all her love, all her hopes and loyalty. George was uncomplicated, an extrovert who accepted with boyish interest, but not boyish greed, that one day all the land would be his. She rejoiced more and more in her grandchildren. Terez was not the son of the house, but she brought strength and light into the manor which sometimes grew dark and gloomy even on the brightest summer days. Her only regret about her grandchildren was that they were not more *hers*. She had tried many times to persuade Adam to let them stay alone in the manor with her—in that way she could teach them to revere their land, instruct them how to behave as Kaldys—but Adam never allowed them to be alone with her. They always came together, the four of them, and for a long time she had raged at Adam, frustrated by his silent obstinacy. Did he think that she, Luiza Kaldy, was incapable of rearing a son of the house in the proper way? Why did he guard his children from her as though she were dangerous, unfit to teach her own grandchildren? But as Felix became more and more estranged from her she forced herself to accept the restrictions imposed upon her relationship with George and Terez. Better an heir of any kind than no son to follow at all.

These two she loved with a righteous pride. These two helped her to forget the bitterness of Felix's betrayal.

He was rarely home during the weekends when Eva, Adam, and the children came. She noticed how careful he was to avoid meeting them, even his brother, and when she reproached him for avoiding his family he screamed—really screamed—at her.

"*My* family! How dare you say that? She is corrupt and decadent, and her children are like her! She has defiled our family. She has turned the Kaldys into a tainted breed!"

"Out! Out!" she had screamed back. "Out! Until you can remember who you are and not disgrace your name by behaving like the rabble you mix with!"

Old and infirm as she was, she had still been able to quell him . . . just. She was still Luiza Kaldy, powerful, strong, with a will dominant enough to cow anyone who defied her. But the strength was fading. When he had left the room, scowling and sullen, her limbs had sagged and she had felt a terrible erratic pounding in her heart that had frightened her badly. Was she going to die before seeing George safely into his place at the head of her table?

Felix had returned later, humble, penitent, asking forgiveness the way his father would have done years ago. But he could not win her any more. He was not the only love in her life, for now she had young George.

She found herself less and less able to control Felix, and once or twice she found, to her amazement, that she was slightly afraid of him. Towards the beginning of March, 1944, there was a new, dangerous air about him, a concealed triumph, something secret and gloating that she did not like. He spent much time upstairs in his study, a room her legs would no longer carry her to, and at night she could see under her door a crack of light that showed down the staircase. He was doing something up there, something secretive and evil. She was sure it was evil, but what?

One evening a party of men came to the manor, five men all in the hated green shirts of the Arrow Cross. She was in the hall when they came. She spent more and more time in her wheelchair in the hall, hoping by positioning herself at the centre of the house to keep control over everything happening there. Tamas, the servant who opened the door, was bewildered by the menacing group outside. He looked towards her with uncertainty in his face and she propelled the chair nearer the door.

"Ask them what they want here," she told the nervous

Tamas. "Ask them what they want, and then tell them we are not at home to visitors."

Her voice was clearly audible to the men outside, as she intended it to be, and she heard a murmured angry response from them. But before Tamas could close the door Felix, running down the stairs, cried, "It's all right, Tamas. They are friends. They have come to see me."

Furious, she swung her chair to intercept him before he could get to the door. "I will not have these *peasants* in my house!" she snarled. "I've told you before: what disgrace you bring on our name outside the estate I can do little about, but here, in my house, we will entertain only gentlemen."

Felix's face was blank, the eyes opaque. "But dearest Mama," he whispered softly, "you are forgetting that this is not your house. It is my house. Open the door, Tamas!"

The door swung wide, pushed from outside, and the grinning green-shirts stepped inside, lounging against the wall hangings, the ornate balustrades, filling up her elegant great sweep of hall with their vulgar shapeless bodies. Fury raged in her, fury made impotent by the curse of the wheelchair, by her body no longer able to be used as a weapon. They were pigs! Only to look at them proved they were pigs, fat and vulgar. Three of them, staring insolently at her, had not even bothered to remove their caps. She wanted to scream, but she controlled herself. She was still mistress of this house and still had sufficient authority to send them away. She drove her chair to the bottom of the wide staircase and turned to face them.

"You will have to excuse me, gentlemen. I am no longer well enough to receive visitors in my house. You will have to postpone your visit to my son indefinitely. Good evening." Her voice had the old icy tone that had quelled so many people in the past. None of the men moved, although one tittered derisively and nudged his companion.

Felix smiled at her. It's going to be all right, she thought with relief. My son will do as I bid him. The men will go away now. Then Felix placed his hand on the back of her chair and slid it along the floor, out of the way of the stairs.

"Go to bed, Mama!" he said slyly. "We have much work to do. Go to bed."

They pushed past, ignoring her, and followed Felix up the stairs, leaving her in a welter of rage, screaming rage that was also tinged with something else, the first threads of fear that came from recognizing her own helplessness.

She did not go to bed. She could not. She sat in the room that had once been the downstairs small drawing-room and was now her sitting-room, and she listened to the murmur of male voices and an occasional burst of humourless laughter. She smelt massed cigarette smoke, saw Tamas take up brandy and glasses, and her rage abated and her fear grew. She waited until they had gone, and then she thrust out into the hall again, intercepting Felix before he could return to his study. His study? It was his father's study and now he was defiling it.

"Why did those men come here?"

"Because I invited them," he answered smoothly. "We had much business—planning—to do."

"What business? What planning?" Trying hard not to scream but hating him because he was keeping something evil from her.

His face assumed the smug, complacent look she was coming to dread so much. "You will know soon, Mama," he gloated. "Soon you and all of Hungary will know."

"I want to know now!" she screamed, and he stared again, then turned his back and began very slowly to climb the stairs.

"Tell me!" she screamed again, but he didn't even turn, and she saw him enter the study—her husband's study!—and close the door.

Three days later, when the Germans had marched in, she knew what the meeting had been about. She knew, and her shame was so great she couldn't look at him or speak to him. She lay on her bed, unable to move herself and unwilling to have Hermin lift her into the chair. She lay there for several days, brooding, worrying, using her bright and active mind to unravel the sinister mystery of her son.

He came to her at last, the old charming Felix, concerned and not a little worried about her physical condition. He brought her tray in himself. There were roses by her plate— he must have telephoned into town to have them sent up—and he was quite his old winning, loving self.

"Darling Mama! You must try to eat something! If you can eat then you will be strong enough to get up. It is very lonely without you. Your Felix wants to see you about, as you have always been. I do not want you to be ill."

"What have you been doing, upstairs in that room? What has been going on up there, Felix?"

"I have been busy, my darling Mama," he said with exquisite charm. "We have had a great deal of work to do, and soon

I must go into town. But I want you to be a little better before I go. I am worried to see you like this."

"Worried in case I die," she snarled. "Worried in case you find yourself superseded by your nephew! That is why you don't want me to die!"

She saw a quick flicker of triumph in his eyes, but it was hastily controlled, extinguished.

"Not at all, Mama. I have no fears about my future. I just wished to see you well again."

"Cha! You are afraid of your nephew, afraid of your heir." Venom began to loosen her tongue. "You are envious, Felix. I have seen the way you look at your nephew—yes, and at your brother too! You have not fathered a son for the Kaldys, and now you are envious of those who have." She was gratified to see a faint flush raised on his cheek.

"I? Envious of that—that trollop and her tainted brats?"

"Envious!" she screeched. "You could have had a son of your own. It could have been your heir if you had done what I told you to do! You should have divorced Kati! Divorced her and fathered a child on someone else!"

"Divorce will not be necessary now," he whispered, and then stopped, the secretive smile she dreaded so much spreading over his features.

That night she lay on her bed, watching the crack of light under the door. Whatever he was doing was doubly dreadful now. Before she had dismissed his madness, his Arrow Cross friends, as no more than an unpleasant diversion. But now she had seen the power of these people; she had seen them in action. The Germans were spreading like disease over the face of Hungary. What fresh evil was he plotting now? What terrifying new developments were being devised in the upstairs room?

Two days later when he went away again, she noticed the pupils of his eyes were pinpointed with concealed excitement, the way they had been when the Arrow Cross men came to see him.

"Good-bye, dearest Mama," he said fondly, stroking her hair and staring out of the window, out across her lands, her farms, her river and trees and soil. "You must try to be more tranquil, accept things as they are going to be. When I come back everything will be right again. We will be the way we used to be. Hungary will be a wonderful country, and you and I will be happy together, just us."

Her body iced over. Fear drained away all strength from

her body, all blood from her heart. She was too afraid even to challenge him, ask him what he meant. She tried to control her body's shivers. Instinctively she felt it would be better if he was ignorant of her fear.

"Good-bye, darling Mama." He bent his head, kissed her, and was gone.

What had he meant, *"just us"?* What fresh terrible denouement was about to be sprung on her? What new disgrace was he going to wreak on the Kaldy name? She was helpless, helpless. *Curse my body, my sick pain-filled body that handicaps my spirit, saps my courage. If only I could walk, go upstairs and see what he does there, see what evil is perpetrated in this house.*

Throughout the morning she propelled her chair back and forth, back and forth, through the great entrance room, staring up at the passage that led to his room—her husband's room. The servants, used to her frustrations, her caged strength, ignored her vigil at first, but after a little while the strangeness communicated itself to them and they scuttled nervously past her, trying hard not to stare at the figure wheeling frantically over the area.

She had to get up there. Somehow she had to see what he had done. She had to know, even if it was too late to do anything. But how? To ask the servants to carry her would be a sign of betrayal in the family. How could she ask Tamas to carry her to her son's desk and leave her? Felix would be sure to learn when he returned, and now—she was ready to admit it—she was afraid of what he might do.

She propelled the chair to the bottom stair, reached out for the rail, and gripped with both hands. She placed her swollen, crippled feet on the stair and tried to heave her body up. The pain screamed through her. She was so used to pain that she had finally come to accept it as a necessary adjunct to her body, but this new, fresh agony obliterated everything else. She gave a small, soft scream and fell back into her chair, sweat breaking out over her body. Hermin came running from the downstairs room.

"Madame! What has happened?"

"Nothing. Go away."

Hermin was her own servant. Could she rely on her loyalty? Would Hermin gossip about the mistress going upstairs to Mr. Felix's study? Yes, Hermin was like all the rest of her kind, no loyalty or respect for the privacy of those she worked for.

Another hour of frenzied wheeling, of tension and conjecture and horrifying speculations. When would Felix come back. Today? This afternoon? When he came back it would be too late. Perhaps it was already too late?

"Just us, the way we used to be." What did he mean? What of George? What of her grandson! Upstairs. She must get upstairs and seee.

She swallowed. No matter what might happen when Felix returned, she had to see.

"Tamas! Hermin!" They came at once, so swiftly it was obvious they had been lurking close by, watching her, wondering what was wrong.

"I must go upstairs. Tamas, you will carry me and place me on the chest at the top of the stairs. Hermin, fetch Tibor and Endre and tell them to take my chair up immediately behind me."

"Madame, yes. Yes, madame!" Eyes round, voice tremulous. Were they all afraid of Felix?

Tamas, his peasant's face impassive, registering no emotion at all, bent and scooped her gingerly from the chair. She felt a flash of agony; then she felt exultation because she was being held by strong arms and her sense of movement, or power, drew added strength from the man's body. Behind she could hear the two men bouncing the chair up the stairs. Hermin, flustered, was trailing along behind; she couldn't see her but she could hear her. "Don't fuss, Hermin," she snapped, with a brief flash of her old confidence, and then she was lowered into the chair and they stood watching her, a quartet of stupid faces, wondering what to do next.

"Don't stand there! Continue with your work. I shall ring when I wish to be carried down again."

They clumped away, and when the last had vanished she turned the chair and wheeled it slowly towards the study.

It was the way she remembered. Several fine antelope heads on the wall, a case of her husband's guns which she had redeemed from a gunsmith when Kati's money had come into the family. There were animal paintings on the panelled walls, a huge seventeenth-century bureau, and Felix's desk, which had a well beneath a flat top. Her chair fitted comfortably into the well.

The stacks of papers on the desk revealed little: lists of names and addresses that meant nothing, circulars, letters and official communications from the Arrow Cross Party. The drawers were sure to be locked. How could she open them?

She tried and was surprised to discover they were all open. Whatever was here he treated with assured indifference. Who of importance would look at anything he had to read? No one would come here who could form a threat to his plans, whatever they were.

The top drawer held a small, smooth, German revolver. It was modern and offensive, the sort of thing gangsters used in the very few American films she had seen. She gazed from the revolver to the beautiful old hunting guns on the wall. That was how a gentleman shot, with a craftsman's gun. Not with this brash, vulgar, killing toy. She clipped back the magazine and saw it was loaded. Had it ever been fired? Had her aristocratic son ever pulled this . . . piece of machinery from his pocket and killed anyone? Did all Arrow Cross men walk around with these things festooned about their bodies like American policemen?

She placed the revolver back in the drawer and opened the one underneath. A brown leather folder was on top. It was embossed with the emblem of the Arrow Cross, another manifestation of Felix's declining taste. She opened it and stared at the typewritten carbon copies clipped inside. She read them and did not understand, the words blurred into something so familiar it did not make sense, a list of names so well known to her she didn't understand why they should be written down.

Zsigmond Ferenc, banker, retired. 74. Jewish.

Leo Ferenc, journalist. 34. Jewish father.

David Klein, banker. 66. Jewish.

Amalia Marta Klein, née Ferenc. 48. Jewish father.

Karoly Klein, currently in Labour Corps serving in Russia. 20. Jewish father. Half-Jewish mother.

Jacob Klein, bank clerk. 19. Jewish father. Half-Jewish mother.

Eva Sarolte Kaldy, née Ferenc. 47. Jewish father.

Terez Amalia Kaldy. 17. Half-Jewish mother.

George Felix Kaldy. 16. Half-Jewish mother.

Katalin Gizelli Kaldy, née Racs-Rassay. 48. Jewish mother.

Nicholas Rassay, son of above. 14. Father unknown but probably Jewish. Half-Jewish mother.

She stared at the list, not comprehending, noting in an abstract way that it had been prepared very efficiently. By the side of each name was an address, even including the school where George was a weekday boarder. Only the spaces beside Karoly Klein and Leo Ferenc were blank, "whereabouts unknown." These people she had known all her life. It was strange; it did not register. Why was Marta Bogozy not there, or Adam, or Felix, or herself?

The horror of what she was reading blanched slowly over her brain, made sense in a dawning of terrible scalding pain. The top of the page burnt into her eyes, the letters jumbled, straightened, plummeted into her belly and bowels.

Those listed below are, with the exception of Zsigmond Ferenc and David Klein, classified as Christians of Jewish origin. They are corrupt and dangerous elements and have tainted the blood of pure-bred Magyar families. Their economic, social, and financial positions have rendered them undesirable in the new society, and it is essential that they be deported before influence can be exerted on their behalf to protect them from due legal processes.

It went on, pages and pages of the report, listing their life records, their income, the dates of their marriages, the names of their properties. And at the bottom, showing clearly through the smudged carbon, was the signature of her son, Felix Kaldy. Her son, on the last page. And on the first page, George Kaldy, her grandson, her heir. The scream bubbled up from deep within her, from a fount of madness that could not, would not, accept what was written before her.

"No! God, no! Aaah!"

Feet on the stairs: Hermin and Tamas, white-faced, frightened. "Madame?"

"No! Wait. Must think. George. Save George. School, phone school. Hermin, my telephone book; get my telephone book. Hurry, hurry!"

The operator spent hours trying to get the number. He was infuriatingly painstaking and came back every few moments to apologize and ask her to hold on. She rocked to and fro, moaning, feeling floods of terror, pain, agony washing over her, threatening to drown her consciousness in merciful oblivion. When the director of the *Gymnasium* came through she was nearly incoherent.

"My grandson, George Kaldy. You are to let no one take him away. You must hide him until my son comes."

"Who is this, please?"

She swallowed. Control . . . calm. Luiza Kaldy, capable of dealing with anything. "This is Madame Luiza Kaldy. My grandson is in danger and you must let no one remove him from school other than his father."

"George Kaldy is no longer here."

"Oh, no!"

"We received a message from his father four days ago. He was sent home then."

She replaced the telephone at once and dialled Adam's number. It rang and rang—oh, God!—there must be someone there; why were the servants not answering? But she must control herself. Yes, control. She couldn't help if she panicked. If George had been sent for it was sure to be all right.

"Hello?"

"Eva? Is George there? Has he returned from school?"

Eva's voice, bored but also a little puzzled. "Yes, Adam recalled him a few days ago. Why didn't he tell you, I wonder? He thought, with the war so uncertain, it would be safer to—"

"I must talk to Adam. At once."

"He's in the granary."

"At once!"

She could still command Eva when she had to. Another interminable wait followed. Control, control. What to do? What to do?

"Mama?"

"Adam." Her voice dried suddenly, went dead. She tried to croak the words out, force them up from her chest, but all that came out was a wild rasping sound. Everything else had settled—her bowels, the sweat—but her voice wouldn't work.

"Mama? Are you there? Are you all right?"

"Get George away, Adam. Hide him. Terez and Eva too."

A pause. She could hear him breathing, slowly and regularly, and she suddenly remembered Adam as a child. Whenever he was nervous he breathed like that.

"What have you discovered, Mama?"

"Papers. In Felix's desk. Papers."

"Who else, Mama?"

"Everyone. The Ferencs, the Kleins, Kati and her bastard."

"Have you telephoned them?"

"No. George—I was worried about George. What—"

"I have made provision, Mama. I will visit you when everything has been done."

The flat voice was abruptly cut and she was alone with the silent receiver in her hand. She was calmer now. Adam would look after everything. He had "made provision." He had always made provision. Quietly and without fuss he had done what had to be done. He would telephone where necessary. He would look after George. Her family, her blessed little family, would be safe, George and Terez too, bright, sparkling little Terez. A wave of affection even for Eva washed over her. Eva had provided George and over the years had proved a reasonable daughter-in-law. They would all be saved. Adam would save them. He was a good son, a strong loyal son who had saved them before; after the war he had saved them. Why was one son like Adam and the other—? A drenching sense of shame, disappointment, betrayed love, shock. What had she done? Adam. Felix. Was the evil already there or did something happen? How were they different? Where had their ways diverged? Felix had been schooled as a member of the nobility, Adam as an artisan. Why?

Hunched in her chair she brooded, until the daylight went and Hermin came in to try and persuade her to go downstairs. She refused and went on thinking—of her youth, her marriage, her widowhood, the years which had been obsessed by one desire, to see her son sitting in his rightful place. She looked back, trying to separate the truth from her years of self-delusion, trying to see herself, to see the woman she had become.

Hermin came again. It was dark outside, and she asked for brandy and coffee and a candle. She did not want to sit under the harsh light of electricity.

"I cannot leave you like this, madame," the girl faltered. "If you are waiting for Mr. Felix, can you not wait downstairs? He may be all night. You cannot stay here all night, madame."

"Leave me. Get out." She poured brandy and sipped. With good brandy she could retain her self-possession for several hours.

The night closed in, and that and the brandy threaded through her brain, making pictures, giving her at last the nightmare of truth that blessedly comes to only a few, the truth of self-knowledge. And with truth she felt her strength —the strength inside her—die. Her body had been tired and crippled for a long time, but she had never given way to age because her spirit had burned fiercely, tugging her body along because it could not be left behind. Now a profound sense of weariness engulfed her. *I am old, an old woman. I do not care any more about my life.* An irrational longing just to sit in the

491

sun and sleep overcame her. How nice to sit on the terrace and think of nothing.

She heard him coming at last. He came swiftly, quietly, entered the study like a cat. In the candlelight he looked shadowed and evil, but then of course he was evil.

"Why, Mama," he said smoothly. "What are you doing in my study? And why are you waiting up so late? Do you want to know what I have been doing? Shall I tell you about my work for the last few months?"

She had the revolver in her lap, hidden below the desk. She raised her hands and rested the gun on the smooth top. Her heart was thumping erratically, loudly, and there were momentary spots of blindness before her eyes. She felt as though she were going to faint, collapse into blackness, drown in the terrible thumping of her heart. *Not yet. Be strong for a moment more. What is one more moment after a lifetime of strength?*

So many years since I fired a gun. . . . Hunting. I was beautiful then. Can I remember how? Am I strong enough? Oh, yes, one more moment of strength and then I can sleep, drown in my black heart.

She saw Felix's face change. He smiled at her, a sly, nasty smile of infinite complacence.

"You are cross with me, Mama. Do you want to frighten me? Punish me a little? But you won't, dearest Mama. You won't because I am Felix. You couldn't possibly want to frighten your darling Felix."

One more moment, just one. Place the revolver squarely. Steady the right wrist by holding it with the left: such old hands, such old trembling hands.

In the candlelight she had a brief illusion of Felix as he used to be: smooth-cheeked, young, infinitely beautiful.

"I have created a monster, Felix," she croaked. "And what I have created it is my right to destroy."

She fired. One last moment of strength and then, blissfully, she went down into the pumping sea of her heart.

35

He had made provision. He knew one blinding moment of panic when he wasn't sure what to do first; then everything settled into place. Eva was standing beside him, a slight frown across her eyes.

"It has come, Eva. Fetch the children. Quickly. As quickly as you can. Then change into your old clothes, the ones I told you to keep ready. All of you. Hurry."

"What's happened? Why do we have to go now, this very moment?" She was frightened. Her small, still very pretty face was white.

"It's begun. The Gestapo are rounding up the Jews."

"But we're not Jews," she faltered. "Why should they take us?"

"Don't argue, Eva. Please do as I say. One suitcase each as I instructed."

He was past her and out of the house, over to the estate office. He unlocked the safe and from a deep pile of seed invoices he took the false papers. They had cost a lot of money and a great deal of time to obtain but they were as authentic as anything could be. Mrs. Szabo with her two children, Mrs. Szabo, widow of a tenant farmer, poor but respectable. The photographs matched the descriptions. He had gone to a lot of trouble over the photographs, making sure that Eva and the children looked less affluent than they were.

He took the car round to the front of the house and they were waiting for him, a sad, frightened little group standing with three suitcases on the veranda. A lump rose in his throat, but he thrust it hastily away. No time for grief or farewells. Concentrate on their appearance. Eva looked wrong—her hair! It was far too stylish for a working-class woman. He must tell her. Terez was all right, hair in plaits and a shabby dark blue coat; so was George, who wore a darned jacket. He had taken great care over the right clothes.

"Get in. . . . Quickly!"

In panic they tumbled into the car, looking over their shoulders in case they should see a German staff car, or maybe even a truck, coming along the farm path. He started the car and drove away from the direction of the village; then he made a wide detour that took him up into the hills before he turned west again. On the county road threading through the mountains he was able to let the muscles in his neck and back relax.

"Terez, your mother's hair is wrong. Make it look less sophisticated. Comb it straight over her ears."

"Yes, Papa." A small frightened voice, but he must not listen, must not let it affect him.

"Where are we going, Papa?" George, trying to be brave and manly. George, who was so normal, such a healthy, ordinary boy, that it seemed ridiculous he should have to hide from persecution.

"I shall take you to a village outside of Eger. You will get a bus into the town, and from there you will take a train to this address." He pushed a scrap of paper into Eva's hand. "There you will ask for Mrs. Ladi. You may recognize her; she is a sister to Janos Marton. You will be her cousin, Eva. You will be Eva Szabo, widow, now homeless because your husband has died on the Russian front and the holding has been taken away from you. Here is money." Another package. "This will serve for your daily needs. You will not need to pay Mrs. Ladi or her husband. I have already paid them, and they will receive more at the end of three months if you are all safe. You will only stay there three months; it is not safe to remain in one place longer. I will send fresh papers and directions at the end of that time. You must never, never try to contact me. They will be watching me all the time. Do you understand?"

"Yes, Papa."

"Eva?"

She began to cry, a silly, sniffling cry that hurt him because of its helplessness.

"Eva, Eva! Don't make it worse! You must do this well or we shall all be in danger. You must try and be sensible."

"What happened, Adam? Why should they come for us so soon? We are not Jews, not registered Jews. Why do we have to go away like this?"

His hands tightened on the wheel. "We have been . . . betrayed," he said tonelessly. "We have an enemy who has seen that we are punished first."

"Papa." His daughter's voice was trembling but controlled. "Papa, what of the rest of the family, Aunt Malie and Uncle David, all of them—Jacob—" The control wobbled and broke a little. He dared not look in the rear mirror at her. He could not look at any of them.

"Them too. As soon as you are at the village I shall telephone them."

"Can't you telephone now?"

"No." His heart was breaking because he had to decide who to help first. If he had stopped to telephone from home his own family might have been lost.

"Have they got false papers too, Papa? Has Uncle David made plans for hiding too?"

"I hope so, Terez. I hope so." He hoped, but he doubted. He had warned Amalia and David several times. He had listened to the secret broadcasts of the BBC and had believed the reports of vast populations of people—Slavs, political prisoners, anyone with Jewish blood—disappearing into a nameless void, "deported" but never heard of again. David had tried to find other escape plans, some way of getting the old people out of the country. But all along Adam had said the only answer was false papers and a plan of constant movement.

He stopped the car once to buy mineral water and fruit which they ate as they were travelling. Every mile away from the estate made him feel easier but made him dread the parting that was coming. He stopped the car just outside the village. "You must walk in, like respectable farming tenants. No one will be able to trace you back to me then."

They stood by the roadside, all four of them. Terez was pulling her mother's hair down flat over the ears and settling the black felt hat more squarely on her head. Eva's huge dark eyes gazed at him, luminous with tears, pleading, miserable. "Oh, Adam, I'm so frightened!" she sobbed. "I don't think I can manage without you!" He held her hard against him, his silly, spoilt, thoughtless little wife who had broken his heart so many times. He held her, aching with love and anguish, not knowing how he was going to be able to send her away.

"Good-bye, Papa. Don't worry, I'll look after her. I'm the man now. I'll see everything goes the way you've planned it." George was trying hard not to cry, looking worried at the responsibilities he felt he was taking on. He reached up and patted his mother on the shoulder, and she turned tearfully and clasped her son to her. Adam pulled Terez to one side. She was calm, still. Only a nerve beating at her temple told of her agitation.

"Terez—" Large soft eyes, just like Eva's, stared intently at him, listening to his words. "Terez, you know you will have to do most of the planning. You will have to watch, guard, see that nothing is done or said that could bring down suspicion."

"Yes, Papa. I know."

"Your mother"—he coughed and stared down at the road —"she's not a very clever woman, but I undertook to look after her when I married her. This is one time I cannot protect her and you have to do it for me. It is not a fair or a right thing to ask a daughter. But she cannot manage alone, Terez. She has to be protected."

"I know, Papa. I understand."

So like Eva, and yet so like Malie too. Strong and honest. A heart full of hope and serenity, trying already to be brave and responsible. His daughter whom he loved, born out of anguish and suspicion, misery and betrayal. His daughter whose heart answered his own on so many occasions.

"Go now, Terez."

She bit her lower lip hard. Not yet eighteen and having to cope with all this. "Papa—" She stared hard, unblinking at him, and then threw her arms round his waist. "Oh, darling Papa!" Unashamedly his face screwed into a mask of pain and grief. Then he pushed her away and ran for the car. He didn't look back, dared not. He drove for several miles, forcing emotion away from him, making himself calm and controlled once more.

He stopped at the first post office he came to and asked to telephone. He waited and waited. The line was dead, the operator reported. He tried again, this time with Leo's number in Budapest. That was all right; the café owner answered and Adam apologized for troubling him and asked if he would fetch Mr. Leo Ferenc downstairs to the telephone. There was a strained, uncomfortable pause. "Mr. Ferenc has not been here since the invasion, since March the eighteenth."

"Did he—did you see how he left? Was he with anyone?"

"He left on his own. He had given up his room. He came back once, the next morning, for coffee. I have not seen him since."

"Has anyone else asked for him?"

Again the pause, then, nervously. "The Gestapo came for him, one week after he had left. I know nothing else. Nothing at all. Good-bye." The telephone was slammed down abruptly. He waited, thought. Of course! How stupid. Kati. He could phone Kati. The operator again reported the line was dead.

He went back to the car, the relief of his own family's escape already being superseded by another anxiety. He turned the car and began to drive towards the town. It seemed strange that the countryside looked exactly the same as it always looked in April. It should have been beautiful, but it was tinged with the atmosphere of nightmares, and the blossoming trees, the young maize, the flowers growing in old wine flasks all had an unreal, sinister quality about them.

When he drew near to the town there were German trucks, tanks, soldiers in abundance. There were also more Arrow Cross men, as though the German invasion had flushed them out of holes and cellars. They had been suppressed and disapproved of by the authorities for such a long time that now, with the power of the Gestapo behind them, they strutted with boorish aggression through the streets and cafés of the town.

The house was empty. He knew before he even knocked at the door, knew while he was driving the car into the courtyard. It had the stillness, the dead emptiness of permanence that is different from the emptiness of a house left alone for a few hours. Several pigeons whirled against the eaves, outlined first against the old brown roof, then against the blue sky. A few leaves and papers unswept from the yard lifted and blew in a gentle spring breeze. He knew it was empty, but he knocked anyway and heard the echo reverberate away inside.

He stared up at the windows, closing his eyes and praying to a reflex god, the same way he used to pray in the first war. What can I do? How can I find out what has happened? He climbed back into the car and drove slowly out of the yard, heading in the direction of the Racs-Rassay house, although he knew what he would find there also—nothing.

He began to let the car drift idly through the centre of the town, looking for someone whom he could trust enough to ask. Finally, on his fourth turn through the square he noticed that some Arrow Cross men were regarding him with surly interest and he hurriedly parked down a side street near the market place and sat in a café, trying to think what to do next.

He must stay away from every official source of information: police, county offices, the newspaper. They would all be interested in his interest, and later, when it was discovered that his wife and family had vanished, they would not believe his story of a visit to Budapest and a subsequent disappearance. Whom could he ask? He must choose with care, someone he could trust and someone whose own well-being would not be threatened by his inquiry. A sense of lethargy began to creep over him, a feeling of fatalistic despair that he knew he must fight. He still had to get home and prepare to answer questions. He had to face his brother and, in some way, try to control him. He had to cope with that mad, bigoted, still-powerful woman who was his mother. He ordered another coffee—filthy wartime stuff—and tried to push everything away for a few more seconds: his wife's frightened little face, his gawky adolescent son trying to be a man, Terez's cry, *Oh, darling Papa!* He hadn't said good-bye to them. It was more than probable he'd never see them again, and he hadn't said good-bye! He wanted to weep as the realization of his loss swept over him. His tiny family, knit together with so much grief and endeavour in the past, all gone. He gulped his coffee, closed his eyes, and forced order back into his mind. When he opened his eyes there was a figure he recognized walking across the market place. Instantly he was on his feet shouting from the café doorway, "Marie! Marie!"

The figure halted, then began to hurry away from him and he rushed across the square, ignoring the waiter's indignant cry behind him.

"Marie! It's me, Mr. Adam! Don't run away!"

Her stout body turned. White-faced she shook her head and whispered, "Quiet, Mr. Adam. Don't draw attention. It is better not to be noticed in the town now."

She was afraid. Every movement of her body, every expression of her face showed fear. He slid his hand under her arm and she flinched away from him. "Marie," he whispered catching the fear from her. "Where are they? Where have they gone? Did they escape?"

She shook her head. "No," she moaned softly. "They didn't escape, Mr. Adam. They had no warning."

It was beginning to grow cold, and he pushed her gently across the market place in the direction of the café. "We cannot talk standing out here, Marie. Please sit down and drink coffee with me. We shall be less conspicuous."

She was embarrassed and awkward, even in the midst of their joint misery and fear; she was still uncomfortable because she was sitting in a café opposite Mr. Adam as though she were his equal. Her plump, work-stained hands clutched at her bag. She sat upright on the chair, her large feet in shabby but well-polished flat shoes placed tightly together.

"There's nothing to be done now, Mr. Adam," she said simply. Her eyes filled with tears and she brushed them quickly away. "What about Miss Eva and the children?"

"They've gone away. I can't tell you more than that. I've sent them away."

"That's good, Mr. Adam. That's good and sensible."

It was the first time in his life he had ever really looked at Marie. She'd always been there, just a servant, but when had she grown old? When had the round-cheeked peasant girl become fat and middle-aged? And what would happen to her now?

"What happened, Marie? Tell me. Perhaps I can do something even now."

"Two days ago. Just a banging on the door and—" She swallowed, and the swollen hands twisted on the handbag. "Two Germans, Gestapo, and four Arrow Cross men. They had a truck and guns. They pushed past me." Her face was yellow and her chin was trembling. "They took them away. They were allowed to put on their coats and pack a small bag."

A groan escaped from her lips and she hurriedly pressed her hand to her mouth.

"Just as they were climbing into the truck one of the Arrow Cross men pushed Madame Ferenc away. 'You're all right,' he said. 'You can go back; you're not one of them,' and Mr. Ferenc shouted down to her to go away. 'Stay with Adam,' he cried. 'Go back. You'll be safe in the house, Marta.'"

"I see." He felt sickness creeping into the pit of his stomach.

"She climbed up into the truck, young Mr. Jacob helping. 'I can't leave you now, Zsigmond,' she said." The old servant began to sob. "She was such a silly lady sometimes, Mr. Adam. The way she laughed—you remember? Like a young girl. It used to annoy Mr. Ferenc; it wasn't right for an old lady to laugh like that. She laughed at Mr. Ferenc when she was trying to get into the truck. 'I can't leave you now, Zsigmond,' she said. 'I've stayed with you all these years. Do you think I could leave you now?'" The dark lines of flesh on her face began to quiver and blur. "Oh, Mr. Adam. I should have gone with them! I was ashamed when I saw how brave she was. I wanted to go with them but I didn't! I stood at the door and watched them drive away! I was afraid. I wanted to be

499

brave like she was, but I was afraid." She covered her face with her hands and he was only able to stare at her, not offer any comfort. Everything had gone too far for comfort. There was only this terrible dread that had settled in the pit of his stomach.

"Amalia? Mr. David?"

She nodded. "Them too. There were others already in the truck: the Maryks, and the doctor, and Mr. Glatz, and Miss Kati. But her son wasn't there. I looked for him and he wasn't there. When the truck had gone I went to Miss Kati's house. I thought I would find the boy and take him to my sister at Szentendre. He would be safe with my sister. My sister would look after him." She began to talk quickly, trying to appear controlled and sensible. "I thought it all out while I was going to Miss Kati's house. My sister could say he was our nephew from Vienna. They're the same age, and no one in Szentendre has seen our nephew."

"And—"

Hopeless brown eyes mourned at him. "No one was there. I waited for two hours, but he didn't come, and then the servant next door said he hadn't been there when the truck came. The . . . the Gestapo searched the house for him, but he wasn't there."

One had escaped. Perhaps. Nicholas Rassay, fourteen, old enough—just—to look after himself for a few days if he was lucky. But how could he exist without papers or work if he didn't have anywhere to hide?

"Where could he have gone, Marie, to school friends?"

"No. He had no friends at school. It was . . . difficult for him, you see, on account of his mother. They used to call her names and he was always fighting. He was very lonely at school; his life was here, with us, the family." She choked, swallowed, gripped the bag again. How extraordinary that she should know so much, although of course it wasn't strange at all. Nicholas had always seemed so happy he had taken it for granted that the boy was content at school. But Marie had shared every miserable humiliation with him, had known of his daily life in the same way that she knew Marta Ferenc's laugh annoyed her husband.

"I'll try to find him, Marie."

"You won't find him, Mr. Adam. If you could find him then so could the Gestapo. I've walked through every part of the town in the last two days and I haven't seen him at all.

wonder—dear Mother of our Lord—if they have found him already and taken him away."

He felt as though lead were weighting his feet, stomach, brain, heart. It was hopeless. A few hours ago he had had a family, friends, people he loved. Now a giant hand had swept them away.

"There was one more thing," she continued wearily. "The next morning, early, Mr. Leo telephoned—but I knew someone was listening on the line. He said he was coming back to save the family and I told him it was too late. I could *hear* someone listening, Mr. Adam. I could hear them. So before Mr. Leo could say anything more I told him to keep away, to run and hide, and then I rang off, packed my clothes, and left the house in case they came for me too."

"Where have you been staying, Marie?" he asked, realizing suddenly that Marie had come under his area of responsibility. She had tied her life to the family, risked her future. Now she must be looked after.

"At the Rheiners' house. I've been helping the cook there. . . ." Her voice trailed away, lost in two days of atmospheric nightmare, walking through the town looking for Nicholas, cooking food for a strange family, sleeping in an alien house. He threw some coins onto the table and then placed a hand under her elbow and helped her to rise. "You must go to your sister at Szentendre," he said. "I will go home now—I have things to do—but I will come early tomorrow and take you to Szentendre."

"Yes." She nodded lifelessly.

"You still have a family, Marie. Now you must think about them: your sister and her husband, your nephews and nieces. These are your family."

But she only shook her head and let tears course unchecked down her cheeks. "The Ferencs were my family, Mr. Adam," she whispered.

He watched her walk across the market place through the evening gloom, ghosts walking with her. He went back to the car and prepared to drive home, back to his mother, who was mad, and his brother, who was both mad and evil. He was tired, sick and soul-weary, and he kept seeing his wife's small frightened face and his two children trying hard to protect her.

501

36

Towards the end of the summer the morning mist was so thick on the mountains it was impossible to see for more than a few yards. Once, waking early, he had stepped quietly from the hut and come face to face with a stag, an old bull, his antlers thick and scarred. Startled, the stag and Leo had stared at each other, and then Leo had retreated into the hut and the stag had turned and slipped away through the trees. Later he had seen a small herd of them on a clearing on the opposite side of the valley.

It was cold in the hut. The nights that he had to retreat there and hide he was always cold, even though it was summer. He could light no fire in case the smoke should be seen and investigated. He had a blanket and a bottle of *barack* to warm him and neither were effective in the early hours of the morning. But the cold and discomfort were more than compensated for by the mornings of peace and the evenings of quiet. He felt momentarily safe up in the mountains. The safety had something to do with his boyhood—memories of expeditions up into the mountains when the world had been a golden progress of sun and trees and hills, all filled with miracles. The nights up in the hut gave him back the dreams of his childhood, which even the far-distant thunder of the Russian guns could not destroy.

In the morning he watched the mist pale, then become luminous with flecks of sunlight. Finally it would wisp softly to the bases of the trees and then the whole air would burst into the golden glow of a September morning. As he gazed over the hills he could see little pockets of mist, clinging round the oaks and birches, giving a dressing of fairy-tale unreality to his mountain hideout. The unreality was worth any amount of cold and discomfort.

The gentle growl of the artillery was deceptive. The Russians were still a long way off, but the acoustics of the Carpathians carried the message over range after range until finally they mellowed into a soft rumble over Leo's mountain hut. Sometimes it was possible to imagine that the noise was

502

the preamble to a mountain storm; sometimes, up in the hut, he would delude himself that there was no war above a certain altitude. When the morning came and he had to start moving, the delusion vanished. He would slip silently down through the trees, avoiding the tracks and open stretches of meadow that flattened out amongst the hills. There was a thick, pine-covered escarpment close enough to the sawmill to make a good viewing point. From here, crouched low amongst the trees and shrubs, Leo could see the entire clearing.

Gabor had worked out a simple method of indicating whether it was safe to return. A huge oak had been felled some months before across an open piece of ground, and if some of the men were working on it, it was safe to come down. If the tree was deserted, he knew he must slip silently up into the hills again, not to the hut—that was safe only at night—but into the trees, constantly moving, keeping eyes and ears open for passing patrols. Once he had seen a German reconnaissance troop threading through the wood, studying possible passes where a defence line could be disposed, or so he imagined. He often heard rifle shots and presumed that someone was out hunting fresh meat. Several times, when the weather was clear, he climbed to a high point in the mountains from which he could see down to a thread of road. He wished he had binoculars—he even thought of asking Gabor to try and find some for him—for convoy after convoy passed through the valley making their way towards the west. "Running, running," he gloated. "They can't hold the Russians back any more! Now it's their turn to be afraid, to have a juggernaut behind them, rolling forward, crushing them!" If he thought about it at night he couldn't sleep. He grew excited and a maelstrom of thoughts and reflexes jostled in his fevered brain. The Russians were coming to liberate his tortured land. They would annihilate the Nazis, both German and Arrow Cross, and then, after the welter of the war had died away, a new Hungary would emerge, a Hungary free from foreign oppression in which the poor could at last live with dignity.

Planning the new Hungary rationalized his thoughts a little, but weaving through was the instinctive hatred of the Germans and the Arrow Cross men who had taken his family away. Where were they? What had happened to them? Rumours of unbelievable evil circulated, rumours that at first he had dismissed as foreign propaganda but that became more and more credible as the summer passed and the Jewish population began to vanish from the land. His hatred for the Germans grew to fanatical, unbalanced proportions, outweighing fear and caution. When he was working back at the sawmill he tried to persuade Gabor to support him in a scheme to blow up the road where the convoys passed. "Kill the Nazis!" he cried to Gabor and then had to listen to Gabor's slow and cautionary reasoning. "Kill them now? When the countryside is still swarming with them? They will tear through every village in the mountains until they find us—and you, my dear Leo, will be easier than anyone to find with your useless papers."

He had papers, the papers of an Arrow Cross man that he had killed while making his way north to the mountains. He had been given shelter in a cottage on the outskirts of a village, hidden by the kindness of a middle-aged carter and his son. He had woken in the morning to the sounds of dispute and shouting. A local Arrow Cross man had come to "requisition" the carter's pig in order to supply the local German unit. The shouted abuse, the arrogance, but above all the seething knowledge of what these men had done to his family broke Leo's control and he found himself in the yard, a shovel in his hand, beating savagely at the head of the Arrow Cross man, who had not even had time to draw his revolver. Later sick and shaken, he realized what he had done. He had no regrets for the death of the Nazi, but what of the carter and his son? Together they had loaded the body onto a cart and taken it up into the hills. Then Leo had dragged it into the forest and buried it under last year's leaves.

He had taken from the corpse's body the papers, the ration card, and a sum of money so large that it was obvious the "requisitioning" of local produce was a profitable private business.

When, finally, he had managed to find his way to the sawmill, the money was depleted but there was still enough to bribe the owner of the mill to keep his mouth shut. Gabor whose name was the last in a series of links that led from the group in Budapest, had examined the ration card and the papers with punctilious care.

"The ration card is good. We can use it," he said slowly "All the men here hand their cards in and we are fed together But the papers—" He stared at the picture of the huge, tow haired Arrow Cross man. "This is no good. You will have to pretend to be this man because of the ration card. But you must let no one see you who wishes to check your papers."

"I can stay here then?"

"For a while. Possibly for good, until the Russians come. They are not far away, I think. The Germans are stripping the country like hysterical locusts. They are up here once a week to see that every piece of timber that is cut goes straight back to Germany. When they come you will have to hide on the mountain."

"The owner of the mill?"

"For this money"—Gabor held up the packet of stolen notes—"he will pretend not to notice you, although you will be expected to work here in return for your food and a place to sleep, over there in the workshop."

"Can he be trusted?"

Gabor shrugged. "He is growing afraid. The Russians are going to win, and he is quite willing to take out a little cautious insurance policy on the future. Can you work a radio transmitter?"

"Yes."

"Can you understand Russian?"

"Yes."

"What was your profession? Your employment?"

"Journalist, translator."

For the first time since his arrival Gabor smiled. "Good, good. We can use you most happily."

He was exhausted and pleased to settle in one place. He had been walking, hiding, back-tracking, and trying to trace people who were links in the chain for five weeks. The weeks had been like a murky dream, for all the time he had been hovering on the verge of madness because of what he pictured in his mind. One morning he had seen trucks of people— Jews—being driven across the country and had thought his head was going to explode. But Gabor had given him back his sanity, had provided a reason for *being* when he knew that the others no longer *were*. He could channel his hate, his fear and despair. It could be used for revenge and the building of a new Hungary. But still the nights were difficult, nightmares of reproach and indulgences of the imagination. Only the nights spent up in the hut gave him peace.

In October he had to spend four days up there. Each morning he went to look at the clearing and each morning the tree was untouched, although he didn't need the sign because the clearing was seething with German soldiers. He knew a moment of panic, and then reassurance. These were soldiers, not Gestapo, and their function was obviously to hasten the loading of timber.

He ranged over the mountains during the day, finding blackberries and nuts to supplement his bread ration, which might have to last a long time. He was cold and hungry, but the enforced break from reality gave him back his sense of balance. He became strong again, knowing that despite what had happened to his family he must follow his own path of reconstruction, must help destroy the Nazis not only for revenge but because Hungary must be liberated and rebuilt.

They came up into the forest one afternoon, five soldiers and a team from the sawmill. Hiding in a thicket of bracken and scrub, he watched them choosing timber and realized what a good woodsman he had become. All the old tricks of boyhood had returned: he knew the best places to hide, how to move silently, how to destroy tracks by using streams and rock faces. This summer and autumn had taught him other things as well: how to ignore the cold, how to manage on very little food, and how to sense when danger, in a German or Arrow Cross uniform, was close at hand.

On the fifth day the Germans went from the clearing. He waited until two men began hacking branches from the tree, and then he slid down through the undergrowth and melted in amongst them. One of the two men on the oak was Gabor.

"Horthy's been deposed," he said, without looking up from his work. "He announced an armistice with the Russians. He's been taken to Germany. The Arrow Cross men are solely in charge now. The news from Budapest is bad, very bad. Do you have anyone in Budapest?"

"Friends, no family."

"It sounds like indiscriminate massacre."

Hatred welled up again. The peace of four days vanished into neurotic dreams of revenge.

"But it will not be long now," Gabor continued dispassionately. "The Germans are pulling out—and have you listened to the guns? They are louder. Much louder."

They were louder. They had been the background noise of the sawmill and the mountains for so long that he had ceased to notice them. But now he listened and realized that the increasing volume was no acoustical trick. The Russians were advancing.

"Things will change," Gabor remarked, motioning Leo to

the other end of the saw. "There will be fewer Germans, but more Arrow Cross." He turned and spat into the withered leaves of the tree. "Madmen and lunatics. Their days are numbered and for a few weeks they will behave like cornered rats. You and I must be ready to hide up in the hills."

"You too?"

Gabor nodded. Beads of sweat flew from his forehead onto the moving saw. "My papers are better than yours, but the Nyilas are unpredictable and kill without reason. You and I are too valuable to be killed."

Two weeks later the lookout down in the valley signalled that Arrow Cross men were coming, and this time Gabor, obeying some instinct of his own, left the camp with Leo. They took with them the radio transmitter, two blankets, what rations they could muster, and their partisan identity cards printed in Russian that had been issued from the central partisan group in the town. They set off eastwards, across the hills, towards the sound of the guns, and as they breasted the first rise they heard behind them, from the valley of the sawmill, the sound of rifle shots. They did not look at each other, but Leo, who was leading, hastened his pace.

As they moved over the mountains it became obvious that Gabor was neither fit enough nor skilled enough to live in the forests. He was a planner, an organizer, but his body was not equipped to stand a hide-and-seek life in the hills. It was very cold. The first falls of snow lay on the trees and open slopes and they had to be doubly careful when camping at night so that their tracks didn't lead others to their resting-place. Leo carried the transmitter and as much of the other equipment as he could. But even then Gabor moved slowly and clumsily.

Finally Gabor himself broached the subject of his inadequacy as a mountain walker. They had found shelter in a cowherd's hut placed high on one of those secret hidden meadows that the mountains abounded in. Gabor, after leaning exhausted against the stone wall for half an hour, had then set up the transmitter. Leo went outside to collect wood and fill their small can with snow. Whenever they were fortunate enough to find a hut, they allowed themselves a small fire after dark. The snow, when melted and mixed with meat extract, made a kind of soup that was at least hot. He stood for a while, watching the flashes in the sky to the east, nearer now, much nearer. The guns could no longer be mistaken for thunder. They were unmistakably guns. When he came back inside, Gabor was sitting by the transmitter.

"I have made contact with them," he said quietly. "With the Russians."

Leo's heart began to pound. The Russians . . . their liberators. It was nearly the end now: the end of the war, the end of oppression, and the end of an era. He should be happy, but always at the back of his mind was the memory of his family. There was also another unease, one he had difficulty in placing. The Russians—there were rumours, but surely they were only rumours. In a war armies behaved as armies, soldiers as soldiers. Whatever happened in the next few weeks—months —was only the final death spasm of the war. His people would ride it out, as they had ridden out so much else, and then the new world would begin. Nonetheless the unease persisted.

"Do you know where we are?" Gabor asked, watching him through the dusk.

Leo nodded. He had known for some days that they were approaching the mountain range that lay to the north of his own town. Somewhere, a little to the south-east, were the hills and woods of his childhood, the farm, the meadow where he and Malie had played, the Kaldy land where Adam still lived —as far as he knew, and Eva and George and Terez. . . . His mind clamped down quickly. If he thought about Eva and her children—and especially if he thought about Terez—the sick screaming rage that made him lose control of himself would take possession once more.

"Good," said Gabor, and then he smiled, a wintry, self-deprecating smile. "I have been a bad traveller, Leo—oh, yes!—I have slowed us both and I do not have the ability you possess to live from these woods. But I knew where we had to come. I can still navigate, and we have come east this way for a very special reason."

Leo watched the snow melting in the can. Without answering Gabor he took their carefully hoarded bread from his rucksack and cut two pieces from it.

"Tomorrow I shall go down into the village south from here. My papers are foolproof enough for that. In the village is someone—a contact—who will give me a map of your town. On the map will be marked all the German gun emplacements and also the site of the steelworks and the arsenal. When I return you will take the map through the German lines and give it to the Russians."

"I see." He tried to appear as cool as Gabor, but excitement was racing through his veins. At last, at last he was able

508

to fight back, to make some kind of mark, however small, against the enemy.

"We should have gone together," Gabor continued slowly. "But I realize I will delay you, Leo. It will be too difficult for you if I come."

"I can go quicker alone." No point in lying, just to save Gabor's feelings. He would go quickly alone, quickly and efficiently.

"You understand the significance of the map, Leo? It means that your town will be treated as a partisan community. The German gun emplacements will be destroyed, but the steelworks and arsenal will be left—and so will the rest of the town. Any family or friends of yours will be comparatively safe."

Safe. Desolation swept over him because for a moment he had believed that down there, in the town, his father and mother, his sister Malie and her family, were all living in the old house just the way they used to. He had envisaged himself riding in with the Soviet army and finding them there just the same. . . .

Two days later, when he began his journey over the mountains, his emotions were still unsettled. He sensed himself slipping into unreality, and so he forced himself to picture the old house as it now must be, empty of everyone, dirt and rubbish blowing into the courtyard, the windows broken. Then he tried to accept the knowledge that they were all dead, each one gone. He went through the list rationally. Mama, Papa, David Klein, his brother Jozsef, his nephews, Eva, Malie, Terez . . . oh, no! The last two he could not bear. Not Malie, who had been closer to him than any other human being, and not Terez, whom he loved because she was warm and bright and like the daughter he had never had. Tracking up through the snow he tried to bargain with God. *Give me these two back and I will try not to bear hatred and venom in my heart. Just these two. I know they are all dead . . . all, all dead . . . but give me a miracle, God, give me these two back and I will bear with humility everything that life offers me from this day forward.*

He was still praying, walking and praying, with the guns thundering ahead of him when something cracked down on the back of his skull and shattered him into darkness.

509

37

From failure to victory. From waking in the snow with blood trickling down his neck and three narrow-eyed Mongols grinning down at him, to the embraces of two Russian "comrade" officers who kissed him and then handed him a water glass filled with vodka. His head, roughly bandaged and aching from the rifle below, exploded into agony with the vodka, and through stars and pain and coloured lights he heard the belly laughs of his grateful hosts.

Lying in the snow he had gurgled "partisan" at them and had been rewarded by three rifles thrust against his chest. He could only just understand them—the Russian he had learned was never like this—and they obviously had just as much difficulty understanding him. Finally he had managed to convey that he had papers—it was a war of papers and one's life depended on always having the right ones at the right time. A moment's panic as a huge hand in a grey glove fumbled at his breast pocket. Supposing none of them could read! But the partisan card in Russian had turned their grins to puzzled frowns and a discussion had ensued which he just managed to follow. Was the card genuine, or was it a Nazi fabrication for spies? Should they shoot him now or later? After more frenzied explanations, the passing round of the map, and the surrender of his wrist watch came another trek through the snow with his head dripping blood and the uncertainty of a trigger-happy Mongol with a rifle in the small of his back.

A hunting lodge swarmed with grey-clad Russian soldiers who looked, extraordinarily enough, just like the pictures one had seen of them in the First World War, and a succession of "comrade" officers, all staring at the map, all suspicious of his motives and surprised because he could speak their language. He was never to understand fully the dialects of the soldiers, but to his relief the officers were perfectly comprehensible. He explained, showed his partisan card, referred to the contact between Gabor and the Russian operators over the transmitter. The map vanished. He was given a chair and a cigarette which he would have happily exchanged for some water and then, after several hours, the officers had returned with smiles and a glass and a bandage for his head. After the second tumbler of vodka he had a curious sense of *déjà vu*—the moment just before the rifle had descended on his head—and, just as expected, he spun forward onto the floor again and lay there, listening to his hosts singing melancholy but tuneful songs of Russia.

His intention had been to return through the lines and make his way south to the town. Gabor had said he would wait there, joining up with the main partisan group and forming a committee to try and bring order out of the disintegrating chaos of the town. But in the morning his comrade revellers of the night before turned stony faces towards him and said, "You. Stay here. Later you can go, when we go." He was not locked in—there was really nowhere to lock him—but as he wandered round the temporary camp he was accompanied by two guards with rifles. If he ventured too far from the camp's perimeter he received a rough nudge in the ribs with a gun. The shelling grew heavier, but now it was nearly all from the Russian side. Had the Germans retreated entirely? Was the map accurate?

Two days later, in the wake of the Russian army, he came down from the mountains and, on a bitterly cold, snow-filled night, entered the deserted streets of his own home town.

It was a place of empty houses and silence. The diminished population was seen only rarely, scurrying from home to food queues and back again. The women were kept firmly out of sight, but the Russians found them anyway and helped themselves in the same way they helped themselves to wrist watches, cameras, and other less understandably attractive items such as chamber pots and family photographs. On the whole it was not too violent an occupation, provided one didn't try to protect the women or the wrist watches, and as the Soviet colonel explained to Leo at the first meeting of the town's newly formed District Committee, the reason for his troops' superb and well-mannered behaviour was that the town had "co-operated" and was listed as a partisan area.

There was, surprisingly, very little damage, and that mainly from the air raids of the summer months. The German gun emplacements had been blown up with remarkable efficiency. The German and Arrow Cross units had speedily evacuated themselves westwards and the Soviet army had marched into a city completely devoid of resistance. Leo, observing the "well-mannered" behaviour of their liberators, wondered what their occupation of German-defended areas would be like, but he hurriedly thrust the thought away, as he was thrusting so many other disquieting questions away.

Why, he reflected gloomily, could he never accept things in a way that was sensible and practical? Gabor, who was importantly forming the town's first committee, seemed to be troubled by no doubts at all. "We have been waiting all these years for liberation, Leo," he cried jubilantly, "and now the hour has come! Remember the years of repression, of starvation for the many, of the cruelty of the *pandur,* of lack of freedom. Hungary has been given a new chance and we must see it is not abused. We must build a land where socialism and democracy become the birthright of every single Hungarian."

"The Russians—"

"The Russians will soon be gone," Gabor had said, waving his hand impatiently in the air. "Once Germany is defeated the Russians will leave us to rebuild our nation in peace. Now—" He shrugged. "Soldiers are soldiers. And we have to pay the price for trying to placate Germany all these years. Be thankful the occupation is not worse than it is."

Gabor was right. No army could sweep through a country without behaving like a conqueror. And surely anything was better than the last nightmare months of the German occupation. But questions still nagged at him. He noticed things that made him uneasy. Their boots, for one thing, and the rest of their uniforms. For so long he had thought of Russia as the land of equality, where peasants were no longer kept in poverty and servitude. The Russian soldiers' boots were made of rubberized linen and their greatcoats of thin cloth. That was all right, except that the officers wore leather boots and coats of pure wool. No doubt there were good reasons; only so much leather and wool, so who should have it? And no doubt there was also a good reason for the Soviet major who pulled out a revolver and shot two of his own men who were coming out of a house with a sack of stolen food. There were reasons, most certainly . . . but was he foolish to be disappointed at the socialist dream in action?

He suppressed his traitorous thoughts and accepted the post that was allotted him as editor of the town's newspaper, which, after some discussion, was called *Liberation.* For the time being the paper consisted of a single sheet written mostly by Leo. There was little paper available and an even greater shortage of staff, but after years of apprenticeship in Berlin and Budapest he was disproportionately proud of his creation. He was suddenly aware of the power of the printed word, of *his* power, and he remembered with a nostalgic affection the little old Jew in Berlin who had employed him in the press translation agency. Mr. Heinlein had behaved as though he were the protector of a message for mankind. Now Leo understood the pride and the principled integrity that had enabled the old man to carry out a war against the Nazi press. Mr. Heinlein. Where was he now?

Another thought to be thrust away. Where were any of them? More and more rumours filtered through from survivors relayed through Russian lines, rumours of mass murders and prison camps. He shut them out. He must look not back but forward, to the new Hungary. He had gone to the old house almost as soon as he arrived in the town. Foolishly he had thought there might be someone, just one person there. But the windows were boarded up and the downstairs apartment had been stripped of everything valuable. The corner of the coach yard was filled with excrement and he had hurried away before loneliness overwhelmed him. He was alive, but there was no one else. Oh, God, please let there be someone still alive! Don't let me be the only one left. Give me back someone of my blood, my flesh, my family!

As the population began to creep out into the streets, he started to ask questions. There were a few, infinitesimally few, old acquaintances who still lived in the places they had always lived, but there was little information they could give.

"My parents? My sister and her husband and son?"

"Vanished. With the others."

"My cousin, Kati Racs-Rassay, and her son?"

"Vanished."

"My sister Eva and her family? Up on the Kaldy estate?"

"Vanished. . . . But, no, not quite." And hope pumped into his heart until the speaker said that Adam Kaldy—and only Adam Kaldy—had still been there during the summer months, before all transport and communications had broken down and severed news from the country.

"Just him?"

"Just him. He was under arrest for a while. His brother was shot and there was suspicion of murder, but they let him out again. They needed the produce from his farm, they needed him to run it. And then there was a rumour that the old lady was involved in the killing, but she was paralysed from a stroke and could say nothing. The last we heard she was living at the farmhouse, unable to speak or see or hear."

Adam. His first disappointment faded and he thought that even if the rest were gone forever, there would still be Adam. Dear, beloved old friend from childhood, a familiar face, shared memories, someone with whom he could be not quite alone. If only Adam had survived he would not ask for anything else.

A week after his return the man who was to be the secretary of the town's District Committee, the man who had been the leader of the partisan movement in their area, arrived from behind the Russian lines: Janos Marton.

Leo had known he was coming, had heard of little else, in fact, for Marton had become the local hero—the man who had led an attack on a German supply column and distributed the arms and ammunition to the local resistance, the man who had operated a wireless transmitter during the dangerous months of the Nazi occupation, the man who had made the map of the German gun emplacements. And—a small voice whispered—the man who had betrayed the family to the Gestapo after the German occupation? Now that theory seemed absurd; so many had gone whom Janos Marton did not even know. And a hero of the people was surely above such methods of spiteful revenge. Reason dismissed the old suspicions as ridiculous, but the animosity that the suspicions had aroused remained with him.

Janos Marton came back dressed in one of the borrowed thin coats of the Russian soldiers. He presided over his first meeting with an efficiency that was frightening because he spoke so little, just short questions and, at the end of an answering report, a nodded "yes" or a silence, a stare, and a scribbled note on a piece of paper.

"Ferenc."

Ferenc? Already the times had changed. The last time they had met it was Mr. Ferenc.

"Ferenc, the paper. You have taken over the old offices of *Hungary Today*. Is there sufficient paper for three months?"

"Yes. If we continue with a single news-sheet."

A scribbled note. "Good. And we must have reports from sources other than your own. It is supposed to be a newspaper, not a daily treatise from the editor."

How dare he! The jumped-up son of a peasant who knew

nothing of journalism, who would not even be able to write if it hadn't been for Adam Kaldy educating him.

"I don't think you understand the problems, Marton," he snapped. "Members of the committee are too busy to write editorials. And everyone else in the town is too frightened. What is said now may prove incriminating in the future."

A stare from the glacial eyes and a scribbled note on the paper before him. Once, long ago, he had felt pity for Janos Marton, a lonely, loveless, underprivileged child who had grown into a solitary and unlovable man. Now he aroused nothing but anger and resentment. He tried to rationalize his resentment. Was he really still so bourgeois in outook that it was impossible for him to accept, in practice as well as theory, that a peasant could be the intellectual equal of anyone else? Was he really as hypocritical as that? No, some warring voice within him cried, it is not that. Any peasant but this one! I would take orders and reprimands from any peasant but Janos Marton!

"Ferenc! Would you wait, please! I have something to say to you."

A reprimand, no doubt, for implying that the aims of the committee were not necessarily reliable ones and later might be dangerous. He stood by the door, watching Gabor and Julius and all the others shaking Janos Marton by the hand and congratulating him on his courage and leadership. Adulation at last: the peasant turned into a prince, the local charity schoolboy a hero. And still he did not smile. He thanked his supporters courteously, but his thin face registered none of the usual human expressions of gratification or pleasure. Janos Marton was a cold, efficient political machine.

When the others had gone he watched Janos struggling into the Russian coat. Leo remembered him as a thin child, and a thin man, but now he seemed to carry no flesh at all on his whipcord frame. He was—how old? Twenty-eight? Twenty-nine? And there was no youth in him at all. A machine.

"I would like you to come with me, Ferenc. I have some good news for you."

"If it's about the paper—"

"It is not about the paper." They left the icy County Offices and trudged out into the snow. "Ferenc, I hope you are not going to find it difficult to accept that one of your former family servants is now directing you in your work." He said it gently, quietly, but with cold authority. "It would be a great pity if, after we have worked for the same cause through all these difficult years, you now discover you cannot forget your —antipathy."

"I never—"

"Oh, yes, Ferenc. Antipathy. Even as a child. But what you and I feel is unimportant, is it not? The fact remains that I am able to govern a committee and you are not. I understand what has to be done in Hungary, and I know how to do it. You understand too, but you do not know how to do it. You are a dreamer, an idealist. Whatever happens you will always be looking beyond, looking for the nirvana that does not exist."

"That is unfair," he burst out. "I have done as much as you during the bad years. I fought fascism too. I stood trial for Communist activities when you asked me to lecture to the steel workers. I worked with the resistance in Budapest—"

"But you are an idealist, Ferenc. Useful and necessary in the years of persecution, but now is the time for the realist. Already you are beginning to wonder if our way is the right way. You look at the Russians and see they are not perfect and so you begin to doubt and dream again. We have no time to dream now. We have to feed a country in which no crops have been sown and where the land has been ravaged by the Germans and by the Russians. We have to lay down roots of government that will rebuild our economy and independence. There is no time to dream now."

"You think, because people must be fed, we should throw away our consciences?" He was angry because so much of what Janos said was true. And he resented that the peasant child should be able to read his thoughts.

"Conscience is the privilege of those who are not hungry," Marton replied quietly. "I too would like to be a dreamer, Ferenc, but I have settled for realism because I never again want to see my people hungry, or humiliated, or dying without comfort and help."

He remembered Janos Marton's mother and was suddenly ashamed. Not a political machine, a machine with a memory.

"I endeavour not to allow any emotional memories to influence me now," Janos continued, uncannily reading Leo's thoughts again. "But the lessons one learns in youth are there to be analyzed, sifted, used where necessary. It is difficult to have a conscience when you are hungry and poor."

"But the Russians . . . you have seen the Russians. It is not

516

what we thought, Janos Marton. They still have their rich and their poor."

"The Russians do it their way, Ferenc. Once they have gone, then we shall do it ours. I hope you will still be here to work with us. I hope your conscience will not make it necessary for you to . . . leave the committee."

He was threatening to replace him! After everything he had done—rebelled against his background and family, joined the party in the years when he could have been imprisoned if caught. Was this the reward for his years of endeavour?

Marton turned into a cobbled yard filled with puddles of dirty snow. They had walked a long way and were now in the poor area of the town, down by the steeelworks. The bomb damage was worse here—piles of rubble partially covered with soil and snow, and several rows of apartment buildings ripped open like doll's houses. An old man with a bundle under his arm hurried away from them, down into a cellar under one of the devastated buildings.

"Why are people still living here?" asked Leo, puzzled. "The town is half empty, plenty of good houses abandoned by the Germans or Arrow Cross . . . or by the Jews. It is unsafe for them still to be living here."

"Their homes are here." He began to pick his way over the rubble. A few frightened faces peered out from doorways and cellar steps. Then blankets and sacks were hastily dropped over the various openings.

"Come, Ferenc. We must hurry if you are to get home before curfew."

He led the way to a tall apartment block. The top floors were gutted and open to the sky, but the ground floor was still whole and weatherproof. The windows were boarded up and the brickwork was pitted and scarred with shrapnel wounds. Janos knocked quietly on the door and Leo heard a chain and bolt being drawn back. The door opened and a thin, brown-eyed face came into view, a face made sallow from months of hiding in cellars and attics but a dear, beloved face that was home and family and memories of a life that had died centuries ago.

"Nicholas! My boy! My dear good boy! Oh, God! You're safe! One person . . . safe!"

"Uncle Leo." The thin, nervous face crumpled and began to cry. "Uncle Leo, Uncle Leo!" Caught in each other's arms, gripping each other because they were the only two left.

517

"Where's my mama? Is she safe? Have you heard anything about my mama? Nobody in the town knows anything. Janos asked. Do you know where they are? What happened to them when the Gestapo—?" His thin, leggy frame began to shake. He had grown tall in captivity, tall and white like a hidden plant. Sobs racked his body and over his head Leo's eyes met those of Janos Marton. "They're all dead, aren't they, Uncle Leo? They're all dead?"

Leo suddenly pushed the boy away and turned into the wall, his hands over his face. He had buried the knowledge of his family's obliteration as best he could, but Nicholas's raw emotion was about to unhinge him.

"Perhaps they are dead. Perhaps your mama is dead," said the cool voice of Janos Marton, "but perhaps they are not. And now, young Nicholas, you have one person of your own back. It is not your mama—no, not your mama—but you have someone. Now you can come out of hiding and go and live with your Uncle Leo."

The boy brushed his hand across his face and then smiled, the beautiful smile that had lit his face when he was a child, the smile that reminded Leo of Terez. Terez—where was Terez?

"Where—what happened to you, Nicholas? Why weren't you taken with the others?"

The brown eyes glazed over, a nervous tic began just under the left one.

"I came back from school and I saw the truck—and the Gestapo—driving away. And I ran all the way to Grandma Ferenc's house. I thought if I told Malie she would know what to do; she would know where they were taking Mama and know where I could find her. But before I got there the truck passed me again and . . . they were all in it. Mama saw me—I'm sure she saw me because she shook her head, very very slightly—and then the truck was gone. I ran after it but it was gone." Tears ran down the sallow features. Nicholas had been such a beautiful child and now he looked like everyone else who had survived the war.

"I dared not go back to school, so I ran and hid near the steelworks. The houses there had no locks on the gates and I hid in one of the yards for two nights. And then I saw Janos, in the morning, and I remembered him because we had gone to see him, Mama and Aunt Malie and I." His face screwed up again. "Where is my mama, Uncle Leo? What have they done to them?"

"I kept him hidden in my apartment for a few days." The voice of Janos Marton was cool, sensible, the voice of reason amidst too much emotion. "Then it became dangerous. I was not—unknown to the authorities. There was never any proof, but it was not safe. He came here, in the attic until it was bombed, and then in the cellar. An old woman, dead now, whom I could trust; she helped. I brought food, books. He survived, as you see."

Survived. One infinitely precious person, son of his cousin, blood of his blood, Cousin Kati's bastard child—family, someone against whom he could measure himself. He was Uncle Leo again. He had a place and he had a pale, underfed youth to care for. He wanted to hold the boy in his arms, be reassured of a presence, a survivor, someone who should be loved.

"You're thin, boy," he said hoarsely, "thin and pale, but we'll soon get you well again." They stared at each other, held together by all the faces that were not there, a tiny lost oasis of family on a bombsite. "Come, Nicky, let's go before the curfew."

Nicholas turned and, to Leo's astonishment, put his arms round Janos Marton. "Can I come and see you, Janos? Tomorrow? And you'll come to see us?" His voice had the desperation of someone clinging to the small fragments of a familiar world. He had two people left, and he needed them both. Marton hugged the boy back and then softly made a fist to his face. "You'll see me, Nicky. Don't worry. You can come tomorrow. Perhaps you can help with some paper work. Go along now."

Leo found he could not speak. He should feel gratitude to Marton for saving the life of his family, his minute family. But the debt was too great. He could think only of Nicholas—his child now, all that was left.

"I—"

"That's all right. Go now." The blue eyes glittered, not with tears but with some deeper emotion that Leo didn't try to understand. He placed his arm round Nicky and propelled him through the yard, looking back once to see Janos Marton watching them, solitary, lonely. Leo had a curious sensation of guilt, as though he were stealing Nicky from him.

"We must hurry, Nicky." They began to trot over the wet cobbles. After the curfew the Russians shot anyone they saw. Nicky was clinging to his arm and he felt the thin body trembling against him. "Are you all right?"

The boy nodded, too breathless to speak, and Leo realized that he was not only unwell but also afraid of the streets. He had been in hiding for so long he was nervous of sky and spaces. A lump formed in Leo's chest and with it a determination to get the boy well again. I can get black-market rations. There must be some things left in the upstairs apartment I can sell. If I can buy good food—some meat and butter, perhaps —he'll soon grow well again.

They reached his apartment, the apartment of an Arrow Cross man who had fled before the Russians, three minutes before curfew. Nicholas stared up at the house, confusion registering on his face.

"Aren't we going home, Uncle Leo?"

"This is home for me, Nicholas. The other house—the old house—it's empty, and Grandpa Ferenc's apartment has been ransacked. It's better here."

"But that's where they'd come, Uncle Leo! Mama and Aunt Malie and all of them. That's where they'd come. We should go there in case they return and find it empty. We should be there with food and a fire. We should put a light in the window so they know we are there. We—" Leo led the weeping boy through the door and closed it behind him.

Nicholas's words prevailed. It was foolish to hope that any of them would come back—but if they did, the boy was right. They would go to the old house. He spent several weeks making up his mind, weeks in which he adapted his life to sharing with a fifteen-year-old boy. Together they worked out a new pattern of living, dividing the tasks of queuing for food and keeping their clothes as clean as possible and their bodies as warm as the lack of fuel permitted. Nicholas had been very quiet for the first few days, and then had begun his two recurring themes, their return to the old house and the sayings of Janos Marton. A dozen times a day his sentences began with "Janos says" and "Janos believes," and although it was natural—so Leo consoled himself—because Janos Marton had been the only human contact Nicky had had for several months, he became increasingly tired and resentful of Janos's place in his nephew's life.

But Nicky's other concern made sense.

The Russians were moving swiftly over the land now. Budapest was taken in January, and as the spring advanced more and more territory was "liberated." Great sections of the population that had been displaced by the vagaries of war began to drift back to old and familiar haunts. It was difficult not to hope, and with hope came an urge to go back to the old house, to prepare a welcome for anyone who might arrive.

They cleaned out the yard that had been used as a latrine and they washed the stairs and the floors of the upstairs apartment, Malie and David's apartment. Leo had sold what could be sold for winter food, but there were beds and carpets, chairs and cooking utensils. He even managed to find some unbroken glass which, inexpertly, he put into one of the drawing-room windows. The light streaming into the familiar room gave them a fleeting confidence. Some of them will come back—surely some of them will come back?

It was impossible to travel without the blessing of the Soviet army or some kind of official permission. There were no trains or buses, no postal service or telephones, but in March a miracle happened. They received a letter. The letter was delivered by a huge grinning Cossack who waved it in Leo's face and then asked for payment. The sight of Adam's handwriting induced such delirium in Leo that he let the soldier come in and pick what he wanted: an evening coat of Malie's, a cuckoo clock, and three bottles of wine from Papa Ferenc's cellar that had somehow been missed during the looting. There was little else to take that could be carried but the Cossack ambled off, seemingly content. The letter, devoured in the light from the single window, spread the family net wider, made them three instead of two.

Dear Leo and Nicholas,

The local committee visited me today to assess my land and, unwelcome as they were, they brought news of you that made me forget their purpose and rejoice. I feared it might be a rumour and no more than that—God knows the world is full of rumours at the moment—but I think it cannot be. You are on the District Committee, Leo, and editing the town's paper. These details were so prosaic I knew they must be true. They said also that Nicholas was with you. Thank God, my dear, dear friends! You cannot know what this news has meant to me, for if you have survived then perhaps so have others. The knowledge of your safety gives me hope again. I know no details of your survival, only that you are there. It is enough. Please God my beloved wife and children are alive and will come home soon! Your family

521

too, my dearest friends! I try not to think of what the Germans have done—surely some of them have survived.

I will tell you what little there is to tell of myself. Felix and my mother are dead. I have 100 *hold* of land and the rest has been distributed to the peasants. This you know, of course, Leo, and I do not wish to enter into discussion upon the subject with you. But I have one thing to say—what use is the Kaldy land to the peasants when the trees have been felled for firewood, when every animal has been stolen, when the seed grain has been eaten, and when the Russians are using the old manor as their headquarters? My 100 *hold* are as useless as everyone else's and this coming year will see famine in our barren land. God help us all.

News of my family. Eva and the children escaped just before the Gestapo came, but now they are lost to me. They moved west before the Russian advance and I cling to the need that they must be safe—they must be safe. The last time I had news of them, they were with the sister of Janos Marton outside Magyarovar.

Leo, I think if they return it will be to you—to the old family house. I hear that sometimes, where the Russians feel so disposed, they will send back a convoy of refugees and deposit them at some central point. This is the only hope for them until we are allowed to travel again. If they come I beg you to use your influence as a Party man and try to get a message to me.

One of the committee men has agreed to take this letter part of the way in return for a bag of flour. I have told him that whoever delivers it will be rewarded lavishly and can only hope you have something that will fit that description. Take heart, my dear friends, for if some of us are still alive then others will be. The war is over and nothing matters—not our differences in ideas, nor the decimation of our land—except that those we love will return to us. Give me news as soon as you can, Leo, and take good care of our beloved cousin, Nicholas Rassay.

                                        Adam

"You see, Uncle Leo, we were right to come back! Otherwise we would not have received the letter. And Uncle Adam says himself that they will come here. They will come back soon, Uncle Leo. They will, won't they?"

His face was alive, smiling and excited. Leo was suddenly

overwhelmed with depression. They both hoped, prayed and hoped, but Leo knew that the hope was thin. The family were not going to return. Inevitably Nicky's faith was going to be destroyed, his grief was going to be twice as shattering, because he still believed his mama—and all of them—would come back.

"Nicky," he said tonelessly, "you are fifteen. At fifteen there are some things it is difficult to accept. You still believe that if you want something badly enough you can have it. At fifteen you cannot that believe God could be so cruel as to take your mama when you have done nothing to deserve it."

The pallid face with the huge brown eyes was anguished, determined not to listen.

"Nicky, we must both try to accept that they are gone—all of them. It is finished. There is just you and me and Uncle Adam."

"No!"

"Yes, Nicky. What you do with your life from now on must be for the future, a future in which the only family you will have will be me and Uncle Adam, no one else. You understand?"

"I don't believe you!" He jerked round and ran across the room. "I don't believe you!"

"Where are you going, Nicholas?"

"To see Janos, my friend Janos!" He was fumbling at the door, trying to grasp and turn the handle. It never had opened properly; Leo could remember Malie's having trouble with that door. "Janos won't tell me lies like that! Janos won't say those things . . . those terrible things!"

He went, and Leo sat looking down at the letter in his lap. He could tell Nicky that he must not hope. Surely he should tell himself the same thing, make himself accept the loss of all of them. He didn't want to think about it and so he clung to the one point of positive energy that coursed through his brain, an increasing and jealous resentment of Janos Marton.

38

When he heard Nicky's feet on the stairs outside his room he experienced, as he always did when the boy came, a soft implosion of pleasure. Emotional reaction, quickly brought under control, shrank into a tiny pinpoint of something that was warm and yet at the same time painful. He recognized the pain, a fragment of an old and much larger sensation. It was the pain of loving someone. He had learned to master it years ago.

The door of his neat, bare room was flung open and young Nicky, red-faced and out of breath, hurtled in. "We have a letter from Uncle Adam, Janos! He's alive, and he thinks Terez and George and Aunt Eva are alive too!"

"I have told you to knock, Nicky," he said mildly. "You have no right to enter other people's rooms like that."

The boy flinched and rapidly blinked his eyes. His thin wrists sticking out from the sleeves of his too-short coat twisted and he slumped a little, embarrassment in every gawky angle of his body.

Janos shared his humiliation, partly from empathy and partly from memories of his own rejections, and said quickly, "It doesn't matter. I'm very pleased to see you and I am pleased to know that Mr. Kaldy—your uncle—is safe."

"Uncle Adam says that Terez and her mother and brother escaped before the Gestapo came. He says they are near Magyarovar with your sister!"

"One of my sisters. The first sister they lived with was in the north."

Nicky glared at him. "They've been with your sisters all the time and you didn't tell me?"

"No."

"Why didn't you tell me?"

"Supposing you had been caught by the Gestapo, Nicky?" he asked gently, and watched the changing thoughts fleet across the boy's face: anger, insecurity, pride, and finally hopelessness.

"You are right, of course," he said at last. He slumped

across the room, bumping awkwardly into the wooden rail at the foot of the bed and then tripping—on nothing—and overbalancing onto it. "I wouldn't have been brave enough to keep silent. I would have betrayed them. And your sisters too." A failure, a coward, the Judas of his family. Then he looked up and smiled. "You looked after me very well when I was hiding, didn't you, Janos? You thought of things like that. I wouldn't have thought of that."

The implosion of pleasure and pain again. He had never intended, never wanted, to let anyone be in a position to cause him pain again, and now this gawky adolescent whom he had protected for eight months had become his friend, had made him vulnerable once more. He felt irritated with himself. He should have seen what was happening and used his intellect to guard his emotions as he had on previous occasions when someone threatened to come close. Because the boy had been helpless, afraid, and above all (oh, how well he understood!) nearly insane with worry about his mother, he had allowed a bond to form, a giving and a taking that held them together. And if he was honest he had to admit that it had begun even before he had found Nicky hiding in the derelict yard. It had begun on the day his mother and aunt had brought him to Janos's room. The misery had begun then, when he watched the boy and his mother and had been reminded of another child with a similar obsession.

And perhaps the roots of the disease went even deeper. It was the family, this particular Ferenc–Kaldy–Racs-Rassay family which he hated but which fascinated and absorbed him. Only this family could have produced a child capable of twisting into the soft underbelly of Janos Marton.

He could have friends now if he wished—unlike the earlier years of his misplacement between two societies—friends who shared his intellectual exercises and admired his achievements. But he had learned, at school and at college and at his uncle, the shoemaker's, to manage without friends. He had been rejected then; now, without bitterness, he in turn rejected. He had sisters, but he was just as isolated from them as he was from his colleagues. They were awed and a little afraid of him. His sister near Magyarovar had worn her best dress every time he visited her, and once she had almost called him excellency. He didn't belong to his family any more. They didn't want him other than as a totem, a symbol of their superiority over the other simple people about them. Once the isolation had been accepted, the condition of belonging neither to one world nor the other had been absorbed, he had discovered that he could manage without family and without friends, that indeed one was stronger without these encumbrances. And then Nicholas Rassay had needed help and suddenly he had found the old remembered craving back in his heart—the need for warmth and intimacy, for love to be both given and received. He had discovered that there were no barriers between him and this child because their conditioning had been the same, isolated from school friends and at the same time separated by circumstances from their own backgrounds. And Nicky had found the same refuge from bastardy as had Janos from poverty, a fierce possessive clinging to his mother.

Their hardening process had been the same, their escape hatch identical, but Nicky had the final and ultimate lesson to learn, the one that refined and hardened and threw out the polished mould of a man. He had to accept the maiming blow of his mother's death.

"They'll come back—to our house—as soon as they can," Nicholas was saying. "Uncle Adam believes they are alive and so do I. They are *all* alive, I know they are."

"Nicky—"

"They're alive! All of them!"

Janos remained silent. The lesson was something you could not teach anyone, or even prepare them for. Nicky had to learn this one all on his own. He gazed at the boy and under the thoughtful blue eyes Nicky grew uncomfortable. He fidgeted slightly on the bed.

"Don't you want to know if your sister near Magyarovar is safe?" Nicky asked finally.

"Yes."

Nicky was suddenly off the bed, bounding across the room like a young dog. "Then can't you go to see her? *You* could get passes to travel, Janos! You're important, a hero! And the Russians respect you and let you do all kinds of things that we can't do. They'd give you passes to get to Magyarovar, I know they would!"

"I can't possibly go to Magyarovar." His voice was cold because he was afraid. Nicky was making him become involved with people again.

"Why can't you? Please, Janos!" Nicky drew breath and then began to speak quietly, controlling himself and trying to talk as an adult instead of an adolescent. "You have done so much for me that I know I have no right to ask more. But I am asking more because I cannot think of anything else. Every night I try to imagine what has happened to them: my cousins, Aunt Malie and Uncle David, my mama. And now Uncle Adam says Terez may be safe! That is why I ask you to go to Magyarovar—please, please, dear Janos! I will do anything for you if you will go and find them!" Young, demanding, proud in so many ways, but not yet proud enough.

"How can I find them?" he asked, suddenly angry. "You know what the country is like. You know what this town is like. How can I find them?" His composure had vanished and he had forgotten how to be impersonal. The judgment that he brought to everything had been destroyed in a sea of panic. Nicholas was hugging his arm, gazing at him with huge pleading eyes. This close he could see just how thin and ill the boy looked. The veins were visible under his skin and there was a transparent appearance about him.

"You don't have to go around looking," Nicky said humbly. "I know you can't do that with the Russians there. But if you just went to your sister's and asked what had happened to them—"

"I can't go!" he shouted. "You must ask someone else. Your Uncle Leo, ask him to go."

"Uncle Leo wouldn't get papers quickly enough; he's not as important as you. You'll get everything. They'll let you use the trains and probably give you rides in their trucks. And if—if they are in trouble with the Russians, Uncle Leo would only make it worse. He would lose his temper and begin fighting. Please, Janos." The boy's hands pressed hard into his arm. "I would do it for you," he said simply. "If you wanted me to go to Magyarovar and look for your sister, I would go." He smiled again, that warm endearing smile that twisted into the breast and hurt. "I would go. Because you are my friend and I love you."

Janos closed his eyes and drew a deep breath. "I cannot go," he muttered, knowing that already it was too late. Whatever he did, whether he went or not, the pain was there and would remain. And because he was a rational man and did not believe in wasting energy in futile effort, he gave in, opened his eyes, and said coldly, "Very well, Nicky. If I can get passes and papers I will go."

The smile exploded over the boy's face again. The hands gripping his arm hugged and pulled. "Thank you, Janos! Thank you!"

Janos pulled his arm away and stood up. For a moment he hated Nicky. He was disturbed and unsettled. His calm, abstract pattern for the future had been destroyed and Nicky must be punished.

"Go home," he said curtly.

"You're not angry with me, are you?"

"I've told you to go home."

Uncertainty on his face, Nicky took a step towards the door. "I'm sorry, Janos. If you really cannot go—"

"I've told you I will go to Magyarovar. I have also told you to leave here."

Tears stood in the boy's eyes (yes, there had been a time when he too would have cried over such a rejection). Janos turned away and picked up a book from his desk, any book. It was his volume of verse, the poetry that he had written just before and after his mother's death, and quickly he put the book down again. He heard the door close and footsteps on the stairs. The implosion of pleasure that marked Nicky's coming was now matched by an explosion of misery. He held his body rigidly controlled for a moment and then rushed across to the window and threw it open.

"Nicky!"

The figure just emerging onto the road looked up.

"Good-bye, Nicky," he shouted.

There was a pause, then a nervous smile appeared on the upturned face.

"Good-bye, Nicky," he shouted again, and the nervousness disappeared. Nicky waved up at him and began to walk away. He looked back, waved again, tripped over nothing, and faded into the distance, a tall, gangling youth who had not yet learned how to live alone.

A hundred times during the journey to Magyarovar he cursed himself for surrendering to emotional involvement. He was an important man and he had urgent and difficult matters to attend to; instead he was rattling 200 kilometres across the country on a fool's errand searching for three people for whom he cared nothing, just because a boy had made the very worst kind of sentimental appeal to him. He was angry, but he was sensible enough to admit that he could blame no one but himself for his irrational behaviour.

The journey would have taken less than a day including changes before the war, but now it took him three days to get there. Bridges had been destroyed, tracks blown up, and the Russians inspected passes and issued delaying instructions at every station and checkpoint.

Hungarians had been forbidden to use railway stations, and although his pass gave him a dispensation, he thought it safer not to wait around at night when trains were unlikely to run. It was warm and he spent one night curled against his rucksack in a field of grass—grass was all that was left anywhere this spring—and another night sleeping in an ammunition train waiting for the morning departure. As he moved west the evidences of war were more prevalent, for as the Germans had been pushed back against the Austrian border, they had tried, once more, to launch delaying tactics. With only one more country, one more border before the Russians were on German soil, pockets of resistance had tried to hold for a few days. He learned that the German garrison had been cleared from Magyarovar on April 3 and that the town was still in post-battle chaos. The train was halted some 20 kilometres outside and soldiers began to unload ammunition. He was offered a ride in a jeep into Magyarovar but decided that from this distance it would be easier to walk across country direct to his sister's village. His sister had married well—all his sisters had married well—to a landed peasant with a small but fertile patch; at least it had been fertile once. Now, as he looked about him, he supposed it would be like anywhere else, stripped, unsown, and devoid of cattle. So much to do, so much to do. . . .

The last time he had visited here the fields had been full of sunflowers, moving their great dinner-plate heads round to gaze at the sun, a good rich crop of seed and oil. He was still, for all his early exile from the country, a child of the soil, and as he struck off across the fields he stared down at the ground, hoping that perhaps some of the flowers had seeded themselves for this year. There had been fighting in Magyarovar and, inevitably, some evidence had carried over into the surrounding countryside: an abandoned tank, a crater in a field, a bombed farmhouse. These things were nothing compared to the neglected fields, the lack of cattle, the things that meant no food next winter. What was he doing trekking across the country looking for the wife and children of his old master when he should be at home, trying to plan how they were going to cope with the bad months that lay ahead?

Madame Kaldy—the young Madame Kaldy—Terez, George: what were they to him? They were not the same peo-

529

ple that young Nicky described to him, for Nicky had created an image of a pretty, silly, rather sharp-tempered Aunt Eva that bore no resemblance at all to the languid, distant lady he remembered from his youth. He could recall her sitting on the veranda, sipping juice from a long glass, playing tennis in a white dress, or alighting from a car or carriage carrying parcels and smelling of city perfume. Terez he could remember, a jovial baby up at the farm whom he once prevented from falling into the river and, after that, a schoolgirl who always smiled when they met in the town and said, "Good morning, Janos Marton," making it plain that in spite of the age difference, and the fact that he was a schoolteacher, she still considered him the Marton boy from her father's estate. George was a schoolboy whom he knew only by sight. What were these people to him? Why had he come to look for them?

During the months that Nicky was in hiding, the boy had talked incessantly of his family, relating stories and family jokes. At first he had listened because he could not be cruel. And then, in spite of himself, he had become fascinated by the incredible descriptions that in no way matched up to his memories of the amoebic country family. Uncle Adam—who had set the *pandur* to beat the truth out of his father—a dull, fair, and kindly man? Uncle Leo—that weak, over-emotional pseudo-liberal—a brave and adventurous rebel? Nicky's mother, Kati Racs-Rassay—a timid mouse who had disgraced her family—a brilliant, talented cosmopolitan? And so it went on, the people whom Janos had watched from childhood, watched fascinated because they had lifted him from his world in a careless amused way just as they put out crumbs for birds or fed stray dogs, revealed as many-faceted humans, not gods to be hated or revered. There was only one where Nicky's description matched his own recollection, "Aunt Malie." He too remembered her as kindly, gentle, concerned; even that time she had visited him, accusing him of being in league with the Germans and Arrow Cross, even then he had recognized her gentleness. But of the others, none were the same.

In the distance, across the fields, he saw the smudge of buildings and he swung his rucksack to the other shoulder and wiped sweat from his neck. Soon he could complete this ridiculous mission and go home, to a future he had carved for himself and where Nicky could be his friend or not as he pleased. He stared at the village—something wrong—and realized that the shape and colour of it had changed. It was dirtier, flatter . . . bombed. His heart quickened, as did his pace. He did not want his sister to be dead—even though they meant little to each other he did not want her to be dead. He did not want the others to be dead either; if he found their bodies he would have to tell Nicky—he shut the thought down and ran towards the ruined houses. The main street was flattened, just walls and chimneys rising from heaps of rubble. There were still some houses in the side streets, whole houses, and some that could be lived in even though they were damaged. He ran into the maze of smashed clay and earth, finding his way unerringly amidst the blurred roads to the house that had been his sister's. It wasn't there.

He stared, unbelieving. It wasn't the first time he had seen a battered village, but this was his sister's home, and now there was nothing, just some remnants of wall and fireplace, not even broken furniture—nothing. He clambered over the wall and began to tear at the rubbish. "Elza? Elza?"

"They've gone." Behind him an old woman—why did the war seem to leave nothing but old women?—leaned on a stick and watched him over the wall. "They went before the Russians came; quite a few did. They decided to go back behind the German lines."

Fool! Elza had always been a fool. Did she think by continually moving back before the advancing line she could miss the war? The nearer they got to Germany the worse it was going to be. Why hadn't she stayed and got the unnerving transition over with?

"If she had stayed," the old woman said cannily, "she would have been killed when the shell hit the house."

"Of course. Thank you," he said coldly, and then, as she began to move away, "Do you know what happened to the—the people who were staying with her, a dark-haired woman with her daughter and son?"

The old woman's eyes glittered maliciously. "The Jews, you mean?" she asked. "The Jews with false papers?"

Shock again. Jews? The family he had feared and hated and thought of for so long, dismissed merely as Jews with false papers?

"What happened to them? Did the Gestapo—"

"No." She shrugged. "We knew they were Jews but we never told; we never told the Germans anything. And they paid well—your sister had money arrive every month—but when the Germans began to retreat your sister said that the

Jews could not go back with her. It was too dangerous. The Gestapo would have killed her for helping them."

"So they went . . . somewhere else?" he asked. She was already walking away, shuffling along between the rubble, bending now and again to see if there was anything worth salvaging on the road.

"They stayed here. They're living in what is left of the Dobi house, up on the left, next door to where the butcher used to be."

He began to run, and as he did so he felt that old familiar implosion of happiness. He had succeeded; he had found them. Nicky, Nicky, I've found them for you. Your family, a little more family for you so that you will not be quite alone when you realize your mother will never come back. For a moment, as he ran, jumping over heaps of dirt and clay, he *was* Nicky, running to meet them, Aunt Eva, Terez, George. They were safe, and he had found them.

There were two walls, a mountain of rubble, a chimney, and part of a roof. Someone had piled up pieces of stone to form a fourth low protection against the wind. The makeshift wall obviously kept falling, because that someone was trying to rebuild it, filling a basket with broken stones and trying to block up the holes.

"Terez!" She turned, and his stomach twisted suddenly and he couldn't say anything else. That face again, that thin, ill, but smiling face with the bright brown eyes and the hope not yet killed, the face he thought he had left behind him back in the town, the face of a happy child who had been made desolate by the war. The face, framed by thick curly hair in braids, stared at him, unbelieving. It crumpled, and then the eyes widened, just the way Nicky's did.

"Janos! Janos Marton! From home! You've come from home!" The girl's body—how tiny she was, how thin and tiny —was against him, her arms clinging round his neck, her face buried hard into his chest. "You've come from home," she sobbed. "You'll help us! That's why you've come, to help us!" Her arms had dropped from his neck and were riveted around his waist, her head boring into his chest. "Dear, dear Janos! From home!"

He had never comforted anyone except his mother, but for a moment he found he knew how to do it—you put your arms back round them and rocked a little—only for a moment, and then the astonishment and horror of what was happening became uppermost and, gently, he pushed the girl away.

"Terez? Who is it?" The querulous voice helped. It came from behind the shelter and it was curious to hear it like this, the voice that he had only heard distantly before, talking to servants, now coming from a ruin while he held the voice's daughter in his arms.

"It's Janos, Mama! Janos Marton from home! He's come to help us. He'll get us better and then take us home again. You will, won't you?" she asked anxiously, suddenly afraid that he'd come for a different reason. "You can't help your sister; she's gone. You'll help us, won't you?" One large tear rolled softly down her face. "I can't manage any more on my own."

He clambered over the improvised wall into the makeshift shelter. There was a broken chair on which her mother was sitting. It was supported underneath by bricks that extended out to form a kind of couch. Aunt Eva—Mrs. Kaldy—yellow and petulant, huddled into herself. In the corner on a blanket, very very still, the boy George was lying.

"What's wrong with the boy?"

"He's broken his leg. I've done the best I could. I tried to set it with splints, the way Papa used to sometimes with the horses—do you remember? But he's getting worse. He has a fever. I don't know what else to do." The eyes huge and a rising note of hysteria in her voice. He knelt down by George and pulled back the coat that was over him. Above the knee and on the shin were two huge, misshapen swellings. Strips of black cloth held a broom handle down the side of the distorted limb.

"How did it happen?"

"He fell and—"

"Fell?" shrieked Mrs. Kaldy. "Fell? He was pushed and beaten by those—those pigs. He behaved like a true man, my poor little boy." She began to sob. "He saw what those filthy animals were going to do to his mother and sister and behaved like a hero! A hero, I tell you! My poor little boy, poor brave little boy."

Terez's face had drained of colour, ugly in distress, eyes huge again, and he looked away.

"Never did I think we would suffer like that. My poor child, my poor daughter, so sheltered—and those filthy Russians! What kind of animals are they? They have destroyed me. Destroyed me, I tell you. What shall we do with ourselves? I ask you, what shall we do?"

One of the bricks supporting the chair became dislodged, mostly because Eva was swaying back and forth in dramatic frenzy. When she felt the chair slip she gave a little shriek and began to moan again.

He could feel Terez beside him, strung taut like a cat, and because he understood he made no effort to look at her or touch her. He examined the leg, then lifted one of George's eyelids.

"I think you have done everything that could be done for the leg," he said softly. "But I don't like the fever. I think he has something wrong with his chest."

"I tried to get medicine from the Russians." She stared hard, down at the ground. "One of the officers finally gave me two pills—aspirin, I think." In the background Mrs. Kaldy was working up to a fresh paroxysm of screams. The screams were interposed with details of what had been done to her by the Russians and what had been done to her child.

He saw Terez shudder, watched something in the eyes blank out and be replaced by an embryonic madness. He put his hands on her shoulders and felt her flinch, then stiffen. "Excuse me one moment, Terez," he said courteously, and then he crossed to Mrs. Kaldy and slapped her across the face. "Be quiet!" he snapped.

Her jaw dropped open. She stared, then drew breath.

"Please don't speak or moan any more, Mrs. Kaldy, otherwise I shall be forced to hit you again. We are trying to get you and your son away from here. I have come here to do that. So please help, and if you can't help, be quiet."

She gave a further wailing shriek and then turned a face of venom at him. "You're the same! A peasant! Like the rest of them who raped my daughter and did not even have the grace to leave her mother alone! You're the same, Janos Marton! I remember you and your father; he was a thief and you're no better! You think you can have my daughter just as they have had her, and—aaah!" The final shriek was swallowed into a gasp because this time the slap had come from Terez.

"Be quiet, Mama," she cried. "You're not helping us! You're not helping us at all!"

"Mrs. Kaldy," he said icily, "I came here specifically to look for you and your family. You have suffered, but no worse than many others. I do not intend to take a screaming, insane woman back through the country when it is in its present condition. If you do not behave, remain quiet, and do exactly as you are told, I shall leave you here. It would be far easier for me to leave you here, and I will happily do so."

Eva stared. She had never spoken to him since he had

534

grown up, only greetings and gracious nods. She stared and was a little afraid because he reminded her of—whom? Adam! He reminded her of Adam when he was cross or unable to be coaxed. He was like Adam, only more so.

"Who are you to speak to me like that?" she asked feebly, but he was sick of her and climbed over the wall away from the ruin. Emotion, emotion. It was no good. For a moment he had wanted to punish that stupid, selfish woman, to show just who he was: the head of the District Committee, a man with papers, power, to whom she must bow and say please and thank you. And it was no good; that kind of emotion was as bad as the other kind, the kind that hurt you because you loved.

"Janos." Terez touched him lightly on the arm. Thin, frail little face, pleading, humble. "Please ignore her. She's been spoilt and now it has all gone wrong and she is afraid. She didn't mean any of those things. She's just afraid." She smiled, ashamed. "My mama has no character. Papa tried to tell me, but he loved her too much to admit it openly. She is just a poor, silly creature and she cannot accept what has happened."

"I understand." He suddenly wished he had a cigarette, although he had learned—because of the cost—to do without such luxuries. "Are you all right?" he asked, staring over her head at the ruined village.

"Yes."

"The Russians—"

"I don't talk about it," she said quickly. "I want to get home as quickly as possible. You have come across country. How can we get home with George so ill?"

"Can your mother walk?"

"I don't know." She sighed and pushed a strand of hair away from her dirty face. "She moans and says she is ill. When she has to go outside she leans on the wall and on me. I don't know if she can walk."

How very thin she was! The veins showed in her face too, the way they did in Nicky's. "Have you any food?" he asked.

"Your sister gave me a sack of beans before she left. Some we have eaten and some I exchanged for other things—the blanket for George. Last week the Russians gave soup away one day."

He placed his hand gently on her shoulder and this time she did not flinch. "Then first we shall eat, Terez. Do you know how to light a fire?"

535

"Of course!" Just a glimmer of indignation that made him smile.

"Then light a fire. There's wood enough I think and, if not, burn your mother's chair. We shall have hot soup with beans and sausage and bread." Her eyes widened greedily. "I have a little sausage and bread, and I have an onion for the soup. Then, when we have eaten, I shall tell you about the rest of your family and we shall discuss how to get home."

He watched Eva Kaldy wolfing down the food, and he decided there was nothing wrong with her and that tomorrow she was going to be made to walk and possibly help carry her son too. She was a small woman but a strong one. Beside her daughter she looked like an amazon and she must be made to help with the journey instead of dragging on Terez. George drank some of the soup and seemed a little better. Terez lifted his head and explained that Janos Marton had come to take them home and George smiled, quite rationally, and said, "Good, good."

Just as dusk was drawing in three young Russians came sauntering up the road. Terez pressed back against the wall. He took his papers out of his pocket, just in case, and climbed into the road, smiling at them from a long way off. They paused, glared, smiled back in the irrational way he had come to expect from them—rape and violence one day, distributing soup another—and one of them peered over the wall at Terez and said something that made the others stop and look too.

He had learned the merest superficialities of Russian, but with a peasant's instinct what he had learned was peasant's talk. He lurched over to Terez and pulled her up against him, arching his body crudely into hers. Then he looked over his shoulders at the Russians and winked, brandished his Party card and bundle of passes, and said, in the obscene guttural of soldiers everywhere, that now it was the turn of loyal Hungarian Party members. A pause—how strange that he was not really afraid at all of these dangerous schoolboys—and then a guffaw, a further volley of obscenities, a good-natured wave, and more shouting as they continued their journey through the village.

"That's all," Terez said quietly. "They do that once every night. They won't return again now. It will be quiet."

Eva Kaldy, made comatose by the unexpected quantity and quality of the hot soup, had fallen into a deep sleep. George

536

hovered between consciousness and fever, and Janos put the blanket out of his rucksack over the boy.

"Janos, will we be able to get home?"

"Yes."

"Tell me again about Nicky, and Uncle Leo, and my papa."

He was tired, but he went through it all again, sensing through the darkness her need to picture them back at home. She didn't ask about the others, the ones who hadn't come back yet, although he knew they were there in her mind. When he had finished telling of her papa and Unce Leo and cousin Nicky, she sighed and then reached out and took his hand. "How kind you have been to us all, Janos Marton," she whispered. "How very kind. Whatever happens to us you will always be my friend and I shall never forget you."

Young Nicky, and now Terez. He was becoming enmeshed in sickly bourgeois sentiment made worse because of his own emotional weakness.

The journey back, which took eight days, assumed at times the proportions of a nightmare. The biggest of their difficulties was Eva Kaldy. He could—and did—cope with the Russians, with breakdowns of trains, with the lack of food, and with official red tape that dogged them all the way. But Eva Kaldy made him lose the steeled control it had taken him years to acquire. Once he nearly placed his hands round her still surprisingly fat neck and squeezed. He and Terez quarrelled bitterly about her, and during the course of the eight days he ceased trying to be polite to the old woman; he shouted, ignored, and swore when he felt it would release the pent-up hatred and frustration that she fermented inside him.

On the first morning he had applied to the commander of the village for permission to take the three Kaldy refugees back with him. He had stressed his party function and had indicated that these three were important—they had special information about Arrow Cross activities and could denounce hidden fascists. He hated himself for resorting to such blatant propaganda methods—and for such a purpose!—but after several hours of waiting, arguing, persuasion, and a personal examination of the three by a Russian lieutenant, he had been given passes beginning 20 kilometres away, at the same point where he had been put off the train. They had to get there by themselves and then, if they were lucky, they might find a place on a train going somewhere towards the east.

He had made a stretcher with two uneven bars of wood and

the blanket. George, when lifted on to it, had groaned and then fainted. Fortunately, for most of that long, jolting trek across cart tracks and shell-pocked roads he had remained unconscious.

He didn't even have to ask Terez if she was strong enough to bear the other end. She had already bundled up her few belongings and stationed herself at the foot of the makeshift stretcher. Then she looked from him to her mama, who was sitting crying quietly in the broken chair.

"How do we persuade her to walk, Janos?" she asked.

"She not only has to walk, she has to carry your bundle and my rucksack. So, Madame Kaldy, we are leaving now. We have to walk for the first part of the journey and then, with fortune, we shall be able to find a place on a train."

"You must leave me." Eva sniffed. "I am a sick and crippled woman. Those Russians—what they did to me. No one will ever understand. Go and leave me."

"Don't be silly, Mama," Terez said irritably. "You know we shouldn't leave you. But we cannot carry both you and George—and George is sick."

"And I? Your mother who has suffered at the hands of those beasts? I am not sick? I am a well and healthy woman?"

"No, Mama." Terez sighed. "We none of us are well. But we are better than poor George. Come now, you must try. Put the rucksack and bundle on your back—I will help you—and then try to walk with us."

"Carry those things!" shrieked Eva. "How can I carry anything when I can scarcely move my legs?"

That was the first time he wanted very badly to hit her, but instead he had gone outside and waited, fighting for control and trying not to hear the persuasions and plaintive replies coming from the other side of the wall.

"Come now, dearest Mama. Just stand and try to walk a little way with me supporting you. Once you have your legs working you will see it is easy. Come now, a little practice and then away we can go, back home. See? It is easy!" And then a small cry of misery and anger. "Oh, Mama!"

"I told you, I am a weak and injured creature. Helpless. You must leave me. Take my son home but leave me here."

"Oh, Mama!" He could hear the frustration and tears in Terez's voice and suddenly he could bear no more. He stepped over the wall and and walked to the stretcher.

"Your mama is right, Terez. We must leave her."

"Janos!"

538

"If she wants to walk, she will. All she has to do is pick up those bundles and come with us. That is all. We can waste no more time. Take the other end of the stretcher, please, Terez."

"Janos, we cannot."

"Do not argue!" he shouted, and stared at the old lady who wasn't an old lady at all. "You're a vulture, Madame Kaldy," he shouted, "living on the flesh of your children. Why I am wasting my time with you when Hungary is full of good, strong, worthy people who need to be saved, I cannot think! We are going now, taking your son home to where he can see a doctor and be cared for. If you want to come, get up and walk and bring those bundles with you. Because if you do not bring those bundles you will not eat on the journey. And—" He paused, shaking with rage. "If I see that you have left them behind I shall come back here and tie them to you!"

Terez was trembling. She looked at her mother, then at him, and he waved one hand peremptorily at the other end of the stretcher. "I shall lift it onto the wall, then climb over and slide it forward." He glared at her, daring her to say one word about her mother. "Then you can climb over. Try not to jar him. We shall stop and rest every fifty paces."

She wasn't strong enough to carry it, but there was no other way. He heard her panting, felt her slowing down, and they had to stop and rest long before fifty paces.

"Just until I get used to it," she breathed. "I'll get used to it very soon." And then she whispered, "Janos, Mama is coming after us."

"Is she carrying the bags?" he snapped.

"Yes."

"We'll continue then."

It took them two days to get to the rail point, and to their stumbling, halting progress was added the groans of George and a continual litany of whined miseries from Eva Kaldy. Again and again he reproached himself for what he was doing, the energy he was spending on saving this useless piece of humanity who represented everything he had always despised. If he wanted to indulge in nepotism he could have found worthier causes almost anywhere. Anyone was worthier of salvation than this spoilt, hysterical woman who was immersed in her own discomfort.

At the rail point they had to wait several hours, and when the train finally came, Eva, with exceptional agility, sprang aboard just as Janos was trying to slide the stretcher in. She kicked it slightly to one side and George groaned again as his body was jarred. When he finally had the boy settled and was in himself he lay down as far away from her as possible.

"Janos, about Mama, I—"

"I cannot bear to talk about your mother, Terez. She disgusts me."

Her dirty face crumpled. The huge shadows under her eyes were nearly obliterated by filth but he could still see how tired she was, how her shoulders were hunched forward from the pain of carrying the stretcher.

"You've done well, little girl," he said softly. "You have all the courage your mother has not. I don't mind what I'm doing when I remember it is for you and for my young friend Nicky."

She tried to smile but was so tired she failed. He pulled her down beside him and cushioned her head on his arm.

"Try to sleep. This journey will take many hours and we shall have to walk again before we find another train."

They were both sinking into sleep when he heard the whine, the moaning demand for attention that had grated on his nerves for the last two days.

"Terez. Terez, my baby, help me. Your poor mother is sick."

"Go to sleep, old woman. Do not disturb us."

"I'm sick!"

"If you do not stop I shall hit you, old woman."

She was silent then, so silent he became frightened and finally moved away from the sleeping Terez and crawled over. Eva Kaldy was cushioned against the knapsack, snoring gently, looking stronger and fatter than any of the rest of them.

They jolted, stopped, moved forward, and finally after nearly a day had passed the train came to rest in a siding for the night. They climbed out the following morning and carried the stretcher into the nearest village, where he hoped he might be able to get help. They had left the frontier towns and villages where the fighting had been bad and this far back there had been no total destruction, only the usual deprivations of cattle, women, and wrist watches.

He finally found a farmer who would lend him a hand cart. Anything else would have been useless anyway as there were no horses to pull. The farmer told him that if they could get along the road a few kilometres, to the stone quarry belonging to Geza Gluck, a truck sometimes ran from the quarry to the next rail point. The hand cart was better. He'd become worried about Terez because it was obvious she couldn't carry her end of the stretcher much longer. They got to the quarry by the road, all three exhausted. He opened his rucksack to divide the last of his bread and sausage and discovered that during the night on the train Eva had eaten everything. That was when he wanted to kill her. His rage mounted so strongly that he had been unable to control himself and he towered over her, shouting and waving the rucksack in her face.

"You deserve to die! You are a fat, greedy sow—but even a sow makes provision for its young! If I had caught you stealing our food I would have killed you, you understand? I would have killed you!"

Eva began to whimper and he felt Terez pulling on his arm. "Janos, don't," she whispered. "Leave her. We can buy food in this part of the country. It is not so bad. Leave her."

"Leave her? I cannot leave her! She is a vulture, a leech, and she deserves to die. All my life I wondered what it must be like to be born a Kaldy or a Ferenc or a Racs-Rassay, and now I have learned what it is like. My own mother—" He choked into silence. What had happened to him, to his control, his self-discipline, his iron rules that nothing and no one ever disturbed? He never spoke of his mother in passion, not to anyone, and now, so overwrought was he, he had nearly shared her with these people, compared her—her loyalty, courage, and sacrifice—with the disgusting, greedy, slug-like thing that sat before him at the side of the road.

"Do not speak to her like that," Terez cried. "I don't like it. She is weak and irritating, but don't talk to her like that."

"I shall talk any way I like while she hampers us from getting home."

"You think, just because you are important and some kind of hero, you can treat her as though she is filth!" Terez shouted, crying with anger, tiredness, and also shame, because her mother had disgraced them all. "She is my mother, and I will not have you shout at her or bully her!"

"Then take your brother home by yourself."

She had tried to strike him, an ineffectual floating blow that died at birth in her weak body. In fury she ran away, into the quarry, and he heard her steps run across the loosened stone.

"Are you satisfied, old bitch!" he snarled at Eva Kaldy, and felt no satisfaction because Eva wasn't listening, just sitting whining about her feet, the Russians, her sickness, everything.

Later Terez had come back, slipped her hand in his and

pressed her forehead against his arm. They could neither of them speak—they were too tired, too strained—but they were friends again, of sorts.

The truck took them into the next village and at last they were able to find a doctor to set George's leg and confirm that two of his ribs were broken.

"He is sick, very sick. He should not travel when he is like this. He should rest in bed, warm, and with whatever drugs we can find."

They discussed the matter in detail and finally agreed to stay for a couple of nights, until George was a little better. Again he had to use the power of his Party card to find a bed for the night and he had refused to use it other than for George. He, Terez, and Eva had taken shelter in a barn just outside the town, and he had spent two nights listening to Eva's reproaches because he had found a bed for her son but not for her. At last, unable to bear it any longer, he moved outside and slept huddled against the barn wall. He was cold, but his spirit was left in peace.

George was really not better on the third day, but he heard there was a train leaving for home sometime during the afternoon. He could wait no longer; he had become obsessed, as they all had, with the belief that once they were home everything would be better. In the morning he and Terez went to visit George. He was weak but lucid. In the mornings his fever seemed to abate. He could recognize them, could smile and talk a little. During the journey he had become to Janos not a person but a stretcher, a burden that had to be lifted, carried, moved at difficult angles over walls, rutted roads, and the edges of cattle cars. But now, as he looked at the boy, he felt a grudging approval for his courage and for his lack of complaint. George and Terez, they were worth saving surely. Somehow the despicable creature left sleeping back in the barn had spawned a pair of changelings. Or perhaps it was just that this new young generation had been tempered by the war. They were no longer Ferencs or Kaldys, no longer to be called excellency or sir. They were "Jews with false papers" and the young ones had grown up with a courage and endurance that commended them to him. Nicky, Terez, George—it was worth saving these three, for they had the iron and the will to help rebuild the new Hungary.

"We are going to try and get on another train today, George," he said quietly. "This should be the last part of the journey. Do you feel well enough for us to begin again?"

542

The boy smiled, nodded, said a whispered "thank you," and then tried to say something else but was too weak and the words died in a sigh. They lifted him back onto the home-made stretcher, watched the blood drain from his face as the movement sent fresh pain through him, and carried him outside the cottage. Janos paid the smallholder with money. The man did not look pleased but it was all Janos had. Money was growing increasingly more useless—a chicken or bag of grain would have been more valuable—and as a sop Janos scribbled a note on a piece of paper commending the man to the authorities for the help he had given to the Party. The smallholder stared dispassionately at the paper but Janos could waste no more time or give anything else.

"Let us go," he said to Terez. He debated asking the man to help carry George so that Terez could be relieved, but he felt he had pushed his Party card as much as he dared.

"Can you manage?" he asked her.

"What about Mama?"

"We will take George to the station, then go back for her." Or leave her. That's what he would like to do, leave her. She would survive—people like Eva Kaldy always did survive—by stealing the last of the food, by pushing onto a train ahead of everyone else and getting the best place, by battening on others whose consciences couldn't quite let them abandon these useless leeches. But he had no conscience—not of that kind anyway—and he could happily desert the old trollop and let her make her own way back home. *And what would you say to young Nicky? To Terez?* his other self asked, the new emotional self that he despised. *What of these two young ones who say they are your friends? How would you face them?*

As they arrived at the rail point one of the unpredictable nightmares of the war occurred—the train was already there, was about to leave. Oh, God! They should have started earlier. Every other train had taken hours to arrive. There had been hour-long—day-long!—waits, and now, when they still had to go and collect the old woman, the train, only a few hours from home, was about to depart.

"Hell!" Without realizing it he began to hurry forward, pulling the stretcher, pulling Terez behind him. "The last car is still open!" he shouted. "We can still get him in!" He loped along, right up to the train, conscious with some blanked-out part of his mind that someone was crying very quietly behind him.

"Hurry!"

"Janos, Mama. We can't go without Mama!"

He looked over his shoulder, viewing her awkwardly against the pull of the stretcher on his shoulders.

"Please, Janos. Don't go without Mama!"

He wanted to spit. He put the stretcher down, remembering to do it gently even in his anger. Then he turned and faced her. "There might not be another train for days!" he shouted. "We could be home by tomorrow. George may be dead by the time the next train comes!"

"Please don't leave Mama!" Huge agonized eyes pleaded with him. She was afraid of him too, because she recognized his anger. He felt his hands trembling. He wanted to push her in, tears, protests, and all, and then bundle George up beside her. Fury exploded in his head and suddenly he found he was doing exactly that, throwing her into the open car, ignoring her feeble protests and struggling limbs.

"Janos!"

"Help me with the stretcher, damn you!" he shouted. "I'll go back for her. You'll have to manage as best you can; there'll be someone at home who'll help you off the train." It began to move away, the stretcher only half in, and he gave a violent last push, trying not to hear George's cry as the door slid against his side.

"Don't hurt her!" she cried, staring out at him as they moved away. "Come as soon as you can. Don't hurt her!"

Dirty face, filth-encrusted braids of hair, and two huge dark eyes fixed on him as the train gained speed. It was the way young Nicky had looked at him during the months of hiding. Every time he had to leave Nicky locked in the attic that same dirty, frightened face had stared at him. And he suddenly wanted to reassure her, to comfort her the way he had done when she'd clung to him in the derelict building.

He turned and spat. The train disappeared and now resentment descended upon him again. God knew how many days he was going to have to wait with that old woman before they could get home again.

They were lucky. It was only two days before another train came, but the two days were a purgatory of complaints and hysterical screaming. For now Eva had another grievance to add to all the others. Her daughter had deserted her, left her to the mercies of a brutal and sadistic peasant who swore at her and on one occasion, when she refused to get up and walk to the station (he made her go with him three or four times a

544

day in case the fiasco of the departing train was repeated), actually pushed her. That was when she had enjoyed a bout of hysterics, screaming at him and at the Russians who had raped her. How dare he touch her! Wait until her husband heard about it; he would punish the peasant child, just as he'd punished his father! Oh, yes, she knew about that. Marton had been a thief and his son—his son was a rapist and a bully. He had abducted her daughter and son. Terez would never have left her, not her darling Terez! She'd never forgive her if she had just left her. No. That was gratitude for you: you spent your life sacrificing everything for your children and then they went off and left you. . . . The litany progressed.

Finally he walked out of the barn. He returned at mealtimes with food, and whenever they needed to check at the station, and every time he returned he hoped she had gone. But some hideous instinct of self-preservation in Eva made her acknowledge that this man—sadist, rapist, peasant, bully, son of a thief—was her best chance of getting home again. For some reason, no matter what she screamed at him, no matter what she said, he wouldn't abandon her, and she was clever enough to stay where she was still his responsibility.

There was one more violent outbreak of emotion between them, when they heard at the station that a train was expected to come within the next few hours. Eva wanted to go back to the barn—which had now taken on the aspects of a cosy retreat—and sleep until it was time for departure.

"We don't go away," Janos snapped. "We move a little way up the line—far enough away from the station to avoid trouble—and we wait!"

"No! I cannot wait there, in a field. I shall be sick, die. Hasn't my body been abused enough? Haven't I suffered enough that you—you should do this to me?"

He had walked away up the track, leaving her to follow, and because she knew it was unsafe to remain alone in the station without the protection of his Party card, she had been forced to run after him, screaming abuse and finally pounding him on the back. The face he turned on her was so virulent that she had suddenly cowered away in terror. The old Eva—the clever knowing-how-to-handle-people Eva—realized that she had done something very unwise.

"Don't touch me!" he snarled. "If you touch me I think I shall kill you!"

And from then on she remained silent, quite still throughout the long wait and the ride on the train. She didn't think he *would* kill her, but she knew that he was prepared to leave her behind. Whatever cause had bound him to her before had now been outweighed by her behaviour. She knew she must be quiet—well, just a little whimper, a little moan from time to time, but no more screams and accusations. And after all they were on a train going home, home to Adam, who would care for her and treasure her and make up for all the dreadful things that had happened.

When they finally pulled into the station he thought he was going to choke for they were all there, had been waiting for hours ever since the rumour of the train had circulated round the town. It was something that had never happened to him before, being met by a group of people at the station—eager expectant faces turned upwards, smiles, arms outstretched, figures hurrying forward to help, to take bundles, to cry and kiss—oh, not him, but the charged atmosphere affected him as well as Eva.

Adam had somehow got down from the farm. Young Nicky had sent a message to him saying that his dear friend, Janos Marton—hero, partisan, leader of the District Committee—had gone to bring Eva and Terez and George back home, and Adam, walking most of the way, had arrived in town at the same time as Terez and George. There was an impression of great crowds, of a huge noisy family clustering round Eva when she had clambered down, but in reality there were only four and the best of these was Nicky, whose face glowed with pride because his friend, Janos Marton, had brought about this miracle.

Mr. Adam—Uncle Adam?—was crying, unashamedly crying as he clasped that nauseous greedy woman in his arms, and then, to Janos's astonishment, he saw a complete metamorphosis take place in Eva Kaldy, a change not of character but of physical appearance. He couldn't believe it and he watched in something akin to horror as she sloughed off the form of a fat caterpillar and turned into a butterfly. During the last nine days he had come to regard her as fat, shapeless, half-witted, and uncontrollably greedy. She had seemed fat because she never moved when she could help it and ate more than anyone else. But now the lethargic lump suddenly drew herself up and, on tiny, dainty feet, fluttered into her husband's arms where she looked small, shapely, and incredibly helpless.

"Oh, Adam, my dearest husband!" She smiled bravely through a face of tears. "Oh, Adam! Thank God it is all over! Now we can be happy again. Now we can forget the war!"

Nothing about the Russians or the hunger or her health or the vicious peasant who had brought her home. And nothing either about the health of her son. Nothing about Terez, or young Nicky, or her brother Leo, who all stood there smiling and embracing her and talking at once.

They turned and began to troop alongside the rail, still talking, still hugging each other. Their emotion, their pride in each other, their happiness, was all enveloping, complete; they needed nothing else at this moment, although later they would begin to worry about the others who had not yet come home. And their happiness, their absorption in each other, left no room for Janos Marton.

He stared after them, standing alone with his rucksack on the ground beside him, and an old, well-remembered bitterness stirred in his heart. No. No place for bitterness now; he had rooted it out years ago as a useless and wasteful emotion. Why should they thank him? They were the kind of people who never did say thank you. They said please but not thank you. He had been asked to do something and he had done it. No one had forced him to go to Magyarovar, and therefore he could not expect thanks. He picked up the rucksack and brought his intellect to bear on the hurt within his heart.

And a few moments later, just as his intellect was winning, as cool logic was suppressing mere feeling, he heard a shout and saw two figures running back towards him, two figures that became Terez and Nicky, shouting, smiling, and then hugging his arms, one on each side.

"I knew you'd do it!" gloried Nicky. "I knew if anyone coud find them and bring them home, you could."

No answer—there was no answer unless it be something sentimental, foolish.

"How is George?" he said to Terez.

"A little better. The fever has broken. His leg is still bad, but he is happy to be home. And so am I, Janos Marton. And I shall never forget what you have done for us."

It was terrible! All the emotion, the gratitude, the hugging on his arms and the two faces, so alike, staring up at him, smiling, happy. He was confused, ashamed, worried, and the sheer physical contact of their bodies disturbed him.

"Good," he said coldly. "You must ensure he rests. Presumably he will stay here, in town, until he is better?"

"I shall stay too." She smiled. "Mama will go back to the farm and I shall stay here and look after George."

The implosion of pleasure again. She would be here, in

town, living with young Nicky and Leo Ferenc. He would see her—inevitably he would see her.

"A sensible arrangement," he said coolly.

Terez smiled again, and he noticed she was clean. He had grown so used to her with a dirty face and hair that to see her clean and pretty was surprising. He saw, too, that although she was like Nicky, yet she was not, for her face had feminine fullness where Nicky had angles, and her eyes, now that she was happy, narrowed at the corners in a disturbing, seductive way.

"How very alike you two are," he mused softly.

"Do you think so? I am supposed to be very like my mama."

"You're not a bit like your mother," he snapped. "Not at all. In no way are you like Madame Kaldy!"

"She was pretty when she was young," Terez invited naughtily. How quickly they recovered, the young ones. How quickly their spirits revived. She was a girl again; in spite of what the Russians had done, she was a girl.

"I would like to go home now," he said, suddenly longing for the quiet asceticism of his room, his bed, his books, the picture of the stag on the wall.

The naughty, flirtatious girl vanished and the young woman who had carried the other end of the stretcher said quietly, "I want to thank you again, Janos Marton. I am sorry my mother made everything worse than it needed to be. She will not thank you; she has forgotten it already because it was unpleasant and my mama does not remember things that are unpleasant. Especially she does not remember when she has been unpleasant. My papa, as soon as he has recovered, will come and thank you himself. He is old-fashioned and he does not approve of you—or Uncle Leo—but he will thank you, and he will never forget your deeds and your discipline with Mama. He knows her well enough to understand that only someone like you could have got her home."

She squeezed his arm, tilted her face towards his, and for one horrifying second he thought she was going to kiss him. She must have felt him flinch because she smiled again, the smile that narrowed her eyes, and then removed her arm from his.

"Come now, Nicky," she cried. "Let us go home. Janos Marton, would you like to come with us and tell everyone your adventures?"

"No," he said, horrified.

"Then good-bye."

They left, and he shifted the rucksack to make it more comfortable and then began to walk home. In his room he would be restored to order, discipline, and the controlled purpose to which he had dedicated his life. He would be calm, quiet, and—he smiled—he would be able to lie back on his bed and hear . . . nothing! The wonder of hearing nothing after days and days of Eva Kaldy!

But strangely, when he got there, when he had washed and unpacked the rucksack and stretched himself on his bed to try and sleep, the tranquillity would not come. His room was empty, and he felt an uneasy need that he could not at first define. After concentrated thought and rationalization he realized that his need was one of conditioning that could soon be overcome. It was for people—human contact—people he liked and who liked and needed him. George perhaps, young Nicky, Terez.

39

Once there had been money, unlimited money. There had been the farm and Papa's bank and all the securities and shares and land that the Ferencs and the Kaldys and the Racs-Rassays had amassed between them. And now, now there was nothing—no, not quite nothing, for Adam had 100 *hold* of stripped, grainless, cattleless land and the Kaldy farmhouse, and Leo and Nicky had the gutted Ferenc house and the salary from Leo's post as editor.

It was the way it should be, Leo told himself. A man should not be blessed with more than his neighbour when that neighbour was starving, ill-clothed, and ill-housed. Oh, yes, it was fair, the new system, but how was he going to keep them all— Nicky and George and Terez—on his salary? There were the taxes on the house (and how long would the house still be considered theirs?), medicine for George, and the price of food soared out of all proportion to his useless, inflated, newly printed money.

He began to understand—for the first time really understand—about poverty. It wasn't just hunger or cold or no shoes or sickness and death. It was constantly working out, sometimes on pieces of paper and sometimes in one's head, how to keep four people on one crazy, varying salary. (Money was useless; there was one morning when he had to price the paper at 20,000 *pengo* a copy!) Poverty was his feeling of relief when Adam managed to send from the farm a little food that somehow the Russians had overlooked; it was constant anxiety about young Nicky, who got thinner, coughed badly, tired easily, and obviously needed more than the lentils and black bread and dried beans that was their staple diet.

He knew that some of his comrades on the committee were taking advantage of their authority to steal, coerce, and buy extra food from black-market sources. But he had been told he was an idealist, and idealists did not do such things. Janos Marton didn't, and therefore neither would he because whatever that peasant child could do he could do also. In his mind Leo had a curious division of ethics. He could buy from the black market, or even cheat and steal, provided it did not infringe on his position as editor and committee member. If he could get hold of money or exchangeable goods in any way, he would happily pander to the joint Russian-Hungarian underground market that seemed to be flourishing in certain quarters. But how to get the money?

The burden grew. He felt like a married man with an ever-increasing family of dependents, for in July Adam brought Eva to the town, a tired, over-worked Adam and a frightened and fractious Eva.

"I think it best that Eva stay here with you, Leo," Adam said heavily. "It is growing difficult at the farm. The local Communist agent constantly harasses us, and the Russians up at the manor. . . . Eva's nerves are bad. After her terrible experiences she cannot bear the strains and pressures. Now that you are the important one of the family, the powerful one"—it was said without rancour, without bitterness, merely a bald statement of fact—"you are obviously the best person in the family to provide protection."

Oh, yes, true. But did Adam think that the importance and protection enabled him to feed yet another mouth?

"I'll send down some food, whatever I can find," Adam continued, "but I expect you don't have too much bother with extra supplies in your position." And now there *was* bitterness. "The Party men up at the farm do very well indeed, at my expense."

How could he explain to Adam that he did not do very well

indeed? Adam—poor, loyal, trustworthy old Adam—didn't understand at all about the new ways that were coming. He just thought that now there was a new aristocracy. Before the war, *he* had been one of the rich ones, and now the others, the peasants and Leo, were the rich ones. And because Leo was family he would provide for them all, just as they had provided for Leo in the old days.

He tried to explain; then his voice died away. A vain, foolish pride refused to let him ask Adam for money or food. He felt torn between his loyalty to the code of family and to his ethics of Party incorruptibility. He kissed his sister, promised to do his best, and then escorted his brother-in-law back to the bus station. It was surprising—shocking—to see Adam (younger son of the land-owning Kaldys) climbing onto a bus amidst peasants, workmen, and the odd Russian soldier. But that was the way it would be from now on, for all of them. No favours, no special treatment.

"Thank God we have some transport again," he said to Adam through the glassless window. "Everything is getting back to normal. Soon we shall be able to plan ahead, decide how we are going to live in the future." He smiled but his brother-in-law did not smile back. As the bus pulled away he wondered why he felt so very miserable, and on the way home he realized it was because he was worrying about the cost of feeding his sister.

It was Terez who helped. She understood, more than all the others. She came into his room that evening and shut the door so that no one else should hear what she was saying.

"Uncle Leo, I have found myself work—or rather Janos Marton has found it for me—in the Department of Agriculture at the County Offices. From now on we shall have two salaries to help keep us. And later—who knows?—we may even be able to persuade Mama to go out and try earning a little money."

She smiled, and his first reaction was one of infinite relief. He had to control himself from jotting down her prospective income on a piece of paper and allocating it to various expenses. And then he remembered the way she had been brought up, and the way his sisters had been brought up, and who she was—a Kaldy.

"Will you be able to manage, Terez?" he asked weakly. "I mean, you have never worked—not like that. What will your mama and your papa say?"

"Oh, Uncle Leo!" she said impatiently. "Do you think we don't know the world has changed? I'm nineteen years old and I've lived through the war! Do you think I'm going to sit at home waiting to get married like Mama did?"

"Will you know how to work?" he asked, realizing it was insulting as soon as he saw her flushed face.

"I wasn't exactly idiotic at school," she said stiffly. "If the war hadn't come I was going to persuade Papa to let me go to university, to study biology. I've not worked before—not like that in an office—but I think I'm bright enough to learn."

"Yes, of course," he apologized. "It will help considerably, Terez. I don't have to tell you how it will help."

"Nicky and George and I talked about it," she said. "George said that as soon as his leg was better he would get work too. And Nicky—" She paused. "Nicky came with me to see Janos. He wanted work too."

"And what did Comrade Marton say to that?" he asked coldly, resenting the way Marton was interfering in his family affairs.

"He told Nicky that he wanted him to go back to school, George too. He said that they would be of more service to him in the future if they were trained and educated."

Service to him! Not service to the country or their family but to him, Janos Marton!

"And afterwards, after they'd gone, he told me that he didn't think Nicky was strong enough to go to work or to school. He thinks Nicky is ill."

"Yes." The fear again, the fear that went with money and food and inflation. "Yes, Nicky is ill."

"He's going to find a doctor to come and see Nicky. A chest doctor."

"I see," he answered bleakly.

"I'm telling this to you now, Uncle Leo, so that when Nicky begins saying he wants to find some work, you will say what Janos has said—that he must go back to school in the autumn."

"Very well."

Her frown vanished. She smiled and hugged him. "Uncle Leo, I think I'm going to enjoy going out to work for my living!"

Eva shrieked and cried, lay on her bed with a wet cloth on her forehead and said her daughter had betrayed her. "Going out just like a factory girl or a streetwalker!" she screamed.

552

Leo wondered how it was possible that his sister was still living in a dream that had died before the First World War. She had spent a year disguised as a peasant, hiding from the Germans. She had survived bombing, the Russian liberation, and the stripping of her husband's family estate. And yet she was still behaving as though life consisted of nothing more than meeting friends for coffee and going to the dressmaker, the hairdresser, and a succession of balls and parties. He listened, astonished, to her tirade, and he listened, with even greater astonishment, to the way Terez handled her.

"Don't be ridiculous, Mama," she said coolly. "No amount of screaming will prevent me from working. If you want to eat, then I must provide food for you, must I not?"

Eva sobbed, dissolved, said how cruel the world was when a mother couldn't even afford to indulge her pretty daughter any more. Terez just patted her hand and said, "That's better, Mama. Much better. Don't make things difficult for us."

"Difficult!" Another shriek. "How could I make things difficult when the Russians have already done that?"

Another pat, affectionate but also admonitory. "No more noise please, Mama. It will be very enjoyable, going to work every day. And besides"—her dark eyes flashed wickedly—"I may meet some suitable young men at the County Offices! Where else am I to meet men these days?"

"A fine kind of man you will meet there," grumbled Eva, but she was quieter, more thoughtful, and later she asked Leo to see if there were any trunks left in the cellars, any of their old clothes that the ransackers had missed.

"My poor little girl," she moaned. "No pretty clothes to wear. Going out into the world with no pretty clothes. I want to alter some things, make her a dress—some blouses—anything pretty."

An occupation! Something to keep Eva busy and stop her from wailing all the time. He watched her cut and alter, stitch and furbish all the old garments of twenty and thirty years ago. Her complaints changed to reminiscences and he realized that Eva had blotted out the knowledge that her daughter was going to work "like a factory girl or a streetwalker." Terez was going into society. That her debut involved her going to the County Offices every day at eight o'clock was part of the changing times. But at least she would go in suitable garments.

From his Party office in the main square he watched her

every day, watched her treading lightly along the cobbles, her slender bare arms swinging out in the sun. Some mornings he could see she was singing. He couldn't hear, but he could see her lips moving and could tell, from the way she walked, that a special rhythm was sending her along.

It became part of his day, looking at his watch at about 8:25 A.M. and then rising from his desk and going to the window, watching her in the morning sunlight. One morning the phone rang just as he was about to rise and without waiting to hear who it was he just said, "Marton here. Please ring me back in a few moments," but when he got to the window he had missed the best part of her and she was disappearing into the County Offices.

She was young, full of hope and energy, and yet there was something old-fashioned about her, something that reminded him of the Ferenc and Kaldy ladies sitting on their verandas, that reminded him even of his own mother, although Terez was dark, brown-eyed, tiny, where his mother had been fair and tall.

She still wore her hair in braids at a time when every other girl had short hair curled into the neck. The braids were piled up high and wound round on the top of her head. It made her look just a little taller than she was. And her clothes were old-fashioned. Everyone's clothes at this time were old and shabby, but Terez wore frocks that looked like dresses of thirty years ago. There was a cream one with a lace collar that made him remember—still with a faint stab of pain—his mother, although he could not think why, because his mother had never owned a dress like that. And then one day, as the sun slanted onto the lace collar, making everything yellow and light, he remembered the cottage and the sunlight shafting in through his mother's lace curtains, and although the lace of the curtains and that of the girl's dress were different, the sunlight, the golden shafts, and the feeling of happiness were the same.

At 12:30, she left the County Offices and walked across the square to the terrace café that had once been the Franz-Josef and was now (as a tribute to their liberators) the Café Moscow. There she ordered a coffee and took from her bag a carefully wrapped parcel containing black bread. He couldn't see if it were a sandwich (perhaps she had a little cheese?) or just bread, but she bit into it with all the gusto of a healthy nineteen-year-old who never had quite enough to eat. At 1:10 she finished her coffee and walked back to the County Offices. He didn't see her any more after that because he became very busy in the afternoon and often had to go out on business. But the mornings, and then the lunchtimes, became isolated moments of his life in which he drifted into a past of sunlight and lace that was also the presence of a young woman who had said she was his friend.

Summer came, the warm, soft, dry weather. It was more difficult to be ascetic, rational, all the time in summer. He had always found it harder to bear his restrictions in the hot months. As a child, sent away from home, the miseries, the loneliness, the insults and laughter had always been harder in the summer. And then as a man, disciplining himself, he had found it encouraged self-indulgence, found it harder to ignore outside distractions and concentrate on plans and policies. One summer he had even indulged in a brief, somewhat torpid affair with a visiting Party member, a thick-set young woman who was five years older than he. The affair had taken excitement from the shared secret fear of arrest and imprisonment that faced them all in those days. But he knew it would not have developed at any other time of the year except the summer.

And now, this summer, the summer of his success, his climax of achievement after years of ideological struggle, he was drifting into foolishness again—foolishness that he recognized, deplored, but that made him walk down to the Café Moscow one lunchtime and stand beside her table.

"Hello, Janos," she said through a mouthful of bread. "Are you going to have coffee?"

He sat, not answering, disgusted with himself. How pretty she was, how bright and cheerful—no problem of rejection or insecurity—how very much like Nicky.

"How is your cousin?" he asked abruptly. "How is young Nicky?"

"He's resting, like your doctor told him to. He lies in bed all the time and we've asked Papa to try and send some fresh food down from the farm if he can."

"It would be better if he went and stayed on the farm. He needs to rest where the air is good."

Terez stopped chewing, and her eyes clouded a little. "He doesn't want to go. He gets agitated every time we mention it and makes himself ill—his temperature rises and he doesn't sleep. Uncle Leo and I thought it better that he stays."

"He's waiting for his mother to come home," Janos said slowly.

555

Terez nodded, staring agreement at him. How huge her eyes were, how soft, like Nicky's.

"Why are your clothes so old-fashioned?" he heard himself asking, and then was shocked—shocked because he had asked so personal a question and shocked because it had obviously upset her. A flush spread up from the lace collar and she put a hand up and straightened it needlessly. "I'm sorry," he said, flustered. "It was impertinent of me. I should not have asked."

"They're my Aunt Malie's old clothes cut down," she answered, looking down at the table. "They're very old—it's the best Mama could find. I lost my clothes when we went to Magyarovar, and when I came back all my old things were too small."

"I'm sorry," he said again.

"I expect I look very funny."

"You look beautiful!"

She was as astonished as he was.

For a moment they stared at each other across the table, too stunned to say anything more. And then, "Excuse me," and he rose stiffly from the chair. "I must return to my office."

Back in his cool, safe office, with the telephones and the tray of Party papers and the files of everything that had happened in the town, he drew a deep, tranquillizing breath and determined never to speak to her again. When he walked across to the window she was still there—it was 1:15; she would be late!—and when she finally rose and walked back across the square she stopped briefly and stared straight up at his window. She raised her hand in a shy, half movement of acknowledgment, and fully intending not to, he found that he had answered her salute with a wave of his own hand. It was the summer, and the fact that she looked like young Nicky and wore a dress with a lace collar that the sunlight turned to yellow.

Everyone looked strange and shabby that year. Clothes had been destroyed, stolen, and had worn out, and there were no more. Occasionally you saw a smart, well-dressed woman, but always she was with a Russian officer or in a café with fat men exchanging wallets of mixed currency. Everyone else was worn, tired, and dingy. Women who had been elegant before the war looked like peasants, and peasants looked like beggars.

Leo, trudging home from the printer's on a hot September afternoon, wished he still had some of the lightweight alpaca

suits, flannel trousers, and canvas shoes of pre-war summers.
He was all right. He had a suit—he had found it in the Arrow
Cross man's apartment—but it was thick winter-weight and
even without the jacket, just wearing the trousers as he was
now, it made him feel heavy and lethargic.

Mustn't complain, he thought to himself. How lucky I
am, how lucky. He watched an old woman in front of him
and thought how hot she too must be, wearing a man's army
greatcoat tied round the waist with string and a shapeless
black beret on her head. She looked like a beggar but was
probably, he reflected sadly, a peasant or smallholder who
had lost everything in the war. She had a bundle—black cotton—that was dragging on the ground beside her. Thin wisps
of white hair frayed out from the pulled-down beret.

The war . . . the war. That is how we all look, how we all
feel, he thought tiredly. She's worse than some of us, but not
really. We're all like that inside.

The sight of her dragging along suddenly depressed him
and he turned his head away and rushed past her. Repeatedly
he found himself unable to believe in the new wonderful
Hungary that was going to emerge. There were too many people like the old beggar woman, too many untilled fields, too
many wrecked factories, mutilated families. How could any
kind of phoenix arise from ashes like these?

He hurried home, nearly racing, until the sweat ran down
his face to lie in thick salty patches around the inside of his
collar. Get away from them all—from the newspaper, from
poverty, from the shouted unrest of the world—get home to
where he was cocooned for a while with people he knew and
loved.

As he opened the door he could hear, whining down the
stairs from the upper apartment, the complaining voice of
Eva. He screwed his eyes into a grimace of pain, leant against
the door and sighed. It had been many years since he had
spent any length of time with Eva, since he had gone to Berlin, in fact, and he found it hard to reconcile the transformation of Eva the girl, vivacious if a little spoilt and sharp, to the
whining, querulous woman who now filled the apartment. The
war again . . . the war had done this to her.

He was still leaning against the door when someone
knocked on the outside. It was so unexpected it made him
jump away, swearing crossly at yet another irritant in the hot
day. When he opened it the old beggar woman was standing
there. She's followed me all the way home, he thought angri-

557

ly. Someone to beg from. I lok as though I'm rich so she thinks she can come here and ask for food and clothing. He glared at the greatcoat tied up with string, at the feet breaking out of a pair of cracked shoes, at the lined walnut face with a complexion as weathered and rubbery as a man's.

"Yes?"

She stared at him, not speaking, but with her lower jaw working and her face breaking down into a welter of ridges and lines. Something cold moved in his stomach.

"What do you want?"

A croak that sounded like a word emerged. The terrible face moved and writhed again, toothless, but even in ugliness growing increasingly familiar, frighteningly familiar. And then—

"Leo," the face said finally. "Leo . . . Leo . . . Leo . . ." and the old woman stretched her hand out and touched his shoulder.

"Oh, my God!" he whispered. "Is it you, Malie? Is it you?"

She nodded. That was all, just nodded. She didn't touch him again, or try to come in. The hand that was holding the bundle curled tighter round the cloth.

Malie, bending over his bed with a napkin of delicacies stolen from a party. . . . Malie with her shoes and stockings off, paddling in a mountain stream with a young hussar officer. . . . Malie laughing, running through the acacia woods in a soft lawn dress. . . .

"Malie!" he cried, tears and sweat breaking out together all over his body. "Oh, my God! Malie, Malie!" She stumbled over the step, the terrible face still moving, and he threw back his head and screamed, "It's Malie! It's Malie!" and then he pressed his face into the door and groaned, feeling such anguish and pain that he wanted to hurt himself, bang his head against the door until his senses became dead, obliterated in physical sensation.

Nobody heard. Surprisingly nobody heard. Eva's voice whined on and no sounds of movement came from upstairs. He sobbed into the door and then felt the old woman's hand on his shoulder again.

"Leo." The voice was the same, soft, gentle, the voice of Malie, his beloved and beautiful sister, and the voice destroyed all the fear and shock. He drew her into his arms, his heart filling with shame, swelling with pain. She was tiny now, his big sister was a little old woman, and gently, gently, he rocked her to and fro, crooning as though she were a child.

"Malie, Malie." The smell of old clothes and dust and malnutrition. The feel of a small body, knotted with swollen joints, destroyed. What had they done to her? "Oh, God, Malie! My dearest, darling Malie! You've come home. You'll be safe now. You're home with your Leo and we'll never let you go away again."

He took the beret from her head. Thin, sawn-off hair, dirty white. *Malie with her brown hair piled high for a party, then falling round her shoulders when she came to say good night....*

"Leo, my sons—have my sons come home?"

"No, darling," he wept. "No, no."

"Karoly? Jacob?"

"No, darling! No!"

"Have you heard? Has anyone sent news?"

"No, Malie. No news."

"Aaiee!" her head tilted back, eyes closed, mouth open, and she began to weep. "Aaiee! Aaiee!"

He could feel the pain of sobbing deep down in her body and he held her close, rocking and soothing. "Hush, Malie. Hush, my darling!" *Malie, the young matron, stately, smiling, presiding over her husband's table in a green silk dress....*

He found they were sitting on the bottom stair and through the open door he could see into the courtyard—the sun pouring down onto the stones, the dust piled thickly where no one had had time to sweep. It was hours since he had walked through the courtyard and opened the door, hours.

"Hush, Malie. Quiet now. You are home, home with your family."

"Who?" she whispered at last. "Who has come home?"

"Eva is safe, and Adam and the children—George and Terez. And young Nicky."

She nodded slowly, with sad but fatalistic acceptance. "Nicky, yes. How pleased Kati would be, to know her Nicky survived."

He had to know—to learn what had happened to the others, to her. She was old and tired and should be put to bed, but before the family came down he had to know.

"What happened to you?" he asked hoarsely. "To you and David and Mama and Papa. All of you?"

"You know what happened, Leo," she breathed, staring out into the sunlight in a queer disorientated way. "Everyone knows what happened."

559

"Where are the others?"

Her face screwed into pain again.

"Dead, all except my sons." Her eyes opened suddenly and entreated Leo. "If you have heard nothing, perhaps my sons are still alive!"

"Perhaps, Malie," he said heavily.

"I saw Jacob," she said, staring at nothing. "When we were going into Auschwitz, we saw men in prison clothes working on the electric cables. And Kati pulled me and said, 'Look, there is Jacob.' 'No,' I said, 'Jacob is in Germany. They took him straight to Germany.' But Kati is sure it is Jacob. I shout to him and the S.S. guard with the dog tells me he will set the dog on me if I shout again. I say to him, 'What sort of man are you? That is my son! Have you no feelings? You do not have a mother?' I shout again and Jacob calls to me, 'Go on, you will be all right.' " She stopped, and her hands dropped suddenly in front of her, down between her knees, and she stared at them.

"What happened, Malie?"

"What?" She looked at him, uncomprehending. "That is all."

"What happened to Mama and Papa, to David, Kati, and all the others from the town?"

"Dead. Now I know they are dead. At the time I thought we were divided for different reasons: health, or for baths. Mama, Papa, David—they were sent away. Too old, you see? Kati and I—they kept us, first to Bergen Belsen, and then to the factory . . . Germany."

"And Kati? What happened to Kati?"

Malie stared into the air again. "She stole a tin of meat."

"Yes?"

"Kati is dead."

"Are you sure of this, Malie? Because of Nicky, you must be sure."

"Kati is dead," she said tonelessly.

He could ask her no more, but already he was thinking about the next thing that would happen. Nicky. Nicky would want to know if—how his mother had died.

"Malie, listen to me." He took her hands between his and tried to infuse steadfastness into her body with his eyes and hands. "Nicky is very ill. He has tuberculosis and he must rest all the time and not be upset. He refuses to believe his mother is dead; he has been convinced, right from the beginning, that she would come back here. Malie, are you listening?"

She was. At last he knew he had her attention; she had begun to listen to him at some point after he said Nicky was ill.

"Malie, if you know how Kati died—and if it was bad—I beg you not to tell Nicky."

"She was beaten to death by the woman S.S. guard," Malie said dully.

He gripped her hands again and whispered, "Malie, you have suffered so much. It is cruel to ask you to have to pretend, to make up lies to protect others, but tell Nicky his mother died . . . easily. Later, when he is cured, you can speak the truth."

"What can I say?" she cried. "What can I tell him that will make it any better? What can I say to any of them?"

"Nothing, my darling. I will tell them. I will tell them everything."

"Yes, yes!" she began to cry again. "I'm so tired, Leo, so very tired . . ."

"I will say to Nicky that his mother died of a heart attack —at night—and you were with her. She didn't wake and it was over in a second. All you have to do is say yes when Nicky asks you if it was so. That is all."

She nodded, crying quietly into her hands. He kissed her, stroked her, fondled the sparse hair and the coarse-grained skin of her neck.

"I want you to wait here, Malie," he whispered. "Just for one moment while I go and prepare them. Then you can go to bed. We will make some water hot for you to bathe, and you will sleep."

She was slumped against the wall as he pushed past, up the stairs, with a heavy heart. The happiness of Malie's return was tempered by her ravaged body and by the news she had brought with her.

Later, when the evening of gladness and sorrow had passed, when Nicky and Malie had been talked away into sleep and when everyone else—shocked, stunned, tearful, afraid—had finally been tired into silence, he lay on his bed, closed his eyes, and tried not to see the memories that Malie had given him.

She lay on her bed for a long time, staring up at the ceiling and then turning her face into the pillow and weeping. They could hear her all over the apartment when she wept. It was terrible and it was worse when it happened at night. It didn't sound like a woman crying, it was like the noise of an animal in pain.

Within a few days of her return the old women began knocking on the door, dreadful old women with ravaged faces and stained hands. "Did you see my sister? My brother? My parents? My child? What happened to the Maryk family, to the Jacobys, the Kohns?" Old women who all looked the same, who had huge eyes and trembling mouths. And every time they came Malie would drag herself from the bed and sit quietly, listening to names and descriptions, shaking her head. "No, no, I didn't see them, I don't know what happened to him—" and on one occasion, after a pause, "She is dead. I know that one is dead."

Sometimes, with no prompting or questioning, she would begin to talk. They would be eating their meal or cleaning the apartment and she would begin talking about Lili or Marta or Suzi—women they did not know but who were intimate friends to Malie because she had shared misery with them.

"On the train. . . . Going to the factory . . . one morning there is an explosion. We hear bombs dropping and the guard is shouting. And the bombs grow worse. It is hot and Lili falls on her knees and begins to pray: 'Let the doors open. Oh, God, let the doors open.' We push, it is a cattle car, and together we push from inside until the bar breaks open. The factory is in flames, the Germans lying dead, and in the sky are noises of cannon—"

She stopped then, abruptly, the way she frequently did. "Yes, Malie, what happened then?" and her blank puzzled stare.

"What happened?"

"Yes, Malie. What happened when you saw the factory burning and the guards dead?"

"We hid. Until the Red Cross came in three days later." Said without interest, as though it had happened to someone else. And again: "When the guard beat Kati I tried to help her. I was beaten too." She remembered then and looked at Leo, afraid. "I'm sorry, Leo," she whispered. "I forgot."

"'It's all right. Nicky is in his room. He cannot hear." But he was afraid that this maddened and melancholy woman would one day forget and speak the truth in front of Nicky, who had grown thinner, more feverish, more flushed since he had heard that his mother was dead.

The day following Malie's return, Janos Marton walked into the house with Terez. It was the first time he had been there since—as a child—he had visited the kitchen. Now, with cool disinterest, he walked through the shabby rooms to stand by Nicky's bedside.

"Why did you bring him?" Leo hissed furiously at his niece. "Why did you bring him at this of all times? Strangers in the house with your aunt just returned to us and Nicky shocked and ill. Why did you have to let him come here?"

"I asked him," she replied, "because of Nicky."

"What do you mean, because of Nicky?" Already the familiar angry spasm twisted through his chest. Janos Marton was part of his life outside the family, part of his work, part of the town and government. He had no right in this house.

"Nicky loves him."

"Don't be foolish, Terez. Nicky is grateful to Janos for hiding him during the war. He doesn't love him."

"Nicky loves him." She shrugged. "I thought you knew that. And Janos loves Nicky, in his funny, cold way."

He hurried into Nicky's room and saw the pair of them there, Nicky's eyes bright with unshed tears and Janos, sitting by his bed, cold, expressionless, not saying anything at all.

"Nicky is ill," he said hurriedly. "He is upset and he must not talk or be disturbed."

"Oh, Uncle Leo, let him stay! Let Janos stay!" The boy's voice wobbled unhappily, tears nearly ready to unman the slight composure.

"I have come to talk about the election," said Janos distantly. "Nicky lies here in bed all day. It is time he learned what is happening to his country—the first free election in the history of Hungary, the first time we have a secret ballot. Nicky should learn of these things and be proud."

"Let me listen!" Nicky cried, and Leo, strangely miserable, left the room without answering.

"You should not have brought him in!" he whispered again to Terez. "He is nothing to do with us, nothing to do with Nicky or you and me."

"Nicky's mother is dead, Aunt Kati is dead," she said tonelessly. "And whether you like it or not, after his mother, Janos Marton is the most important person in Nicky's life."

"No, no, that is not true. Why should Nicky like him better than his own family?"

"Because he is strong, loyal, and because"—a slow flush

spread up from the collar of her dress—"because he is a poet and understands about—"

"About what?"

"About how Nicky feels about his mother."

"And I—we don't understand?" he asked bitterly.

"Not in the same way."

He felt again the sour twist of jealousy. He had accepted that Marton was more successful than he at administration, at cool planning and mathematical precision. But now Terez was trying to pretend that the man was also a dreamer, a visionary, the very things that Marton had accused Leo of being.

When Janos came out of Nicky's room he nodded politely to Leo. "How is your sister?" he asked.

"She will be all right," Leo replied curtly. He wanted no more of Janos Marton's interference in his family life.

"I will come again, to see Nicky. I will come as often as the elections allow," he said, and strode down the stairs without waiting for an answer.

"How young he looks from the back," he heard Terez murmur beside him, and he stared at the retreating figure, noting the bony shoulders and the dark blond hair curling in at the back of his thin neck. "He looks rather sad from behind," she continued dreamily. "He doesn't look important or strong when you see the back of him, does he, Uncle Leo?"

Leo didn't answer. His heart was too full of wild and varying emotions.

40

He came to see Nicky two or three times a week, and all he ever did was talk about Hungary, the election, the future of which Nicky must, one day, be a part. To Nicky, trying to escape the sound of his Aunt Malie's weeping, the visits of his friend were an escape from his own misery and from the misery of those around him.

His grief for his mother was not assuaged by the kindness of his family. Aunt Eva's sentimental tears—"You still have us, my darling boy! You have lost your dearest mama, but you have your old aunts who love you just as well!"—served only to emphasize his loss. His Uncle Leo's admonishments to "try not to grieve too much, Nicky" and even George and Terez's silent sympathy did nothing for him, only served to refresh the memories of the woman who had been his one tie with warmth and love for the early and most important part of his life. Only his friend, Janos Marton, gave him brief respites of peace from his memories: Marton's dispassionate greetings and casual farewells, his impersonal discussions about the election (which *were* emotional, but in a safe and abstract way), these things gave him hope, lifted him from his misery—made worse because of his forced inactivity—and encouraged him to believe that there was a future without pain, a future in which he could take interest and heart.

After a few such visits it became the custom for first George, then Terez, to join the little parties in Nicky's room. It was as though Janos Marton was holding a youthful seminar, lecturing on the future of their country, on the new emancipation and legislation that would soon take place. Leo, joining them once, had been filled with such rancour that he was never part of them again. Everything that Marton had said to the children was right and true—he could not have said it so well himself—and therefore he could not argue or correct. But his resentment was such that he needed, in some way, to remove the adoration from Nicky's eyes and the interest and warmth from Terez's. There was nothing he could say, nothing that would not bring disrepute upon himself, for any criticisms he levelled at Marton would have to be personal. Even in his jealousy he was not small enough to ridicule the many things available to ridicule—the clothes and accent, the mannerisms of the country that Marton had not entirely succeeded in throwing off.

The election consumed them both, in time and energy and emotional endeavour. Leo's articles and editorship of *Liberation* became more ardent. There were constant meetings in which he was by the side of—but slightly subservient to—Janos Marton, and even while his own enthusiasm was keen, he was able to observe that Marton's became almost frenzied. The man was tireless, his thin body hurrying from one meeting to the next, organizing, directing, giving his heart to a cause as he had never, since childhood, given it to a living person.

The Party did not get in. In their town they were successful, and in fact their defeat made little difference to the overriding power of the Party—the Russians were there to see the Party was never . . . overlooked—but the defeat was a strongly psychological one. Could it be that Hungary did not want a Communist government?

When the national results of the election were known he watched Janos Marton crumble, and though he should himself have been sorry, his first reaction was one of deep gratification.

"So," he said, trying to hide his satisfaction, "your prognostications have not come true. We shall have to wait a little longer for your perfect Hungary."

The blue eyes turned to stare at him and he was suddenly ashamed. They had both worked hard. Was his dream, his ideal, so much less than Marton's that it could be swept away in momentary revenge?

"Perhaps . . . next time," he mumbled, but Marton's blue eyes continued to stare, cold, calculating, and in their depths something of hurt, the betrayal of a child.

"Next time, or the time after that," he said slowly. "It must be so."

When he came to talk to Nicky after that there was no more of the election. But still the talks were of the future, of the proud new Hungary that was going to emerge.

They got through the winter of '45–'46 somehow, as everyone else did. There was only just enough food, just enough fuel, just enough money. The gutted downstairs apartment was requisitioned by the authorities and given to a refugee family from Pozsony. George went back to school, an unheated and thinly staffed school, and Nicky continued resting—and coughing. The worst of that winter was Malie.

After the first weeks of madness and isolation from them all, she began to eat . . . and eat . . . and eat. There was little except black bread, potatoes, and beans, with sometimes a few eggs and a small ration of cheese, but Malie ate everything that came her way and then went out and found—somewhere—more rations, extra food. Automatically they saved the best for Malie and Nicky. The rest of them, even Eva, left the biggest portions, the few delicacies, for these two who by their very condition needed more than the rest. Malie ate, and still it was not enough. In her room she kept a tin containing bread that she sprinkled with sugar from their joint rations and ate throughout the night. His room, that he shared with George, was next to Malie's, and at night he could hear the lid of the tin being removed, or the rustling of paper if she had won some special treat during the day. Throughout a winter of thin, tired, sallow-looking people, he had to watch his sister (she had been so graceful) swelling with the unhealthy fat of a badly balanced diet. The thin, stick-like legs changed within months, feet swelling over her cracked shoes, clothes straining across her bulging stomach and thighs.

"Malie, my darling, why do you eat so much?"

"I am hungry."

What could he say? What could any of them say? The eating was better than the weeping, though sometimes he thought it was the same.

In January she came out of her room one morning dressed in the greatcoat tied up with string.

"I need money, Leo," she said quietly.

He thought she was going in search of food again. "How much?"

"I need the fare to Budapest."

"Later, Malie. Perhaps in the summer I will take you to Budapest. It is not a good place to go now."

"You think I am mad, Leo," she said gently. "I am not mad. I am going to look for my sons. Mrs. Hofer has said there is a place in Budapest where one can find news of soldiers who went to Russia. Karoly—remember he was in the Labour Corps—he was in Russia. Perhaps he has come home, perhaps he is sick somewhere, or a prisoner. I must go and look for him. And then Jacob. Someone must have news. I can ask everyone, all those who came back."

"You can't go now, Malie. Wait until the weather is warmer."

Very gently she began to cry. "All the time, in the camp, in the factory, I prayed to God: 'Please let one of my sons be alive, just one.' I did not pray for David or for Mama and Papa—even then I knew it was no good—but if only one son is left, I said, just one son—" She put her hand to her mouth. "Give me the money to go to Budapest and look for my son."

He was afraid to let her go alone, so he gave them both the money, Eva and Malie. Eva made her remove the man's coat and wear something she had bartered from the refugee family below. He saw the two of them to the station, wondering just what fresh catastrophe might occur to them in the war-torn capital, and with the Russians still swarming over the land. He was mad to let them go, but it would have been worse to have prevented her.

They were gone for two weeks and returned tired and sad. There was no news, but Malie had heard of someone at Debrecen whose son had returned from Russia, from Karoly's Labour Corps. She rested a few days, then went to Debrecen, and returned without news except that a man in Eger had been a prisoner of the Russians, captured just where Karoly was stationed.

She stopped eating now. She became thin again and every few days—weeks—he saw her to the station, sometimes with Eva, sometimes without. Every time she returned she was a little more tired, a little more sad, and yet with each hopeless trek he sensed that something of the old Malie was returning. She was tired and old now—she would always be that—but beneath the sorrow and hopelessness was sanity.

There came a day in April when she said to him, "Your chest is better now, isn't it, Leo?"

He looked at her carefully, wondering if once more she was thinking of her year in the camp, of some old ailment that had afflicted one of her fellows.

"Your chest," she said again. "Don't you remember, Leo, when you were a boy you had a weak chest and had to go and spend the winter with Eva and Adam at the farm. Don't you remember?"

Relief flooded over him, relief and with it joy, because this was the first time she had spoken of anything except her sons or what had happened to her.

"It was Nicky coughing in the night," she said. "It reminded me of when you were ill and I wondered if we could send Nicky to the farm."

"Adam says it is not safe. The Russians are headquartered in the old manor and everything is very difficult." The difficulties that he did not want to worry her with were the increasing bad feelings between Adam—a relic of the old aristocracy—and the local committee. There was no knowing how long Adam would be in possession of what remained of his land.

"Why don't you speak to your influential friend?" she asked gently. "He has done so much for us—for Nicky—perhaps he would help us now."

"Janos Marton?"

She nodded. "I was so foolish, such a silly woman," she murmured. "I thought it was him giving us away to the Nazis. I went to ask him to leave us alone. I was so foolish. Nothing could have stopped what was happening, nothing." She began to cry again and he wanted to calm her, before the weeping brought back madness.

568

"All right, Malie, I'll talk to him." He wanted to ask no further favours from Marton, but against his sister's melancholy and his nephew's sickness he had no choice.

There had been changes at Party Headquarters throughout the winter. He had been so busy with *Liberation* and with his family that the changes had only made a dim impression on him. A new comrade had come down from Budapest, and then another. He had met one but his appointment with the other had been cancelled, he could not remember why. There had also been a guard placed on the door of the Party offices, some kind of security check, but again he had thought little of it during the passing months.

When he went to see Janos Marton he was surprised to see two guards on the door, neither of them the rather genial middle-aged man who had stood there throughout the winter.

"Where's Mikos?" he asked, surprised, but received only a demand to show his card. He began to grow annoyed. It reminded him of the war when one was constantly having to show one's papers.

When he went into Marton's office he attacked without preamble. "Why do we have the *pandur* on our doors now? I thought the old days were dead!"

Marton didn't answer, but Leo caught a fleeting spasm of annoyance cross his face. Annoyed with whom? With him or with the guards?

"It's a new . . . precaution," he said tonelessly. "Comrade Lengyel gave orders."

"Lengyel?"

"From Party Headquarters."

"Oh. I see."

He didn't see, and they stared at one another blankly for a moment.

"What did you want?" Janos Marton asked.

"Ah, yes." He sat down. Marton had not asked him to but he put that down to forgetfulness, or the fact that his manners were bad. "It is about . . . about young Nicky. His chest is still very weak. My sister—my sister who was in Germany—she noticed it this morning and asked if there was no way he could be sent to the country. She wanted him to go to my brother-in-law's farm, the Kaldy farm. Ah! But of course you know where I mean." Sometimes when he was in Marton's office he forgot that they both came from the same family estate. It was a genuine mistake but Marton stared coldly, as though suspecting him of jeering.

"Of course I know it," he replied coolly. "And I do not think it would be wise for Nicky to go there. Quite apart from anything else the farm is not high enough. He should go to the mountains, to a sanatorium."

Leo snorted. "A sanatorium? In these times?"

"It may be possible. Not a sanatorium, no, but a place to live up in the mountains." He paused and stared down at his desk. "Matrafured. It is possible I could find a place for Nicky to stay in Matrafured. But one of your sisters—or Terez—would have to go with him. Two rooms in a house. They would cost nothing; that I could arrange. But someone must go to look after him."

"When will you know?"

"A week, possibly less. I will come and tell you."

He hurried home, a plan fizzing at the back of his mind, a plan based not on logic or even hope but on a vague instinct that this—this of all things—might help not only Nicky but also his sister Malie.

Over the supper table he explained Marton's proposition. Before anyone else could say anything, he rushed on. "I do not think we can spare Terez. She is earning money here and if Nicky is to go to the mountains we shall need money. The rooms may be free, but the food will not be. Someone must work and send money for Nicky. So that leaves you, Eva, or Malie."

Eva looked unhappy. "I'll go, of course, Leo. But then I have my duty here, to my children. Who will look after them? George is still at school, and Terez—Terez is of an age when a girl needs a mother's care. But of course I will go where my duty lies . . . if only I knew where my duty lies!"

"Your children are hardly babies, Eva," he could not refrain from saying. "Terez is nearly twenty and George is eighteen."

"But they need a mother's care, a mother's love!"

"Nicky needs someone too," said Malie quietly.

"Will you go, Malie?" He looked straight across the table at her. "I know you are afraid of going away, but who else will look after Nicky?"

"I don't want to go," she faltered. "I don't want to go away again."

"For Kati. Can't you do it for Kati?"

He watched her eyes withdraw into some secret world, saw her remembering, and wished he had not been so cruel. They were blurring a little, her memories, not much, but a little, and now he had forced her to look back again. The silence and her staring grew interminable, and then came the noise of Nicky coughing, and for once the sound was welcome.

"I suppose I must go," she whispered. "He *is* sick, isn't he?"

"Yes, Malie."

"And no one else can go?"

He could have lied to her, but he hoped that enough of the old Malie was there for him to tell the truth. "Eva *could* go. We all, including Eva, know that she *could* go."

"But my children—"

"She *could* go," he cut in, "but Eva is not the nurse I would choose for Nicky—not when he has to pass several months alone with her."

Surprisingly there was no retort from Eva, and he looked to see her sitting red-faced but relieved. A tiny shadow of a smile crossed Malie's face and a pain moved through his chest. It was the first time Malie had smiled since her return.

"I must do it, then," she said. "He has no one else."

The two of them, the weakest of his family, going alone into the country to look after each other. The pain in his chest grew worse.

"When must we go?" she murmured.

"It is still unsettled. Janos Marton will tell us, probably the next time he comes to see Nicky."

"I think I'll go and prepare him," she said, rising suddenly from her chair. "It will be a shock for him. He will not want to leave you all."

She left the room, a bent, elderly woman with thinning hair, and though the ache in his heart would not disperse he believed that he had given her once more a little pattern to her life.

Janos Marton, their protector, their saviour in the new democratic system of things, gave more than he had promised. The rooms in Matrafured were obtained, and so was a car in which, he stated, he would drive Nicky, Malie, and one other up into the hills. He looked at no one when he asked for a fourth occupant and gave no sign of either pleasure or annoyance when Terez asked if she could go. And on a Sunday morning in early June he drove them up to Matrafured.

571

At last the country was fertile again; fields of wheat, maize, cabbages and root crops stretched away on every side. The winter was behind and nothing would be quite as bad again. This year the fields had been sown and with the new growth came hope—hope that suddenly communicated itself to the four people in the car.

"Such a lovely day," Malie murmured. "Like going up to the farm when we were young."

There was no one there who could remember or understand what she spoke of, but her voice was dreamy, not unhappy, and something of a past life communicated itself to the others.

"We had Uncle Sandor then," she mused. "Uncle Sandor and . . . Sultan. That was the name of the horse. And we were so excited when they came to take us up for the summer—so many trunks and boxes, so many dresses. The boys were always afraid of Uncle Sandor. Such a long time ago. Poor old man, he was killed by the revolutionaries in 1919."

A moment's discomfort filtered through the car. Janos Marton gave no indication that he had heard and Terez fidgeted in her seat.

"I think you will be comfortable in the house," Janos said when the moment had passed. "It is outside Matrafured, on the Matrahaza side. There is a lake and a clearing where you can sit and watch the pine trees."

"I shall like going to the country again."

Janos put the window of the car down, and the hot smell of the asphalt began to give way to other smells: warm grass, earth, the dry scent of grain.

"I'm sure to get well up in the country," Nicky enthused from the back seat. "I didn't think it would be like this. I know I'll get well again now."

They all knew that everything would be all right. Nothing could go wrong when the sun was so bright and the ground was fertile once more. Malie suddenly felt that she was going to be contented again one day, that the demented thoughts that raced through her head at night would grow less. She did not feel afraid of summer in the country any more. She knew she could make Nicky well again, knew she could look after him, perhaps—later—earn money enough to send him to college. But before that there was the summer, at peace in the mountains.

And Janos Marton knew that everything would be all right with the Party and with Hungary. His recent fears, the uneasiness that something not quite right was happening, that the Russians would not leave, all vanished into the sun. Little teething problems, soon settled, not to be worried about too long. He was confident today—helping Nicky, his friend, and with the girl in the lace collar by his side. It was summer. He could relax a little; it was summer.

Terez had no worries to evaporate in the country air—at least, no more than those she had lived with since the war began. There was Aunt Malie and Nicky, and worrying about Papa up at the farm, and being irritated with Mama and concerned about money with Uncle Leo. But apart from these ever-present things she had no worries. The thing the Russians had done to her had been pushed away into the darkest part of her mind, pushed so far that she was able to feel young and excited again, excited because she was sitting next to a man whose thin, whipcord body roused a tensing desire in her own. She glanced sideways at him and thought, not for the first time, that if only he would smile he would be handsome. He had removed his coat and his tie, and the open neck of his shirt revealed a tanned skin and smooth throat. His arms reaching out to the wheel of the car were muscular and covered lightly with dark blond hair. The sight was disturbing—both disturbing and exciting. Coming back she would be alone with him. Would he be silent, uncommunicative? Or would the summer thaw his customary icy control?

They came to the house and it was exactly as he had described: a lake, a clearing, and pine trees growing up a knoll that masked the side of the mountain.

"The woman is the widow of a partisan member," he explained. "He died a hero. Now she makes a living by selling cheese—the Party presented her with a goat as tribute to her late husband—and she also has rooms which the Party use when they wish." He paused and added in a distant voice, "She is a peasant, a smallholder, Mrs. Klein. You will find her . . comfortable to be with."

He was kind, Terez thought. He didn't approve of the way they had lived before the war, but he understood that Aunt Malie was too old to absorb new ways. A woman described as a Party member's widow would only have frightened her. A peasant woman sounded comfortable and familiar.

The rooms were ready and Nicky walked slowly to his bed and climbed in. It faced the open window, and he could see the lake and the pine trees and the mountain behind. He was asleep when they left. Terez kissed her aunt good-bye, trying to conceal the mounting excitement in her heart, telling herself that in all probability he wouldn't even speak to her on the return journey.

Just past Matrafured, on the south side, he stopped the car and climbed out. "We've time to walk up a little," he said, staring over her head. "There used to be a meadow at the end of this track. I shot a pheasant there once."

He didn't wait for her answer, just began to climb the track, through rocks and stubby grass. Quickly she followed him. "Don't you want to lock the car?" she cried. The back of his neck reddened a little and he came back and locked both doors. When he caught up again she let her hand brush against his. They neither of them looked at each other and they spoke as strangers, but their hands clasped and held fast, the fingers caressing and warm, saying things they could not say with words. They moved on two separate planes, the state of Janos Marton and Terez Kaldy who did not speak, or spoke only coldly, and the being of their hands that longed and stroked and made love. They did not know how to bridge these two planes and make them one, so they were careful not to confuse words with touch in case the one should destroy the other.

The sun beat down on the side of the hill, and they came to a place where three arms of the track faced them. He hesitated a moment and then turned into the most overgrown of these.

"Are you sure this is the right one?"

"Quite sure."

There were flowers—oh, how long since she had seen wild flowers!—and birds in the undergrowth at the side. They forded a stream and followed its path up the hill into a small wood that filtered out into a ravine.

"Is this where you meant to come?"

"Yes. Up the slope and we are there."

She had to let go of his hand while she scrambled up the side of the ravine, holding on to the boles of trees, but at the top, as though he were picking up a pen or a book, he took her hand in his again.

"This is the place." A meadow, quite high, looking out over the hills and distant plains that they had driven through earlier in the day.

They stood, holding hands, not speaking and afraid to move. The moment came when the touch of his hand was not enough for her and she turned to look at him. He was staring out over the plains, his body rigid and controlled, only his hand caressing and moving against hers.

"Janos." She could wait no longer. Her body demanded the pressure of his; surely he could sense the strain of every muscle, every tendon in her?

"Terez?" The voice was just as cold, as controlled as always, but he turned his head to look at her, blasted her with brilliant eyes and, not understanding quite why, she very gently put her other hand up and touched his cheek.

The moan was from both of them, stifled between their bodies as soon as it was born. He was strong, incredibly strong, for all his thinness, and now, if she had wanted to move away, she could not. One hand behind her neck holding her mouth to his, the other at her back pressing, forcing her into him. It was like the Russians but it was not like the Russians because this time there was no resistance in her own body, only a longing to press back, to be used by this man who did not know how to be a lover.

She bore with his roughness, his awkwardness, even when he hurt her. Tomorrow there would be bruises on her arms and legs, but some old instinctive wisdom told her that now was not the time to check his clumsiness. She waited, a little afraid of his strength and also of the violence she had released in him. He did not kiss her a second time, just pressed her down onto the ground, using her acquiescent body to destroy the first hurt, the first uncontrollable emotion of his body.

When he lay still, before he could grow ashamed or turn away from her, she began to kiss him, cradling his head into her neck and brushing his eyes, forehead, cheeks with her lips. "Janos, Janos!" She stroked his hair, his neck, let her hand wander lightly, tenderly, over the rest of his body, told him she loved him, called him darling and beloved. She felt him stiffen against her, go rigid as though about to pull away, and then his body relaxed, fell against hers, began to respond, moving and stroking, and finally he pulled himself up on one elbow to look down on her. "Terez . . . Terez."

No more than that, but the voice was everything, the voice of the poet and of the man who loved her but wouldn't be able to say so, perhaps not ever.

He kissed her then, and this time it was slow, and became sensual. This time he was confident of her, and she of him, Lazily, in a world of grass and sun and fluttering moths, they smiled at one another while their bodies loved.

They lay a little while, sleeping, then dressed and wandered down the hillside. No words, but now there was no need for words or for the strangeness of their hands saying things their tongues could not. They stumbled because their arms were wrapped around each other, and when she shivered a little in the evening air he pulled her closer, protecting and comforting.

They had been driving for some time when he asked, "Terez, what do they think of me?"

"Think of you? Who?"

"Your family. Your mother, father—all of them."

There was a long silence and then she asked, "Does it matter what they think? Does it matter to us?"

"Yes. Not to me, but to you. It will matter to you. You are a child of your family."

She was silent again, then said, "Uncle Leo is jealous of you. Nicky adores you; so does George. My papa disapproves of you—your politics—but is in your debt because you have helped us. Malie, poor Aunt Malie doesn't think of you or anyone else much at the moment. Mama—" She began to laugh. "Mama has forgotten that she hated you on the journey from Magyarovar. Now her complaint against you is much more convincing and relevant."

She felt him tense again, and she quickly put her hand down on his thigh and let it rest there, a gesture to assure him of both affection and intimacy.

"Mama does not like you because you do not bring roses."

"Roses!" he cried, aghast. "What time is there for roses?"

She loved him but was suddenly hurt because he had said that. So foolish and romantic to be hurt. Who could be hurt by such a thing? She tried to drown the thought in laughter.

"Mama has a great belief in roses. When she was a girl Papa kept one that had fallen from her dress. And Uncle David sent her roses the first time he met her in Budapest; he was always sending roses to the ladies."

"She can't expect me to bring her roses!"

"No, of course not. Roses are just a symbol to Mama. She means that you don't bring flowers—to anyone—and you don't pay compliments or ask people to have coffee with you or take little walks or go out. All those things to Mama are 'bringing roses.' "

"It's foolish. Embarrassing and foolish!" Strangely the criticism had affected him more than Leo's jealousy or Adam Kaldy's disapproval. Later, coolly and analytically, he was able to define why: the other criticisms had been those of personality

576

or politics, but Eva Kaldy had pinpointed his background. Peasant boys cannot afford "roses," and when they have grown up they do not know how to give them.

"Foolish," he repeated angrily, and sadly Terez echoed his voice.

"Foolish, Janos. Mama is very foolish."

He spent the summer suspended between self-loathing and an explosive happiness that at times threatened to destroy his reason.

He hated himself. He had diverged from his painless path of logic, forgotten the cardinal truth, learnt so cruelly years ago, that to love inevitably brings pain, makes one vulnerable, destroys the clear, pure path of reason and dedication. He had not wanted to love her—or had he? Even when they were climbing the mountain, her hand in his, he had not intended to touch her more than that—or had he? There was no moment, no point of realization when he had thought, I will take this girl. She likes me and it will be easy so I will take her. And yet from the moment he knew she was coming to Matrafured with him, the warmth had been there in his heart, the warmth of knowing that they would be alone together with a car in the country. And that one act in the hot scented afternoon, loving her, had destroyed his invincibility, made him weak again.

There was no place for love if you were an idealist seeking to fulfil a dream. Look at that fool Leo Ferenc, torn in all directions because of emotional ties of family and friends. Everything he had ever done in his life had been motivated by emotion. Even now—Party member and editor—he was torn between duty and worrying about the condition of his landowning Kaldy brother-in-law, hovering between the two and making a good job of neither. That was what love did to one.

And this love, this embryonic tie, must be destroyed before it could root securely. He would not see her again, would not look out of his window at 8:25 every morning or join her at the Café Moscow for the lunchtime interval.

He maintained his isolation for a week and one morning could not bear it any longer and waited by his window from eight o'clock to see her crossing the square. Her small body was so dejected, the youth destroyed, the face so sad and hopeless, that he was unable to work all the morning and at lunchtime he hurried across the square to stand by her table.

When she looked up at him he was lost. Her face was transformed from misery to happiness in the second that it took to register his presence. Never—not since his childhood—had he had power like that over anyone.

"'Janos!" she cried softly.

He had to sit, quickly, because the breath left his body and his legs were weak. How could he be that important to her? How could just seeing him make such naked joy appear on her face?

"Why haven't you come before? Why haven't I seen you?"

Staring at her, wanting to be alone with her, remembering her gentleness, her voice, her body. . . . "I don't know," he answered tonelessly. "I've been busy."

"Oh." Her shoulders slumped a little, the joy went from the face. She picked listlessly at her portion of bread. He longed to reach across the table, fold both her hands in his, kiss them, close his eyes and know she would be smiling when he opened them.

"I love you." The words came from some part of his brain over which he had no control. They said themselves, boiled up from a place of warm, flooding emotion. "I love you, Terez. I love you."

"Oh, dear God!" She leaned back and closed her eyes. "Oh, dear God! I thought you hated me, thought you had used me and then forgotten. I thought—I don't know what I thought." Two tiny beads of moisture welled from beneath her closed lids and rolled down her cheeks. The madness seized hold of him again and he did what he had wanted to do, reached over and took her hands.

"I must see you, Terez. This evening, I must see you!"

"Yes, yes. Where?"

"Here. No—yes, I'll meet you here. Then we can walk—the Kossuth Gardens—anywhere. I want to be with you, anywhere."

"Can't I come to your room?"

"No!" A spasm of fear. His room was inviolate, a retreat where he could not be hurt. And there was the Party. He did not want them sniggering, admiring, envying Comrade Marton who had staked a claim to a fallen daughter of the gentry.

They met. They walked in the Kossuth Gardens, speaking hardly at all, touching briefly when the evening grew soft and the people drifted away.

"I must go. Mama will be angry. She will want to know where I have been."

"Will you tell her?"

A pause. "No."

Was she ashamed to tell her mama that she had been with Janos Marton? Did the attitude of that selfish, petulant woman still affect her daughter?

"I will walk with you to the square," he said coldly. Reason asserted itself again, cold logic balancing against the summer madness that obsessed him.

He went back to his room calling himself a fool, an adolescent, and all the other names he could think of. But the next morning he watched her cross the square, and when she looked up at his window and smiled he could think of nothing else but her for the rest of the day.

Once that summer they went to his room. He smuggled her past the porter and spent the evening worrying how he was going to get her out again. It was not a success, not like the day on the mountain. They were embarrassed, made awkward by the need to conceal what was happening. There was no joy or spontaneity between them.

"Why do we have to be so careful?" she asked. "No one cares what Party men do. Gabor has a woman; everyone knows about it."

"I do not want people to think I have a woman."

"Why?"

Why? He couldn't answer. Sometimes he thought it was because he wanted to protect her from his colleagues' ribald groupings of whores and mistresses. But also he was afraid—afraid of men knowing that he was human, was as weak as the rest of them. Once they knew he would no longer be strong and impervious to hurt. "Why do you not want your mama, your papa, your family to know?"

And now she was silent, unwilling to admit that she did not want to face the storm of disapproval and shocked disbelief that would inevitably ensue when her family knew of her attachment.

He tried to pull away again from her after that night, but it was hopeless. Whatever he did, thought, reasoned, he could not keep away from her, could not stop the wild joy in his heart when she smiled and said she loved him.

One morning, in the autumn, she did not come across the square, and at lunchtime she was not at her table in the Café Moscow. He descended into near madness, alternating between fear that she had gone from him because of sickness or disaster, and fury that she should be so careless of his feelings. By the time the evening came he had ceased to think clearly, and he snatched his hat from behind the office door and strode, like a blind madman, through the streets to the old Ferenc house. The refugees on the ground floor opened the door to him, and he thundered up the stairs and through the door into her apartment without thinking of what he was going to say to Leo or Eva Kaldy. The fates, for once, were kind to him. The apartment was empty of everyone except Terez. She was in her room, lying in bed, her skin slightly yellowed and dark circles round her eyes.

"Why didn't you come today? Where have you been? You should have let me know what was wrong. Are you ill? Why didn't you send a message to me?"

"I did, Janos! I asked George to take it to your office before he went to school."

His anger evaporated. She had cared, bothered about him, and at once he was concerned. What had happened to the note? What was wrong with her?

"Are you ill?" A twist of fear. She was so like young Nicky. Supposing she had caught tuberculosis. She was small, not strong, even though she had carried the end of George's stretcher. What if she were ill? An old nightmare: his mother, shrunk into a pain-stretched skeleton with the blue eyes faded and dull. Oh, God! This was what loving someone did to you, hurt and destroyed your reason. "What's wrong?" he breathed, frightened to touch her in case his control should break.

"Nothing!" she flushed a little. "I just couldn't go to work today, that's all."

"Why?"

"It's nothing. You know, I just wasn't well. I'm like that sometimes . . . fainting. It happens . . ."

"What happens?" he shouted. "Tell me, have you a weak heart? Why do you faint? People don't faint unless they are ill. Why didn't you tell me? I sent a doctor to Nicky, didn't I? I would have found one for you!"

"Oh, Janos!" She flushed, furious with him. "Don't be so ridiculous. I don't want a doctor. It's just—the way women are sometimes."

It took a moment even then for him to understand, and when he did he felt foolish and annoyed, as though she had done it deliberately to humiliate him.

"Is *that* all?" he said contemptuously.

Her eyes grew watery and her tiny heart-shaped face crumpled a little. "Yes, that's all. I'm sorry you've been bothered and concerned about me."

How could he have been so unkind! Why did he hurt her, snarl at her when he loved her so much? And suddenly the dilemma, the ambivalence of the last months, vanished. Fatalistic acceptance swept over him. He threw away the caution of years, understanding at last that he had lost the battle with himself and could now only go one way.

"Terez." Now that it was clear to him he could speak quietly to her. "It is no use, the way we behave with each other, hurting, pretending, and trying to hide things. It must stop. We must be married."

He thought she had not heard, and then the smile began—a huge, slow, spreading smile that took away her pallor and sunken eyes.

"It is the sensible thing to do," he murmured, unable to take his eyes from her face. Was that what he could do to her, make her as happy as that?

"Oh, Janos, I don't think it's sensible at all. I think it's wonderful!"

The door slammed, and Eva's voice shrilled through the apartment. "Terez! Are you all right? The door was wide open. Did I leave it like that?"

"Don't tell Mama yet," she whispered. "Let me tell her first. I'll wait until I feel better. Don't tell her yet."

"Why was the door—oh." Eva scowled and stared at him. "What are you doing in my daughter's room, Janos Marton?"

"He came to see how I was, Mama. He heard I was ill and came to see me and there was no one here so I called him in."

"You should not have done that, Terez."

"It was kind of Janos to come, Mama."

"Mmm. . . ." Her dark eyes raked over Janos, then flashed quickly round the room as though looking for something. "Yes, it is pleasant to have visitors when one is ill. I remember when George was born and I had to come into the town to the hospital; your papa visited me every day, Terez. Every day."

"I know, Mama. You've told me before."

"Every day," Eva repeated complacently. "And every day he brought a bunch of roses. There were enough to fill the entire hospital by the time I came home."

It was incredible to think that anyone could be so shallow. She believes I should have brought flowers or something, he thought, astonished. She really does judge me on whether or

581

not I bring flowers! The rebuke was intended for him but it didn't act the way she meant it to, for he had a sudden memory of his own mother, pregnant, with her legs and feet so swollen she had to hoe the patch sitting down. He remembered being sent out of the cottage when the children were born, and his father caring only about how soon she would be able to work again.

"Good-bye, Terez."

"Janos!"

No, he must not be cruel to Terez because her mother was a mean and selfish woman. He forced himself to smile, then switched the smile away as he turned to Eva. "Good-bye, Madame Kaldy."

Walking home he was at first irritated, then nervous. He had committed himself, had admitted that he was as weak as other men, had placed his pure code of ethics on the altar of passion. There was a moment of regret in his heart for the asceticism he had renounced, and then he remembered her face and was engulfed in love.

41

Even though the world had changed, though men and women had died and the social order was uprooted, the family were still shocked at Terez's news.

They did not shout or storm at her, but their dismay expressed itself in a thousand ways. Eva, surprisingly, had not given way to hysterics or shouted protestations. Her face had blanched and, horrified, she had whispered, "Oh, this dreadful war! What it has done to us all . . . that my child should mate with a peasant boy!" After that she had said no more. But she stared at Terez as though her daughter was suffering from an incurable disease and was soon to die.

Adam, who visited his family once a month, came down before his time and took her gently to one side. "Terez, my child. I don't know why you are doing this, but if it is because you think it will help the family, marrying a Party man, I beg you not to make such a sacrifice. Times may change—it is too early to tell. What if the old ways came back and you awoke to find you were tied to Janos Marton, a peasant school teacher with a Communist record! What would your life be then?"

"It's nothing to do with politics, Papa. No one understands that. I care about Janos Marton. I want to marry him, no matter what he is or what he may become."

He seemed not to hear her, or at least not to understand. "The boy has been good to us. I do not deny that. He has proved his loyalty to his old master; he has more than repaid the debt he owed us. But to marry him? I knew you were his friends, all of you, you young ones, and I made a point of not interfering because I believed he had earned the friendship, and when a man has been as good as he has been, then old prejudices must be put aside. But Terez! You cannot completely ignore the old ways! The son of a peasant! His father was a thief, a constant trouble to me on the farm. I kept him only because of *his* father, the old man who was with me in Russia."

"Janos is the grandson of that old man, Papa."

She was angry with her father, but sad more than angry, because until now he had always understood, had always known her heart, followed her dreams. Now he was expressing standards and creeds that meant nothing to her. He was preaching customs that she believed had been discarded long ago. She tried to explain her heart to him, her feelings and admiration for Janos. She tried to tell him how brave and gentle he was, how patient, how fair. But her father only shook his head and begged her to reconsider.

Uncle Leo had hurt her most of all. He had ignored her for a week, refusing to listen when she talked about it, pretending that it had never happened. And when her father had gone back to the farm (taking George with him, ostensibly to help on the land but, Terez suspected, because he did not want Janos Marton to steal any more of this children), Leo had called her quietly into his room.

"I want you to look at this photograph, Terez," he said, holding out a picture of a girl with short hair and a funny old-fashioned droopy dress. "I don't know if you will remember her—you were only a little girl when she came here—but I want you to look at her."

"Yes, Uncle Leo." Obediently she looked, wondering what great influence the picture was supposed to wreak on her.

"She was German, the daughter of a shipyard labourer. She worked in a shop in Berlin when I was a student there."

"Yes, Uncle Leo." Fragments filtered back to her, half-

583

heard pieces of conversation that had hardly interested her at the time.

"I was in love with her, Terez. We lived together in Berlin for over two years. I wanted to marry her in spite of all the differences between us. Grandpapa Ferenc was against it, but it made no difference to me. I was in love with her."

She was interested in spite of herself. She guessed that the story would only illustrate some point as to why she shouldn't marry Janos, but the image of Uncle Leo, twenty and in love, was an intriguing one.

"She loved me too, I know she did. But one day she discovered that Papa was a Jew, and even though she loved me, she found she was unable to overcome the barriers and marry me."

"What's that to do with Janos and me?" she snapped. "Janos doesn't care what I am, and I don't care what he is. We just love each other, that's all."

"Terez." He sighed. "I have told you this because I want you to understand that it never works, to marry someone too different from yourself. You think it is all right, and then one day a gulf yawns, a gulf that no amount of love can bridge."

"Uncle Leo, it's no good trying to tell me these things. If you had been told the same things at twenty you would not have believed them either."

He put the photograph down and sat in silence for a moment. "Terez, your father would not forgive me if he knew what I am about to say. But Adam is an old-fashioned man in many ways. He doesn't understand what it is to search and seek for what is new in life. Terez, if you love this man you do not have to marry him. Please, I beg you. Make no permanent commitment yet. Do what you must, what you want, but don't marry the man—don't marry him!"

"I want to marry him!" she sobbed. "I hate you for saying that, Uncle Leo! It's none of your business what I do! You have no right to tell me how I should conduct my life!"

She ran out of his room and he sat down on the edge of his bed, allowing his careful restraint to evaporate in hatred for Janos Marton. He had forced himself to talk to her without prejudice, trying to put aside the fact that what especially nauseated him was the knowledge that it was Marton whom she loved, not another peasant turned successful leader, but Marton who had shadowed him from childhood. Every way he turned the man was there, at work and now in his private life. Terez, his favourite, the golden girl who was like him in so many ways, to be ruined by the ambitious desires of a murderer's son!

He couldn't speak to her again for several days, but he could think of nothing else, nothing else but her and Marton. When he received a message to go and see him he felt relieved because at last he could fight without having to consider feelings and family. He walked along to the Party offices shaking with a mixture of rage and delight, knowing that he was going —at last, at last—to say the things he had stored away for so many years.

"Sit down, Ferenc." Leo could see that Janos was embarrassed. He felt a surge of wild elation. Already the man was uncomfortable, knowing there was going to be a quarrel, a lancing of the bitter emotion of years.

"I would rather stand. What we have to say cannot be discussed across a table like a Party matter."

Janos looked surprised. "But it is a Party matter."

"No! This is to be treated differently. This has nothing to do with our varying levels in the Party. This is a personal matter, between you and me!"

Marton rustled some papers on his desk and stared without expression at Leo. "It has nothing to do with us," he said. "Whatever I feel personally about your editorship of the paper, I would take no steps to remove you on my own authority."

"The paper?" What was he speaking of? What had the paper to do with Terez?

"I tried to warn you, Leo. I tried to tell you that the paper wasn't right for Party needs. But you've continued to do it your way, and now the leaders in Budapest have noticed. They have stated that"—he consulted the papers before him —"'Comrade Ferenc's early participation in the production of the paper was timely and in the spirit of that period. It is now considered that Comrade Ferenc's many and special gifts can be put to better Party use in a different sphere of activity. The Party thanks Comrade Ferenc for his early work in founding Liberation and asks that he will report to Budapest for duties of equal importance to the creation of our social and democratic state.'"

It filtered through a stunned brain still obsessed with thoughts of Terez. What was Marton saying, that they were taking the paper away from him? His paper. His own special task that had come to be so important to him.

585

"I don't understand," he cried. "What do they mean, the production was 'in the spirit of that period'?"

Marton rustled the papers again. "It means that you are not doing what they want. And with the new election every paper is going to be of vital importance. This time we must win. And it is felt that you are not an editor to help us win."

He sat down, feeling that his life's energy was draining away from him. He could hardly believe it. He was being dismissed!

"But they can't do it! *Liberation* is *my* paper. I created it. I have made it from a single news-sheet into a comprehensive, well-balanced journal. They can't take it from me!"

He noticed that Janos Marton wouldn't look at his eyes. He stared down at the desk and, if it had been possible for Marton to look uncomfortable, he would have done so now.

"No, Leo. It is not your paper. That is the trouble. You have been behaving as though it were your paper instead of the Party's."

"I shall not accept this decision! It is a slight to me personally and I do not believe you had nothing to do with it. This is a personal thing, Janos Marton. You want me away from this town because of Terez!"

Silence, the cold silence that Marton was so skilled at creating. And then, as though Leo had not spoken, "Your duties in Budapest could prove to be exciting and interesting. You are to act as translator at the preliminary talks on setting up a trade mission. Possibly you will travel with the mission to countries of both West and East. It is a post in which the Party places great trust and responsibility in you."

"A translator!" The blood began to pound in his head. He could have accepted many things—a junior place on a national paper, an editorial post of any kind—but this was a calculated insult. He was to act as a glorified clerk to a band of civil servants and bureaucrats!

"I refuse! This is more than a Party decision. This is a personal vendetta, and I will not countenance it. I demand to see Comrade Lengyel!"

"I do not advise it, Leo. Comrade Lengyel is . . . a different kind of member from the rest of us. He is stricter, Moscow trained. I suggest you do not speak to him."

"I insist! If you block this I shall file a complaint against you!"

"Very well." A small pulse beat in the side of Marton's brow. He lifted the telephone and spoke to someone at the other end. There was a long wait, then a voice. He replaced the receiver. "If you wait outside Comrade Lengyel's office, he will try to see you sometime later this morning."

Leo turned and flung out of the room, hating Marton so much he could not even throw a final vitriolic word at him. He was shattered. The paper was the culmination of his editorial life. He had spent time and energy in composing what he considered exactly the right mixture for a socialist party in a county town: some simple but intelligent editorials, poems by local patriots and writers, a small column of theatrical and arts criticism, and a diary of the social progress being made by the Party. He had felt the way old Heinlein in Berlin must have felt, as though he were creating a mouthpiece for the truth to be presented to the world. And now it was to be taken away, because he would not accept his niece's affiliation with a dangerous political rival.

He had to wait for an hour outside Comrade Lengyel's office and during that time his anger had a chance to evaporate a little. In its place grew a slight unease. Could it be entirely Marton's fault? No, Marton was not that powerful. Some remaining spark of judgement made him admit that neither would Marton stoop to personal vengeance. There was something else behind it, something he didn't quite understand. By the time Comrade Lengyel opened his office door, a chilly premonition had superseded everything else in his heart.

"Comrade Ferenc, I understand you are dissatisfied with the decision to transfer you to new duties in Budapest?"

Lengyel was plump and had a bland round face sheltering behind thick pebble glasses. He smiled, but the smile was solely a movement of the lips. Behind the glasses magnified pale eyes observed.

"I cannot understand why now, when I have achieved my aims with *Liberation,* I should be taken away. I have worked to create a balanced socialist paper that everyone can read and appreciate—"

"Perhaps a well-balanced paper is not what the Party requires at this time, Comrade Ferenc."

"The principles of the Party must always be the same, to build a new, free, socialist Hungary!"

The glasses glinted. The eyes were blanked out by reflected light. "I think you must allow the Party to know what it wants, Comrade Ferenc, and what it does not want is the rather ... bourgeois, ineffectual medium that the paper is now."

587

"Bourgeois?"

Another joyless smile. "That is the criticism, Comrade Ferenc. And, sadly, it has been pointed out that your background is obviously affecting your judgement. You come, I believe, from a family closely related to the old landowning gentry. Headquarters does not like that, Comrade Ferenc. That is not at all a good background for a Party editor."

"But I have spent years overcoming my background!" he shouted. "Was it for this I broke away from my family, risked imprisonment in the Horthy years, fought the fascists in Germany and here in Hungary? Does all this count for nothing?"

"The Party appreciates your efforts, Comrade Ferenc. That is why you have been appointed to the trade mission. Your services to the Party will not go unrewarded."

"I have no wish to go to Budapest as a clerk! I have responsibilities here, my family are here—"

"No, I think not, Comrade Ferenc. You have a sister and an illegitimate nephew at Matrafured to whom you send money each month. You can do that from Budapest. Your brother-in-law—Kaldy—and his son are on their farm trying to work it together. Our report from that area is that they are having difficulties. They should leave, Comrade Ferenc. Sooner or later they will have to leave. This means that you live with your other sister, Eva Kaldy, and her daughter, who works at the County Offices. Neither of these ladies is in any kind of dilemma. There is no reason why you should remain here when the Party requires your services in Budapest."

The chill spread down Leo's spine, a vaguely familiar fear; it was the fear he had had during the war, hiding from the Nazis and the Arrow Cross.

"Things are to be done differently in Hungary very soon," the soft voice continued. "When the election is won—and this time there will be . . . precautions taken to see that we win— things will be very different. There will be a place for you in the new Hungary, Comrade Ferenc—the Party is never ungrateful—but you must try to overcome your unfortunate background. Practise the rule of obedience." Another eyeless smile. "What use is a Party member if he is not obedient?"

He had enough sense and enough control to remain silent, even though he felt the bottom had fallen from his world. He was shocked, betrayed, but he was also afraid, and he knew he must keep his protests to himself until he had had time to absorb the fear.

"You will enjoy Budapest," purred the fat man. "You will be allocated a very pleasant apartment and your allowance will be most generous. And what work could be more rewarding than helping to re-establish the economy of our country?"

He couldn't answer. If he did as he felt he would first of all weep, and then lean across the desk and squeeze the fat man's neck until he died. Where had the dream gone? All the years of planning, the visions that were talked of in the Balasz, the war, the political persecution—what had happened? Where was the dream they had pursued for so long?

"There is no hurry for your departure, my friend. You need not be in Budapest for a couple of days. Take a little holiday before you go."

Where had he heard that before? In 1939, on the newspaper, when the editor was trying to get rid of him because he was politically undesirable.

"Good-bye, Comrade Ferenc. I hope you will take every advantage of your stay in Budapest."

The pebble lenses flashed again, and then Comrade Lengyel padded softly round the desk and opened the door of his office.

"Good-bye," he said again, most pleasantly. Leo swallowed, nodded, and crossed in front of him. The door didn't close immediately behind him and he was aware of the glasses observing him along the passage, could feel the spot on the back of his neck where they rested. When he left the building he noticed consciously, for the first time, that there were now three guards on the door of the building—three guards holding rifles—and a Russian soldier.

42

In the spring Malie and Nicky came back from the mountains. The year in the country had healed them: Nicky was strong enough to return to school, and Malie had regained her calm, her gentle tranquillity. She was older, much older than the rest of them, but some of her composure had returned. The tranquillity was needed, for she walked into a house where mother and daughter lived alone in sullen resentment

589

over the question of Janos Marton. Once the warm welcomes were made, the invalid cosseted and admired and Malie's careful nursing congratulated, the travellers were divided, Eva taking Malie into her room for a long complaint, leaving Nicky and Terez together in the cluttered kitchen.

"Where's Janos, Terez? I thought he might be here to meet me. I haven't seen him for a year—not since he took me to Matrafured—and apart from one postcard he has not written either." He was hurt, and his voice was slightly plaintive. Janos had not fulfilled all the functions of a hero. Terez swallowed, took a deep breath and explained.

It took a moment for him to absorb. At first he didn't believe, and then he did and looked puzzled and vaguely disapproving.

"Oh, no, Nicky! Not you too! I thought you would be on my side!"

"Oh, I'm not against you," he answered airily. "I just think it's a shame, that's all—that Janos should want to get married. Everyone gets married. I thought he was different. But I suppose it's all right." He smiled at her, then came round the table and hugged her. "Of course it's all right, Terez. If he wants to marry someone I'd just as soon it was you."

So the younger members of the family were on her side, for George on his visits to the town with his father was moved to discreet indignation on his sister's behalf.

Malie, listening to her sister's voice rising and falling in a series of illogical and unco-ordinated resentments, suddenly wished herself back in the country. There she had mourned and buried her parents, her husband, her sons. She had come to a point where she had managed to rise above personal grief, where the flight of a heron over the lake, where clouds moving across the mountain, gave her peace and a sense of the continuity of her life. The continuity had included the steady improvement of her nephew and the knowledge that once again she had a responsibility to someone. The year had made Nicky her own, for if Janos Marton had become his father (and she came to understand that indeed this was so), then she, most certainly, was his mother. She had felt strong enough to return to the old house and adapt herself to a changed environment. She had felt strong enough to face the full responsibility of caring for her nephew. And now it appeared she had walked into a house divided into two camps, the older generation against the younger.

"What does Adam say?" she interrupted gently. Eva

stopped her flow of complaints, which consisted mostly of a description of Janos's bad manners and the fact that he didn't bring them any black-market food.

"Adam is *heartbroken!*" she cried.

"But he hasn't forbade it?"

Eva sniffed. "How can he? The war has changed all that. They do as they like now. No one is obedient to their parents any more."

"'What you mean, Eva, is that while Terez's salary is keeping the apartment and you, no one has any right to forbid her to do anything." She looked coolly at her sister, feeling the same irritation with her she had felt since they were girls. "Why haven't you been out to find work? You could have helped if you'd wanted. You obviously don't do very much to keep the apartment tidy."

The rebuke was justified. The apartment was in chaos and when she and Nicky had arrived they had discovered Terez (who had hurried home immediately after work) preparing a meal for them. She had apologized for the untidiness but had pointed out that the bedrooms *were* tidy and that she had made the beds with fresh linen that very morning.

"How could you, Malie?" Eva whimpered. "I do what I can, but you know I never was any good at housework."

"You ran the farm all right."

"But I had servants," she wailed. "I know how to organize things, but I get tired so quickly if I have to work!" She sniffed again, then cheered a little. "It will be better now you are back. There'll be two of us in the house all day long to do things."

"No, there won't." Eva looked hurt. "I've applied for a kiosk, Eva. Tobacco and tickets—" She broke off as an expression of horror slowly spread over Eva's face, the blood draining away and then flooding back in outrage.

"But you can't, Malie! You can't sit in a street kiosk all day selling cigarettes as though you were a war veteran!"

"That's exactly what I am," she answered sadly. "And that is why I shall almost certainly be granted one."

"But Malie, you can't!" Eva began to cry. "What would Mama and Papa say? A granddaughter of the Bogozy selling tobacco on a street corner!"

"How strange. It's so long since anyone said that: a Bogozy granddaughter. It doesn't seem to matter any more."

"But why, Malie?" Eva sobbed.

"For Nicky. Someone has to keep him, to buy his clothes

591

and schoolbooks. He is going back to school, and then to college or university, however it can be managed. Janos Marton has told him the same thing and he is prepared to work and catch up with his schooling because of this." She saw Eva stiffen at the mention of Marton's name. "I know you do not like him, Eva. But I try to remember what he has done for Nicky—and what he may do in the future. I am told it is going to be difficult for children of bourgeois background to find places in the colleges. We need every help that Janos can give him."

"He won't give anything, anything! I told you, he never brings presents, never an extra pound of butter or fresh coffee. And don't tell me he cannot get them, of course he can." The tirade continued, the same grievances and moans that she had begun her litany with an hour before.

"And Leo? What does Leo say to all this?" The letters from Leo had been solicitous but uncommunicative. They had told her nothing of his own feelings, of his work in Budapest, of his opinions about Terez and Janos Marton. Sometimes, during the past year, she had worried about him a little—but not too much. Up in the mountains her sense of isolation had protected her from the emotions of others. She had needed the year and had deliberately tried to detach herself from the abrasive disturbances of others.

"Leo?" Eva shrugged. "You know what Leo is like, a big Party man now with an apartment in Buda and the use of a car. He hasn't been home once. Not once. He said he would visit us when you and Nicky came back, if he wasn't too busy with the election. He doesn't like Janos Marton either."

"How do you know?"

"Because he told me he didn't wish to discuss him in his letters. I had written, you know, about Terez, asking for a little help, asking him to speak to Janos—and he said he wished never to hear the man's name again. Do you think I should write again?"

"Leave him, Eva, leave him. I will talk to him when he comes to see us. He will come now, I'm sure of it, and I will talk to him then."

Just before the elections he came. She hadn't seen him for a year and she recognized at once the old signs in him: the restlessness, the rebellion, the air of barely concealed excitement. It was the election, she supposed wearily. He was absorbed with seeing that the Party finally and completely mastered the land.

At thirty-seven he seemed to have changed hardly at all from the boy who had gone off to Berlin and fought the Nazis, only now he was respectable, a Party man, for once on the right side, the winning side.

But as his time with them passed she grew at first puzzled and then concerned. He didn't behave like a Party man. For one thing he didn't go and visit any of his old comrades, and whenever any mention of the election was made, he spoke in a manner that was openly derisive. "Election? What election? I hope no one is foolish enough to believe they are about to choose a government. The Russians have chosen it already. Last time they were careless. This time it has all been arranged exactly the way they want. It will make no difference if you vote or how you vote; the result will be exactly the same."

He shrugged his shoulders and walked away from the window (he spent a lot of time just staring out of the window) back to where she was sitting on the old French settee.

"How shabby this is," he murmured, stroking the threadbare damask. "And I remember it as so pretty. It was in Mama's drawing-room. I remember you sitting on it when David Klein first came. You were so unhappy then, do you remember?"

She nodded, and he reached over and took her hand. "Malie, will you really be all right now? You have Nicky, and you have Eva and her family. Will you be all right? If anything happened to me, would you be all right?"

"Why?" she asked, her heart beating and a flicker of fright moving in her stomach. "What is going to happen to you?"

"I don't know yet," he muttered, and then he sprang away from her and walked back to the window. "I only know I cannot continue in this way any longer. My life here is finished, useless. I have to change it."

"You are not to do anything foolish, Leo!" she cried, afraid, remembering how he had lectured to the steel workers and plotted in a Budapest cafe to bring about the downfall of the government. "Please don't do anything foolish. This time there will be no one to help you, no David to find a barrister, no influential friends to help. We have only Janos Marton, and even he would not be powerful enough to save you now."

"Janos. Ha!" He flung the windows open and grasped the frame. Dirt came off onto his hands, and he stared at his blackened palms, then brushed them against his trousers. "Marton? He would not help me. He is one of Them, one of those who believe that any means are justified if the result fulfils their dreams. He believes that Hungary can still be saved and he would sacrifice me or Terez or anyone to bring about that dream."

She didn't know how to answer. He was so angry, and she didn't fully understand his argument anyway.

"You're all worried about Terez marrying him. She won't. When she sees what he and the people like him are doing, when her father finally loses his land, then she will understand and hate him."

"Oh, no, Leo," she whimpered. "No more hate, no more hate!"

He was sorry. He hurried over and held her in his arms, smoothing her hair and comforting her as best he could. When she was calm again he said, "Malie, in my room is an envelope full of money I have saved during the last year. I shall leave it there when I return to Budapest. It is to be used for you and for Nicky. No one else, you understand?"

"Why?"

"I can't tell you why. But the money is there."

"What are you planning, Leo? Please tell me!"

"I can't, Malie. But I promise no one here will come to any harm. And you must not talk to anyone about the money, or about this conversation."

She felt the way she had in 1944, afraid, uncertain, but not knowing where to look for the source of her fear. "Don't do anything foolish," she begged. "Please, be wise now—you are a man, not a boy. Be sensible."

"I can't be sensible any longer, Malie."

She thought he was going to say something more, but he stopped himself and just gave her another gentle hug. "It will be all right, little Malie. Nothing will happen, I promise you."

"Why do you have to be so restless, Leo?" she whispered. "Why can you not settle, be content with what is here? If you had married, perhaps. . . . I don't know. We always hoped you would marry and be contented."

"Well, maybe I will. One day, maybe I will." He would say no more. For the rest of his visit he was gentle and spent his time with her and Nicky. He was pleasant to Terez but her link with Janos had broken the old tie between them. She was no longer his favourite child, and he was no longer her idolized uncle. There was a rift between them.

When he left, Malie knew she wasn't going to see him again. She knew by the way he held her in his arms and whispered, "Good-bye, little mother. How kind you have been to me always. The one I loved most, better than Mama and Papa or anyone. Good-bye, little Malie." She tried to speak, to beg him not to do whatever was in his heart, but a sense of futility buried her cry before it was born. He kissed her, then picked up his case and hurried down the stairs. She watched him from her bedroom window, saw his tall frame springing away along the street, and then he had vanished round the corner without once turning round to wave.

The election was a farce; even to unpolitical people like Malie who did not understand, it was a farce. There were those, like herself and Eva, who could not vote at all because there had been a "mistake" and they were not registered where they should be registered. And there were those—mostly in trucks and buses—being driven from poll to poll with green cards that registered them in several places at once. The result, as Leo had predicted, was inevitable. The Party emerged as the single largest group and, without waiting for any niceties of overall majorities, seized power quickly and irrevocably.

One month after the election Janos Marton, white-faced, stern, came to call and report that their brother, Leo Ferenc, was listed as a renegade from the state. He had taken advantage of his first foreign assignment and was now—so it had been reported—on his way to London via Vienna and Paris. If ever he set foot on Hungarian soil again he would be arrested.

While Eva wept, Malie felt only relief. He was safe, alive, and his act of rebellion was so much milder than she had feared.

43

At night he lay awake, staring at the picture of the stag that hung on his wall and trying to define why he felt unease, why every day brought a fresh disquiet to his work and beliefs. Sometimes, in the shaft of light from the road lamp outside, the stag appeared to move, turn his head a little and gaze longingly at a different angle of the Bukk Mountains, and at those moments Janos would be seized by a longing, long since mastered, for the country of his childhood—the hills and rivers and woods that surrounded the Kaldy land. Here, in this room, he sometimes allowed himself to be nostalgic about the pastoral background of his youth. Sometimes, but not too often. Nostalgia was at best wasteful, at worst dangerous.

He had been offered a different apartment on more than one occasion, one near the town's main square, a more splendid and luxurious home, a tribute to his place in the local Party hierachy. He had refused. He told himself that it was because that kind of privilege was exactly what he had spent his life fighting. But a deeper truth was that this room had been his oasis for a long time. He had made it what he wanted it to be: plain, unsentimental, pure, a refuge where he cast away the shell of pretence and considered himself and the world as it was.

He tried very hard to see the world as it was, especially now, because he was constantly perturbed about his work and about the work of the Party. The voluntary exile of Leo Ferenc had jarred his pure beliefs—yes, the man was an indulgent romantic, unstable, spoilt, but he had served the Party in his own way for many years, had survived the Horthy persecution, the Nazis, the war. Why did Leo Ferenc choose to exile himself after all this? Was it simply because he was a selfish and frustrated child?

What was it that troubled him; when had his unease begun? He thought back. The days after the war had been courageous and constructive. They had been given a task to do and had done it well. The Party, and no one else, had rebuilt the factories, put industry and government into working order, given the people work and bread. Now, only two and a half years after the war, they could look proudly about them and say, *No one starves; there are no poor; at last after a thousand years there is bread and meat for everyone.* Surely this was enough? This had been his life's desire—to see that a child ate, that a woman did not die untended, that a man could not be beaten by the *pandur* for no other reason than that he wanted to eat and see his children eat.

Was it the election, the "arranged" election? It had bothered him, but he had considered carefully and realized that the end justified the means. If this was the way it had to be done to ensure that there were no poor, so it must be. Stifling his conscience, he had taken his part in the voting fiasco, keeping his sights firmly on the ultimate aim: a country where no one was poor or hungry or beaten, where the greatest freedom of all prevailed, the freedom of fear from want.

So where did his doubts begin? He could not remember, but now when he walked to his office past the guards at the door he felt unease. When the sealed orders came from Budapest for Comrade Lengyel and no one else, he felt unease. When he was asked for secret reports on the private lives of old comrades like Gabor, he felt unease. Surely these men who had suffered before and during the war for their beliefs could be trusted now? Surely the dignity of privacy could be accorded them?

He drowned the horrifying thought that someone was probably also writing a report on his private life, giving times and details of when the girl, Terez Kaldy, visited his apartment and how long she stayed. He shrank from this thought, recoiled the way he had recoiled all his adult life from any intrusion on his secret self.

She came to his apartment quite openly now, and she stayed for as long as she could. What questions and suffering she endured at home he never asked. The last year had put such a strain on their relationship that at some point the knowledge that she would be labelled as Marton's whore had ceased to matter. There were so many strains between them, so many things they had to avoid discussing, from Leo's dismissal as editor to her father's pathetic attempts to hold his patch of land, that the quiet time of loving each other in his ascetic room was the only thing that gave them hope and reassurance. Several times he tried to break the bond between them, for her sake as well as his. He grew angry when he thought of how loving her had confused his clear-cut path of action. Perhaps that was the cause of his present unease. It was nothing at all to do with the Party; she had destroyed his ability to devote his mind and being to dispassionate reason. And he? What had he done for her? He had never, other than that first time at the Café Moscow, told her he loved her. He never laughed with her or took her to the country or—or brought her roses! She was pretty and young—oh, yes, she was very pretty, soft and gentle and pretty—and there were still enough young men left who came from lives less harsh than his, young men who would be pleasant and easy to be with. They were wrong together, the peasant and the Kaldy daughter. He could not make her happy, and she was pulling him into bourgeois confusion.

All these things he told himself, and he knew all the while that nothing—ever—would make him relinquish her. She was his, irrevocably his. Nothing he could do to her would drive her away. He had been cruel to her, ignored her, given her none of the outward signs and gestures of love, but she had stayed with him, crying sometimes, but always assuring him before she left, "Janos, I love you. I love you so much!"

"Why do you love me?"

"'Because . . . I trust you. You are like my father. You would never betray me or lie to me."

"That is no reason to love me."

A smile, her small wicked imp's smile that made him long to be young with her except that he did not know how.

"No? Well then, perhaps I don't love you!"

He could not see himself, could not see how his face steeled over and the blue eyes blazed, even though it was only a joke. Now she knew him well enough to recognize that the stony face covered fear. Quickly she put her hands up around his neck and pulled his face down to hers. "Of course I love you, Janos. I love you because you need me."

Little by little he told her things about the past. Not the bad things; he did not wish to remember those. He told her about the picture of the stag. And he told her about the first day he had gone to the village, his mother belonging to him again, and the flowers he had picked that matched her eyes. He could talk of these things when he was close to her, lying near in the darkness, learning how to be with someone, to trust, to open a little of yourself and reach out, hoping she would not strike and hurt the open place.

In the autumn, soon after Leo had gone to the West, she came to his apartment one evening and, after a long silence, asked him if they could be married very soon.

"Why now?" he taunted. "When I wanted to marry you last year you made me wait."

"You know I had to!" Her eyes filled with quick indignant tears. "There was Mama and me, no one else! I had to look after her. You would not have wanted to look after her if we had married."

"No. I wouldn't. So why is it all right now?"

Brown eyes fixed upon his face, she whispered, "Because Papa is coming to live in the town. He has given up the farm; he cannot fight any more. They have beaten him—the taxes and inspectors and threats of legal action—they have won. I love him, Janos. But I cannot stay in the same apartment with him, not when I love you too."

Her pain was his. He never jeered at her when he knew she was genuinely distressed. He had known too much hurt himself to do that, and now, although he could not sympathize with her father's loss of land, he could understand her sorrow.

"My poor little Terez," he murmured. "What trials I have brought into your life."

"Not you, Janos. Papa would have lost his land anyway, whether you and I were married or not."

"He should have left a year ago," he murmured. "He should have lived here with his family, sent George to school, and found work for himself."

"You understand, Janos? I cannot see him every day, hurt and not understanding why he has lost everything, and then let him see me come to you."

"I understand."

"Can we be married soon?"

He waited, thinking. "Yes. But first I shall come to see him."

"Oh, no! Don't do that. Please don't do that." She giggled, a sound in which mirth was mixed with hysteria. "The days of asking my papa if you can marry me are over! They ended long ago, after the war—and when we took Nicky to Matrafured."

His blue eyes fixed unseeingly on her. "I have to see him, Terez. I have to make him understand that you and I are nothing to do with politics, with him losing the land, with your Uncle Leo running away to the West. All these things have nothing to do with our marriage. I cannot take you from him without even speaking to him. Don't you see how cruel it would be, as though I were seeking to humiliate him and revenge myself?"

"I don't want you to see him."

"I must." His voice was crisp, curt. "When does he return?"

"Tomorrow."

"Good. Tomorrow I shall see him."

He hadn't been to the apartment since reporting Leo's defection to the West. He was led by Terez into the shabby drawing-room with the bed in the corner for George. They were all there, dressed as neatly as they could be, sitting stiffly on their chairs, and for one moment he felt he was still the humble peasant child in the presence of the great Kaldys. Eva, strangely quiet, the roots of her dyed hair showing through a little; Malie, also quiet, hoping there would be no distressing scenes; Nicky and George, who smiled at him and then left the room; Adam, his old master . . . his excellency.

He saw at once that the old man was broken. There was no need to protest anything, no need to explain. Adam Kaldy had lost his land—his pitiful tenure of the old estate—and with the land had gone his strength. He felt a swift pang of pity, unreasonable but there nonetheless. Adam Kaldy was too old a man to learn the new ways, too old to take his loss with stoicism. He should have learned the lesson years ago that no man could depend on anything material for his life's impetus. He had nothing now, nothing that counted.

"Mr. Kaldy," he said sternly. "You know that Terez and I are going to be married."

"You have taken my land. Why not take my daughter as well." It was said not bitterly but tiredly.

"We have . . . a great affection for each other." It choked him to say that in front of these three. The two ladies were staring at the floor, but he felt as though he were undressing in front of them. "Whatever events have occurred, however different our connections, our affection is genuine. That is why we shall be married."

He was saying it badly, but it didn't matter. Whatever explanations he made the old man would not accept the marriage. His land . . . his daughter—the loss of the two was somehow the same. And Janos Marton, a peasant who had betrayed his master, was responsible for both.

"I can do nothing any more," the old man said. "You people will do what you want to do."

"I wish you would understand—"

"Go away!" Adam suddenly put his hand up before his eyes. "My little girl . . . to go and live with you? You are so hard, Janos Marton. You will destroy her."

Janos turned away and groped for the door. Why had it seemed so important? Why had he wanted them to accept it? Not to like him, just to accept that he loved Terez as he had loved only one other woman in his whole life.

"What happened?" Terez whispered. "What did they say?"

"Nothing." He was curt, and down the sides of his cheeks the muscles moved. "I will arrange the necessary papers for the marriage as quickly as possible. We shall stay in my room until we find a bigger apartment." He swallowed, unable to look at her unhappy face without hating the people in the other room. "I quite see you cannot remain here for any longer than you have to."

He forced himself to walk slowly down the stairs. He didn't touch her or kiss her. He heard the door of the drawing-room open and close and then the sound of her father's voice speaking to her. He stepped out onto the cobbled yard, feeling once more the son of a thief, knowing that nothing he had ever done, or would do, would change these people. He would always be Janos Marton, who had stolen their child.

In the sitting room the two sisters remained in silence. Eva, her hands trembling, suddenly said into the quiet, "I do love Adam, Malie. I know you thought I never did, and perhaps, when we were first married, I wasn't too sure. But I do love him."

"He doesn't know it," Malie said softly. "He has grown used to loving you, Eva, but he gave up expecting anything years ago."

"I hate to see him like this." Quiet tears, so unlike Eva, flowed down her face. "I always knew he loved his farm—I used to tease him about it—but I didn't think he would be like this because he had lost it."

"Poor Eva," Malie whispered. "You never did understand anyone very much, did you?"

"Do you think I could make it up to him, Malie? If I told him how much he meant to me, if I tried to be a good wife, do you think I could make him happy?"

"Perhaps. You could try." She reached across and patted her sister's hand, knowing how impossible it was for Eva to change at this time of her life, but also knowing that she had spoken the truth when she said she loved him. "How strange," she murmured. "History repeating itself . . . First me, then you, now Terez."

"What do you mean, Malie?"

"All of us so unhappy with our first loves. Remember Karoly? And how cruel Papa was when I loved him so much? And when at last he consented, the war—" She sighed. "And you were in love with Felix, and you married Adam. And my poor darling Kati, who knows who she might have loved, but she had to marry Felix."

"Felix was evil!" Eva flushed. "He was wicked and evil!"

"And now," Malie continued, "Terez cries herself to sleep

every night. I hear her from my bed. I pretend to be asleep so that she can save her pride. She loves the boy, Eva. Is it always to be this way with us?"

"He's a peasant, Malie! His father was a thief, and he has no manners, no charm, no way of making my little girl happy."

"He is a brave young man," Malie chided gently. "Have you forgotten all he did? He hid Nicky from the Nazis, rescued you and Terez and George from the Russians, arranged for Nicky to have doctors and rooms in the country. He is a good young man, and Terez loves him. She loves him the way I loved Karoly and you loved Felix. There's nothing you can say to alter that."

"Well, she's going to marry him." Eva sniffed. "She's luckier than we were. I don't see why she cries at night."

"Remember the ball, Eva? Cousin Kati's birthday party when it all began?"

"Oh, yes! I had a dress with roses and you were cross because it was cut so low."

"Remember what they called us, the enchanting Ferenc sisters?"

"Yes." Eva smiled and clasped her hands together; then the smile faded and she stared down at her hands. "Look at us now. We're old and ugly. We're not the enchanting Ferenc sisters any more."

Malie smiled and patted Eva on the shoulder and said briskly, "Yes we are, Eva. We can still be the enchanting Ferenc sisters if we wish. Eva, if Janos Marton comes here again will you try—for Terez's sake—to be gracious to him, enchanting, the way you used to be?"

"To Janos Marton?"

"To your daughter's sweetheart!"

"Oh, Malie!" She began to giggle, and Malie knew that if she closed her eyes the giggle would sound the same as it had thirty-four years ago.

"Promise?"

"Oh—all right."

"The enchanting Ferenc sisters?"

"You're a silly old woman, Malie!"

"And your hair needs re-dyeing at the roots. But in spite of it all we're still the Ferenc girls, are we not?"

And Eva smiled and wiped away a romantic tear, knowing she had been handled but enjoying it just the same.

The following morning Comrade Lengyel sent for him. It was a rare occurrence. Usually they sent memoranda to each other or spoke on the telephone. Sometimes, in the café, they would courteously drink coffee together, their conversation limited to short comments on Party trivia. Now, his thoughts of Terez driven away by the unaccustomed summons, he hurried up the two flights of stairs to Lengyel's office.

A pot of coffee waited, two cups, cream. Comrade Lengyel beamed affably behind the glinting glasses and beckoned him to the seat on the other side of the desk.

"Comrade Marton! We must speak together. We speak so rarely, do we not? We are busy men, but sometimes a little . . . conversation is necessary. Your coffee. You like to take cream?"

He shook his head and reached his hand forward to take the cup. As he did so he caught a glimpse of Lengyel's eyes behind the lenses, and the old sense of unease descended on him once again.

"We have worked hard, all of us, have we not? And now, Comrade Marton, our vision is in sight, a *fait accompli*. We are proud—but not too proud, because there is still much to be done . . . much to be done. . . ." His voice trailed away and he spooned several layers of cream onto his coffee.

"You may not be aware, Comrade Marton, that you are thought of very highly in the Party. Yes, very highly. I have heard it whispered that Comrade Rakosi himself has noticed you. Did you know that, Janos Marton?"

"I am honoured," he replied tonelessly.

"So are we all. To think that one of our comrades in this humble town may be singled out for greater glories to the state. It is not impossible, Comrade Marton, that you have a future—in Budapest, of course—a great future."

"Thank you."

"Of course"—Lengyel suddenly pushed aside the cup and pulled a folder of papers towards him—"to succeed in the Party must mean sacrifices. We have all made sacrifices. You too, Comrade Marton, must make sacrifices in the cause of the Hungarian state."

He knew what was coming. Lengyel had to say no more. He knew what was in the folder: every meeting with Terez recorded, every moment she had spent in his room carefully checked and double-checked.

"We—the Party—are unhappy about your connections with a certain family, a bourgeois family—dangerous—and

603

particularly with the daughter of that family. It is a great pity. You remember Leo Ferenc, of course—if only he had not betrayed the Party perhaps his family would not now be considered quite so . . . bourgeois."

"What are you trying to say, Comrade Lengyel?" he asked icily. The glasses glinted, as though faintly shocked at his peremptory tone.

"I am saying that disquieting rumours have reached me. I hear you have not only indulged in a liaison with this girl but are considering marriage. Furthermore, you have, on frequent occasions, assisted her family in a variety of ways, the most recent the arranging for her cousin to be given convalescent rooms in the country."

"That is quite true."

"Comrade Marton." The bland tones melted, as though some of the cream still lingered in his throat. "Don't you see that is exactly why the Party frowns on these liaisons with bourgeois families? It begins with a little . . . amusement . . . and it ends with favours that should only be granted to Party members."

"It is not improbable that Nicholas Rassay will one day be a Party member."

The fat man shrugged, bored with such a dialectic notion. "The fact remains, Comrade Marton, that it would be most foolish of you to entertain any idea of marrying this girl. You have a brilliant future before you. You are a rarity in Hungary, a peasant who has achieved distinction under most difficult circumstances. It would be tragic to destroy all this— the success of your future career—by linking yourself to a woman who is the niece of a renegade and the daughter of a kulak." The fat hand closed the folder, stroked it, and pushed it away. Then it reached for the coffee again. Janos watched and hated—first the hand, then the man—hated everything that Lengyel represented, hated the corruption and distortion of ideals that had once bound together a group of men in courage and endeavour.

"Where did you spend the Horthy years, Comrade Lengyel?" he asked coldly.

The hand paused over the coffee pot. "Moscow, Comrade Marton. You know that."

"Then you know little of what we suffered here during that time?"

Lengyel turned the glasses full onto Janos's face. The eyes were dangerous, embedded in fat and pinpointed with malice.

"I see no connection between your question and the matter we are discussing."

"No?" He rose suddenly. He was angry, terribly angry, but strangely he was also relieved. The unease of months had dropped away, the unease of not knowing what was wrong, of wondering how far to go in a cause one believed in. He still believed in his cause. He had fought for freedom from want, bread for the masses, and that cause had been fulfilled. But somewhere along the way the purity had been lost—the purity and dedication and a belief in the building of the Hungarian nation. He was angry but excited, the way he had been excited before—coolly, dispassionately, knowing exactly what he believed in, knowing what principles he must embrace no matter what happened.

"Thank you for the coffee." He stood, looking down on the fat man before him, not underestimating his capabilities or training but knowing that he was wrong—completely and absolutely wrong—for what Hungary needed.

"Comrade Marton—"

"Goodbye."

He closed the door quietly behind him. All his control, his cool sense of balance had returned. He could hold hard to his ethics, and everything else became natural and right. Terez, her bourgeois family who only yesterday had had the power to hurt and intimidate him—all these things fell into place because, once more, the truth had blazed in his heart. No, not his heart, his brain.

He returned to his office and sat quietly, thinking of all that might happen and knowing it was unimportant. What a stupid, cowardly fool Leo Ferenc had been. How could they continue to create their country when people ran away at the first setback? He had betrayed his own ideals, sacrificed them because of personal frustration and hurt pride. What good was it to run away? One must stay in the place allocated for as long as possible, deviating not at all from the truth discovered in one's own heart, endeavouring, believing, fighting, the way he had fought for years against the *pandur,* the Nazis, the Arrow Cross.

He would have liked to see Terez at lunchtime, but Lengyel had kept him too late and he had missed her. He sat at his desk, working happily at the suggested plans for re-schooling in the area. There will be trouble with Lengyel, he prophesied to himself, and then with wry humour reflected that he was unlikely to fulfil the promise of a rising career in the Party—

at least not this time, not until everything had been cauterized, fought against, rediscovered, and put right. . . .

When it was time to go, he carefully tidied his desk and put out the new work for the next day. Schools, more schools. He was still a teacher in many ways; that was probably why he had enjoyed talking to Nicky and George so much. Possibly, if the Party had no further use for him, he could teach again. He shrugged, thinking it unlikely he would be allowed to but not worrying too much. It didn't matter what one did as long as one went on fighting for the right things.

He went home, washed, shaved, put on a clean shirt and then caught the tram to the main square. He hadn't arranged to meet her this evening but, like a young man in love—the way he had never been before—he prepared to go and see his bride.

The door of the apartment was open; so was the door to the drawing-room. The two old aunts were there, Malie doing the accounts from her kiosk, Eva unpicking an old dress that looked like a crumpled curtain.

"I'd like to wait for Terez, if I may," he said courteously. They stared at him. "Will she be long?"

Malie recovered first. "Not long, no. Please sit down and wait."

Eva looked at his face, then at the bundle he carried in his hand. "What do you have there?" she breathed.

He flushed a little and placed the bundle on the table. "Roses," he said coolly. "Roses, for Terez."

"May we look?"

He nodded.

Her wrinkled old hands undid the paper. Across her face spread a smile of gloating delight. "Look, Malie! Roses! Red ones!" She fondled them, bowed her head into the blooms, smiled at them. "How many?"

"Twelve," he answered, staring hard across the room.

"Twelve roses!" She gulped and stroked one of the petals with a caressing finger. "Twelve roses, for Terez."

The two old ladies sat one each side of the table, looking down at the flowers. He leaned back in his chair, embarrassed but happy, and listened for the sound of Terez's feet upon the stairs.

Bibliography

Clark, Alan. *Suicide of the Empires: The Battles on the Eastern Front, 1914-18.* London: BPC Publishing (Unit 75), 1971.

Cruttwell, C. R. M. F. *A History of the Great War, 1914-18.* Oxford: Clarendon Press, 1936.

Czebe, Jeno, and Tibor Petho. *Hungary in World War II.* Pamphlets of "New Hungary," Budapest, 1946.

Edwards, Tudor. *The Blue Danube.* London: Robert Hale & Co., 1973.

Erdei, Ferenc. *Information Hungary.* Oxford: Pergamon Press, 1968.

Faludy, George. *My Happy Days in Hell.* London: Andre Deutsch, 1962.

Horthy, Admiral Miklós. *Memoirs.* London: Hutchinson & Co., 1956.

Ignotus, Paul. *Hungary.* London: Ernest Benn, 1972.

Illyés, Gyula. *People of the Puszta.* Budapest: Corvina Press, 1967.

Kállay, Miklós. *Hungarian Premier: A Personal Account of a Nation's Struggle in the Second World War.* New York: Columbia University Press, 1954.

Liddell Hart, B. H. *History of the First World War.* London: Cassell & Co., 1970.

Listowel, Judith. *The Golden Tree: The Story of Peter, Tomi, and Their Family. . . .* London: Odhams Press, 1958.

Macartney, Carlile A. *October Fifteenth: A History of Modern Hungary, 1929-1945.* Edinburgh: Edinburgh University Press, 1956-57.

Newspapers of the First World War. Newton Abbot: David & Charles, 1970.

Roth, Ernst. *A Tale of Three Cities.* New York: Charles Scribner's Sons, 1971.

Seth, Ronald. *Caporetto, the Scapegoat Battle.* London: Macdonald & Co., 1965.

Shirer, William L. *Berlin Diary: The Journal of a Foreign Correspondent, 1934-1941.* New York: Alfred A. Knopf, 1941.

_____. *The Rise and Fall of the Third Reich: A History of Nazi Germany.* New York: Simon & Schuster, 1960.

Taylor, Alan J. P. *War by Time-Table: How the First World War Began.* New York: American Heritage, 1969.

Watt, Donald C., Frank Spencer, and Neville Brown. *A History of the World in the 20th Century.* New York: William Morrow & Co., 1967.

Zeman, Z A B. *Twilight of the Habsburgs.* London: BPC Publishing (Unit 75), 1971.

The incident described on pages 140-145 is based on a factual reportage from the First World War, although the place and time have been altered. This reportage appeared in *20 Riport Bemutalja a Vilagot* and was written by Pásztor Arpád.